HEROES DIE

Matthew Woodring Stover

A Del Rey® Book

THE BALLANTINE PUBLISHING GROUP • NEW YORK

A Del Rey® Book
Published by The Ballantine Publishing Group
Copyright © 1998 by Matthew Woodring Stover
Map copyright © 1998 by Matthew Woodring Stover

www.randomhouse.com/delrey/

Library of Congress Cataloging Card Number: 99-90141

ISBN 0-345-42145-0

Manufactured in the United States of America

First Trade Paperback Edition: August 1998
First Mass Market Edition: June 1999

10   9   8   7   6   5   4   3   2   1

For Charles,
for being Caine's best friend;
and for Robyn,
for making it all possible

THERE ARE MANY, many people whose support made this novel possible, stretching back over more years than I am willing to admit.

I can only hit the high points:

Charles L. Wright, without whom there would be no Caine.

Robyn Fielder, who told me I had to write this book, and supported me both emotionally and financially while I did.

The above, Paul Kroll, H. Gene McFadden, Eric Coleman, Ken Bricker, and Perry Glasser, each of whom generously read at least one early draft of this story, and offered opinions and advice.

Clive A. Church, for technical advice and inexhaustible patience with my bitching.

My agent, Howard Morhaim, for tireless enthusiasm.

My indefatigable editor, Amy Stout, for making me do it over until I got it right.

And my mother, Barbara Stover, for one particular kindness among a lifetime of such.

Thank you, one and all.

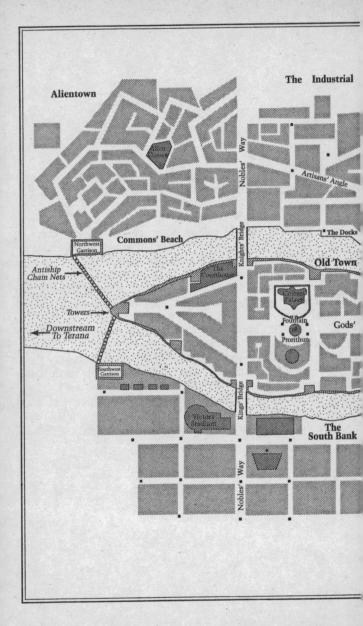

PROLOGUE

1

WITH MY HAND on the doorjamb, some buried-alive instinct thumps within my chest: this is going to hurt.

I take a deep breath and step inside.

The bedchamber of Prince-Regent Toa-Phelathon is really pretty restrained, when you consider that the guy in the bed there rules the second-largest empire on Overworld. The bed itself is a modest eight-poster, only half an acre or so; the extra four posts—each an overcarved slab of rose-veined thierril thicker than my thigh—support lamps of gleaming brass. Long yellow flames like blades of spears waver gently in the breeze from the concealed service door. I close the door soundlessly behind me, and its brocade paper–covered surface blends seamlessly into the pattern of the wall.

I wade through the billowing carpet of silken cushions, a knee-high cloud of vividly shimmering primary colors. A flash of maroon and gold to my left, and my heart suddenly hammers—but it's only my own livery, my servant's dress, captured briefly in the spun-silver mirror atop the Prince-Regent's commode of lacquered Lipkan krim. The reflection shows me the spell, the enchanted face I present: smooth, rounded cheeks, sandy hair, a trace of peach fuzz. I tip myself a blurry wink and smile with my sandpaper lips, ease out a silent sigh, and keep moving.

The Prince-Regent lies propped on pillows larger than my whole bed and snores happily, the silver hairs of his mustache puffing in and out with each wheeze. A book lies facedown across his ample chest: one of Kimlarthen's series of Korish romances. This draws another smile out of my dry mouth; who would have figured the Lion of Prorithun for a sentimentalist? Fairy tales—simple stories

1

for simple minds, a breath of air to cool brows overheated by the complexities of real life.

I set the golden tray down softly on the table beside his bed. He stirs, shifting comfortably in his sleep—and freezing my blood. His movement sends a puff of lavender scent up from the pillows. My fingers tingle. His hair, unbound for napping, falls in a steel-colored spray around his face. That noble brow, those flashing eyes, that ruggedly carved chin exposed by careful shaving within his otherwise full beard—he's everybody's perfect image of the great king. The statue of him on his rearing charger—the one that stands in the Court of the Gods near the Fountain of Prorithun— will make a fine, inspiring memorial.

His eyes pop open when he feels my hand grip his throat: I'm far too professional to try to stifle his shout with a hand over the mouth, and only a squeak gets past my grip. Further struggle is discouraged by his close-up view of my knife, its thick, double-edged point an inch from his right eye.

I bite my tongue, and saliva gushes into my mouth to moisten my throat. My voice is steady: very low and very flat.

"It's customary, at times like this, to say a few words. A man shouldn't die with no understanding of why he's been murdered. I do not pride myself on my eloquence, and so I will keep this simple."

I lean close and stare past my knife blade into his eyes. "The Monasteries kept you on the Oaken Throne by supporting your foolish action against Lipke in the Plains War; the Council of Brothers felt, on balance, that you would be a strong enough ruler to hold the Empire together, at least until the Child Queen reaches majority."

His face is turning purple, and veins in his neck bulge against my grip. If I don't talk fast, I'll have choked him out before I'm done. I sigh through my teeth and pick up the pace.

"They have discovered, though, that you're an idiot. Your puni-tive taxes are weakening both Kirisch-Nar and Jheled-Kaarn— they tell me ten thousand free peasants starved to death in Kaarn alone last winter. Now you've bloodied the nose of Lipke over that stupid iron mine in the Gods' Teeth, and you're making noises like you want to fight a full-scale war over two crappy little eastern provinces. You have ignored and insulted the Lipkan trade delega-tion and have dismissed the Council of Brothers' admonitions. They've decided that you're no longer fit to rule, if you ever were.

They are tired of waiting. They've paid me a great deal of money to remove you from the throne. Blink twice if you understand."

His eyes widen stiffly, bug out staring from his head as though he'd make them lidless if only he could, and his throat works under my hand. He mouths words at me that my poor lipreading skill can't follow beyond the initial *please please please*. He'd like to argue with me, no doubt, or perhaps request leniency or asylum for his wife and two daughters. I can grant neither; if a war of succession follows this murder, they'll have to take their chances along with the rest of us.

Finally his eyeballs begin to dry, and he blinks—once. Funny how our reflexes conspire to kill us, sometimes. In terms of my contract, I'm to ensure his comprehension; if I'm to do this properly, I should wait for his next blink. All proprieties should be observed, in the death of a king.

His gaze shifts minutely—the old warrior is going to make a try for me, a last desperate convulsion of his will to survive, calling on other, more recent reflexes to rescue him.

When it's a choice between observing the proprieties and getting caught in the Prince-Regent's bedchamber, nine infinite floors up the spire of the Colhari Palace, the proprieties can fuck off.

I jam the knife into his eye. Bone crackles and blood sprays. I use the knife to twist his face away from me: a bloodstain on this livery could be fatal, on my way out. He flops like a salmon that's found unexpected land beneath an upstream leap. This is only his body's last unconscious attempt to live; it goes hand-in-hand with the release of his bowels and bladder. He shits and pisses all over himself and his satin-weave sheets—another one of those primordial reflexes, a futile dodge to make his meat unappetizing to the predator.

Screw it. I'm not hungry anyway.

He quiets after a year or so. I brace my free hand against his forehead and work the knife back and forth. It comes free with a wet scrape, and I set about the grisly part of this job.

The serrated edge slices easily through the flesh of his neck, but grates against his third cervical vertebra. A slightly altered angle of attack puts the edge between the third and fourth, and a couple seconds' sawing loosens his head. The copper scent of his blood is so thick I can smell it through the stench of his shit; my stomach twists until I can barely breathe.

I uncover the golden tray that I'd carried up from the kitchens, gently set the plates of steaming food to one side, and put Toa-Phelathon's head in their place, picking it up carefully by the hair so that none of the gore that drains from it will stain my clothes. I replace the golden dome and strip off my bloodstained gloves, tossing them carelessly onto the body beside the discarded knife. My hands are clean.

I lift the tray to my shoulder and take a deep breath. The easy part's over. Now I have to get out of here alive.

The trickiest part of this escape is the first hurdle: getting away from the body. If I pass the pair of guards at the service door cleanly, I'll be out of the palace before anyone knows the old man is dead. My adrenals sing to me a potent tune that makes my hands tingle and raises goose bumps up my back. My heartbeat thunders in my ears.

In the upper left corner of my vision, the red Exit Square blinks. I ignore it, even as it moves with my eyes like an afterimage of the sun.

I'm only halfway across the room when the service door swings open. Jemson Thal, the master steward, starts talking before he even clears the doorway. "Your pardon, Majesty," he begins in a hasty breathless gabble, "but there is a rumor of an impostor among the serv . . ."

Jemson Thal takes in the headless corpse on the bed, he takes in me, and his gabble trails into gasping. His eyes go round and the color drains from his face; his mouth works like he's strangling. I close the distance between us with a long, smooth *croisé* and kick him in the throat. It drops him like a bag of rocks, and now he's strangling for real as he tries to breathe around the splinters of his larynx, clawing at his throat and writhing on the service-passage floor.

I didn't even tip the tray.

One of the guards is, will be, easy. With a wordless exclamation he drops to one knee beside Thal and tries stupidly to help him. What's he think he's gonna do, thump the poor bastard's back until he coughs up his windpipe? The other isn't in sight; smarter than his partner, he's pressed against the wall of the service passage, waiting for me.

Both of these guards wear long sturdy hauberks under their mantles of maroon and gold, with padded chainmail coifs reinforced by studded steel skullcaps. Toa-Phelathon spared no expense in outfitting his Household Knights; my knives are useless against them, but hey, that's all right—I'm deep in it, now.

The waiting is over. I'm happy again.

The smarter guard has a brainstorm and begins to shout for help.

I uncover the tray and gravely regard Toa-Phelathon. The lower third of his flowing hair is soaked in blood, but his face isn't too contorted; even with the ruin of his eye he's still clearly recognizable. I thrust the tray through the doorway about chest high; the sight of its cargo cuts off the shouted alarm as efficiently as an arrow down the throat.

While the portion of the guard's brain that handles signal processing still struggles to assimilate the concept of the disembodied head of his king, I skip out into the service passage; I have two seconds, maybe more, before Smartguard there can use his mind for anything beyond saying, "Huh?"

The guard on one knee claws at his sword as he surges to his feet. I drop the tray with a clang, and the head bounces away as I get a hand on the dumb guard's wrist and keep that blade where it belongs. I follow with a sharp headbutt that rings in my ears with a slapstick *bonk*; Dumbguard's nose spreads like deviled ham, and his eyes drift together. I wrap both forearms around his coif and pivot away from him, twisting him sideways into a hangman's throw that sends him tumbling forward to crash into Smartguard. The padding behind his chainmail coif didn't give his neck enough support to save him: his neck bones parted with a sharp pop as I levered him over my back. He twitches out the last of his life as I leap lightly across Jemson Thal's convulsing body to go over and kill Smartguard.

That's when Toa-Phelathon gets his piece of me, a bit of petty revenge that must have him snickering in the afterlife.

I'm coming down—it's just a little jump—but I've got my eyes on Smartguard, who's disentangling himself from Dumbguard, and my foot lands on Toa-Phelathon's head.

It rolls out from under me, and I upend like Elmer Fudd.

I barely manage to take the fall on my shoulder instead of the back of my neck, and only the narrowness of the service corridor saves my life: when Smartguard swings his broadsword at my head, its tip hangs up in the woodwork. I try to roll away, but I come up against Jemson Thal, who's still choking, and this time Smartguard gets it right. Instead of swinging his sword, he lunges with a stiff arm and drives a foot of steel through my liver.

A sword in the belly is a disconcerting thing: it doesn't really hurt, much, but it's really fucking *cold*, it radiates freezing cold that surges through your whole body and drains the strength out of your legs, like the brain freeze you get from chewing up an ice cube only you feel it all over, and you can feel the blade sliding around in there, slicing things up, and frankly, the whole process sucks, if you ask me.

A couple of pounds of steel in the belly also plays fuckass with the forcepattern of the spell that makes me look like a teenage eunuch. The magick flickers like a dying CRT, and the discharge lifts hair on my neck and makes my beard tingle.

Smartguard pulls the blade instead of twisting it around in there—a mistake of inexperience that I'm going to kill him for. It scrapes a rib on the way out, a sensation that's analogous to fingernails across a blackboard combined with having your teeth drilled without anesthetic; screaming clouds of blackness bloom inside my eyes. I moan and shudder with pain, and Smartguard mistakes these for death rattle and convulsion—more inexperience.

"There, you bastard, an easy death is better than you deserve!" he says.

Tears well in his eyes for his fallen lord, and I don't have the heart to tell him that I agree with him. He bends toward me a little as the enchanted disguise finally fades, and his eyes go wide. There's awe in his voice when he says, "Hey, you could be . . . you look like, like *Caine*! You *are*, aren't you? I mean, who else would . . . Great K'hool, I've killed Caine! I'm gonna be *famous*!"

I don't think so.

I hook my right toe around his ankle to hold his leg while I stamp his knee with my left. It snaps, loudly, and he collapses into a wailing heap. That's the trouble with chainmail: it's no defense against joints bending in ways they're not designed to bend. He doesn't drop his sword, though; the kid has heart.

I come to my feet with an acrobat's kip, tearing something inside my wounded belly. He jabs at me with the sword—but from the ground he's slow, and it's easy to slap my palms together around the flat of the blade, kick his wrist, and take it away from him. I flip the sword end-for-end and neatly catch the hilt.

"Too bad, kid," I tell him. "You'd've been pretty good, if you'd lived."

I shortarm the swing, and it takes him across the top of the ear, half an inch below the studded rim of his skullcap. The edge doesn't penetrate the chain coif, but it doesn't have to; I'm good with swords, and the impact alone is enough to fracture his skull and kill him.

I pause a bare moment to get my breath and take stock of my situation. I'm bleeding, front and back where he ran me through, and no doubt internally as well. I figure I've got ten minutes of useful action before I hit shock. Could be longer, could be a lot less; depends on how much damage that broadsword actually did and how badly I'm hemorrhaging.

In that time I must descend eight heavily guarded floors of the Colhari Palace and lose myself in the crowds of Ankhana's Old Town—all while carrying the head of the Prince-Regent. The alarm's been raised, and I'm probably bleeding to death, but that's no reason to leave him behind; without the head, I don't get paid, and besides, carrying a severed head won't make me any more conspicuous than I already am. With blood running down my legs, I can't bluff, I can't hide, and I'll leave a trail behind wherever I go. Now I can hear the pounding of booted feet approaching at a run.

The red Exit Square is back at the upper left corner of my field of vision, flashing on and off.

Yeah, all right. Time to go.

I get the rhythm of it and start triggering my blink reflex in synch with the flashing. The service passage and the dying men around me fade into nonexistence.

2

HARI MICHAELSON'S EYES ratcheted open when the Motorola rep swung back the helmet, and he ground his teeth against the sliding non-pain of the IV needle that the rep's assistant slowly drew out of his neck. He lifted his hand and hacked a cough against the thick callus that ridged his knuckles, and the Motorola rep hastily produced a paper cup for him to spit into. He stretched slowly, with much creaking and joint popping, and sat forward in the simichair, elbows to knees. His straight black hair was glossy with sweat, and his eyes of the same color were rimmed in red; he turned away from the reps and rested his face on his hands.

The Motorola girl and her assistant both looked at him with the kind of hopeful puppy-dog eyes that sickened him.

From the depths of an immense, genuine calf-leather lounger, Marc Vilo asked, "Well? How was it, Hari? What do you think?"

Hari took a deep breath, sighed it out, scratched his beard, rubbed the sallow scar that crossed the bridge of his crooked, twice-broken nose, and tried to find the energy to speak. He called this, privately, his post-Caine shits: a shattering cocaine-crash depression that hit him every time he came back to Earth and had to be Hari Michaelson again. Even today—not even a real Adventure, only a three-year-old recording—had been enough to trigger it.

And let's be honest: There was more going on here than post-Caine shits. There was a sizzling hole in his guts—like he'd swallowed acid and it had burned its way out through the skin, right alongside the scar Smartguard's broadsword had left on his liver. Why *this* cube, out of all Caine's Adventures? What in Christ's name was Vilo *thinking*?

To bring him here and put him through part of *A Servant of the Empire* again—even a small part—was an exquisite refinement of cruelty, a lemon squeezed into an already-salted wound. It chewed at him, gnawed that hole in his guts like a little fucking rat.

Most of the time, he could kid himself along, pretend that he wasn't really hurt, pretend that this empty burning ache that took over his chest whenever he thought of Shanna was just indigestion, just an ulcer. Most of the time, he could pretend the pain came from a hole in his guts, instead of the hole in his life. He'd gotten good at kidding himself: for months now, he'd had himself believing he was getting over her.

What the fuck, huh? Practice makes perfect.

"Hari?" Vilo leaned forward in his lounger, an edge of dangerous impatience sharpening his voice. "Everybody's *waiting* on you, kid. Let's have it."

Slowly, Hari managed to force words from his throat. "It's illegal, Biz'man. This is illegal tech."

The Motorola rep gasped like a Leisurewoman meeting a flasher. "I assure you, I *personally* assure *both* of you, this technology was developed entirely indepen—"

Vilo cut her off with a smoke-trailing *shut up* wave of his cigar, a thick black ConCristo almost as big as he was. "I know it's *illegal*, Hari, shit. Am I an idiot? I just want to know if it's any good."

Mark Vilo was a little salty-haired fighting cock, a self-upcasted Businessman pushing sixty from the far side, a swaggering bowlegged bastard who was the majority stockholder in

Vilo Intercontinental—ostensibly a worldwide transport firm. He was the lord and master of this sprawling estate in the foothills of the Sangre de Cristos, and was the Business Patron of the super-star Actor whom everyone called Caine.

"Good?" Hari shrugged, sighing. Why argue? "Yeah, you better believe it. Next best thing to being there." He turned to the Motorola rep. "Your neurochem feed—that's a fake, isn't it?"

The rep made protesting noises until Hari cut her off with a weary, "Ahh, shut up."

He was glad, really, that the Motorola rep was an idiot; it gave him something to think about beyond the cold hurt that lived in Shanna's eyes whenever he pictured her face. It had been months since he'd been able to even imagine her with a smile.

Keep your mind on fucking business, he snarled at himself.

He turned to Vilo and tried to stretch some life back into his voice by flexing his aching shoulders. "Don't let them shit you, Biz'man. This whole Exit Square business, what do they call that? Blink in Synch?"

The Motorola rep offered a glassy, professional smile. "It's only one of the cutting-edge features that make this unit the best value on the market today."

Hari ignored her. "So you trigger your blink reflex to exit the program," he went on. "It's not a mechanical trigger. It reads the impulse as feedback on the inducers; this is wholly owned Studio technology, and the Studio takes this kind of shit seriously. The neurochem feed is just camouflage. Nothing's going through that line but the hypnotics—and not much of them, if you want to know: they pooched the feed. They're playing all the sensation through the same kind of direct neural induction that the Studio uses in their first-hander chairs—and they've got it turned up too high. The smell, when I cut off Toa-Phelathon's head? The real thing's not that potent. And they had the adrenal level jazzed so high I could barely breathe. Finally, the sword in the guts, it *hurt* too much."

"But, but Entertainer Michaelson—" the rep sputtered, exchanging a quick worried glance with her assistant, "—we have to make it *believable*, you know, I mean—"

Hari rose slowly; the post-Caine shits made him feel boneless, as if only extreme concentration kept his head on his shoulders—but a little bit of Caine's edgy threat began to leak into his voice, into the cold darkness of his eyes.

He lifted the hem of his tunic to expose the brown lines of the twin scars, front and back, on his left side below the short ribs, where Smartguard's broadsword had pierced his liver just less than three years ago. "You see these? You want to *touch* them? So who should know better? You?"

"Hari, Jesus Christ, don't be such an asshole," Vilo said. He waved his cigar dismissively at the rep. "Don't mind him; it's not personal, y'know. He's like this with everybody."

"I'm telling you," Hari said lifelessly, "they screwed it up. If that sword scraping my rib had hurt as much when it really happened as it did just now, I'd have spent a couple more seconds stunned. When something hurts that much, there's not much you can do except moan or scream, writhe around, or pass right out. That poor bastard guard would have put his next thrust into my throat. All right?"

He opened a hand toward Vilo and sighed. "You want to invest in proprietary tech, that's your business. But I'd think you wouldn't want to deal with idiots who can't even tune an induction helmet."

Vilo grunted. "Invest, nothing. I'm just gonna buy the goddamn thing, Hari; this is a quote-unquote prototype. Not even a dinosaur like Motorola is gonna freemarket tech that pirates Studio effects. I just wanted to have one so I can go over cubes on my own time, without blowing a couple weeks on a first-hander berth."

"Yeah, whatever. Do what you want."

"Hari . . ." Vilo said mildly, returning his ConCristo to a corner of his mouth. "Attitude."

It was a mild chill that settled into the silence Vilo's admonition left in its wake, just enough that the rep and her assistant exchanged a flickering glance—no one actually shivered. Vilo blandly nodded toward the reps, indicating *put on your company manners, son.*

Hari lowered his head sullenly. "Sorry, Biz'man," he muttered. "I'm out of line. But I've got one more question—with your permission."

Vilo gave his lord-of-the-manor nod, and Hari turned to the woman from Motorola. "The cubes this chair plays—they're not standard Studio-issue recordings. They can't be; standard cubes don't carry scent or touch/pain data, and I can't believe your inducers can read off the neurochem channel and compensate for time lag and dosage and everything else. You're getting bootleg masters from somewhere, aren't you?"

The Motorola rep smiled her best corporate smile and said, "I'm afraid I can't answer that. But, as guaranteed under the purchase contract, Biz'man Vilo will receive cubes appropriate for this equipment—"

"That's enough," Hari said disgustedly. He turned back to Vilo. "Look, it's like this. These idiots have another idiot inside the Studio processing labs who's feeding them bootleg masters. First, that means that what you'll get is gonna be, most likely, *uncut*. A two-week Adventure is going to run two weeks in that chair, just like if you were sitting in the Cavea in a first-hander berth, only worse. This chair doesn't have twitch-response units, comfort hookups, or an internal food supply. Second, they'll be feeding you a steady stream of these bootlegs. There'll be records of regular delivery, that kind of thing, and one of these days, their idiot is gonna get caught. Then before they cyborg him and sell him for a Worker, the Studio cops will get enough out of him to roll up the whole network, which they'll turn over to their friends in the government. And these won't be friendly and courteous CID guys knocking on your door, because this isn't just tech violation anymore. By now, it's about intellectual property, and copyright infringement, and all of a sudden you're looking at the Social Police. Even you, Businessman, do not want to get on the short end of the fuckstick with Soapy."

Vilo leaned back in his chair, snugging his head against its gel-pack headrest. He puffed a couple rolling mushroom clouds of his stinking cigar smoke, then sat up again, a half grin wrinkling his crow's-feet. "Hari, you still think like a criminal, you know that? Twenty years later, you're still a street punk at heart."

Hari stretched his lips into a humorless smile in response; he didn't know what that was supposed to mean, and he didn't want to ask.

Vilo went on, "Why'nt you go on up to the pond and have a drink while I wrap things down here, hey?"

There was a time, Hari reflected dully, that to be dismissed like a child, like a little fucking kid, would have felt like a slap. Now, it produced only a blank amazement that he still seemed to be going about his business, going on with his life, as though it still had meaning.

But it was an act, as hollow a pretense as was Caine himself.

Without Shanna, the world was empty, and he couldn't really manage to care about anything at all.

He nodded. "Sure. See you there."

3

HARI PROWLED THE sunlit rocks that surrounded the shimmering pond and the twin waterfalls that fed it. The pond was a beautiful piece of work: only the faint scent of chlorine and a sneaking conviction that nature wouldn't have arranged stone and water with so much attention to human comforts betrayed its artificial origins.

Hari paced back and forth, sat down, stood up. Once or twice he started out toward the scrub desert, into the gritty wind and barren mounds of slag and tailings from the surrounding mines. Each time, he stopped at the fringes of Vilo's artificial oasis, came back, and started the cycle over again. He stared out at the toxic sludge of the barrens with a kind of wistfulness; he could imagine himself walking among the heaps, all the way up into the dead rock of the mountains. He wasn't sure that tramping through the poisoned waste would make him feel any better, but he knew it couldn't make him feel much worse.

Take it easy, he told himself over and over again. *It's not like she's dead.* And each time, a dark whisper in his heart told him that maybe he'd be better off if she was. Or if he was.

With her death, he could start to heal; with his, he'd be beyond pain.

What the fuck was taking Vilo so goddamn long?

Hari hated waiting, always had. Nothing to do but stand around and think—and there were too many things in his life that didn't bear thinking about.

He looked around for something, anything, he could use to distract himself. He even looked up the wall of the artificial cliffs down which the waterfalls streamed into the pond, thinking that maybe a fifty-meter free climb up a vertical water-slickened face might be just the thing to take his mind off Shanna.

This had been his tactic ever since the separation: Keep busy. Divert the mind. Don't think about it. And it was a good tactic, one that worked, day to day. Sometimes hours would pass, days, even a week, during which he barely thought of her.

But he'd always been a better tactician than he was a strategist. He won every battle, but on days like today he couldn't help realizing that he was losing the war.

Even climbing the fucking waterfall wouldn't help; his experienced eye picked out innumerable handholds and footholds that could only have been put there by intention. This cliff had been *de-*

signed to be climbed, and he could go up it more easily than most men could climb a ladder.

He shook his head disgustedly.

"Hey, Caine!" called one of the girls who swam in the pond. "Want to come in and play?"

In the pond a couple of the ubiquitous Vilo Intercontinental party girls had been swimming and splashing and dunking each other. Long-limbed, lean, athletic, with perfect teeth and breasts that were better yet, their job was to be available to Businessman Vilo's guests. They both were staggeringly beautiful. Surgical glamour was part of their bonus for their five years' service, at the end of which they'd be released to seek their leggy fortunes elsewhere. They were playing up for him now, arranging lovely flashes of thigh and butt, the graceful arc of a well-toned back thrusting a nipple toward the sky; if it hadn't been so deliberate it might've been appealing.

Now the one who had called to him slid behind the other and drew her into an embrace; one hand cupped her breast while the other slid below the water's surface toward her crotch. She bent her graceful neck to kiss her partner's shoulder, all the while inviting him with her eyes.

Hari sighed. He supposed he might as well jump in; at least fucking a couple party girls would have a certain honesty. Unlike the celebrity-hungry women who put themselves in his way wherever he went, these girls were professionals. There wouldn't be any pretense that they cared about him, or he about them.

A few years ago, sure, he would have done it. But now, so late in his life, after he had finally found someone who had loved him, whom he had loved, who had made truth of the ancient euphemism *making love*, he couldn't. He couldn't even get interested. Fucking those girls would be like sticking his dick in a knothole: a complicated, slightly painful way to masturbate.

A waistcoat-and-cummerbund servant slid silently up beside Hari and offered a tray with a snifter of scotch.

"Laphroaig, right?"

Hari nodded and took it.

"Uh, Caine?"

Hari sighed. "Call me Hari, all right? Everybody forgets I have a name."

"Oh, okay, uh, *Hari*. I just wanted to say, y'know, I'm a big fan of yours, I even, well, y'know . . . ah, never mind."

"All right."

But the servant—Andre, Hari thought his name might be—still hovered expectantly at his elbow. Hari took a slow pull from the snifter and watched the girls swim.

The servant coughed and said, "I only get cubes of your stuff, of course. I only been a first-hander once, a few years ago when Biz'man Vilo took a bunch of us for vacation. It was kinda wild, because, y'know, we didn't first-hand *you*—that's really expensive—but the guy we did, he was Yoturei the Ghost. You remember him?"

"Should I?" Hari said, bored. Why do people think that all Actors know each other?

"Well, yeah, I mean, I don't know. You killed me—I mean *him*. In the Warrens in Ankhana."

"Oh, yeah." Hari shrugged, remembering now the ruckus at the Studio when he'd transferred back after that Adventure. "He tracked me for a day or two before I caught him. Hell, how'm I supposed to know the kid's an Actor? He should've had enough brights to stay out of my way."

"You didn't even remember?"

"I kill a lot of people."

"Jeez." The servant leaned closer, conspiratorially, offering a whiff of the red wine that was giving him the balls to keep talking. "Y'know, sometimes I even dream of being you . . . being Caine, y'know?"

Hari grunted a laugh. "Yeah, sometimes I do, too."

The servant frowned. "I don't get it."

Hari took another pull from the snifter, warming to the conversation. Even empty chatter with a fan was better than standing alone with his thoughts.

"Caine and I, we're not the same person, all right? I grew up in a San Francisco Labor slum; Caine's an Overworld foundling. He was raised by a Pathquan freedman, a farrier and blacksmith. By the time I was twelve I was a sneakthief because I wasn't big enough to be a mugger; when Caine was twelve, he was sold to a Lipkan slaver because the whole family was starving to death in the Blood Famine."

"But that's all, like, pretend, right?"

Hari shrugged and sat down on the rocks, making himself comfortable. "When I'm on Overworld, being Caine, it seems real enough to me. You train yourself to believe it. Overworld is a different place, kid. Caine can do things I can't; I mean, he's not a spellcaster, but the principle's the same. He's faster, stronger, more ruthless, maybe not as bright. It's like magick, I guess. It's imagination, and willpower: you make yourself believe."

"That's how the magick works? I mean, I don't really get it, magick, but you—"

"I don't really get it, either," Hari said sourly. "Spellcasters are crazy. They, sort of, hallucinate on command . . . Ah, I don't know. First-hand one sometime. They're all fucking bughouse nuts."

"Well, then, uh—" The servant offered a clumsy boys'-club laugh. "Then why'd you marry one?"

And, somehow, it always comes back to Shanna. Hari emptied the snifter, swallowed hard, sighed, and with a blurred whip of the wrist fired the empty snifter over the pond to shatter on the rocks on the other side, a shimmering crystal shower echoing the waterfall's rainbow spray. Hari rolled his eyes up to meet the consternation on the servant's face. "Maybe you better go sweep that up, huh? Before the Businessman gets here."

"Jeez, Caine, I didn't mean to—"

"Forget it," Hari said. He leaned back on the rocks and laid his elbow over his eyes. "Go sweep."

Lying there, he could only think of the end of *A Servant of the Empire*. He could almost feel Shanna's lap below his head, almost smell the faint musk of her skin, almost hear her whisper to him that she loved him, that he had to live.

The happiest dream he could dream, lying on the rocks beside Marc Vilo's pool, was of lying on the shit-stained cobbles of a narrow Ankhanan alley, bleeding to death.

A shadow fell across his face and woke him up.

His heart leaped, and he started upward, shading his eyes, breathless—

Vilo stood over him, haloed by the afternoon sun. "I'm goin' into Frisco. Come on, Hari, I'll give you a lift home."

4

VILO'S ROLLS LURCHED slightly on insertion into the slavelanes. The Businessman unbelted his pilot's straps, walked back to the passenger lounge, and poured himself a long shot of Metaxa. He drained a third of it at a gulp and lowered himself onto the love seat that formed a corner with the sofa where Hari sat.

"Hari, I want you to get back together with Shanna," Vilo said.

Long years of practice in dealing with the upcastes kept Hari stone-faced. He'd anticipated it and thought he was ready, but the sizzle in his chest told him he'd never be ready for this.

It seemed like, somehow, she was all around him, like he couldn't turn his head without seeing something that reminded him of her, like every word spoken in his presence was some kind of a jeering reminder that he had been tried and found wanting—that, in the end, he just wasn't good enough for her.

He stared out one of the broad windows that sided the Rolls, watching the snowcapped peaks of the Rocky Mountains flow past far below. "We've been over this," he said tiredly.

"Yes, we have. And I don't want to have to talk about it again, understand? You patch things up with her, and I'm not kidding."

Hari shook his head wordlessly. He looked down at his hands, folded now between his knees like a sullen child's, and with a sudden twist popped his knuckles hard enough to make his joints ache. "Can I have a drink?"

"All right," Vilo said. "Help yourself."

Hari went to the bar and kept his back to his Patron while he pretended to scan the liquor display. Finally he stabbed a code at random, and the dispenser whirred and hummed and burped up some evil-smelling crimson frozen fruit concoction—and eliminated Hari's last delaying tactic. He sipped it and made a face.

"Exactly what is your problem?" Vilo asked. "I think this is the third time I've told you, straight out and no dodging, that I want you two back together. So what's the holdup?"

Hari shook his head. "It's not that simple."

"My ass. The only reason I let you marry her in the first place was she's good for your image. And mine. I need to soften a little so I can cozy with Shermaya Dole; she's a little leery of selling GFT to me."

The Doles were a Leisure family, but it pleased Shermaya to dabble in Investing, and occasionally in Business; she sponsored a number of Actors, including—most prominently—Shanna.

Vilo took another long pull of his brandy and went on musingly. "Green Fields Technologies . . . Y'know, I've been trying to crack into agriculture for five years now, and GFT has some new synthetic something or other that's supposed to let us recover the Kannebraska Desert for farming. Dole's worried about the GFT Laborers and Artisans, though; I've almost got her convinced that I won't postacquisition downsize at all. Silly bitch. Anyway, I've been talking to her about Shanna, and she says she won't press for a reconciliation; she's got this thing about letting you two work this shit out for yourselves. I say, screw that. Dole's a twitch, and a softhearted one, too. She's teetering. I get you back together with Shanna, it just might trip the wire on this deal. So do it."

"She left *me*, Biz'man," Hari murmured, and was again surprised at the sudden twist of pain that followed saying this. It always surprised him, every time. "There's not much I can do."

"Well, what's up *her* goddamn ass then?" Vilo snapped. "There's probably five billion women that'd sell both their tits and an ovary to spend *one night* with you! Jesus Christ!"

"The nights weren't the problem."

The Businessman chuckled crudely. "I'll bet."

Hari stared down into the creamy crimson head of his drink. "She, ah . . . shit. I don't know. I think she figured that I'd be a little less like Caine. It was—" He took a deep breath. "It was the Toa-Phelathon thing that started it, if you really want to know."

Vilo nodded. "I do know. That's why I picked that cube for you to audit today."

Hari stiffened, and muscles at the corners of his jaw suddenly bulged.

"She left you because you're an *asshole*," Vilo told him, jabbing his finger at Hari's chest. "She left you because she couldn't stand living with a homicidal shit-heel who treated her like dirt."

A red mist began to coalesce in Hari's vision. "I *never* . . ." He clenched against his temper and said, "It wasn't about how I treated her. I treated her like a queen." The glass trembled in his hand and slopped a bit onto the Rolls' carpet. The spreading stain looked like blood.

Vilo followed his gaze and snorted. "You can clean that up later. Right now I'm not done talking to you."

He drained his glass and leaned forward, creases in his face deepening with his frown. "I know you're a little wrought up, but you listen now. I want you back together with Shanna, and no fucking around on this. You do whatever it takes. If she thinks you're too . . . whatever, you make goddamn sure that you're *less*. You follow? I don't care what it takes. You do it."

"Biz'man—" Hari began.

"Don't 'Biz'man' me, Michaelson. I give you a lot of fucking slack. I let you talk up, I let you play studman for the public, and I give you a lot of fucking money. You start paying back now. You ever don't feel like it, you just remember that you're not the only motherfucking Actor that fronts for VI." Vilo sat back to let Hari think about it.

Hari's ears rang with the tension in his neck. Slowly, carefully, he set his glass down on the bar, watching his hand all the way. Then, just as slowly and carefully, he turned back to his Patron and said, in a voice held very soft and very calm, "Yes, Biz'man. All right."

5

HARI STOOD BY the tall chain fence that surrounded the grass court behind the Abbey and watched Vilo lift the Rolls expertly from the lawn, its turbocells rotating toward flight position before it cleared the trees. He squinted against the backblast but held his position respectfully until the Rolls slid into the thick, rolling clouds over San Francisco, clouds that now reflected the bloody glow of the streetlights from the city below.

He walked to the broad armorglass doors of the sunroom, put his hand on the scanner, and said, "Honey, I'm home."

The pause was as brief as money could make it, while the scanner read his palm and matched it against his voiceprint, then disengaged the security system and magnetically unlocked the door. Actuators hidden in the walls took up much of the work of opening the seventy-odd kilos of armorglass that made up the doors; they seemed as light as old-fashioned plexi.

The lights came on as he entered the sunroom, and the Abbey said to him, "Hello, Hari. You have fourteen messages."

The furniture in the sunroom was a beautifully matched set of antique bentwoods; Hari moved through the room uneasily, touching nothing. The drawing room lit up as he approached the door.

He said, "Abbey: Query. Messages from Shanna?"

"No, Hari. Shall I replay messages?" The voice followed him; the housecomp phased the sound from tiny speakers hidden in each wall to make the Abbey's voice seem to speak softly from just behind Hari's left shoulder. Shanna had found the placement creepy; she'd never liked to talk to the house, and she had pestered him to change it until they'd once nearly come to blows.

Hari sighed. He stopped on the rose-veined marble floor of the front hall and looked up the wide empty sweep of the stairs that rose to the second-floor loggia. "Yeah, fine," he said. "Abbey: Replay messages."

The nearest wallscreen—the one beside the service elevator behind the stairs—lit up. Hari couldn't see the face as he turned away and climbed the stairs, but he knew the voice—the deferential whine of his lawyer. Even though they were of the same caste, both Professionals, his lawyer insisted on bootlicking; Entertainers have some theoretical social precedence over Attorneys.

As Hari walked through the echoing halls of the Abbey, each wallscreen behind him flicked off and the next one ahead flicked on, all showing his lawyer's sweating face as he explained that Hari's petition to upcaste to Administration had been denied yet again; the lawyer believed that the Studio was blocking him, because Caine was still so popular that Hari's retirement from Acting would represent a substantial fiscal burden et cetera et cetera.

Hari went into the gym and stripped off his Professional's suit and slacks. He didn't have much interest in what his lawyer had to say; he hadn't really expected to be allowed to upcaste, anyway. The lawyer's only other news was that Hari's request for an appeal of his father's sedition sentence had been denied yet again.

The balance of the messages were of even less interest, from his local Professional's Tribune asking for his endorsement in the upcoming election, to eight different begging calls from various charitable organizations, interspersed with requests for appearances and interviews on a number of magazine netshows. He made a mental note to have the Abbey's secretary subroutine upgraded to include a precis function; it would be painfully expensive—all AI functions were—but more than worth it, if it would allow him to avoid hearing their whining voices and seeing their eager, sincere, puppy-dog eyes.

Much of his time at home he spent here, in the gym. The exercise rooms, and the track that circled the second floor of the Abbey, were the only parts of the Abbey that hadn't been refurnished under Shanna's direction. Everywhere else, Hari felt like a guest in his own empty house.

Clad only in his shorts, Hari went to work on the gelbag without putting on gloves or foot guards. The harder it was hit, the stiffer the gelbag became, up to approximately the resistance of human bone, then it gave way with a sharp pop. Long before Hari had worked out the pressure of the frustrated anger that boiled behind his ribs, each blow he struck penetrated deep into the gel with a satisfying *crack* that sounded a lot like the snap of a human neck.

His shoulders gradually began to loosen as his body warmed up—with a painful slowness that forcefully reminded him of the approach of his fortieth birthday. It only made him hit harder. He barely even saw the bag, after a while; shifting images of the Toa-Phelathon assassination played tag behind his eyes.

That was one of Caine's murders that stayed with him, hung around the back of his head like an upcaste guest: no matter how sick of him you get, you can't make him leave.

He couldn't even blame the Studio for it: Caine had taken that job, accepted the Monasteries' commission, even though the Studio had told Hari that they were leaning in favor of war between Ankhana and Lipke, Overworld wars being very good for business, very fertile ground for young Actors to make their reputations. Hari had gone before the Studio's Scheduling Board to personally argue in favor of the assassination. He'd argued that the murder of the Prince-Regent would destabilize Ankhana's federal feudalism; he'd argued that civil wars are bloodier and far more bitter than war between two empires on opposite sides of the Continental Divide could ever be.

He'd never wanted to be proven so conclusively right.

The bloodshed that had followed, as the various Dukes of the Cabinet jockeyed for power and slaughtered each others' adherents, was appalling even by Overworld standards. The poor, bewildered little Child Queen Tel-Tamarantha, in regency for whom Toa-Phelathon had ruled, had survived her uncle by mere hours; none of the competing Dukes could take the risk that another would control her, and so the first casualty of the Succession War had been a beautiful, slightly dim-witted nine-year-old girl.

Sometimes, now, as he slammed the gelbag with fist and elbow and shin, it was his own face he imagined on the bag's surface, his own neck that he wanted to hear snap.

A Servant of the Empire was unusual for a Caine Adventure, nearly unique. Despite his reputation, Caine rarely murdered his targets outright, in blood that cold; the audiences didn't like it. They wanted more action, more risk—some few even liked a fair fight. The murder of the Prince-Regent was still a popular rental, even now—three years later—largely because of the extraordinary violence of Caine's escape from the palace. Caine had killed four more men and one woman beyond the two guards, the master steward, and the Prince-Regent, a total of nine; he'd also nearly died himself, and the increasing desperation of his attempts to get out of the Colhari Palace while hanging on to consciousness added suspenseful spice.

If he had been what he pretended to be, an Overworld native, he would have died that day. Even the state-of-the-art medical technology of the Studio infirmary had barely sufficed to save his life after his emergency transfer back to Earth. He'd stumbled into that alley in Ankhana's Old Town as his vision faded to black, sure that the Studio would leave him there to bleed to death because he hadn't made it back to his designated transfer point.

The exception they'd made for him had been approved at the highest level; it had to be. No one below the Board of Governors, in Geneva, can pass down such decisions. Arturo Kollberg, the Chairman of the San Francisco Studio, had personally pleaded with them; when Studio CEO Turner added his voice to the plea, they had finally approved the emergency transfer that had saved his life.

Emergency transfers are more rare than flawless diamonds. After all, where's the suspense, if Actors can be pulled back to Earth anytime they get in a little trouble? Even stars of Caine's magnitude get killed from time to time; it's what keeps the first-handers coming back. You never know if the Adventure you're passing up might be the Actor's last. Among the Leisurefolk and Investor families that make up the bulk of the firsthand audience, there's a whole bag of cool derived from having been on-line with a major star when he or she is violently killed—in real time, seeing what he sees, feeling the life drain from his body as though it's your own.

And that's where he'd been, lying among rags and scraps of food, his blood pulsing through his fingers onto the shit-stained cobbles of an Ankhanan alley, when a shadow had fallen across his face and woke him up.

He leaned his forehead against the impact-warmed poly of the gelbag and draped his arms around it, like an exhausted boxer going into a clinch to hold himself on his feet. The memory had him in its jaws, now. It shook him like a terrier shakes a rat, trying to crack his spine with the whiplash.

That filthy little cul-de-sac, and the shadow on his face, opening his eyes to see the haloed silhouette above him . . .

Shanna had stood over him, a full eclipse of breathless horror.

She'd been in Ankhana on an unrelated Adventure of her own, as Pallas Ril; Ankhana before the Succession War had been a

popular environment. The uproar at the palace, the shouts of panicked guards and blaring trumpets and the massive, desperate manhunt through the streets of Old Town, had drawn Actors like flies to
a three-day corpse, all hoping to inject a little excitement into their
second-rate Adventures. Of the hundreds of men and women in
Ankhana who'd been looking for him that morning, only Shanna
had taken that narrow turn into the stinking shadows of the cul-de-
sac where he lay, the head of Toa-Phelathon still held by a snarl of
bloody hair in his fist.

Only Shanna had knelt beside him, had cradled him on her lap,
had stroked his hair as light had faded from his world.

They had been married less than a year.

He would have been better off if he *had* died that day. Instead,
the emergency transfer had finally been approved, when it was almost too late, bringing them both into a reality far colder than a
lonely death in a filthy alley.

It brought them to Earth, and to each other.

She had believed—when they met, as he courted her, even when
they married—that Caine was only an act. She had believed that inside somewhere, within his heart of hearts, he was a fundamentally
good and decent man. She had believed that no one could see in
him what she saw, until that morning when she knelt with his head
on her lap.

When she looked down and saw the old man's head on the
cobbles like a discarded ball, ragged shreds of neck below the
bloody ruins of its eye, she finally began to suspect that she was
wrong about him, and the world was right.

That wasn't the end of their marriage, no: that would have been
too easy. Neither of them were quitters. They hung on to each other
like grim death, fighting and making up and fighting again, both of
them pouring their guts into each other, no matter what the cost. It
was Shanna, as usual, who had done the right thing, the smart
thing, the practical thing: she had let him go.

When she left, she took with her everything that had been right
with his life.

He pushed himself off the gelbag and whipped into a side kick
that folded it in the middle like a car around a bridge pylon. He
grabbed the bag and tried to rip it off its shock cords; he hammered
at the bag with fists and stiffened fingers, elbows and knees, forearms and shins, toes and heels and forehead. But no matter how
hard he hit, how long he worked, he couldn't touch the anger. He

couldn't get at it, not this way. And the anger was only the shield of the pain.

Finally he stopped, panting. This wasn't what he needed. He knew what he needed.

He needed to go back to Overworld.

He needed to be Caine.

He needed—finally, inescapably—to *hurt* somebody.

And as always, when lacking a better target, he turned on himself. He said, "Abbey: Call Shanna. Audio-out only."

The wallscreen lit up with her face, and the soft green hazel of her eyes stabbed him like a knife.

This was her message dump, of course; she no more answered her screencalls personally than he did.

"Hi there," her image said brightly, cheerfully, sincerely glad-to-see-ya. "I'm Pallas Ril, adventuring mage. I'm also Shanna Leighton, Actor."

Shanna Leighton Michaelson, Hari said silently.

"If you have a message for either of me, start talking."

His mouth tasted of dust. He could only stare: at the subtle curve of her neck, the line of her jaw, the thick curls of her short-cut hair. His fingers twitched with the memory of its softness. If he closed his eyes, right now, he could fill in every line of her body, every faintest freckle.

I'll change, he told her digitized image, but silently; he knew this was hopeless. Perhaps she'd help him put up a pretense, just a few days to satisfy Vilo, perhaps she still cared enough for him for that, but he couldn't even ask.

It'd hurt too much to be refused, and it'd hurt more if she went along with it.

She'd claimed, more than once, that their separation was painful for her. He didn't know if that was true; he didn't know if she still hurt as much as he did. He hoped not.

And here he was, and the tingling in his hands and the stutter in his chest told him that he'd been wanting this for a long time. He'd only been waiting for an excuse.

The pressure from Vilo gave him something to say that would gloss over the unspoken truth: that no matter how hard he tried to pretend otherwise, no hour passed in which he did not ache for her. He didn't know what to say, how to put it that wouldn't sound too cold, that wouldn't sound like *My Patron and your Patron have decided we should be together.*

But he had to say something. He cleared his throat. "Uh, Shanna, this is Hari, and I've—"

"One moment," her image told him, and it swiftly morphed into a new view of her, in her rich blue and steel gray Overworld costume, the one she wore as Pallas Ril. "Congratulations! You've made my Friends File."

Friends? he thought. *Is that what we are?*

"Being in the Friends File means I can tell you that I'm currently on Adventure, and I expect to be back on the evening of November 18. Don't expect a return call before then, and you won't be disappointed."

Hari sagged, defeated. He'd forgotten; today's avalanche of memory had buried it entirely. She'd left for the latest installment of her ongoing Adventure a week ago. He canceled the call with a weary slap against the wallstud. She wasn't on Earth. She wasn't even in the same universe.

My life, he thought, *is a short dive into deep shit.*

6

THE SQUEAL FROM his wallscreen stabbed him like a knife in the ear. He started upright, head spinning. He'd been drinking into the late hours of the morning, sitting alone in his empty house, and now his eyes were crusted shut and he couldn't make sense of that shrieking. He rubbed his eyes until the lids parted with a dull ripping sensation that brought the taste of blood to the back of his throat, and the brilliant sunlight that streamed in through his bedroom window threatened to burst his skull.

What the fuck time is it? Noon?

"Abbey," he croaked thickly. "Polarizers. Twilight."

"Please rephrase your command, Hari."

He cleared his throat and spat a wad of phlegm into the disposall under the nightstand. "Abbey: Polarize the windows. Twilight."

As the room gradually darkened around him, he raised his voice so he could hear himself over the shriek. "Abbey: Query. What is that fucking noise?"

"Please re—"

"Yeah, yeah. Abbey: Delete word *fucking*. Retry."

"That noise is your priority alarm, Hari. It indicates a screencall coded *Extremely Urgent*."

"Abbey: Query. Which code?"

"It is the code labeled *King Bleeding Studio Asshole*, Hari."

"Shit." He shook the cobwebs out of his head. *King Bleeding Studio Asshole* was the label of the code he'd given to Gayle Keller, the personal assistant of the Chairman of the San Francisco Studio, Arturo Kollberg. It meant this was bad news. "Abbey: Audio only. Answer."

The shrieking suddenly cut to creamy silence. Hari said, "Yeah, Gayle. This is Hari."

"Entertainer Michaelson?" The Chairman's secretary sounded uncertain; like most people, he was uncomfortable talking to someone he couldn't see. "Uh, Administrator Kollberg wants you in his office ASAP, Entertainer."

"In his *office*?" Hari repeated stupidly. Kollberg never saw people in his office. Hari hadn't been in the Chairman's office in ten years. "What's this about? My next Adventure isn't until after the first of the year."

"I, ah, don't really know, Entertainer. The Administrator wouldn't say. He only told me that if you asked, I should tell you it's about your wife."

"My wife?" *What* isn't *about my wife?* he thought sourly, but that was only his hangover talking. "What is it? Did something happen?" His heart thumped once, heavily, and kicked into a faster beat. "Is she all right? What happened?"

"I can't really say, Entertainer Michaelson. All he said is to tell you—"

"Yeah yeah yeah," Hari snapped. He swung his legs out of bed and stood up, and suddenly he didn't feel hungover at all. How fast could he shower and dress? No, fuck showering; he had no time. Brush his teeth? See the Chairman with stale scotch on his breath? *Shit, pull it together.* "I'm on my way. Tell him half an hour. Tell him . . . just tell him I'm on my way."

DAY ONE

"Hey, I'm not the only guy who kills people."

"Nobody said you're the only one, Hari. That's not the point."

"I'll tell you what the point is. The point is: that's how I became a star. The point is: that's how I pay for this house, and the cars, and get us a table at Por L'Oeil. That's how I pay for everything!"

"It's not you who pays for it, Hari. It's Toa-Phelathon. His wife. His daughters. Thousands of wives, husbands, parents, children. They're the ones who pay for it."

1

"HIS NAME IS, ah, Ma'elKoth," said Administrator Kollberg. He licked his thick, colorless lips and went on. "We, ah, believe this to be a pseudonym."

Hari stood stiffly before the Chairman's massive desk. Inside his head he snarled, *Of course it's a pseud, you moron.* Out loud, he said, " *'elKoth'* is a word in Paquli that means 'huge,' or 'limitless,' and the *Ma* prefix stands for the nominative case of *to be*. It's not a name, it's a boast."—*and if you weren't a fucking idiot you'd know it.*

None of his commentary showed on his face; years of practice kept his expression attentively blank.

The wide, rectangular Sony repeater behind the Chairman's desk showed a view that roughly corresponded to what a window would have shown—the late-autumn sun sinking toward the bay—had this vaultlike office not been buried deeply beneath the Studio complex.

This inner office was a sanctum that few ever saw; in the eleven years that Kollberg had been Chairman, even Hari—San Francisco's number one star and perennial member of the Studio Top Ten in earnings worldwide—had been in here only once before. It was small, with curving walls and ceiling, and no sharp corners; climate control kept it nearly cool and dry enough that Kollberg wouldn't sweat—but not quite.

The Chairman of the San Francisco Studio was short and sloppy, not fat so much as soft and thick. Pale grey strands of hair strung themselves across a scalp pitted with the scars of failed transplants, and his watery eyes were surrounded by rolls of flesh the color and consistency of spoiled bread dough.

Hari had seen flesh like that once before, when Caine had liberated some human slaves of an ogrillo tribe in the Gods' Teeth. The ogrilloi had been breeding them as cattle, underground in their stinking lair; there were teenage boys there who had never seen the sun—and they'd been gelded to keep their meat juicy and sweet. Their skin had looked very much indeed like Kollberg's.

If Hari let himself think about it too much, it could give him a serious case of the shudders.

Kollberg's star had risen along with Caine's; he'd gotten behind Hari when Hari had pitched the Adventure that later became known as *Last Stand at Ceraeno*. That was Caine's big break, and Kollberg's—with *Last Stand*, Caine cracked the Top Ten, and Kollberg was the Chairman who had put him there. Since that time, Kollberg's almost preternatural sense for the rhythms of public taste had driven San Francisco to its current world prominence; he was popularly considered to be the heir apparent to Businessman Westfield Turner, the Studio President and CEO. Kollberg, more than any person save only Hari himself, was responsible for Caine's success.

Hari despised him with the sort of personal loathing most people reserve for cockroaches in their breakfast cereal.

Kollberg had been babbling on about this Ma'elKoth, who called himself the Ankhanan Emperor. "You might pay a little attention to this, Michaelson," Kollberg was saying. "After all, you put him on the throne."

This was vintage Kollberg: the clammy bastard might waste an hour building up to the real reason he'd summoned Hari. On his way in, Hari had tried the usual downcaste whispering gallery, casually questioning doormen, security, secretaries—even that smug worm Gayle Keller. Nobody knew anything about Shanna; whatever had happened, the Studio lid was screwed down tight. Kollberg hadn't so much as mentioned her name. Hari's palms burned with a suicidal lust to beat it out of him.

"First," he said tightly, "I didn't put Ma'elKoth on the throne. He did that for himself."

"After you murdered his predecessor."

Hari shrugged; he'd had his fill of that subject already this week. "And second, I don't do assassinations anymore."

Kollberg blinked. "I'm sorry?"

"I. Don't. Do. Assassinations. Anymore." Hari articulated every word slowly and clearly, skating on the dangerous brink of caste-violating insolence. "I'll only do straight Adventures, like *Retreat from the Boedecken*."

Those heavy lips pressed together. "You'll do this one."

"Are you a betting man, 'Strator?"

Kollberg's chuckle was as moist as his watery eyes. "Quite, ah, impressive, this Ma'elKoth is—military sorcerer, fine general. Here, look at this."

The repeater behind his desk flickered and relit with a computer-stabilized view through some anonymous Actor's eyes. Hari knew the scene: it was the travertine-faced address deck, three stories up the sheer wall of the Temple of Prorithun, shining in the rich yellow glare of the Ankhanan sun. The Actor who'd viewed this had stood with his back to the Fountain—from the angle, he must have been practically leaning on the statue of Toa-Phelathon—and it was clear from the lower fringe of the view that the Court of the Gods was packed shoulder-to-shoulder with folk of all description.

The man who stood on that deck and exhorted the crowd dwarfed the Household Knights who flanked him; he was as tall as their blood-colored halberds. The fist he shook in anger could have crushed coal to diamonds.

He wore some sort of armor that gleamed with the black semi-translucency of obsidian, and to his shoulders was fixed a cape of pure and gleaming white that spread behind him like the wings of an eagle. Hair the color of burled maple curled across his shoulders and rippled in some unfelt breeze, and a beard shot through with bars of iron grey and shimmering with oil framed a face wide-browed and clear-eyed, a face of obvious honesty and translucent nobility.

Even without the sound, Hari couldn't look away. When Ma'el-Koth's brow clouded in anger, it seemed that the sky did as well;

when he looked down with love upon his subjects, his face brought light to them like the first dawn of spring.

Someone there was subtly manipulating the sunlight, Hari realized; a good illusionist can do it, even over a substantial area like this, but making it look as natural as this did—

Hari grunted, impressed despite himself. "He's good at this."

"Oh, yes," Kollberg said. "Yes, indeed he is. He's also, ah, rather frighteningly brilliant."

"Yeah?"

"It seems, well . . ." Kollberg coughed into his hand. "It seems that he's independently rediscovered the police state."

"Good for him," Hari murmured absently, still watching. He'd glimpsed Ma'elKoth once or twice before, on victory parades after the stunning campaign that had won the Plains War, but he'd never seen the man in action. There was something vaguely familiar about him now, though, about the way he moved, the way he gestured. This would bug him until he worked it out, a little finger poking at the back of his mind.

Where had he seen these mannerisms before?

". . . an *internal* enemy," Kollberg was saying. "The Nazis had the Jews; the Communists used the 'counterrevolutionaries'; we have the HRVP virus. Ma'elKoth has hit upon, ah, a rather novel internal enemy. When he needs an excuse to eliminate political enemies, he, ah, well, he accuses them of being 'of the *Aktiri*.' "

Aktiri was a Westerling word having a number of pejorative meanings: insane, evil, homicidal, alien baby-eater, and endless variations on that theme. *Aktiri* are evil demons who take the form of men and women to deceive honest folk into trusting them so that they can rape and steal and murder with mad abandon; when slain they vanish in a burst of shimmering colors.

The word was a linguistic borrowing from English. The early Actors, making the transfers to Overworld in the cruder, more direct Studio style of thirty years ago, had left a lasting impression on the culture.

"A witch-hunt."

"Aktir-tokar," Kollberg corrected. "An Actor hunt."

"Not bad," Hari said. He touched the spot on his skull, just above and in front of his left ear, over his brain's language center. "The only way to prove you're innocent is to let them dig around in your brain until they decide they won't find a thoughtmitter. By that time you're dead anyway. Then if your corpse doesn't slip out of phase, I guess they apologize." He shrugged. "Old news. The Studio's put out a couple circulars on updated Ankhanan protocols. I'm still not going to kill him for you."

"Michaelson—Hari, please understand. It's not only that he's actually caught some Actors—no one very successful, at least not yet— but that he's using the *Aktir-tokar* in a rather decidedly cynical fashion, to eliminate his political opposition, folk that he knows quite well are entirely . . . ah, well, *innocent.*"

"You're talking to the wrong Michaelson," Hari said. "You want my wife."

Kollberg put a chubby finger to his lips. "Ah, well, your *wife*, . . . mm, in her capacity as Pallas Ril, she's already taken a certain interest in this problem."

Just hearing her name finally come out of Kollberg's mouth felt like someone had slipped a needle into the back of his neck. "Yeah, I heard," he said softly, through his teeth. "She's been doing her Scarlet Pimpernel act."

"I feel I must make this entirely clear, Hari. Here at the Studio, we must look to the long term. This *Aktir-tokar* business will blow over soon enough, and the Ankhanan Empire will be safe for Actors once again. Entirely *too* safe, if you see my meaning. If the Empire were to become truly organized, they would certainly put down the ogrilloi and the human bandits, and kill the dragons and trolls and griffins, possibly the elves and dwarves and all the other things that make Adventuring entertaining in the first place. Do you see? If Ma'elKoth is successful, the Empire will be essentially lost to us as an Adventuring environment. Already, Ankhana itself is hardly more exotic than, say, New York. This, ah, *trend* cannot be allowed to continue. The Studio System—and this Studio in particular—has far too much invested in the Ankhanan Empire. Fortunately, this Ma'elKoth has gathered most of the reins of power to himself; you could call it a classic cult-of-personality thing. If he is eliminated, the Empire should balkanize in a very satisfactory way."

"Shanna's heated up about this; why don't you have her do it?"

"Oh, come now," Kollberg murmured. "She's a save-the-innocents type; you said so yourself. You know very well that Pallas Ril doesn't do assassinations."

"Neither does Caine. Not anymore."

"Michaelson—"

"If you have a problem with that," Hari said heavily, "you can take it up with Biz'man Vilo."

The mention of Hari's powerful Patron didn't make Kollberg so much as blink. In fact, it brought a faint smile to his rubbery lips. "I don't believe that will be necessary."

"Believe what you want, Administrator," Hari said. "And you still haven't explained what this has to do with my wife."

"Haven't I?" He rose and clapped his hands together, rubbing them against each other with a mock-regretful sigh. "Perhaps you'd better come with me."

2

THE 270-DEGREE FLOOR-TO-CEILING screen that faced the simichair in the Chairman's private box showed only a uniform grey when Kollberg led Hari inside. *Another first,* Hari thought, scuffing his sandals across the burgundy cashmere of the deep-pile carpet.

The Chairman's simichair was done in walnut and kidskin, filled with bodyform gel and more comfortable than your mother's arms. Reach-around swingarms held a bewildering variety of refreshments—from beluga on toast points to Roderer Cristal on tap—for those occasions when the Adventure feed was directed to the screen, rather than the induction helmet that hung over the back like the cap on an electric chair.

Kollberg directed Hari to the chair with a butler's one-hand sweep and said, "Don't bother with the comfort hookups; this cube only runs twelve minutes. And there'll be no hypnotics. I, ah, assume that you can tolerate direct induction without any chemical suppression?"

Hari shrugged. "I've done it before."

"Fine, then. Please be seated."

"Are you gonna tell me what this is about?"

"This cube is, ah, self-explanatory," Kollberg said, his mouth twitching as though he tried to suppress a smirk. "Please," he repeated, and it was not a request.

Hari lowered himself into the simichair in the grip of a dizzying sense of unreality. He'd never even seen the Chairman's private box before; now he was sitting in the Chairman's personal simichair. This was tantamount to putting on the man's underwear.

He reached behind his head to grasp the helmet and found that it was already moving into place. The shields covered his eyes, and he snugged the regulator over his nose and mouth, breathing deeply of its tasteless, neutral air supply.

He brushed the arms of the chair with his palms, searching for the tuning switches, but the Chairman's simichair already had begun the process. Light flared inside his closed eyes as the induction helmet stimulated his brain's vision center; the shapeless blurs within the light slowly resolved into simple shapes: lines, squares, circles, gradually gaining depth and solidity as the helmet's feedback circuits monitored the flow-patterns of his brain activity and adjusted the inducers to fit his individual characteristics.

Similarly, the simple bell tone that began faintly in his ears split into chiming melodies that gradually developed into Bach's *Jesu, Joy of Man's Desiring*. The melodies expanded into shimmering chords, added instruments and voices, became the chorale of Beethoven's Ninth; before his eyes was the late-summer view from atop Copper Mountain in the Rockies. He felt the crisp breeze on his skin, felt the rough texture of a hemp rope coiled over his shoulder and the pressure of boots, smelled the scent of the tiny yellow and white wildflowers and the faint musk of the marmots that live in homes on the mountain.

At the same time, he was aware of the kinesthesia of being seated in Kollberg's simichair. While adjusting the induction feed, an ordinary chair would have also been dripping chemical suppressors into his bloodstream, hypnotic medications that would have dampened his sense of self and opened his mind to pure experience, unfiltered by his own consciousness. The Chairman's chair was not equipped with a hypnotics feed; he couldn't afford the luxury of being someone else so completely that his own responsibilities were forgotten.

The Rocky Mountains faded into a slow cross-dissolve with a scene already in progress.

Sight came first, a room flooded with sunlight that is warmer and yellower than the sun of Earth. Coarse wool blankets over palliasses prickly with straw, and huddled on them a man and a woman who cling to each other, two young girls beside them, all four wearing what look like beekeeper's nets of some dull-gleaming metal.

Scents and sounds followed; smells of distant horseshit baking in the sun and bodies sweating under armor, the shouts of drovers in tangled traffic and the splash of nearby water, voices—

"*. . . why? I cannot understand, I have always been loyal,*" the man was saying in Westerling, the predominant tongue of the Empire. "*You must understand how frightened we all are.*"

The simichair was connected to the Studio mainframe, which ran an AI translation protocol on it so that the sense of the words registered in English. Hari didn't need it; he spoke fluent Westerling, as well as Paquli and Lipkan and smatterings of several other tongues, and the AI's translation differed just enough from his automatic comprehension to be distracting.

He ground his teeth and concentrated on the kinesthetics of the Actor he rode.

Slim, not muscular, but very fit; body armor of light, flexible leather, cape, bracers, boots; perfect and constant awareness of body position, like that of a dancer or an acrobat—no codpiece on the armor, nor need of one, none of the male's instinctive and permanent consciousness of external genitals.

Hari thought, *It's a woman,* even as he became aware of the pressure on his/her breasts, tightly constrained by the armor.

And the package came together: his awareness of the precise curve from breast to hip, the slight tilt of the head to shift the hair away from the eyes, the rotation of one shoulder in her unmistakable shrug. Before she ever spoke, before he heard her voice through her own ears, he knew.

"*We're all frightened. But I swear that we can save you, if you'll help.*"

It was Shanna.

3

"OF COURSE I'LL help," he snaps. "Think you I want my wife and daughters given to the Cats?" His wife flinches; the two girls don't, but they're probably not old enough to understand what that means.

"Not at all," I tell him through my best smile. It's a good one; he's already softening. "Konnos, there's no need for you to explain anything if you don't wish to, but I'm wondering how you got this far. You were denounced four days ago; how have you avoided capture? Anything you feel you can tell me might help me save others. Do you see?"

I fold my legs beneath me to sit on the splintery floor. Konnos casts nervous glances at the others in the room, and I follow his eyes. "You trust me—you've trusted me enough to send for me; I trust these men. The Twins"—a matched pair of brawny youths, golden haired, with eyes much older than their faces, stolidly sharpening identical broadswords—"escaped from the gladiatorial pens; you can believe they have no love for Imperials. Talann, here"—a woman, legs folded in lotus on the floor, muscular under loose linen tunic and pants, her eyes a manic violet glitter within a ragged halo of platinum hair—"there's an Imperial price of a hundred royals on her head. As for Lamorak there by the window, well, you've probably heard of him already."

Lamorak? Hari thought with an uncomfortable twinge of surprise. Lamorak was an Actor. *Son of a bitch! I knew Karl and Shanna were friends, but . . . Jesus. How deep does this go?*

Lamorak mutters a short phrase under his breath, and I feel the pull of his magick as a small flame springs from the palm of his hand; he draws it up to the rith-leaf cigarette between his lips, and soon the sharp scent of burning herb drifts over from the window. **He's showing off,** Shanna's subvocalized Soliloquy runs, **he should know better than to do a magick here, even a tiny one that probably can't be felt outside this room.**

The Soliloquy—the tiny motions of tongue and throat that the translation protocol transformed into quasi-thoughtlike internal monologue—would ordinarily fade behind the screen of hypnotics that would drip into the bloodstream of a first-hander until it became indistinguishable from actual thought; without the hypnotics, the Soliloquy was nearly as distracting as the AI's imperfect translation of Westerling. Pallas'—Shanna's—voice whispered constantly in his ears. Hari shifted in the chair, gritted his teeth, and reminded himself that this cube only ran twelve minutes. For that long, he could stand anything.

Lamorak winks and turns back to watch the street, one hand on the leather-wrapped hand-and-a-half hilt of his sword Kosall. Sunglow backlights his perfect profile with a golden halo, and as usual I can't quite get mad at him; it's an effort to turn my attention back to Konnos.

"I'm not political," Konnos says, pulling the netting away from his face so that he can mop his mouth with the back of his hand. "I never have been. I'm a scientist, that's all. I've spent my life in research into the fundamental nature of magick—the nature of reality, because, y'know, they're the same thing. This netting? Silver, you see? Silver is a nearly perfect channel for magickal force—gold is better, but I'm only a poor researcher; whatever gold which found its way to my purse always went to feed my family. But, you see, nearly all charged amulets, floating needles, pendulary indicators—all that run of seeking items—detect a characteristic pattern of essence that emanates from their targets: the Shell you adepts like to talk about. These items are charged, after all, by contact with our homes or personal items that would resonate in our own unique pattern. This silver net turns our patterns in upon themselves, making us effectively invisible to items of this sort, and it also serves as an admirable defense against compulsions. In fact, if one can connect the net itself to a Flow source, such as a griffinstone . . ."

He keeps babbling, but his words fade behind my admiration for the elegance of his defense. *He's invented a variant of a Faraday cage; that means he's been doing some pretty basic scientific-method-style research. Natives aren't supposed to be able to look deeper than the immediate magickal surface of an effect. Our social scientists have been saying for years that the operation of magick stunts the "scientific sense." By that theory, he should only be able to think of blocking a spell with another spell, instead of taking advantage of a general principle underlying a whole branch of magick. Hah. I'm impressed.*

And I'm going to get myself a few of those silver nets.

". . . of course without the griffinstone they're hardly proof against a determined effort by a powerful thaumaturge," Konnos continues, "but for that eventuality I have this little friend, right here." He pats the knob of a polished ivory scroll case that pokes out from a pouch on his belt. "I wrote it myself; I call it the Eternal Forgetting. It's the most powerful nondetection spell ever devised, but very much a last-resort kind of thing—"

"Let's hope you don't need it," I cut him off. We might not have time for another lengthy explanation. "Now, I must ask you to remove the netting. Only temporarily," I add hastily, when he gasps a wordless protest. "The King's Eyes try to send spies to us from time to time—"

"I am no spy! Would a spy bring wife and daughters with him to do his work?"

"No, no, no. You don't understand. I know that you are a good and honest man," I lie gracefully. "That's not the issue. But there are enchantments that can be put on a man to make him betray himself against his will, and there are others that may call out to a searching mind to reveal a place of hiding. I must examine you now, to ensure that none of these have been laid upon you without your knowledge. Others, who are hunted just as you are, also wait where I am taking you, in a place that I have made proof against all kinds of seeking magick. It is they that I protect by examining you, as well as ourselves."

Konnos looks at his wife, she looks back at him fearfully, and before either can speak Lamorak says from the window, "Trouble."

I'm at his side in an instant; behind me come faint rustlings as Talann and the Twins rise and prepare themselves.

The sun-washed street outside looks utterly normal, crowded with ramshackle tenements, its center still churned mud from the rains two days ago. Traffic is light, mostly on foot, day laborers picking across the rotting boardwalks toward a chance of work in the Industrial Park across Rogues' Way.

I frown; what's wrong with this picture? I'm about to ask Lamorak what he sees when I realize that it's what he *doesn't* see that alarms him: our stooges are missing.

The alley mouth half a block down that should have sheltered a sleepy drunk yawns emptily; the stoop where a ragged leper should have been sunning himself sports a wetly gleaming splotch of blood.

My heart stutters. This is bad.

"How?" I say numbly. "How is this possible? How could they get so *close*?"

No need to say who they are; we both know it's the Grey Cats.

Lamorak shakes his head and mutters, "Some kind of spell; I don't know. I didn't see a damned thing."

"But I should have felt a current in the Flow . . ."

"We knew this could happen someday," he says, taking my shoulders and gently turning me toward him. He looks down into my eyes with that glorious crooked smile. "We knew when we took this job that we couldn't beat the odds forever. Maybe I can lead them away, give you a chance to get Konnos and his family out."

"Lamorak—"

"No arguments," he says, and stops my mouth with his lips.

The kiss stabbed Hari like a knife in the balls—not just that Pallas let him kiss her, not just that she liked it. She wasn't surprised, and she wasn't tentative, and this wasn't even nearly the first time.

Hari thought in sudden toneless blankness, *Lamorak's been fucking my wife*.

Shanna's audience—all her first-handers, every person who would ever rent the secondhand cube—they'd all know it. They'd all experience it.

Hari's heart smoked within his chest.

I push him away gently; his reflexive heroism catches at my breath, even though it's futile—I'm not ready to sacrifice him uselessly. We'll save heroism for a last resort. I turn to the others.

"It's the Cats," I tell them shortly, brutally. Konnos and his wife clutch each other, and one of the girls begins to cry; she sees how frightened her parents are, and she doesn't need to know more than that. "They've taken our stooges. That means we're already surrounded and they're closing in for the kill. I'm open to any brilliant ideas."

The Twins exchange an identically grim glance; they shrug and one of them—probably Dak, he does most of the talking—says, "We can hold the room—fight them off until the Subjects of Cant can mass against them."

I shake my head. "The Subjects aren't ready to come open. And with the stooges gone, they don't even know we're in here. Talann?"

She stretches like a cat and pops the knuckles of both hands in swift succession. Her eyes spark with an uneasily familiar fire. "What would Caine do?"

I wince. "He wouldn't ask stupid questions," I snap.

Talann the groupie—at least half the reason she's with me is she hopes she'll meet Caine someday. Somehow his shadow still darkens my life. Now I know why I recognize that spark in her eye—it's the look Caine used to get when we were cornered, when the thread of our lives spun through our fingers. It's the closest he ever came to being happy.

On the other hand, I do know what Caine would do: attack. Crash their line, somewhere in tight quarters where they couldn't use their crossbows. Smash through and run like hell—but that would be almost certain death for Konnos and his family, and protecting them would slow us until we couldn't protect ourselves. I glance at Lamorak, at the noble resolution on his face as he waits for my answer. Sure as death, Caine wouldn't sacrifice himself in a gesture like Lamorak proposed—but Caine also wouldn't stand there and wait for me to give him permission.

They're all looking at me. For an empty second I wish that someone else would make this decision.

"All right," I say heavily. "The Twins and I can hold this room. Lamorak, head east."

"Over the rooftops?"

I shake my head. "Through the tenements. Kosall can cut through. Talann, go south into the river. If you get clear, either of you, head for the Brass Stadium and tell the—"

"Oh, crap," Lamorak breathes. He's looking out the window again. "I think . . . Gods, that could be *Berne*."

"Count Berne?" Talann says, her eyes on fire. "Himself?"

I crowd close to Lamorak and follow his gaze and there he is, leaning insolently against a grey-weathered wall across the street, holding a flame to a hand-rolled cigarette.

The recorded chill that Hari felt shooting down Pallas' back at the sight vanished in the surging fury that blazed up his own spine. *Berne.* His hands knotted into convulsive fists, and he cracked his wrist painfully against the simichair's swingarm. *Berne, you vicious shit-sack bastard, if I was there . . . Oh gods, oh gods, why can't I be there?*

It's Berne, all right; I recognize him instantly. He's not wearing his Court rags, the slashed-velvet blouse and leggings he's made fashionable again. Instead, he's in scuffed and faded heavy serge that once was scarlet but now has the patchy strawberry-cream shade of a half-washed bloodstain. His slender, gently curved sword hangs in its scabbard from a handsbreadth leather belt. The planes of his face are so sharp they should gleam like metal in the sun, and now his toothy grin cracks them like a mirror.

My heart plummets; I know him too well. Worse: he knows me.

It's wrong, I shouldn't feel this way . . . but right now I really wish that Caine were here.

"Change of plan," I say quickly, turning back toward my friends, the faces that ride the lives for which I am responsible. "Lamorak, you and Talann take the Konnosi—" I point at the south wall of the tiny apartment. "—that way, and down. Stay off the stairs and out of the corridors. The Twins and I will rearguard the retreat."

Lamorak stiffens. "Pallas—"

"Do it!"

He still hesitates for one naked second, and his eyes speak poetry to mine.

Then he draws Kosall, grasping it by its quillions and clearing the blade from its scabbard before activating its magick by taking the hilt, and the enchanted blade comes to life, its high buzzing whine making my teeth ache. Its edges waver like heatshimmer off a sun-baked sidewalk, and I can feel its pull on the currents of Flow.

Lamorak stands at the south wall and puts Kosall's point to the wall at head height; he leans on the pommel, and Kosall slides smoothly through the planks, its whine dulled to a hum. He draws the blade downward in an arc, not sawing, just pressing it through the wood as though the wall were soft cheese. With this sword he can cut his way through the tenements all the way to the river, if need be; Kosall can cut stone, or even steel, given enough time.

Time is what I have to provide.

Below us, Berne gestures.

Men in the dove grey leather jerkins and breeches of the Cats stream from alleys and sprint toward our tenement.

I take a deep breath, let it trickle out from my lips, and take another; my hands flit over my clothing of their own will, from pocket to pouch, from scabbard to sheath, checking all of my graven gems and intricately worked knots of precious metals, my wands and my wires, bits of glass and packets of powders, while my breath-control technique shifts my vision to mindview.

In mindview, Berne's Shell—the shimmering aura of life power that surrounds him—is as large and eyeburning-bright as an archmage's, and I fight down a rising panic that would throw me out of mindview.

This isn't *possible*; Berne's a warrior, not an adept, he's a Monastic-trained swordsman—*he has no magick*. He never did! But now—

Now, through the tangled ribbons of multicolored light that represent Flow in my mindview, I see another ribbon, a shaft of power bigger in diameter than my doubled fists. It neither twists nor tangles as do those of the raw Flow, and its color is the pure crimson of hot steel in a forge. It bathes Berne's Shell, and it runs straight as a spear from him to the southwest. It vanishes into a tenement there, but mere brick and wood is no impediment to Flow, and I know what's in that direction. That shaft of power aims toward Old Town, the island in the Great Chambaygen that is the heart of Ankhana.

That shaft of power springs from the Colhari Palace.

This son of a bitch is *channeling*. Never mind that it's impossible—he's channeling from bloody *Ma'elKoth*! That explains the magickal

Cloak that let him invisibly take our stooges without my feeling the pull of the spell: the power for the spell comes from a mile away, and it doesn't draw local Flow at all. As all this runs through my mind I fail to notice Berne stretch his hands up toward my window until it's almost too late.

I throw myself back from the window. The entire wall explodes with a splintering roar and a wash of fire. Even as I sprawl on the floor and cover my eyes against the flames, my other hand seeks out the miniature shield modeled of faceted quartz in my breast pocket. My hand tingles with the charge it carries, and mindview shows me the lattice of glowing lines enchanted onto its surface. I force that image into my consciousness, visualize it so powerfully that I can actually see it filling the yawning gap that was once the wall.

Sunlight streams through the ragged hole, and flames lick its edges; the ceiling sags, cracking now that the wall's support is gone, and on the rooftop across the street, ten Cats swing cocked crossbows up over the lip of the roof and fire on me.

Their quarrels sing across the street and stop where the wall once was, quivering as though they'd struck wood, though the only thing that holds them hanging suspended is my imaginary Shield, which fills the hole. Four Cats swing down on ropes from the roof of the building—it's a beautifully executed maneuver that would have brought them gracefully through the hole into the apartment. Instead they hit my Shield and bounce, though their impact feeds back enough to make me grunt like I've been gut-punched.

The Shield looks in mindview like a decimeter-thick matrix of golden force; to them it's a wall of semisubstantial glass with the texture of vulcanized rubber. Flow streams through the quartz model. There's plenty of power here, and I can hold this Shield as long as I can keep the visualization going. The Cats hanging from their ropes outside kick off the Shield to hit it again, and again it hurts.

At least Berne can't channel another of those firebolts without frying the Cats outside; I take my time getting to my feet, concentrating on holding the Shield.

Over my shoulder, through the arch Lamorak cut in the wall, I can see Talann lowering the younger of Konnos' daughters through a similar hole in the floor. She clenches her fist in the catspaw "We're okay" sign and beckons for us to follow, then leaps lightly down through the hole.

The Twins have been using the planks Lamorak cut from the wall to angle-brace the hallway door—a dagger pounded into the floor foots the planks, and the tops are wedged beneath the handle. This might slow the Cats for a few seconds, but no more. "Come on, move it move it *move it!*" I yell. I'm going to have to give up the room, retreat through the cut, and shift the Shield from the outer wall breach to the cutaway arch, because I can't hold the breach and the door at the same time.

As the Twins pound the last plank into place, the door and the wall around it explode into smoking splinters and blow them sprawling across the room. The room fills with choking sulphurous gas, and through the hole, from the corridor beyond, pour the Cats.

They come in fighting.

The jerkins they wear are reinforced with wire, but that is their only armor; their acrobatic mobility and stunning speed are their defenses. They're at their best in small groups on open ground; that's why I've chosen our battlefield in the most constricted quarters I could find. It may not be enough.

Berne's bell-toned tenor comes from the corridor outside. "Get the adept! I want him alive!"

Both Twins are bleeding as they struggle to get up. The lead Cat dives at them and pays for it—Jak has his broadsword out, and he spears the Cat through the throat. The Cat's impact lays Jak on his back again, and Dak has to cover him from one knee. Then I see no more because I have problems of my own.

A pair of Cats spring for me. I drop the Shield—four more won't matter, in this crush—and draw the finger-length boltwand from my left wrist sheath. I barely have time to trigger it with a caress of my Shell before they're on me. A lance of light springs from the end and spears through a knee of one of the leaping Cats. He goes down in a heap, but the other hits me like a charging bull and slams me against the wall.

He slaps the wand out of my hand with the flat of his blade and gives me the pommel hard upside the head. I roll with it enough to escape a skull fracture, but fireworks shower across my eyes. He pins me against the wall with his off shoulder and holds the point of his blade against my throat and snarls, "Now, y'cunt traitor, whatter y'gonna do?"

He's justified in his confidence; most adepts are helpless in hand-to-hand range, and I'm a small, slender woman who clearly is no physical threat. On the other hand, when you've spent a couple years married to the man who's popularly considered to be the best infighter alive, you pick up a bit here and there.

I bite my tongue, and saliva floods my mouth. I take a deep breath, and spit in his eyes.

He blinks, that's all—but it's enough. In that bare instant while his eyes close and open again, I lift a foot, put the edge of my boot on top of his kneecap, and stomp down. Ligaments tear as the kneecap shifts. The pain is stunning, and while he's deciding whether to scream first and then stab me or the other way around, I twist out from under his shoulder and dart away; he won't be able to follow.

The Twins are up and back-to-back; they're breathing hard and bleeding, but five Cats lie draining their lives onto the floor around them. Dak and Jak grew up in the gladiatorial pens, they've been fighting as a team since they were six years old: in this kind of crushing close-quarters fight they're unbeatable.

But now the Cats are backing away from the breach in the outer wall, leaving the Twins exposed to the crossbowmen across the street—and now the Cats notice that their companion doesn't hold me anymore.

It's a second's work to return to mindview; their Shells shimmer around them, and the drifting lace of Flow fills the room. My hands find a tiny pinwheel, only the size of a copper coin, in a pouch that hangs from my belt; it's layered of platinum and gold, and the sigils I enchanted onto it glow with the green of new leaves. The pattern fills my consciousness as I bring the pinwheel to my lips and blow.

The pattern expands outward from my eyes to layer my Shell, then it reaches to the shattered planks and splinters that litter the floor, their tiny faded Shells reflecting the life that once flowed through them. It takes me only a second to link the pinwheel's forcepattern to the faded Shells of the planks, to forge a sympathetic identity between them and the pinwheel's vanes. The planks lift off the floor, and when I blow on the pinwheel again, the planks spin.

They spin *fast*.

They spin like propellers, like buzzsaws; I wave the pinwheel through the air, keeping it spinning faster and faster, and the planks match its speed. The link to the pinwheel will keep them spinning; now I can use my own Shell control to direct their flight.

I send them whirling into the Cats. The whining roar of the wood mingles with the Cats' cries of pain and dismay; the larger planks hammer with crushing force, and even the tiniest splinters draw blood.

"*Retreat,* you idiots! Fall *back*!" Berne barks from the safety of the corridor. The Cats scramble for the gaping hole where the door once was, and I send half the wood roaring after them. The other half I send whirling toward the opposite roof, to cover the Twins' retreat from the crossbowmen, and for half a wild, exhilarated second I start to believe we might actually get away.

The crossbows' flat whacks are barely audible through the roar of the spinning wood. Only two quarrels make it through the cloud of wood into the apartment—but one of them slams into Dak's shin. These quarrels mass roughly two hundred-fifty grams of solid forged steel, and they hit like a sledgehammer; Dak's shin shatters, and he goes down with a cry, clawing at his brother's shoulders. Jak turns to take his arm and carry him, and that's when Berne dives into the room like a bloodstained thunderbolt.

His dive becomes an acrobatic roll, and he comes to his feet with his sword in his hands. I frantically reverse the direction of the flying wood, but long before I can bring it back into play, Berne spins and his blade opens a gaping wound across the nape of Dak's neck before the wounded Twin even knows Berne's in the room. Dak's head flops forward, spraying blood across his brother's face, and Jak howls like a damned thing, trying to drop his brother and bring up his sword at the same time. Berne's already reversed his blade for an over-the-elbow backstrike, and he drives its chisel point through Jak's open mouth and out the back of his head.

In just over a second, he's killed two of the best swordsmen in the Empire.

He says, "Shield. Personal."

As my roaring wood finally spins into him, a globe of semisubstantial glass has already surrounded him. The wood batters uselessly against it.

"You'll have to do better than that," he says. Within the globe, he whips his blade in a short arc that sprays blood, and smiles.

I don't answer; instead I send the wood flying out into the corridor among the Cats, then I smash the pinwheel into the wall at my side, exploding the planks into what I hope is a blinding cloud of splinters and sawdust. Outside, the Cats respond with a satisfying chorus of shouts.

Berne looks at me, frowning, then his face clears. "Pallas!" he says with a broad grin of recognition. "It *is* you! Pallas Ril, fuck me if it isn't! Does this mean that *Caine's* with you? No, no, I don't need to ask. If he was, he'd be at your side like a loyal puppy."

I back away, through the cut into the next room, as he paces toward me.

"Does this mean you're on your *own*? Is it . . . is it *you*? You're Simon Jester? *You?* The Infamous Simon Jester, the Elusive Thorn in the Paw of the Ankhanan Lion, is Pallas fucking *Ril*. Fuck me like a goat."

He licks his lips. "I've *dreamed*," he says, his voice becoming thick and wet, "of meeting you again. I have *plans* for you, Pallas. Who knows? You might even like them. If you like them enough, you might live through them."

I hold my tongue and keep backing slowly away; the longer Berne talks here, the farther away get Lamorak, Talann, and the Konnosi.

His grin spreads even more. "It might actually be fun to keep you alive. That way you can tell Caine all about what I did to you."

I shake my head. "That's pretty weak, Berne. Caine and I—we had a parting of the ways. He doesn't care what happens to me."

He nods judiciously. "All right. I'll just please myself, then."

"After you catch me." I follow the words with breath control, shifting back to mindview as my fingers fumble for the drawstring of a pouch at my belt.

He snorts. "I've caught you already."

The polished buckeye that comes into my hand starts to trail smoke and pulls a huge swirling cloud of Flow as my patterned concentration triggers the enchantment. Berne sees the smoke and gives me a pitying look. "You don't have to be smart to be a pretty good thaumaturge, but I can't believe you're stupid enough to think you can hurt me. This Shield is powered by *Ma'elKoth*, you stupid cunt. Nothing you've got can get through it."

By way of answer, I flick the buckeye at his feet as though I'm shooting a marble. I can't resist a cheesy line, Caine style, because my adrenaline's high and I still don't quite believe that I will die here.

"See you in the fall," I tell him, and then jump down through the hole at my back as the buckeye erupts into a ball of fire that shatters the floor and blows Berne, Shield and all, out through the breach in the wall.

We're only on the third floor; it won't kill him, but the three-story drop to the street might break a bone or two and shake him up some. And the hole in the floor should slow the Cats a little. I hope.

I land in the apartment below, and pause just long enough to catch a whimper coming from under a bed in the corner. Some poor guy got awakened out of a sound sleep by fire and explosions and people cutting through his roof. I shrug; he's as safe under his bed as anywhere else in this building.

Following through three cutaway walls, it takes only seconds to catch up with the others. Lamorak's working on the brick wall that adjoins this tenement to the next one south, but it's slow going; sweat darkens the end of his ponytail. Talann, covering their backs, nods to me. "Where are the Twins?"

"Dead." I turn back toward the hole I came through and pull another carved shield of quartz out of a pocket.

"Dead?" Talann sounds stunned. "Both of them?"

I don't answer her until I have another Shield in place to seal this hole; even as the Shield resolves into existence the Cats are dropping through the ceiling in the farthest room and pelting toward us with swords in hand.

"Yes," I tell her. "They bought us this time. Let's not waste it."

Both of Konnos' daughters cling to their mother and sob soundlessly. Konnos shakes his head, stricken. "I should have given myself up. I should have surrendered. I've brought this upon all of us."

"Shut up," I tell him. "We're still alive, and we're going to get you out of this. All of you. Lamorak—how long?"

Cords bulge in his neck as he forces Kosall through the brick to the bottom of one side of the arc. "Thirty seconds," he says, hoarse with strain.

"Make it fifteen. This is my last Shield, and I don't know if I can hold it against Berne."

Cats pound booted feet and blades against my Shield, and feedback makes me dizzy. A splintering crash comes from the outer room of this apartment: the Cats have found the hall door.

Talann draws a pair of long knives and salutes me, wearing a manic grin. "I believe they're calling my name."

"Talann—" I begin, but she's already gone into the outer room. It's not for nothing that she idolizes Caine: in battle she becomes a berserk chainsaw of feet and fists and blades, and the shouts of alarm and pain from the room beyond confirm that the Cats weren't ready for her. I find myself praying that she kills a lot of them before they bring her down.

Lamorak pulls Kosall out of the bricks and kicks the center of the arc. It falls away into a cloud of dust, and he helps the Konnosi through the gap. He takes my arm and pulls me close. "No more cutting—you can run straight down the corridor, through to the alley that curves to the river. Go."

"Lamorak, they'll kill you—"

He shrugs. "It's me, or it's you. You can get the Konnosi away by yourself. I might not." He taps the cut brick with Kosall. "And this is a gap I can hold for a long, long time. If you get to the Subjects, send a rescue."

As I start to protest, a blazing wash of flame punches through my Shield, and pain scatters ragged patches of black across my vision.

Berne is coming.

My knees buckle, and Lamorak pushes me through the gap. He says, "Please believe that I never wanted it to turn out this way. I'm sorry, Pallas. And this is where I pay for it."

"Pay? Lamorak—"

But his back is to me, and his shoulders fill the cutaway arch, and Kosall sings as it shears through steel and bone. "Go!"

Konnos and his wife—I'm struck by a sudden absurd embarrassment that I don't even know her name—wait for me to lead them. "Pick up the girls," I say. "Now we have to run."

They each gather up one of their daughters and fall in behind me as I race through the apartment and out into the mercifully empty hallway. It's long and straight and lined with doors. The window at the end gleams with golden sunlight like the promise of salvation. We run like hell.

From the window, I look down into the alley below.

It's full of Cats.

There must be ten of them at least, two groups of five closing off the visible ends of the alley. Ten Cats, and I don't have anyone left to fight them with.

Konnos catches the look on my face. "What? What is it? They're *out* there, oh great gods, they are."

"Not dead yet." I reach into a pocket on the inside of my tunic and pull out a silver key. It takes only a second to summon mind-view and pattern my mind to the glowing sigils. I stick the key into the lock of the nearest door, and the lock snaps open sharply. I pull everyone inside.

It's a two-room, and it's empty, thank all gods.

"All right," I say. "We've got a few seconds to figure out what to do next. As long as I do no magick, no one will detect us in here; they'll have to open every door."

"Can't you . . . can't you," Konnos' wife stammers, speaking for the first time. "Can't you turn us all invisible, or something?"

"Don't be a ninny," Konnos says severely. "A Cloak cannot work when there's no other magic being done around it. Any device and quite a few people can feel its pull on the Flow."

"But maybe," I say, "maybe a Cloak in conjunction with a powerful *nondetection* . . ."

His eyes widen.

"Give me that scroll of yours."

"But, but—"

Booted feet batter the floor of the hallway outside. That means Lamorak has already fallen. The realization stops my breath, and tears begin to well up in my eyes; the burning knife that this drives into my chest hurts so much that I can't think.

I shake the tears violently off my face. I'll have time to cry for him later, if I live long enough.

I reach out and tangle my hand in Konnos' tunic and jerk his face close to mine. "Give it."

Without waiting for his answer, I yank the scroll case from his belt. I give him a shove, and he stumbles back while I unscrew the bone knob and shake the scroll out into my hand.

"But, I'm not sure this is—"

"You have a better idea?" I unroll the buttery lambskin of the scroll; the markings on it are painted in ink of gold, and they instantly burn their way into my brain. I barely have time to summon mindview and open my Shell before the eldritch chanting begins to spill automatically from my lips. The words ring in the air, and then there was no more light, no more sound, no more Pallas; there was only Hari Michaelson sitting in Chairman Kollberg's simichair with sweat pouring from his hairline. The eye shield was blank before his staring, and all he could hear was the harsh rasp of his breathing and the trip-hammer slam of his heart against his ribs.

4

IT SEEMED LIKE minutes that he sat rigid and sweating, convulsively digging his fingers into the leather of the simichair's arms. He couldn't think, he couldn't make himself move to shift the eye shield, he couldn't swallow past the giant hand that squeezed the breath from his chest.

"That's, mm, all we have." Kollberg's voice came from somewhere outside Hari's universe.

This must be what panic feels like, Hari thought disconnectedly. *Yeah, that's it: this is panic.*

The induction helmet lifted away, and Hari had nothing to look at in front of him except Kollberg's moonface with its rubber-lipped smirk.

"It's, um, pretty, pretty *intense*, isn't it?"

Hari let his eyes drift closed. The longer he looked at that smug bastard's face, the closer he came to felony forcible contact. Kollberg was an Administrator; while forcible contact with an upcaste man was no longer a capital crime, it still carried a mandatory downcaste to Labor and five years' commitment to a public camp. When he was sure he had control of his voice, he said, "Is she alive?"

"No one knows. The end of that cube marks our last contact. We have no telemetry, nor do we detect her transponder signature. We, mm, we believe that this scroll, the spell on it, severed the thought-mitter link."

Hari pressed his fingertips against his eyelids and watched the phosphenes explode showers of sparks across his vision. "How long does she have?"

"Assuming she's still alive—"

"How long?"

Kollberg's voice became chilly. "Don't interrupt me, Michaelson. Mind your place."

Hari opened his eyes and leaned forward in the chair. Kollberg stood before him and waited. The invisible hand that crushed Hari's chest tightened its grip until it nearly strangled his voice. "I apologize, Administrator."

Kollberg sniffed. "All right, then. So: this sequence, that you have just second-handed, this occurred near ten hundred Ankhanan time this morning. The energy cell in her thoughtmitter carries sufficient charge to maintain amplitude match for one hundred seventy hours, give or take ten. At the very least, she has one hundred fifty-seven hours remaining. If she presents herself at a fixed transfer point before then, well and good. Otherwise . . ." He let his voice trail away.

Hari sat motionless, his mind flooded by horrific visions. Amplitude decay is every Actor's nightmare. Young Actors in training at the Studio Conservatory are shown a series of holos of what is left of Actors who slip out of phase with Overworld; usually all that returns is a bubbling mass of undifferentiated protoplasm, or a twisted array of half-crystalline splinters, or something entirely indescribable—and those are the good ones, the easy ones, the ones that don't hurt you to remember.

Once in a while, you can recognize one as having once been human.

Hari asked quietly, "Does she even know she's off-line?"

Kollberg's rounded shoulders lifted in an eloquent shrug. "Frankly, Michaelson, she's most likely dead."

"Get me there. I know that city. I can find her." *Or her body.* Hari forced the thought away by promising himself that if her body was what he found, he would also find Berne. *Let's see you channel, you fuck. Let's see you channel with my fingers jammed through your eye sockets.*

"I beg your pardon?" Kollberg's eyebrows twitched upward, and his whiny\schoolyard-hectoring tone brought Hari back from his bloody fantasy. "I, ah, don't think I heard you correctly. And I think you should get up from my seat, now."

Hari lowered his head and reminded himself that Kollberg held Shanna's life in those soft corpse-pale hands. He slowly pushed himself up out of the Chairman's simichair and stood, head still lowered with eyes downcast. He put as much sincerity into his voice as he could shove past the fire in his chest.

"Please, Administrator. Can we make some deal? Please send me to Ankhana."

"That's better. That's, ah, that's what I've been hoping you'd say. Come with me to the Contract Center."

5

HARI AND KOLLBERG nearly filled the soundproof plexi cubicle in the middle of the Contract Center. Seated outside on tall stools were a pair of Studio Attorneys who were also registered witnesses. Kollberg fidgeted and played with his notepad while Hari slowly scrolled through the contract. In other cubicles scattered through the room, lesser Actors scanned standard contracts in the company of other lawyers.

The contract spelled out Caine's obligations in the euphemistic terms of "colorfully and suspensefully attempt to remove the current Ankhanan Emperor from power." Even in its most privileged and secret documents, the Studio never openly ordered an Actor to kill.

Hari looked up from the screen. "This doesn't say anything about Shanna at all."

"Of course not," Kollberg said easily. "You want to go to Ankhana. We want Ma'elKoth eliminated; I've already explained why. It's a very straightforward proposition."

"If you're so hot to have him killed, why don't you just transfer six guys with assault rifles into the Colhari Palace?"

"We, er . . ." Kollberg coughed wetly into his fist. "We tried that; except it was eight, not six. We, ah, still don't know precisely what happened."

Hari looked at him, blinked, blinked again, then said, "Oh," and turned back to the contract.

"Yes, well, after that incident, Ma'elKoth has, mm, done something to the palace. We don't know what, exactly, but it seems to prevent our scans. Within the palace grounds, we're completely blind and deaf. Any Actors who get past the gate are cut off until they leave."

"I see." Hari leaned his elbows on the desk and lowered his face into his hands. "Before I sign this, I want more information."

"Certainly everything pertinent will be in your faxpack."

"I mean, for example, what happened to Lamorak? Is Karl dead?"

Kollberg lifted his notepad and tapped a query onto its screen. He read its response with pursed lips and said, "We're not sure. On the basis of Pallas' cube, we assume he was killed."

"How can you not be *sure*? Did that fucking spell cut *him* off too? Can it do that?"

"As to the effects of this spell," Kollberg said, "there's no way to know. I've queried Archives, and they have no record of a spell with this effect. That, ah, Konnos fellow, his claim of having originated that spell must be accepted as genuine. We don't know the operation of this spell; all we can really say is that it seems to be, ah, singularly powerful. But, mm, that's nothing to do with Lamorak. He was never on-line."

"I don't understand."

"It's a, ah, pilot program of my own devising. I call it the Long Form. Lamorak is on freemod."

Kollberg rose and began to pace the two steps back and forth he could take within the cubicle. "Lamorak—Entertainer Shanks—his career hasn't developed to the satisfaction of his Patron. He volunteered for this Long Form program. Instead of having first-handers coexperiencing his Adventures in real time, and thus restricting his Adventure to the usual ten-day average, he's had a prototype thoughtmitter implanted that contains a microcube and a graver; it will record his experiences for up to two months, at which time he'll transfer back to Earth. The cube will then be edited into a standard second-hander format. This will allow for a much more extended story-arc, and—"

"This is *insane*," Hari said. "You're telling me that nobody knows whether either one of them is even *alive*? Good *Christ*, Administrator!"

Kollberg nodded agreement. "Yes, I know, it's terrible. The real pity is that Pallas' Adventures have been relatively dull lately—her Simon Jester operation, smuggling fugitives out of the Empire, has been entirely too easy. As soon as it starts to become interesting, *this* happens. Terrible."

"Simon Jester," Hari murmured. A pounding headache built between his temples. Simon Jester was an imaginary revolutionary in a banned twentieth-century novel. Hari had secret copies of a number of banned books, and he'd introduced Shanna to the guilty pleasures of reading the works of unpersons like Heinlein. Those books were banned for a damned good reason—shit, for all he knew, it might have been Heinlein's libertarian propaganda that started Shanna on this antiauthority fling. If he'd never given her *The Moon Is a Harsh Mistress*, would she still have set herself against the Imperial Government?

Cut it out, he told himself. Things were bad enough already; he didn't need to invent ways to make it all his fault.

He pressed his knuckles against his throbbing temples and said, "So, we know nothing. There's nothing you can tell me."

"I can tell you this," Kollberg said, standing over him. "If you want to find out anything, if you want to help your wife, if you want to go to Ankhana at all, you'll have to contract to eliminate Ma'elKoth."

"What makes you think I even *can*? Administrator, a special ops team with assault rifles couldn't handle him; what am *I* supposed to do?" Hari said desperately.

"I have infinite faith in your, ah, *resourcefulness*."

"This isn't like going after Toa-Phelathon—have you *seen* the cube you just showed me? The kind of power Ma'elKoth must have . . . I mean, all I can really do is hit people. How am I supposed to counter that kind of magick?"

"But you *do* have power," Kollberg replied smugly. "*Star* power."

He sounded like he actually believed Caine could do anything, as long as he stayed in the Top Ten.

"Administrator—" Hari fought for words that wouldn't come out hot, for a tone that wouldn't trigger Kollberg's petty casteism. "Why? Why can't I contract to find Pallas and Lamorak and bring them out? Why can't I go for Ma'elKoth after she's safe?" The plaintive weakness in his voice nauseated him, but there was no help for it.

"For one," Kollberg said mildly, "I don't think you *would* go after him, once they are safe. But more than that, don't you see the kind of *story* this makes? Do you have any idea of the kind of audience you'll command, going to Ankhana without knowing if your beloved is alive or dead, but sworn to slay her enemies or die trying? Do you have enough romance in your soul to understand how this will *play*?"

"My beloved?" Hari shook his head. "You haven't been keeping up with the netleads on my personal life."

"None of that *matters*, don't you see?" Tiny white flecks of foam showed at the corners of the Chairman's lips, and his hands clutched words from the air; there was a vibrancy in his voice that Hari had never heard before.

"You don't understand what your life looks like from the outside. Street-raised Labor boy from the Frisco slums, rising to the pinnacle of the Studio . . . you're a vicious and hardened killer whose heart is finally softened by a refined Tradesfolk debutante with a spine of steel. It's perfection; I couldn't *pray* for a better story. Whatever problems you two have are only *obstacles*, from the public's view. Everyone knows you'll live happily ever after."

"If she's not already dead," Hari muttered. The words came out effortlessly; it was remarkably easy to twist the knife in his own belly.

"That would be, mm—" Kollberg pursed his lips and chose the word with precision "—*tragedy*. But it wouldn't hurt the story. My god, Hari, this could be bigger than *Retreat from the Boedecken*—love, murder, politics . . . and *Berne*."

Kollberg leaned close and lowered his voice to a reverential hush. "Hari, this may be bigger than *Last Stand at Ceraeno* . . ."

Hari looked into Kollberg's moist, bulging eyes and knew that there was nothing he could say, nothing he could do, no leverage he could use except to appeal to whatever stunted sense of decency the Chairman had left.

"If I do this," he said slowly, "if I commit to taking Ma'elKoth, I want a commitment from the Studio, from *you personally*, that the Studio will flood Ankhana with Actors. That you'll use every resource to find her and bring her out. Please, Administrator?"

Kollberg appeared to think it over. He stretched his mouth downward and mopped sweat from his upper lip with two fingers, then shook his head. "No. No, I don't like it. It's a better story if everything depends on you."

"Administrator—"

"No. It's final. Sign the contract or go home. Your choice."

Blood hammered at Hari's headache. His vision misted red, and his hand trembled as he brought the pen to the screen. *What choice is there?* Even if he'd wanted to refuse, he couldn't; Pallas' voice kept repeating in his head:

"He doesn't care what happens to me."

Did she believe that? Could she? He kept thinking of Lamorak holding the gap in the wall with steel and guts. He wanted to believe that he would have done the same, or better—that he would have gotten her to safety without sacrificing himself. But it wouldn't have been the same: put his life, and Shanna's, at risk for some native family he didn't even know? Not fucking likely.

Caine would have thrown the Konnosi to the Cats without one second's thought.

But when I thumbprint this contract, I'll be stepping into that doorway right beside Lamorak.

Kill Ma'elKoth or die trying; the third outcome—to fail and live, or not really to try—would be a contract violation that could have consequences Hari couldn't even bear to think about.

I knew what kind of ride this was before I sat down, he thought, and: *Will she hurt as much for me as she did for him?*

He signed his name on the winking line and held his thumb against the DNA scanner.

"Ah, good," Kollberg said with deep satisfaction. "The net releases are already prepared, and you'll be the lead story on *Adventure Update* tonight. Visit Media on your way out and pick up your interview kit; we'll put you on *DragonTales* with LeShaun Kinnison, and you'd best be prepared. Plan on transfer at oh eight hundred tomorrow."

"*Tomorrow?* But—" *But that's eighteen hours,* he thought. Eighteen out of Shanna's precious reserve. Almost a whole day lost.

"Of course tomorrow," Kollberg said briskly. "Even with the worldwide publicity blitz we're preparing, it'll take at least that long to pull enough audience to cover expenses. And you are expected to attend the reception for the subscribers. No need to be on time; let some anticipation build. Shall we say twenty-one thirty tonight? In the Diamond Ballroom, of course."

Hari held himself motionless. *If I lose her . . . If I lose her because of this, because of you, you will be entered on a short list.*

A very short list. Right under Berne.

He said quietly, "Yes, Administrator. I'll be there."

6

THE SOBBING MOANS from beyond the double door slanted up into shrieks of agony with the relentless regularity of the waves of an incoming tide.

His Grace the Honorable Toa-Sytell, Imperial Duke of Public Order, sat forward on the edge of a comfortable chair across the anteroom, elbows on knees and fingers laced together, and looked at the newly created Count Berne with bland contempt. He tried to ignore the screams that came from the room beyond; had he not found a scapegoat, those screams could well have been his own.

Toa-Sytell examined Berne, from his thick brush of platinum hair to the bloodstained leather of his soft calf-high boots, and tried to imagine what he must be thinking now, as the pair of them waited outside the Iron Room for the judgment of Ma'elKoth. Count Berne stood at the beautifully glazed window that filled the wall of the anteroom and chewed at his thumbnail as he stared out over Ankhana.

The Duke had an intensely detailed and vivid imagination, but of a very literal sort; he had trained himself not to indulge in fantasy. He could imagine very clearly what Berne saw out that window.

From this vantage point high in the Dusk Tower of the Colhari Palace, the financial district on the western tip of the island of Old Town would lie spread below like one of Ma'elKoth's models—baroque and decorative, backlit blazing red by the setting sun. Nearing twilight, the sun would now strike fire from the slow boil of the Great Chambaygen, hiding the garbage and filth of human waste that Ankhana poured into it, and would gild the immense anti-ship nets of heavy chain that stretched from the northwest and southwest garrisons across the channels of the river to Onetower at the westernmost tip of the island. Bonfires on the Commons' Beach south of Alientown would be flickering like stars on a clear night, welcoming the throngs of subhuman and semihuman workmen and beggars and street vendors that would be crowding across Knights' Bridge to beat the curfew. Only purebloods were allowed on the central island after sundown.

Toa-Sytell suspected that Berne's thoughts tended toward the east, where a similar flood crossed Fools' Bridge onto Rogues' Way between the Warrens and the Industrial Park. Those with money would be turning left to their grimy tenements nestled between the manufactories; those without would be turning right to take their chances on the streets of the Warrens.

It was in the Warrens that Simon Jester had once again slipped through their fingers, and neither of them yet understood how.

Muscles bulged at the corners of Berne's jaw, and he clutched the scabbard of his sword until his knuckles popped. Toa-Sytell hadn't seen Berne wear this particular sword before. It was longer than Berne's usual style, and broader as well, and he wore it across his back with its hilt jutting above his left shoulder. Berne's usual quality of boneless relaxation was conspicuously absent; Toa-Sytell guessed that the Count was actually frightened. This was unsurprising, and Toa-Sytell didn't fault him for it. They both had sufficient reason for fear.

Berne still wore the bloodstained clothes he'd worn all day, through this dusty and exhausting and finally futile search. The blood that had dried in a ragged splotch across his chest belonged mostly to that gladiator brat whose neck he'd sliced in the tenement, although some of it had leaked from wounds his Cats had suffered.

None of it was his own, more's the pity.

"I don't like to be stared at." Berne had never turned from the window, and his normally petulant tone held a thin edge of danger.

Toa-Sytell shrugged. "Sorry," he said tonelessly.

"Keep your eyes to yourself, if you want to keep them in your face."

Toa-Sytell smiled thinly. "I've apologized already."

Berne now came away from the window, and his pale eyes burned. "You apologize too easily, you spineless cocksucker."

"You're ahead of yourself," Toa-Sytell murmured. His eyes held Berne's, while his fingers unobtrusively caressed the hilt of the poisoned stiletto that he wore in a sheath strapped to his wrist beneath his sleeve. "Perhaps if Ma'elKoth judges against me, he'll give me to you. Until then, have a care with your words, catamite."

His colorless tone, as much as the words themselves, brought rising purple to Berne's face. Toa-Sytell was fairly sure that he couldn't survive an attack from the Count; before his ennoblement a few months ago, Berne had been a notorious freebooter whose swordsmanship was legendary. On the other hand, with his fingers on the stiletto, he was fairly sure that Berne wouldn't survive it either.

Some of this assurance must have shown on his face, for Berne chose not to pursue the discussion. He spat on the pale limestone floor at the Duke's feet and stalked back to the window.

Toa-Sytell shrugged, and continued to stare.

The screams built toward a climax.

Toa-Sytell was a man of average size and average appearance, with one of those blandly regular faces that one forgets a moment after looking away; only the keen brain behind his forgettable eyes was extraordinary. He had been in service to the King's Eyes for twenty-three years, in that time rising from an apprentice shadow-pad to the apex of the organization. Born with the common name Sytell, he had been privileged to take the prefix after he was ennobled by the late Prince-Regent Toa-Phelathon. In the yearlong chaos of civil war that followed the murders of the Prince-Regent and the Child Queen, he had survived by making himself equally indispensable to all sides, never seeking power himself but gathering resources and men into the agency he led.

He alone of the Council of Dukes had survived Ma'elKoth's coup with life and power intact; the new Emperor had been already well aware of Toa-Sytell's value. It was, in fact, at Toa-Sytell's advice that Ma'elKoth had taken the title *Emperor*: the restless and quarrelsome nobility would never have tolerated a King who bore no trace of royal blood, but an Emperor was a different matter. Perhaps Emperors were *always* commoners who ruled by fiat, backed by a loyal military; who could say different? Ankhana had no Imperial traditions—the nation had, after all, *become* an empire largely through Ma'elKoth's astonishing successes as Toa-Phelathon's most trusted general.

This transparent rationalization could be used by the nobles to satisfy their liegemen. They didn't have to believe it themselves; their own cooperation was ensured by the diligence of the King's Eyes.

Under Toa-Sytell's leadership, the King's Eyes had grown from a simple gang of spies and informers to a full-fledged secret police with nearly unlimited discretionary powers. Rare was the Duke, Count, or even provincial Baron who would dare to whisper treason, even to his own wife in the privacy of their bedchamber; the King's Eyes could see, so it was said, even through the thickest stone.

But the mere knowledge of treason was never sufficient to quash it. The nobility had traditionally woven tangled nets of alliances and blood bonds to protect themselves from the power of the Oaken Throne; to attack any single one would invite full-scale civil war. These alliances had made the nobles untouchable until Ma'elKoth devised his most brilliant stratagem: the *Aktir-tokar*.

A Baron who whispered against the Imperial Government now might well find himself denounced as an *Aktir*. Certainly, the unfortunate fellow's allies would know that the charge was fraudulent, but that knowledge bought them nothing. The Empirewide *Aktir-tokar* had spawned such a frenzy of suspicion and fear that any noble who openly supported a denounced man would face sudden hot rebellion from his peasants, and not a few of his arms-bearing liegemen. One by one, the nobles fell, slowly, in a carefully calculated progression; soon, only those nobles who supported Ma'elKoth would remain, along with the dregs of their fellows, too cowed to give the Emperor so much as a sidelong look.

Toa-Sytell was not concerned only with the upper reaches of Ankhanan society; he also directed the Imperial Constabulary and was on his way to running the criminal elements of the Empire as well. He had already unobtrusively assumed control of the most powerful of the Warrengangs and had his men busily infiltrating the rest. The King's Eyes were spread throughout the Empire; they reported only to Toa-Sytell and took only his orders. He could almost certainly have controlled the Empire himself, in secret; he did not. His ambitions did not tend in that direction.

The bloody sun sank into the horizon, smearing crimson across Berne's too-pretty face.

The screams within the Iron Room faded with the light; as the giant brass bell in the Temple of Prorithun tolled the curfew, the sobbing from behind the door was buried under a new voice, a dark and savage throbbing that Toa-Sytell could feel vibrating in his guts; the words meant nothing, but the mere depth of the tone was like a finger that jabbed into the notch of his collarbone. Toa-Sytell shuddered and made no attempt to listen.

There was only one man alive that Toa-Sytell feared; but the beings that Ma'elKoth trafficked with, behind that door, were not men. Nor were they, strictly, alive.

That voice became difficult to ignore in the silence of the antechamber. Toa-Sytell rubbed his forearms, to make the hairs on them lie down once again, and spoke mainly from a desire to fill the quiet. "One of the prisoners—Lamorak—he's been asking for you," he said.

Berne snorted. "I should think so."

"Oh?" Toa-Sytell said mildly. "Why is that?" Berne suddenly coughed into his fist and turned his face away from the Duke. Toa-Sytell waited for him to elaborate, watching him with the unblinking patience of a snake coiled at the mouth of a rabbit hole.

The silence, underscored by the voices from the adjoining room, stretched thin. Berne coughed again. "Well, I have his sword, don't I?"

"Do you?"

Berne drew the blade smoothly over his shoulder. Its edges shimmered in the crimson twilight, and a whining hum came clearly to Toa-Sytell's ears. "The enchanted blade Kosall—you've heard of it?"

"No."

"Well, it is. Enchanted, I mean. It's packed to the eyeballs with magick." He held it slanted at garde to admire it in the fading light. "Cuts through anything. Huh, he nearly killed me with it. He dropped two of my boys, and when I came against him myself his first stroke sheared my blade in two, a handbreadth above the guard."

"How did you take him?"

"I grabbed this blade with both hands, and held it while I kicked his lamps out." Berne smiled with adolescent smugness and flexed his fists before him like a stretching cat. He opened his unmarked palms and turned them toward Toa-Sytell as though to say, *See? It cuts through everything—except me.* "Being Ma'elKoth's favorite comes with bonuses."

"But this is no answer," Toa-Sytell said. "I questioned him, and the other, for hours. Why would he insist that he will speak only to you?"

"Maybe it's because I beat him," Berne suggested with a shrug. "A point of honor, between *men*. You wouldn't understand."

"I see," Toa-Sytell said blandly. "It's clear enough that there is certainly something here that I do not understand. Yet."

Berne only smirked and whirled the enchanted blade through a complex arc that ended with it once again within its scabbard. He went back to the window.

The distant-thunder rumbling of the savage voice faded after a time, and there came an explosive *pop*, like a giant's handclap. Ma'elKoth's negotiations were complete.

Berne came hesitantly to the inner door, a great black slab of cold-worked iron. On that door hung a massive ring forged in the ancient symbol of the serpent devouring its tail. To lift and drop it would be a simple thing, a second's work that would produce a resonant clang, but Berne's hand, reaching for it, trembled like an old man's. He swiftly shot a glance over his shoulder, to see if Toa-Sytell had noticed.

Toa-Sytell allowed himself another smile.

A swirling wind came from the center of the closed anteroom as though someone had opened the window where Berne had stood, as though the calm night outside had become a gale. The wind pushed the great door smoothly open with a hollow rushing sound like a distant waterfall.

"Berne. Toa-Sytell."

The Emperor's voice was richer and more resonant than the temple bell that had recently rung the curfew. Toa-Sytell never thought to wonder how Ma'elKoth had known they were out here: Ma'elKoth always knew.

"Join me, my loving nobles."

Toa-Sytell exchanged a glance with the Count he despised—a sudden kinship of apprehension between them—then together they crossed the threshold.

The Iron Room, in which they now stood, had been built more

than a century before, early in the reign of Til-Menelethis the Golden, the last Ankhanan king to dabble in sorcery. The windowless interior of the room was plated with interleaved sheets of hammered black iron, the joints worked with binding runes of silver. Silver runes ringed the doorway and the only two places where the palace's stonework was exposed: the matching mystic circles, one at the center of the floor and the other on the ceiling above.

The room had been sealed by order of the Council of Dukes in regency for Til-Menelethis' heir after that unfortunate experimenter descended into wailing madness; the Wards had been set by the legendary Manawythann Greyeyes, and had stood inviolate against all attempts until broken by Ma'elKoth himself.

In the northern quadrant of the mystic circle, the naked body of a middle-aged man lay across the altar of native limestone, now greyed with soot and crusted with ancient brown blood. Toa-Sytell knew this man, knew him well, had eaten with this man's wife and had patted his children's heads; he didn't allow himself to think of his name.

An intricate web of wetly pulsing ropes stretched upward above the man's torso to hang suspended from a treelike metal rack, the arms of which ended in silver hooks that were driven through the ropes . . . But the ropes, they weren't ropes: ropes aren't slick with blood, and they don't twitch with the rhythm of a slowly beating heart.

In a single dizzying instant, Toa-Sytell's vision seemed to come finally into focus as he understood what he saw: these ropes were the still-living guts of the man on the altar, withdrawn through a gaping slice below his navel and hung from these silver hooks like chitterlings in a smokehouse. Toa-Sytell's stomach twisted, and he risked a sidelong glance to see Berne's reaction.

Berne had leaned forward and to the side, craning his neck for a better view.

The Emperor stood within the mystic circle, bare to the waist like a wrestler, his hands dripping blood to the elbow. Ma'elKoth's eyes were as black as a clouded sky at midnight, and they glittered with indifferent perfection, neither warmth nor chill. He nodded toward the low sofa against one wall, and his voice seemed to rumble from the roots of mountains. "Sit, while I cleanse my hands."

They did, and they both watched as the Emperor went to one of the lazily smoking braziers that provided both reddish light and a juniper-oil scent that nearly covered the sulphurous fecal tang that always hung in the air within this room. Ma'elKoth stared at the brazier, without word or gesture, and yellow flame now leaped crackling from it to the height of his head. He thrust his hands within it, and the flame turned brilliant green around them; the blood on his hands caked, charred, and flaked away.

The Emperor Ma'elKoth, Shield of Prorithun, Lord of Ankhana, Protector of Kirisch-Nar, Lion of the Northern Waste and a host of other titles, was the largest man Toa-Sytell had ever seen. Even Berne, tall by ordinary standards, barely reached Ma'elKoth's stiffly waxed beard. His spreading curls of chestnut hair gleamed rich red in the light of the flame before him and draped across shoulders like the rock of the Shattered Cliffs.

The Emperor worked his hands within the flame. His biceps bulged like barrels, and the massive swelling muscles across his chest might have been carved of individual stones and joined together like a puzzle. His growing grin showed perfect teeth as the blood crackled from his fingers. The flames faded away from his hands, and he brushed them together briskly, scraping away the last of the burned blood. When he looked down upon his seated nobles, his eyes now shone with the deep blue of a late-summer sky.

The Emperor was the one man that Toa-Sytell feared.

"Do not trouble to report," Ma'elKoth said. "I have tasks for you both."

"You, ah . . ." Berne said, straightening, coughing harshly to clear his throat. "We're not going to be punished?"

His brows drew together. "Should you be punished? How have you betrayed Me?"

"I, I ah." He coughed again. "I haven't, but—"

"But Simon Jester once again escaped," Ma'elKoth said equably. He stepped out of the mystic circle and over to the sofa, where he crouched before Berne and put a hand on his shoulder like a father gently correcting his young son.

"Berne, do you know Me so poorly? Am I a maniac, to punish men for My own failure? Was I not with you at every moment? I do not yet know what this Simon Jester did, what magick it is that still dances within us all. If I can neither break nor avoid this power, how should I punish you for that same inability?"

Berne looked up, and Toa-Sytell was astonished to see on his face an almost pathetic eagerness to please. "I only . . . I didn't want to disappoint you."

"And that is why you are My favorite Child," Ma'elKoth said warmly. "Here, scoot, both of you. Let Me sit between you."

Toa-Sytell hastily shifted to the end of the sofa. This was part of why he feared Ma'elKoth: the man was as changeable as a summer storm. One moment he could terrify you with a mere glance from the mountaintop of his regal majesty; in the next he might sit familiarly beside you like a boyhood friend on the stoop of your house.

"It is My lust that has undone Me," Ma'elKoth said, leaning forward onto his knees. "I have made this Colhari Palace proof against all magicks that are not of My own making. In the crucible of My desire to capture Simon Jester, I forged the knife that now trembles within my belly. It was the channel that joined us, Berne, that was the fatal chink through which Simon Jester's dart has stabbed Me. The Power that I summoned this eve—to ask what can be done to break this magick—laughed. It laughed at Me! It said the magick is easily broken, once I lay hands upon its caster."

Ma'elKoth shook his head slowly, with an inward-looking smile as though deeply amused at this irony. "Can you feel it? Berne, you met Simon Jester face-to-face—what did he look like?"

Berne shook his head miserably. "I don't remember. I have tried . . . I think I may have even recognized him."

"I know you did," Ma'elKoth rumbled. "Since this morn I have worked to deduce who Simon Jester must be, based on what I know of whom you know. It cannot be done; each time an inkling comes, I feel the pull of that cursed magick and the inkling is driven off. I have even tried to use the spell against itself, working through the alphabet for initials, for names at random, and waiting to see which trigger the pull—and I find myself, again and again, staring at a sheet full of letters with no memory of which pulled and which did not. Were I a man given to fury, I would find it infuriating."

"But you seem, Imperial Majesty," Toa-Sytell said delicately, "almost pleased."

The smile that Ma'elKoth turned on him held an irresistible heat; despite the Duke's apprehension, the smile warmed him to his core. "But I am! This is *new*, Toa-Sytell. And a challenge. Do you have any conception how rare it is for Me to be surprised? To be frustrated? This Simon Jester is the most *interesting* opponent I have faced since the Plains War. He's outfoxed my entire pack of hounds; the solution to such a problem is, of course, to find a better hound."

"Better?" Berne said, frowning.

Ma'elKoth smiled and engulfed Berne's shoulders with a titanic arm. "Do not take the metaphor personally, dear boy. I apologize for the misspeech; I should have said, one more suited for this particular task."

"And that would be?" Berne said sullenly.

"Come. I will show you."

Ma'elKoth rose and entered the mystic circle. Toa-Sytell joined him instantly, but Berne hesitated, looking at the man who lay stretched across the altar. "He, uh, he looks familiar."

Ma'elKoth said, "He is. Duke Toa-Sytell, you may explain."

Toa-Sytell took a deep breath and looked away. "His name is Jaybie. I think you've met him once or twice. He was a captain in the Eyes." Toa-Sytell studiously avoided looking at Jaybie's slow rise and fall of breath, at the heartbeat that could be seen in the woven net of his intestines. "He is the man who tipped the artificer, Konnos, that he'd been denounced."

"Indeed," Ma'elKoth murmured indulgently. "And so I turned his treachery to a useful purpose: the Outside Powers with which I deal usually arrive hungry. I should be a poor host if I did not offer at least a . . . snack, shall we say?"

Berne nodded his understanding. "He's still alive?"

"Only his body," Ma'elKoth rumbled. "Now come."

Once Berne joined them within the circle, Ma'elKoth laid a hand on each man's shoulder and lifted his eyes to the bare limestone of the ceiling. In no more time than it takes to draw a breath and release it again, the solidity of the stone misted and faded to a ghost of itself. Through the stone itself Toa-Sytell could see the roll of oncoming clouds and the first strengthening stars of night.

An instant later, the floor fell away beneath his feet and the three of them rose in effortless silence through the ceiling. The stone beneath them regained its substance, and the three men now stood on the very parapet of the Dusk Tower.

This was another reason that Toa-Sytell feared Ma'elKoth; it was not only the stunning range of his power, but that he could summon it without a word, without a gesture, with no more than a thought. Toa-Sytell knew enough of magick to appreciate the level of concentration required for the simplest operation; even the finest adept could do only one spell at a time. Most depend on enchanted items to supplement their abilities. Not so Ma'elKoth; on him there seemed to be no limit.

It was not the cool of the night breeze that made Toa-Sytell shiver.

Ankhana lay spread below them like a carpet of jewels, from tiny diamond chips of lamps to blazing ruby bonfires. The freshening breeze carried snatches of song from alehouses and cries of newspages as they trailed back to their offices for evening accounting, the savor of meat stewing with onion and garlic, and the wild clean scent of the grassland that stretched to the sea.

Clouds built in the west and rolled majestically toward the city as the moon breasted the Gods' Teeth range far to the east.

Ma'elKoth spread his arms wide and threw back his head. He lifted his voice above the rising wind. "I asked of the Power to show Me who can pluck this thorn from My flesh, to show Me the man who can rid the Empire of this seditious Simon Jester. It dug its answer from the depths of My own mind—I had known this, without knowing that I knew. Now we ask the wind, and see it written on the clouds!"

He pointed at the wall of approaching thunderheads. "Look there, and see the face of My hound!"

Toa-Sytell followed the Emperor's finger with his eyes, anticipating an image to appear on the cloud where Ma'elKoth pointed, like a drawing on parchment. The thunderheads rolled and boiled, swelling and pulsing as though they themselves lived, as though they were slaves cringing under the lash, and again Toa-Sytell felt that disorienting blur in his vision, that dizzying alteration of perspective as he realized that there would be no image on the cloud.

The cloud was itself the image.

Under the relentless knife of the Emperor's will, the thunderhead that towered above the rest writhed and carved itself into the face of a man—a face larger than a mountain, framed with a fringe of beard and short-cropped hair. Its mouth was contorted into a snarl of fury, and lightning flickered within its eyes.

Berne breathed, "Fuck me like a virgin goat . . ."

Toa-Sytell coughed and said in a thin voice, "You couldn't have drawn a picture?"

Ma'elKoth laughed like a drunken god. "Power unused is not power, Toa-Sytell. Beautiful, isn't it?"

"It's, ah, yes," Toa-Sytell said. "It's beautiful." He could only stare in awe.

Berne said harshly, "It's *Caine*."

"Oh, yes," Ma'elKoth rumbled with bone-deep satisfaction. "Oh yes, it is indeed. He shall be in Ankhana tomorrow morning."

"Caine the assassin?" Toa-Sytell said, both awe and fear vanishing behind sudden interest. "The Caine who murdered Toa-Phelathon?"

He studied the cloud face more intently, now; he had seen crude drawings of Caine in the past, but this modeling was so lifelike that he felt he might know the man on sight. Even as he looked, the face dissolved and became once again an approaching thunderstorm.

"Mmm, yes," Ma'elKoth sighed. "That is another service he has done Me, though not at My direction. Your task, Toa-Sytell, and that of the King's Eyes, is to find this man and bring him here to Me. Bend every resource to the task, and know that he may not wish to be found. He has both contacts and friends here. Perhaps some one or more of them will come to you, if they know—what would make an enticing sum, without being excessive?—if they know that, let us say, two hundred golden royals await their word. Also, set the Constabulary on collecting citizens for the Ritual of Rebirth—we may catch him by accident, where design might fail. I want him within the palace gates by sundown tomorrow."

"Two hundred royals reward," Toa-Sytell repeated, nodding. "Is he in the city already?"

"No. I do not know where he may be. But he will be here by two hours after sunrise tomorrow."

"Prophecy?"

Ma'elKoth smiled. "Magick. I shall Draw him as a goat draws a panther, and he will come."

"But—" Toa-Sytell frowned. "—if he is a thousand leagues away tonight—"

"It would not matter if he were a million," Ma'elKoth said. "It would not matter if he were beyond the walls of Death. You, Toa-Sytell, are a blind man thrust stumbling along the narrow corridor of Time; I am a god who holds Time within his hand like a child's rag ball. Reality orders itself to My convenience. If Caine were a thousand leagues away, months ago he would have begun his journey to answer My call. Should I choose, tonight, not to Draw him . . . then months ago, he chose to stay where he was. Do you understand?"

"Well, actually, no," Toa-Sytell said. "If you, mm, *Draw* him so powerfully, why must we search for him like a thief? Won't he come to you of his own will?"

Ma'elKoth's smile became indulgent. "He may. It may also be

that he must be dragged; that is why I have ordered your task. Either way, he will come; the call will be answered. The mechanism is irrelevant."

Toa-Sytell frowned. "If this magick is so potent, why can you not simply Draw Simon Jester himself?"

"That is," Ma'elKoth said, "precisely what I am doing. The less I know of a man—the less of him I can image within My mind—the longer and more complex becomes the Drawing. Caine is only the component, the focus, like a bit of crystal or a handful of sulphur. Once I have Caine, I will Draw Simon Jester into My grasp like a woodcock on a string."

Through all this, Berne had stood with arms folded, staring off out over the city, lips pressed into the down-curved line of a sulking child's. Now he finally burst out, "And what am *I* supposed to do?"

Ma'elKoth turned to his Count, and his smile faded. "Take the day off."

"What?" Veins pulsed in Berne's forehead, and his mouth worked as though he couldn't decide whether to burst into tears or leap at the Emperor's throat.

"Berne, you must," Ma'elKoth said, his tone soothing but never suggesting the possibility of argument. "I know too well the history between you and Caine; I was the cause of some of it. I know too well that your next meeting may be fatal for one of you. Take the day, relax, enjoy the sun. Go to Alientown; gamble, drink, and whore. Stay out of the Warrens; he has friends among the Subjects of Cant, and he'll likely surface there. Forget Simon Jester, forget the Grey Cats, the cares of state. Forget Caine. If the two of you meet while Caine is in My service, you will treat him with the courtesy due another Beloved Child of Ma'elKoth."

"And after?"

"Once Simon Jester is in My hands, Caine's fate is of little interest to Me."

"All right," Berne said, breathing deeply but quickly. "All right. I'm sorry, Ma'elKoth, but you know . . . you know what he did to me."

"I know what you did to each other."

"Why *Caine*? I mean, what's so special about him?"

Now Toa-Sytell recognized the tone in Berne's voice, deeper than the petulance that usually colored it. He thought in wonder, *Why, the man's jealous!* Although he kept his face carefully blank, he graved a note on his mental tablet to investigate the possibility of a deeper personal relationship between Ma'elKoth and his favorite count.

"I am not sure," Ma'elKoth said. "He's had a spectacular career, certainly."

He shrugged massively and laid his huge hand upon Berne's shoulder. "Perhaps his peculiar quality can be summed in this way: he's the only man ever to face you in single combat, Berne, and escape with his life."

A smile flickered onto Berne's thin lips. "Only because he can run like a bastard jackrabbit."

Ma'elKoth took Berne's other shoulder as well, and looked searchingly down into the Count's face. "I tell you this: you are not that same man. With the Gifts that I have given you, he will not escape you again."

Berne reached up to stroke the hilt of Kosall; it answered his touch with a dangerous buzz, muffled within its scabbard. "Yeah. Yeah, I know."

Ma'elKoth turned his head only far enough to fix eyes grey as steel upon Toa-Sytell. "You have much work ahead, My Duke. Fare you well."

Before Toa-Sytell could answer, his feet sank through the stone beneath them. The tower's stone was still solid beneath Ma'elKoth and Berne; expressionless, they watched him sink. He let out a startled yelp as he went down, and the last he saw, before the stone closed over his eyes, was Ma'elKoth gathering Berne's head to his bare chest.

Whatever force it was that supported him let him down gently into the center of the mystic ring of the Iron Room. He brushed himself off, slapping imaginary grit from his sleeves while he looked up at the blank stone overhead.

He grunted once, softly, and shook his head. He went silently to the altar and looked down upon Jaybie, the man he'd—in effect—put there. He stared for a long time, watching him breathe; watching the pulse of his heartbeat in the tangled net of his guts; watching it stutter, race, then slow near to stopping.

Jaybie had been his friend—a good friend, a loyal friend. Loyal to a fault: Jaybie had been a friend to Konnos, too. He had chosen friendship over duty. The choice of a good man.

The choice of a dead man.

His loyalty had cost him more than his life. Toa-Sytell could still hear the echoes of his screams, the agony and terror that had baited the Outside Power, that had brought it close for Ma'elKoth's binding. He wondered if whatever might be left of Jaybie lay here, within this dying body, or if it howled in uncomprehending pain in whatever unimaginable hell to which the Power had returned.

Whatever the truth was, this breathing corpse had served Ma'elKoth's purpose; the Emperor had no further need of it. Toa-Sytell was not, himself, as good a man as the one who lay before him, but he was still a man; there was one mercy he could give his friend. The end was near, anyway, but he could hasten it this much.

Gently and very precisely, he pinched Jaybie's nose shut while his other hand covered Jaybie's mouth.

Jaybie didn't even struggle. His chest heaved once, and again, and shortly he expired without a sound.

Toa-Sytell wiped his hands on his breeches and sighed. He had a great deal of work to do.

Before he left the room, he glanced again at the bare stone of the mystic ring on the ceiling and once more grunted softly.

He'd survived the last Lord of Ankhana. He wasn't at all sure he'd survive this one.

7

THE COMMON FOLK in the great city of Ankhana, capital of the Empire, rarely look at the sky, especially after dark. On the north bank of the Great Chambaygen in the Warrens they are, as a rule, too concerned with who or what might be lurking within the next shadowed doorway or the mouth of a nearby alley. In Alientown, the wretched subhumans are too drunk or drugged, or too deep within their particular hustle upon whatever slumming purebloods might be spending the night. In the Industrial Park that separates the two, the manufactories belch smoke and flame that swallow the stars.

On the island of Old Town, honest folk are indoors after sundown, unless they're on the Watch. Constables patrol the streets with lamps that are mainly used to light the cobbles, so that they don't step in the occasional mound of horseshit that some lazy mucking-crew missed before curfew.

On the South Bank, where the houses of the wealthy and the noble surround the ducal estates, the servants are too occupied with their tasks, and their masters sleep the sleep of the just.

But here and there, folk do look up. A sailor, on a barge moored alongside the steelworks, smells the oncoming rain and glances at the sky. An elvish whore in Alientown wraps her shawl more tightly around her thin, translucently pale shoulders, and snarls a human obscenity at the approaching clouds. Two brothers, teenage sons of the Baron of Tinnara, hoist their pants after the casual rape of a kitchen girl they caught behind the garden of their father's city home, and stretch their arms in satisfaction over the bleeding girl. One sees the cloud and nudges the other.

These and the others like them, who glimpse the snarling face carved upon the thunderhead, shudder once, briefly, at the omen. An instant later the cloud is just a cloud again, and they shake their heads and smile at their own superstitious imaginations.

8

THE CAB GLEAMED in the last of the sunlight, then winked out as it dove into earthshadow and swooped to a landing at the gate on the edge of the Abbey's airspace. Hari was already there, waiting for it.

The door slid open, and Hari stepped in. He took a seat next to the minibar and tried to ignore the widened eyes and slack mouth of the driver within his armorglass compartment.

The driver's voice sounded faintly metallic through the speaker. "Holy Christ, it's you! I mean, you're Caine!"

Hari nodded. "Yeah. You know where the Buchanan Camp is?"

"The prison? Sure, Caine. Jesus Christ, I mean, when I got the call, y'know, to the Abbey, but no name, I thought maybe, but I din't wanna get my hopes up. With no name on the call, maybe you coulda been one a your girlfriends, like, or just a friend or something, but, holy cock, Caine—wait'll I tell my kids!"

"Do me a favor?"

"Sure, Caine, anything."

"Shut the fuck up."

"Well, um . . . sure, Caine, whatever, you're tired. I understand, no problem. But couldja sign my book, though?"

Hari squeezed his eyes shut. "Didn't you hear me?"

"Come on, just sign the book. It'd mean a lot to my kids, y'know, they'll never believe I really metcha if you don't sign it, y'know?"

"If I sign it, will you leave me alone?"

"Sure, Caine, anything. It's under the top of the bar, it folds up like the cover of a notepad."

The cab lifted smoothly into the air while Hari located and signed the cabbie's faded little autograph book. Hari grunted. It was real paper—must have cost a stack.

"So, ah, what're you goin' to the Buke for?"

Hari swallowed anger; to lose his temper here would be humiliating. "Listen. I don't want to talk with you. I've signed your book, and I'd really appreciate it if you'd just be quiet."

"Sure, whatever." The cabbie turned his head away from the glass, but Hari could still hear him mutter, "Yeah, what the hole, a fellow gets to be Professional, he forgets where he come from—"

Hari stared out the window at the sun setting behind the Pacific horizon. *Not me,* he thought. *I never forget. No one ever lets me forget.*

Storm clouds built themselves to the southwest. The cab lurched a little on insertion into the slavelanes, and the cabbie leaned back in his chair and stretched. "Hope you don't mind if I watcha little screen, huh?"

Hari didn't answer. The cabbie touched a sensor plate, and the windscreen of the cab lit with a closeup of LeShaun Kinnison's oversharp face on heads-up display. Hari winced—this would be *DragonTales.* The cabbie pressed his seat back to half-recline and tucked his hands behind his neck.

Kinnison's bullshit nodding slopped over with played-for-the-camera sympathy. She was saying: *". . . could explain for my viewers what ammod really is, and why Pallas Ril is in so much danger?"*

Hari closed his eyes again as the shot cut to his own face. It was bad enough to have to say the fatuous crap that the Studio forced on him; it was a level of magnitude worse to have to watch himself say it.

"Whoa, Caine! That's *you,* there! Hole, right there with Le-Shaun. She's a honey, huh? A honey."

"She's a fucking crocodile. After the show, I almost had to break her fingers to pry her damn hand off my crotch."

"No, come on, really? Right there at the show? LeShaun Kinnison grabbed your dick?"

"Shut up."

". . . people in the world who really understand the physics of it, and you might guess I'm not one of them."

(Audience laughs)

"But I can explain it to you—and your viewers—the same way it was explained to me. You see, Earth and Overworld are the same

planet in different universes. Each universe, the whole thing, sort of vibrates in its own way—what they call the Universal Constant of Resonance. Now, it doesn't really vibrate, that's just the easiest way to think about it. We go from one to the other by changing our Constant of Resonance to match the other universe. Is everybody confused yet?"

(Audience laughs)

Now, on the screen, the shot would show him pulling an antique pocket watch from inside his vest; he couldn't stand to look. Hari's face burned with humiliation, and he ground his teeth together.

He could see it in memory: he held the pocket watch by the end of its chain, its bottom rim touching the palm of his other hand.

"Pallas Ril is like the watch, here. My bottom hand represents Earth. See, when the watch is at rest, it's stable right here on Earth. Now, let's say that Overworld is a different height, see, a higher level of reality—say halfway between my hands. So, if we want to raise the watch to that level, without moving my hands, there's two ways we can go about it. One is to shorten the chain, like this. Simple, isn't it? This is kind of like freemod—that's short for 'frequency modification,' which isn't even the right term for it, but anyway . . . This is what we do for trainees who go to Overworld for a long time, sometimes years, to finish their training and develop the personas that they hope will make them stars someday. When they decide to come home, they go to one of our fixed transfer points, and the equipment there lengthens the chain again. Just like this, see? They're back on Earth. But there's a problem with this. When you're on freemod, you're just like a native. You're completely a part of the Overworld universe, and you're completely cut off from the Studio. No first-handers, not even a recording for second-hand cubes. You wouldn't like that a whole lot, would you? We get all the fun, and you can't share it."

(Audience roars agreement)

"Now, ammod—amplitude modification, which isn't the right term either, but there you go—that's a little more complicated. It's what happened to Pallas, what happens to me and every other Actor you ever enjoy."

Here his wrist snapped in a little arc, and the pocket watch whirled in a circle as centripetal force drove it up and out to midlevel.

"See, it's a whole different way of getting to Overworld. To keep the watch up here, I have to keep spinning it. That's the same as

adding energy, you see? That's what we do through the thought-mitter link. The same link that carries our experiences back here to Earth for you to enjoy, carries energy from the Studio reactor to us, to keep us on Overworld."

Hari, eyes closed, remembered the veneer of concern on Kinnison's face as she leaned toward him, and he remembered his urge to slap her.

"And so," she asked, *"can you tell us what happens if the link gets broken?"*

Hari had held his hand still then, and he, Kinnison, and the entire audience watched in silence as the pocket watch spiraled down to his other palm.

"So, she slides back to Earth."

Hari had followed the script flawlessly; this was the spot for him to turn grave.

"It's a lot more serious than that. See, Overworld isn't what you'd call adjacent to Earth's universe. Just the opposite; it's so similar to Earth because, you might say, it's a harmonic of Earth, like an octave. There are any number of different universes that lie at energy levels between ours and Overworld's, and most all of them are so unlike our own that I can't even describe them. They're all hostile to life as we know it. In some, for example, the element carbon, the element that makes up pretty much your whole body, can't even exist there, by the physical laws. When an Actor slips out of phase with Overworld, it's death. It's the most hideous death imaginable. Most of them are never seen again. Some eventually slip into phase with Earth, and it's, well . . . gruesome. I don't even want to describe it."

"And this is what will happen to Pallas Ril if you don't find her?"

His best hardguy voice: *"It might've happened already."*

The sick twist in Hari's stomach forced his eyes open to see his own face staring back at him from the heads-up on the cab's windscreen.

The cab lurched from one slavelane to another, swinging, so that for an instant his projected face overlay the building storm clouds out on the Pacific.

"I know that when you slip that helmet over your heads, you are me. You feel what I feel. I know that you love her, too. And I swear to you, that if anything has happened to her, no power in any universe will save the men responsible. I will make Berne pray for death;

Ma'elKoth will curse the day his parents met. No one whose hand was in this will escape me. I swear it."

It was all scripted, all written by the pros from Studio Hype, but at the end it hadn't mattered. That oath was as honest as any words he'd ever spoken.

"Hoo, mama," the cabbie chuckled. "Sure wouldn't want you mad at *me.*"

9

THE ATTENDANT HELD the door respectfully, to allow Hari to pass. As he entered the tiny room, Hari shook the attendant's hand; this bit of upcaste-to-down contact, though unusual, was not unheard of, and it served to cover the passing of a small packet of pure cocaine from Hari's hand to the attendant's. All flows of credit were electronically monitored, but cocaine and other stimulants could be purchased legally by anyone of Professional caste or above; it and other drugs had become the preferred medium of black-market exchange and were absolutely de rigueur for unobtrusive bribes. Hari always brought a substantial supply on his visits to the Buchanan Social Camp; a steadily descending series of bribes—from the Director on down to the Laborers who oversaw the surgically deafened cyborg Workers that attended the internees—was the only way Hari could buy a chance to speak with his father.

The attendant pointed silently to the touchpad on the wall, where Hari would press to signal that he wished to leave, and then spread his hands, fingers up and out.

Ten minutes.

Hari nodded, and the attendant closed the door; it locked with a heavy mechanical *chunk.*

"Dad?" he said, coming to the edge of the bed. "Dad, how are you feeling?"

Duncan Michaelson lay twisted beneath sheets of sweat-soaked synthetics, his eyes rolling like misshapen marbles. Veins writhed across his hairless skull; his wasted arms strained spastically against padded straps, and the soft mumbling moan that bubbled from his lips echoed his perpetual nightmare.

Dammit, he'd been promised Duncan would be *awake.*

Hari shook his head angrily and almost went to the touchpad to signal the attendant, then shrugged and went to the small window instead. He was paying a lot for this window—a 20 percent surcharge to his monthly debit. He might as well get some use out of it.

That monthly debit, which supported the expense of maintaining Duncan in the Buke, was all that stood between Hari's father and a cyborg's yoke; that yoke, and the Worker's life that went with it, would have killed Duncan in months even years ago, when he'd been vastly stronger than he was now.

Hari had been paying to keep him in prison for more than ten years.

Rain streaked the window, blurring and dimming the grey world outside. A stroke of lightning shattered a small tree into glowing flinders only a few meters away; the crackle of energy and the splintering crash of thunder triggered Hari's reflexes, and he dove for the floor with a startled shout. He rolled into a crouch next to a small desk, shaking his head and disgustedly waiting for his pulse to normalize.

On the bed above him, Duncan Michaelson opened his eyes. "Hari?" His voice was thin and querulous, barely above a whisper. "That you, Killer?"

Hari steadied himself with a hand on the bedrail and stood. "Yeah, Dad."

"God, you're getting big, Killer. How's school?"

"Dad, I . . ." He pressed his hand to his forehead. "Fine, Dad. Just fine."

"Your head hurt? I tolja t'stay away from those Artisan kids. Hoods, all of them. I'm a Pr'fesh'nal, goddammit. Better get y'mom t'stitch that up."

Hari shifted his hand so that his fingers brushed the ancient ridged scar that twisted just above his hairline. When he was ten years old, he'd fought a whole gang of older Artisan boys; six of them had been pushing him and singing one of those tuneless songs that boys can make up on the spur of the moment. This one, they called "The Crazyman's Kid."

A brief smile flickered over Hari's face at the memory—one boy rolling on the ground cupping his crushed testicles, another howling as he pressed his hand to his face, trying to stem the blood that spurted from the ragged mess Hari's teeth had made of his nose. For a moment, he wished he was ten again; he wished he'd gotten a couple more of them before their leader—Nielson, something Nielson—had ended the brawl with a brick.

But nostalgic reflection had never been Hari's habit, and this passed swiftly away. His mother had not stitched the gash Nielson's brick had left in his scalp; by that time, she'd been dead for three years.

And Duncan had been completely fucking bugnuts for two of them.

"I will, Dad."

"That's good . . ." Duncan's strengthless hand scratched at the straps. "Can you loosen me up? Gotta terrible itch."

Hari loosened the straps, and Duncan scratched himself around the edges of the nutrient patches on his chest. "Oh, that's good. You're a good kid, Hari . . . a good son. I wish I hadn't . . . I just, y'know, could have . . . I . . ." Duncan's eyes rolled up under their flickering lids, and his voice slurred back into throaty, incoherent muttering.

"Dad?" Hari reached out to his father, to shake him gently. His hand closed over Duncan's shoulder. He could feel every tendon, every detail of bone and joint; Caine's training rose from his subconscious and whispered the exact simple twist that would dislocate that shoulder, separate bone and ligament.

Hari yanked his hand back as though his father's flesh were hot iron. He stared at his palm for one long second, as though expecting to see a burn.

He pushed himself away from the bed and turned again to the window, to rest his forehead against the chill smooth glass.

Nearly everyone on Earth knew the approved version of Hari's life, the classic Studio success story of the tough kid from the Labor ghettos of San Francisco. Only very few knew that Hari hadn't been born a Laborer. His father, Duncan Michaelson, had been a Professor of social anthropology at Berkeley, and was in fact the principal author of the standard texts on Westerling and the cultural mores of Overworld. Hari's mother, Davia Khapur, had met Duncan when she took his Principles of Linguistic Drift seminar for her masters in philology. The union of two traditionally Professional families had been too good to resist, and Hari's earliest memories were happy ones.

Hari now knew what had triggered his father's breakdown. After Hari had clawed his way up to stardom, he'd finally been able to afford the medical tests that pinpointed Duncan's progressive neural degeneration. Duncan Michaelson had an autoimmune disorder that ate away at his synaptic chemical receptors, essentially causing random short-circuiting throughout his central nervous system. As one meditech had brutally put it, "Your father's brain has spent the past twenty years gradually turning to pudding."

But when it had begun, all those years ago, Hari'd had no idea his father was sick. He'd barely noticed Duncan's increasing moodiness and brooding, lost as he was in the bright world of learning that a six-year-old Professional child had open to him. He remembered the first beating—the backhanded slap that had buffeted him across the carpet in his father's study, the hands that had crushed his shoulders and shook him until his eyes filled with shooting stars.

He remembered the screaming, back and forth between his parents—shouting filled with names he didn't know, names that Duncan had been using in his seminars and lectures, names that frightened his mother until her teeth chattered. Many years would pass before Hari could afford to purchase the black-market banned books that told him who these names belonged to, names like Jefferson and Lincoln, Voltaire and John Locke. At the time, all he knew was that his father wouldn't stop talking about these men, and it was going to get him in trouble.

He remembered the brisk, businesslike manner of the silver-masked Social Police when they arrested Duncan. Six-year-old Hari had been long abed, but Duncan's snarl had awakened him; Hari had watched through the barest crack of his bedroom door.

Duncan must have been either too proud or already too crazy to lie; after he'd been gone for a week, more soapies came and moved Hari and his mother into a two-room apartment in the Mission District Labor ghetto.

For years Hari had tried to believe that the reason his mother hadn't divorced his father was that she loved him too much to leave him, even when his madness carried them all downcaste to a Temp slum. In other families, a divorce would have protected the innocent spouse's caste status. It wasn't until Hari was a teenager, many years after his mother's death, that he'd realized a divorce wouldn't have protected her. She hadn't turned Duncan in for sedition; as far as Soapy was concerned, that made her his accomplice.

She'd had nowhere else to go.

His father was allowed to join them only a month later. Their assets had been confiscated, as Laborers can neither possess nor receive income from Professional work. Neither Duncan nor Davia had Labor skills; the best they could do was Temp at unskilled jobs. And Duncan grew worse, more erratic, more violent, more prone to bellowed declamations of the "rights of man."

Hari didn't know what had killed his mother. He'd always sort of figured that Duncan had beaten her a little too hard one day, and that some Labor Clinic medical aide had been too zoned on Demerol to give her proper treatment. Hari's strongest memory of his mother was of her lying on her bed in their tiny apartment, soaked in sweat, her palsied hand gripping his without strength. "Take care of your father," she'd said, "because he's the only father you'll ever have. He's sick, Hari. He can't help himself."

A few days later she died in that bed, while Hari played stickball a few blocks away. He had been seven years old.

Duncan's hold on reality was intermittent. On his lucid days, he was almost pathetically kind to his son, struggling with all his might to be the good parent that he knew in his heart he wasn't. He did his best to educate Hari, teaching him to read, to write, and to do simple arithmetic. He managed to scrape together enough cocaine to not only purchase a screener but to bribe a local tech into illegally hooking it into the library net; Duncan and Hari spent many hours together before that screen, reading. But those were the good days.

On the bad ones, Hari swiftly learned that he was safer among the dregs of the Mission District than he was with his father. Hari became almost preternaturally sensitive and adaptable; he was able to scent a shift in his father's sanity from upwind and over a hill, and he could instantly fall in line and play along with the delusion of the day—could make himself see the world the way that Duncan saw it. He'd been taught early and often that any denial of—or deviation from—his father's private reality was a short road to a savage beating.

And he learned to fight back. By the age of ten or so, he'd discovered that the beatings would be just as bad whether he fought back or not. Fighting gave him the chance to escape.

When he could escape, the only place a Labor kid could go was the street. His intelligence and adaptability let him survive out among the whores and the thieves and the addicts, the upcaste perverts and the prowling sexual predators. His unhesitating willingness to fight anyone, anytime, any odds, earned him a reputation for being as crazy as his father, and from time to time it saved his life.

By the time he was fifteen, he'd had the world pretty well figured out. His father went crazy, he'd decided, because he kept trying to fool himself. His father'd read books by these guys that he kept ranting about. They told him that the world was one way, and he wanted to believe them, and so when the world showed him that it was something else he couldn't handle it. He'd pretended so hard that he could no longer separate pretense from reality.

Hari swore a private oath he'd never do that. He'd keep his mental balance by looking the world straight in the eye, for exactly what it is; he'd never pretend it was different.

A childhood on the streets of the Mission District had pretty well shattered any illusions he might have inherited about the sanctity of human life, or the fundamental goodness of people. By fifteen, he'd already killed two men and had been supporting himself and his father for five years as a petty thief and a courier for the local black-market dealers.

It was less than a month after his sixteenth birthday that Hari had contrived to catch the attention of Marc Vilo; two weeks after that, he'd packed his few possessions and moved out. On Hari's last day under his father's roof, Duncan tried to open his skull with a pipe wrench.

Vilo prided himself on the care he took of his undercastes. Unknown to Hari, Vilo saw to it that Duncan was provided for throughout the next six years as Hari grew, entered the Studio Conservatory, and spent three years in freemod training on Overworld. When Hari returned to take up his Acting career, Duncan had been in specialized care for several years. With continuing drug therapy, he was consistently lucid.

His only remaining problem was that he'd never learned to shut up.

Stripped of his Professional privileges, he could no longer legally teach. Instead, he'd gathered a following of young Labor men and women who met in secret in his apartment for discussions on banned philosophies culled from Duncan's prodigious memory; they in turn disseminated these antisocial ideas among their own acquaintances. The soapies had known about this, almost certainly, but in those days they were somewhat more tolerant. It wasn't until the crackdown that followed the Caste Riots that Duncan was convicted of sedition and placed under a standing sentence: either permanent restraint in a Mute Facility like the Buchanan's or the cyborg yoke and life as a Worker.

In the Buke, nothing Duncan could say or write would ever reach the outside world. The only human contact he could have was with a surgically deafened Worker who tended his personal needs. He was allowed full net access, but incoming only. Any personal requests were submitted to the Director by E-mail on a closed-circuit system designed specifically for that purpose; not only could Duncan not communicate with the outside world, he could never even converse with the other Buchanan campers.

These rules, though, like all rules, could be bent—or broken—for the right price.

And these rules made Duncan the safest man on Earth for Hari to talk to. When the winds that howled through the holes in Hari's life became too bitter, he'd come here for a moment of stillness, for a moment of peace.

The chill glass of the window had grown warm with the heat from Hari's forehead. "They've really got me this time, Dad," he said softly. "They have really got me by the balls."

Duncan's mumbling had faded away; the only sound Hari could hear above his own breathing was the pittering raindrops on the window.

"They're making me kill another Ankhanan king. I barely survived Toa-Phelathon—I shouldn't have, really. I should have died in that alley. If Kollberg hadn't pushed through the emergency transfer . . . And this guy, this Ma'elKoth, he's . . . he's so . . . I don't know. I have a bad feeling about this. I don't think I'm gonna make it, this time."

It was easier to say when he knew no one was listening. "I think they're finally gonna get me."

Hari pressed his palms against the glass and stared out at the smoldering embers of the tree. "It's not like I didn't know what I was getting into. I mean, even at the Conservatory they tell you straight: *Your function in society is to risk your life in interesting ways.* But the Adventures, they just keep getting worse and worse; they're *trying* to kill me, Dad—each one is a little tougher, the stakes a little higher, the odds a little worse. From their point of view . . . I don't know, I guess they have to; I mean, who'd bother first-handing an Adventure they think'll be easy for me?"

"Quit, then. Retire." The voice was ragged and thin but unquestionably *present*; at least for the moment, Duncan's mind was here. Hari turned from the window and met his father's milky stare.

He coughed into his hand, suddenly embarrassed. "I, ah, didn't know you were awake."

"At least you'll be alive, Hari." Duncan's voice was barely above a whisper. "That counts for something."

"I, ah . . . I can't do it, Dad. I've already contracted."

"Forfeit."

Hari shook his head. "I can't. It's, ah, it's Shanna, Dad. My wife."

"I remember . . . I see her with you on the nets, sometimes. Been married . . . what, a year?"

"Three."

"Kids?"

Hari shook his head silently and examined his knotted fingers. He said, "She's there, in Ankhana." His breath caught in his throat—why was this so hard to talk about? "They, ah . . ." He coughed harshly, turning his face back toward the window. "She's lost on Overworld, and they're gonna let her die there if I don't try for Ma'elKoth."

For a moment, the only sound was the thin whistle of Duncan trying to inhale.

"I get it. I caught some of . . . *DragonTales* . . ." Duncan seemed to struggle for breath, for the strength to put conviction into his voice. "Bread and circuses, Hari. Bread and circuses."

It was one of Duncan's catchphrases; Hari understood it only abstractly, but he nodded.

"Your problem," Duncan went on with difficulty, "isn't Overworld, or this Emperor. Your problem . . . you're a slave."

Hari shrugged irritably; he'd heard this many times before. To Duncan's hazy eyes, everybody looked like a slave. "I've got just about as much freedom as I can handle."

"Hah. You've . . . more than you think. You'll win." Duncan sank back into his pillow, exhausted.

"Sure I will, Dad."

"Don't . . . *humor* me, Hari, dammit . . ." He spent a few seconds only breathing. "Listen. Tell you how you beat 'em . . . Tell you?"

"All right, Dad." Hari came close to the bed and bent over his father. "All right, I'm listening. You tell me how I can beat them."

"Forget . . . Forget *rules* . . ."

Hari fought to keep his rising exasperation off his face and out of his voice. "What do you mean?"

"Listen . . . they think, they think they own you. They think they own all of you, and you have to do what they say."

"They're damn close to right."

"No . . . no, *listen* . . . your wife, you love her. You love her."

Hari couldn't answer, couldn't push words past the constriction in his throat.

"That's their hold . . . their grip. But it's their only one . . . and they don't know it . . . they think they're safe . . ."

Hari stiffened and scowled, but said nothing.

"Hari, *listen*," Duncan whispered, his eyes fluttering closed. "The smartest . . . the smartest man in the world once said, 'Anything that is done out of love takes place beyond good and evil.' You get that? You understand? *Beyond*."

Hari sighed. What had he been thinking? That his crazy father might really have advice for him? He shook his head disgustedly and said, "Sure, Dad. Beyond. I got it."

"Tired now. Hrr, sleepy. Mm, Hari?"

"Yeah?"

"You ever . . . you ever tell her . . . about me?"

The truth is the truth, Hari thought. *Look the world in the eye.* He said, "No. I've never told her about you."

Duncan nodded, eyes closed, his freed hands blindly seeking their usual tie-down positions. "I wish . . . I'd like to, after you save her, I'd like to meet her. Just once. On the nets, she seems so nice."

"Yeah," Hari said, suddenly hoarse. "Yeah, she is."

10

THE DIAMOND BALLROOM on the Studio's twentieth floor glittered and shone with scintillant color, flashing prismatic splinters of light across the faces of Caine's subscribers. Most of them were Leisure faces, some here with their loyal Investors; few in Business could wield either the cash or the clout to walk among the elect. Caine commanded the highest subscription rate of any Actor in North America: one thousand upcaste subscribers paid a round hundred thousand marks each for a year's rental of a luxury box, with seven Adventures guaranteed—barring the unexpected death or maiming of the star, of course.

This was an elite club; the Studio collected a thousand marks per year from ten thousand hopefuls, merely for the privilege of staying on the waiting list. One of the privileges of subscribing was meeting the star at pre-Adventure receptions like this one.

This reception, like so many of them, was done up as a costume ball; the theme this time was "The Enemies of Caine."

Hari circulated through the crowd wearing a costume mock-up

of Caine's black leathers, playing at being Caine, growling hard-assed responses to the wet-eyed well-wishers and backslapping advice offerers.

Playing at being Caine made this almost tolerable; at least he didn't have to smile.

Kollberg bustled up to him and took his arm. The Administrator wore the maroon and gold of Ankhanan royal livery; it took Hari a moment to realize that Kollberg was supposed to be Jemson Thal, Toa-Phelathon's master steward. Hari had a fleeting impulse to kick him in the throat.

"You have your speech?" Kollberg asked.

"Yes."

"Did you look it over? It's not quite the, ah, usual." Kollberg sweated with his night-before nerves; something about being among all these upcasters always made him edgy. Hari figured it was because Kollberg was the only Administrator present; no Administrator would ever be privileged to rent a box for a Caine Adventure. Everyone in the place was upcaste of him, far upcaste.

Everyone but Hari.

Hari looked down at the Administrator's hand, which still held his elbow. If only he really were Caine right now—Caine would break this fat fuck's arm. He said, "Yes, Administrator. I have it, all right?" He looked pointedly down at Kollberg's moist hand. "No offense, Administrator—but people are staring."

Kollberg let go of Hari's arm like he'd been stung. He licked his lips as he straightened his tunic. "Well, we're going to be sitting down to eat in about fifteen minutes, and you've barely been on the north side of the room at all."

Hari shrugged. "On my way."

He threaded through a clot of Investors all dressed like the Bear Guard of the Khulan Horde; the two Leisuremen to whom they were attached both wore the skins and winged helmet of Khulan G'thar himself. He accepted a handshake from some Leisureman under about five kilos of putty; this idiot had spent probably sixty marks to look like an ogrillo chieftain Caine had killed in the Adventure called *Retreat from the Boedecken*—more money than most Labor families get in a week. Hari dodged around any number of pudgy, slack-muscled Bernes, ducked one creative soul who'd costumed himself as one of the mantislike Krrx warriors from *Race for the Crown of Dal'kannith*, and found himself face-to-face with Marc Vilo.

The little Businessman had done better than most: He wore gleaming platemail modeled of lightweight plastic, lacking only the helmet. He'd sprayed his hair platinum blond. He had a gruesomely realistic prosthetic that made him look as though his left cheekbone and eye socket were freshly shattered: bone splinters stuck through the skin and dripped gleaming blood; a half-deflated eye dangled by the optic nerve.

Hari admired it with a low whistle. "Marc, that's beautiful. Purthin Khlaylock, right?"

"Bet your ass, son," Vilo said with a broad grin. "Picked him because he's about the only one who's still alive, and I don't have the figure for Berne. Not that it stopped any of *them*." He snorted as he gave a nod that included the entire room. "What's the matter, kid? You look like you're not having a good time."

"I, ah, guess I'm a little tense, Marc."

He nodded, absently understanding. "Listen, I got a special guest here I want you to meet. Come on and . . . Wait, listen, before we go—that little talk you and I had the other week, about you getting back together with Shanna?"

"Yeah . . . ?" Hari said warily.

"Well, I just wanted to say that this is *great*. This is better than I hoped for."

A knot tied itself into Hari's stomach. "It's not like I planned it this way."

"Oh, shit, I know, I know. But this is absofreakinglutely spectacular—I can't *lose*, y'know?"

Hari understood exactly what he meant: he'd heroically save Shanna, heroically avenge her death, or heroically die in either attempt. No matter what the outcome, it would reflect admirably on his Patron. "Yeah," he said thickly, "I guess things look pretty good for you."

"Bet your ass. Here, come on."

Vilo led him over to where a fiftyish, fleshy Leisurewoman stood amidst a gaggle of admirers. She wore brown suede chest armor over her steel grey tunic and breeches, and a flowing cape of blue completed the costume: she was dressed as Pallas Ril.

Vilo cleared his throat importantly. "Caine, I'd like to introduce you to Shermaya Dole. Leisurema'am Dole, this is Caine."

Her eyes lit as she turned, though of course she didn't offer her hand. "Oh, yes, Marc. We've met."

"The Leisurema'am," Hari said with a slightly stiff bow, "honored Shanna and myself by attending our wedding."

"Yes indeed," she said. "If you'd been there, Marc, you'd remember." Vilo's ears turned red. Dole went on, "Entertainer Michaelson, how are you?"

"As well as can be expected, ma'am, thank you. And yourself?"

"Oh, well, you know, I'm terribly distressed about Shanna," she said, one palm pressed against her ample chest. "Marc was *so* kind, to invite me to share his box. I so hope that you can find her."

"I intend to, ma'am."

"And please, Entertainer, please forgive my choice of costume. Marc told me the theme this evening, and I know," she said, leaning close with a self-conscious giggle, "that Pallas Ril isn't Caine's enemy; please, how well I know that! But I want to remind everyone what's really important here—what's really at stake. You're not upset?"

Hari was astonished at the sudden rush of warmth he felt toward this woman. "Leisurema'am Dole," he said seriously, "you are maybe the most gracious person I've ever met; it's impossible that your concern would upset me. I couldn't agree with you more."

"I only wish that I could do something to actually *help* you," she sighed. "Please know that I'll be with you the whole time; I'll be first-handing in Marc's box, and my prayers will be with you and Shanna. God be with you, Entertainer."

She turned away, dismissing him, and spoke over her shoulder to Vilo. "He's so *polite*, Marc. I can't thank you enough. Really, *very* well behaved."

Vilo allowed her to take his arm and lead him away. As he went, he shot a look back to Hari, his eyes alight and his lips silently forming the words *I'm in.*

Hari forced a smile and a nod, and then the crowd closed in around him again.

In only minutes it was time for his speech, a brief predinner address. After dinner would come the nearly endless speeches from Marc Vilo, as his Patron; Arturo Kollberg, as Studio Chairman; and whatever broken-down retired Actor they'd roped in for this. Hari pulled his notepad out of his front pocket and tapped open the cover. Its screen lit up with the text of his speech. He made his way to the west end of the ballroom, where the huge curving staircase provided the dais.

He mounted the steps and turned to face the ballroom. The lighting subtly changed to get everyone's attention and to bring a golden glow around him, and concealed shotgun mikes aimed at his face from across the room. He coughed, and the cough's amplified reproduction sounded like distant thunder.

A thousand faces and more turned toward him in anticipation. Hari looked out over them, his stomach roiling: more than a thousand men and women dressed as his enemies. There was only one missing: among them all, no one had costumed himself as Ma'el-Koth. Hari gave his head a little shake. The Ankhanan Emperor was too recent; no one thought of him as an enemy yet.

He cleared his throat again, and began.

"They tell me this evening's theme is 'The Enemies of Caine.' I'm looking out at you now, though, and I'm thinking that a better name would have been 'The Victims of Caine.' I don't think there's ever been a room with so many dead people in it outside of Hell."

As called for in the script, he paused for his audience's appreciative laughter and scattered applause.

They think they own you.

Hari felt sweat trickle from his hairline down the back of his neck.

"I know that some of you have first-handed Pallas Ril's Adventures, that some of you feel like it might even be *you* over there, lost and frightened in Ankhana . . ."

Shanna, lost and frightened? Who writes this crap? His heart began to boil within his rib cage.

". . . but I swear to you, I'll find her. I'll find *you*. And I'll bring you both safely back to Earth."

They think they're safe.

The words on the screen blurred. Hari pretended to cough, and he wiped his eyes, squinting at the screen. "Y'see, these guys in Ankhana, they don't really know what they're messing with. They don't really know what kind of trouble they're in . . ."

Singing wires stretched themselves tight up the back of his neck.

I've got just about as much freedom as I can handle.

Something took over Hari's hands: they snapped shut the cover of his notepad and dropped it to the stairs. His feet got into the act: before he completely understood what he was doing, his heel came sharply down on the notepad and cracked the cover.

"*Fuck* this," he said harshly.

A ripple of murmurs passed over the surface of the crowd.

He said, "All night long, I've been pretending to be Caine. You know, walk around, give you the eye, give you a line or two, a little thrill. It's all a fucking act."

He let a little of Caine's blood-hunger leak into his flat-eyed grin. "You want to know what Caine would really be saying to you, here tonight? You want to?"

Hari picked out Kollberg's face, pasty and goggle-eyed with panic, shaking frantic negatives. He saw Vilo, looking dubious, and Dole, squinting as though she couldn't quite see him. Most of the rest of the faces wore looks of anticipation so intense they might have been lust.

"He'd say: She's my woman and this is my fight. He'd say: You flock of shit-eating vultures should get lives of your fucking own."

He walked down off the stairs and stopped at the edge of the crowd—a mob of the most powerful men and women on Earth. "Get out of my way."

They slowly parted for him.

He walked to the door, and left.

His boot heels clicked on the marble of the anteroom, and before he could reach the outer door, applause began within the Diamond Ballroom like the surf of an incoming tide.

He kept walking.

Kollberg slammed through the outer doors while Hari waited for the elevator. "Michaelson!" he barked, a little thinly from shortness of breath. "Don't you move!"

Hari didn't look at him. He just watched the baroque indicator arrow of filigreed bronze creep toward the number of the floor.

"That was not acceptable!" Kollberg said. His eyes bulged, and his face shone with sweat over strawberry mottling. "I covered you—*just barely!*—and most of them think this was part of the schtick. But you're going to march your butt right back in there and pretend it was all a *joke*, you understand me?"

"You know what?" Hari said softly, still looking up at the arrow. "We're alone here, Artie. No guards, no security cameras. No witnesses."

"What? *What did you call me?*"

He now met Kollberg's gaze, and Caine looked out from behind his eyes. "I said we're alone here, you fat fuck, and I know three different ways to kill you that won't leave a mark."

Kollberg's mouth opened, and a sound came out like air escaping from a balloon. He took a step back, then another. "You can't speak to me this way!"

The elevator doors opened, and Hari stépped on board. "...tell you what," he said flatly. "If I live through this, I'll apologize."

Kollberg gaped, his hands trembling from the adrenaline that makes rage and terror so much alike. The doors closed between them, and the elevator carried Hari down to ground level.

I'll pay for that tomorrow, Hari thought as he paced toward the outside door. He put a hand on the armorglass, and looked up at the storm clouds that glowed sickly orange from the streetlights below.

Shit, he thought. *Tomorrow, I pay for everything.*

DAY TWO

"What's wrong with you? You never even get angry! Even a shout would be better than this, than this, this calm . . . nothingness."

"Come on, Shanna, Jesus Christ. What would shouting prove—who has the loudest voice?"

"Maybe I'd just like to be able to believe that you have a passion for something besides violence. Maybe sometimes, I wish I were as important to you as killing people—"

"Dammit, that's not fair—"

"Fair? You want fair? Let me quote you: 'I believe in justice, as long as I'm holding a knife at the throat of the judge.' "

"What does that have to do with—"

"Everything. It's all part of the same thing. I suppose I shouldn't expect you to understand."

1

A TOO-YOUNG, TOO-PRETTY man with artfully curled hair stares earnestly out from the main screens of homes all over the world.

"For those of you just joining us, this is *Adventure Update*, your only Worldwide Twenty-four-hour Source for Studio News. I'm Bronson Underwood.

"Our top story this morning: in less than one hour, the legendary Caine will make the transfer into the City of Life, the capital of the Ankhanan Empire, on the northwest continent of Overworld. His real-life wife, the well-known Pallas Ril, is lost somewhere within the city. The graphic that you see in the lower left corner of your screens is our best estimate of the number of hours remaining until Pallas Ril's amplitude match fails and she slips out of phase with

Overworld. As you can see, if Caine cannot save her, Pallas Ril will die, hideously, in one hundred thirty-one hours—only a little more than five and a half days.

"*Adventure Update* will run this graphic twenty-four hours a day, as long as we have any hope remaining, and we will offer hourly updates on Caine's progress in his desperate search.

"In our next hour, we'll have the tape of LeShaun Kinnison's interview with Caine himself, and let me tell you, it's really *something*. But now, we go to our chief analyst for Ankhanan affairs, Jed Clearlake."

"Good morning, Bronson."

"Jed, what can you tell our viewers of the current situation there in Ankhana? How much do we actually know?"

"Well, Bronson, more than you might think. First of all, the one hundred thirty-one hours is only an estimate; a number of factors can affect the phase-locking capability of . . ."

And this is barely the beginning.

2

THE MOUNTAIN OF stone and steel that was the San Francisco Studio towered above the broad plain of landing pads and carports. The eagles that circled the mountaintop were the limousines and flying coupes of the Leisurefolk and Investors, soaring through endless loops of holding patterns.

The weather had broken overnight. The rising sun painted the polished Gothic arches of the windows and glittered in the eyes of gargoyles that crouched among the arms of massive flying buttresses. High granite walls—the first line of defense against undercaste intrusion—ringed the entire compound.

Outside the iron-toothed mouth of the enormous gate, the hordes of undercastes—the Laborers and Artisans and even some Professionals who were not too proud to mingle—shifted and stamped and flowed toward the wide road, restrained by the linked arms of the red-suited Studio Security force who lined the curbs.

Within the hour, Caine himself would pass through these gates.

In the Cavea, the great hall of five thousand firsthand berths, a battalion of ushers fiddled and fitted and plugged the wealthy clients into their simichairs.

In the subscription boxes, the Leisurefolk and their guests enjoyed the delicacies and exotic wines that each box's waiter had to offer and talked about Caine's extraordinary performance at the Subscriber's Ball. Opinion was divided: most believed that it was a particularly inspired piece of Studio theatrics, but a stubborn minority maintained that what they'd seen was entirely unplanned—that something *real* had happened.

All agreed, however, that it had powerfully captured their interest. Many had passed a sleepless night in anticipation, and of those who had slept, many had dreamed of being Caine.

In the techbooth that overlooked the ebony ziggurat of the Cavea's transfer platform, Arturo Kollberg snapped useless orders and fumed and brooded on his humiliation the night before, on the brink of his greatest triumph. It was intolerable, and something had to be done.

Something *would* be done, and he would certainly do it.

This wasn't personal, he assured himself. It wasn't some fit of pique, a need to salve his wounded vanity. Kollberg thought of himself as a bigger man than that; he'd always understood that his personal needs must be subordinated to the necessities of his position, and he'd always done so. The humiliation he'd suffered, the insult to his person, the *threat*, was irrelevant; he could let it pass unrequited, if he chose. That was a matter between Michaelson the man and Kollberg the man; it was personal, and it could be forgotten.

The insult to his *position* was another matter entirely.

That was between Michaelson the Professional and Kollberg the Administrator. To ignore it would begin to unravel the very fabric of civilization.

Administrators the world over have two mottoes, two simple principles to guide them in their lives: *Deference to Those Above, Respect from Those Below,* and: *Service.*

All Administrator children learn early that they are the guardians of society, that they are, in fact, the axis upon which turns the world. Ranked below them are the Professionals, Artisans, and Laborers; ranked above are the Businessfolk, the Investors, and the Leisurefolk. Administrators are the center, the fulcrum, the balance point, and their role is nothing less than the maintenance of civilization. Administrators take the directions of the upcastes and translate them to reality by their direction of the downcastes. Administrators allocate the distribution of Earth's dwindling resources. Administrators manage the enterprises; Administrators promulgate the regulations; Administrators create the wealth that is the engine of the Earth.

Administrators carry the world upon their backs and ask for nothing in return.

One of the most basic skills of the Administrator, an essential element of his education, is the maintenance of the dignity of his position. The moral authority of an effective Administrator is so powerful that undercastes—and even lesser Administrators—follow his directives without question; great Administrators have undercastes that actually *compete* against each other in the performance of their functions, for no other reward than an approving glance and a firm *Good job*.

But when errors and weakness erode the authority of the Administrators, undercastes become surly and shiftless—sometimes goldbricking and malingering to the point of sabotage, to where it actually harms the corporation. This was no myth, no ghost story to frighten Administrator children; Arturo Kollberg had seen it in action.

Kollberg was the product of a mixed marriage. His father—a competent if unexceptional Administrator of a Midwestern hospital—had married below himself, had taken to wife one of the Professionals he supervised. Kollberg's mother had been only a thoracic Surgeon, and the other Administrator pups, cruel as children are the world over, had never let him forget it.

Kollberg's childhood had been spent watching helplessly while the parents of his schoolmates had risen in status and position, had been transferred away to challenging and glamorous posts all over the world. Kollberg's father, in his foolish weakness, had condemned himself to the obscurity of his provincial hospital, largely because he never understood how to keep his undercastes in their proper place. He'd even allowed Kollberg's mother to continue to work—but as long as she did Professional work, she could not upcaste to Administration; to come from reduced circumstances was no shame, but to *prefer* those circumstances was criminally selfish. She'd gone on performing her surgery, heedless of the damage this did to the career of her husband and the life of her only son.

But the blame couldn't be laid entirely on her head. His father had never understood the importance of dignity, of Administrative image. Fundamentally weak-spirited and easygoing, he'd preferred to be liked more than respected. He'd never insisted on proper deference; even now, Kollberg could raise a burning blush of shame when he remembered how his father would let his mother speak to him in public without use of his courtesy title, how he would let her *touch him in front of other undercastes*.

Kollberg had defined his life in opposition to his father's. He'd never married, had no interest in family—in fact, he never intended to marry. A wife would take up too much of his attention, would interfere with his ascetic devotion to the performance of his duties. He insisted upon—and got—precisely proper deference from those below him, and he offered precisely proper respect to those above. He knew exactly where his place was in the hierarchy of reality, and he knew exactly the vector of his life.

Upward. Slowly, perhaps, but ever upward.

Through devotion and skill he'd risen throughout his career, from an assistant departmental supervisor in his father's hospital to his father's own job. One of the proudest moments of Arturo Kollberg's life, one of his most cherished memories, was the day he had entered his father's office to personally hand-deliver the Notice of Forced Retirement. He'd proven what could be accomplished by a skilled Administrator, and he'd proven that he had every one of those skills, despite his miscegenetic birth.

But conquering his father hadn't been enough for him. There was only so far an ambitious man could rise in the health-care system. Now, twenty years later, he was among an elite of which the average Administrator could only dream. He'd outstripped every one of his schoolmates, their parents, every Administrator he'd ever met: he was not only a Studio Chairman, but Chairman of *the* Studio, San Francisco, the one that had started it all, the one where the first Winston Transfer equipment had been built by the hands of Jonah Winston himself. This Studio had transformed not only the nature of entertainment, but the structure of society itself.

It had been crumbling when he took it in hand, practically a derelict, a joke, a backwater final resting place of Peter-Principled incompetents. His peers had shaken their heads gravely when they'd heard of his transfer there, and they'd clucked solemnly about the self-destruction of a promising career.

They clucked no longer.

San Francisco was now the jeweled diadem of the whole Studio system, the flagship operation, the prestige market; San Francisco took in fifty million marks a year from the mere *waiting lists* it maintained for hopeful subscribers to its top ten stars.

And when one speaks of the top ten stars of San Francisco, when one speaks of the top ten stars of all time, one inevitably comes around to Caine.

Say what you will about Burchardt, about Story and Zhian and Mkembe, bring up any name you want; there was only one Caine. Never been anyone like him, probably never will be again; often imitated, never duplicated. There were any number of conflicting theories about Caine's continuing popularity, giving the credit variously to his eloquence, to his curious combination of ruthlessness and passion, to his peculiar quirks of honor; Kollberg knew all these to be empty rationalization.

In a word, bullshit.

There were two reasons that Caine continued to dominate both the firsthand and secondhand markets. The first was his snarling bare-knuckle brawling.

Throwing spells is one thing—feeling the power of magick surge through your body. Hacking into an enemy with a steel blade is something else—something more intimate, more brutal. But even that can't compare with the erotic power of the snap of bone beneath your bare hands, the smack of flesh on flesh and the sudden, delirious surge that takes you when your enemy gives that faint sigh—that gasp of the consciousness of defeat—when his face goes slack and he sees his death in your eyes. It's the fighting itself that Caine's fans live for, and Caine throws himself into combat with the abandon of a cliff diver: he springs out into space, to live or die, just for the rush.

The second reason was Kollberg himself.

Kollberg had *made* Caine, had managed his career with the sort of personal attention that most men reserve for their sons. Anyplace on Overworld where a situation was reported that would make a thrilling backdrop for a Caine story, Caine went. Kollberg had even sent him to places where other Actors were at work— even when it meant dropping him into their story lines and having him take them over. Kollberg had been criticized for this favoritism, and he'd been criticized for pandering to the public, for damaging the stories of the other Actors and destroying their artistic validity.

He had answered every charge with a gesture, a chubby finger pointed straight at the Studio's bottom line. Even the lesser Actors gave up grumbling; after all, the chance that Caine could show up unexpectedly in their Adventures boosted the subscription rates for every single Actor in San Francisco.

But this matter of Caine setting himself against Kollberg, defying him to his face, even threatening him—this could not be allowed to pass. Michaelson shouldn't even really be considered a Professional—this current fad for pandering to the egos of Actors had gone too far. Professionals, indeed. If anything, Actors should be Artisans, at most; their trade was a simple exchange of handiwork for money. A true Professional is a member of an elite society with a self-enforced ethical code; a true Professional is accountable for the results of his work.

Kollberg smiled grimly to himself. Now that would be amusing— if someone held Caine accountable for his actions, if he ever really had to face the consequences of things he'd done. It was a happy fantasy, but one he couldn't afford to indulge. Caine was too valuable.

And really, he reminded himself, it wasn't Caine who had threatened him: it was Michaelson. Caine was the one who brought all this wealth into the Studio; it was Caine who was Kollberg's greatest success.

It was Michaelson he'd find a way to punish.

3

HARI FINISHED HIS workout with a series of spin kicks against the head-sized holographic target that danced in the electrostatic mist at one end of the Abbey's gym. Back-spins to both sides, hooking kicks, side kicks, crescents: Hari spun until sweat sprayed out horizontally from his hair.

He shook his head and made a mental note to be cautious about his left lead; some change in the weather had stiffened the old sword cut on his right thigh, slowing him enough that he was only landing about three in five of his back kicks on the bobbing target. This was a bad trend: he wasn't a kid anymore, and experience compensates for speed only up to a point.

He went straight to the screen without bothering to shower. He toweled away most of his drying sweat while he spent a few minutes with his lawyer, making sure that his affairs were in order, and especially that the annuity he'd arranged for his father's upkeep was unbreakable. That done, he clicked off. There was no one else he had to talk to.

He draped the towel across his shoulders and headed for the vault. The Studio limo would be landing in fifteen minutes.

It was time to become Caine.

The vault in the Abbey's basement drew enough power to light a small town. This vault maintained an Overworld-normal field that allowed him to store Caine's outfit and weapons so he'd never have to change at the Studio vault with lesser Actors.

It was only the size of a small closet: exactly twice as big as he needed.

With the door open, the empty left side of the vault stared back at him. Occasionally he entertained masochistic fantasies of buying duplicates of Pallas' costume, just so there'd be *something* there, in place of this mocking emptiness. Sad dreams of a desperate man—he could never hang his own costume there, just as he still slept to one side of his king-sized bed.

He pulled out his gear.

The black leather tunic was faded and cracked—white salt rings of ancient sweat circling the armpits, rawhide laces stretched and stiff. He put it on the immaculate upholstery of the dressing room couch, next to the soft black breeches that were covered with slices and tears crudely sewn; the coarse brown thread showed like old bloodstains against the leather. On the floor he set the pair of supple boots, cut low to the size of the high-top tennis shoes of a different era.

He stood naked before the full-length mirror on the outside of the vault door. The flat muscles of his chest, the ridges of his abdomen, the bunched cords of his thighs and arms, all stood out like they'd been cut into stone. He turned slightly and narrowed his eyes, regarding the slight thickening just below his waist with critical distaste. Maybe this was an inevitable consequence of pushing forty—or maybe he'd been slacking. Only the faintest twinge of vanity colored his disapproval; nearly all of it was caused by the certain knowledge that four or five extra pounds could slow him fatally at the critical cusp between victory and death.

He had the build of a middleweight boxer, somewhat tall for his weight. His skin was a swarthy map of crisscross scars on which could be traced the high points of Caine's career. Here was the puckered circle of the crossbow quarrel he'd taken at Ceraeno; here was the diamond scar of the sword thrust through his liver outside Toa-Phelathon's bedchamber. Up at his collarbone was the jagged axe cut where Ghular Freehammer had nearly decapitated him; there on his back were parallel scars given him by a puma in the cat pits of Kirisch-Nar. He had a story for every major scar and not a few of the minor ones; now in the mirror he touched each scar and let each story flood his mind, reminding himself once again who he was.

I am Caine.

The big scar, from his right hip down his thigh, the one that slowed those kicks—that one he'd gotten from Berne.

He shook off that memory and slipped into his supporter—a leather jockstrap padding a steel cup sewn within. He pulled on the leather breeches and drew the pair of throwing knives from his thigh sheaths to test their razor edges against his forearms. He stepped into the boots, and checked the small leafblade daggers in the ankle sheaths. Inside the tunic were sewn the sheaths for three more knives—two long ones below the armpits for fighting, and another throwing knife between the shoulder blades. He laced the tunic up to his sternum and belted it with a supple garroting-rope cored with steel cable.

Now again he looked in the mirror, and the image that returned his glare was Caine.

I am strong. I am relentless. I am inescapable.

The knots of worry that had tied themselves into his guts slowly uncoiled and fell away; pain and resentment eased down from his shoulders and rolled off his back. He grunted a grim chuckle at the cold freedom he now felt. Hari Michaelson's problems, his weaknesses and insecurities, his whole claustrophobic life, would be left behind here on Earth.

He let Shanna's image boil to the surface of his consciousness. If she was alive, he would save her. If she was not, he would avenge her. Life is simple. Life is good.

I am invincible. I am the Blade of Tyshalle.

I am Caine.

4

IN THE TECHBOOTH, Arturo Kollberg licked his lips and rubbed his hands together. Not only was every first-hander berth filled, he had already fielded overnight requests from the Studios in New York, London, Seoul, and New Delhi for satellite simulcasts.

This Adventure had taken on a life of its own, before Caine could even enter the Studio. This would be bigger than he'd dreamed. While techs throughout the Studio ran down their flat-voiced checklists, Kollberg hummed to himself and imagined the titles he might attach to this. *Against the Empire?* No, too common. Perhaps *Seven Days in Ankhana*—but that would only work if Pallas lived that long. *For Love of Pallas Ril*—now that, that had a nice ring to it, in an old-fashioned, slightly overripe sort of way.

The smile this brought was still on his lips as a tech's colorless monotone reported that the satellite links checked out perfectly. He pushed himself to his feet and headed for the green room.

5

IN HIS PRIVATE box, Businessman Marc Vilo gave one last sidelong glance at Shermaya Dole—*of the Leisure Doles of Kauai,* the phrase rolled warmly inside his head—at her torso, at least. Her head was already concealed beneath the induction helmet, and her hips were covered by the privacy shield of the simichair's comfort hookups. He'd decided she was really very attractive, in a fleshy sort of way, and he figured on tearing off a piece of that before the two of them left his box. He'd gotten a tremendous amount of ass in this room; it almost never failed—first-handing Caine always made them horny. A little jazz, a little jizz, and she just might sponsor him on an upcaste to Leisure. He smiled as he pulled down his own induction helmet.

6

OUTSIDE, THE MURMUR of the undercaste mob was joined by the low-voiced growl of the long black ground-effect limo that swung up the curving drive. The murmur rose, peaking toward orgasm as Security pressed the mob back from the gate, clearing a path. The limo settled, and the crowd sighed. Actors almost always flew directly in to the Studio's landing pad; they almost always dodged the crowds and hurried directly from the landing pad to the Studio's green room; almost all of them did.

Except Caine.

Every person in the crowd knew his story, the story of the street kid from the Mission District. He was one of them—they believed—and he never forgot where he came from, he never forgot his people, as the Studio marketing flacks relentlessly reminded them. The Studio chauffeur sprang from the front, but the passenger door of the limo opened before he could get his hand there; Laborers open their own doors. The crowd held its breath as Caine climbed into view.

He stood beside the limousine, his back to the gate, surveying the crowd in its sudden silence. They saw what they believed to be lines of worry in his face; many of them nudged each other to point out what seemed to be added grey in his hair and beard.

His stillness held them, and the moment stretched until even the coupes of the last arriving Leisurefolk seemed to pause in their swooping flight. Then his back straightened and his eyes flashed; his teeth gleamed through a smile that held neither joy nor humor.

He slowly raised his knotted fist to them in a gesture older than the Colosseum of Rome.

The crowd went wild.

7

CAINE STRODE INTO the gaping maw of the gate, and its iron jaws clanged shut behind him.

God's bloody balls, he thought as he walked toward the main doors. *I hate that shit.*

At the Overworld-normal vault, similar to but vastly larger than the one at the Abbey, he was issued the six silver coins that were Caine's cash reserve.

Kollberg met him in the green room. Two red-suited secmen stood at attention by the door. "Nice, ah, timing on the crowd out there."

"Yeah, whatever."

"About our, hmm, little *disagreement* last night—I understand that you're under a great deal of stress. As far as the subscribers, well, we'll wait and see, shall we? If it doesn't turn out to be a, mm, problem, we can forget all about it."

Caine looked at the pair of secmen, their faces masked by the smoked shields of their helmets. "Yeah. I can see that you've forgotten already."

Kollberg harrumphed nervously. "Just a last-minute note or two. Feel free to investigate Pallas' disappearance a little before you go after Ma'elKoth, to make it look good. No one is to know your actual mission. And, ah—" He coughed into his hand. "—about

Lamorak. If he's not dead—if, for example, he was captured—you are under no circumstances to attempt a rescue."

"I'm sure Karl appreciates your concern."

"Think about it from our point of view. You are a vastly more bankable star; it would be frankly, ah, *silly* to endanger yourself for the sake of a man whose audiences have been dropping for three years, and they were never large to begin with. However, if you have an opportunity to recover his thoughtmitter without, ah, undue *risk*, go ahead. We're all interested to find out how the Long Form works, and you'd be in line for a percentage of its cube rentals."

"I'll keep that in mind." He pointed at the clock. "Five minutes."

"Oh, yes, well, mm, break a leg."

He nodded. "Probably several."

8

IN THE CAVEA, the lights dimmed and the mountain scene of the helmet test pattern faded from the techs' screens. A soundless shadow passed through the ranks of reclining firsthand berths, the figures they held made faceless by the blank ceramic shields of the induction helmets. The shadow mounted the steps of the ziggurat transfer platform and crossed to its geometric center. The massive overhead bank of the stage lights known as sunbeams flared to life, perfectly framed to the platform's edge.

Caine stood, motionless, in the stark white glare.

9

ONCE AGAIN IN the techbooth, Arturo Kollberg moistened his already-wet lips. *My masterpiece,* he thought. "Engage thoughtmitter."

A tech stroked a sensor, and the wide, domed screen at one end of the techbooth flickered on, showing the rising rows of firsthand berths through Caine's eyes.

"Engaged."

Another tech frowned at his monitor and reported an unusually high number of adrenal reactions to the sensory-deprivation sequence. Kollberg himself adjusted the neurochem feed and then thumbed the microphone sensor.

"Leisurefolk and Investors," he intoned, his words echoing through the Cavea and into the aural sensors of induction helmets around the world, "Businessfolk, Ladies and Gentlemen. I am Administrator Arturo Kollberg, Chairman of the San Francisco Studio. On behalf of the entire Studio System, I welcome you to the birth of this extraordinary Adventure. And now—brought to you by Vilo Intercontinental, *We Carry the World for You*—I give you the Blade of Tyshalle, the Right Hand of Death Himself . . ."

A long, pregnant pause.

"Caine!"

With his own hand, Kollberg stabbed the switch that fed the holoview from the Cavea into thousands of induction helmets. The sigh that went up was like the first breath of a hurricane. Kollberg flicked the mike to inactive.

"Establish transfer link."

Beneath the Studio the powerplant hummed. Techs glared at readouts with total concentration. "Established. We've got an alley in the Warrens. Clear."

"Good. Whenever he's ready, then." Kollberg patted the tech on the shoulder and left the booth, heading for his own box.

10

ON THE TRANSFER platform, Caine stood with the focused stillness that implies the capacity for instant violence. He held this stillness for a long breath before he spoke.

"I don't have any high words for you," he said slowly. "She's my wife, that's all. I'm going to hunt down any bastard who even thought about doing her harm, and I'm gonna hurt him till he dies like a dog in the street. I hope you have fun."

His hands folded into fists of stone. "I know I will."

He lifted his eyes to the glass panel that fronted the techbooth high above.

"Let's do this thing."

11

ARTURO KOLLBERG SNUGGED his head against the gelpack in his simichair. The helmet automatically covered his head, and the preset adjustment instantly matched his field patterns. He breathed out a long sigh of perfect contentment.

He honestly believed he was going to enjoy this.

12

AN ALLEY TAKES shape around me. Daylight. Smells—heavy spice, curry and green chilies, water-soaked charcoal, dung, rotting flesh . . . To my left there's a weather-bleached wooden bin against the wall, piled high with body parts that are mostly human, some ogrillo or troll: rat-chewed legs, arms with fingerless hands, sections of rib or pelvis: leftover scraps from the business alongside, the Zombie Rent-to-Own. I know this alley; I'm in the Warrens, near the Kingdom of Cant's border with the Face.

I should say, near where the border *was*, the last time I was in town, almost two years ago. The politics of territory in the Warrens are fluid, to say the least; in the absence of any outright turf wars between the various and several Warrengangs, borders are even more imaginary here than they are in the wider world. Borders in the Warrens are mainly an expression of where, street to street and house to house, members of a particular Warrengang can do business without getting themselves killed by the neighboring gang.

Which isn't so different, really, from the wider world with its nations and principalities, treaties and surveyors. We're honest about it, here; that's all.

An enormous slack-jawed dog, filthy brown coat patched with mange, creeps tentatively toward me, keeping to the morning shadows along the wall. I step politely back to let it pass; damn Warrendogs carry diseases I haven't even heard of. It looks me over with its one good eye—the other's webbed with milky cataract— while it considers its options.

My fingers tingle with adrenaline as I raise my fists.

This is the best thing about being Caine, by far the best: this almost sexual rush of perfect confidence, the conviction that I'm the toughest kid on the block. On any block.

"You want a piece of this, pooch?" I say, showing my teeth. "Come and get it, you wormy sack of shit."

I speak in Westerling without hesitation; the Studio-conditioned blocks on my voice wouldn't let me speak English even if I wanted to.

The dog decides I'm too much trouble and passes me by for the easier meal at the used-parts bin. Big damn dog, shoulder as high as my ribcage. The severed arms and legs in the bin squirm and press themselves blindly away in their imitation of life as the dog roots into them. A low moaning comes from deep within the pile; some lazy mucker must have left a head attached to a torso. Or maybe there's a live one in there—a bum snuggled in for the warmth of the decaying flesh around him, or a victim of one of the Warrens' countless daily muggings. I chuckle, and shrug.

Time to get to work.

I stroll out of the alley toward the heart of the Kingdom of Cant, into the bazaar that surrounds the ancient, crumbling hulk of the Brass Stadium. The sun is brighter here—a richer yellow—and the sky is more deeply blue; the clouds are more full and whiter, and the breeze that pushes them carries a faint undernote of green and growing things. It's a beautiful day; I can barely whiff the shit trodden into the well-churned muck that passes for a street, and the flies, swarming in blue-shimmering thunderheads over the heaps of random trash, sparkle like gemstones.

I weave between the pushcarts and the tentstalls, smilingly refusing steaming chunks of river trout and nets of fruit cunningly displayed to hide the wormtracks and blotches of mold, ignoring vendors of charms and amulets, avoiding rug dealers and pot sellers. This is my ground; I worked this city and the surrounding provinces for the first ten years of my career.

I've come home.

On walls, here and there, I see the Simon Jester graffito, very much as it was described in the book Shanna stole it from: an oval for a face, a stylized pair of devil's horns, and a simple curved line to make his crooked grin.

None of the beggars look familiar, and I don't see any Knights; where the fuck is everybody? I stop at a stall half-shadowed by the towering, smoke-etched limestone curve of the stadium wall.

The sweating vendor bends over the handle of a spit that holds legs of mutton over a bed of red-black coals. "Leg of lamb, hot mutton," he calls dispiritedly. "Fresh this morning, worm free. Leg of lamb—"

"Hey, Lum," I say. "You look a little down this morning. Something wrong?"

He looks at me, and the heatflush drains out of his face. A second or two later he remembers to try to smile, but it doesn't last. "Caine?" His voice squeaks a little. "I don't know nothin' about it, Caine. Swear on my *balls*, I don't!"

I reach into the stall and casually hook one of the cooling shanks that hang from the guy ropes. "You don't know nothin' about what?"

He leans toward me and lowers his voice. "Don't play with me, here, Caine . . . My woman's got the fever, y'know, and my boy—Terl, you remember?—he's off with the Dungers, could be dead, I don't know." He's trembling now, casting furtive glances at my expressionless eyes. "I can't take any more trouble right now, all right? I don't know you, I haven't seen you, all right? Just walk."

"Well," I say flatly. "Aren't you friendly?"

"Please, Caine, I *swear*—" He flicks sweaty glances at the oblivious crowd around us. "If you get taken, I don't want you thinkin' it was me turned you in."

"Taken," I murmur. Well, well, well. I bite a chunk out of the mutton. It's tough as an old boot. I chew on it to give myself time to think this over, and before I can swallow it I feel someone coming up too close behind my left shoulder.

"Trouble, Lum?" the someone says. "This guy giving you hard times?"

Lum shakes his head, wide-eyed. I've got the newcomer in my peripheral vision now: black scuffed boots, red cotton breeches, the bottom edge of a knee-length chain shirt painted black, and a scarred but young-looking hand resting on the hilt of a scabbarded broadsword. One of the Knights of Cant. Finally. He'll have a partner nearby—they always travel in pairs.

I tongue the mutton into my cheek and say, "Just passing time. Don't get pissy."

The Knight grunts a laugh. "That's a kinda fresh answer, there, dinky. I'm gonna have to levy an insolence tax. Five nobles. Pay up."

I wink at Lum, then spin like I'm delivering a backfist. The mutton shank catches the Knight behind the ear and bends him over. I forehand the meat into his nose; blood spurts, and he goes straight and then over backward to measure his length in the mud. Lum gasps and disappears behind his grill, and the thick traffic of passersby transforms into a curious crowd.

I take another bite of mutton while the Knight shakes his head and tries to get up. His blood improves the flavor.

"Here's a hint, big fella," I tell him in a friendly way. "Don't charge what you can't collect. Makes you look bad. You lose the respect of the crowd."

His partner charges toward us through the chattering press. I smile and wave to him, and he scabbards his sword.

"Sorry, Caine. New kid. You understand."

"Not a problem. Tommie, isn't it? Yeah, from the Underground Tap. How's business?"

He grins, pleased that I remember him. "Yeah, shit, I'm all right. You know you're hot?"

"I'm hearing that word. What price?"

"Two hundred. In gold."

I swallow the second chunk of mutton with difficulty. "A lot of money."

The kid finally gets himself to his feet and is trying to draw. Tommie clouts him on that same swelling ear. "Stop it, y'fool. This here is *Caine*, all right? He's an honorary Baron of Cant. Even if you live through drawing on him, which you won't, His Majesty'd have your balls for lunch."

The kid decides he's got better things to do with his hands.

"Speaking of that," I say, "I need to talk to the King."

Tommie looks at me, his eyes suddenly clouded. "He's busy right now."

"It's life or death, Tommie."

He stares into the distance while he imagines various reactions, weighing the King's anger at being interrupted against the debt the King might still feel he owes me. Abruptly he makes up his mind. "All right. Follow me."

"Hey, Lum? It's all over," I say. He pokes his head up from behind the grill, and I toss him one of my silver nobles. I'm not a thief. "Your mutton's shit, by the way. Keep the change."

He blinks. "Uh, thanks . . . I guess."

Tommie leads me off around the curve of the stadium. The kid follows, pinching his nose shut with a crusted handkerchief. We stroll out of the bazaar and into the narrow winding alleyways that give the Warrens its name. I can get only the most occasional glimpse of the sun, but I don't need it to know what direction we're going: toward the triple border of the Kingdom, the Face, and the Rathole.

The real business in the Warrens takes place in the heart of each gang's turf; the borders are too vulnerable, too susceptible to suddenly lethal accidents and casual arson. Each border comprises at least a couple of blocks of no-man's-land, sometimes five or six, whose unfortunate residents are usually forced to pay off both sides. The triple borders—there are four of them; the Kingdom of Cant holds the center of the Warrens, around the stadium—are the poorest patches of bottom-feeding scum in the poorest part of Ankhana. Often the only shelter is the shell of a burned-out tenement. Many of the residents sleep on the street.

I like it here. It reminds me of home.

Tommie stops four paces from the sun-washed mouth of the alley we've been following for a few minutes now. "This is as far as I can go." He nods out toward the border, then indicates his chainmail, painted black with the silvered borders of the Knights of Cant. "The kid and me, we're in colors. His Majesty's running a game out there today, and we'd blunt the hook."

I nod my understanding. "Where is he?"

"You can't see him from here. You know the alley between the Working Dead and where Fader's Whores used to be?"

"Used to?" A twinge of nostalgia—I've spent some happy hours at Fader's. "What happened to Fader?"

"She was entertaining too many Rats," Tommie says with a shrug. "She had a fire."

Life in the big city. "All right," I say. "I'll tell His Majesty you took good care of me."

"You're straight, Baron. Thanks." Tommie nudges his kid partner with a sharp elbow and gives him a *Get with it, idiot* look.

The kid snorts blood and mumbles, "Thanks, uh, for not killing me, Cai—uh, Baron."

"My pleasure."

I leave them there and walk out into the sunlight.

The buildings that were once in the midst of this border have burned to low-sloping mounds of rubble, leaving a wide-open area of breeze and sun. A couple of places around the plazalike clearing hold lounging Rats in their colors of shit: brown and yellow. That's not unusual—this is their border, after all. A few of the shuffling street-people might be Rats as well, covert.

There's a considerable traffic through here: men with sharp prods driving roped-together strings of zombies from the Working Dead, which is the only thriving business for blocks around. I guess the owners want to be close to their source of supply. The zombies don't bother me, with their grey-leather skin and filmed-over eyes. Our Workers are worse, really; with the zombies, you can't see the buried spark of life—intelligence, will, whatever—that makes Workers so tragically creepy.

No sign of any Subjects, although you can never really tell. Any of these loafers who are taking the sun, any of these winos in this alley or the sleepy-faced rith smokers on that stoop, any could be Subjects of Cant. I can't count on recognizing them—I've been out of Ankhana for a while.

The alley Tommie directed me to is full of garbage—food scraps, rotting clothes, bits of broken furniture—and rats, the four-legged kind. There's a leper lying on a makeshift bed of rags, bloody pus draining from open sores into his ragged patches of yellowed grey beard. I squint at him.

He says, "For fuck's sake, Caine, get off the street, you stick out like a fucking boil on my ass."

"Hey, Majesty," I say as I drift casually into the alley. "How's business?"

The King of Cant's ravaged face splits open into a grin of unalloyed joy, and mine answers him. He's just about my best friend on Overworld. On any world. "Caine, you son of a bitch! How'd you find me?"

I dig down behind his pile of rags and settle in, my back against the wall. "Your boy Tommie sent me over. He's a good man. Hey, those are some killer sores."

"You like 'em? They're yours. Lamp oil with candle wax and bread dough, chicken blood half curdled with willow bark to keep it from clotting, and some pine gum to hold them on. Look nice, but they stink like a bastard. What brings you to Ankhana, you shit? Who are you killing?"

I shake my head and give him a serious look. "It's personal, this time. I'm looking for—"

"You know there's an Imperial warrant on you?"

"Yeah yeah yeah, I heard. Listen, I need to find Pallas Ril."

He frowns. "Pallas?" he says slowly, then he suddenly brightens. "Hey, look there, the boot's about to drop." He waves a rag-wrapped hand toward the plaza.

"Majesty, this is important," I begin, but my eyes follow his gesture in time to see a loose zombie shuffle up to one of the lounging Rats on the far side of the plaza. The Rat gets up to kick the zombie away, and the zombie suddenly moves a lot faster than zombies can really move.

It grabs the Rat and pulls him close, then steps into a shadowed alley mouth like a trick with his favorite whore; when it lets him go the Rat has a bloodstain spreading below his solar plexus. He drops to his knees and then pitches forward onto his face.

A very professional job: if you can rip the heart good on your first stab, you don't get the messy spray, and the gut-punch that accompanies the stab drives air out of the lungs. He's dead before he can draw enough breath to shout. As the zombie shuffles off, another man in Rat colors steps out into the dead Rat's place.

"Smooth, eh?" Majesty chuckles and cups a hand to his ear. "I don't hear any alarum. Got 'em all."

I nod. "What's this about?"

He smiles. "I got a tip that Thervin Backbiter is meeting a certain captain of the King's Eyes in that tenement across the way."

"You taking him?" Thervin Backbiter is King Rat, the leader of the northwestern rival of the Kingdom of Cant. I know him. I don't like him. "Hey, long as I'm here, maybe I could do him for you?"

"Thanks," Majesty says with a grin, "but not this time. I don't want war with Rats right now—and besides, you'd have to kill the Eye captain too, and nobody needs that kind of trouble. But, y'know, I also don't want Thervin to climb into bed with the Eyes; the Rats've been entirely too frisky lately as it is—if they line up some Imperial backing they'll be out of control. So instead of killing him, I'm sending a friendly message—all three of his stooges."

Three dead men equals a friendly message. That's the kind of math I understand.

"Best part is," Majesty goes on, "he won't even know anything's happened until he comes out of the meeting. That's when my fake Rats out there'll give him my regards. He'll hear the word. 'If there's a next time,' y'know?"

"So who gave you the tip? You got an ear in the Eyes, or in the Rats?"

His grin turns smug. "Trade secret, buddy-o. Let's say times are good in the Kingdom, and leave it at that."

Huh. If times are all that good, he wouldn't be hanging his ass out here for on-site supervision, but I let it go. Why waste breath arguing?

"Pallas Ril," I remind him. "Where is she?"

His eyes go vague on me again. "I hear she's in town," he offers.

"I hear that too. That's why I'm here talking to you. I also hear she's running a game and some Subjects are playing."

"I don't think so. I'd know about it. Pallas and me, maybe we're not close, exactly, but she would come to me straight for that kind of help, wouldn't she?"

"She did."

He gives me a long look, and his voice cools. "You think I wouldn't tell you?"

I shrug.

"Caine, I'm telling you now, all I know is she's in town. I seem to recall some report of contact—she talked to one of the boys, or something—but nothing serious."

"Who's Simon Jester?"

"The guy who's smuggling these poor mopes that Ma'elKoth thinks are *Aktiri*? How should I know?"

"You lost at least two of your boys about this time yesterday morning, down in Dunger territory by the river. What were they doing there?"

"How should I know?"

"That's twice you asked the same stupid question. They were stooging for Simon Jester, and you fucking well know it."

He sits up suddenly and gives me a hard look. "You're working, aren't you? Who's paying? The Monasteries or the Imperials?"

"Majesty, I swear to you, my only interest in this is finding Pallas Ril."

"I heard you broke up."

"Is that your business? Where is she?"

"But—" He shakes his head and looks honestly confused. "—what does Pallas Ril have to do with Simon Jester? Is she working for him?"

I squint at him without answering. He takes it for a long time, then lowers his face and scratches his head. "All right, shit. I've been supporting Simon Jester a little. Those boys, yeah, they were stooging. I mean, what's the harm? A little jab in Ma'elKoth's ass, that's all. But I guess the Cats took them; I don't think any lived."

"What's the next leg on the trip out?"

He frowns. "I don't know."

"When's the next time Simon Jester should make contact?"

"I don't know." His frown deepens. "I should know this."

"All right, listen." I scratch my head in furious exasperation, rub my eyes, and ask, "How'd you get into this in the first place? Did you meet, ah, Simon Jester . . . in person? Who came to you?"

Slowly, very slowly, he shakes his head, and his frown clears into something like awe. "I don't remember . . ."

"This is a problem."

His expression instantly congeals into stony belligerence. "Don't try and make it *my* problem, Caine. I've got too many guys on this street, you'll never—"

"Relax." At least I'm starting to get a handle on how that damned spell works. Funny that it doesn't seem to work on me. "I believe you."

Majesty now looks honestly disturbed, and more than a little frightened. "Are you ever gonna tell me what's going on? I mean shit, Caine, this is creepy! Am I losing it? I should *know* this shit. It's some kind of magick, isn't it—somebody fucking *hexed* me, is what happened, I'm thinking."

"Yeah," I say.

"I'm hexed? That's what you're telling me? I'll fucking kill them."

"Don't take it personally."

"You say. Nobody puts magick on me, Caine. Nobody. Don't they know I'll *kill* them? Do these fumbledicks have any clue who they're fucking, here? I've got Abbal Paslava the freaking *Spellbinder*—he'll do these bastards till their dicks stick up their own assholes and they fuck themselves with every step!"

I hold up a hand to cut him off. "How's our politics with the Faces, these days?"

"Not so good," he says, subsiding. "Why?"

"Hamman's got the best connections into the palace. I have to talk to him."

"You'll need a damn loud voice. He's been dead a year."

"You're kidding! Fat Hamman? I thought he was indestructible."

"Yeah, so did he. Nobody knows who took him, but the smart money's on the new leader of the Faces—that elf bitch from the Exotic Love in Alientown. Kierendal."

"The dyke? Holy shit."

"Yeah, it's bad enough to have to deal with a lapper, but a sub? Running a Warrengang? She's bringing in all kinds of subs—elves, dwarves, sprites, the works. The Faces practically own Alientown, now. She moved all the fittings from Hamman's old place, the Happy Miser, over into Exotic Love; it's the top casino in the

Empire, now. Calls it Alien Games. And she is no one to screw with, no pun intended. Word is, she's got her hooks on Hamman's spellbook, and you know what elves are like—they fucking *invented* magick. Hey, is *she* mixed in this? Is that mothersucking dyke the one who put magick on me?"

"How're her connections?"

He shrugs. "Good as Hamman's, maybe better. He only got the gamblers, mostly. She gets the gamblers, the addicts, and the perverts who like to wet their wicks in a subhole. Hey, you wouldn't want to kill her for me, would you? I'd make it worth your trouble."

I shake my head. "Not today. Listen, I gotta go. I'll be in touch."

"What, already? It's been two years—you can't catch up a little?"

"Sorry. I'm on a deadline. And, hey, if I'm as hot as all that— you got a spare cloak, or a cowled robe or something? Something that'll get me as far as Alientown without being tagged?"

He points with his thumb. "Take mine. It's behind that broken cabinet. Y'know, it'd help a lot if you'd just shave. Without that beard, you'd be a different man."

"That's just it. Sometimes I need to be me."

He shrugs. I get the robe and shrug into it, and pull the cowl up to shade my face.

Majesty extends his hand; I take it. He says, "You know my house is open to you. Come by after the Miracle, any night. You can stay with me."

"I'll do that. See you."

I stroll off, whistling like a malingering Laborer until I'm out of the game field; then my face sets and I start to move with some serious speed. So this is going to be a little tougher than I'd thought; so what? Here in Ankhana, it's impossible to be depressed.

The soft west wind blows the smoke and stench of the Warrens off behind me as I head out of the borderlands toward the Face, and the sun warms the light cloth over the leather on my back. Whores and beggars look me over as I trot past, maybe sizing me for a lift or a strongarm, but I'm moving too fast; I'm gone before they can make up their minds. I ignore them.

The fire-gutted rubble of a building provides a shortcut into the Face, the section of the Warrens that borders Ankhana proper and was once the home ground of Hamman and his Faces; a filthy man dressed in scorched rags snarls at me from under a tarpaulin stretched between beams that are tumbled like cornstalks after harvest. Farther back in the shadow behind him a dull-eyed woman cradles a silent infant at her sagging, empty breast. I smile and shrug an apology for intruding in their home and move on.

I'm comfortable here, more easy in my heart than any place I've been since I was eight years old. Maybe after I find Pallas, I'll have a couple of days to enjoy it.

The warming sun raises a slight prickle of sweat. I itch all over. I smell like a goat.

I love this town.

I'm free.

13

KIERENDAL THE FIRST FACE looked up briefly from her book at the coded knock on her apartment's outer door. Tup's tiny doll-sized hands continued to dig into the cords of her shoulders and neck. "Don't get up," Tup's whistling voice fluted in her ear. "Zakke will get it."

"That will be Pischu," Kierendal sighed. He'd never intrude, lacking an emergency.

"Tell him to go away." Tup now added lips to fingers on the nape of Kierendal's neck and drew warm shivers up from the base of her spine.

"Mm, stop." Kierendal reached back over her shoulder and drew the lovely little treetopper forward; Tup rode the palm of Kierendal's hand as though bareback on a horse. Though only twenty inches tall, Tup was a marvel of feminine perfection; perfect breasts that need never fear the pull of gravity, flawless skin, golden hair that seemed to shine with a light of its own. She might have been a beautiful human, were it not for her height, and the large translucent wings that were folded behind her, and the back-folding thumb of each foot that enabled her race to perch. And charming, too, as well as incredibly responsive; her nipples hardened as Kierendal watched. She squirmed in a deeply suggestive way and wrapped her trim and lovely ankles around Kierendal's forearm.

"No time to play now, sweetling. Business calls. Fly along—and get dressed. Pischu likes his women tiny, and we don't want to put ideas in his head."

"Oh, you're terrible." Tup giggled. She spread her wings and flew into the gloom of an inner chamber, silent as an owl.

Pischu coughed from the doorway. "Janner's cheating again."

Kierendal slowly and lovingly stroked shut the manskin cover of her massive book, and only then lifted her steel-colored eyes to meet the gaze of the daytime floor boss of Alien Games. The pupils in those eyes slitted vertically: nighthunter eyes.

Pischu coughed again and suddenly looked away; Kierendal, as was her habit when studying, reclined nude on a vast expanse of piled silken cushions. Pischu was one of only three Faces who were allowed within her chambers, but this privilege didn't ease the man's discomfort. Kierendal enjoyed it; that discomfort lent an attractive lemony tint to the otherwise bland earth-tones of Pischu's Shell. Like all of her people, the First Folk, she never needed to concentrate to summon mindview; it was simply another sense, like smell or taste.

With heavy brocade curtains drawn closed over the wide windows, her chambers were lit only by artfully placed lamps that painted rose highlights into her spun-silver hair, and across her lead-white skin.

She was tall even for a female of the First Folk, who commonly outgrew their males, and so lean that the articulation of her hip joint could be seen through the swell of her ass as she stretched her endless legs behind her. She lifted herself up on one elbow to expose the nipples of her nearly absent breasts; she'd painted her nipples silver this morning to match her intricately coiled hair. The money-colored flash caught Pischu's eyes, and his face reddened while the lemon shade in his Shell deepened sharply.

"How bad today?" she asked in a voice husky and languid enough to make Pischu wince.

"Worse than usual. He's gumming the dice, and he's so damned *clumsy*! Two of our . . . guests . . . have already tipped, and I had to toss them to stop a fight."

"Anyone important?"

"No. Both losers, but low rent. They're no loss, but Berne just came in."

"Berne?" Her thin lips, the color of calf liver, drew back enough to expose her overlong and oversharp canines. If that maniac caught Janner gumming . . .

Berne liked the dice and was a bad loser from the first roll. If he found someone to blame for it, Janner's head would be rolling across the floor in the fraction of a second it took Berne to draw. And Janner was the proprietor of Ankhanan Muckers and Manure, one of Kierendal's more profitable partnerships.

"I'll deal with it. Is Berne in the pit yet?"

"Not yet, but it won't be long. He's at the Crystal Bar, chatting on Gala. He still thinks one of these days he'll get her for free."

"If he does, he'll be disappointed." Kierendal rose and stretched, arching her back. "Actual passion interferes with her technique. Zakke?"

Her stonebender houseboy instantly appeared in the doorway, all broad shoulders and neatly shaved weak chin; he'd been eavesdropping, as usual—it was part of his job. "Yes, Kierendal?"

"Tell the kitchen I'll be wanting brunch. Whatever they have that's alive—oysters will do. And a fresh comb of honey—Tup will be joining me, I think." As she spoke, a mist swirled and coalesced around her, draping like cloth from her bony arms.

Zakke nodded and ticked his fingers, making mental notes. He was a sweet boy, really, if not too bright. And he was very strong and loyal; Kierendal decided impulsively on the spot to finally let him grow in his traditional stonebender beard to cover that unfortunate chin.

Now she stood motionless and built her image; it was a simple process, especially now—the page of Hamman's book she'd studied that very morning had provided an interesting twist in substantiating a Fantasy. She opened her Shell to the Flow and drew it around her as a lesser woman might draw silk. It wrapped her lovingly, gently concealing, enveloping, coloring the air in which she stood with sheer and translucent pastel.

While her hands pulled the mist into the apparent solidity of cloth, they also stroked her body into the shape she desired. As she did this, her coiled metallic hair seemed to unbind itself and flow in beautiful curls—now definitely golden—about shoulders that had a touch of human color to them now, and a soft roundness that matched the breasts she had massaged into a swelling feminine curve.

When the process was complete, she still appeared exotic—still obviously of the First Folk, unquestionably primal, with the slant of her now violet eyes and the pronounced points at the tips of her ears—but there was a gentle quality of innocence in the fullness of her lips, a softer texture to her gold-touched cheeks, a sweet arc to her hip that would catch at the heart of any man. She now hid behind a face that had never been touched by the frown of thought.

She smiled as she altered the drape of her illusionary clothing with a twist of her mind and a hand that followed it. It would amuse her to walk naked among her unsuspecting staff and clientele. And it would amuse her even more that Pischu would have to follow her, knowing she was naked.

"Well. Let us see if we can convince Lucky Janner that this is not his lucky day."

Zakke opened the door; Pischu stepped respectfully aside. After only a short walk down two flights of stairs and along a guarded corridor, Kierendal entered her kingdom.

Alien Games was a fairyland of vice. Rails of gleaming brass surrounded the gaming pits that dimpled the floor. Three wide steps of glistening purple-veined marble circled each pit like a bull's-eye. Swivel-hipped girls and flat-bellied boys—all in scant clothing revealing their astonishing grace and beauty—ferried trays of cocktails and various other intoxicants over carpets of crushed red velvet. These servers, human and primal, were no less intoxicating than the contents of their trays, and no less available—and in some cases, substantially less expensive. Five huge crystal chandeliers held no candles but radiated a soothing amber light that seemed to have no definite source. Even now, well before noon, the gaming pits were largely filled with crowds of sweating men and women watching the tumble of dice or flip of cards with the bloodshot concentration of hungover hawks.

Those clients not engaged in gambling, or in drinking themselves blind at one of the seven bars, all watched the show. Up on the narrow thrust stage that projected above the gaming floor, an apparently human female with a glorious spray of raven hair took well-acted pleasure from a pair of male treetoppers. Nearing the end of this particular performance, she was already nude and bathed in sweat, trembling with feigned passion, while the treetoppers swirled around her on the blurs of their diaphanous wings like oversize hummingbirds. They carried silken cords and trailed them across her body—binding and unbinding her, slithering knotted silk over the translucent purity of her flesh.

This "girl" was one of Kierendal's best performers; even now, men and women both were rising from their seats to take the hands of nearby whores. Kierendal watched the show for a moment, smiling to herself and shaking her head; if only those guests who'd become so aroused in watching her knew that she was actually a fifty-year-old ogrillo bitch with flaccid dugs and finger-sized warts all over her body.

Similarly, the purple-veined marble was in truth splintered pine, weathered to the color of dirt; the gleaming brass was actually rusty cast iron, and the service staff were pox-raddled and dull eyed, most of them broken-down ex-whores.

All this illusion stirred the Flow into fantastic whirls of energy, but did not deplete it; it all was powered by a single shiny black griffinstone no larger than the first joint of Kierendal's thumb—which, she reminded herself, she'd need to replace later this month.

Kierendal paused in the doorway long enough to be joined by her three overt guards—massive ogres with unfiled tusks, wearing light chainmail painted with the scarlet and brass motif of the house and carrying wickedly spiked morningstars slung at their waists. All of Alien Games' overt security staff were ogres, or their nocturnal cousins, trolls; they were uniformly stupid, but huge and terrifically strong—and the sure knowledge that troublemakers would not only be killed but eaten helped Kierendal maintain an orderly business. She had never been robbed.

The overwhelming menace of the ogres also allowed her to let her guests go armed, as disagreements rarely became fatal before the ogres could break them up. And letting men keep their swords improved the whoring; men are universally friskier when they have their steel penises belted at their sides.

She extended her Shell and twitched the Flow in currents toward three of her coverts—two humans and one fey who were flawlessly impersonating innocent guests. The fey and one human looked up at what they perceived as her whisper in their ear. *At the Crystal Bar,* she sent. *The one in the slashed-velvet doublet and shoulder-draw sword is Berne. Get close and stick there.* She sent the other human to stand behind Lucky Janner in the bones pit.

Even as her coverts approached, Berne pushed himself away from the bar, giving up on Gala for now; he strode toward the bones pit, the diagonally shoulder-slung scabbard that held a long straight blade slapping at his back. The coverts were too experienced to announce themselves by a sudden change of direction, and so Kierendal hurried to reach the pit first, ogres stomping at her heels.

Janner, the deep, slanting scar across his nose glowing white against a face flushed with victory, grinned fiercely at Kierendal as she approached.

"I'b habing a gread day, Kier! Gread! Can'd *belieb* id!" Due to the hatchet wound that had destroyed his sinuses, Lucky Janner perpetually sounded like a man with a severe head cold.

Kierendal modulated her voice into the aristocratic tones she used for guest contact. "Of course we are very pleased at your success, Janner. Today, your nickname is well deserved. Can I perhaps tear you away from the table for a minute? Business of mutual interest . . . ?"

"Innda minnid. I'b onnda roll."

Kierendal watched Janner's clumsy gumming of the dice with distaste. What in the world was he using? Snot?

Berne glided down the steps into the pit just as Janner made his point. A cold ball gathered in Kierendal's stomach; Berne walked with the loose-limbed dangerous grace of a puma, and his pale eyes had the fixed reptilian stare of a reflexive killer. His Shell flickered scarlet and white with barely repressed violence.

He'd been created Count only a few months before, but Kierendal's sources informed her that he was one of the new Emperor's closest confidants—some reports claimed he was Ma'elKoth's personal assassin—and he was known to command the Grey Cats. Every time she looked at him, Kierendal well believed the tale that Berne had received Monastic training—his instinctive weight-forward balance and perfect kinesthetic awareness were both convincing and unsettling. His swordplay was already legendary: he never wore armor in battle or duel, depending solely on his blade-skills for defense.

Whatever the truth about him might be, he was unquestionably one of the most dangerous men in the Empire. It was widely said that no one had ever lived to cross him twice.

He nodded expressionlessly to Kierendal as he slid into a place at the table; he didn't spare the ogres even a glance. He laid a stack of royals against Janner's next throw.

"Play or pass, buttface. Let's go."

"Buddface . . . ?" The color that rose up Janner's neck was a deeper scarlet than the flush of victory.

"Has a crack in it, no?" Berne laughed. He was always his own best audience. "Tell you, though, if my butt was that ugly I'd never get laid again—be ashamed to take my pants off." Now the two coverts were finally coming down the steps behind him, much to Kierendal's relief.

"Oh, comb ond," Janner said, a wild look in his eyes, "if your boyfriend realdy loved you, he'd make allowances . . ."

Other men around the table snickered into their hands, none of them foolish enough to laugh openly. Berne's face froze. He stepped back from the table, his left hand drifting up toward the hand-and-a-half sword hilt above his right shoulder. Janner squared off, grasping the hilt of the shortsword at his belt. Berne's Shell had gone crimson—Janner might be dead in a heartbeat.

"Gentlemen." Kierendal gestured and stepped smoothly between them. Only the barest flicker of Berne's eyes betrayed the fact that the two coverts at his back each now held the point of a dagger against his kidneys.

"Berne, Lucky Janner is an honored guest, as well as a personal friend. You will not kill him within my establishment." Berne's only reply was to rake the illusionary curves of her body with his eyes, from knees to neck, with slow and deliberate insult. *Mm*, she thought. *So that's how it is. All right.* She turned to Janner.

"As for *you*," she said in her most scathing tone, "if you must give your life simply to score a *point* off this man, at least be witty enough that I'll get a laugh when I repeat it in your eulogy."

Janner began to protest; Kierendal ignored him. A sudden clatter near the street door drew her eyes. One of the new Faces, a stonebender female she'd recruited since taking over and moving operations to Alientown, had come sprinting up to the fey who worked in the coat check. With no more than a thought, Kierendal extended a tendril of her Shell to touch his, drawing only enough Flow to power the effect, and shifted her consciousness to his body so she could see and hear the stonebender. He expressionlessly acknowledged her presence with a welcoming swirl of Flow.

The stonebender's mouth was painted with rich crimson blood that still trickled from her nose, which looked broken. Her neatly trimmed goatee was caked with clots. Her Westerling was thick with the accent of the Gods' Teeth. ". . . askink me which were Kierendal's chamber, which door, which winder. He wanted se knock codes . . . he t'ought I was unconscious, so he left and I ran, I ran . . ."

"All right, it's all right," the fey said soothingly, his slim hands on her powerful shoulders. "Who was he? Can you describe him?"

Here the Faces' training paid off; she had memorized her

attacker's appearance even while she was being interrogated and beaten. "Half again a foot taller san me. Straight black hair, shot grey at temples. Dark skin, black eyes, mustache and jawline beard. Broken nose, wis a slantwise scar. And fast. Faster san I've ever seen. He had knives, but he used his fists."

Kierendal thought, *that sounds like Caine,* and slowly it dawned on her that it could *be* Caine. She'd heard about the sudden Imperial bounty on his head, had suspected that he must have been in town—and only then did she connect the thoughts that swirled around her.

Caine was asking about me!

With a gasp she found herself back within her own head; her knees were weak and her bowels loose. Panic-thoughts yammered a stunning babble: Who could have hired him? The Imperials? No, they would have sent the Cats for her. The Monasteries, Caine usually worked for the Monasteries, but she had done nothing to attract their lethal disfavor—had she? No, it must be—ah, it was the King of fucking *Cant*! That bastard! Wasn't Caine supposed to be hooked into the Subjects? But why? Why *now*? Or was it the Monasteries after all? Had she told one too many truths about Ma'elKoth?

Stern mental discipline swiftly mastered her panic; she had more immediate issues with which to deal. First things first.

Kierendal prided herself on her ability to think and act in an organized fashion in the midst of a crisis. In only the time it took to breathe deeply in and slowly out again, she had sketched out the rudiments of a plan of defense. She once again reached into the Flow and established contact with the fey in coat check.

In minutes Alien Games would be surrounded, outside, by an invisible army of Faces in teams of three, one member of each three either primal or treetopper for swiftness of communication. The pissoir in the street outside would be covered inside and out, as well as the shaft that sank below it into the limestone caves that underlay the city. The roofs of the surrounding buildings would be scattered with Faces either present or in clear line-of-fire with loaded crossbows. Every combat-capable staff member within the casino would be alerted, and pairs of guards would be placed in every corridor in plain sight of each other. She'd already rejected the idea of calling the Constabulary; worth more than the two-hundred-royal reward would be the knowledge of who wanted her dead badly enough to hire Caine. The coat-check fey met her eyes across the room and nodded his acknowledgment.

She sent: *"Use her story for the current description. Pass it through the ranks. Keep me informed. I'll be in my apartment; use the five-code when you knock. Now* move!"

He moved. She let the link dissipate and returned her attention to the immediate events here in the bones pit.

Janner was still talking. She had no idea what he'd said, and less interest. She flicked a finger at the ogre who stood near her right shoulder, and he clamped his massively taloned hands around Janner's arms and lifted the struggling little man off the floor. "Hey! Hey—!"

"You're done for the day. Get him out of the pit."

The ogre hoisted Janner and ponderously carried him up the steps onto the main floor. Kierendal paced beside him.

"You can'd do dthis!"

"I don't have time to handjob your wounded feelings," she said, low enough that Berne wouldn't overhear. "Have a drink at the bar. Grab a bite in the dining room. My treat. Just watch your mouth and stay away from Berne."

"I can handle himb—"

"No, you can't. Shut up." She reached up, took his chin in her surprisingly strong hand, and dug her fingernails into his cheeks. "And stay away from the dice pit until you learn to cheat *properly*, you stupid shit." She waved a hand, and the ogre let Janner go with a shove that sent him stumbling off toward the Silver Bar.

"Kierendalll . . ."

Berne leaned motionless on the edge of the knucklebones field, wearing his mocking smile. The pair of coverts were still at his back, daggers still pricking his kidneys. "Can I move now, Kierie? Do I stand here all day?"

She made a sound in her throat that was almost a whine of frustration. "Apologies, Count Berne," she said. With a wave of a hand she instructed the coverts to release him.

He shrugged once, like he was shaking tension out of his shoulders, and then he paced toward her with that hungry-puma walk of his.

"I have to kill him, y'know," he said easily. "He insulted me, and I'm obliged to pay him out. It's the, ahh, *honor* of the *nobility*. You understand."

This, at least, she knew precisely how to handle. She took a step to meet him and looked up meltingly into his eyes. "Please, my lord," she said with her hands resting on his heavily muscled chest, "I would take it as a personal favor if you could let this pass, forgotten."

His mocking smile took on a twist of contempt as his arms slid around her slim back and he forced his lips down onto hers. His tongue pushed into her mouth, probing with slimy insistence, and she knew well how to pant and squirm as his hand cupped her illusionary breast.

This was insult deeper than the last, but she had once been as good at her former profession as Berne was at his current one; he never suspected how revolting she found him. When his hand slid roughly down between her legs, she released the tactile part of her illusion of clothing. He found his hand pressed directly to the lips of her vagina, while his other felt the smooth and flawless skin of her back.

He stiffened, then lifted his head and stared down at her with moist surprise. The contempt in his eyes now mingled with sudden lust—contempt and lust that seemed to feed on each other so that both grew together.

"You know what?" he said thickly. "I think I like you after all. I'll do you that favor, this time. Just remember what you owe me."

She demurely lowered her head to his shoulder. "Oh, you know us elves—" Using the human slur name for her people gave her not the faintest twinge. "—we have long memories. Allow me to sponsor your morning's recreation. Tallin, five hundred for the Count."

The click of the tiles as the croupier pushed them across the field drew Berne's eyes, but then he looked back down into hers. "A difficult choice," he murmured.

"You're very gallant," she said. "Please, enjoy yourself."

He shrugged. "Another time, then."

"Of course."

She turned crisply and headed for the service door as Berne returned to the pit and warmed the dice. She felt a certain sense of accomplishment: a bit of quick, efficient lick'n'flick to keep Berne happy and Janner alive? Cheap at twice the price.

But she had no time to enjoy minor victories.

Her ogres were close on her heels in a liquid rustle of chainmail; subtle gestures summoned four coverts and the pair of treetopper showboys, who were now on a break. She stopped in the doorway and spoke in the clipped, decisive tone of a feya accustomed to obedience, repeating the orders she'd sent to the fey in coat check.

"What is it, though?" one of the coverts asked. "Are the Rats coming against us? The Serpents?"

"Worse." She swallowed through a painfully dry throat. "I think it's Caine. Now move."

They scattered at a run.

She rubbed her hands together and found that her palms were damp and her fingers slightly tremulous. A drink, she decided. That's what she needed, a drink to steady her nerves and smooth her roiled consciousness, then more time spent in study of the book. She strode upward toward her apartment, taking steps three at a time, wondering urgently if she had time to charge a Shield.

She reached the door of her apartments and knocked lightly, twice and then once again, and waited for Zakke to open the door.

She knocked again: two, one. The intricately silver-inlaid door had no external keyhole, and she herself had laid the wards that prevented it from being magically opened. The lazy shit was probably asleep, and she had no time to waste. She hammered the door with her clenched fist.

"Zakke, you worthless prick!" Her shout resounded in the empty hallway. "If this door isn't open in ten seconds you are one dead dwarf!"

Finally she heard the rasp of the bolt being drawn. When the door cracked open she stiff-armed it back with a thump and strode into the room, heading straight for her private dry bar next to the huge stone fireplace. The heavy brocade curtains were tightly drawn, and every lamp was dark; the pungent odor of smoldering wicks hung heavily in the gloom. "You *were* sleeping, you shit! I'll skin you for this!"

The closing door cut off the last of the dim light from the corridor. Kierendal, nearly blind until her eyes could adjust, slammed her shin into an errant footstool hard enough to bring tears to her eyes. She hopped about on one leg, cursing and trying to keep her balance while holding her throbbing shin with both hands. "And get some light in here!"

The only response was the dry, rasping click of the door bolt locking home.

She stopped. She put her foot down gingerly, testing her weight. There was another smell underlying the thick smolder and the tang of lampblack: old sweat—a sharp, goaty odor of unwashed human.

Kierendal stood motionless, not daring to breathe.

"Zakke?"

"He's out."

The voice was flat and lethal.

Every joint in her body turned to water.

Kierendal, like any primal, had exceptional night vision and could move as silently as a ghost, and she was in her lair. If this had been anyone but Caine, she might have made a try for him—but he'd been in here who knew how long, he was dark-adapted and probably ready for anything she could do. And from the sound of his voice, he was no more than a long stride away from her.

"Don't take a deep breath," he said softly. "If you do, I'll think you're about to yell. I might kill you before I realize my mistake."

She believed him.

"I . . ." she said thinly, breathing only from the top of her chest, ". . . ah, you could have killed me when I came through the door."

"That's right."

"Then I'm not your target."

The darkness gave no answer.

She could see his outline now, a blacker shadow against the black-shadowed wall. Still she could not see his Shell—and this absence terrified her. How was she to know what he intended if she couldn't read his Shell?

Slowly the glittering points that were his eyes came clear.

She said, "I've . . . I know I've said some things about Ma'elKoth, but, but I've done nothing—nothing that the Monastic Council would want me dead for! Have I? Tell me, you have to *tell* me! I know the Council supports Ma'elKoth, but, but, they don't have to *kill* me . . ."

His response was a dry, hollow chuckle, then: "I can neither confirm nor deny the presence or absence of any policy or viewpoint of the Council of Brothers, or the several and individual members thereof."

"Then it's the King of Cant, isn't it? I know you're hooked into the Subjects—"

"You have a nice place, here. A lot of knickknacks. Mementos." From the darkness came a slow *scrrt* of steel on flint; an amber flame grew from a shoulder-high fist, red-shading a high-cheekboned face that might have been carved from ice. The flame touched the end of a thin cigar—stolen from her desktop humidor, like the lighter.

Now she could see his Shell: it was black, smoke-dark, without any color she could read.

"Caine . . ." Kierendal's hoarse whisper sounded to her ears uncomfortably like a plea for mercy.

"Nice lighter."

"It was a gift," she replied, a little stronger now, "from Prince-Regent Toa-Phelathon."

"I know. Says so right on the side, here." He touched the flame to the wick of a lamp on a small side table, then turned the lamp down to a bloody emberous glow. "We both know what happened to *him*, don't we?"

He pinched the lighter's wick between his thumb and forefinger, and the flame extinguished with a fading hiss.

She had never given a lot of credence to the rumors that Caine had been involved in Toa-Phelathon's assassination; it had smelled of an in-palace affair. Now she believed without question. In his presence, it was impossible to doubt.

He pointed to a chair. "Sit down."

She sat.

"On your hands."

She tucked her hands beneath her thighs. "If you're not here for me, what do you want?"

He stepped around the sofa, only an arm's length from her. He crouched before her and stared into her eyes. The silence stretched until she had to consciously restrain herself from babbling just to break it.

She forced herself to silently return his regard; she studied him with the profoundly detailed attention that came of staking her life on her ability to observe.

She found herself comparing him inevitably with Berne: each had made his name and fortune spilling blood for pay. Caine was much smaller, less heavily muscled, and carried an array of knives instead of a sword—but the differences went far deeper than that. Berne had a feral quality, a wildness of lust and dangerous unpredictability that went with the loose and relaxed jointless way he walked and held himself; he was potently, almost fiercely, *alive* at all times. Caine, too, had a quality of relaxation, but there was nothing loose about it; instead it was stillness, a meditative readiness that seemed to flow out from him and fill the room with capacity for action, as though all around him ghosts of imaginary Caines performed every movement that was possible within the space: every attack, every defense, every leap or flip or roll.

He watched her watch him with concentration that equaled

hers, and he was as full of potential violence as a shining blade fresh from the forge. There was the difference, in a nutshell: Berne was a wildcat.

Caine was a sword.

"You done?" he asked quietly. "Don't let me interrupt."

Her eyes flicked up to meet his, and she found no humor there.

He said, "I'm looking for Simon Jester."

The relief that flooded through her unstrung her nearly as much as had her earlier panic; she had to struggle not to laugh out loud.

"You and the King's Eyes. Not to mention the Grey Cats and the entire Constabulary. What makes you think *I* know anything?"

He went on as though he hadn't heard her. "Just about this time yesterday, the Grey Cats ran a game in the Warrens. How'd it come out?"

She licked her lips. "Really, Caine, you can't imagine that I have sources within the Cats themselves—"

"I ask you again. I'm not a patient man, Kierendal."

"I, ah, but—"

There came the barest whisper of wings, and Caine moved.

He gave no warning of any kind, no hitch of breath, no preparatory tensing of muscle, not even a shift of his eyes. Kierendal had been watching for those signals with seamless concentration, those indicators that any creature gives before violent action. In one instant, he was perfectly motionless; in the next he spun and his hands blurred and a silvery flash sped through the gloom and struck wood with a humming *chunnk*.

Tup gave a fluting cry of pain and despair—she hung from the lintel of the doorway, Caine's throwing knife pinned through one wing. A yard-long birdlance of needle-pointed steel slipped from her hands and chimed faintly as it bounced on the parquet threshold.

Kierendal surged to her feet with a cry that was instantly stifled by Caine's hand on her throat. The thin cigar clamped in his teeth came perilously close to her eye as he yanked her toward him. She couldn't see what he was doing with his other hand, but she assumed it was something potentially lethal.

And his Shell still pulsed a smoky, seamless black.

"You might have difficulty believing this," he said through his teeth, "but I don't want to hurt you. Or your little friend, there. All I want is to hear what you know about Simon Jester. That's the easy way to get me out of your living room and out of your life."

He let go of her throat and the unseen other hand poked her just below the navel, gently but firmly, not hard enough to hurt but exactly the right amount of pressure to fold her in the middle and sit her back down in the chair.

"All right," she said thinly. She couldn't even look at him; her eyes were consumed by struggling, weeping Tup pinned to the lintel. "All right, but please, first, please get her down from there. She'll shred her wing—*please*, you'll cripple her!"

Caine said, "Hands."

She hastily tucked her hands once more beneath her thighs. Caine gave her a long look, his lips faintly compressed; then he breathed a sigh out through his nose and turned to free Tup.

"Touch me and I'll kill you, you bastard," the little treetopper shrilled. "I'll cut out your eyes!"

"Yeah, whatever," Caine said. He took her head and shoulders in one hand, her neck between his first and second fingers; his hand wrapped around to pin her arms but avoided her delicate wings. He carefully, even gently, worked the knife loose; Kierendal shuddered at the faint squeal of metal in wood as the blade came free. Tup kicked at his forearm again and again, but he didn't seem to notice. Pale rose-colored blood leaked from the gash in her wing.

"One hand," he said, holding the treetopper toward her. "Keep her under control."

It wasn't until she actually had Tup's firm warmth within her hand that she really believed Caine was doing this: that it wasn't some sort of cruel trick, that he wasn't pulling the knife from Tup's wing so that he could snap her neck, or something even worse, something unimaginable.

She gathered Tup to her breast, and the treetopper bent her head and moistened Kierendal's nipple with crystalline teardrops. "I'm sorry, Kier, I'm so sorry." She gulped sobs back into her throat. "He, he came through the window—and Zakke, he killed Zakke . . ."

"Hush now," Kierendal told her softly. "Hush, everything's well." She looked at Caine, and her eyes asked him to make this true.

He shrugged irritably. "If she's talking about your dwarf, he ought to be just fine, once he wakes up. He might have a headache for a couple days, but he's alive."

She met his cold, flat stare with dawning wonderment; perhaps those eyes were neither as cold nor as flat as they appeared. Perhaps they were only veiled . . .

She said, "You're different than I thought you'd be. The stories, they make you sound so . . . well, rather—"

"Simon Jester," he reminded her.

"Yes." She stroked Tup's curly hair. "That game in the Warrens was expensive: six Cats killed, and a lot more wounded. I don't know how many of Simon Jester's men might have been killed, but the Cats captured two of his followers."

"Two?" Something kindled in his expression, some emotion that Kierendal couldn't name for sure, because it made no sense; it looked like the wild hope-against-hope of a prisoner expecting a rescue on his walk to the gallows. "Their names. Who are they? Is one of them—"

He said something, finished the sentence, but she couldn't quite make it out—a sudden current in the Flow distracted her. She snapped back to herself. "I'm sorry—I'm sorry, I missed that. Could you repeat it?"

"Pallas Ril."

She frowned. Pallas Ril? Wasn't Pallas Ril some human thaumaturge? What did she have to do with . . . whatever they'd been talking about? That current in the Flow was back again, swirling around her, and she found she couldn't quite remember what the subject had been.

"I, I guess, I think I heard that she's in town. Is she important?"

His reply was as solid and definite as a word carved in a slab of granite. "Yes." He leaned closer. "Is she one of the prisoners?"

"What prisoners?"

Caine sighed in a way that hinted he might be struggling to keep his temper, and Kierendal's throat closed with swift new fear. What if she didn't have the information he wanted? What would he do then?

He said something else, and again she missed it.

"What?" she asked thinly, flinching against an imagined blow.

"Those two prisoners the Cats took in the Warrens yesterday, Simon Jester's followers—was one of them Simon Jester himself?"

She shook her head, praying he'd be satisfied with her half ignorance. "I don't know; all I've heard is that it's a man and a woman. Perhaps they're not quite sure themselves who it is they've captured; there's been no announcement from the pages."

His voice tightened. "Where are they held? The palace?"

"I think—in the Donjon, below the courthouse."

"Can you get me in there?"

She goggled at him, leaning back away from the flame that seemed to light his face from within. "What?"

"Come on, Kierendal. Bloody *Hamman* got me into the damned palace; if you're not better at shit than he was, the Faces would never follow you. Get me in there."

"I can't," she said. "The palace—that was a long time ago. Things are different, now. And the Donjon—Caine, it's carved into solid rock. If you have a few hundred royals to spread around in bribes, we might be able to get you in within a week or two. It's the best I can do."

His eyes smoldered. "Maybe you can do better with the right kind of encouragement."

She struggled to keep herself calm. "It cannot be done, Caine. No one has ever been broken out of that place; the only way is to bribe a judge or suborn the guards. That takes time, and money." She let him search her face; she was telling the truth, and soon enough he saw it.

He looked away from her. His disappointment was so palpable that she almost felt sorry for him. In some subtle way their relationship had shifted. She found, with surprise, that she was now much less frightened, and more than a little interested.

He said, "I don't want to be your enemy, Kierendal. I might need your help, sometime soon. You should realize that I can repay any favors fivefold."

"All I want from you, Caine, is the assurance that you'll never trouble me again."

"I could make that promise," he said with a shrug. "But it would be meaningless, and we both know it. Let me instead offer you a piece of information: somebody high up in the Subjects of Cant is an informer for the Eyes."

The lift of her eyebrows was sufficient to feign surprise. "Oh?"

"Yeah. Here's another: the Subjects are supporting Simon Jester."

This time the surprise wasn't feigned. "Now," she said, "that I *didn't* know . . ."

"I think it was the informer in the Subjects who fingered Simon Jester for the Cats. If you can find out who it is, I'll more than make it worth your trouble."

She snorted. "Why don't you ask His Majesty the King?"

He stared at her, unmoving, unspeaking, as expressionless as a death mask.

Now it was her turn to look away. She clutched Tup's trembling form more tightly to her chest.

"I don't have evidence. I don't even really have rumor. All I know is that the Eyes are looking hard at me, at the Rats and the Dungers and the Serpents, but they seem utterly blind to the Subjects of Cant. Maybe His Majesty will explain to you why that is."

"Yeah," Caine said, low and harsh. "Yeah, maybe he will." He said nothing more for a long moment, then he shook his head with the manner of a man deliberately turning his mind aside from unpleasant contemplation. He nodded toward the waist-high bronze statue and the darkened votive candles in the shrine corner of the room. "What's the story with that?"

Kierendal shrugged. "It's a shrine to Ma'elKoth. What of it? Everybody has them."

"You worship him? Like a god?"

"Me, personally? Be serious, Caine."

He nodded distantly. "Mm, yeah. I'm surprised you'd have one in your house, though. I hear he's a little down on the subs."

Subs, indeed—if it weren't for us, you humans would still dress in skins and bay at the moon, she thought, but she let it pass. She spread her hands and shrugged again. "There's a proverb, perhaps you've heard it: to get along, you go along."

His eyes went farther away. "Yeah," he murmured, and said no more.

Kierendal finally broke the silence. "If you truly wish to make peace between us, you might start by telling me how you got in here."

"That's no mystery. Your boy—Zakke, that his name?—he'll tell you all about it when he wakes up. A third-floor window isn't secure when the alley it opens onto is narrow enough to jump across. You should have bars put in."

"I have two men in the opposite apartment." She realized what she'd said, and her eyes widened. "Maybe I should say, I *had.*"

Caine shook his head. "They're all right. The alarm you put out drew them out of the apartment. I didn't touch them. They never even saw me."

She became curiously aware of her own breathing. "Then," she said softly, "you let the stonebender girl go *on purpose*—you planned the confusion, to cover you . . ."

His answering smile looked as cold as the others, but now Kierendal began to suspect how much heat the furnace doors of his control held shuttered within. She said, "And you haven't killed anyone . . ."

"Not today. Although the only reason your sprite friend's still alive is that I'm a little rusty with the knives."

"You leave a lot to chance, Caine."

"It is better to be rash than timid," he said, his smile becoming oddly distant, "for Fortune is a woman, and the man who wants to hold her down must beat and bully her." From his tone, he was quoting someone, although Kierendal had no idea whom.

"Why, Caine," she said, faux-coy, sensing an opening, "are you making a pass at me?"

His reply was a derisive snort. "One last question—"

"I know my reputation," Kierendal said, looking up at him from under her impossibly long lashes, "but I'm not really homosexual. It's just that I don't enjoy having foreign objects jabbed into my body; I'm sure you can understand that." She arched her back to give him a good look at her inflated breasts; maybe he'd be as easy to manage as Berne was, in the end. "This doesn't mean we can't have fun together."

"You're right, it doesn't. But there are plenty of other things that do. Last question: that warrant on me—you've heard about it. What do they want me for? And how did they know I'd be in town?"

"This is a mystery. The word went out on the street at sundown yesterday, that's all I know. And that they want you alive."

"You can't do better?"

She shrugged and offered him a cynical half smile. "Hey, if you're that desperate, Count Berne's on the floor right now playing knucklebones. Maybe you could ask *him*," she said pointedly.

"Berne?"

Kierendal's growing insouciance vanished like smoke before a gale; the black and lethal fury that flooded Caine's face when he spoke that name terrified her more than had his earlier threats. It was as though all of those ghost-Caines that had filled the imaginary air suddenly turned and whipped faster than thought back within his body, to make him so ferociously *present* that he seemed to burn with a scarlet flame.

"Berne is *here*? *Right now?*"

He slowly lifted his hands up before his face and stared at his fingers as they curled into fists, his eyes burning red in the lamplight.

"Yeah, maybe I *will* ask him. Maybe I will do exactly that."

And again without the faintest shift of shade in his Shell, without any hint of anticipatory breath, he moved: he was gone from the room, an inhumanly swift rush of absence like the darkness that closes in around a snuffed candle. A briefest flicker of brighter, yellower lamplight—the door opened and closed with the speed of a single blink.

Kierendal sat quite still for a long moment, as she tried to catch her breath and stroke away Tup's trembling.

"I *hate* him," the treetopper said, her voice muffled against Kierendal's breast. "I hope Berne kills him!"

"They could kill each other," Kierendal said softly, "and I don't think the world would be any less for their passing."

She gently touched the pink-rimmed rent in Tup's wing. "Can you fly?"

Tup lifted her tearstained face and rubbed at her cheek with a tiny fist. "I think so. I think I can, Kier, but it will hurt."

"Fly, then. Go to Chal. He will tend your wing. Have three of your folk fly with the word that Caine is here: one to the garrison, one to the constable post, and one to Count Berne's townhouse, for the Cats."

"You're turning him in? I thought . . ." She snuffled back more tears. "I was thinking you sort of *liked* him."

Kierendal smiled distantly. "I do. But he's about to reveal himself in my casino, and we can't have the King's Eyes thinking we'd shelter a fugitive. And the world is dangerous enough already, without men like Caine in it. Once he's dead, we'll all sleep easier."

She looked around the room. "Besides, the sonofawhore stole my lighter."

14

ARTURO KOLLBERG SQUIRMED wetly in his simichair. *At last, some action,* he thought, as he/Caine skidded down the two flights of stairs and sprinted past the startled guards in the corridor. He/Caine had gotten enough details from that dwarf whore to know which turns to make, and he was at the service door before anyone could possibly know he was coming.

Kollberg's heart pounded with anticipation. Only four hours into the Adventure, and already Caine was about to confront Berne. It might make up some for the plodding dullness of this first day so far; Studio-sponsored focus groups had determined that an average of 1.6 lethal combats per day was optimum for a Caine Adventure, and Caine had barely thrown a punch, yet. Dropping the houseboy, knifing the pixie, big deal. Beating up a whore had a certain old-fashioned charm, but it hardly qualified as actual combat. Confronting *Berne*, on the other hand . . .

He licked his already moist lips and smiled into the face shield.

Live or die, this was going to be great.

15

I PULL THE service door closed behind me and lean against it. No one on the crowded casino floor seems to be paying any attention to me, yet. One of the little leafblades from an ankle sheath should serve to slow down the guards who are coming after me along the service corridor. I lean casually on the door, gazing blankly out into the casino, while I work the leafblade into the crack between door and jamb alongside my thigh; I pound the knife in tight with the heel of my hand. The muffled thudding this makes is barely audible, even to me, over the music and babble that fills the seething room.

Damn good business she does here: it's only noon.

The bones pit, that's what she said. The knucklebones . . .

And there he is, warming dice with his breath, his brush-cut hair shimmering above his classic profile. That's a new sword he's got—Berne never favored the shoulder-draw before; it's slow and desperately clumsy. And what's with the clothes? A slashed-velvet doublet and magenta *hose*, for shit's sake.

The scenarios spin out of my subconscious:

I walk deliberately, grim as death, across the room; a hush falls as heads silently turn. Scuttling crablike, gambler's hands scrape coins off tables. Whores slowly take cover behind the bars.

Berne knows something's happening—the floor goes too quiet too fast—but he's too cool to look. He pretends that his attention is on his pass of the dice.

I stop, ten feet away. "Berne. Long time. I've been looking for you." He doesn't turn, doesn't even blink; of course he knows my voice.

"I've been waiting for you to find me, Caine. Time for one last roll." He tosses the dice: snake-eyes.

He shrugs and draws his sword as my fists come up . . .

Or:

He doesn't even know I'm there until he feels my arm go around

*his throat for the choke. He freezes, knowing I can kill him before
he can move. I whisper in his ear: "Funny how shit works out
sometimes, isn't it? Now, tell me what I want to know, and this won't
hurt." And he pretends he doesn't know what I'm talking about as
his hand creeps toward the dagger in his boot . . .*

Or: . . . anything I want . . .

These sweaty macho fantasies take almost no time: this isn't
something my mind creates, these are scenes that live there, permanently circling just below the surface like curious sharks, waiting
only for features to be painted on the blank faces and names to be
wedged into the dialogue. I could stand here all day, stretching time
by enjoying the endless play of ROM scripts patterned into my
brain by too many books, too many films and plays and Adventures
and *DragonTales* teasers—but now a huge shadow darkens the
wall at my right, and I look up into a pair of protuberant yellow
eyes that are each the size of my fist.

It's an ogre, maybe nine feet of one, and he's got shoulders about
equal to my elbow-to-elbow wingspan. He's wearing some expensive chainmail, a nicely painted hauberk that makes only an au-
tumnal rustle like dry leaves as he comes up—too close to me. The
morningstar in his hand has spikes that are as long as my little
finger and not much sharper.

He rumbles, deep in his throat, "I'm sorry sir. This area is staff
only. You have to move on."

His breath smells of old meat.

"All right, I'm going. Don't push." The floor trembles faintly
beneath my boots—those guards must be running right up to the
door. The ogre squints at me like he's suddenly remembered my
face, and a breastplate-sized hand lowers like a drawbridge toward
my shoulder.

Guards hammer on the other side of the service door behind me,
and their shouts come thinly through it. This draws the ogre's eyes
for the fractional second I need to duck aside from his hand and run
like hell.

I could make the street door—sunlight shines its golden freedom
only twenty meters to my right—

But, on the other hand, Berne has his back to me.

I'm nimble enough, even at a flat sprint, to dodge around the
bigger men on the floor, and I'm strong enough to flatten and
overrun the smaller. I trail a spreading wake of shouts and confu-

sion, but I've gone hypersonic, as it were: I outrun the noise of my passing.

Berne has warning enough only to barely begin the turning of his head before I reach the brass rail around the bones pit and launch myself over it like a javelin.

I stiffen my neck in the air and spear him, the top of my head to the side of his jaw. My arms tangle in his, and we tumble over the bones field scattering gold and dice in all directions. The other players scatter, shouting incoherent surprise, and the table goes down in splinters. By the time we skid off what's left of it to hit marble steps on the other side, I can hear the pit boss' silver whistle piping a shrill alarm that'll bring the ogres at a run.

I don't care: I landed on top.

The edges of the steps crashing against his spine had to hurt like a bitch, and his muscles loosen into stunned slackness. I lock up his legs with mine and get a forearm under his chin to force his head back and cut off his wind. His eyes go from glaze to focus almost instantly, and he mouths: *You,* and the half-buried flicker of fear that passes over his face calls to something elemental inside me, a volcanic surge up from the base of my spine that thunders in my ears and shades my vision scarlet.

"You bet your fucking ass it's me."

I create additional emphasis with a hammer-hand that crushes and spreads his perfect nose wide across his cheekbones. Blood sprays; it's on my fist, all over his face, it's on my lips, I can smell it and taste it and I no longer care if I die in the next breath so long as I go to my grave with my teeth in his throat.

So I hit him again.

He struggles beneath me, but I've got him now and there's no way I'm gonna let him go. I slam his head into the curving step, and again, and again and again; the purple-veined marble is now artistically spattered with the crimson of Berne's blood.

But he's still conscious, and now he's smiling up at me with those smeary lips and reddened teeth, and I have to choose between continuing to beat on him or just cutting his throat because those ogres will haul me off him in about ten seconds, and having to make that choice brings me back to something resembling rationality.

At about this time I realize he's been pounding the side of my head with his doubled elbow. He can't get any force behind it, lying down like that; he's doing it mostly to distract me from his other hand, which is sliding up my neck to hook a thumb toward my eye.

As he swings again I rear back out of his elbow's path and grab his upper arm, twisting him on around so his back's to me now, pinning his scabbarded sword with my chest. The hair on the back of his head is matted with blood from a single cut where his scalp split against the edge of the step. I lock my legs around his again and roll us both over faceup just in time—the pair of ogres, who were winding up for free shots at my back, lower their morningstars uncertainly.

My left arm snakes around Berne's face, over his eyes, to pull his head back while my right hand draws one of the long fighting knives from its sheath along my ribs. I put its point against his external jugular; it'll take a single second to drive it straight in the side of his neck and slice out though the front, parting carotids, external and internal jugular, and windpipe. He has no chance to survive, and he knows it.

I whisper in his ear, "Tell them to back off."

"Back off," he croaks. He coughs a wad of blood out of his throat, and his voice gets stronger and more confident. "Caine's an old friend of mine. We're not really fighting—this is just how we say hello."

I murmur: "You got a nice sense of humor, for a dying man." The shoulder-twitch of his shrug feels careless against my chest. "Keep your hands where I can see them."

He extends his hands blindly in front of him and wiggles his fingers. "Pretty, aren't they?"

"What happened to Pallas Ril?"

"Your bitch? How should I know? I've been busy with this Simon Jester asshole."

"Berne, Berne, Berne," I whisper in his ear like a chiding lover. "There's no reason to lie: Think of this as a deathbed confession."

He chuckles. "Then there's also no reason to tell the truth. But I am, anyway. You're not worth lying to."

I believe him, even though I have Pallas' memory of their confrontation. I've been figuring that the outripple of that spell she did—the information threshold that spread outward at whatever-the-hell the propagation speed of magickal energy is—sort of randomized everyone's most recent memories of Pallas, or something like that. But Berne and the Cats must have had some contact with her after the spell was cast—they had surrounded her, after all. If he still can't remember, the spell must still be operating somehow. And if the spell is still operating . . .

Pallas is still alive. She might be one of the captives in the Donjon, after all; but for now, at least, she's *alive*.

This certain knowledge spreads such warm and fuzzy feelings from my heart out into the whole world that for almost half a second I'm tempted to let him live.

"Last question: What am I wanted for? And who tipped the Eyes that I was coming to town?"

His tone is mocking. "That's two questions."

I don't really need to know these answers badly enough to make listening to his shit worth my time, so I jam the knife into his neck.

The knife's point skids off his skin as though his flesh has become tool-grade steel.

Stupidly I try to stick him again in the same place—I just can't believe it didn't work—and when it skids off again I waste a full second staring like an idiot at this blade that has betrayed me.

I begin to understand why he's not scared.

I think I'm in trouble.

Berne says in a voice bright but silky soft, "And now, for my *next* trick . . ."

He reaches back and takes my left shoulder with one hand in a grip so crushing it doesn't even hurt: my whole arm goes numb. Then he peels me off him with irresistible strength—no art involved, just a long, smooth yank—and he comes to his feet and holds me dangling in the air.

"I always was better than you," he says. "But now I'm the favorite of Ma'elKoth. He's made me faster, vastly stronger—and *invulnerable*. Ma'elKoth created the spell just for me; he calls it Berne's Buckler. You like it?"

I kick him in the face, a short Thai-jab that smacks the ball of my foot into his broken nose, and he laughs at me. He catches my crotch with his free hand and lifts me flailing up high.

And he throws me over the heads of the crowd.

Up, out of the bones pit, arcing high—he must be stronger than the ogres that stand staring dumbly at my flight. I tumble through the air while people try to duck out of my path.

My body can sort out the landing on its own; my full attention is consumed with how I'm going to beat him.

By the time I crash into a knot of gamblers and we all go down to a surprisingly soft landing, I've come to a couple conclusions.

One, strength alone won't help him for shit against my knives, and—

Two, if this invulnerability of his was all he'd like me to think it is, I wouldn't have been able to break his nose.

I can still beat him; I just have to alter my tactics to meet a changed situation. I have a hypothesis about this magick that protects him—and like any good scientist, I have an experiment in mind to turn this hypothesis into a theory.

The people I've landed on thrash away from me in a tangle of limbs, knocking me around a little, so I'm still fighting to gain my feet as the crowd parts and Berne vaults the rail of the bones pit. He wipes his bloody lips with the back of his hand and stalks toward me.

"You're a lucky man, Caine," he says. "I made a promise—"

The best time to catch a man off guard is while he's talking— too much of his attention is on what he's going to say next. Still on my knees, I cross-draw my throwing knives from the sheaths on my thighs and flip them both spinning backhand.

There's no force behind this kind of throw, but force isn't what I need. The one from my numbed and weakened left goes high, toward his face, and he slaps the whirling blade irritably aside— but it doesn't cut his hand because that's where he's instinctively focused this defense of his. The other knife, that's the one that warms my homicidal heart: it hits his leg an inch above the knee, slices his magenta hose, and cuts the skin beneath.

It's only a little cut, a thin line of swelling crimson droplets, a hardly noticeable scratch—but he looks down at it, and I look at him, and when his eyes come back up I see the faintest perceptible twitch of uncertainty at their corners.

That unlocks a rushing within my mind, a waterfall of wind like God sucking in an endless breath, as the entire universe narrows down to Berne, me, and the three meters of open floor between us.

I stand.

I draw my one remaining fighting knife.

"He that lives by the sword shall die by my knife," I tell him. "That's prophecy, if you like."

And I can see something else in his eyes now: the frenzy. He's gone blood simple.

It's like looking into a mirror.

He says, inexplicably, "Fuck Ma'elKoth."

He springs at me, and I leap to meet him.

He makes the over-the-shoulder draw so fast his hands are barely a flicker of motion. No subtlety here: he's slicing at the joining of my neck and shoulder. My knife meets his sword in a two-handed rising parry that forces the arc of his blade over my head. The knife buzzes in my hand, sending unsettling shock through my arm and shoulder to my teeth.

I backhand the knife with my right to rake the point across his eyes, and miss by a handbreadth. I continue the motion into a diving side roll, and Berne comes after me, slashing, the air singing a tooth-grinding whine as his blade cuts through the carpet and into the floor beside my head as though the planks are soft cheese. I hook his ankle with my toe and kick his knee; he bends his leg to take it so the joint doesn't break, but it brings him to the floor.

I kip to my feet and now I understand why my backhanded slash missed his eyes—my knife is about five inches *too short*, its blade sheared off three fingers above the guard, bright new steel gleaming like chrome along the cut edge.

His sword—sweet shivering fuck, that's *Kosall* . . .

The realization freezes me for a scant second, long enough for him to reach his feet. A smooth *croisé* brings me into range and I chamber my leg for a side kick to knock him down again—

And a huge, blunt-clawed hand grabs my arm from behind and yanks me back and up into the air.

I drop the useless stub of knife and flail desperately—I was so consumed with Berne, I never even *saw* the ogre who now holds me—but Berne has the same problem: two of them hold him. One has both huge hands on his sword arm, and the other holds him tight around the waist.

And I feel like I'm swimming up to the surface of a dream. What in all gods' names was I *thinking*? Wasting my time here with Berne, maybe throwing away my life—I must have been *crazy*—

Somehow I got sucked down into that feral blood lust again. Shit, that's part of why Pallas left me, this mindless thirst for death. Master Cyrre, the Abbot of Garthan Hold—almost twenty years ago, he used to tell me I think with my fists.

And the sonofabitch is *still* right.

Now Kierendal is coming toward us across the room, the perfect image of icy command. "That's about enough of *that*," she says. "Now I think we'll all wait quietly for the constables to arrive."

Berne's eyes meet mine. He's not struggling anymore, and his sardonic grin briefly contracts as he blows me a kiss and mouths *Next time.*

The ogre lifts me higher and gives me a little shake. My feet dangle an arm's length from the floor, and the ligaments that hold my shoulder together start to hurt. My head's straight now, though, and everything's clear—if I get taken by the Constabulary, it won't matter what they want me for. By the time I can get shit sorted out, I'll be too late for Pallas.

The ogre gives me another shake, a not-so-gentle warning. "Don't get ideasss," it rumbles wetly, slobbering around its tusks. "You s'ould know I won't mind hurting you."

"Yeah," I say softly. "Likewise."

I jack my knees up in front of my chest and then buck like a wild horse, a whip-crack arch of my back that sends my feet backward into the ogre's midsection. It's like stomping on a stone floor. The ogre barely grunts, but this wasn't the part that was supposed to hurt.

I kick off its chest and swing up around the pivot of my shoulder joint like a footballer doing a wheel kick, up and over; I wrap my legs around its head with a wrestler's ankle lock. The ogre snarls and instinctively turns its head to rip the inside of my thigh with those wicked tusks. One punches through the leather and into my flesh.

This is the part that is supposed to hurt.

I twist and drive a handspear past my butt, right into the tearduct at the corner of its eye. Ogre's eyes are hard-shelled, kind of like a snake's, but they pop out just as easy as a man's. I drive my hand in there and blood sprays; I scoop its baseball-sized eye right out of its head with a wet ripping sound as the muscles around it give way. It dangles from its long ropy optic nerve onto the leathery cheek, and the ogre screams into my thigh, releasing my arm to clap its hands to its face. I untwist my legs and buck again, and the ogre's tusk tears free of my leg.

I land clumsily but keep my feet. The swiftness with which scalding wetness spreads down my leg tells me the ogre nailed me good. It's almost funny—I come through fighting Berne without a scratch and get the shit ripped out of me by the fucking bouncer.

The ogre screams like an air horn while it tries to fit its eye back into its socket. The people in the casino flinch away from me, covering their ears. Berne is struggling now, furiously twisting and snarling grim threats, but the two ogres holding him show no signs of letting go.

I shoot a glance toward Kierendal, who looks like she's thinking seriously about casting a spell. I draw my last throwing knife from between my shoulder blades and show it to her, and she changes her mind.

In the brief silence that comes when the ogre stops for breath, I say loudly, "I'm leaving. The first three creatures—man, woman, or sub—that get in my way, they die. Right here on the floor. Die."

They believe me. A path clears to the door, and I take it at a dead sprint, out into the sunlight and the smells of the city.

Berne's screams of frustrated rage fade into city-sounds behind me.

Sometimes, y'know, that passion for violence serves me well.

A squad of constables pounds toward me, far away along Moriandar Street. I go the other way. I'm going to need somewhere to go to ground until I can get this wound properly dressed. The Subjects are out, at least for a while, until I can learn whether Kierendal's right about Majesty and the Eyes. Majesty's my friend, but that doesn't mean I trust him.

The answer's obvious. There's still one place in Ankhana where I can claim Right of Sanctuary. I just have to live long enough to get there.

Three paces within a convenient alley, I lean against a clapboard wall to pull the tear in my breeches closed over the wound and tie a couple loops of my belt around it. This'll do until I can get stitches and a real bandage. The leg is swelling already, and starting to throb, and I know I'd better keep moving, get out of Alientown before it stiffens. Looking back along my trail of left-foot prints outlined in blood, it's clear that I'm losing a dangerous amount, and I'm limping enough to guess that the tusk tore deeply into muscle.

On through the alley and along one of its branches to another curving street. Away northwest along the curve there's another constable squad. This one has fanned out in teams of four, knocking on doors and entering shops. Only now does it become clear that Kierendal gave me up as soon as I left her chamber. I should have known. I don't hold it against her—I would have done the same—but it's gonna make getting out of Alientown kind of a problem.

I fade back into the alley and take a different branch, picking around piles of garbage. I find a reasonably sheltered place near the alley mouth where I can watch the street, and I scan the passersby for humans or elves close to my size, looking for someone I can persuade to donate their clothes to a hunted man.

16

ARTURO KOLLBERG SLAPPED his face shield up, away from his eyes. As the induction helmet automatically retracted, he rummaged through the swingarm pharmacopoeia for a trank and an antacid. His nerves thrummed like overwound guitar strings. Caine *still* hadn't killed anyone, though this hunted-fugitive-in-Alientown business was promising.

Caine apparently didn't understand how important it was to make this Adventure a success. Good *God*, there were live feeds going out to Studios all over the world! If he continued to lay back like this, he'd ruin Kollberg's reputation, and with it his chances of upcasteing to Business and eventually succeeding Westfield Turner as Studio President.

Didn't Caine realize that Kollberg's whole career rode on this? Didn't he *care?*

At the very least, he could have done that ogre. Christ, he'd already *maimed* the poor creature; how much more trouble would it have been to kill it? People—*Leisurefolk*—around the world had spent millions of marks to be him while he took some lives; what in the name of God was holding him back?

Kollberg heaved himself up out of the chair and mopped sweat from his brow. He peered briefly at the picked-over leavings of the snack foods on the other swingarm, made a face, and decided that he should eat a real lunch while he had the chance. He keyed the wait service and ordered a cart of whatever they had that was hot and fresh and could arrive in his private box within five minutes.

Then he paced heavily around the tiny room while he dictated the next *Adventure Update* release. Though he couldn't control Caine's actions, he certainly could control what the public thought of them.

17

THAT EARNEST FACE on the world's wallscreens says:

"Well, by the numbers on the *Adventure Update* Pallas Ril Life-clock, it's time to get a report on Caine's progress in Ankhana. Once again, Jed Clearlake."

"Thank you, Bronson. There's been some action since our last update, in fact. I've received reports of an inconclusive fight with—can you believe?—Berne!"

"That would be the swordsman who murdered two of Caine's partners in *Race for the Crown of Dal'kannith*."

"That's correct. This is a blood-feud that's been running for quite a while. We caught up with Caine only hours before his transfer into Ankhana, and we asked him about Berne . . ."

A shimmering white line crosses the screen in a diagonal wipe to reveal Caine as a talking head against a neutral smoke-dark background. *"Berne?"* His recorded voice has an odd combination of cynicism and husky emotion. *"Yeah, we have history."* A sense of shifting in his chair, a deep breath to organize potent memory, a hesitation before opening a painful subject—all combine to make a truly pregnant pause: Caine's a pro, and he does interviews as well as anyone in the business.

"Laying hands on the crown of Dal'kannith turned out to be a lot harder than anyone expected. My team—it included Marade and Tizarre, the only two other survivors of Retreat *from the Boedecken, as well as Pallas Ril—we were turned back twice, with nothing to show for it but wounds and exposure. Berne, well, he had a team of his own, and they decided that the easiest way to get the crown would be to take it away from us.*

"I came back from a two-day scout in the mountains, not in a good mood—I'd had to bury a partner up there. I was carrying a pair of barbed ogrillo quarrels that I'd had to dig out of my shoulder and thigh with a knife. I was exhausted, I was frostbitten, and I found my camp empty except for a semiliterate letter from Berne. He wanted me to turn over the crown to his boyfriend t'Gall; each day I made him wait he was going to torture one of my partners to death.

"Problem was, I didn't have the damned crown.

"I knew Berne's reputation. I didn't waste any time with the truth.

"I got my hands on t'Gall and spent a couple hours persuading him to tell me where Berne was holding my friends. T'Gall didn't survive the experience. I hit Berne's camp hard and fast enough to free Pallas, and between the two of us we fought our way out.

"I didn't get there in time for Marade and Tizarre.

"Anybody wants the details, he can rent Race for the Crown of Dal'kannith. *It was ugly.*

"Berne is a disease that sickens the world; his breath poisons

the air. If I get the chance, I'm going to do the world a big favor. He's a cancer. I'm a knife."

The screen cross-fades to Jed Clearlake's earnest gravity. "And Berne is now, as you may recall, Bronson, a Count of the Empire and the de facto commander of the Grey Cats, the elite Imperial special-operations division."

"That sounds like quite a fight, Jed."

"Well, Bronson, we have a clip—"

. . . and through Caine's eyes the knife skids off skin, and again . . . The twisting disorientation of being lifted and thrown . . . and Berne vaults the brass rail and wipes blood from his mouth below his broken nose . . . Caine's Soliloquy: * . . . like any good scientist . . . * The cut on Berne's thigh . . . *He's gone blood simple.*

"He that lives by the sword shall die by my knife. That's prophecy, if you like."

The image freezes for an extended discussion of magickally enhanced strength and reflexes, and the curious "Berne's Buckler" effect, and joking references to Caine's either astonishing daring or extraordinary foolishness in facing an obviously superior opponent.

"And our latest report indicates that Caine is wounded and on the run in Alientown, the subhuman ghetto that comprises the red-light district of Ankhana. Studio analysts predict that he'll try to cross Knight's Bridge into Old Town, and take refuge at the Monastic Embassy."

"That's an interesting choice, Jed."

"Well, Bronson, Caine can claim Right of Sanctuary there, seeing as how he's still technically a Monastic citizen, though he's no longer a sworn friar."

"But can they actually protect him against the Empire?"

"A lot depends on just how much pressure the Ankhanans are willing to bring; as you know, Caine still hasn't managed to discover why they've issued a warrant and a reward for his capture. But I should certainly say that the Ankhanans will *under no circumstances* use force to settle a dispute with the Monasteries. Whenever this has been tried in the past, the results have been shortterm success, shortly followed by appalling disaster. As Caine fans will remember, several of his earliest Adventures involved the Monasteries' complex revenge against those who foolishly violated their sovereignty on one pretext or another; their standard policy in such matters is to appear to give way, and later inflict the harshest of punishments. In an area such as the Ankhanan Empire, where the Monasteries have been well established for hundreds of years, this lesson has been learned the hard way. I don't think that anyone in the Imperial Government will make that sort of mistake."

A polished, professional chuckle. "So the Monastics are not quite like, say, Franciscan friars, tending gardens and healing the sick?"

"No, Bronson, that's true." An answering chuckle. "While the Monasteries do comprise a 'nation without borders' not unlike the Catholic Church in the Europe of a thousand years ago, they're not actually a religious organization. *Monastery* is the word we use for the Westerling *Khrasthikhanolyir*, which translates roughly as Fortress of Human Future. The Monasteries are centers of learning, primarily, and serve as schools for the children of nobility and such of the common folk as can pay their fees. They attempt to spread a familiar philosophy of the brotherhood of man, and that kind of thing. This all sounds very peaceful, you might think, but remember: they preach the brotherhood of *man*, in a world where there are no less than seven sentient humanoid species and more than a dozen species of sentient nonhumanoids. They also teach a number of very advanced fighting arts, and several Monasteries are well known for their schools of magick. The Monasteries are aggressively political, and are certainly not above toppling a government that they perceive as being dangerous to their long-term goal, which is nothing less than the survival and dominance of the human race on Overworld. You might recall Caine's adventure of two or three years ago, *A Servant of the Empire,* when at the instigation of the Council of Brothers, Caine assassinated Prince-Regent Toa-Phelathon . . ."

18

I REFUSE THE offered wheelchair, even though dodging the garrison soldiers' crossbow quarrels on that dash across Knight's Bridge reopened my thigh, and with each step my left boot squishes blood out like a sponge. It's an irrational prejudice, I guess, but I'd rather limp exhausted along behind the puzzled novice who leads me to the infirmary than sit on my ass and leave my progress in someone else's hands.

I walk with my palm brushing the rich paneling of the corridor wall—this gives me support against the occasional waves of dizziness that seem to be coming with increasing frequency, and it also keeps me close enough to the wall that my blood won't stain the exquisite Ch'rannthian runner that decorates the floor.

Friars, novices, and students all glance at me as we pass, most of them trailing toward the dining hall for supper. The embassy in Ankhana does a brisk hospital business; there's nothing unusual enough about a blood-soaked man limping along their halls to draw undue attention. I wonder how many of them suspect who I am . . .

Down in the vaulted bedlam of the infirmary, the Healing Brother's eyes widen when I identify myself: "Caine of Garthan Hold."

"Oh, my," he says, lips pursed with prim dismay. "Oh, oh, my. The Ambassador must be—"

"I claim Sanctuary. I am a Citizen of Humanity and Servant of the Future. I have broken neither oath nor law. By law and custom, Sanctuary is mine by right."

The Healing Brother looks decidedly cross. "I'm not sure that I—"

"Horseshit. You know who I am. What are you waiting for, the goddamn secret handshake?"

I can read his face like a billboard: he doesn't want to do anything without the Ambassador's approval, and he'd really much prefer that I have a stroke and die right here before he has to answer me. But I gave him the formula, and he knows the Law: he doesn't have any choice at all.

"You are welcome, Caine of Garthan Hold," he says sourly. "The arms of your Brothers enfold you, and you need fear no prince of the world. You have found safe Sanctuary."

"Swell. Now who's on call that can sew up this damn leg?"

"Combat or accident?"

"Combat. Hey," I say, brightening, "does that mean you've got a Khryllian here today?"

He nods, his lips going even thinner. "He's donating his services for three days as a minor penance. Cell three. Await him in meditation."

"Sure, whatever."

I limp through the infirmary, enduring glares from the sick and broken people who line the bare wooden benches waiting their turns; their resentment stings my flesh nearly as much as, oh, say, the pittering raindrops of a summer shower.

I pause at the candlerest near the mouth of the corridor and pick out a fresh one, fitting it into a brass holder with an adjustable oval breeze-shield. The lamp nearby provides flame, and I move off into the unlit corridor.

The halls and cells of the Monasteries across the world have no lamps of their own, and often not even windows. A friar must carry his own illumination, you see, never depend on the efforts of others to push back the darkness. Symbols, always symbols, to remind us of our Sacred Mission.

Horseshit.

There may be, I guess, a few idealists and other gullible types who still believe that the Monasteries are devoted to the Future of Mankind; the rest of us know that their true function is to acquire and wield power: naked force, political and otherwise.

Down through the years, the *otherwise* has been, occasionally, me. And I'm far from the only one, nor am I the best or most successful— I'm only the most famous.

Cell three is a rectangular box, two meters by three and maybe two and a half high. I shut the door behind me and lean against the wall, slowly sliding down it to lower myself to the chill limestone flags of the floor without having my leg buckle under me. I set the candle on the floor next to me and look up at the beautifully detailed low relief that's carved into the cell's end wall.

Brought to life by the slowly wavering flame of the candle, the limestone eyes of Jhantho, Our Founder, gaze sadly down at me. His cupped hands cradle the world between them like a thin-shelled egg of a dragon—something infinitely precious and astonishingly fragile.

"There was a time you had me suckered, too, you sonofabitch," I say softly. "I remember what it felt like to believe."

And in the corner of the cell stands a small bronze of an impressively muscled man with flowing hair and piercing eyes; the statue's feet are surrounded by offering plates and stubs of candles. Another shrine to Ma'elKoth, just like Kierendal's, but this one's seen some use.

This shrine shit is starting to creep me out.

It's not long before the priest of Khryl shows up. He's probably having a slow day; Khryllian healing works only on wounds sustained in battle. He clanks in through the door in his full armor—I think they even sleep that way—and the steel of his breastplate is so incredibly polished that it reflects the candle flame like chrome.

We exchange only enough words for him to understand the wound. Although I detect a brightening of his eyes when I tell him it came from an ogre's tusk, this brightening darkens again when he learns the ogre survived the encounter.

He stands tall and stretches his arms wide to pray; the last time a priest of Khryl ever kneels is when he receives his Order of Knight-hood. His chant rings in the tiny cell, on and on.

It would be easy to envy him his faith, but I don't; that'd be a prejudice left over from my other life. He doesn't have faith, he has certain knowledge: he feels the power of his god every time he prays. I hold the torn leather of my breeches wide, for him to lay hands upon my wound.

The ragged flaps of skin, lipped with yellow globules of fat and strung through with torn muscle, slowly draw together. Khryl is a god of war, and his healing is intended for use on the battlefield; it is fast and certain, but savagely uncomfortable. A wound this deep would take a couple of months to heal fully, and in the meantime it would throb, and itch, and shoot the occasional stinging stitch up the leg. Khryl's healing takes every scrap of the discomfort of those months and compresses it into five eternal minutes of agony.

My vision fades under the onslaught. My ears ring, and I taste blood; it feels like he's poured sulphuric acid down my crotch and it's eating the flesh through to the bone.

I probably pass out at least once, maybe twice; it's hard to tell—it never seems to end—I'm greying in and out, and every time I come back it's still going on.

When I get back full consciousness, I'm alone in the cell, and I have hazy memories of the priest taking his leave. There's a jagged V-shape of new pink and puckered scar tissue on the inside of my thigh. A deep ache in the muscle sharpens instantly when I try to put weight on it, but I get up anyway and start to stretch it out.

Fatigue sinks steel hooks into every muscle and drags them toward the floor. I feel like I've been lost in the desert without food or water for a year or so. What I really need is a side of beef, a gallon of whiskey, and a bed for about three days; but I lost the whole afternoon dodging the damned constables and Shanna has maybe five days left to live.

The constables might have already presented themselves at the gate and been turned back—I can't have been difficult to track. They'll be watching, but there are ways out of this embassy that the Constabulary doesn't know about. If I move fast, I should be able to be off the island and back in the Warrens before the bridges go up at curfew.

I push on the door, and it barely rattles.

I push harder. It shifts just enough to let me know it's barred from the outside.

"Hey!" I shout, hammering on the door with both fists. "Open this fucking thing!"

"Er, Caine?" The boy outside sounds a little nervous, with good reason. If I could somehow get into the corridor right now I'd beat him to death on my way out. "I have to keep you here, for just a few minutes. The Ambassador wants to see you—he, uh, he wanted to make sure you don't leave before he has a chance to talk with you."

And there's no point in arguing. The word *Ambassador* doesn't suggest the full range of his powers; in matters concerning Ankhana, he's kind of a minor pope. This kid out there could no more disobey the Ambassador than fly to the frigging moon. The cell is now a cell in the other sense as well.

I sigh and lean my forehead into the cool oak of the door. "He could have asked . . ."

"Uh, well . . . I'm sorry . . ."

"Yeah, whatever."

What would Dartheln want with me? It's not likely to be a friendly chat—we weren't on the best of terms, last time we met. He'd opposed the Council of Brothers' decision on Toa-Phelathon; the Prince-Regent had been something of a personal friend.

Dartheln's a man of principle, though. Despite his personal feelings and principled objections, his Oath of Obedience had taken precedence: he'd bowed to the Council's orders and given me the full support of the embassy's resources. I couldn't have succeeded without him. I have a great deal of respect for him, even though he's never bothered to conceal that the feeling isn't mutual.

They don't keep me waiting long. When the door swings out, four friars stand outside, and they're all armed. The short, shoulder-high staves they carry are ideal close-combat weapons, and I wouldn't be surprised to find that each of these guys is my equal in a fight, or close to it. They relieve me of my last two knives—the thrower from my back and the little leafblade from my boot. I've got a bad feeling about this.

They lead me along the corridor away from the light, so that we won't pass through the common room of the infirmary. We go up a couple twisting flights of stairs and along another hallway so underused that we leave footprints behind us in the dust—but only briefly, as the nervous and bemused novice trails us with a broom.

They open a small service door for me and bracket me into the room: two ahead and two behind. The novice closes the door behind us, and before him—he stays out in the hallway.

I recognize the room, even though the decor has changed: this is the private office, just off the Ambassador's chambers. Instead of the massive dark wood furniture of the sort produced by the friars at Jhanthogen Bluff, this room's full of the light, curving, graceful sort of thing produced by the best Ankhanan craftsmen; every piece gleams, rich veneer layered with transparent varnish.

And in one corner, candle flames wavering at its ankles and offering plates piled high, is another shrine to Ma'elKoth.

The only piece of furniture I recognize is the bulky, scarred old writing table of the sort Exoterics use for drafting and copying manuscripts. And the man sitting at it with his back to the five of us, though he's wearing the Ambassadorial robes, isn't Dartheln—Dartheln is a hefty man who'd be nearing seventy, and is as bald as an egg. This guy's skinny enough that he'd blow away in a high wind, and his head's full of curly brown hair. He glances back over his shoulder, nods to himself, and lays down his pen.

"Caine. I've been hoping you'd come here first." His face is familiar—those cheekbones that look sharp enough to cut cheese—but it's the voice that triggers my memory, even though I haven't heard it in maybe eighteen years.

I squint. "Creele?"

He nods and flicks his wrist toward one of the chairs. "Good to see you. Sit."

I take the offered chair, more than a little amazed. Creele was a couple years behind me at Garthan Hold. I tutored him in Applied Legendry and Small-Group Tactics. Now he's the Ambassador to the Empire.

Shit, am I that old?

"How in the name of Jhantho's Fist did you get a post like this at your age?"

He smiles thinly. "The Council appoints by merit, not age."

That doesn't answer the question—or maybe it does. The Creele I recall from school was a natural politician, a master of telling you what you wanted to hear, even then. A manipulative little skunk, but good company, intelligent and witty; I can remember many hours spent laughing over wine filched from the hold's cellars.

It's hard to look at him; my brain keeps trying to see him the way he looked at eighteen. We don't spend much time in small talk. He knows most of my career already, and I don't have much interest in his—the unspoken details would be depressingly familiar, the kind of backstabbing politics that drove me away from the Vows in the first place. And the four staff-armed friars are still here; they're standing at parade rest in a short arc behind me, which puts a damper on chatty conversation.

Shortly he gets to the nub. He twists the ring with the Seal of Mastery around his finger to its proper place, and he puts on his Important Business voice.

"I don't know by whom you've been hired, and I don't need to know. But you should know that the Council of Brothers won't tolerate any action against Ma'elKoth, or against the Empire generally."

"Against Ma'elKoth?" I say, frowning. How does he *know?* "I'm not working. This is personal business."

"Caine, you might remember I'm not an idiot. We know that Ma'elKoth is not popular with some rogue elements within the nobility. I know that the Eyes have been anticipating that you'll surface in Ankhana, and they've issued a warrant for your arrest on unspecified charges. This reads like your employer is compromised, and they know what you're up to. And here you are. Don't bother to pretend."

I shrug. "All right."

He looks like he's expecting me to continue. I stare at him blandly. He gives his head an irritated little shake and works his lips like there's a bad taste in his mouth.

"You should understand that we support Ma'elKoth; we couldn't have *handpicked* a better successor to Toa-Phelathon. He's brought the common folk together like no ruler since Dil-Phinnarthin himself, and he's solidified the Empire into a stable nation. He's holding the subs at bay on the borders and controlling the ones within; he's reached an understanding with Lipke that may bring the two empires together within our lifetime."

As he speaks, his eyes keep flicking past me toward the shrine in the corner, his gaze drawn there like a moth to a candle. "Ma'elKoth may be the most important man alive—he may be the man who will ensure the ultimate survival of our *species*, can you understand that? He may be able to bring together all the human lands; if we can stop fighting among ourselves, the subs will never stand against us. We think he can do it. He's the horse we're riding, and we won't let you cut him out from under us."

"We?"

"The Council of Brothers. The whole Council."

I give him a derisive snort. The Council of Brothers, as a whole, can't decide what day it is. "I tell you again. My business in Ankhana is personal."

"If you could only *meet* the man, you'd understand," he says. His eyes spark with messianic fire—he's a believer. He pushes his hands toward the shrine as though offering worship. "His presence alone is overwhelming, and the power of his intellect—! The way he's taken the entire Empire into his hand—"

"By murdering his political enemies," I murmur, and an expression of fleeting satisfaction crosses his face, as though I've confessed to something.

Maybe I have.

Or maybe I'm just contrary, but I can't help it. His tone of uncritical awe makes needling him irresistible.

"Enemies of Ma'elKoth are enemies of the Empire," he insists. "They're enemies of humanity. Should he deal gently with traitors? Would that make him a better Emperor, or worse?"

I give him a thin smile and quote, " 'Those who make peaceful revolution impossible will make violent revolution inevitable.' "

He rocks back in his chair. "I thought that might be your attitude. Dartheln said almost the same thing, only in different words."

"Yeah, well, he's pretty smart," I tell him. "And he's a better man than you'll ever be."

Creele waves a weary hand. "He's a fossil. He doesn't see that Ma'elKoth is our chance at the bold stroke, the final success. He thought we should stick with our tried-and-true methods; now he's applying his tried-and-true methods to growing corn at Jhanthogen Bluff."

I'm becoming acutely conscious of how much time this is wasting. I lean forward and put my elbows on my knees and give him a pretty fair Earnest Look.

"Creele, listen. I'm happy for you, getting this post, and I understand your concerns for Ma'elKoth. But, really, if everything I hear about him is true, he wouldn't be in much danger even if he *were* my target. The truth is, I've heard that my old girl is in town here, and she's in trouble, and I'm trying to find her. That's my real interest here."

"You'll give me your word that you will take no action against Ma'elKoth, nor against anyone in his government?"

"Creele—"

"Your word." He's learned the command voice well; his tone makes it clear there's no room to wiggle.

You have my word—it's a simple phrase, and easy on the lips; my word is nothing more than what I am, and it's broken as easily as men are.

But it's also nothing less than what I am, and it has the same lust for survival that I do. I spread my hands in a disparaging shrug. "What would my word mean?" A rhetorical question. "It would place no chains upon my arms that could prevent the raising of my fist."

"I suppose that's true." He looks tired, as though the Ambassadorial robes drag on his shoulders like anchors on his spirit. The zealotry that smoldered in his eyes has faded, and his mouth takes on a cynical twist. "I suppose I would have had to do this, anyway. You're only making it a little easier."

He rises like an old man, and goes to the chamber door; with a brief glance of something like regret over his shoulder at me, he shoots the bolt and swings the door open. "Thank you for waiting, Your Grace. Caine is here."

Six men in the blue and gold tunics of the King's Eyes' dress-livery file into the room, shortswords slung at their waists along with identical daggers. As they come in, they crank back the crowsfoot mechanism on small, compact crossbows and load steel quarrels into the bolts. The seventh is an ordinary-looking man with mouse-brown hair who wears a stylish burgundy velvet blouse with a baldric of gleaming white silk. He offers the corner shrine a cursory nod as he clears the door. The slim jeweled sword that depends from his baldric appears purely ceremonial, and from his hand dangles a bulging drawstring purse of black velvet—my head-price, no doubt.

"Creele," I say, "I've said some bad things about you in my time, and thought worse, but I'd have never believed you'd give me up."

He doesn't even have the grace to be embarrassed. "I told you," he says, "we're going to help Ma'elKoth every way we can."

The man in velvet steps forward. "I am Toa-Sytell, the Duke of Public Order, and you, Caine, are my prisoner."

I get out of my chair quickly enough to make the friars behind me heft their staves, and the King's Eyes close into a defensive screen before their Duke.

"I don't have time for this."

Toa-Sytell says blandly, "Your time is mine. I'm pledged to deliver you to Ma'elKoth, and I will do it."

I spare him not so much as a glance; my eyes are only for Creele. I step over to him, close enough to see the soot-clogged pores of his nose, to see the black squid ink caked in the Seal of Mastery.

"Y'know, there's nothing more dangerous than an intellectual with power," I say in a light and conversational tone, as though we were back arguing over a jug of wine at Garthan Hold. "He can rationalize any crime, and he's certainly not going to let abstractions like justice, loyalty, or honor get in his way."

Creele flushes, just a little. "Oh, grow up, will you? You knew this could happen; we can't let you endanger Ma'elKoth."

"Fuck Ma'elKoth," I say mildly, quoting Berne with a tiny disbelieving smile. "This is between you and me."

"Caine—"

"You have violated Sanctuary, Creele. I am Sanctuaried here, and you have delivered me into the hands of my enemies. You know the penalty. Did you really think I wouldn't kill you for this?"

He sighs, almost contemptuously, his eyes flicking toward the four friars and the six King's Eyes. "I hardly think I'm in much danger, Caine, if you know what I—"

The edge of my hand cuts off the rest of his sentence, a forehand chop across the bridge of his nose. The sudden stunning shock unstrings his limbs and slackens the muscles in his neck. I get my hands on his head, a sharp twist: his cervical vertebrae separate with a wet driftwood squelch and slice into his spinal cord. Before anyone else in the room can move, he flops kicking and convulsing to the floor.

I say into the blank silence, "And here I thought I'd get through the whole day without killing anyone."

With a shout the friars' paralysis breaks. They spring toward me, staves raised—and stop before the dully gleaming pyramidal heads of the Eyes' crossbow quarrels that are suddenly pointed at them, rather than me.

Duke Toa-Sytell says, "This man is my prisoner, and I am

pledged to deliver him to Ma'elKoth." His colorless voice leaves no doubt that he'd give the order to fire. "Stand back. A cocked crossbow is a delicate mechanism; if my men become nervy, one may fire by accident."

One of the friars, older than the others, maybe even my age, extends his staff horizontally, like a barrier. "Let us waste no time. You, go to the Healing Brother. The Khryllian may be able to save the Ambassador's life."

The younger friar bolts through the hall door, and his footfalls fade away.

I say, "He won't make it."

The older friar meets my eyes, and shrugs.

We all stand there for a minute or two and watch Creele die.

In some of my old books, I've read about certain blows that are supposed to cause instant death—especially one to the nose that's supposed to drive bone splinters from the fragile sinus into the brain through one of the strongest bones in the human body, the frontal bone of the skull. This is a puerile fantasy, but sometimes I wish it were true.

In reality there's no such thing as instant death; different parts of the body shut down at different rates, in different ways, shuddering and jittering, spasming, or simply relaxing into lifelessness. If you're unfortunate enough to be conscious, it's got to be a pretty hideous experience.

Creele is conscious.

He can't speak, because his larynx shattered when I broke his neck and his lungs are filling with blood, but he's looking up at me. There's raw terror in his eyes; he's begging me to tell him this isn't happening, not to him, not now, as he feels himself bounce and shudder, smells his bowels and bladder releasing. But it's too late, and I wouldn't take it back if I could.

Sometimes dying men ask, either with words or only with their eyes: *Why? Why me?* Creele doesn't ask; he knows the answer.

It's because I'm an old-fashioned guy.

Toa-Sytell says musingly, "You are an extraordinarily lethal man. Don't bother to hope that you'll catch me within arm's length."

I meet his eyes, and we measure each other.

His lips show the barest ghost of a smile, and he glances down at Creele's stilling body. "It's so rare as to be almost unique, to meet a man who lives up to his reputation. Which do you think is more dangerous: the intellectual—" His gaze flicks up to match mine once again. "—or the idealist?"

"Don't insult me. Or him."

"Mm." He nods. "We'll be going, then."

One of the younger friars speaks, his voice level and in-placable. "You'll never be safe, Caine of Garthan Hold. There is nowhere you can hide from Monastic vengeance."

I meet the eyes of the older friar. "He violated Sanctuary. You saw."

He nods.

"And you'll speak truth."

He nods again. "I would not dishonor myself by lying for such a man."

Toa-Sytell drops the black velvet purse on the floor beside Creele's body. One gold royal bounces jingling from the purse's neck and rolls in a slow and lazy circle around Creele's head to pass the feet of the friars. All eyes follow it expressionlessly, and for a moment no one moves as it chimes to rest.

Toa-Sytell says in that colorless voice of his, "At least he can afford a sumptuous wake . . ."

He gestures, and the King's Eyes swing their crossbows to point just above my head, where they won't kill me if one triggers by accident, and as we leave I can hear the growing clatter of the approach of the Healing Brother and the Khryllian priest, far too late.

With Creele dead, no one has the authority to order that a Duke of the Empire and his men be detained, and so we walk right out of the front gate of the embassy without incident.

Just outside, they very professionally lay me down in the street to put shackles on my arms and a pair of bilboes on my ankles. The cobblestones are cold and shining wet. I don't bother to resist. It's pretty clear that none of them would mind putting a quarrel into my knee if I try anything foolish. Toa-Sytell himself helps me to my feet, and we set off.

We walk slowly along Gods' Way toward the Colhari Palace. The moon is rising, casting an oyster-shell glow over the misty drizzle that nightfall has brought to the streets, polishing the cobblestones and painting cool moisture across my brow. It's awkward, walking with the bar of the bilboes scraping between my ankles, and Toa-Sytell holds the chain attached to their end tight in his fist. Nobody seems to have anything to say.

I figure it's about fifty-fifty, whether the Council of Brothers will order my death in retaliation for Creele's. Shit, they should give me a medal. The oaths of Sanctuary are among the most sacred vows a friar ever takes, and the penalties for violating them usually include death.

But I'm only rationalizing, inventing defenses before an imaginary Monastic judge.

The truth is, I would have killed him anyway: for betraying me, for keeping me from Shanna, for letting the headsman's axe swing closer to her neck.

No one, *no one* will do that and live.

And the glittering arch of the Dil-Phinnarthin Gate looms, gleaming silver through the mist, the awesome tower of the Colhari Palace rising behind it. Toa-Sytell gives the recognition to an expectant captain. The gate swings wide, and we walk toward the arch.

Huh. Well, at least I don't have to spend a lot of time figuring out how to get myself into the Palace. Maybe I can take this—

19

" 'STRATOR? MM, 'STRATOR Kollberg?" The voice of Arturo Kollberg's personal Secretary came over the screenlink as a hushed, almost reverent whisper.

Kollberg swallowed—he well knew what that tone probably meant. He swiftly swept his desk clear of the crumbs of his supper, rubbed a napkin furiously across his mouth, and wiped his hands as thoroughly as he could. He took a deep breath, trying to slow his stuttering heart. "Yes, Gayle?"

" 'Strator, on line one, it's *Geneva*."

When Caine had entered the palace grounds and his transfer link had been severed, Kollberg had had a thousand things to do at once—from ordering adjustments in nutrient drip for the first-handers to editing decisions on the clip release to *Adventure Update*. When the cutoff had occurred, the first-handers all over the world had gone into an automatic sendep cycle, and the Studio comm nexus had flooded with calls ranging from curious to outright panicky from the technical directors of the linked Studios around the globe. In the midst of chaos and confusion, Kollberg had forcefully resisted the urge to handle every problem at once.

The very first thing he'd done was put in a call to the Studio Board of Governors in Geneva.

He'd turned to other business while waiting for his call to be returned; it had taken only a bit more than an hour to mollify the other Studios, get the Caine first-handers into peaceful induced-sleep cycles, order his own supper, and catch up on some other work—some marketing decisions on two of San Francisco's lesser stars, and a judgment call on scheduling for an up-and-coming Actress. This was mostly his way of pretending that *For Love of Pallas Ril* hadn't consumed his entire attention.

But now his supper curdled in his belly and he tried to shake the tension out of his shoulders. All for Caine, all for Caine's success. If only Michaelson knew how hard Kollberg worked, what Kollberg put himself through to take care of him!

He keyed line one, and his screen lit with the Adventures Unlimited logo, an armored knight brandishing a sword, mounted on the back of a rearing winged horse. The screen didn't clear to visual; when the Board of Governors called, it never did.

The modulated, artificially neutral voice of the Board started in without preamble. "We are reviewing your application for emergency transfer authority. There are some concerns that you should clear up for us."

The Board of Governors had a shifting membership of seven to fifteen high-ranking Leisurefolk who were charged with the responsibility of setting policy for the Studio system as a whole. There was no appeal of the Board's decisions, and there was no politicking or playing one member off against another when no one outside the Board really knew who was on the Board at any given time; the blank screen and artificial voice prevented Kollberg from even knowing whom he was talking to. Kollberg was fairly sure that there was a Saud on the Board right now, as well as a Walton and a Windsor, but that was useless knowledge: it did nothing to moisten his lips or level his voice.

He rapidly, almost breathlessly, reeled out his prepared speech. "Based on Caine's experience on the previous occasion that he entered the Colhari Palace on a mission, I believe that emergency transfer authority is a reasonable precaution, to protect the life and profitability of a major star. In fact, due to the severance of his transfer link and loss of transmission, we wouldn't even get the usual death surge in sales of this Adventure—"

"We have little interest in this Actor's life or profitability. Our concerns are of matters far more grave."

Kollberg blinked.

"I, ah, I'm not sure that I—"

"We were assured by you personally, Administrator, that the termination of this Ankhanan Emperor would be nonpolitical."

He swallowed and said cautiously, "Nonpolitical . . . ?"

"We've questioned your judgment from the beginning regarding these recent Adventures of Pallas Ril. Do you understand the danger involved in allowing a heroine to be shown subverting civil authority? The danger involved in *encouraging* her fans to cheer her on as she defies the *lawfully constituted government*?"

"But, but she's, well, saving innocent *lives* . . . Surely, that's acceptable subject matter—"

"Guilt or innocence is irrelevant, Administrator. These natives were condemned according to the laws of their society, and the government that Pallas Ril defies is legally constituted. Do you wish to be responsible for the actions of her Earthly imitators?"

"But, but but, I hardly think—"

"Precisely. You hardly think. It's been ten years since the Caste Riots, Administrator. Have you learned *nothing*? Have you forgotten how fragile our social fabric can be?"

Kollberg hadn't forgotten—he'd lived though those terrifying days huddled in his Gibraltar Homes condominium.

A charismatic Top Ten Actor named Kiel Burchardt had inadvertently triggered the Caste Riots while preaching on Overworld; he played a priest of Tyshalle Deathgod, and the gospel of radical liberty and personal responsibility he'd preached to foment a peasant rebellion against the robber barons of Jheled-Kaarn had become the rallying slogans of spontaneous riots in cities across Earth. Disaffected Laborers turned on the upper castes, the midcastes, and eventually themselves.

Fortunately, Burchardt was killed by one of those robber barons while leading an assault on his keep, and the Social Police rapid-response squads had eventually crushed the rioters, but the Caste Riots remained a chilling reminder of the mesmeric influence Actors could exert over their audiences.

"But," Kollberg said, wiping with the back of his hand at the perspiration that bubbled out across his upper lip, "but she's *failed*, you see? And she needs Caine—the completely *nonpolitical* Caine—to either rescue her or avenge her death."

"That was our understanding. But how, then, do you explain this?"

The Studio logo vanished from the screen, replaced by the face of the Monastic Ambassador seen from Caine's POV, and Caine's recorded voice came over the speaker. " 'Those who make peaceful revolution impossible will make violent revolution inevitable.' "

Kollberg thought, *Oh, Christ. Oh my god.*

The logo came back on. "That is *decidedly* political, not to say subversive, even treasonous. Do you know whom he was quoting?"

He shook his head hastily. "No no no, not at all."

"Good."

Kollberg looked down; dark patches of sweat stained his pants where his trembling hands had rested. He laced his fingers together and squeezed until they hurt. "I, ah, I first-handed that scene, you know, and I don't believe that Caine meant this as a political—"

"You do understand the pernicious effects of allowing an Actor of Caine's popularity and influence to turn to politically motivated violence against an authoritarian government? Allowing him in Soliloquy to self-justify overturning a police state? This has echoes of the Burchardt business; Earthly parallels of this attitude would be explosive."

"But, but really—"

"Caine often swears by Tyshalle, the god whose gospel Burchardt preached."

Kollberg said nothing; there was no possible reply.

"Caine has begun to undertake subversive social criticism."

"What?"

Once again the screen changed, this time to the scene before Caine's eyes as he walked through the burned-out borderland of the Kingdom of Cant. Caine's Soliloquy: *Our Workers are worse, really; with the zombies, you can't see the buried spark of life— intelligence, will, whatever—that makes Workers so tragically creepy.*

The logo returned. "Workers are convicted *felons*, Administrator, who are cyborged to repay society for their crimes. This could be interpreted as a plea for sympathy, that death is preferable to life as a Worker."

"But the Soliloquy—"

"Death may be better for them; their death is *not* better for us. Workers support a substantial fraction of the world economy."

"The *Soliloquy*," Kollberg said more forcefully, belly quivering at his own boldness, "is purely stream-of-consciousness; it's part of what makes Caine such a powerful and effective Actor. It reflects his emotional and preconscious instinctive reactions as well as his rational thought processes—if he must stop and consider the political implications of his every thought, it will cripple his performance!"

"His performance is not our concern. Perhaps Actors should be found whose *emotional and preconscious reactions* are more socially responsible."

There came a pause, and then the neutral voice continued more slowly. "Do you know that Duncan Michaelson, Caine's father, has been interred in the Mute Facility in the Buchanan Social Camp for more than ten years? That his crime was sedition? The seed does not fall far from the tree, Administrator."

Kollberg's dusty tongue clove to the roof of his mouth, and a single drop of sweat rolled stinging into his left eye. He looked down, squinting against the tear the sweat brought, and bit his tongue hard to moisten his mouth so he could speak again. "What do you want me to do?"

"We authorize the emergency transfer. You will find that the emergency key in your Cavea techbooth is already active. We had considered ordering Caine's immediate recall, but we are not unmindful of the potential profitability of this Adventure."

The voice hardened. "There will be no more suggestion of subversion in this Adventure, do you understand? We direct you to personally monitor every second; delegate all other responsibility. You will be held personally responsible for the political and social content of this Adventure. When Caine kills Ma'elKoth or dies in the attempt, it will be the result of a *personal vendetta*, do you understand? There will be no further discussion of political motivations whatsoever. And there will be no discussion of Caine's contract; the Studio is not in the business of sponsoring assassination. We provide *entertainment*, nothing more nor less. Do you understand?"

"I understand."

"It is not only your *career* that's on the line, Administrator. Any serious breach of this directive will be turned over to the Social Police for investigation."

The spreading coldness in his chest felt like someone had slipped an ice dagger into his heart. "I understand."

The screen went blank.

Kollberg sat staring at the flat grey darkness of the screen for a long, long time. Then suddenly he twitched like a man jolting awake from a nightmare—Caine might have come back out of the palace already, might already be on-line, might already be doing or saying or thinking something that would destroy Kollberg's life.

He jerked to his feet and brushed crumbs from his blouse; he slicked over his pale hair with the sweat from his palms and heaved himself toward the door of his private box.

Michaelson had threatened him yesterday; today the threat came from Caine. It was time, Kollberg decided, to smack that little bastard's hand.

Just give me a reason that'll stand up for the Board, he thought. *Just one excuse. You'll see what you get. You'll see.*

DAY THREE

"Sometimes I wonder if you really respect anything besides power."

"What else is there?"

"You see? That's what I mean, that's a flip, glib, toss-off answer. It's because you don't care about what I care about. The things that are important, that are really important—"

"Like what? Justice? Give me a break. Honor? Those are abstractions we've invented, to make the reality of power easier to face, to con people into voluntarily limiting themselves."

"What about love? Is that any less abstract than justice?"

"Shanna, for Pete's sake—"

"Isn't it funny how we always end up fighting about the abstractions?"

"We're not fighting."

"Yes, we are. Maybe we're not fighting about justice and love, but we're sure as hell fighting."

1

RING UPON RING of crumbling stone benches and walkways rose step-built above the bull's-eye of rain-damp sand in the center; the whole titanic structure might have been a target offered for a game between gods. The inner wall that separated the sand from the seating had once been three times the height of a man. Though it was crumbling now with age and the decay wrought by the corrosive coal smoke from the steelworks in the nearby Industrial Park, on its raddled face could still be seen curved parallel scars left by the diamondine claws of draconymphs, ameboid chemical burns

161

from the acidic venom of wyverns' tailstings, and pockmarks left by crossbow quarrels that had struck through the flesh of fleeing gladiators.

A third of the way up the arc of the seating stood a ring of pissoirs that had been built an age ago for the use of long-dead spectators. They were similar to the pissoirs that were scattered throughout the city, relics of the Brass King, Tar-Mennelekil, who'd nearly bankrupted his nation with his public works.

The public pissoirs of Ankhana were built above shafts sunk through the limestone that formed the bedrock beneath the city; within these shafts are three screens of progressively finer bronze mesh to capture the solid wastes and allow the liquid to drain into the bottomless caverns below the city. A parallel shaft descends alongside each. The muckers make their rounds about once in a tenday, to collect the valuable shit and cart it away to Lucky Janner's Ankhanan Muckers and Manure on the outskirts of Alientown.

This much any citizen of Ankhana knows; what is less well known among the respectable citizenry is that concealed doors in these mucker shafts can lead one into those bottomless caverns, through which one who knows his way can move freely beneath the city.

It was up from these pissoirs that they came—the deformed, the blind, the crippled, amputees on their crutches and lepers in their pus-moist shreds of rags. They'd walked through the cloaca of the Empire to get here, and now the Knights of Cant, who stood in pairs at each pissoir door, swept them downward through the broken rings of crumbling stone benches with gestures of welcome.

Happy babble and snatches of song shivered in the night's freshening breeze as the mass of beggars swarmed down from the pissoirs, scrambling over seats their ancestors could have only gazed at in envy, never touched—only the landed gentry ever sat so low, so close to the arena. They reached the high wall that surrounded the arena sand and flowed over it like sheep, like lemmings, like a wave of ravenous vermin.

The sand of the arena floor, still damp from the evening's misting rain, now churned beneath sandals and rope-tied scraps of boots, beneath the iron ferrules of their crutches and the calluses of their naked feet. For two hundred years this sand had absorbed the blood and shit of mortally wounded gladiators, ogres, trolls, ogrilloi, and dwarfs; the half-digested bowel contents of gut-slashed lions; the ichor of throat-cut wyverns and the aqueous humors of draconymphs stabbed through their vulnerable eyes. For another hundred years it had stood abandoned to squatters, but no more: now oilskin tarpaulins were pulled off stacked cordwood in mounds taller than a man, and snapping bonfires leaped toward clouds so low that they reflected a dull orange toward the fires beneath.

Around the bonfires the cripples danced, for this hulking ring of stone was the Brass Stadium, and these beggars were the Subjects of Cant, and this night was the Night of the Miracle.

And among them a presence passed, a ghostly feeling of *here*-ness that could not be explained.

A leper paused in his grinning tale of a fat purse stolen while its owner handed him a coin; he'd felt a brush along his own rags, but no one stood beside him. He shrugged and finished his tale. Warm breath on a blind woman's neck caused her to turn and shift the filthy bandages over her eyes that she might see who'd stood so close. She rubbed her eyes and shook her head at her active imagination. Once, briefly, what must have been a trick of the shadows made footprints seem to appear in a clear patch, away from any feet that could have made them, but the Knight who saw this only sighed—his sharp suspicious wonder had instantly faded into bored forgetfulness.

A Cloak is a fiendishly difficult spell to maintain under the best of circumstances; among a constantly shifting crowd of suspicious and cynical professional thieves and beggars it's nearly impossible. A Cloak doesn't affect the physical world, it doesn't alter the path of light or prevent its reflection; it works directly, and solely, on the mind. Holding a Cloak requires that the adept maintain a constant mental visualization of the surrounding environment, including the positions and postures of every single person present, saving only himself—in other words, the adept must carry in his mind a perfect image of the scene as it would look *without him there*. As long as this concentration is maintained the adept may still be visible to the eye, but not to the brain: an onlooker is magickally prevented from mentally registering the sight. It's fairly simple when only one person is there to deal with, not too bad with two or three.

In the midst of the Subjects of Cant, no ordinary adept could hope to hold a Cloak. No ordinary adept would even attempt it—to be an outsider caught within the Brass Stadium on the Night of the Miracle was certain death, delivered instantly and ruthlessly without trial or appeal of any sort.

No one of Pallas Ril's acquaintance would describe her as ordinary.

Forty hours, murmured a tiny niggling voice in some distant and disconnected part of her mind. *I've been on the move for almost forty hours.*

Her teeth felt fuzzy, and her eyes seemed to scrape within her skull every time she blinked, but she moved silently through the press, listening here, watching there, letting herself drift wherever her feet took her. It might have been foolish of her to trust these people in the first place, but she was not so foolish that she didn't realize she'd been betrayed.

On the Night of the Miracle, all the Subjects of Cant gathered here. That meant that somewhere within this crowd was the man who'd betrayed her, who'd killed the Twins, and Talann—and Lamorak. She wouldn't have to kill him herself; she knew that Majesty would be grateful for the honor.

Unless, a cold internal voice reminded her, the traitor was Majesty himself; she was not so naive as to eliminate the King of Cant as a suspect simply because she liked him. She needed evidence, she needed a finger to point out a target, and this need had brought her here. The nature of the evidence she'd find, she had no idea.

A restless, oppressive lust for motion had driven her here, a feeling that something she couldn't see was gaining on her from behind. She had no real plan; holding a Cloak, which she'd been doing for several hours now, consumed so much of her attention that she was mostly confined to absorbing sense impressions for later examination. In what was very nearly a Zen state of meditative awareness, she'd opened herself to the radical present—and trusted that the moment itself would provide what she needed.

The moment provided a drumroll by an unseen hand, somewhere in the northern quadrant of the stadium seating.

There a ziggurat stood—nine ascending steps built above the stone benches, culminating in a massive high-backed throne that was carved from a single block of the native limestone. The drifting lace of Flow, that filled Pallas' mindview with translucent veins of color, suddenly whirled up toward the ziggurat and dove down through it. Pallas nodded to herself; inside the ziggurat was where Abbal Paslava the Spellbinder would be standing, weaving the effects for Majesty's entrance. Caine had described this to her once, and she knew what to expect.

Single-foot braziers of bronze flared into sparkshowers with no hand to ignite them. Dense billows of white smoke poured from the bronze bowls and down the platform, thickening until they utterly obscured the throne.

The scattered laughter and conversation among the Subjects died swiftly away; lamb shanks and wineskins were laid respectfully aside. Faces, rosy from the heat of bonfires, turned toward the swirling cloud. The drumroll stuttered into a marching cadence: down, out of the smoke, strode the nine Barons of Cant.

Pallas squinted at them, only half curious; she was familiar with the name and reputation of a couple of them, but she had no reason to suspect they even knew of her connection to the Subjects. They took up positions on the lower third of the nine steps, seven men and two brawny women, grounding the points of their naked blades into the stone and resting their hands upon cord-wound hilts.

Now the mist began to thin, slowly revealing first the shadowy silhouettes, then the motionless forms, of the Dukes of Cant arrayed on the third step from the top. Pallas knew both of these men: the skeletal figure in robes was Paslava, still pulling Flow; on the opposite side stood Deofad the Warlord, once of the Lipkan Imperial Guard, white-bearded and stolid.

She had met these two men shortly after approaching Majesty with the concept of the Simon Jester operation; either of them could be the traitor.

Then from the thinning mist at the apex of the ziggurat rang Majesty's voice, deep and clear as a temple bell. Pallas heard no suggestion of strain, of raising his voice to fill the Stadium—the lateral swirl of Flow that whirlpooled outward from the apex suggested to her that Paslava was tricking up Majesty's volume.

He said: "My Children. We gather tonight in this, the discarded arena of empire. And we, too, are discarded. We are the forgotten, the maimed, the crippled, the blind!"

The answering choral shout of the Subjects rang from the crumbling walls: *"We are!"*

"We are the thieves, the vagabonds, the beggars!"

"We are!"

"But we are not alone! But we are not helpless! We are powerful! We are brothers!"

"We are!"

"This Arena of Despair shakes before our brotherhood! The power of our brotherhood transforms the Arena of Despair into the Stage of Miracles! Here with your brothers, cast off your crutches!

Cast off your slings, your bandages! Let the crippled walk, let the blind see! Rejoice! My Children, you are healed!"

"WE ARE!"

And throughout the arena, crutches fell to the damp sand; limbs sprouted from empty sleeves; milky cataracts popped free from clear and sparkling eyes; and the dripping sores of leprosy peeled off from smooth skin as the last of the mist cleared and His Majesty the King of Cant sat on the throne in a coronal halo—a scarlet backlight from braziers that leaped to life above and behind him— as he motionlessly oversaw the transformation of his subjects.

Pure theater, Pallas well knew—no real cripple or leper would ever be allowed here—but she couldn't deny the power of this simple ritual, the rush of joy from every side as all their masks fell away at once.

Caine had tried to explain to her how the Subjects were vastly more than a mere street gang, tried to describe their almost religious devotion to each other, their sense of family, of belonging to something greater than the sum of its parts; Pallas had seen this devotion in action, but now she was beginning to understand it. She also understood how this simple ritual made it thoroughly impossible for an outsider to conceal himself and blend in here, without the use of magick.

And, looking up at Majesty as he descended the ziggurat, smiling and relaxed, bringing his Dukes and Barons with him to receive tithes at the retaining wall, Pallas had to admit that he knew everything there was to know about making a star entrance.

She drifted toward the wall, carefully slipping aside from Subjects moving in the same direction, and got close enough to overhear as he accepted gifts, money and otherwise, from the Subjects that trailed past. Three Barons carted the loot away when all was done, and Majesty vaulted lithely into the arena to mingle and laugh with his people. The Dukes and the Barons all followed him, and soon the arena had become a sprawling party, as wineskins passed from hand to hand and voices rose in boisterous song.

Pallas stayed close by Majesty's side, vaguely hoping for an opportunity to get him alone where she could speak with him, and so she heard Abbal Paslava's low-voiced warning as he pulled Majesty to one side.

"There's magick here; someone other than myself is pulling Flow within the stadium."

Majesty's answering smile was grimly humorous. "Well, point him out, and we'll spank the naughty bastard."

"I cannot."

"I don't understand."

"Nor do I. I feel it tug at my mind, but when I turn my attention onto it, it seems to skitter away like a sun-flash in the corner of the eye. This is definitely cause for concern."

"Keep working on it. And meanwhile, cover my exit; the tithing took too damned long and I'm late for a meet."

"Done." Paslava's head tilted back, and his eyes rolled up; Flow spiraled into his Shell as he pulled a tiny doll from a pocket and rolled it between his fingers. A tendril of violet power clung to Majesty as he drifted away, and Pallas followed on his heels.

Not too closely; many a Cloaked mage has given herself away simply by bumping into someone. Once or twice she had to move quickly to avoid clumps of Subjects, and each time she stepped clear Majesty seemed to have inexplicably gained ground, nodding and speaking a word or two here and there among the Subjects that he passed. He never seemed to move quickly, but somehow she could never quite catch up with him.

Even in her dissociated, meditative state, it took her barely a minute to realize what Paslava had done. This must be a sophisticated variation of the Cloak she herself was under—anyone looking for Majesty would see him off on the other side of the arena somewhere, always just a bit too far away to interact with. She tipped a mental nod of professional respect for Paslava's creativity. It was a clever spell, though she could break it with ease, if she chose.

Paslava might be clever, but for raw power he was not remotely in her league.

Breaking the spell, however, would require concentration that she needed to maintain her Cloak. Instead, she glanced around the arena; as her gaze passed the half-open gate on one of the beast chutes, Flow swirled more strongly around Abbal Paslava's Shell, and she felt the faintest increase in the tug of the spell's pull. She needed no more than this, and she let her desire to speak with Majesty draw her more strongly toward the chute, still drifting— she felt like she was floating, her legs obeying her desire for direction, but not for speed.

The darkness of the beast chute closed over her eyes as she moved away from the light of the bonfires and into the dusty scent of rotting wood and ancient urine. Here in the darkness, in unfamiliar surroundings, she couldn't visualize accurately enough to maintain her Cloak; it collapsed around her and she sagged against the wall, suddenly trembling.

Mindview—the mental state necessary to perceive Flow, to cast and maintain spells—is a meditative state, almost transcendental. When in mindview, you don't feel tired, you don't feel fear, you don't feel much of anything at all; you're aware only of your environment and your will, what adepts call your *intention*. For hours, Pallas' mindview had held at bay all the fatigue of protecting the Konnosi and the exhaustion of two days of running from the Cats, all the fear and horror of the fight, all the stomach-gnawing grief for the Twins, for Talann and Lamorak, the swelling ache of having led them to their deaths. But these emotions had circled her like hyenas: they hadn't lost interest, they hadn't gone off to seek other prey. Their patience was nearly infinite.

Now that her defense was gone they mobbed her; they sank needle teeth into her throat and dragged her gasping toward the floor.

For a moment faces flooded her, driving out all other thought: the terror and desperate hope of Konnos' two daughters, so much like what she saw on the faces of all the *tokali*, the hunted, who huddled together beneath that abandoned warehouse in the Industrial Park, with no one but her to depend on. The manic confidence of Talann, the grim trust of the Twins . . .

And, of course, the face that stung her eyes with a single tear: Lamorak with his gentle smile, tapping the fresh-cut brick arch with the blade of Kosall. *"And this is a gap I can hold for a long, long time."*

Oh, Karl . . . His name, the name she couldn't say out loud, couldn't murmur in her Soliloquy, the name that Studio conditioning wouldn't allow her to so much as whisper until she returned to Earth.

Until she returned to Earth, alone.

He'd held that arch for perhaps a minute, no more.

All these hyenas chewed into her belly, but she was an adept: she lived and died by her control of her mind. It took only seconds for her to strangle these carnivorous thoughts, and soon she pushed herself upright. There was no forgetting the danger she was in, simply by being here. Now as she picked her way up the incline, one hand against the crumbling stone of the chute, the images she'd stored from the Miracle began to organize themselves within her brain.

A meet, she monologued. *A meet during the Miracle. When every Subject of Cant will be inside the Stadium. The one moment out of the entire week when you can walk the Warrens without being seen by a Subject of Cant.*

A pounding rumble like distant surf began to grind in her ears; blood rose into her face, and she picked up speed.

Majesty, I swear . . . If it's you, Majesty, I swear I'll eat your rotten heart.

Her practiced hands flitted unconsciously over the pockets on her tunic and within her cloak, searching by feel for something that would put her on Majesty's trail without subjecting her to the foot-slowing necessity of mindview. She had plenty of artillery left, even without the boltwand she'd lost to the Cats: four of the charged-buckeye fireballs, two hunks of charged amber for Holds, a powerful Teke and a bladewand, as well as a less aggressive crystal Charm. This Adventure so far had consisted of mostly running and hiding; her defensive and evasive spells were depleted save only a single Chameleon, as were her few scrying devices. Without those prepared spells, she'd have to do everything in mindview—as she had the Cloak—which was dangerous and time consuming, at best.

When the inspiration came, she smiled to herself and swallowed a chuckle. The solution was so simple and elegant it was almost funny. She drew out from a pouch at her belt a small faceted chunk of purple quartz and patterned her mind to the sigils inscribed upon it. It was a process as simple as turning a key—no need to maintain mindview. The quartz grew warm in her hand, and as she held it out, an intermittent stripe at shoulder level along the wall began to fluoresce a dully ruddy magenta, as did faint, vaguely boot-shaped blotches along the floor. The Cloak variant Paslava had used on Majesty would be shedding magick continuously until it wore off, like a battery leaking charge—until then, she could use this simple detection spell to track his footprints and the places he'd brushed his hands along the walls, to follow his path through this Stygian maze.

The crystal caused trace magick to fluoresce at a range of only three to four meters; she had no fear of alerting Majesty, and the trace magick was visibly fading even as she began to follow it. When necessary, Pallas could move like a river, fast and smooth, and with only as much noise as her surroundings could absorb and cover. Moving at speed, she cleared the stadium in seconds and glided onto the streets of the Warrens.

Blessedly the clouds above parted, and the moon shone through. She could see him now, only forty or fifty meters ahead of her, moving at a steady lope. He'd picked up a hooded cloak somewhere along the way, but he must have been telling the truth to Paslava when he'd said he was late—he was moving too fast to conceal his natural gait, which was as distinctive as his voice. He didn't appear to worry about being followed; why should he? He'd hear the boots of anyone who'd try to match his pace.

Pallas smiled grimly as she put away the detection crystal. She slipped off her ankle-high boots and held one in each hand as she ran after him lightly, springing along silently on the balls of her bare feet, staying close to the buildings at her side; the hard-packed dirt of Warrens streets was substantially higher and drier along their edges than in their centers, and the litter of stones, wood scraps, and potshards tended to drift downhill toward the streets' centers. Along the side, she could sprint barefoot with little to fear.

Ahead, Majesty slid into the darkness of a doorless arch. Instead of following him within, she slipped back into her boots and slowly worked her way around the building. There, near a corner of the third floor on the far side from the arch Majesty had used, a sliver of lamplight leaked through weather-sprung shutters, the only light showing on the faces of this darkened hulk.

Controlling her breathing, she summoned mindview and scanned the twisted alleys around her, the faces of the buildings and what she could see of their roofs. The tangled lace of Flow drifted undisturbed, and no aureate Shells larger than those of rats shimmered in the shadows.

This meant that there were no stooges to watch this place, no guards to protect it; this meant that secrecy, even from his own men, was more important to Majesty than safety.

The distant surf of fury that rumbled in Pallas' ears drew closer.

But she held on to mindview and the surf faded. Of their own accord, her nimble fingers found the tiny model of a Chameleon in a pocket of her cloak. The beautifully sculpted platinum shone in mindview with complex whorls of power. These whorls spread into her mind, then downward across her body; to an observer, her skin and clothing would take on the grey-black moon-dappled appearance of the wall against which she stood. She paused a moment longer, to fix the image more strongly in her concentration, then she faced the wall and scampered up it with the ease of a lizard.

She hung effortlessly from the wall beside the splinter of light, and listened.

". . . before Berne catches him. This is vital," an unfamiliar voice was saying. "Berne has, already, entirely too great an influence over Ma'elKoth, and I believe that Berne is a deeply sick man—sick within his mind. It's vital that Berne does not succeed, here, and that I do. Don't try to tell me you're not involved: three of the five dead lookouts were known Subjects. The other two probably were as well."

"If I had him to give, he'd be yours, Your Grace." Majesty's voice was oddly humble, even obsequious. "I don't ask the Subjects for full accountings of their actions, only of their incomes. If some of them have chosen to supplement their incomes by stooging for Simon Jester, it's really none of my affair, unless they fail to pay their full tithe. They were my people, though, and I expect compensation."

Your Grace? That's probably Toa-Sytell himself! Pallas monologued, a sickening dread sinking into her stomach. Suddenly it was all too clear why this particular, private hour had been chosen for this meet. *So it's him. The King of Cant betrayed us all. I should have suspected: he's Caine's best friend. But . . . ahh, gods, I was really hoping he'd be innocent.*

The blood-smeared faces of Dak and Jak, of Lamorak and Talann rose up before her eyes.

I could frag them both. Right now. Right here. Trigger a fireball and poke the buckeye in through this gap in the shutters. I could drop to the ground, be well out of the blast radius. I wouldn't even have to hear them scream as they burn.

She shook the image out of her head. *I lived with Hari way too long,* she thought. She understood too well the trap of fury to give in to it here; that it was a righteous fury made it more dangerous, not less.

She monologued, *But I won't. I'll wait, and I'll listen. If there's killing to be done, I can do it after I understand what's going on.*

"I don't think you understand the gravity of this situation," said the unfamiliar voice, as tonelessly as a man ordering breakfast. "Simon Jester has already embarrassed the Emperor. Not only does he seem to operate with impunity, even here in the capital of the

Empire, but this graffito of his has appeared on walls within the Colhari Palace itself."

Hah. I've become a fad.

"I'm doing everything I can, Toa-Sytell. No one seems to know who Simon Jester is, or where he'll appear next."

And I can thank Konnos and his fancy spell for that.

"I believe," Toa-Sytell said, "that these accusees are still within the city limits of Ankhana. They number seventeen men, and many of them have taken their families—as many as thirty-eight persons altogether. Perhaps your energies may be more profitably spent searching out their hiding place?"

Pallas swallowed and hooked a buckeye from her hip pocket. She couldn't see the sigils of power that scribed its surface, not being in mindview, but she seemed to feel them scorching the flesh of her palm.

She might have to frag these men after all.

Majesty knows where they are; Konnos' spell wouldn't have altered that at all. Take two lives, to save thirty-six. She drew in a deep breath, preparing physically, while she clamped a mental hand down upon her emotions.

Majesty said apologetically, "It's a big city."

Hah?

He went on, "I'll put my people on it right away, but I can't make any promises. There's lots of places to hide, and more than a few of them aren't open to the Subjects."

"Do what you can on this. There is vastly more than money riding on it, as you might understand. If the Barons of the outlying marches see that defying Ma'elKoth is easily and safely accomplished . . . I believe you can imagine the possible consequences."

"Yeah. Another civil war, we don't need."

Pallas found herself panting, white-knuckled fingers crushing the buckeye within her grip. What kind of game was Majesty playing? And she'd almost *killed* him, almost killed them both; only by the grace of some kind god had she waited long enough to hear this last . . .

She barely half listened while the two men went on to other, less pressing business, dealing with the day-to-day politics of the Warrengangs and tidbits of rumor that Majesty had picked up from the Subjects. This Chameleon that held her to the wall wouldn't last forever; she'd begun to move away when she heard Majesty say,

"One last thing. I need to know what this warrant on Caine is about. What's he wanted for?"

Caine? Pallas' heart thumped painfully in her chest; she stopped moving, stopped breathing, and squeezed her eyes shut to listen harder.

"I do not believe that this is any of your concern."

Majesty's tone of nonchalance sounded faintly forced. "He's a friend of mine. I don't want this . . . arrangement between you and me to get in the way of that friendship. I also don't want that friendship to get in the way of our arrangement, you follow? I don't want to turn him in without knowing what he's in for."

Turn him in? Hari's here? *He's here now?* Pallas' mouth went dry and her stomach clenched and her heart skipped into a triphammer beat. Her fingers tingled uncomfortably, as though she'd just slapped someone.

"Don't concern yourself with this. I took Caine into custody earlier this evening, but he's not in any sort of trouble. Not from *us*, at least; although I do believe that the Monasteries might be a wee bit upset with him. In fact, I've been told in no uncertain terms that Ma'elKoth plans to hire him."

"Hire him? For what?"

"What else? To find Simon Jester and kill him, of course."

Of course, Pallas thought disconnectedly. *Why else would he be here, if not to fuck up my life again?*

She missed the two men's friendly leave-taking while images and thoughts whirled scattershot across the surface of her mind. Caine would know, of course—he'd know who Simon Jester was and where Simon Jester was and where the *tokali* were—the Studio would have simply shown him her cube. And she knew, too, that he wouldn't really hunt her down; not even Caine was *that* low. It was clear, it was all too fucking clear exactly what was going on.

The Studio had decided she'd bitched it up, this time. They'd decided that she couldn't do this on her own. They'd decided they could make a bigger bang by sending in The Mighty Caine to save her useless, incompetent, female ass.

With Caine to ride in at the last moment and save the day, they'd make a hundred million more than they would if she somehow managed to pull this off on her own.

All her stifled rage roared into her chest like a waterfall. Didn't they understand that this wasn't some stupid *game*? That this wasn't just entertainment? That *lives* rode on this, *real* lives, lives of real people who loved and grieved and laughed and bled?

And he had to be just *loving* this; she knew that too. Hari must be grinning right down to the scurf between his toes. She could almost hear his smugly patronizing voice say it: *See? You can't make it without me. Why even try?*

And she heard her own response, too, or rather her lack of one, her inarticulate rage at being treated like a bit player in her own life, like a sidekick, nothing but a motivation for someone else's Adventure. They weren't going to give her the chance to have a story of her own.

The light had gone out behind the shutters.

She pattered sideways around the building, moving across the wall on all fours at the speed of a fast walk. Down below her, at the archway where Majesty had gone in, she could see the top of the hood of his cloak as he stood by the wall. He worked his tinderbox to light a cigar, little *scrrt*ing sparks drifting down toward the street. No one else was in sight; Toa-Sytell must have left by a different door.

She waited until the cigar was well lit, then she canceled the Chameleon and fell on him like an old building.

Her feet slammed into his shoulders and he went down hard; she bounced off and rolled into a low, balanced stance. Stunned by the unexpected attack, Majesty couldn't do more than shake his head dazedly before she put her bare hand against his cheek and said, "You know me."

This was how Konnos had told her she could cancel the effect of his spell.

First the haze cleared from his eyes, then she watched amazement grow there as her canceling of the Eternal Forgetting allowed the different things he knew about her to slowly relink themselves within his mind.

"P-Pallas," he gasped, "great stinking *Curse!* What did . . . How did . . . And Caine . . . Caine—"

She crouched over him. "I know all about it. This is a dangerous game you're playing, Majesty."

"I, I, uh, shit . . . What did you hit me like that for?"

"I had to hit somebody," she said. "You were available. Now listen while I tell you what we're going to do."

He sat up and began dusting himself off. "You know, I'll take a lot from you. But you've really pushed this too far. Nobody lays a hand on me—"

Pallas interrupted him with a forehand slap on his ear. "You mean like that?"

Half-stunned again, he could only shake his head in disbelief.

She held her open hand up in front of his face. "You don't like being touched like that? Just imagine what kind of touch you'll get from *Caine*, after he finds out you're in bed with Toa-Sytell when you're supposed to be helping me."

She crouched there and let him think about it.

It didn't take him long. "Hey, uh, hey," he said hastily, "I've been helping you all along; I'm even juicing Toa-Sytell to keep him out of your way."

"Maybe I understand that," she said. "You think Caine will?"

"Well, but, yeah, but . . . you don't have to *tell* him, do you?"

"Maybe I don't. But I want you to understand that I'm kind of angry about this."

He rubbed his ear and slowly nodded. "I guess I can follow that. But it's got nothing to do with you. It wasn't me that fingered you to the Cats, don't you see?"

"No, I don't see. What I see is that you're holding me in the bag until you get a better price from Toa-Sytell."

"Pallas, I swear—!"

"Don't swear. You know what I've been doing these last forty hours or so?"

"I, uh—"

"In between staying a step ahead of the Cats and the King's Eyes and generally trying to stay alive, I've been examining an innocent family, probing them in some ugly and extremely uncomfortable ways, to make sure none of them was a spy, or had a telltale planted on them—or in them. The father's name is Konnos. You'd like him, Majesty. He works for the government." She leaned close and bared her teeth. "Just like you."

"Pallas, hey, Pallas—"

"Shut up." She found herself suddenly short of breath and sweating, and her heart thumped inside her chest as she imagined pulling the bladewand from her wrist sheath and just slicing his damned head off. She shivered with cold fury, and she wondered fleetingly if this is how Caine felt, just before he killed someone. "I *trusted* you, Majesty. I trusted you, and you lied to me, and people I care about died."

"Think about what you're doing, Pallas," Majesty said, licking his lips, shifting his legs to scoot back from her.

"You," she said, "will never lie to me again."

"Pallas, really, this isn't necessary—"

"I think it is. I have no one left to depend on, Majesty, and I have thirty-six people counting on me to save their lives. There were some people, three or four, that I knew I could trust. They're dead now. I'm taking no more chances." She shut her mouth abruptly. Why tell him any of this? She was only talking to herself, really, trying to justify to herself what she was about to do.

She dipped into a pocket on the inside of her belt and brought out a prism-shaped crystal of quartz, slightly smaller than one of her fingers. It rode within a platinum cage, attached to a platinum chain from which it dangled; she twirled the chain between her fingers to make the crystal spin and splinter off shards of moonlight.

"Don't do it," Majesty said hoarsely, trying to sound fierce. "Don't put magick on me, Pallas. *Nobody* puts magick on me."

A single breath slid her into mindview and kindled the glow of the force-pattern within the crystal; the briefest caress of her Shell triggered the Charm. The moonsplinters off the planes of quartz took on a phantom solidity in mindview; the splinters shot outward, carrying the force-pattern of the Charm like poison upon a blade. They pierced Majesty's Shell, and the shining net of the Charm spread over his Shell's dangerous yellow-shot orange like oil poured upon rippling water. One scant breath later, the shades of anger and fear faded into the greens of serenity and the warm, solid earth tones of absolute loyalty.

"You're sure?" she asked lightly, surfacing out of mindview. "It's just a little spell."

Majesty took a deep breath, visibly steeling himself. "All right," he said. "I trust you. Do what you think is right."

I deserved that, she thought, wincing. It made her feel a little sick.

Forget that she didn't really have any choice. Forget how many lives depended on her—and on him. She had reached into his heart and made herself the best friend he'd ever had, closer than a sister, closer than his mother. It was a terrible thing to do, even to an animal; to do this to a man—how had she come to this, all of a sudden? The woman she had been, only a few days ago, would never have considered such a thing. She'd enchanted that crystal against an emergency, a desperate situation, where she'd have no other choice. Did this qualify?

She shook herself; she'd worry about hypothetical erosion of her morals after the people in her care were safely away from Ankhana. "Come on, Majesty, get up," she said. "We have some work to do."

Majesty rose obediently and gazed at her like a loving puppy. "Whatever you say, Pallas."

2

THE STINGING YELLOW glare of the Ankhanan sun stabbed through Caine's eyelids like the flash of a bomb and brought him bolting upright out of the chair where he'd finally slept.

For a second that stretched toward the infinite, he struggled with the gluey mess inside his head, trying to fit together where he was and what was happening; then his eyes finally focused on the six men in the livery of the Household Knights who formed a sort of human wall between him and His Grace the Imperial Duke of Public Order.

Toa-Sytell stood by the window, his hand still on the curtain that he'd just now thrust aside. Sunlight streamed past him, filled with swirling motes of dust. "How are you feeling?"

Caine scratched at his tangled hair. "That depends. Did you bring coffee?"

"I'm afraid not."

"Then I feel like shit." Caine squinted at the Duke, who now moved away from the window into the light. Purplish smears trailed downward from the Duke's eyes, which were themselves bloodshot and puffy. "You're not looking too well yourself. Late night?"

"That's not your concern. I've come to take you to the Emperor."

"We could have done this last night."

"No, we could not."

"And the reason for this is—?"

Toa-Sytell spread his hands. "Ma'elKoth did not choose to summon you until this morning."

Caine nodded, scratching disgustedly at his beard; keeping others waiting is a privilege of power everywhere, but he didn't have to like it. In fact, he'd probably be pretty damn angry, once he was fully awake.

"You don't think you still need these guys, do you?" he said, waving a dismissive hand at the guardsmen. "I thought we'd reached a sort of understanding."

A sere smile barely bent the Duke's mouth. "Perhaps I should be confident that I can depend upon your good nature; I imagine that Creele was."

Last night, when Toa-Sytell had cautiously installed Caine in this room in the Colhari Palace, a room already provided with a generous platter of cold meats, bread and fruit, a carafe of wine, and a piping-hot bath freshly drawn, Caine had shaken his head and given a bitter laugh. He'd said, "And to think I just now killed a man for turning me over to you."

Toa-Sytell, watching from the doorway as Caine's shackles were removed by the King's Eyes who'd accompanied them, had replied without a hint of humor, "Perhaps you were somewhat hasty."

While Caine picked at the food, Toa-Sytell had revealed why the reward had been issued, why he'd been arrested and brought here. The stinging irony of it left Caine speechless.

The Emperor wanted to hire him to find Simon Jester. Wanted to *pay* him to do what he was already doing, wanted to offer all the resources of the Imperial Government to help him in his search.

Creele, all unknowing, had been doing Caine a *favor*.

Caine had very slowly and carefully laid aside the sandwich he'd made, swallowed, and said, "Sure. What does it pay and when can I start?"

But here was the sticking point: Ma'elKoth wished to personally interview him. Toa-Sytell didn't know why. Caine was invited to bathe and wash his clothing, and to hold himself in readiness. He'd eagerly done so, even mending the tear in his breeches from the ogre's tusk; his fingers had trembled, shook with the anticipation and the astonishment he felt at this swift surge of fortune—palace access, an excuse to meet privately with his target, and the full resources of the King's Eyes to find his wife.

Then he'd waited.

After that, he'd waited some more.

Alone in the sumptuous room, he'd paced up and down, growing impatient and angry, then furious. The door was locked from the outside, and when he'd rattled it, the solicitous voice of a guard posted in the hall had inquired if there was anything he needed. He'd checked the concealed service door, remembering its location from the week he'd spent in this palace masquerading as a servant before the murder of Toa-Phelathon, but that too was locked. He could, he had supposed, break a window and have a chance of escape, but to what?

He was imprisoned here more by his own wishes, his own hopes and desires, than by the locks on the doors. This was an opportunity he couldn't bear to let pass.

His thoughts had twisted around the axis of the female prisoner in the Donjon like a pinwheel in the hand of a running child.

Shanna could be in that cell.

She could be safe.

She could be in his arms within an hour, or less.

Because of that spell, it was certainly possible that Berne could have captured her without understanding who she was, just taken her into custody for her proximity to the scene, arrested her because she was there. It was possible.

It was also possible that the prisoner in the Donjon was this Talann woman. Shanna could be anywhere. It could be she was having a lavish dinner at a club on the South Bank. It could be she was cornered in an Alientown back alley, fighting for her life against the Cats.

It could be she was already dead.

The uncertainty had chewed at him like a rat trapped inside his skull.

Ma'elKoth had never come, had never sent for him. As the night crept by he had only been able to pace angrily and watch the level of rose-scented oil in the lamp's base shrink by the millimeter; he'd counted with the beating of his heart each minute of Shanna's life that he wasted in this room.

Sometime past midnight he had gotten over any regret for Creele's murder.

Finally exhaustion had dragged him into a soft overstuffed chair. He had sat, brooding on his helplessness, until that brooding passed seamlessly into sleep.

Now he preceded his escorts into the corridors of the Colhari Palace. The six Household Knights followed him in a shallow arc, and Toa-Sytell came last, his hands clasped behind him and an expression of thoughtful attention on his face. Their boot heels made no noise on the deep teal runner that half covered the pale, vaguely peachy marble floor. Toa-Sytell directed Caine verbally— turn here, here again, take these stairs.

The stairs were near an open archway that led onto a vertical shaft with oiled ropes at the back and sides that stretched upward and downward out of sight. Near the arch was a bellpull. Caine nodded toward this arrangement as they passed. "Too many of us for the Shifting Room, eh?"

Toa-Sytell replied, "Yes, the ogres on the donkey wheel in the cellar cannot manage more than three or . . . But then, you'd know all this, I imagine." In his voice whispered an odd huskiness, a thickness of some unidentifiable emotion.

Caine shrugged and walked on to the stairs. They went down two floors in silence, and along another corridor, and Caine could now detect a growing carnal scent, a coppery, meat-locker kind of smell.

"You and I are nearly of an age, Caine," Toa-Sytell said abruptly. "You cannot be more than four or five years my junior. Do you have children?"

Caine stopped and squinted at the Duke over his shoulder. "What's it to you?"

"Sons are a man's pride, Caine, and daughters are the comfort of his age. I am only curious."

Caine shrugged. "Maybe someday."

"I had two. Sons that I loved, Caine. Who grew into men of honor, strong and fierce. Tashinel and Jarrothe. They were both killed, only a month apart, in the Succession War."

He said this as though he were reporting a rise in crop prices in the markets, but something dark and potent flickered behind his face.

Caine's eyes held those of the Duke for a moment, gravely acknowledging his loss. *Another knife aimed at my conscience,* he thought. But compared with the other wounds his conscience had taken, this was barely a scratch.

Eventually, he dropped his gaze as though ashamed, then turned to walk again. *Let him think I feel it more than I do, if that's what he wants. Let him take what comfort he can.*

And I should remember that Berne might not be my only enemy in the palace.

Toa-Sytell said, "Your destination is through that archway at the hall's end. Take care not to speak, or in any way interrupt the Emperor. He's engaged in what he calls his Great Work, and will address you when and if he so desires."

"Great Work?" The capitals had been audible in the Duke's tone.

"You will see. Go, now."

The bloody scent grew thicker. By the time Caine reached the doorway he could *taste* it, like raw meat a couple of days old.

This room had been the Lesser Ballroom in the days of Toa-Phelathon, an intimate space for fetes of less than a thousand guests. Sunlight strong enough to singe the eyeballs glared in through the huge windows that dominated the south wall, narrow Gothic-arched windows ten meters high and separated by sturdy columns of imported granite. The center of the parquet dancing floor had been cut away, and a shallow bowl half a stone's throw across had been scooped from the limestone beneath.

The resulting pit was lined with coals that glimmered red and cast a wilting heat, but no smoke or scent of any kind; supported on legs of brass above it was a massive cauldron, shallow as a stew bowl but broad enough to swim laps in. The cauldron was tended by pages who raced around its edges, stirring with long wooden poles held high above their sweat-soaked heads or pouring hods of this or that into the brew, while pairs of others roamed from side to side, bearing massive leather-lung bellows. These they rested on the floor and leaned upon with all their weight, to breathe searing yellow life into the coals below.

Within the cauldron appeared to be boiling mud, or very wet clay; it was from here that Caine thought the blood-scent—as well as some bitter, acidic undernote—might be coming. The entire room rippled and shimmered with heat.

Barefoot across the surface of the boiling mud walked the Emperor Ma'elKoth.

His size alone made him unmistakable. Caine stood just within the archway and studied him from there, mindful of that finger poking at the back his head, that nagging sense of familiarity to the way the Emperor had moved, had gestured and spoken in the recording Kollberg had shown him.

The Emperor wore only a kilt of crimson velvet bordered with a weave of cloth-of-gold, and there was something of the dinosaur, of the dragon, in the slow, majestic grace of his movements, the way he would flow from pose to pose with evident satisfaction, as though the play of muscle in his massive arms and shoulders, chest and back, gave him some deeply spiritual joy to be savored; as though it answered some personal aesthetic need in a fashion as primal as sex.

This wasn't it—Caine couldn't find that tug of familiarity here.

These movements were as stylized as a bodybuilder's, and as precise as ballet.

The boiling clay beneath Ma'elKoth spat smoking gobbets up
his legs; he paid them no more attention than he did the breeze from
the pages' bellows. His eyes shone pale shamrock green and more:
fluorescent emerald. He raised his hands like a priest extending
benediction, and from the boiling clay there rose a formless mass,
still spitting steam and roiling with its heat.

The mass of clay, a hundred kilos or more, hung in the heatshimmer, two meters above the surface, supported only by Ma'el-
Koth's will. Pseudopodia squirmed outward from the mass, five
limbs that stretched and seemed to form themselves of their own
accord. Clay fell away from the mass, dropping like fresh shit back
into the mud beneath; four of the limbs stretched and thinned while
one contracted, and the mass took on the shape of a man.

The man-shape looked small, even tiny, beside the Emperor's
bulk. It rotated in the air, its features refining. Ripples and folds of
what would represent clothing passed in waves over its surface. Its
face slowly swung through Caine's view; this face had a close-
clipped mustache and thin jawline beard, a nose with the slight
bend of an old break and a scar across it, and his mouth went suddenly dry.

He lifted a foot to step forward, to get closer, and Ma'elKoth
said, "Please do not move. This is, you might imagine, difficult."

He had never even glanced toward the archway. There was no
way he could have seen Caine standing there; not with his eyes,
anyway.

Caine stared at the statue, barely daring to breathe. *Tyshalle's
bloody Axe,* he thought.

That's me.

And by the time this thought was completed, it was true: it was a
replica, perfect in every detail save only that it still had the color of
the clay—it even matched his posture in the doorway. It hung in the
air, rotating slowly like a body on the gallows, while Ma'elKoth
studied his handiwork. The Emperor's voice had the warm and distant rumbling tone of a father heard through the walls of the womb.

"You may move now, Caine. Please come in."

The pages who scurried around the cauldron, stirring and pump-
ing the bellows, barely spared him a glance as he entered the room.
Caine's step was tentative, and his chest ached with some emotion
that he couldn't at first identify because he really couldn't remember

ever having felt this before—seconds passed before he realized
that it was awe.

This had been the most astonishing display of total mastery he'd
ever seen: it was impossible for him to conceive of a man more
completely in control of every element of his environment.

And I've contracted to kill this man, Caine thought. *I'd better
catch him in his sleep.*

Ma'elKoth strode across the boiling surface of the clay, oblivious
to the steam and the heat, the Caine-manikin he'd made bobbing
along behind him like a puppy. His smile of welcome warmed
Caine like a shot of whiskey, and he said, "I cannot quite see where
this piece fits. What do you think?"

"Piece?" Caine said hoarsely. What piece? Piece of what? "I
don't understand."

An Olympian chuckle: "Of course not. You look on this—" He
nodded toward the clay statue. "—as a finished work of art. To Me,
it is only a single piece: of *that.*"

Ma'elKoth swept up a hand to point behind and above Caine's
head. Caine turned and looked up, and up, and up. His mouth hung
open like a child's does, as he stared up the side of a skyscraper.

It was a face.

It could only have belonged to a Titan, to Atlas who carried the
sky on his shoulders. From just above the arch to the very ceiling of
the ballroom, thirty-five meters above, stretched this Gargantuan
relief of a face.

It was less than half finished. Some parts were still bare wall;
others had the structure of bones building slowly outward. Only
the brow and one eye were truly complete.

It was built out of people.

Like the jigsaw puzzle of an insane god, it had been constructed
of human bodies, layered and pieced and interlaced like corpses in
a mass grave; an instant later Caine realized that these weren't
bodies, of course, not actual corpses, but were clay statues like the
one of him that floated at Ma'elKoth's shoulder.

The sheer immensity of it was staggering; when he thought of
how much work it had taken to form each perfect manikin and fit
each into place, when he thought of how much work remained to
be done, that earlier awe swelled into his throat, choking off any
real hope that Ma'elKoth was just another thaumaturge, merely a
man of power writ large.

Caine could only stare.

"Do you like it?" Ma'elKoth boomed. "I call it *The Future of Humanity*."

At these words something clicked within Caine's mind, and he saw it: he had an instant's prophetic vision that built the bones outward, and fleshed them, and painted them with color.

The face was Ma'elKoth's.

Caine whispered, "It looks like you."

"Of course it does. It's a self-portrait."

Ma'elKoth's voice came now from just at his side, and Caine turned to find himself nose-to-collarbone with the Emperor's immense chest. He must have leaped down from the cauldron's rim as silently as a cat. Caine could smell him: rich masculine sweat over the lavender-scented oil that gleamed in his hair and beard, and the thick, meaty odor of the clay that caked his bare flesh. Ma'elKoth showed his perfectly white, perfectly even, and impressively large teeth.

"All great art is ultimately self-portraiture, Caine."

There was something so daunting about being within the reach of those bulging arms that Caine couldn't speak, could only nod in response.

The Caine manikin was beside him, perfect in height and every feature: Caine looked into his own eyes modeled in clay, and could see now that even individual hairs were modeled into the beard.

Ma'elKoth said, "And this is the piece with which I'm working right now, but I cannot quite see where it needs to go. Every piece must have its own place; every piece must contribute to the whole. I have been working with this one from time to time for two days now, and I still do not see it. Perhaps you have a suggestion?"

Caine shook his head and forced words through his constricted throat. "I wouldn't presume."

"Just so," Ma'elKoth sighed. "Well, then. If no proper place can be found—"

The Emperor lifted his hand up before his eyes and suddenly made a fist; the Caine manikin convulsed and squeezed out of shape, squirting its clay-flesh out between the fingers of some invisible giant.

For just one instant Caine thought he saw an expression on his face of clay, of some hideous and inexpressible agony, and then it too was crushed. Another gesture from Ma'elKoth, and the irregular ball of clay lofted up over the rim of the cauldron like a child's ball to splash down into the clay from whence it had come.

Ma'elKoth said, "Any questions?"

"You," Caine replied slowly, "are not subtle."

"Subtlety is for the weak. It is a wheedling tactic they use to achieve their desires, when they lack the power to do so directly."

Funny, Caine thought. *I can remember saying almost the same thing, more than once.*

A page walked by carrying a large bucket of dark liquid, which he then poured over the rim of the cauldron. Caine watched him do this, then squinted up at Ma'elKoth.

"Here's a question: what's this stuff they keep pouring into the clay? It smells like blood."

"It *is* blood," Ma'elKoth replied gravely. "All Great Works are built with blood; did you not know this?"

"That's, ah—" Caine cleared his throat uncomfortably. "That's usually just a metaphor."

"Is it?"

He rubbed his hands together briskly and suddenly clapped a comradely hand on Caine's back, hard enough to make him stagger. "Come. I must wash, and you, of course, are hungry and should eat. We have much discussion ahead of us."

He strode off through the arch with a swinging gait so fast that Caine had to jog to keep up.

3

THE BREAKFAST TABLE looked to be laid out for a banquet, loaded with everything from vegetable soufflés to stuffed quail. Caine sipped from a tall frost-rimmed goblet of iced coffee and tried not to think of Greek myths and pomegranate seeds.

Ma'elKoth lay on a curving couch at the far end of the table, reclining with leonine ease. He'd made skillful small talk while Caine had sat beside his bath; the three lovely girls who'd shared the bath with him, scrubbing away the hardening clay, had drawn no more of Ma'elKoth's attention than had the table alongside the tub.

Caine hunched over the table so that the hilts of his new knives poked into his ribs; he was acutely aware of the presence of all seven of these blades. On the stroll from the baths to the breakfast chamber, Ma'elKoth had suddenly turned to him and said joyfully, "I must beg your pardon for a poor host. I have only now realized why you seem so uncomfortable and reticent in conversation. Please follow Me."

The Emperor had led him to the Arms Gallery on the second floor and ushered him into a bedchamber-sized room whose walls and floor were filled with rack after rack of every conceivable style of knife, from bent-blades like *khukris* to fan-hilted *mains gauche*, *katar*-like punching daggers, *tanto*-style chisel blades, even a few with the foot-long isosceles blade of an Arkansas Toothpick. "Please," Ma'elKoth had said. "Help yourself."

Caine had picked up a rippled-blade dress dagger similar to a Florentine flame stiletto and turned it in his fingers. They were alone, together, in a small room with a thick door, and the place was full of knives.

"You know," he'd said, "Creele believed that someone had hired me to kill you. You might be well advised to keep me unarmed."

Deep amusement had sparkled within the Emperor's brilliant green eyes. "Am I a fool? You, Caine, are never unarmed. I could cut your arms from your shoulders, and you would still kill with your feet. Please, accept My hospitality. It is My Wish that you be completely at ease."

At ease? In the presence of Ma'elKoth?

"That's a joke, right?"

"Of course."

And so Caine had sat down to breakfast with every sheath full of fresh steel.

Caine had been waiting all morning for Ma'elKoth to get down to business. Now, finally, he could wait no more.

"Duke Toa-Sytell explained what you want of me. I'm willing. I only want to know what resources I can use, and what you'll pay me."

He knew he was overplaying, showing too much eagerness, but he couldn't help it and he no longer cared: that sharp need was there, in his guts, pulling him along. He had to get out of this place, had to get onto the streets and onto Shanna's trail.

"Caine, please," Ma'elKoth said languidly from his couch. "It's vulgar to discuss business during a meal, and bad for the digestion."

"You're not eating," Caine pointed out.

"I no longer eat," Ma'elKoth said with a heavy shrug. "Nor do I sleep. In small, peripheral ways like these, power such as Mine can be a burden."

So much for catching him napping, or slipping a couple drops of arsenic into his stew, Caine thought. He let a little of his impatience creep into his voice. "Well, if we're not going to talk business, why are we wasting our time?"

"This time is not wasted, Caine. I am using it to study you."

Caine carefully set down his goblet; he didn't want to slop coffee onto the linen tablecloth if his hand should start to shake.

"Oh?"

"Indeed. It was a Power, Caine, that drew your name and image from My mind, a Power from Outside that answered My query: Who shall bring this pestiferous Simon Jester into My grasp? Initially, I was inclined to trust this happy accident, that the Power showed me a face I knew so well that Drawing you here required less than two full days."

"Drawing me?" Caine said, frowning. "You think I'm here because of some kind of—"

"Let's not quibble, dear boy. I desired your presence, and here you are. These are facts; the mechanism behind them is irrelevant. Furthermore, while I am gratified that you now feel enough at your ease to interrupt Me, it is discourteous to do so. Even rude."

The surface of Ma'elKoth's tone remained light, but subterranean echoes beneath his contrabasso rumble hinted that some large and hungry creature slept fitfully, down within his chest. He waited, outwardly calm, staring at Caine with limpid hazel eyes—

Hey, Caine thought, *weren't his eyes blue, before? Or green?* Momentarily distracted, Caine let the silence stretch to a painful length before coming back to himself. He met the Emperor's gaze somewhat sheepishly. "Apologies, Imperial Maj—"

"Accepted," Ma'elKoth said briskly. "I do not stand much on ceremony here, as you may have noticed. Ceremony is for insignificant men who lick others' pretended awe like spittle from their chins. As I was saying, My original intention of simply allowing you to undertake this task has fallen by the wayside because I, Caine, am a man cursed with curiosity. I asked the fatal question: Why *you*?"

Caine spread his hands. "I'm wondering the same thing myself."

"My quest for the answer to this question led Me to consider your career." Ma'elKoth suddenly sat upright and laid his palms upon the table between them. His eyes burned. "Do you have any conception of how extraordinary a man you are, Caine?"

"Stop, you'll make me blush."

"Don't be ridiculous. Of the six crucial turning points of the history in this Empire over this past turbulent decade, you were a central participant in *four* of them. The only tangible links between the four are their magnitude, and the fact that you, personally, affected the outcome."

"Really?"

Ma'elKoth ticked them off on his fingers. "One, the assassination of Prince-Regent Toa-Phelathon—" He held up a hand. "—do not bore Me with protestations of innocence—that triggered the Succession War, which ended in the destruction of the Menelethid Dynasty and My accession to the Throne. Two, you led the small party of adventurers who, at great personal risk, came out of the Boedecken Waste with news of the rise of Khulan G'Thar, and his unification of the ogrilloi, in time for Ankhana to fortify its border cities and raise two armies against his onslaught."

"That was kind of by accident," Caine said. He and his partners had been looking for artifacts and treasure among the ruins of an age-old primal metropolis—from the days thousands of years before when the elves still built and lived in cities—when they'd been captured by a nomadic ogrillo tribe. The bloody games the ogrilloi had played with them, and Caine's bloodier escape with his two surviving companions, made *Retreat from the Boedecken* still a popular rental, after nearly a decade.

"Nonetheless. More than a year later, as incompetence among the Ankhanan generals allowed the Khulan Horde to threaten the very existence of humanity on this continent, it was you, Caine, who infiltrated Khulan G'thar's personal guard. Not only did you furnish the Ankhanan army with G'thar's complete order of battle in time for our armies to link with the Monastic Expeditionary Force and meet the Khulan Horde at Ceraeno, but you reentered the Horde, engaged the Khulan himself in single combat, and killed him."

"Single combat," Caine said with a slow smile, "is a little bit of an overstatement. I snuck up behind him during the battle and stabbed him in the back. The old bastard was tougher than I thought—he broke my arm with that morningstar he carried for a scepter. I can still feel it every time it rains." The warm pride that snuck into his tone was only peripherally related to Ma'elKoth's praise; *Last Stand at Ceraeno* was popularly considered Caine's greatest Adventure.

Ma'elKoth shrugged. "Details are only trivia. On that particular occasion, you certainly saved the Empire single-handedly. In fact, as I glean stories and rumors from across the continent, you are involved almost constantly in great doings of one sort or another . . ."

His voice went deadly soft, a silken garrote sliding across a soft throat. "And I wonder how it is that one man can be so relentlessly *important*. Curious, isn't it?"

It's because the Studio sends me where the action is, he thought, and he didn't have a better explanation. He was painfully aware of how treacherous had become the ground on which this conversation walked; it had suddenly shifted from dry and pleasant flattery to hungry quicksand.

How much did Ma'elKoth really know about these *Aktiri* he hunted so ruthlessly?

"Now a Power has told Me that you are the only man who can catch Simon Jester. I spent all of last night attempting to determine why that is so. While you slept, I subjected you to every test at My command."

Caine's mouth went entirely dry. "And?"

"And I found nothing. Whatever power it is that drives you to the center of these events, it is not magickal. The only peculiarity I found was the color of your Shell—it's black, you know, and quite unreadable. This perhaps explains some of your success against thaumaturges—I know you've killed quite a number of adepts, in your day—and other magick-using creatures. Must be a substantial advantage, when your emotions and intentions cannot be read."

"Sometimes," Caine said, letting out a long, slow breath.

"But this is hardly unique; it is only rare. Lacking the resources to satisfy My curiosity by Myself, I have come to another course of action: to *ask* you."

"Because you assume I know."

Ma'elKoth nodded ponderously. "Indeed. I hope you do; frustration I find intolerable. In My frustration of last night, I nearly killed you."

Caine blinked. "Oh?" he said thinly.

"A spell. A power. I closely considered taking your life so that I could absorb some of the memories of your departing spirit."

"That, ah," Caine said carefully, "seems a little extreme . . ."

"Well, yes," Ma'elKoth said with a dry chuckle. "Understanding *how* you can catch Simon Jester might have done Me little good without having you here to perform the task."

"I guess I still don't understand why you can't find, uh, this guy yourself," Caine said.

"It is a spell of concealment that Simon Jester has done, that is still in action. I have been able to analyze its effects, but I cannot counteract it—not yet, perhaps not ever. The Power from Outside told Me that this spell is easily broken once I lay hands upon its caster. It operates directly on the mind, splintering off the bits and pieces of knowledge I have about him; it prevents Me from connecting one to another, or even noticing that a connection is possible. It is infuriating to think that I may already know who Simon Jester is, and that I'm simply prevented from putting a face to the name."

Oh boy, Caine thought. *Oh, holy shit.* It wasn't a flash of inspiration, rather it was more of a slow dawning: he came to realize that the answer to this question was the same as the answer to the previous one.

It's because I'm an Actor.

Everyone here, the way their eyes would go vague whenever he mentioned Simon Jester, or Pallas Ril—the reason this didn't happen to him was that in his heart, in his mind, in his cherished dreams of happiness, there was no Simon Jester. There was no Pallas Ril. There was only Shanna. He didn't love the abstraction, the Scarlet Pimpernel game she'd been playing; he didn't love the character, the persona of Pallas Ril. It was Shanna, had always been Shanna.

Would always be Shanna, forever.

There was no answer that could be made, even if he'd wanted to. If she'd been his worst enemy alive, the Studio's conditioning would strangle his voice, even kill him, before the truth of her could pass his lips. And the closer Ma'elKoth came to the answer of his questions, the closer he came to the truth of Caine.

Truth that was, in this case, lethal.

I'm going to die, here, Caine thought. *Eventually, he's going to realize what's going on, what I am, and then he's going to kill me.*

And even if he doesn't, I've contracted to take him down. When I try, he'll snuff me like a candle.

Death, like the sun, was something that not even Caine could stare at too steadily; he wondered fleetingly if Creele and Toa-Phelathon and his countless other victims would be waiting for him, then he put it out of his mind.

The best I can hope for is to get Shanna back to Earth alive. Win or lose, live or die, I don't give a shit so long as she's all right.

"What is it?" Ma'elKoth asked, leaning forward and studying Caine's face. "You've come to some realization, I can see it. Tell me. Now."

"I have," Caine said, "come to the realization that I don't really need to be polite to you anymore."

"Oh?" Ma'elKoth looked more amused than offended.

He shrugged, and gave the Emperor a cynical half smile. "If you didn't need me to catch Simon Jester for you, I'd be dead already. You said so yourself. So maybe I'm thinking it's stupid to worry about staying on your good side."

Some of the amusement in the Emperor's eyes began to fade, and his rumble sounded faintly dangerous.

"Stupid?"

"Be reasonable: accept the facts, and let me get on with it."

"Reasonable, indeed," Ma'elKoth purred. He rested his elbows on the table and steepled his fingers before his face. " 'The reasonable man adapts himself to the world: the unreasonable man persists in trying to adapt the world to himself. Thus all progress depends on the unreasonable man.' "

That's Shaw! Caine thought, thunderstruck. That particular quote was a favorite of Duncan's—where would Ma'elKoth have come across a quote from an Earth author? And a banned one, at that . . .

"You know," he said carefully, "my father used to say that to me."

"I know." Ma'elKoth's smile broke like the dawn. "You quoted him to Me once before, and I never forget."

This shit has gone far enough, he thought, and said, "All right, I give up."

"Eh?"

Caine shook his head irritably. "I've been trying to figure out where I know you from. I mean, I know your reputation, from the Plains War and the Succession War, and I've seen what you've done here in Ankhana, but I keep getting the feeling that we've met, that I *know* you. Your manner—the way you talk, especially, the way every other sentence is some sweeping statement about the Nature of Reality or something—I know we've met before, somewhere, but I'm damned if I remember. And I'm damned if I can understand how I could forget meeting a seven-foot, three-hundred-forty-pound adept who looks like a sculptor's wet dream."

"Mm, flattery." Caine could feel Ma'elKoth's answering laugh vibrate against his chest. "We do know each other, Caine. You might say that you met Me in My former life. Once before, I hired you to do a job of work."

"Really?"

"Indeed. And We worked rather closely together for a time. It was, oh, seven years ago, I'd say, shortly before the Plains War. I hired you to retrieve the crown which once belonged to Dal'kannith of the Thousand Hands."

Caine stared, openmouthed. "You're kidding."

The Emperor shook his head smugly. "I am not. You knew Me as Hannto of Ptreia, and I believe by My rather uncomplimentary nickname 'the Scythe.' "

"Hannto . . ." Caine breathed, unbelieving. "You're *Hannto the Scythe?*"

The man who'd hired Caine to steal Dal'kannith's crown had been a thaumaturge, all right; he'd been a rat-faced little weasel with bad skin, maybe ten years Caine's senior. Hannto was fairly adept, but not spectacular; he specialized in necromancy to support his hobby, which was collecting relics of various historical figures. The crown was the only surviving relic of the legendary Lipkan warlord Dal'kannith, who later came to personify their god of war; it had been missing since Jhereth's Revolt, more than three hundred years before, when Hannto had gotten a lead on its whereabouts. But Hannto . . . He was nothing, really; Caine could have broken him in half with one hand—he was known as the Scythe for his physique, his sunken chest and crooked back.

And Ma'elKoth was, well . . .

He was *Ma'elKoth.*

"I am not," the Emperor said, "Hannto the Scythe. I *was* Hannto the Scythe, some years ago. Now, I am Ma'elKoth. Emperor of Ankhana, Shield of Prorithun, Lion of the White Waste, and so forth and so on."

"I can't believe it . . ."

The Emperor grinned, obviously enjoying Caine's awe. "What is so difficult to believe? With the power of the crown—and some few other bits and pieces I'd acquired over the years—I transformed Myself." He stretched like a sleepy lion. "I made Myself into the man I had always wished to be. Is this so very odd? Have you, Caine, not done the same?"

"Maybe," Caine allowed slowly, "but for me the results weren't so, ahh, *spectacular* . . ."

"You're too modest. Your acquisition of the crown, by the way, that's the fourth of those crucial turning points of the history of the Empire of which I spoke. And the most important, if I do say so Myself."

Caine continued to squint at Ma'elKoth, still trying to glimpse the whiny, neurotic little necromancer he'd known, somewhere within this mountain of granite assurance.

"What are you? I mean what are you, really?"

Ma'elKoth spread his hands. "What you see before you. I have no secrets, Caine. Can you say the same?"

There was no safe answer for this; Caine only continued to stare. After a moment Ma'elKoth sighed and pressed himself up onto his feet.

"You're done eating?"

The plate before him had barely been touched. Caine shrugged. "I guess I don't have much appetite."

"Fine. Follow me."

Ma'elKoth made for the door. Caine quickly mopped the corners of his mouth, and then surreptitiously swiped the napkin over the cold sweat that had moistened his forehead. *At least I managed to change the subject.*

He wadded the napkin and tossed it onto his plate. He rose and followed in the Emperor's wake.

4

THE GREAT HALL of the Colhari Palace was vast, a titanic echoing space floored with marble and walled with travertine. Caine remembered walking that floor as he'd paced up to the Oaken Throne almost a decade ago.

Tel-Alcontaur, the elder brother of Toa-Phelathon, had offered Caine a barony for his heroism against the Khulan Horde at Ceraeno. The Studio had had no interest in their fastest-rising young star settling down to run a backwater holding on Overworld, and furthermore it was traditional for Monastic citizens to refuse titles and decorations offered by temporal monarchs, and so Caine had come to respectfully turn down the old King's offer, a ceremonial formal refusal.

He remembered how empty the Hall had felt, despite that it had been packed nearly shoulder-to-shoulder with nobles and dignitaries and officers and prominent citizens of all descriptions. The towering opalescent arches of the ceiling shot back hollow echoes of every sound and made the place feel empty no matter how crowded it might be.

The Oaken Throne, where Ma'elKoth now sat, still stood on its broad rectangular dais, twenty-seven tall steps above the vast floor of the Hall; narrow tapestries with the dust- and lampblack-smokiness of age still hung between the soaring buttresses, but this was the extent of the Hall's resemblance to Caine's memories.

Ma'elKoth had made some changes around here.

The dusty light from the south windows vanished into the magmatic glow of twelve bronze braziers, each wide enough for a tall man to recline within. Coals of the same sort as the ones beneath the cauldron in the Lesser Ballroom burned there, light and heat without smoke. They did not seem to consume themselves, but their light was not so steady as that cast by lamps might be; rather it shifted and pulsed until the shadows it cast seemed alive, and purposeful.

In the center of the floor a gigantic platform had been built, a square nine feet high and hundreds of feet on the side; it was draped with enough maroon-and-gold bunting to clothe the entire palace staff.

Over it all towered a statue of Ma'elKoth, nude, cast in bronze.

The shining bronze nude stood with arms akimbo and feet spread in a stance of authority and power, its crotch a meter or so above the level of the platform's floor. Not even the faintest tint of verdigris dulled the shine of its mighty musculature, and the expression on its face was one of perfect benevolence and warmth. From his angle, Caine could see that the statue was double-sided, so that there was another face staring back over the platform.

Caine nodded to himself; he took the statue's double face as a warning omen.

Between the legs of the statue was a short, angled slide, also of bronze, that led down from the platform to a shallow basin at the foot of the steps to the throne. Caine could just barely make out the shadow of a Herculean penis on the opposite front of the statue; on this side there was only a swollen fold at the crotch that seemed to be a stylized representation of a vagina.

He had a feeling that things were going to get weird.

He sat in a tiny curtained alcove just behind the throne. There were a pair of chairs in this alcove; Caine sat in one, his eye pressed to a tiny judas gate in the wall at Ma'elKoth's back. Ma'elKoth had installed him here, explaining that he had no desire to forgo the pleasure of Caine's company simply because the hour had come for Ma'elKoth to give audience.

So Caine sat and watched, while delegation after delegation from around the Empire was ushered into the Great Hall. One spokesman from each group would come forward and mount the steps to the throne to present their supplication. Ma'elKoth would listen and nod, and when they were finished he'd direct the delegation to the platform. The delegations would go beneath the platform, and there remove their clothes.

A line of naked men and women, from humble Squires to Dukes of the Empire, climbed the stairs to the platform.

They joined the growing crowd there, a crowd of naked shivering men and women of all ages, who waited and watched—understandably, a little nervously—while Ma'elKoth dealt with each of their successors.

Through this all, Ma'elKoth kept up a running sotto voce commentary for Caine's benefit, speaking of this Baron or that Knight, and the troubles in their lands, their past political connections, their current ambitions, and what use Ma'elKoth might find for them in his Great Work. Sometimes the conversation ranged widely, but it always seemed to come back around to Ma'elKoth, to his accomplishments and his plans.

Caine suspected that Ma'elKoth held him here, told him all this, largely because Caine had known the man he'd once been, and thus could appreciate how far he'd come and how much he'd done; the underlying desire for approval this implied might have been his only human weakness.

Caine slowly—and uncomfortably—decided that he really, kind of, *liked* Ma'elKoth. There was something immensely attractive in his effortless and unlimited confidence; his arrogance was so fully supported by power that it became almost a virtue. Whenever Caine let himself forget why he was here, and what he would have to do, his trepidation dwindled and he found himself drawn to the man; not, perhaps, in the sense of human attraction, of friendship, but rather more in the sense that some men are drawn to the sea, and others to mountains.

How could he not like someone who took such obvious joy in simply being alive, in being who he was?

"I destroyed the crown, of course," Ma'elKoth was saying. "It was only a key to unlock the gate that restrained the power I now wield, and I saw no sense in allowing anyone else access to this power. And I could use this power—" He passed a hand over his robes as though to say, *Voila!* "—to remake Myself in any image I chose. First, I made Myself beautiful—recalling how Hannto looked, you might understand why. Then I gave Myself brilliance, an intellect that borders on the omniscient. Next, I gave Myself another form of power: nearly unlimited wealth. Latterly, I have become the Ankhanan Emperor: political power, real authority. But I'm not finished yet."

"You're not?" Caine asked. "What do you do for an encore, become God?"

"Precisely."

And the very next delegation had come from the free farmers of Kaarn; they'd traveled a thousand miles to ask the Emperor to break the drought that was searing their fields. Ma'elKoth gave his word in agreement and sent the men to the platform.

As they walked with stiff dignity under the bunting, Caine whispered, "That's quite a promise."

Ma'elKoth answered with his infectious Olympian chuckle. "And I'll keep it. I'd be a piss-poor god if I cannot even make rain."

"That's a joke, right?"

"Mmm. Perhaps."

He spent a moment settling a land dispute between two Kirischan Barons. He did it well, so far as Caine could see; both Barons appeared satisfied as they ducked under the bunting below the platform. Then Ma'elKoth returned to the subject.

"Ironically, it was the *Aktiri* who inspired Me in this."

Caine was glad to be behind the wall and out of sight; he swallowed and steadied his voice before he said lightly, "The *Aktiri*? Aren't you a little old to believe in *Aktiri*?"

"Mmm, Caine, if you had seen what I've seen . . ."

"I thought," he said carefully, "well, to tell you the truth, I thought this whole *Aktir* hunt was just a dodge to wipe out your political opposition."

"And so it was. I am a tyrant, after all: I hold the throne without any legitimate claim of succession. I am, in fact, a commoner."

He settled back into the Oaken Throne and looked darkly out upon his subjects. "Despite My ability, and My popularity with the common folk of the Empire, the nobility has been arrayed against Me since the day I took power. Denouncing this Count or that Baronet as an *Aktir* not only destroys the credibility of his opposition, but it gives Me a perfectly legitimate excuse to have him killed.

And yes, I thought that the *Aktiri* were no more than stories, convenient phantoms to shade the features of My enemies.

"Until they tried to murder me.

"Eight men, with weapons such as no one has ever seen, that spit pellets like slingstones in a stream like rainwater from a gargoyle's mouth; they attacked Me within the very halls of My palace. Twenty-six of My household died in that attack, only seven of them Household Knights, only three others of Armiger rank; the rest were *unarmed*: servants, men and women, and three pages who were no more than children."

Caine winced behind his concealing wall. *Eight men with assault rifles . . . Kollberg, you're a real hero.*

"I took six of them alive. Three died in the Theater of Truth, under the care of Master Arkadeil; it was there that I learned much of the *Aktiri*. They are as human as you are, Caine, as human as I once was. Some geas of their masters stops their breath if they attempt to tell of their world, but I learned much from them nonetheless, and more from the other three that I killed with My own hands."

Learned much? Caine thought. He knew the limits of Studio conditioning very well, the hand-to-his-throat choking sensation of trying to so much as speak English here on Overworld. The Studio claimed that it was impossible for an Actor to reveal himself or others as Actors, no matter what the duress—they would die if somehow they were forced beyond their capacity to keep silent.

"It was that spell we spoke of, the one I nearly used on you, Caine," Ma'elKoth went on as though aware of Caine's thoughts. "I developed and refined it in experiments on a number of enemies of the Empire. When in the mindview trance, holding this spell, I can trap the fading essence of a man's memories—his soul, if you care to call it that—if his body no longer has the life to hold it within. In this way I learned much of their world."

A freezing hand stroked down Caine's spine. *I'm one of the most famous men on that world.*

"There, humanity is ascendant. They own the world and have only fading legends of the subhumans. They all speak a single language, and have magick that would beggar your imagination, Caine, if I were to try to tell you of it. You would think Me mad."

He paused, his eyes distant as they ranged over the wonders of this alien world. "And I sought, among their memories, the reason for humanity's success, there, why they have become so much while we have remained so little, and I believe that I have found it."

Caine coughed into his hand to clear his throat. "Oh?"

"It's our *gods*, Caine. The gods who rule us, they hold us back. Even though they are restrained from direct intervention in human affairs by the Covenant of Pirichanthe, they continue to squabble and fight through their priests and followers; they spark no end of conflict, wasting forces that should be used to defend the race. The *Aktiri*, though—more than four thousand years ago, a small band of desert raiders on their world originated a stunning idea. They decided that their god was the only *real* god; all others were either figments of the imagination or demons that had duped their followers. After two thousand years, the followers of this One God became evangelical, but not in our sense; they did not merely persuade folk that following their god would bring them greater happiness or better luck. *They would not allow any other gods to be worshiped.* They would often murder the priests, and their followers, and destroy the temples of competing gods. Over time, these tactics brought success. The extraordinary thing is, *none* of these Aktiri were certain that this god *had ever existed*—! Do you see? If so much can be done with a god who may be only an *intellectual concept*, how much more powerful would be the concept of a single god who is *present*, who is *potent*, who can unite every human soul to stand against the threats we all face? I am that god, Caine. I have become that god, so that I can save the human race from extinction."

I don't know if you're completely fucking bugnuts, or I am, Caine thought, *because I almost kind of believe you.* He said, "Wow."

"Wow, indeed."

"Excuse an impertinent question?"

"I already have. Several times."

Caine took that for a yes. "Did you become a god because you wanted to save the race, or do you want to save the race because it gives you an excuse to become a god?"

Ma'elKoth's laugh boomed out through the Great Hall, bringing startled flinches from the crowd and most of the guards.

"This, Caine, is part of why I so value your company. I have pondered that question Myself, from time to time. I have decided that the answer is irrelevant."

The next petitioners came up the steps with clear reluctance, and no wonder: as far as they could see, Ma'elKoth had been muttering silently for some time, and just now had laughed out loud at a joke he'd told himself.

This wouldn't improve his reputation for sanity.

He dealt with their request swiftly and neatly, and as they retreated down the steps he went on.

"And perhaps the greatest threat that humanity faces today is these selfsame *Aktiri*."

"I, ah . . ." Caine said. "That's, mm, don't you think that's a bit of an exaggeration?"

Ma'elKoth turned his massive leonine head to meet Caine's gaze through the judas gate, and his eyes burned with righteous fury, with hatred so passionate that Caine felt it in his guts.

"You can have no concept of the evil of these creatures," he said. "They are deadly enemies of mankind, and of Myself in particular. Tell me—try to guess why they come here, why they kill My people and try to murder Me, why they rape our women and slaughter our children. Try."

Caine discovered that he had no voice. His stomach knotted.

"It's *entertainment*, Caine. They're worse than demons—even the Outside Powers that prey upon men do so to feed, to sustain themselves upon our terror and despair; the *Aktiri* do so to *divert their idle hours*. Just for *fun*."

The loathing in Ma'elKoth's voice hit Caine like a slap. "If that is not evil, I don't know what is."

Caine coughed wetly and found his voice. "Well, it seems, I mean, you make it sound like, they're kind of . . . like gladiators, really."

"Gladiators do not slaughter children. Gladiators do not murder Kings. And even gladiators I find disgusting. I have banned such pursuits from the Empire."

There was a disturbance in the Great Hall below, a murmuring among the naked throng on the platform and the few remaining delegations on the floor. A door had been thrown open, and striding toward the throne, boot heels clacking loudly on the marble floor, came Berne.

A large dove-grey plaster spread its wings across his nose, and both his eyes were shadowed with purple bruise; this gave Caine a passing warmth inside.

"Speaking of evil," he said quickly, grateful for a chance to change the subject, "here comes your newest Count."

Berne shouldered aside the next delegation and took the steps two at a time. He dropped to one knee before the throne and spoke with low urgency. "Ma'elKoth, I'm sorry, I know I should have been here an hour ago, but—"

Ma'elKoth gave him an indulgent smile. "You are not too late for the Ritual, my lad. What news?"

"I've found the *Aktiri*," Berne said breathlessly. Caine studied him through the judas gate as he told Ma'elKoth about it. His source had identified the hiding place of the fugitives—an abandoned warehouse in the Industrial Park—and the Cats now had the place surrounded. They were waiting and watching, so far, not wanting to move before they were sure they would snare Simon Jester in their net.

But Shanna's in the Donjon already, Caine thought. *At least, I hope she is—if she walks into that trap, I don't think I'll be out of here in time to save her.*

And, belatedly: *Who the hell is this "source?"*

Watching Berne he found that, for now at least, he felt no burning need to rush out onto the dais and beat him to death. Maybe being off-line from the Studio, not feeling the pressure to entertain, made him less reckless; maybe it was a sudden uncertainty, an unfamiliar maybe-I-really-can't-beat-him dread that dampened the kindling of his blood-lust.

The hate, though—that still burned hot as ever.

As Berne finished his tale, the indulgence faded from Ma'elKoth's smile, and his voice became paternally correcting. "You have broken a promise, Berne."

"Heh?" He seemed startled, and puzzled, but then his expression cleared and he touched the plaster across his broken nose with an apologetic hand. He dropped his eyes and clasped his hands before his crotch like a repentant schoolboy. "I know. I know I promised, Ma'elKoth, but . . ."

"But what?"

"When he came *at* me like that . . . I lost my temper, Ma'elKoth, that's all. But I didn't really hurt him."

That's what you think. Caine's whole shoulder still ached where Berne's preternaturally powerful hand had gripped it, down to the bruised bone.

"You will treat Caine with respect and deference while he is in My service. You would regret making Me remind you again."

"I'm sorry, Ma'elKoth. I really am."

"You will also apologize."

"Ma'elKoth—"

The Emperor's chin lifted a centimeter, and Berne's protest died in the womb.

He lowered his eyes. "I, ah, I heard you caught him . . ."

"Indeed. In fact, he's watching you now." Ma'elKoth inclined his head fractionally to his left, toward the judas gate; Berne's eyes followed the gesture and locked onto Caine's. His lips pulled back from his teeth.

"He's . . ." Blood rose up Berne's neck. "Fuck me like a goat. You put him in *my chair*?" He strangled this to a throaty whisper.

Caine said with soft mockery, "Hey there, raccoon boy."

The bruises around Berne's eyes blackened against the scarlet that surged into his face, and veins bulged at the sides of his neck.

Ma'elKoth said, "Caine, that was childish, and beneath you. Berne, you will apologize."

"But—"

"Now."

Berne could barely push the words out through the clench of his teeth. "I apologize. Caine."

Caine grinned at him, even though Berne couldn't see his face. "I accept."

"Caine, you are under an identical restriction. Respect and deference, while you both are in My service."

"Sure, why not?" Caine said. "I won't be in your service forever."

"That, dear boy, is an open question. Berne, take your place at the slide. I shall begin the Ritual in very few minutes."

"Ma'elKoth—"

"Go."

Berne turned swiftly and stalked down the stairs. Caine watched him go, then said, "I don't understand how you can use that sick fuck. He's barely human."

"Some would say the same about you, Caine." Ma'elKoth waved a hand dismissively. "I have made him the, so-to-speak, High Priest of the Church of Ma'elKoth, largely because he is efficient. He will do whatever I ask of him—he would kill his own mother for Me."

"Yeah? You think he had a mother?"

Ma'elKoth chuckled. "Come now, Caine. I confess it: he was not My first choice. You were."

"Hah?"

"Oh, yes. I was hoping I could find you in person; the Drawing that I have lately done upon you consumes entirely too much of My all-too-limited time and attention. Berne has proven an acceptable substitute. Ever since the business with the crown I have been most impressed with your tenacity and resourcefulness—not to mention your ruthlessness. I hope, even now, that you, Caine, will become My most trusted companion. You can hardly refuse ennoblement now, after all; I daresay the Monasteries can have little claim on your loyalties, not after last night."

This would be a very bad idea.

"So, you want to give me Berne's job, huh?" he said, trying to change the subject and still sound like he was considering it. "In a way, you already have. He's hunting Simon Jester, right?"

"Oh, you won't be taking over for him, Caine. I want you to operate independently. I have found that two agents, working separately— even in competition—toward the same end, achieve that end much faster and more reliably."

"Yeah, kind of like . . ." Caine's voice trailed away. —*like me and Berne in* Race for the Crown of Dal'kannith, he finished silently.

He said, "You've always worked this way, haven't you?"

"That did not sound like a question."

Caine swallowed anger. "It wasn't. You did that to me, before. The crown," he said evenly. "He was working for you, wasn't he, working for you the whole time . . . You hired Berne at the same time you hired me."

"Mm, not so. I hired him after your initial attempt had failed."

"You know what he *did*? You know what that pig-fucking shit-sack bastard *did* to me?"

"I know what you did to each other."

"But you got the crown, and that's all you cared about."

"Precisely. I know you find this upsetting, Caine, but I know also that had you been in My position, you'd have done exactly the same. Which, in the end, is more important, the power itself, or the method used to acquire it?"

Ma'elKoth smiled indulgently. "That's a rhetorical question, dear boy. Now, be silent. I have only three more delegations, and then I shall begin the Ritual."

"What's this ritual?"

"You'll see. They bring Me greater gifts than mere tribute or taxes, and the Ritual is how I accept them. Hush now."

He dealt with the last three delegations neatly, justly, and with dispatch, and when they had left their clothes beneath the platform and joined the nervous crowd atop it, Ma'elKoth gestured, a lazy wave toward a captain of the Household Knights. The captain saluted, then turned and issued crisp orders to his squad. Some of them mounted the platform to chivvy the naked throng into a rough square, while the others opened a smaller door and led in more naked men and women.

Caine guessed that whatever this ritual was, there was a specific minimum number of people needed for it: these newcomers looked like they could very well be unwilling volunteers, just terrified townsfolk press-ganged in here to fill out the numbers. The echoes grew in the hall as they all tried at once to ask each other, ask the Knights, and ask the waiting delegations above, *What the fuck is going on?*

Ma'elKoth stood, and the babble took on a frightened edge. He raised his arms.

Silence dropped like a bomb.

An electric tension built in the hall, a yellowish breath-catching shimmer in the air like the light before a summer storm.

Into the silence, into the tension, Ma'elKoth began to speak.

His voice rolled out like thunder to match the lightning that shone from his eyes, long sonorous phrases metrical and unpredictable together, a slowly developing and growing rhythm like the plainsong of the elves: a long verse to love, to brotherhood, to hearth and family, the meter seeming to time itself to the beat of Caine's heart, its sweeping rhythmic power washing away the individual words. Caine couldn't follow the words, not exactly—they skittered away across the surface of his mind—but they hooked images out of the depths: his mother's lap warm beneath him, the sweet huskiness in her voice as she read to him from a book spread wide before his uncomprehending eyes, the dry strength of his father's hand on his arm as he frantically tried to balance on his first bicycle. He found unexpected tears stinging his eyes for what he'd left behind, and for the incredible promise of what he might find ahead.

Ma'elKoth's upraised arms came to sway, gently at first, oak boughs in a freshening breeze, then they stroked the air like the

wings of an eagle swimming majestically upward into the limitless
sky. He turned first one way, then another, then his stance shifted
and Caine's breath left him.

The Emperor began, incredibly, to dance.

To only the spare, resonant music of his own voice, Ma'elKoth
danced: a slow and powerful eurythmy of impossible grace, moving
with the invincible elegance of a kabuki demon.

Caine knew enough of magick to have a fair notion of what was
going on; with effort he tore his eyes away from Ma'elKoth. He
was able to do so, he guessed, only because the ritual was directed
not at him, but at the crowd on the platform. The guards below, he
noted, kept their faces carefully averted; the crowd on the platform
swayed in openmouthed awe, perfectly in time with the irresistible
surge of Ma'elKoth's dance. They began to moan softly, unconsciously, low and potent chords that beat in counterpoint to his
rolling voice.

Ma'elKoth's gestures became broader, his steps more sweeping,
his voice charged with cresting energy until it hummed like a dy-
namo, everything building toward a shattering climax—and then
he suddenly, shockingly, stopped.

Into the stunning silence a beat continued, a nearly subaural
iambic rumble; Caine closed his eyes and filtered out the surge of
blood in his ears. He listened: *a'fum, a'fum, a'fum* . . .

Breath.

It was the breathing of the hundreds of people on the platform,
sighing in perfect synchronization.

When Caine opened his eyes again, Ma'elKoth was looking at
him over one massive shoulder. The Emperor's lip quirked toward
a wry half smile, and one eyelid drooped in a sly, sidelong wink.

Some undetermined time later, Caine remembered to start
breathing again.

Ma'elKoth turned back toward the mass of naked people, who
waited openmouthed in spellbound anticipation.

"These are the words you shall say to bind your souls forever
to Mine:

By this, my heart's blood, I am baptized a Child of
  Ma'elKoth.
I serve the dream of One Humanity with all my heart.
I pledge the service of my body and my eternal spirit to the

Justice of Ma'elKoth, the True and Living God, the Father
  Almighty.
By this passage to a new life, I am Reborn.
I am Reborn without stain or allegiance save to the Holy
  Church.
I proclaim now and forever that there is no God but
  Ma'elKoth, and I am his living Child."

The guards on the platform passed out tiny golden cups to the
throng, who accepted them mechanically. The straight handles of
the golden cups had been sharpened into blades, and with these the
soon-to-be Children of Ma'elKoth each opened a vein in his or her
left wrist and caught the sluggish, brightening blood as it flowed
down their wrists.

And shortly the guards pulled a man from the mass, and there
was no blood on his wrist. Ma'elKoth nodded, as though to himself, and beckoned for them to bring him forward.

"You have not offered blood," he said. "Will you not swear?"

The man had the shaved head of a priest and the bearing of a
warrior. He stood naked and unafraid, not deigning even to struggle
against the grip of the guards.

"My Lord Emperor," he replied, "I serve Rudukirisch Storm-
god, as I have since my naming day. No power can induce me to
deny Him, and His glance shall strike lightning death against any
who would do me harm."

"Yes, yes, yes," Ma'elKoth said testily. He glanced over his
shoulder toward Caine and muttered, "This happens from time to
time, in the random sweeps. It's convenient, in a way."

He turned back toward the platform and spoke with his usual
resonance. "I understand your reluctance, but I do not permit it.
You shall be killed."

The priest shouted some words in a Kirischan dialect that Caine
didn't speak, and a sudden clap of thunder sounded outside, while
within there came a blinding flash of light; when Caine's vision
cleared, the Kirischan priest gleamed with fantastically baroque
armor, and he held in both hands a warhammer with a haft nearly
as long as he was tall.

The Household Knights who'd held his arms stretched their
lengths upon the platform, and smoke rose from their armor.

The priest glowed with power—a crackling aura of blue-white

lightning that stretched upward and outward into a flailing serpentine lash of electricity, casting reddish shadows across the faces of the spellbound throng.

"Now, learn what it means to anger the God of Thunder!"

"Yes, yes," said Ma'elKoth, sounding eager. "Get on with it, then."

The priest extended his hammer toward the throne, and the lightning lashed out. Ma'elKoth made no move or gesture of defense, raised no spell of warding. The lightning scorched a smoking hole in the breast of Ma'elKoth's robe; the robe itself caught fire with more than natural intensity. Even through his little spyhole, Caine could feel the heat baking his eyes as the robe flared up around the Emperor.

Then it had burned away, and amidst its ashes stood Ma'elKoth, bare chested and barefoot, only a pair of leather kneebreeches protecting his modesty.

He had not so much as blinked.

Cords rippled in his forearm as he lifted his open hand toward the ceiling, then closed it as though grabbing power from above. He stroked his fist toward the priest below as though cracking an invisible whip.

The priest lifted his warhammer to ward the blow, and his lightning shield flared bright with his god's defense. All his priestly power, his devotion to his god, his courage and his god's love for him made no difference whatsoever: when whatever power Ma'elKoth had summoned struck him, the warhammer that he held, the very symbol of his faith, exploded in his hand like a short-fused grenade.

Blood fountained from the shattered stump of his wrist, and the shards from the hammer ripped through his flesh like shrapnel. Household Knights closed in around him, and they pulled him out of sight on the other side of the statue.

"Your courage earns you this honor," Ma'elKoth boomed. "You shall smooth the way for the faithful."

Blood now began to drip from the statue's stylized vagina, and Caine caught a glimpse of the priest's legs as the Knights apparently upended him as though to force him headfirst into the statue's belly; there must have been some kind of a channel cut through the torso of the statue, and the blood must have been the priest's. The legs moved out of sight, and Caine heard a muffled grunt. Then the priest's head and shoulders emerged downward from the statue's vagina and he stopped there, held suspended while his blood flowed down his face and dripped onto the bronze slide beneath.

A tall, broad-shouldered man wearing the dark brown dress of an Ankhanan midwife stepped out from beneath the platform; in his hand was a short straight sword, thick bladed and single edged, and on his face was a smile of sexual anticipation.

It was, inevitably, Berne.

The priest caught sight of him and shouted, "I confess the power of Rudukirisch! I confess—"

His cry was cut off by the silver arc of Berne's cleaver. The blade sheared into his neck, crunching through vertebrae and slicing out the other side. Berne cleared the blade of blood with a single, professional flick of the wrist as the priest's head, mouth still wide open, tumbled onto the slide in a shower of blood and rolled down into the basin. His heart, far above, pumped furiously, fountaining crimson jets from neatly severed arteries, and it seemed a very long time until the fountain tapered to a trickle. Whatever held the body released it, and it slid smoothly down the blood-slick slide and lay limp in the basin.

And through this all, the spellbound crowd on the platform watched silently.

Now the Knights herded them into a queue at the statue's side, and they each willingly followed in the priest's path, pausing briefly to pour the small cups of their own blood over their heads, intoning their oath and then sliding headfirst into the statue's belly and out through its vagina, down the slide and into the basin, from whence other guards would lead them away to wash away the blood and bandage their wrists.

Occasionally, for no reason and with no signal that Caine could see, one of them would be caught, head down; Berne's blade would flicker, and another head and body would enter the basin separately. The twitching bodies were left there, a grisly cushion for the living ones that followed.

Ma'elKoth stepped away from the pile of ashes that had been his robes and seated himself again in the Oaken Throne. He sighed and said meditatively, "Well, then, what do you think?"

Caine was mesmerized by the endless flow of men and women down the slide. "It's, ah, pretty gruesome, isn't it?"

"As is any birth," Ma'elKoth said.

"How do you decide who lives and who dies, down there? Who decides who gets caught and chopped?"

"Each decides for himself," Ma'elKoth said, and now a smile grew slowly across his face.

"What do you mean?"

"I won't tell you."

"Huh?"

"I spoke clearly enough. It is not for you to know, not yet. If you survive it, you'll understand."

"If I survive it? You're gonna make me go through that?"

Ma'elKoth answered with only a smile.

"How will you approach your quest for Simon Jester?" he asked thoughtfully. "I am certain you've already given this question some thought."

"Some," Caine said. He'd spent all of the night before thinking about it and had come up with a plan both simple and elegant, perfectly in character and, he hoped, daring enough to be irresistible. "I want to break your prisoners out of the Donjon."

"Oh?"

"One of the accomplices of Simon Jester that Berne captured chances to be an acquaintance of mine, a minor adept named Lamorak. You get me into the Donjon, and I break him and the other one out. That should be enough to get me close to Simon Jester."

"How did you know of this? That this Lamorak is in our custody?"

"You're not the only one with sources," Caine said, hoping that Ma'elKoth wouldn't press.

Ma'elKoth's mind was working along other lines. "I see problems with this. Isn't it somewhat extreme? Won't Lamorak be suspicious, to be suddenly rescued? Are the two of you so close that he will believe you'd risk your life for him?"

"Oh, he'll believe it, all right." *Not that it matters a damn if he doesn't.* "We're close enough. And I'll tell him straight off that I'm doing this to get next to Simon Jester."

"And for what?"

Caine glanced down toward the ongoing ritual, where Berne had once again just neatly decapitated someone.

"To get a shot at Berne."

"Mmm," Ma'elKoth said, thinking about it. "Mm, I think I see."

"Lamorak is Berne's prisoner, right? The whole operation against

Simon Jester is Berne's baby. Breaking him out will be a major embarrassment, and will put me in with Simon Jester, the perfect place for me to lay a trap to draw Berne out where I can kill him."

Ma'elKoth chuckled. "And it will make a substantial addition to your legendary career. No one has ever escaped from the Imperial Donjon; if there is a man alive that folk will believe could do it, it would be you."

"Nobody will dream I'm working for you; shit, nearly everybody in town knows there's a warrant out for me. Just give out that I got away from Toa-Sytell and the Eyes."

"*Will* you be working for Me?"

A cold hand reached into Caine's chest. "Of course I will. What's that supposed to mean? After all this, you don't trust me?"

"I remember . . ." Ma'elKoth mused, "I remember a Caine who'd rather kill a man than lie to him . . ."

"Killing's simpler," Caine said, with a thin laugh that tried to sound hearty. "You do it, it's done, it's over. A lie is like a pet—you have to take care of it, or it'll turn on you and bite you on the ass."

"Are you still that Caine?"

He made his voice as flat as his thumping heart would let him. "I'm as honest as circumstances allow."

"Hmpf. A truthful answer, that. Very well. Remove your clothes."

Something seemed to catch in Caine's throat; all he could say was "Hah?"

"You cannot serve Me in body unless you serve Me in heart, Caine."

The Emperor waved a lazy hand down at the platform. Below, pages in livery ladled blood out of the basin into bronze bowls—the same bowls Caine had seen them carry in the Lesser Ballroom, to mix into the clay of the Great Work, and his stomach twisted.

What did you think, you fucking ninny, he snarled at himself. *Where did you think that blood came from?*

He said, "You seriously expect me to go down there and put my neck within reach of Berne's sword?"

"I do. If you do not trust Me, Caine, how am I to trust you? Pledge yourself to Me, place your faith in My justice, and serve Me now. Or deny Me this honor, and never serve Me again."

It wasn't even really a choice. Echoing inside his skull he heard Shanna's words: *He doesn't care what happens to me.* And this might be his best, his only chance to save her life.

There was no reason to hesitate.

"Yeah, sure," Caine said. "Let's do it."

5

THE RIVER BARGE was every bit as disreputable as its captain, a grizzled old rummy with drooping red eyes and a permanently dripping nose, but when Pallas inspected the barge's bilge, a dark dank space full of an eye-watering stink of urine and decay—like a dead turtle sun-baking in its shell for four days while being pissed on by a succession of tomcats—she found something that made her smile: a little horned face with the familiar sly grin, scratched into the sloppily pitched bulkhead recently enough that the wood exposed beneath still showed blond.

She jerked a thumb at it. "Simon Jester," she said. "You know, you can buy some trouble, flying that particular flag."

The captain wiped his nose on the back of his grimy hand. "Can't say as anyone'd find me responsible. I crew this thing temporary, y'know? Can't say who mighta scratched the little face."

"I'd bet there's any number of things you can't say," Pallas ventured.

The captain shrugged. "I mind my manners, if that's what y'mean."

"I'd bet you can't say why that scratching's a couple of weeks old, and it's still there."

"You'd lose that one, girlie," the captain growled. "Gave passage to Baron Thilliow, him of Oklian, and his whole family, fifteen year ago and more, when days was better for us both. And he was a good man, and no bloody *Aktir*, no matter what th'Emperor says. Nothing against th'Emperor; I figure there's some as is tellin' him some lies, and puttin' good folk to the axe, and I'd just as soon Simon Jester gets 'em away as see 'em dead. And that—" He reached up and touched the crude little carving. "—that's just to remind me, that's all. Don't really mean nothing."

Pallas extended her hand, and a shining gold royal appeared between her thumb and first finger. She flicked her hand and another appeared, then another flick and another coin. They gleamed like the sun in the steady lamplight.

She'd gotten his attention with the first one; by the time the third appeared, it was all he could do to keep the drool behind his lips.

"You can use these for provisions. Forty people for a week. Don't buy it all in one place. Use the rest to crew up. Whatever money's left over, keep for your trouble."

"I, ah . . ."

Flick. Now there were four. "This charming little family has relatives downstream. Forty of them. One for each of my friends who'll be riding here in your bilge, provided they make it safe and healthy down to Tinnara, plus a few extra. A gratuity for exceptional service."

He mopped at his face furiously, until the grease and dirt on the back of his hand was streaked with snot. "That's, ah, that's tricky work. Maybe a bit more up front would, ah, steady my nerves . . . ?"

"You'll have to trust me," she said with a quick shake of her head. "We'll have to trust each other. If I don't come through with the gold, there'll be forty people wandering around Tinnara that'd be worth a noble or two apiece to any Eye or army officer."

"Forty *royals*, though . . ." he murmured. "Could really fix up m'old lady, here, get a real crew again . . ."

"We'll call it a deal, then." She handed him the four royals.

"We will, that," he said, and followed her up the ladder into the warm afternoon sunlight. "Gimme two days to crew and provision, and get your friends here by midafternoon on the second—we'll wanta be a few miles downstream by sundown." He accompanied her to dockside and held out his arm to help her up the ramp.

"Do you," he murmured softly, hesitantly, with a furtive look around at the busy docks to make sure no one was within earshot, "d'you really work for the Jester? Is he really, y'know, really *real*?"

"Yes," she said. "Yes, he's really real."

"Is he really wantin' to bring down Ma'elKoth, like they say?"

"No. No, that's not it at all," she said gravely. "He's only trying to save some lives. These people aren't *Aktiri*, Captain. They're just people, innocent people, who have to get out of the Empire, or they'll be killed. Killed because Ma'elKoth doesn't like them."

"Well, then . . ." He dropped his arm and looked at the deck beneath his feet, then spat into the sluggish brown waters of the Great Chambaygen. "Well, then, power to the Jester. And power to you, lady."

Pallas forced a little smile and touched him on the shoulder. "We both thank you. Look for me in two days."

She walked away along the dockside, past the steelworks and the long rows of warehouses that accepted river cargo from all across the Empire.

This should be easy; she'd seen no flicker of betrayal on the captain's Shell, and even though she'd never tried to move this many *tokali* at one time before, she was confident.

This spell of Konnos' had become so incredibly useful—she could pack all thirty-six of the *tokali* into the bilge and Cloak the whole lot of them. Any suspicious Imperial, even an adept, would see only dirty water and black-pitched wood, and the Eternal Forgetting would prevent this hypothetical suspicious adept from connecting any pull he might feel with the possibility of a Cloak. To make it work, she'd have to ride with them all the way to the coast to get them past the toll points on the river, but that was all right.

She could use the rest.

The important thing, right now, was that she could *do* it, she'd get them safely out of the Empire by herself, and those greedy bastards back at Studio Scheduling could just screw themselves.

And when this was over and she was back on Earth, she and Hari were going to have a little talk about staying the hell out of her life. She should never have let him talk her out of filing divorce; this separation was foolish. It wasn't doing either one of them any good, just drawing out the pain, that's all, their own little improvised Death of the Thousand Cuts. She should have trusted her instincts and gone for the clean break, all at once, like ripping away a bandage.

Or amputating a limb.

And that's what this really was, she told herself, this ache that seemed to poke low into her belly when she thought of him looking for her, when she thought of how she would ditch him and head downriver: phantom-limb pain. There had once been a part of her that had tied her to Hari's life, that was now cut away; the twinges she felt from it once in a while were only psychological revenants of the amputation.

And Hari was part of why it was so easy to be ruthless with the King of Cant; Majesty was one of Caine's best friends. He made a pretty good surrogate when she couldn't hit back at Caine directly. As she'd continued to use him, though, she'd surprised herself with a growing sense of contempt; she'd caught herself thinking that this man was only a thug with a gimmick, after all, really just a street punk like Hari once was—but Hari had grown into something more, she'd grant him that much. Hari or Caine, neither would have let anyone treat him like she'd treated the King of Cant; Caine would have gone for her throat the second he caught a glimpse of the Charm crystal.

On the other hand, she wasn't blind to herself: she knew that part of her contempt for Majesty was a reflexive self-justification for using him so badly. But still . . .

Caine had a peculiar integrity, a stubborn attachment to his self-respect, however misplaced it might be. Integrity wasn't a word that came to mind when one thought of Majesty; the man was a weasel on two legs. Useful, even necessary, but a weasel nonetheless.

As twilight drifted down through the deepening blue of the sky, she made her way toward the warehouse beneath which she'd hidden the *tokali*. Her mind wasn't on the crowds that thickened around her as curfew neared and folk of all descriptions flooded across the bridges from Old Town; she was absorbed with the melancholy realization that even now, she still compared every man she met with Hari.

Shaking her head sadly at this sentimental foolishness, she walked into the expanding shadows of the Industrial Park's side streets.

She rehearsed for the millionth time all the reasons that they would never be able to work it out, all the fights and the jealousies and suspicions. They should never have married in the first place; they'd been great as lovers, their affair was passionate, tempestuous, consistently unpredictable, thrilling—but all the things that had made them great lovers made them shitty as husband and wife.

Opposites attract, but similarities bind.

They were the opposite poles of Acting, for one thing. She'd gone into Acting in the first place because on Overworld, she could have the kind of power that would be forever denied her by her Tradesman subcaste in Earth's remorselessly rigid social system: the power to help people, to make a real difference in people's lives, a *positive* difference. She could truly say that her career had helped make Overworld a better place, and she was justly proud of it.

Caine, on the other hand, was just in it for the blood.

She saved lives; he took them.

And his Adventures outsold hers three to one.

In her honest moments, she was able to admit that this was part of the problem, too. She wasn't proud of it, but she couldn't deny it, either.

She sighed and tried to haul her attention back onto the problems at hand. She'd deal with Caine later, when he could no longer be avoided. It was the fatigue, the endless hours of running and hiding and fighting, that made it nearly impossible for her to keep her mind on business; but now, as she neared the bolt-hole where she'd stashed the *tokali*, a lapse in concentration could be fatal.

The *tokali* were hidden beneath the rotting, treacherous floor of a fire-gutted warehouse; it stood in a block with a number of other warehouses in states of similar disrepair. Dry spots here and there—where slanting remnants of charred rooftops leaned against a sturdy wall to keep off the rain—had become shelter for a number of families of squatters.

She'd posted no stooges here who might betray it, had left no sign. The dry, cavelike basement here was her third fallback; she'd prepared it with the help of the Twins and Talann and Lamorak, enchanting sigils across the walls and doors to divert seeking items and other magick of that sort. Majesty himself, in disguise, had helped her move the supplies inside; though he despised physical labor, her Charm had ensured that he'd work without complaint and would die before he gave up its location. Pallas believed that everyone else who knew of its existence was dead.

The entrance was concealed within a former interior office; getting to it required threading through a maze of collapsed walls and treacherously rotten flooring. At the last moment she turned aside instead of entering, drifting past its charred facade as though still lost in thought.

Something was wrong here.

The trickle of day laborers heading home was steady as ever, no more nor less than usual. Glancing at their faces and clothes gave Pallas no explanation for her sudden nerves, but she trusted those nerves, her instincts; they were all she had left to save her life.

She found a solid-looking piece of wall to lean casually against and scanned the street. *What's wrong with this picture?*

There was no smoke.

The squatters ... There were two families in particular, one across the street in what once had been a grain store, and one further down in a former smithy. Now, here, at twilight, they both should have had small, protected fires burning, heating up whatever scraps they had scrounged for their dinners. The intermittent, almost daily rains that came with late autumn in Ankhana would have dampened all the scrap wood there was to be found—but there was no smoke.

It might be nothing. They might both have moved on to some drier and more windproof shelter.

Or: they might be tied down, even dead, while Grey Cats crouched beside them, watching her through fire-sprung chinks in their borrowed walls.

Not for nothing did they identify themselves with cats; they might have been there for hours, slowly creeping into position, watching intently for any sign of movement around the mouse hole where the *tokali* huddled. But they couldn't know that both these families cook at twilight.

She kept moving, kept drifting, until the spire of the Colhari Palace swung into view through a gap in a collapsing wall. She breathed herself into mindview, and the twisting lace of Flow filled her vision, slowly stirred by the dim Shells of the passing townsfolk. She saw no beam of channeled Flow from the Palace, but this was no assurance that she was safe; the Cats themselves wouldn't attack her on sight, having no idea who she was, but if Berne was here with them . . .

The Imperials knew that Simon Jester was a thaumaturge; this was proven by the spell that frustrated their search. In seeking to trap him, Berne and Ma'elKoth wouldn't hold that channel open; it'd be like sounding a trumpet and waving a flag to any adept in mindview.

But Berne, he had reasons to pounce on her unrelated to his hunt for Simon Jester. If he was there, coiled to spring from one of those buildings, and he saw her on the street and recognized her, his own cupidity, his lust for blood, for any way to injure her or Caine, would probably drive him to—

And there it was: from the spire of the Colhari Palace that shaft of crimson power sprang to instantaneous life.

She had only seconds to live.

Surrounded. Alone. The Subjects would help her if they knew she was in danger, but there were no Subjects here to be found.

Alone, but not helpless.

If Caine were here, he'd quote Sun Tzu: "On deadly ground: *fight*."

From a pocket at her breast, her hand pulled a lovingly carved model of itself in miniature: a tiny hand of the same glittering quartz she used for her Shields.

The lines of power shone upon it and spoke to her mind.

The shaft of channeled Flow ran straight as the beam of a laser from the palace to the crumbling warehouse across the street: there was no way Berne could hide from her.

The lines scribed upon the hand of quartz spread like a net, spun like a whirlpool, a massive vortex of Flow that made her flesh shimmer with power. No matter how much power Berne channeled from Ma'elKoth, he was himself no thaumaturge: without mindview, he had no way of knowing the depth of trouble he was in right now.

On her lips was a feral grin that Berne would have recognized, as she extended her hand and made a fist, and the invisible force of her Teke crushed the building like an eggshell.

It fell in upon itself with an avalanche roar and a spreading cloud of choking dust. If Berne wanted her, first he'd have to dig himself out.

The flat whacks of firing crossbows sounded from all around her, but Pallas was already moving, diving away deep into the screening dust. Quarrels sang by her, *spang*ed off cobblestones and thrummed quivering in wood. Shouts and screams from the city folk filled the air as they scattered, running for their lives.

Pallas rolled to her feet and flicked her hand, doing the same trick she had for the captain of the river barge; instead of coins, what appeared between her fingers were her charged buckeyes—one, two, three, four.

Blood hummed in her ears, and a savage exaltation filled her chest. Teeth gleamed through her happy snarl as she triggered a buckeye and fired it along the street with her Teke, directly into the building from which most of the crossbow fire had come. Flame roared out though shattered windows; the building front crumpled and collapsed.

That, she guessed, *should be enough to get their attention.* She turned and sprinted away at a dead run, heading toward the Warrens.

Come on come on come on, move it, you bastards, she chanted inside her head. *It'll take all of you to make sure I don't get away. Come on!*

And come they did, breaking from cover—ten, fifteen, thirty hard-eyed men in grey, running behind grimaces of fury, pursuing at a ground-eating lope as she led them away from the *tokali* and into the Kingdom of Cant. Behind her, the building she had crushed, the building she had brought down on Berne's head, began to pitch and heave and bulge in the middle like a caterpillar carcass birthing a brood of wasps.

Berne was coming.

She put her head down and ran.

DAY FOUR

"You have no principles at all."

"That's bullshit and you know it."

"No, it's true. You're a contrarian. You have to have your own way, but you define it by what people tell you not to do. The problem is that underneath all your macho crap there's this sneaking suspicion that everybody else is right. It has nothing to do with principle—you reject authority because it's fun to break rules. You're like a little kid, being naughty with a grin on his face."

"Do we have to talk about this now?"

"You're not for anything, you're just against everything."

"I'm for you."

"Stop it. I'm serious."

"So am I."

1

SERGEANT HABRAK HAD been in the Ankhanan Army for more than twenty years, so he instantly recognized the look in Berne's eyes as the Count came to the steel bars of the gate; he'd seen it too many times on the faces of officers about to order suicidal charges, on foot soldiers who'd been pushed to the point of bloody mutiny, on peasants about to run screaming against ranks of armored Knights, scythes and pitchforks upraised to avenge rape and slaughter. The sergeant sprang to his feet, fumbling for the jingling hoop of keys at his belt.

Berne rasped, "Open this fucking gate before I cut it down."

"Only a second, m'lord, only a second." Habrak managed finally to shove the key into the lock, and he swung the gate back.

Berne stalked past him, and Habrak coughed wetly: the Count

stank, reeked like a closed stable on a hot summer's day—and what was this filth that caked the heavy strawberry serge he wore? He looked—and smelled—like he'd spent the night rolling in *manure*—!

At Habrak's cough, Berne stopped and looked back over his left shoulder, his face bisected by the long diagonal hilt of his shoulder-slung sword.

"You got a problem?" Berne asked, his voice low and lethal. "Maybe you *smell* something?"

"Oh, oh, oh, oh no, no, my lord. Not at all."

"That's peculiar, considering I'm covered with shit."

"I, ah, ah, my lord, I—"

"Never mind. Open the fucking door."

"Your, ah, your weapon, er Count . . ." Habrak said hesitantly.

"Don't even think you're going to disarm me, Habrak. Not tonight."

Habrak, like any sane man, was bone-deep leery of Count Berne's erratic temper and lightning blade, but he'd been sergeant of the guard here in the Imperial Donjon for five years, and he felt he was on firm ground. "This is, er, standard procedure, m'lord. Security."

"You think one of your starving pukes down there is going to take this sword away from me?"

Either answer to a question like this was liable to hook more trouble, so Habrak sidestepped. "The Emperor hisself leaves his weapons here with me, before he goes through that door. It's by his word that only the guards bear arms in the Donjon. If y'think he's wrong, y'oughta take it up with him."

Berne gave in with a snarl, unbuckling the sword belt and throwing it into Habrak's hands as though daring the sergeant to drop it. Habrak, gratefully, clung to the scabbard like a leech and gingerly hung it on the rack behind his desk.

"And you'll be wanting a lamp, if y're going past the Pit. Patrol snuffs the last torch at midnight."

Berne looked, if it were possible, more angry now than when he'd entered. He took a lamp in his white-knuckled hand and waited by the door. He stared downward as though he could see through the door, down through the living stone from which the Donjon had been carved, and there found the face of a man he despised.

Habrak unlocked the door and held it for him as Berne descended the long, narrow shaft of stairway, down deep into the darkness. The hot reek of fermenting shit and unwashed bodies, air that had been breathed too many times by men and women with rotting teeth and decaying lungs, boiled up out of the stairwell in Berne's wake; Habrak was as glad as ever to shut that door and move away from it, back to his desk.

The Imperial Donjon of Ankhana lies in a series of tunnels cut into the limestone of Old Town beneath the courthouse, excavated over decades by teams of convict stonebenders. The central common room, known as the Pit, had been shaped from a natural cavern three stories high; twenty feet above the floor, it is girdled by a ledge that forms a natural balcony, which is patrolled by guards bearing crossbows and iron-bound clubs.

The Pit is always crowded with men and women awaiting trial— some for months, even years—and those convicts who have already been sentenced, who are awaiting transport to a frontier garrison or the eastern mines. It is the only area that is permanently lit, its ceiling blackened by decades of smoking lanterns. Sloping tunnels carved into the living rock radiate outward from the Pit's balcony like spokes in a wheel, at intervals connected by narrow crossways. These tunnels lead to the private cells, which are inhabited by minor nobles and members of Warrengangs and any others who have the money or influence to bribe their way out of the Pit, and only those.

Solitary confinement is a luxury in the Imperial Donjon; prisoners who cause trouble are condemned to the Shaft.

The Donjon is a place of deep shadow and bad air; the bitter, bloody smells of despair and brutality thickly struggle with the reek of human shit and rotting flesh. The sole entrance or exit is the single flight of stairs down which Berne now strode, from the courthouse cellar to the Pit balcony; a prisoner in the Imperial Donjon has as much chance of escape as does a damned soul in Hell.

Suspicious, hard-eyed guards squinted at Berne as he stalked past them around the arc of the balcony; they trusted no one but each other. He spared them not even a passing glance.

The doors to the private cells carried two locks: heavy beams mounted on pivots, and smaller keyhole locks. The beams could be swung swiftly into place to bar the door against a prisoner's rush; the keyhole locks were there against the occasional prisoner who did manage to get free of his cell, to prevent him from running along the corridors freeing others faster than the guards could put them away again.

Berne had his own key to the door he wanted. He turned it and slapped the beam to vertical, yanked the door open, and went inside.

This cell was well appointed; by the standards of the Donjon, it was sumptuous: a feather bed with clean sheets and a blanket, a small writing desk, a comfortable chair, even a rack of books to pass long hours of waiting. The cell was clean, and on the desk lay a tray covered with the remnants of a pork shank, some potato, and a bit of gravy-soaked bread. The prisoner on the bed stirred reluctantly out of sleep, drawn up toward consciousness by the noise of the door and the sudden light of the lamp that Berne now set on the desk.

The prisoner rolled over and shaded his bleary eyes. "Huh? Berne?"

"You haven't been giving me the whole story, Lamorak," Berne said. He shifted his Buckler to his feet, short-stepped, and kicked Lamorak's bed to splinters.

Berne's foot exploded through the mattress, and a blizzard of swirling chicken feathers filled the cell. The kick slapped Lamorak bodily into the air, his arms flailing helplessly. Berne's hand struck with the speed of a stooping falcon and snatched Lamorak's ankle.

He held Lamorak out, head down, at arm's length and struggling. This strength, this power that Ma'elKoth granted him, he reveled in it. Being able to lift a bigger man, straight armed and one handed, and never feel the strain—it shortened his breath, and brought living heat to his crotch.

"Just imagine," he said thickly, "what a kick like that will do to your *head*."

"Berne, Berne don't . . ." Lamorak said, arms crossed in front of his face in futile defense—those muscular golden arms would splinter more easily than the bedslats had.

"Can you smell me?"

"Berne . . . Berne, calm down . . ."

With a flick of his wrist, Berne battered Lamorak against the stone wall of the cell. Lamorak left skin and blood behind, smeared across the stone, and rose-white bone peeked through where the impact had split the flesh over his elbow. Lamorak grunted, but did not cry out. For a long count of ten the only sound within the cell was the drizzle of his blood pattering onto the floor.

Berne said, "Let's try this again. Can you smell me?"

Lamorak nodded with difficulty, his face becoming puffy with blood. "What . . . what happened?" he asked hoarsely.

"What part does Pallas Ril play in this?"

"Berne, I . . ."

Berne flicked him against the stone again, this time face first. Lamorak's scalp split at the hairline, and blood slicked down into his long, golden hair.

Berne didn't have time to play at this; the rock of the Donjon impedes Flow. Though Ma'elKoth had gifted him with the splinter of griffinstone that he carried on a chain about his neck to power his strength in situations like these, down here it would not do so for very long.

"How many times will you make me ask this question?"

Lamorak said something that Berne didn't quite catch; his mind had drifted away to the humiliation of the beating his Cats had taken at the hands of Pallas Ril and her goat-fucking beggars.

After the shocking indignity of having a building knocked down on his head, digging his way out had taken him only a minute; with his superhuman strength, he had shrugged aside foot-thick beams the way an ordinary man would handle bundles of straw. Raging, he'd led the Cats charging after her, through the streets of the Industrial Park and into the Warrens.

And the beggars had thrown shit at them.

There was no one to fight, no one to kill, just clods of flying shit spattering them from all directions. Soon the Cats were entirely disorganized, chasing after this beggar or that as they disappeared into the crowded maze of backstreets without a trace.

Ma'elKoth had refused Berne's call for firebolts to scatter the crowds. *"Wanton slaughter in the streets of the capital is counterproductive. Perhaps your attention would be more valuably spent ensuring that the* Aktiri *you located do not escape while you are chasing about the Warrens."*

Cursing, Berne had sprinted back to the abandoned warehouse and broken into the cellar, ready to kill them all on the spot—but the cellar was empty. They'd gone, somehow, in the bare quarter hour their bolt-hole had been unwatched. It was as though Pallas Ril had led the Cats away to accomplish exactly this. If, that is, the *Aktiri* had ever been there in the first place. But she was involved, here, somewhere, somehow, in with Simon Jester, and now so was Caine, and Berne was not fool enough to believe in coincidence.

Perhaps Simon Jester . . . perhaps he was *Caine*!

Berne's mind boiled; Lamorak dangled forgotten from his fist. It was possible, he decided, all too possible. Never mind that he was no thaumaturge—he had Pallas Ril for that. It even made a certain hideous amount of sense; Caine was notorious for burrowing his wormy way into the confidence of his enemies—look at what he'd done to Khulan G'thar . . .

And Ma'elKoth had invited him into the palace, had fed and armed him, had seated him in *Berne's chair* . . . !

Caine had to die.

Right now. Tonight.

"It's useless," Lamorak was saying miserably.

"What?"

"Why won't you understand me? Why can't you hear what I'm *saying* to you?"

Berne's mouth twisted with revulsion as he looked down. "The way you whine, it makes me sick. They weren't *there*, you stupid goatfucker. The *Aktiri* were not in the warehouse cellar. Either you lied to me, or you truly don't know, and either way you're no fucking use anymore."

"I'm *telling* you," Lamorak said, clutching for Berne's knee. "Berne, I *swear* to you, I don't know what's going on, but I'm *telling* you Pallas Ril . . ."

Berne lost the thread of his meaning again, imagining the smooth humming slide of Kosall into Caine's body. Where would he cut Caine first? Sever a leg? Perhaps only take an ear? Maybe a low stab, into his groin—Berne felt stirrings in his own as he imagined this. Maybe he'd finish it off by jamming Kosall up Caine's ass until the point came out his mouth . . .

". . . our deal," Lamorak was saying. "Berne, we have a deal."

Berne shrugged and opened his hand. Lamorak barely got his arms around his head in time to avoid braining himself on the stone floor. Berne watched dispassionately while Lamorak slowly picked himself up.

"Tell you what," Berne said. He held out the key to Lamorak's cell. "I'll give you a chance. Jump me, take this key, and I'll let you go."

"Berne—"

Berne pivoted into a low-line roundhouse kick that brought his shin against Lamorak's golden thigh with crushing force. Lamorak's femur snapped with a wet, meaty pop and he fell to the floor, clutching his broken leg and biting his mouth to hold in a scream.

"Too late," Berne said. "Had your chance. Sorry."

He dropped to one knee and rolled Lamorak roughly onto his stomach; Lamorak groaned as Berne forced his legs apart, using his strength to spread the thigh muscle that cramped hard around his broken bone. Lamorak's breeches tore like tissue beneath his fingers.

"Don't," Lamorak pleaded, hoarse with the strain of holding in a scream. "For the love of god . . ."

"Which god?" Berne asked, digging his fingers into Lamorak's ass cheeks, but then he stopped, and he sighed. This wasn't what he needed. This wasn't even what he wanted.

He wanted Caine.

And Pallas Ril. Together. Strapped to the tables in the Theater of Truth, their eyelids pinned back by Master Arkadeil's silver needles, so that each must watch what he did to the other.

Sadly, this was not to be: he'd better kill Caine tonight. That slippery little goatfucker was just too dangerous to leave alive.

Berne left Lamorak lying there on the floor of the cell, his face white with pain and shock. He locked the door behind himself.

On his way up into the night-darkened courthouse, he stopped at the upper gate to retrieve his sword. He buckled it over his shoulder and said to the sergeant, "Habrak. Send a man to Master Arkadeil. I want Lamorak in the Theater of Truth *tonight*. If you hurry, Arkadeil can use him as the subject for his midnight instructional. Tell him to try to find out what he can about Simon Jester, but it's not too important—I don't think Lamorak really knows anything he hasn't already told. Tell Arkadeil to take his time, enjoy himself, and there's no need for Lamorak to live through it."

Habrak saluted. "As the Count orders."

"You're a good man, Sergeant."

He left, pausing only a moment in the courthouse above to dismiss the Cats who had accompanied him; he needed no entourage to protect him on these streets.

He left the courthouse and stopped in the street to inhale the night. A great breath of darkness filled his chest and teased his lips toward a curving grin.

He spread his arms, smiling up at the brilliant stars. This was his favorite time of day, this still emptiness of midnight; the sleepy hush that spread its blanket over the city, the crystal chill in the air, all the city folk behind their shutters, dreaming of the day. They slept secure in the knowledge that nothing of any importance in their lives could happen from midnight to dawn.

They were wrong, of course; especially tonight.

Berne could happen.

He hooked his thumbs behind his belt, ambled down the street, and thought about it.

He picked out windows as he went along, picturing the solid citizens that slept behind them. Those shutters there, with the patch of silvery weather stain—behind them, he decided, could be a young family, a serious-minded tinker from the smithy down the street, his lovely young wife who took in washing for a couple silver a week, and their precious daughter, now turned six. Maybe her birthday is tomorrow; maybe she lies in bed right now with her eyes open, breathless, praying to the gods for a real dress this year.

Getting in would be easy. With his enchanted strength, he could leap to that window from here; with Kosall he could slice away the hasp. A warm squirming began in his belly—he could see, as though they lay before him now, the restless stir of the tinker's wife as Berne slipped into their bedroom; he could see the slow dawning of light in the tinker's eyes, only a glimmer that would fade swiftly away as Kosall silently drank his life; he could feel the frail terror of the wife's heart beating against his chest as she tried to pull her hips away from him, as he fucked her in the pool of her husband's blood.

And the little girl, the daughter—orphaned at such a tender age, in such a brutal way. He could see the approval on the faces of the respectable townsfolk as he offered to adopt her. He was nobility, after all; no one would think to deny him. And she'd be his, all his, to raise and to train, to perfect her body and her mind, to bend her body beneath his, to enter her virginity with his power as he finally revealed to her how her parents had died . . . and her arms would snake around his back, and she'd whisper in his ear, "I know . . . I've always known . . . I've always loved you, Berne . . ."

Berne chuckled and shook his head. He would do no such thing, tonight.

The point was that if he wanted to, he could.

Tonight, he'd let them go. Another night, he might make another choice.

He felt good, now, *really* good, for the first time since, oh, since he'd killed those two gladiator brats in the Warrens. He felt free, and full of light.

It was because he'd finally made the decision: he'd decided to go ahead and kill Caine. Only now could he feel how much Ma'el-Koth's command to spare the life of that treacherous little snake had weighed upon his spirit; he recognized the weight by its absence.

Oh, Ma'elKoth would be angry, sure, at first—no one likes to be defied—but in the end, he'd forgive Berne, even thank him.

He always did.

Ma'elKoth always forgave, always accepted, always valued Berne for precisely what he was. He asked only that Berne exercise restraint, never asked that he change. This was the difference between Ma'elKoth and every other living being that Berne had ever known.

Ma'elKoth loved him.

Berne stretched like a cat, and his loosening joints shifted and popped beneath his skin. He grinned into the moonlight, measuring the towering black-shadowed wall that enclosed Old Town. In the next breath he burst into a sprint along Ten Street, the wind of his passing sizzling in his ears. Twenty paces from the garrison stables he bounded into the air, his enchanted strength sending him soaring up to the stables' roof; then without even a pause he sprang upward again, to the rooftop of the officers' barracks and from there to the top of the wall. A triple bound had taken him up ten times the height of a man.

Standing openly upon the battlement, he threw his arms wide and shouted, laughing, "Lord, my aching balls! *I love being me!*"

A pair of nervous sentries from Onetower, the massive keep that defended the downstream point of the island, came toward him hesitantly with leveled crossbows. "Don't move!" one of them called. "Identify yourself!"

In answer, Berne unslung Kosall and laid it on the battlement. "I am Count Berne," he said, "and this is my sword. Don't touch it while I'm gone."

With that he threw his arms wide once again and leaped high into the air, an arc of perfect grace as he dove toward the Great Chambaygen; he shifted his Buckler into his hands as he cut the water and slid into its depths with barely a ripple. The stones and mud at the river's bottom bothered him not at all, and he passed a happy interval playing in the water, letting the river wash away the shit that had caked his clothes and the last of the knots of anger that had tied themselves in his back.

This was the great gift of Ma'elKoth. Nothing was denied him. He did as he chose, when he chose, and there was no one with the power to say him nay. Only Ma'elKoth himself could stop him—and he never did. He looked upon Berne's excesses as a proud father looks upon the exuberant youth of his favorite son—with tolerance, and only occasional gentle correction.

Berne's real father, a dour and ascetic Monastic official in a small southern town, had raised Berne with the kind of iron hand only a fanatic can wield. His father had been posted there, in a tiny backwater, at the behest of the moderate Jhanthite faction that had, in those days, largely controlled the Council of Brothers; they'd wanted him far enough away that his extremist views wouldn't trouble their relations with the subhumans.

Berne had been raised to be his father's weapon in the war against the subs, trained from birth to be the perfect warrior—but somehow, in all those years, his father had never bothered to ask what Berne wanted to do, if he *wanted* to be the ultimate weapon.

Berne had always known what he wanted to do.

He wanted to *live*, really live, to fight and screw and eat and drink and gamble and do every single thing he could cram into one lifetime. He knew well that this was the only life he'd ever get, and he was determined not to miss anything.

At the age of seventeen, he'd finally shown his father how well his training had worked. He beat the old bastard into unconsciousness, took the old man's sword, all his gold, a jug of wine, and his best horse and headed for the city. He'd quickly discovered that there were few men who'd even care to stand against him with a blade, and nearly none that could survive to the count of ten; he'd never had any difficulty putting his hands on money.

It had been a good life for more than ten years, but the one he had now was better.

Now, as he splashed within the waters of the Great Chambaygen, he wondered idly if his father knew of his service to Ma'elKoth, wondered if his father appreciated the irony. After all, now that he served Ma'elKoth, he fulfilled his father's dreams for him better than he ever could have if he'd followed his father's path. Berne wondered if his father would think it funny; Berne surely did. He could raise a chuckle just thinking about it.

He went to the wall and pulled himself up out of the water, climbing the wall easily, fingers and boot toes finding the mortared joins between the stones. When he reached the battlement, both sentries still lingered, nervously standing watch over his sword. Berne thanked them with a grin for guarding it as he slung it on; then he shrugged and untied the purse that hung from the sword belt. Why not? He tossed a golden royal to each of them; as they

fumbled eagerly for the coins—more than a week's salary apiece—
he gave them a lazy salute and jumped back off the wall, retracing
his upward path from rooftop to rooftop and finally to the street.

He hummed happily, tunelessly, as he jogged toward the Colhari
Palace. He played out the scenario in his mind:

*I swear, Ma'elKoth, he just came at me. It was like the other day
inside Alien Games. I went to his room to make peace, you know?
That's all. I even brought some brandy, a couple of cigars . . . And he
berserked on me. I had to kill him—it was him or me, Ma'elKoth, I
swear it!*

Easy. Neat and clean.

Even as Berne was, himself, now—clean.

Still kinda horny, though—shame that there's no way he could
justify fucking Caine's corpse. He rubbed the front of his breeches as
he jogged along—mm, horny indeed, horny enough that maybe he
should do something about it before he went after Caine. His story
would become vastly less convincing if he stood before Ma'elKoth
with an enormous erection.

And then the gods gave him a gift: as he paced past the mouth of
an alley, he heard the familiar sucking hiss of a whore's come-on.
Standing within was a thin, frail-looking elvish girl clutching a tat-
tered shawl around her translucent shoulders.

Berne gave her a friendly smile. "Missed the curfew, did you?"

She nodded submissively and looked up at him from beneath
long silver lashes. "I must leave the street. Give me shelter for the
night, and I will teach you—" She rotated her hips suggestively.
"—primal secrets . . ."

"All right," he murmured, "but show me some here, first."

He joined her in the alley, and when he left, sated, only moments
later, her broken corpse still twitched like the legs of a half-crushed
spider on the cobbles behind him.

There *was* a curfew, after all, and as a Count of the Emperor, it
was his duty to enforce the law.

Then to the palace, for a quick change into dry clothes; he sent a
servant for a jug of good brandy and a box of cigars—these would
be the peace offering that would buy his way into Caine's room for
the kill.

Humming to himself, he tripped cheerfully along the halls to the
chambers that had been set aside for Caine. His hand was on the
very grip of Caine's door when Ma'elKoth Spoke to him.

BERNE. WHAT ARE YOU DOING?

Berne winced; this Speaking—Ma'elKoth's ability to roar into the mind of any of his Children, anyone who'd gone through the Ritual of Rebirth—thundered inside his head like the voice of a god and made his skull feel as though it might burst at the next word. He barely managed to hang onto the jug of brandy.

"Nothing," he said to the empty air. "I'm visiting Caine. You know, to make peace—"

WHY IS LAMORAK IN THE THEATER OF TRUTH?

Berne pressed the heel of a hand against his eyes, as though to keep them from popping out of his head. "I, ah, just wanted to get rid of him, you know? He's no use to us anymore—why spend the money to feed him?"

THE MONEY IS NOT YOURS TO SPEND OR SAVE; NOR IS LAMORAK USELESS. EVEN AS WE CONVERSE, CAINE IS WITHIN THE DONJON TO PRETEND HIS RESCUE AND THAT OF THE WOMAN, AND THUS ENTER THE CONFIDENCE OF SIMON JESTER.

"Enter the confidence . . . ?" Berne stared at the closed door in front of him and thought as fast as his blade had ever moved. "Ma'elKoth, I can countermand the order—on horseback I'm only five minutes away."

NO. LET HIM DIE. TO REVERSE YOURSELF WOULD CAUSE SUSPICION AMONG THE GUARD, AND POSSIBLY WITH LAMORAK HIMSELF. SIMON JESTER HAS SOURCES EVERYWHERE; NO ONE MUST SUSPECT OUR PLAN. THE WOMAN WILL BE SUFFICIENT—BUT BERNE, KNOW THAT I AM MOST DISPLEASED WITH YOU.

"Ma'elKoth, I'm sorry, please . . ." Berne murmured, but the Presence was gone from his mind.

Berne took a deep breath and carefully set the brandy and the cigars down at the threshold of Caine's door; then he burst into a sprint and ran like the wind, leaping down stairs and skidding around corners, racing to the small stable where the Household Knights kept their steeds.

He couldn't tell Ma'elKoth what he suspected, what he *knew*, about Caine—Ma'elKoth was obviously infatuated with the fucking little snake—but Berne could, right here and right now, save the Empire.

He could *get* Caine: get him killed without a drop of blood on his own hands.

That was the unfortunate part, that he'd have to leave Caine's death to someone else, but in times like these, all true patriots must be prepared to make sacrifices.

He wasted no time saddling his horse, just buckled on his bridle. A golden royal apiece bought him the silence of the guards at the Dil-Phinnarthin Gate, and Berne galloped bareback off toward the courthouse.

So Caine dies at someone else's hand, so what? With any luck at all, Berne would get to do Pallas Ril in a day or two—this would be a satisfying consolation prize, much more satisfying than that elvish whore.

With Pallas, he could take his time and really enjoy himself.

2

" 'STRATOR? 'STRATOR!" A tentative hand on his shoulder prodded Arturo Kollberg awake. He batted at it gummily, smacking his lips against the ashtray taste in his mouth. " 'Strator, Caine's back on-line!"

"Whuh—?" With a buzzing, humming rush, the world flooded back into Kollberg's brain. The 270-degree point-of-view screen that formed a wall of the techbooth spread before his eyes; he'd fallen asleep here, in the stage manager's command chair, waiting for Caine to emerge from the Colhari Palace.

"Zhe hurt? H'longza been?" He shook his head sharply and massaged his face with both hands, trying to drive alertness in through the skin.

He was acutely, painfully aware of the diode-lit fist button of the active emergency transfer control, shining there on the console before him like a radioactive toadstool; he was painfully aware of the responsibility it implied.

"No, he doesn't seem to be hurt," one of the techs replied. "It's been a few minutes short of twenty-seven hours. He's on foot, heading west along the backstreets of Old Town. He is, ah, has apparently been rearmed, somehow, and he's carrying a heavy coil of rope slung across one shoulder."

"Get them up, then!" Kollberg barked. "We've got a hundred and fifty thousand first-handers in sendep all over the world! If something happens, and they all *sleep through it*—!"

There was no need to complete the implied threat; every man in the techbooth understood. For minutes, the only sound was the muted thuttering of fingertip keystrokes and the whispering rumble of Caine's Soliloquy.

"For Christ's sake, somebody get me some coffee."

A tech bolted out of his chair and scrambled toward the urn while Kollberg scanned Caine's telemetry with a critical eye: Caine's adrenal production was soaring, and though his heart rate was barely above one hundred, it was climbing steadily. He clearly wasn't injured—he moved smoothly through the backstreets, easily slipping into deep shadows to avoid the passing constable patrols.

The tech pressed a cup into his hand, and Kollberg sipped the scalding coffee expressionlessly. This coffee was hardly enough for his needs: he couldn't take the chance of drifting off again. He scribbled a brief note on the armpad linked to the chair's electronics and clicked *send*. In five minutes or so a Studio porter would arrive at the techbooth with the carton of amphetamine sulphate that he normally kept by the simichair in his private box.

Caine's soliloquy ran continuously as he artfully filled in the story line for the missing twenty-seven hours. Kollberg nodded his admiration for Caine's technique; the man really was brilliant at this. He knew he'd been off-line, and now he wove the story in images so vivid that the first-handers would almost believe they'd gone through those experiences themselves, while at the same time maintaining a sense of free-associating disorder to uphold the illusion that the Soliloquy was actual thought.

So . . . he'd massaged Ma'elKoth into hiring him to find Simon Jester; this was lovely irony. It would let Caine save Pallas and kill Ma'elKoth virtually simultaneously, provided Caine worked the plot with the sort of skill Kollberg knew he had.

But what was he up to now?

Caine's POV flickered dizzyingly as he scanned the street before gliding across Noble's Way in the black moon-shadows under Knight's Bridge. He still filled in back-story, with some babble about a giant statue and a blood oath, but he hadn't yet breathed a word of why he was creeping into the west end of Old Town at two A.M.

It was a suspense technique, an old one, one that Caine would have learned at the Studio Conservatory, and it was certainly working on Kollberg. He chewed on a corner of his lower lip and wiped sweat from his palms onto the arms of the chair.

Caine's POV crept toward a hulking structure that loomed as a barely blacker shadow against the thin, moon-silvered overcast, a blocky building taller than the sheer curtain wall that surrounded Old Town.

"What is that?" Kollberg murmured. "Where's he going?"

One of the techs checked Caine's telltale on the virtual map. "I'd have to say that's the courthouse, 'Strator. God only knows what he thinks he's going to do there."

Even as Kollberg frowned his agreement, Caine reached a corner of the courthouse and slid along it into ink-painted shadow: his fingers and toes found the mortared cracks between the huge limestone fascia, and he climbed the wall with the ease and speed of a man going up a daylit stair. In slightly more than a minute he gained the guardwalk that surrounded the courthouse's sloping roof and crouched there in the shadows while he caught his breath and counted chimneys in Soliloquy.

One two three up, two over, there it is.

The chimney Caine watched now belched a thick, white, steam-laced smoke that caught a reddish glow from the lantern of an approaching guard. *That puff of steam came from a cauldron of gruel being dumped on a cookfire about sixty meters straight down,* Caine monologued.

Sixty meters? Kollberg frowned, puzzled. The courthouse was barely half that tall.

Now, for the guard.

The guard had no chance. He rounded the curve of the guardwalk and never saw Caine slip over the wall behind him and overtake him on cat feet. To Kollberg's surprise, Caine didn't cut the man's throat; instead he unstrung the guard's knees with a silent and efficient elbow to the neck, just below his helmet's back rim. The guard pitched forward while Caine caught the lantern in one hand and the guard himself with the other; he lowered them both to the guardwalk in absolute silence. Before the guard could recover himself enough to so much as moan, Caine had looped his cord belt around the guard's neck in a simple garrote; in seconds, he silently strangled the guard into deep unconsciousness.

Another twenty seconds were required to bind and gag him, then Caine padded up the slope of the roof toward the chimney he'd picked out.

The King's Eye who dumped that gruel is the only man down there who knows something's up, and even he doesn't know what it is. All he knows is that Toa-Sytell wants to question the prisoner who preps the morning meal, and that Toa-Sytell wants that gruel dumped on that fire. That's all he knows; that's all he needs to know.

The rest of it, I'm handling myself.

On reaching the chimney, Caine pulled from his belt a bar of blackened steel with a long, long hank of coiled rope tied to a notch in the middle. He laid the bar across the mouth of the chimney and let the rope uncoil into the choking smoke-filled darkness below. He pulled out a pair of thick rawhide gloves and slipped them on as he climbed into the chimney.

Fifteen minutes until the trusties who do the morning cooking arrive. Fifteen minutes to get two friends out of durance vile. Longer than that, and I blow the game—which might cost me my life, but that's not important. If I screw this up, Pallas dies down here.

He leaned out from the chimney for one last good breath, inhaled, then held it and slid down the rope fast enough that the gloves smoked and began to burn the palms of his hands.

I've gotta get this right the first time.

Lamorak, Kollberg thought in sudden panic. *Lamorak's down there—he's going for Lamorak and Pallas! But no, he wouldn't waste his time on Lamorak, would he? He'd best not. Didn't I warn him about that?*

His fist twitched and raised unconsciously over the emergency recall switch; an effort of will was required to lower his fist without striking. He couldn't do it, not yet, not without justification; his dealings with Lamorak were somewhat too delicate to bear the weight of an emergency recall—the Board of Governors might not approve.

As Caine slid down into the smoldering embers of the cookfire in the cramped, darkened kitchen of the Imperial Donjon, Kollberg's eyes were fixed on the pulsing toadstool of the emergency recall switch.

This was no longer a matter of *if,* he realized—only a question of when.

3

TALANN STRUGGLED UP from twisting fever dreams, some of the clouds clearing from her mind, and returned to the world of darkness and pain.

She couldn't recall how long it had been since her last interrogation; didn't know how many days she'd been chained here, naked skin rubbing raw against the chill limestone floor. Iron shackles bolted to the floor encircled her ankles; a length of rusted chain joined her wrist manacles to the same floor bolt, too short a length to allow her to stand erect or lie flat. Wetness and soft slime beneath her told her that she'd again voided her bladder and bowels while she'd slept, curled fetally around her restraints; her sense of smell had long ago overloaded and could tell her nothing.

Gasping, she pulled herself into a sitting position. Her various pains announced themselves gleefully in ascending ranks: torn flesh where the iron manacles cut into her wrists and ankles, the oozing sores across her buttocks and flanks that lying in her own filth had opened, the carelessly stitched sword cuts she'd taken from the Cats, now swelling with angry infection, and the sledgehammer of fever that pounded dizziness into her brain. She suspected that the pulpy swelling over her right ear, souvenir of being clubbed into unconsciousness with a steel pommel, probably concealed a skull fracture.

Great Mother, she thought, half in prayer, *don't let me end like this.*

The interrogations, she'd done right. She was sure of that. She'd held the line, held her tongue, kept to her ideals: they hadn't been able to pry so much as her name out of her. They'd even dragged her away from the Flow-choking walls of the Donjon, to the palace, and the Emperor had interrogated her personally.

She had felt the prying fingers of his will struggling for a grip on the doors of her mind; but she'd resisted as the abbey school had taught her, concentrating her entire meditation-sharpened attention on her surroundings, counting wood grains in the molding of the door, the iron-grey hairs in Ma'elKoth's beard, listening for the melody in the buzzing wings of a trapped housefly.

After Ma'elKoth understood her strategy, his own had shifted, and he had magickally dimmed her senses, leaving her blind, and deaf, without smell or taste or kinesthesia, floating in endless featureless nothingness, with only the pressure of his questions beating like surf upon the seawalls of her mind. Still she had resisted, filling her consciousness with nursery rhymes and scraps of song and half-remembered recitations of Monastic history.

After this had come again the easier task of resisting pain—once again to the Theater of Truth and Master Arkadeil's silver needles.

Even then, she might have broken and told them the truth, but the truth could not have helped her.

The truth was that she had no idea who Simon Jester might be, what he looked like, or what his plans were.

She had a vague sense that she had known these answers as recently as a few days ago, but now they had slipped from her mind like water through cupped fingers. All she remembered was sticking close to Pallas Ril, because she had been Caine's woman, because her life was linked with Caine's, because Talann knew, in her most passionate heart of hearts, that someday she herself would grip Caine's hand, would catch his eye, would fight by his side and perhaps, in dreams so precious that she could only peer at them from a distance and then flick them aside, perhaps lie in his bed.

Now, lying in a pool of her own filth on the jagged floor of her cell, watching the colors in her eyes explode in fantastic geometries against the blank darkness, she struggled to believe that this would still happen, that this was still in her future.

That she still had a future.

She fought to believe that her story, the song of her life, wouldn't end with a fading whimper in this endless night.

Unknown. Unsung.

Dead.

Eyes open, or eyes closed? She could no longer tell, and it no longer mattered. She summoned again her favorite memory: ten years ago, when she'd been an adolescent page running messages for Abbot Dartheln on Thorny Ridge above the great battlefield of Ceraeno, through those three days when the combined might of Ankhana and the Monasteries strove, outnumbered, against the infinite savage warriors of the Khulan Horde and was losing, *had lost* the battle, and desperately tried to organize a retreat in good order.

She would never forget the surge that had slammed up her spine when a shout of dismay had risen from the vast ranks of the Horde, and she had looked down to the battlefield to see the huge banner of the Khulan himself burn with smoking yellow flame.

Among Talann's gifts was extraordinary vision; like an eagle, she could see—even from a mile or more away—the black clothes and fringe of beard on the man who held the burning banner up for a moment longer, then cast it down to the mud-churned earth at his feet. She had watched breathlessly, mesmerized, her duties forgotten, as the Bear Guard closed around him like the jaws of a

dragon, and a tear had tracked through the dust of her cheeks for
the death of this unknown hero—but an instant later, she saw him
again, still alive, still fighting, cutting through the finest warriors of
the Khulan Horde as the prow of a warship cuts through waves.

She'd seen him only once more, a month later, when she'd stood
in the company of the Ankhanan Abbot to watch Caine make his
formal refusal of the Barony offered him by King Tel-Alcontaur.
He'd moved stiffly, still hampered by slow-healing wounds he'd
taken in the battle, a splint on his left arm. Dartheln hadn't missed
the look on her face as she'd watched; he'd smilingly offered to introduce her, and later after the ceremony he'd made his offer good.

Caine had gravely gripped her hand as a comrade in battle, and
had listened with solemn attention to her stammered words of admiration. But there were hundreds of folk more important than she
was all waiting to do him honor, and as he walked away he'd dragged
her heart along with him.

Since that day she'd lived her life in emulation, refusing the offers of Monastic posts, requesting her Release from Obedience,
traveling in search of adventure, endlessly honing her skills so that
someday, when she met him again, they could meet as equals; so
that she would be worthy of the respect he had generously granted
her so long ago.

She'd reached an age now to be embarrassed by the adolescent
passion of this dream, but she'd never been able to bring herself to
leave it behind—she summoned it to comfort her in her darkest
hours.

She had never even approached an hour so dark as this one.

So lost was she in dreamlike contemplation of an impossible future that she only barely noticed the scrape of the bar to her cell
being shifted. It was a series of scratching clicks that caught her attention: this was not the sound of a turnkey.

Someone was picking the lock.

And she heard the door open, and in the dim and distant light
that leaked all the way from the Pit, she saw the silhouette of a man
as he slipped inside her cell; and after the scratch of flint on steel
and a shower of sparks, a lantern was gently puffed to life.

Talann's heart stopped, and her vision swam.

He wore the loose robe of a trusty instead of his customary black
leathers, and his face was caked with soot, but the fringe of beard
and the slight angle of the broken nose were exactly as she had seen

them in ten years of dreams. And she knew that this was a dream, that this could only be a fantasy, that she'd finally lost her senses.

But if this had been a dream, he would have gathered her into his arms; he would have whispered her name as the shackles fell away. Instead, as the light grew in Talann's tiny cell, Caine looked like he'd been clubbed.

He stared at her with shock and loathing, and some kind of stunned disappointment. Then he shook his head and covered his eyes with his hand, resting his forehead against the webbing between thumb and forefinger.

"You're *Talann*," he murmured hoarsely. "Of course. It would have been too easy."

Her heart sang; these puzzling words and wounding expressions meant nothing beyond one simple, surging fact. She said, "Caine— you remember me . . ."

"Hah?" His head jerked up, and his eye fixed hers with a penetrating stare—an instant later he grimaced and began rummaging within the trusty's robe that he wore.

"Yeah, that's right," he muttered. "I remember you."

"And I'm not dreaming. I'm not. You've come to rescue me."

Across his half-averted face flickered the shadowplay of a conflicted interior struggle; it came to some resolve when he found what he'd sought within his pockets. When he spoke to her again, he looked her full in the eye, and his face was grim and set.

"Yeah. Yeah, you better believe it. I'm gonna get you out of here."

He held out a shallow ceramic pot only slightly larger than the circle of his thumb and forefinger, its wide mouth stoppered by a piece of cork. "Grease your wounds with this, and eat a little. It'll take away the swelling and relieve some of the pain. Don't use too much—Lamorak might be in worse shape than you are."

She held the pot while he picked the simple locks of her manacles and shackles; then she swiftly followed his instructions. Whatever magick powered the ointment seemed to be a potent one: almost instantly the redness and swelling of the infected sword cuts began to recede, and she could literally feel the fading of her fever.

"This was," she said, rubbing a last bit of the ointment onto the torn flesh of her wrists and ankles, "not exactly the way I'd imagined meeting you again. I'm not the kind of girl who needs to be rescued very often . . ."

This sounded bad, and the hollow laugh that she forced to follow it sounded worse, but thankfully Caine barely seemed to notice. He pulled the trusty's robe off over his head, revealing his familiar knife-studded costume of leather, and tossed the robe to her.

"Dress. We have less than ten minutes to spring Lamorak and get out of here."

For a bare instant she lost herself in the blessed feel of clothing once again covering her body. "Thank you. Mother's *Curse*, Caine, I can't even—"

"Save it. We'll have time for speeches after we get out of here; shit, you can give me a testimonial dinner. Let's go get Lamorak."

"Lamorak," she said slowly. "Do you know—" *that he's screwing Pallas Ril?* her mind finished, but she couldn't say it aloud, not to his face, not here.

"What?"

"—where his cell is?" she amended hastily. "I haven't seen anyone—did anyone get away? Pallas—did she make it? Is she well?"

"Yeah, I . . . ah, I guess so," he said, looking like his stomach suddenly hurt him. "So far. Come on, let's go."

But instead of opening the door, Caine's fingers opened, and the lantern clattered to the floor; an animal snarl scraped up his throat as his hands went to his head. His face twisted into a rictus of agony, and he doubled over an instant before he collapsed against the wall, clawing at it for support; his fingernails scraped across the limestone, and he crumpled to the floor.

4

KOLLBERG LEAPED BOLT upright from the stage manager's chair, chins quivering. "What in Christ's name was *that*?"

"I don't know, sir," said one of the frantic techs, "but it must hurt like hell. Look at this!"

Caine's brain chemistry had gone berserk, and his pain-response telemetry was off the scale; it was incredible that he was even conscious. On Soliloquy there came only a low back-of-the-throat moan.

"Is it some kind of seizure?" Kollberg barked. *"Somebody tell me what's going on!"*

Another tech looked up from his keypad screen, shaking his head. "For that, sir, we're probably going to have to wait for Caine."

And then Caine's Soliloquy came back on-line with a phrase that shot ice into Kollberg's chest.

Everyone seems to want me to let Lamorak die.

5

BERNE THUNDERED UP to the courthouse at a full gallop, and even as a young and nervous sentry unshouldered his pike and snapped at him to halt and declare himself, he swung from the saddle and stalked toward the sentry like a hunting wolf.

"Look at me. You know who I am, don't you?"

The sentry nodded mutely, eyes wide.

"I'm giving you a *gift*, soldier. I'm handing you a promotion."

"My lord?"

"You haven't seen me. We've never met. This is what happened here tonight. As you were pacing your post, you heard a sound—a muffled cry, the thud of a falling body, it doesn't matter. Make something up. All you have to do is go to your watch commander and get him to send men to check every sentry. Understand?"

The sentry nodded, wide eyed.

"One of your men is probably dead, now, as we speak. The man that killed him is in the Donjon."

The sentry frowned. "I don't understand. If he's in the Donjon, how could he—"

Berne cuffed him on the side of the head hard enough to make him stagger. "He's not a *prisoner*, you idiot. He's helping a prisoner *escape*."

"*Escape?* That's impossible!"

"Only if you make it so, soldier. If this man is caught and killed, I'll be your *friend*, you follow? You understand what it can mean for a common soldier to have, for a friend, a Count of the Emperor?"

Ambition seemed to light the sentry's eyes from within, and again he nodded.

"But if anyone ever learns I was here tonight, I'll be your enemy. You might understand what that means, too."

"I wouldn't know you if you bit me, m'lord."

Berne patted him on his reddening cheek. "Good lad."

The sentry clattered off, and Berne remounted his blowing horse. He wanted to be back at the palace before this particular kettle exploded.

6

THIS WAS THE thunder that threatened to burst Caine's skull:

I APOLOGIZE FOR THE SHOUT, DEAR BOY; THE ROCK OF THE DONJON IMPEDES FLOW, AND SO I MUST ROAR.

FORGET LAMORAK. HE IS IN THE THEATER OF TRUTH, AND YOU CANNOT REACH HIM IN TIME. IF YOU CAN BRING OUT THE WOMAN, SHE MIGHT SUFFICE.

OTHERWISE, RETURN AND WE SHALL DEVISE A NEW AND BETTER STRATAGEM.

The Presence was gone from his mind as thunderously as it had appeared. Caine remembered what Kollberg had said in the green-room before his transfer, remembered as clearly as if he was hearing it now for the first time. *"And, ah, about Lamorak. If he's not dead—if, for example, he was captured—you are under no circumstances to attempt a rescue."*

He couldn't look at Talann, couldn't stare into those deep violet pools of her eyes.

He coughed once, harshly, and monologued, *Everyone seems to want me to let Lamorak die.*

He thought, *Kollberg, you cocksucker,* though his Studio conditioning prevented him from bringing the words to his lips. *If there's any way, any way I can show people what you are, you just better fucking watch out.*

Caine said, aloud, "How do we get from here to the Theater of Truth?"

7

TALANN'S EYES GO wide: violets blooming at twilight. "I, I, I'm not sure," she stammers. "Ah, are you, are you well?"

I rest my aching head against the cool limestone behind me and try to look calm and confident—must have scared the shit out of her, when I collapsed like that. Sure as death scared the shit out of me.

"Have you been there? The Theater of Truth?"

She nods uncertainly and can't meet my eyes. "That's where Lamorak is?"

"Yeah, well, his cell was empty when I got there," I lie smoothly. "Unless you think he's having dinner with Ma'elKoth, the Theater of Truth is about the only choice."

She runs grimy fingers into her matted, greasy hair. "I don't, I don't really know how to get there. When they took me, they tied a sack over my head. I couldn't see."

And we've only got about five minutes left.

So there it is, something snarls in the back of my mind. You win, Ma'elKoth. You win, you other, you grey-fleshed flabby maggot of a man whom I cannot name.

You win. Lamorak dies. Game over.

I don't know how that spell works, I don't know if anyone could hear Ma'elKoth's voice roaring into my mind to say that Lamorak lies in the chamber of horrors, that he's too far away and too well guarded. Not a medieval torture chamber, oh, no; a very modern, very clean and efficient torture chamber, run by a Lipkan expatriate whose very name has become a byword for conscienceless brutality.

And yet, something wet and sticky squirms in my chest, telling me it's easy to leave him. Easy, simple.

He's been fucking my wife.

Leave him, let him die. There's no chance to save him. My hands are clean.

Even Pallas wouldn't fault me for this.

I push up to my feet, swaying a little, my head still ringing from Ma'elKoth's roar.

"How do you feel? Can you run? Can you climb? The rope out of here is a hundred and fifty feet. Can you do it?"

"Caine," she says feelingly, "to get out of here, I can do anything."

"Stay two strides behind my right shoulder, and keep up. You're Monastic, right? You can friarpace?"

She nods. Within her filth-streaked face, her eyes shine with a hero-worshiping promise of a knight's reward. This time it's me that looks away.

"Let's go, then."

I close the door behind us, swing the bar into place, and we run.

Friarpace is a form of meditation as well as a method for moving fast over uncertain terrain. We bend forward from the hips and hold our backs straight, running flat-footed while bringing our knees straight up toward our chests with each stride. The arms go limp at the sides, not pumped for balance, and the hands are kept curled in three-finger shape. I watch the floor three paces ahead in the muted gleam from a bare crack in my lantern's cover. I breathe slowly and steadily—three steps in, three steps out—feeling the universal breath like a current that carries me along. A good pacer can run at marathon speed through a woodland and never tire, never stumble on uneven ground, never trip on a root hidden in underbrush, and make very little noise. In abbey school, we'd open each fighting day with a three-mile friarpace into the forest; the gouges and ridges of unevenly cut limestone down here are no danger, even in the dark.

Talann keeps up without difficulty. "Where are we going?"

"Shut up."

I count side passages as we pace, chanting our path under my breath as a mantra. *Straight straight right straight left straight straight right*—as each leg or turn passes I cut it from my chant. None of the passages down here are quite straight, and some of them curve much more than is apparent as we move along them. I spend substantial concentration on this; if I miss one, we're fucked. Even as it is, we're cutting the timing too damned close.

When my chant reduces to *straight, right,* I stop and hold out an arm to catch Talann at my shoulder.

"Around that corner," I say, low, "there's a door with no bar on it. That's the mess. We go in there; there's a rope tucked up inside the flue. It'll take us right up to the courthouse roof, but we have to hurry. If the day cooks show up and relight the fire, we'll smother. Understand?"

She nods, frowning. "But ... where's the Theater of Truth? What about Lamorak?"

I shake my head grimly. "We can't help him. There's no time. If he'd been in his cell ..."

She seems to shrink a little, to collapse in on herself, and she looks away. "So we have to leave him," she says hollowly. "There's nothing you can do?"

She wants me to tell her she's wrong; she turns back to look at me with so much nakedly worshipful hope in her eyes it makes me want to belt her.

"That's right—" A horrible thought leaks into my brain. "You, ah, you and Pallas, you have a meetpoint? You know, a place you can link up if you've been separated?"

She squints at me. "Of course we do. Why should you ask? Didn't Pallas send you?"

"No. It's a long story." I breathe a little easier—it would have been too harshly ironic to leave Lamorak down here and later discover he was the only one who knew where to find Pallas.

But somewhere, deep in my guts, I feel an unexpected twinge.

It's not just that I know Lamorak, that I even kind of *like* the guy—it feels like, I don't know, disappointment?

I see it now: I was *hoping* Lamorak was the only one who knew the rendezvous.

I'm looking for an excuse to rescue him.

We shouldn't even be having this conversation. I should have taken her into the kitchen and up the chimney and worried about this shit once we were out of danger.

Ma'elKoth told me to let him die; that other maggot gave me the same order.

Everyone wants me to let Lamorak die.

A pretty smart guy said to me the other day: *"They think they own you. They think you have to do what they say."*

And, y'know, there *is* one other way out of here . . .

I set the lantern on the floor and reach for Talann's arms in the deep shadows. Her face seems to glow, faintly; back over my shoulder a hundred paces or so is the torchlight and the constant prisoner-mumble of the Pit. Her breath catches in her throat, and her eyes shine.

"You go up that rope," I tell her. "You find Pallas Ril and say these words to her: Caine says you've been off-line for four days. She'll know what to do."

Her eyes narrow, and she gets a hardass set to her mouth. "Tell her yourself."

"I hope I'll get the chance."

She takes a step back and frees her arms from my grip with an efficient crossblock, her palms striking my wrists. It leaves her in balanced guard stance, from which she jabs a finger at my face. "Don't even think you're going to try this without me."

"Talann—"

"No. Lamorak is my companion—and my friend. If you say there's no chance, I'll go up that rope right behind you. If you're making a try, I'll be at your side."

I study her for a long moment while I entertain a fantasy of beating that hardass look right off her face. Screw it. From the fierce confidence in her eyes, and the memory of the solid cables of muscle in her arms, I might not be able to do it. And, y'know, I can't *force* her up that rope.

Besides, I might need the help.

She can read my decision in the shift of the curve of my silhouette.

"How do we find the Theater of Truth?"

"That's the easy part. We grab a guard and hurt him till he gives us directions. Come on."

8

"Now, BEFORE CONSCIOUSNESS fully returns, we make a final check of our equipment. Any gaps in the cage or your suit can have devastating consequences, particularly as—as we are pretending in this case—we have no idea as to the specific abilities of the subject under the question."

Awareness unfolded in geologic time, a coral island rising beneath a black ocean. Unfocused, undefined discomfort resolved into thirst—desert-parched mouth, mummified tongue, surf like sandstone baked onto the teeth.

"Adepts—thaumaturges, whatever—present their own peculiar difficulties in interrogation. Many can partially or completely block the pain responses of their bodies; we are forced, therefore, to deal with them on an emotional level, a *psychic* level, if you will. Rushall, are you listening? Adepts are extremely difficult to acquire; you should pay attention. To continue: Revulsion and horror are potent tools, but alone they are rarely sufficient. Perhaps the most powerful tool in the process of progressive degradation is the subject's own imagination. It is this which we must always seek to stimulate."

Restraint—straps cutting cruelly into flesh of wrist and ankle and neck, further straps around knees and hips.

My neck, came the thought. *I'm the one feeling this.*

A slight shift toward a more comfortable position produced a searing shout of pain from the left thigh, and the instinctive mindview response to block the shuddering agony brought him up to full awareness.

Even as light returned to his eyes, Lamorak remembered who he was.

An instant later, he realized *where* he was.

His heart began to pound drumbeats that pulsed from his toes to his throat; it tossed him out of mindview, back into the sea of pain.

"Observe his eyes. See the focus return? This indicates that we may now make our first incision."

The man who stood over him, dispassionately lecturing in

Lipkan-accented Westerling, wore a curious costume over his long, gaunt frame: a one-piece suit of bulky, loose-fitting cloth—like a beekeeper's—networked with fine-drawn silver wire. A large hood covered his head, leaving his features dimly visible through a fencer's mask of silver mesh.

In one gloved hand, a tiny scalpel gleamed.

The apparatus to which Lamorak lay bound seemed to be some sort of table, or raised bed, covered with layers of cloth and cunningly jointed or hinged so that his back was supported in a position midway between reclining and sitting upright; he had an ideal view of the knife as its gentle stroke parted the cloth of his breeches above his uninjured right thigh.

"Hey," he croaked, "hey, you don't have to go to all this trouble, you know? I'm no hero—just ask, huh?" His jaw worked strangely, and his mouth stung—still swollen and pulpy from being slammed against the wall of his cell and from the kicking the guards gave his head when they came to carry him away.

The man in the beekeeper suit gave no sign that he'd heard. He sliced the cloth crosswise around Lamorak's knee and again up near enough to his groin that Lamorak flinched involuntarily as his scrotum clenched around his testicles.

"Master Arkadeil?" came another voice. "Why isn't he gagged?"

"A fine question," replied the knife wielder dryly. "You must allow the subject to speak, even to scream, regardless that nothing he says will have any effect on the interrogation. This is to balance the essential helplessness of his position; this slightest ray of hope that something he may say will earn him mercy prevents withdrawal into despair, keeps his intellect present and active. This is vital, particularly to help counteract shock in the later stages of the questioning. In this way, you draw the subject into willing participation in the process: his hope becomes your ally. Understood? Fine. You may even ask him a question from time to time. For example—" He bent his hooded face toward Lamorak. "—are you thirsty? Do you need water?"

"Water this," Lamorak croaked, and tried to spit on him, but his mouth was dry as dust. He assayed a weak smile. "How about a beer?"

"Fine, that's fine." Master Arkadeil turned back to his audience. "You see? Nothing more than this is required."

A ring of tripods bearing lamps with white pottery reflectors surrounded the small circular stage on which the apparatus stood; they cast a strong yellow light and left the rest of the room in shadow. Beyond, he could vaguely see a double handful of seated men on raised benches around the stone floor; they all seemed intent on Arkadeil's lecture. Behind them, more rows of benches climbed toward the shadowed ceiling.

A lecture hall, Lamorak thought; it reminded him of the classrooms at the Studio Conservatory. Halfway between a lecture hall and an operating theater.

He looked within himself next and was pleased to find no stirring of panic. He decided he was handling this pretty well, so far—but it could be that part of his confidence was his inability to believe that this was actually happening, that he really was strapped to a table in the Ankhanan Donjon, about to be used as a medical cadaver in a class for apprentice torturers. Unreality, a sense of dissociation, pervaded the scene for him, like he was second-handing somebody else's Adventure.

He kept searching, down within his mind, for any hint of a belief that he would die here, and was again pleased to find none. He was persistently, endlessly aware of the recording device within his skull, and he had a morbid fear of looking like a coward—this had driven him to take greater and greater risks to prove himself throughout his career, and he'd done some spectacular things; if the Studio had only put the kind of cash into marketing him as they had, well, Caine . . .

"Remember," Arkadeil said, "the key is *progressive* degradation; therefore, we begin with the smallest incision." The knife descended onto Lamorak's thigh just above the knee. "Please don't move, Lamorak. Any movement of the treated areas will only make the cut ragged and more painful. All right? Very well."

"You don't want to do that," Lamorak said confidently and shifted his awareness to mindview. He intended to enforce this suggestion with a substantial nudge at the torturer's psyche; it'd play like nitro on the cube.

He saw none of the dangling strands of color that were his mind's metaphor for Flow, but then, he hadn't expected to: three days of futile experiments in his cell had vanquished that hope. This was part of what rendered the Donjon impenetrable, even to adepts: the minerals deposited in the limestone interfered with Flow, and what little that leaked through was diverted and consumed by the endless fantasies and prayers for freedom of the hundreds of prisoners. Thaumaturgy of any real power was impossible, down here. He knew, however, that the power he needed for such a little nudge he could generate in his own Shell.

The spiny flame-orange matrix of his Shell flared bright, and his vision faded as he fed what power he had into it; he held it prepared as he searched for the Shell that would delimit the outskirts of the torturer's mind.

He found nothing there; Arkadeil's hooded form was as blank as a marble statue's.

He struck anyway, visualizing a thick-jointed insectile arm whipping out from his Shell and anchoring itself to the fencer's mask that covered Arkadeil's face. He tried to force it through the silver net, into the torturer's brain, but some sort of shield appeared, a scarlet counterforce that glimmered along the mesh that covered the queer beekeeper's suit.

Lamorak poured power into his assault, hoping to overcome this resistance with sudden effort. The scarlet field only flared brighter, matching his power, even as his spiked Shell leached color, fading like fallen leaves bleaching in the sun, going yellow, then grey, and finally shredding like cobwebs in the wind.

The curved edge of the scalpel bit into his flesh, not deeply, a shallow slice about halfway around his knee. Arkadeil used a fabric pad from his nearby tray to swab away the welling blood.

"That didn't appear very painful," one of the observers said.

"It isn't," Arkadeil replied. "The scalpel should be extremely sharp—obsidian is ideal, if quality steel is unavailable. This slows and sometimes eliminates the onset of shock."

I'm still woozy from the kicks in the head, Lamorak told himself as Arkadeil brought the knife to the upper portion of his bared thigh. *That's all; I've just gotta keep trying. It'll wear off.*

He began again to gather power, but the icy steel of the scalpel sliding easily through his flesh gnawed at his concentration as Arkadeil made his second cut parallel to the first. The sensation—not very painful, as Arkadeil had said—made his skin crawl, and he spent some attention building a grey mist in mindview that fogged his perceptions, a filmy translucent wall behind which he could prepare his attack.

Arkadeil's third cut was a long vertical slice that connected the centers of the other two. He set the scalpel down in his tray and took up a larger knife with a more pronounced curve, and another item that looked like a pair of fryer tongs.

He said, "It is at this point that you should allow the questioning to begin," and Lamorak's stomach plummeted, dragging him sickeningly down out of mindview.

That's a flensing knife. He's going to skin me.

Arkadeil used the tongs to lift a corner of skin at the intersection of the cuts and began to work the knife beneath it with long, slow strokes. The skin came up easily, exposing twitching red muscle fibers and the butter-colored globules of subcutaneous fat.

Lamorak fought down panic and slowed the sputter of his heart. Something came back to him, faintly and foggily, something about Shanna, and Konnos, and the silver nets he had his family wear over their heads. He should have paid more attention at the time, been less concerned with posing in the sun-glow and more interested in what Konnos was saying, but it was too late now.

He cast his eye toward the students, but knew this would be hopeless—even if his suggestion could be made strong enough to influence one or two of them against their teacher, the others would restrain them. *I should have stuck with thaumaturgy,* he thought bitterly.

He'd given up the study of magick in favor of swordplay shortly after his first transfer to Overworld, on the theory that the Adventures of swordsmen were more viscerally exciting and did very well in the long-term secondhand market; so now he was left with only a fading store of minor tricks and a lot of smooth bulging muscles that did him no good at all.

He wondered how long he could keep it up, this good front, this heroic face he showed; in the end, who would care? If he died here, the cube and graver in his head would be lost. The only people who'd know if he died well, or screaming and whining like a coward, were the people present now, here in this room, and none of them gave a shit one way or the other.

He tried to summon mindview for another assault on Arkadeil, but the easy slide of the flensing knife through his flesh shredded his concentration. And he knew, too, that it was hopeless—the torturer must have some Flow source inside that suit, powering the counterforce that resisted his attacks, and nothing he could do would affect Arkadeil in the slightest.

He couldn't seem to breathe, couldn't swallow past the panic that clawed at his throat, couldn't even maintain the block that dulled the pain from his leg.

Arkadeil now had peeled back both flaps of skin, and he turned to his students. "Here, you are faced with a choice. If you are pressed for time, you may gradually slice away the muscle, being careful to avoid the major arteries and veins, of course. This requires a certain amount of expertise, and I recommend finding otherwise valueless individuals upon which to practice, as a mistake here can allow a subject to bleed to death with dismaying speed. Progressive crippling of this sort is crude, but the psychological effect can be potent. Given time for greater subtlety, there is a simpler technique that, in the end, can be extraordinarily effective."

He lifted a piece of folded parchment, displaying it for their view. "Collect the eggs of any small, swarming insect—certain varieties of wasp are ideal, as are some spiders, and even flies or cockroaches will do in a pinch."

Lamorak said thickly, "Oh, god," and he hacked a convulsive retch that slammed agony through his broken leg again.

"Simply sprinkle these eggs directly onto the muscle, and sew the skin over them, thus," he said, matching action to words. "In a few days, as the eggs begin to hatch, your subject will literally beg to tell you everything you want to know." He swiftly finished sewing the flaps of skin with coarse black thread, then wiped his hands.

"Now," he continued briskly, taking up the scalpel once again, "let us move to the consideration of similar techniques as they apply to the intestinal cavity."

9

I SUCK ON the knuckle I'd split on the guard's cheekbone, warm copperwire taste of blood on my tongue, while I peer around the corner at the two crossbow-armed guards lounging outside the door down the hall, and I try to remember why I decided to do this foolish, foolish thing.

Those guys have been here for a while; they're not even chatting anymore. Now one of them slides down the wall to settle his butt on the floor. A single lamp hangs from a peg driven into the stone over the lintel.

Talann whispers at my shoulder. "What's wrong?"

Without looking back at her, I hold two fingers where she can see them.

"We can take them," she tells me.

Which is true. The problem will be noise. The problem will be getting within arm's reach of them without eating a couple pounds of steel.

L'audace, toujours l'audace. I think that's Napoleon. Doesn't matter—he could have been talking about me.

"Wait here."

I take from her hand the iron-bound club, heavy as a mace, that we took off the guard we left gagged and tied within an empty cell. Neither of us had any use for his armor, which wouldn't have fit anyway.

"What about your throwing knives?"

I shake my head. "It's too far, and they're in armor—I'd have to take them in the throat, and at this range I couldn't be sure of dropping one even if I hit him."

"I can do lots of impressive things," Talann offers.

"Yeah, sure. Just wait."

"Caine," she says, taking my shoulder with a warm hand. "A couple of your knives. Please. If this doesn't work—if we don't make it—don't leave me unarmed. I, I can't go back to that cell . . ."

The image of her chained naked in her own shit rises vivid enough to make me wince; I can still smell it on her. I pull the pair of throwing knives from their thigh sheaths and offer them to her without a word. She takes them with both hands together like she's accepting a communion cup. Her attitude has something of awe in it; taking my knives has a significance for her that I don't understand, and I don't have time to wonder about it.

"Now don't move. The way you look, no offense, but if they see you it'll blow the game."

"I'm not an idiot," she tells me.

May Tyshalle grant that this be truth.

I step out into the corridor and start for the two guards with a measured pace. As their heads swivel toward the sound of my boot heels clicking on the limestone, I say with just the right tone of predatory authority, "Is there a *reason* that a pair of posted guards are lounging on their fat *butts*?"

The one on the floor scrambles to his feet, and the other pushes off the wall; they both come to attention. They try sneaking looks at me as I approach, but the shadows are still too deep back here for them to see more than my general outline. I say silkily, "Don't even think about eyeballing me, you lazy sacks of shit."

I can see the door between them now: it's closed, and solid, with no viewport. Good. Both guards are bareheaded: a man in armor can get uncomfortably hot, even in the cool of the Donjon. Their steel skullcaps are on the floor beside their feet. All I have to do is get close enough to swing this club, a quick horizontal forehand bash to the first guy's head, continue the motion into a spin, peg the other guy before he realizes what's happening—

One of the guards unslings his crossbow and cranks the crowsfoot back to cock it.

My throat clenches, but I never break stride. "What do you think you're doing?"

The guard slides a quarrel into the groove. "General Order Three, sir," he says apologetically. "You're out of policy."

I keep walking. The crossbow comes up. Now the other guard is toying uncertainly with his bow. Go with it: audacity, always audacity.

"And what's *your* problem?" I snarl. "Why isn't that weapon cocked, soldier? Where's your quarrel?"

"Sorry, sir, sorry," he mumbles, fumbling with the crowsfoot.

Ten more strides, that's all I need.

"Present for inspection."

It almost works—the fumbler stretches his crossbow out, but the other swings around and levels on me in a smooth motion that speaks of long practice.

"You're out of uniform, sir. How are we to know you're not an escaped prisoner?"

Five more strides.

"What did I tell you about eyeballing me?"

Now the other guard levels as well. He sniggers. "Yeah. How was we to know?"

Fuck. This is a stupid way to die.

They expect me to bluster or back off: that's my edge.

The guard is saying, "Step back or I'll shoot," even as I come up to him and slap his bow down and to the side with the palm of my left hand. The bow triggers at the motion, and the quarrel *spannggs* off stone as I quickstep to his left, to keep his armored body between me and the fumbler's bow, and overhand the club to crunch down on the top of his head. I pivot on my left foot and kick his collapsing body toward the fumbler, but the fumbler skips back and keeps hold of his bow. I know with sickening certainty that it's only a heartbeat until he shouts an alarm, and a heartbeat later that steel broadhead will leap from his bow and slam into my body. At this range it'll go right through me, and I can't get there before the shot.

I throw the club at him to spoil his shot, but he ducks it; I spring up into a leaping side kick, hoping to take the quarrel in the meat of a leg and praying that he'll miss my balls, but even as I'm going up something whickers by my head, brushing my hair, and the hilt of a dagger blossoms from the notch of his collarbone.

His eyes go wide, and his brows draw together; he drops the bow, and my side kick nearly takes his head off before the bow hits the ground. The quarrel falls from its groove as the bow triggers harmlessly with a flat whack. The back of the guard's skull makes a wet crunch on the stone floor.

And I pause for a moment's astonished wonder that I'm alive.

I pull my knife from the guard's throat and wipe it on his breeches as Talann runs lightly toward me. The lips of the wound bubble and shift ever so slightly in and out with his whistling breath, driving little rivulets of blood across the exposed cartilage. A little blood sprays up across my face and tickles as it drips into my beard. I turn him over on his face so most of the blood will drain onto the floor: he might not drown.

I silently hand the knife back to Talann when she arrives—she's a lot better with it than I'll ever be. She grins at me. "Told you I can do impressive things."

"I've never seen anything like it," I tell her truthfully. Never mind that it almost took my ear off. "That was a spectacular throw. You saved my life."

"We can call it even, then, shall we?"

I take her hand in a comrade's grip, and her eyes glow. "Yeah. We can."

She coughs and turns away, blushing a little, looking down at the guards. "Better cut their throats, huh?"

I shake my head. "I think they'll sleep till we're out of here. With those cracked skulls they might never wake up, anyway, but let's give them the chance. They're not badguys, y'know, just soldiers doing their jobs."

She squints at me consideringly. "You're a little different than I imagined you'd be."

"You're not the first person to tell me that. Can you shoot as well as you throw?"

She shrugs. "Probably."

"Grab those bows, then, and let's get on with this."

While she gathers up the crossbows, cocks and loads them, I can't help but appreciate the very interesting streamlined curves that fill the trusty's robe I gave her. I remember how she looked through Pallas' eyes, but Pallas doesn't have the hormonal responses to make that memory as compelling as this experience—and, y'know, there are few attitudes as seductive as uncritical adoration.

I turn away and pull the lamp down from its peg. "Ready?"

"Always." She holds a crossbow in each hand like twin pistols of a gunslinger, and her grin reminds me of mine.

"You're enjoying this, aren't you?"

"Would you believe me if I said this is the fulfillment of a life-long dream?"

I hope the question's rhetorical; silently I snuff the lamp and plunge the corridor into darkness. I set the lamp on the floor and ease the door open by feel, just a crack, and look down into the bowl-shaped Theater of Truth.

Down in the center of the bowl, Lamorak lies strapped to a table on a platform surrounded by what look like limelights. A tall man in some kind of weird coverall and mask is slicing into Lamorak's belly with a scalpel; there's another wound on his right thigh, an ugly I-shaped thing stitched shut with coarse black thread, and his left thigh is swollen up like a fucking blimp.

Ten men sit on benches down there, their backs to me, and hang on the masked guy's—this must be Arkadeil—every word.

He says, "Now that we have exposed the abdominal wall, we again face several choices. Insect eggs are appropriate here, and are recommended, in fact, unless one has had substantial surgical experience. Opening the wall here is extremely tricky—a slight nick in the small intestine can release digestive acids into the abdominal cavity. While death of this sort is satisfyingly painful, it can come too swiftly for effective interrogation, and we are again faced with the specter of our greatest enemy: shock. On the other hand, if you do feel competent to open the abdominal wall, there is a variety of wasp whose larvae are particularly suited to this area. You will find details on collecting these in your notes. Please review them while I open the muscle."

I grind my teeth together against the rising bile that scorches the back of my throat. "It's a class. It's a fucking torture seminar."

"Lamorak's in there?" Talann whispers at my shoulder. "How does he look?"

"Bad. That left thigh looks like trouble. Is there another door?"

"I didn't see one—I don't think so."

"All right. I'm going in. You drag the guards inside and hold the door. Anyone comes up the corridor, shoot him."

"With pleasure. What are you going to do?"

I take a deep breath, let it out slowly.

"Improvise."

I slip through the door and stroll down the broad flight of steps carved into the limestone, past curving rows of benches, thumbs hooked behind my belt, ambling along as though I've got all the time in the world. The students down there seem to be wearing only fabric, no armor or even leather in evidence, and no weapons, by Tyshalle's grace. Lamorak must have glimpsed my movement— with a gasp, he tears his eyes free of their hypnotic fixation on the glittering scalpel and meets mine, staring in blank wonder.

Arkadeil turns and follows his gaze, his face invisible behind the shimmer of silver mesh.

"May I help you?" he asks politely.

"Sure," I say in a friendly tone. The students jump at the sound of my voice. "One second, all right?"

I stroll down the last couple of steps, down past the students, who still sit and wait obediently and expectantly for their master to explain this interruption.

It'd be swell if I could stroll right up to Lamorak's side, but Arkadeil is smart and wary, and Lamorak himself blows the game: a tear leaks down his face and he croaks, "Caine—my god, Caine . . ."

Idiot. I should let him die.

Arkadeil puts the edge of the scalpel against the twitching flesh above Lamorak's carotid artery. "Mmm. Caine, is it? An honor. I presume you're here about this one?"

I stop and spread my empty hands. "We can negotiate, Arkadeil. I've heard you're a reasonable man. A simple swap: your life for his."

"I think not." He waves a gloved hand at his students. "Restrain him."

Fabric rustles behind me, and I turn to face the students at my back. They shift restlessly, looking at the floor, the walls, each other, anything but me, and you can read the strength of my legend in their downcast eyes.

Several of them have more guts than brains, and they force themselves to unsteady feet, tentatively, each trying to time his rush so that he won't be the first one to reach me.

"Courage is admirable," I tell them, smiling through the guard's blood that still trickles down my face, "but it is not a survival trait."

"Come *on*," one of them says urgently, though he's holding himself entirely still. "He can't take us all at once . . ."

And he's right, of course. A couple more stand up uncertainly.

I show them as many teeth as will fit in my widest wolf grin, my best *Fuck with me, I dare you* expression. "That's what the boys outside thought," I remind them. "*They* were in armor. With crossbows, and clubs. *They* were professional soldiers."

I give them a moment to think this over.

The students' eyes fix on me like jacklighted deer.

I open my arms as though I'm offering them a group hug.

"Where's *your* armor, kids?"

Nobody answers.

"Now sit down."

They sink back onto the benches like sandbagged sailors. I turn back to Arkadeil, fold my arms, and wait.

"All right, then." Arkadeil's words are calm, but his voice is tight with tension. He stands on the far side of the table, and now a thin line of blood trickles down Lamorak's neck from the scalpel's pressure. "I don't imagine that you can be persuaded to give yourself up, but if you do not leave immediately, you will be rescuing a corpse."

"Caine . . ." Lamorak says hoarsely, his eyes rolling white, "make him kill me. For god's sake *make him kill me!*"

"Oh, relax, you big baby. I'm the only one around here allowed to kill people."

"I do not bluff, Caine," Arkadeil says.

I shrug. "Cut his throat and there's nothing to stop me from tearing your head off."

"Then we are at an impasse. Time, however, is on my side."

"You're not the only one with an ally. Talann: in the shoulder."

Whack! without hesitation; she must have been aiming already, clever girl. The students all jump and cry out as the quarrel pounds into Arkadeil's shoulder joint and flattens him like a hammer blow. The scalpel chimes prettily as it skitters across the stone. Arkadeil writhes on the floor, clutching at the quarrel's steel vanes and keening a high, disbelieving whine.

"I could," I say generally toward the shadows above, "really get used to having you around."

"Hey, likewise," she replies softly, then shouts, "Move and you get the next one through the skull!"

Arkadeil slumps, surrendering. I step up to the operating table and start to unbuckle the restraining straps. As soon as he gets an arm free, Lamorak clutches at my hand with desperate strength, and his eyes overflow with tears.

"Caine, I can't *believe* it . . ." he whispers. "They sent you for me, right? They found out I was down here and they sent you to get me out?"

He can't say who *they* is, cannot speak the name, and neither can I; but I can still tell him the brutal truth. "No."

"No? What do you mean, no?"

"I was ordered to let you die. The only reason I'm down here is I need you to get me to Pallas Ril. Think about that the next time you put on that armor and sling your sword. Speaking of your sword, Berne has it, did you know that?"

He doesn't seem to hear me; he's still lost in the cold concept of our mutual employer having so little regard for him that they wanted him tortured to death.

"My god, my god, I've gotta get out of here . . ."

I free the last strap. "Let's go, then."

He looks at me blankly. "My leg—I can't walk. My leg's broken."

"Broken?" I repeat stupidly. Lamorak is a big man, and I'm a small one—he outweighs me by maybe twenty-five kilos, and Talann's smaller than I am.

How in the name of every bleeding god am I going to get him out of here?

10

KOLLBERG GNAWED ON a knuckle. He couldn't believe Caine would be so *stupid*, couldn't believe he would risk his precious, extraordinarily lucrative life for Lamorak, and especially couldn't believe that Caine *leaked out in dialogue* what should have been a privileged backstage communication.

He was beginning to believe that the Board of Governors might have been right about Caine all along: the man might be actively dangerous. He was certainly behaving very strangely, taking unaccustomed risks, foolish chances, being uncharacteristically reluctant to exercise his primary talent—killing people—and now, leaking backstage orders to the public!

Kollberg's fist had come very close to stroking the recall there, very close indeed; the last thing he wanted half a million first-handers to take away from this Adventure was some knowledge of how little an Actor's life was actually worth.

Well, he decided, *let it play out.* Lamorak was crippled, and Caine was too pragmatic to give his own life for another's; Lamorak would almost certainly die here, and the death of an Actor is a sure boost in the secondhand market.

And Caine's references to him, personally, he merely noted with what he thought was admirable dispassion: Kollberg thought of himself as too professional to allow being called a *flabby grey-fleshed maggot* to affect his judgment. The amphetamines had something to do with this, perhaps; he was not unaware of the chemical elevation of his mood. This latest insult he simply, almost lovingly, filed on his growing mental tally sheet, every entry of which chewed away at the nether regions of his pride. Sometime soon, perhaps very shortly indeed, he and Caine would settle up.

11

HABRAK STARED IN grim dismay and gathering anger at the tangled, soot-blackened rope tied to the notched steel bar. The sentry who'd brought this to him and laid it on his desk stood stiffly and spoke of how they'd found their comrade bound and gagged on the roof alongside the guardwalk. "They were untying him when I left. I don't think he saw anything, and I thought it was more important to get this to you immediately."

"You did it right, pikeman."

If he really had a bit of brain, Habrak thought, *he'd have left the rope in place and taken each man as he climbed out of the chimney.*

But, as it was, these intruders, these lawless scum—whoever they might be—who had crept into the Donjon, *his* Donjon, they were trapped. They were trapped, and he could take them.

"Assemble the guards without alarum," he growled. "We'll file down and search every inch. Our friends down there might not yet know we're on to them. Tell the boys not to worry about saving them for questioning. Anyone who's not a guard and not in a cell or the Pit, I want him *dead.* Shoot him down. No mercy."

He rose and reached for his weapons. "I want a whole pile of bodies, you understand? A whole *pile*."

12

"IT MIGHT BE different, had you not shot me," Arkadeil pants with pain-thinned blandness, "but with this wound, no one will believe you are in my custody, and I daresay I haven't enough value as a hostage that a guard will let you pass to spare my life."

"I'm not planning to spare your life," I tell him. "Shut up."

"Caine," Lamorak breathes thinly, as he ties what's left of his blouse around the smile of the skin-deep slice across his belly, "make him take off his hood."

"Don't bother me right now."

Ten very nervous students sit on the lowest bench, trembling and licking their sweaty upper lips. I point at the biggest, strongest-looking one. "You. Come over here."

"Me?" He presses a palm to his chest, looking around and half-heartedly pretending that I'm pointing at the guy next to him.

"Come on, move it."

"Hey, why are you picking on me? I didn't do any—"

"Talann," I say sharply, "shoot this dumb son of a whore."

He springs to his feet like an overwound jack-in-the-box and flutters his hands in the air. "Don't! Don't! All right!" He scurries over to me, wearing a smile of eager helpfulness frozen into a twisted rictus of fear.

"What's your name?"

"Ru-Rushall, if it please your—"

"Shut up. Lamorak—" I turn and offer him my arm. "—I give you Rushall to be your trusty steed. Come on—I'll help you mount up."

Lamorak squints at him, then shrugs and summons a sickly smile. "Beats walking, I guess."

"P-please . . ." Rushall stammers.

"I said shut up," I remind him. "Horses don't talk. Turn around."

Rushall continues to whimper wordlessly under his breath, but he accepts Lamorak's weight obediently enough. They both grunt—Rushall in effort, Lamorak in pain.

"Make Arkadeil take off that hood, Caine," Lamorak repeats with effort. "Then maybe I can help . . . otherwise, deadweight . . ."

His color is bad, corpse-pale and slightly green, and he looks like it's an effort to hang on to consciousness. He's fighting shock with long, slow breaths—the son of a bitch must be tougher than I thought. Even so he looks like he can't spare the effort to explain, so I don't ask. I go over to where Arkadeil huddles on the floor.

"All right, you heard him. Take it off."

He flinches away from me and wraps his good arm around his head to hold the hood where it is. Rather than argue with him, I give a sharp, spiral twist to the vanes of the quarrel that sticks out of his shoulder; the steel vibrates in my hand as it grinds bone inside his shoulder joint. He howls and lets go of the hood to grab at my arm; I pull the hood off his head with my other hand.

He has the craggy, high-cheekboned face of a Lipkan noble and stringy hair now matted with sweat, as grey as his pain-blanched cheeks. He pants through clenched teeth that seal the whimpers inside his chest: he's holding on to Lipkan honor as best he can.

Lamorak says, "Stand up."

Now, it's damned clear to me that Arkadeil has no intention of cooperating in any—but son of a bitch, stand up he does, slowly uncoiling spidery limbs until he comes to his feet. I glance over my shoulder at Lamorak and now I understand. His surfer-perfect face wears a familiar expression: the transcendent concentration of mindview.

"The source for your suit," Lamorak murmurs. "Give it to me."

Arkadeil's good hand slips robotically down through the neckline of his beekeeper's suit. Glassy eyed, he speaks without any seeming awareness of his hand's action. "You cannot imagine that you will escape . . ."

He goes on in this vein while his hand brings out a tiny, glossy black stone about the size of a pea. I've seen ones like it before: it's a griffinstone.

You find them in the crops of the draft horse–sized bird-beasts; they can store an immense amount of magickal energy. Unlike dragons, who can tap Flow as directly as any human thaumaturge or primal mage, griffins are wholly dependent on the power of the griffinstones they carry in their muscular flightcrops. Lacking griffinstones, they're every bit as clumsy and helpless as you might expect from a half-hawk, half-lion abomination of nature; with them, they become swift flyers and fearsome predators—and the targets of stonehunters, who have trapped them nearly to extinction. That makes griffinstones exceedingly rare and hideously expensive, even tiny ones like this.

Arkadeil steps mechanically over to Rushall and Lamorak and puts the griffinstone into Lamorak's outstretched hand. A smile spreads over Lamorak's face, and his eyes drift closed in what might be mistaken for sexual pleasure.

"All right," he murmurs. "We can go now."

"You heard the man," I say to Rushall, nodding toward the stairs. "Giddyap."

By the time we reach the top of the stairs, Rushall's already panting under Lamorak's hundred kilos; a bad sign. I step over the two unconscious guards—both breathing, so far—and nod to Talann.

"Let's get out of here. We can bar the door from outside."

"Wait," Lamorak gasps thinly. "Wait one second."

"For what?"

By way of answer, Lamorak lifts the fist in which the griffinstone is clenched, and his eyes drift closed again. "Pick up the scalpel," he says clearly, and far below us on the platform in the middle of the Theater of Truth, Arkadeil does.

"Thine eye offends thee," Lamorak says, with venom in his voice more potent than I've ever heard from him. "Pluck it out."

With robotic lack of reaction, Arkadeil drives the scalpel deep into his left eye.

Talann gags and says thickly, "Mother!"

"Fucker," Lamorak says, his teeth showing yellow and savage. "That's mother*fucker*."

Blood and thick, clear fluid stream down Arkadeil's cheek as he saws the scalpel back and forth within his eye socket. Rushall moans in terror and revulsion.

"Mmm," I say thoughtfully. "Remind me to stay on your good side."

Once out in the corridor, we bar the door behind us. While Lamorak is busy producing a flame to light the lamp, Talann leans close. "Can we haul him up that rope?" she says, low, nodding at Lamorak. "He'll never climb it."

"We're not going up the rope." I nod back in the direction from which we came. "That's gone—the daycooks'll be in there by now, with guardsmen to watch them. But there's another way out of here."

"There is?"

I grin. "What, you thought I wouldn't have a fallback? Am I an amateur?"

"How do we get there?"

"Well, y'know, that's the trick. We have to go through the Pit."

"Through the *Pit*?" Talann goes goggle-eyed. "Are you *insane*?"

"No choice," I say with a shrug. "Our way out? It's in the Shaft."

Lamorak and Talann exchange a grim look, and Rushall blanches—they all know the Shaft's reputation. Lamorak clenches the griffinstone, and Rushall calms; we put the lamp into his soft-fleshed grip.

"Follow me."

We head off along the corridor, and a four-man guard unit swings into view around a corner ahead.

In the instant of recognition it takes for the guards to register our presence, Talann has already leveled one of her bows. The guard who opens his mouth to shout *"Don't move—"* takes her quarrel right into the back of his throat.

It strikes through his spine and bursts out the nape of his neck, so the impact doesn't knock him down: he stands, swaying, dead on his feet. The other guards fire wildly in their alarm, and their quarrels strike fire from the limestone walls. Something smacks the side of my right knee hard enough to buckle it, making a noise like a slap of raw meat on a wet butcher block. They're shouting for help as they duck back around the corner to reload, and the leader finally topples on his face, twitching.

I start to sprint after them and my leg gives way, sending me sprawling. Talann's right with me: she leaps over my head while I hold on to my knee, finding blood there that leaks through my fingers. She bounds like a gazelle toward the corner. Only one foolhardy guard manages to recock before she gets there, but she's ready for him as he swings back around the corner, and she never seems to miss.

Even as he brings his bow down into line, Talann springs into the air and fires, using the smooth arc of her leap to make her hands as steady as if she stood still. She's maybe three meters from the guard when her quarrel takes him in the heart. From this range, his armor can't even stop the vanes: the quarrel punches right through his hauberk to vanish inside his chest.

She drops the bow and makes the corner without slowing, brushing past the guard who makes thick choking noises deep in the back of his throat. Around the corner, the guards' shouted alarms become shouts of alarm, and the wet bone-on-bone music of close combat swells, just out of sight.

Now I find out what's wrong with my knee: on the floor, close enough that I almost fell on it, is a steel crossbow quarrel, its point bent and blunted. One of the wild shots from the guards must have hit me on the bounce. Even blunted and with much of its force dissipated against the limestone floor, it hit the bone of my knee like the blow of a mace. My whole leg is filled with numb tingling, and I can't feel my toes—probably chipped the bone. This is gonna hurt like a bastard in a few minutes. If it got in under my kneecap . . . I don't want to think about it.

This may not be my best day.

There's no time to find out how badly I'm injured. I'll worry about it after I'm sure I'm gonna live through this.

The sounds of combat cease abruptly, and a second later, Talann comes back around the corner, looking pleased with herself.

"Are you hurt?" I ask her.

"Caine," she says seriously, "I'm just warming up."

She can do lots of impressive things, she'd said.

"You are really something," I tell her weakly.

She shrugs and gives me a smile I'd have to guess would be dazzling if her face weren't smeared with shit.

Still no feeling in my right foot, though little white-hot needles are starting to prick my calf. "Help me up," I tell her. "I'm not sure I can walk, yet."

She takes my hand in hers, weapon to weapon, and lifts me to my feet with easy strength. The look in her eyes goes through me like a spear. When was the last time my wife looked at me like that?

This is something I can't think about right now.

The side of my knee is pulpy and swelling already, making sausage skin out of the tight leather of my breeches—nothing feels broken in there, but between the numb tingle and the swelling, nothing feels much of anything in there.

Better keep moving and hope for the best.

Talann slips a muscular shoulder into my armpit and helps me along. Rushall and Lamorak still stand swaying in the middle of the corridor; Lamorak's barely hanging on, head drooping like a freighter pilot's at the ass end of a two-day run.

Shouts that answer the alarms of Talann's recent victims come from ahead of us, toward the Pit.

Talann glances from Rushall's blankly sweating face to my knee. "We can't outrun them."

"No shit. Lamorak, we need some help, here." I take his shoulder and shake him gently. "Come on. Stick with us, man. We're about to have guards crawling all over us. Can't you do something to draw them off?"

His eyes barely focus. "N'much. Mmm, pretty useless . . . swordsman, y'know . . . shitty adept . . ."

I take my arm off Talann's shoulder and whack him a stinging open-hand slap to the side of the face.

"Wake up! We got no *time* for this, you whining sack of shit! You pull it together—or I just cut your throat right now and we take our chances without you."

His face seems to clear, and a half smile bends his lips. "Easy to be tough . . . unarmed man with a broken leg . . . A'right, I got something."

He shakes his head sharply, struggling to keep his focus. "But you gotta look after, uh, after my horse, here—I can't hold him and do . . . other shit at the same time."

"No fear." I draw one of the long keen fighting knives from the rib sheath within my tunic as the pale cast of thought returns to Rushall's face. I show him the knife's chisel point.

"Think of this as a spur. Don't make me dig it into your flanks, huh?"

Rushall wheezes something incomprehensible, and we limp away, deeper into the Donjon, accompanied by the rising sound of boots clattering toward us.

They're between us and the Pit, and so we try to swing wide. Lamorak mutters "Corner" from time to time and we turn; when one of the clattering patrols sees us, they insensibly point in the wrong direction and hustle off down other corridors at right angles to the one we're in. Whatever kind of illusion it is Lamorak's running, it's obviously working.

Now at various places around the Donjon we can hear them shouting to and at each other: conflicting orders and argument over which way we went. It's working swell, but there's too many fucking guards down here—they're everywhere, and Lamorak's grip on consciousness is loosening.

Now and again one of the rushing patrols points at us. They see us instead of his illusion, once even firing on us, before Lamorak's head jerks up like a narcoleptic marionette's and the guards mill in confusion for a moment before stumbling off the wrong way.

And the prisoners are into the act now, wakened by the yelling. They amuse themselves as prisoners will, by imitating the shouts of the guards—*"This way! That way! The other way! Have you looked up your ass?"*—and by simply howling wordlessly to drown all voices in a rising surf of noise.

We turn aside again and again, dodging back from advancing groups, and finally, blessedly, around the curve of a corridor appears the steady light of the torchlit Pit.

I douse the lamp Rushall carries. In the yellow-rose glow from the Pit, his face is grey and slack—shit, he looks worse than Lamorak. His chest heaves, and tears stream down his face.

I can't, he mouths again and again, and: *Don't kill me.* It's possible to feel some sympathy for the poor bastard until I remind myself what he was studying to become.

I motion for them to wait here, and I slide along the curving wall, limping up to the corridor mouth to get a look.

I don't like what I see.

The door to the Shaft is all the way on the far side of the Pit, across the thirty-endless-meter diameter—a long, long walk around the perimeter balcony—and only a few steps from the verdigris-caked double doors that lead up the steps to the courthouse.

Standing by those double doors are nine very alert-looking men in full armor with crossbows at the ready, with the hip-height stone wall of the balcony rail for cover, and with, no doubt, orders to hold that door with their lives.

I mutter, softly enough that no one can hear, "We are lip-deep in shit."

Is it too late to change my mind about this stupid escape thing?

But, y'know, I'm an optimist, and I can look on the bright side: at least we don't have to cross the Pit floor below, with its surging mass of jeering, hooting prisoners. And better a quick death, choking on the blood that fills your lungs from a crossbow through the chest, than to be delivered alive into the Theater of Truth.

I slip back into the darkness to rejoin the others.

"Talann, you remember what I told you before, what you have to tell Pallas Ril if I don't get out of here?"

Her face hardens, and she shakes her head stubbornly. "No. No, I don't, and don't waste your breath telling me again. We all make it or none of us do."

Idiot child. "Lamorak, listen to me." His eyes are glazed, and he seems to be looking at something deep within the stone over my head. I shake him until his consciousness swims up into view.

"Lamorak, goddammit, you have to tell Pallas she's *off-line*, understand? When you meet Pallas, tell her she's off-line."

"Pallas?" he murmurs thickly. "Caine . . . shit, Caine, I'm sorry . . ."

He's in a world of his own. "No time for that, now. Listen to me: Pallas dies in three days, or maybe less, maybe only two. You hear me? Pallas *dies*!"

Lamorak frowns, leaning his head on the back of Rushall's shoulder; I think some of this is drifting into view through the fog in his mind. But now Talann stares at me with an uncomprehending squint.

"What do you mean, Pallas dies in three days? Is she hurt? Poisoned? What does 'off-line' mean?"

I bite down on my desperation and speak through clenched teeth. "Talann, I swear to you, if there's ever a way for me to explain this to you, I will. But not now. For now, just accept my word."

"I do, but—"

"Fine then. Lamorak, you got it? You have to tell her she's off-line."

His brows slowly draw together. "Off-line . . . Pallas is off-line? Bleeding *god*, Caine . . . she'll *die*—!"

"Yeah." Now she has two chances: if either one of them makes it, she might learn it in time to get to a fixed transfer point and live. "All right, follow me."

I lead them up toward the mouth of the corridor; we all stop just barely far enough in the shadows that the guards on the balcony opposite can't see us.

"All we have to do is get to the Shaft door," I tell them, pointing.

Talann's face hardens as she looks out there, but she says nothing. She understands as well as I do the brutal tactical reality of rounding that long open curve of balcony. I pull her back so that I can instruct her out of Rushall's hearing. We don't have to go far—it's loud as a fucking nightclub in here.

"Once we're through that door, we're home free. At the bottom end of the Shaft there's a sump, just a hole in the stone that they drop bodies down. It's a long drop, but the bottom is full of a couple yards of shit and composting corpses on a ledge, and an underground stream flows right by there. That's how we get out. Understand? Jump in and don't swim; just hold your breath and let the current carry you while you count to sixty, like this: one-ankhana two-ankhana three-ankhana. Then swim for the side—the stream is narrow, just swim hard and you'll bump into stone eventually. Keep hold of Lamorak—he can make a light. You'll be in the caverns under the city. If I'm with you, everything will be fine—I know those caverns. If not, keep moving upward and calling out; you should be able to meet up with the Subjects of Cant—they use the caverns to move around under the city."

"How do you know all this?"

Ma'elKoth showed me a map, that's how, an emergency fallback in case something went wrong at the kitchen. I give her a grim smile. "I know a lot of things about this city. It's practically my hometown."

We go back up to where Rushall leans weakly on the wall, sagging under Lamorak's weight.

"All right," I tell them, "here we go." Rushall whimpers, tears leaking steadily from his eyes. "Relax, kid. Once we're inside the Shaft, we won't need you anymore. And we won't have any reason to hurt you, all right?"

He nods uncertainly, not really reassured.

"Lamorak, we need something from you again here, something to keep those guards busy while we cross the Pit."

His breath rattles in his throat for a second or two before he whispers his answer, barely audible above the roar of jeering prisoners. ". . . I, I got nothing left, I think . . . Caine, sorry . . ."

Fuck. Yeah, that would have been too easy.

"All right," I repeat, "let's try it this way. Hands and knees. Stay below the balcony wall and get as far as you can."

"Call that a plan?" Talann says. "Ever try crawling in a robe?"

"Deal with it. You lead. Give me those bows, I'm bringing up the rear."

She hands me the crossbows and the two quivers and begins knotting her robe up around her hips. Rushall whimpers, "I can't do it. Please. I can't make it."

". . . can crawl," Lamorak offers dully. "Don't need him for that . . ."

"No you can't and yes you do. And *you*—" I point a crossbow at Rushall. "—I'm not interested in your problems. You start to feel too tired, just imagine how you'll feel with this quarrel sticking out your asshole. Move."

Rushall flinches away from me with more energy than I've seen since I chose him for this job, and I turn to Talann. "When you get to that door, don't wait for me, just open the damned thing. I'll be right behind you."

They set out with painful, nerve-racking slowness, creeping into the light. I hang back in the shadows, pressed against the wall with a bow in each hand, and watch the nine guards across the Pit.

Three minutes, that's all I ask. Tyshalle, if you're listening, if you're there, give me three minutes and I'll get us out of this.

Talann's already out of my line of sight, and Rushall's right behind her, crawling close to the wall, Lamorak riding him like a baby chimp clinging to its mother's back.

I hold the crossbows upright, pointed vertically on either side of my head. Their weight makes my shoulders start to ache, and when I shift my balance a knife of pain jabs into my right knee. I hope to god I can run. I start a breathing routine and dull the pain with one of the meditative control disciplines I learned all those years ago at the abbey school.

The Shaft door stands closed and silent. As soon as that door starts to move or the guards give any sign of alarm, I'm gonna jump out, fire both bows to get their attention, and sprint for it. Maybe I'll get lucky and drop one. A target moving at the speed I can run, across the thirty meters of the Pit's diameter, will be nearly impossible to hit.

Or, I should say, at the speed I could run this morning. My knee feels like it's being slowly crushed in a vise.

I only hope none of these guys can shoot like Talann.

No sign of alarm, yet. This is going to work. We're going to make it.

And I, I confess, am loving this.

This is what I live for. This is why I am what I am. There is purity in violence, in the desperate struggle to pull life from death, that surpasses any philosopher's sere quest for truth.

All bets are off, now, all rules suspended: no more grey-scale wandering through the moral fog of real life—this is elemental, black and white, life and death.

And even life, even death: they have little meaning for me now. They are only outcomes, consequences, vague peripheries. The violence itself consumes me, even in anticipation. When I step out from my cover, stake my life and the lives of my friends on my gift of slaughter, the caustic tide of mayhem will wash me with grace: a saint touched by his god.

Rushall interrupts my poesy by suddenly standing: he pops up behind the wall like a paper target in a shooting gallery. He's holding Lamorak's arms to keep the swordsman on his back—Lamorak looks like he's out cold. Faintly over the din I can hear Rushall's panicky scream:

"Don't shoot! Don't shoot! I've got one!"

Did I say we're lip-deep in shit? Make that: up to the eyeballs.

I spring out onto the balcony—I'd shoot that cocksucker if I could be sure of missing Lamorak—and level my bows on the guards across the Pit. They have no such reservations; even as I'm bringing my bows into line, eight of them fire. Some miss, but about five quarrels slam into Rushall's chest and drive him spinning back against the wall. He slides to the floor with Lamorak beneath him.

I fire both bows from the hip. One quarrel strikes fire from the balcony wall as it glances upward, and the other takes a guard in the ribs. At this range, chainmail is no protection: the quarrel chops in till it's stopped by its vanes, and the guard sags against the bronze doors—*which are opening!*— and now even more guards press through—

I duck behind the balcony wall to recock and reload, and one of the guards blows some kind of brief tattoo on a bugle that echoes through the Donjon.

This is about to get kind of hairy.

I have to run the opposite way, draw the guards off, but even as I'm uncoiling to stand, something snaps past my head and something else hammers my shoulder from behind. I roll with the impact, and a red-smeared crossbow quarrel clinks to the floor at my feet, even as I spin and see for the first time the four guards pounding up the corridor I was just in.

Fuck going the other way—I'm not feeling heroic enough to get pincered on this balcony just to provide a five-second diversion.

Two of the guards sprint toward me along the corridor walls; the other two stop in the middle of the corridor and take aim on my head.

I drop my bows and shoulder-roll to my feet, simultaneously drawing the little leafblades from my ankle sheaths and flipping them both backhand down the corridor. There's no force behind the throw, but it's enough to make them flinch and duck and spoil their shots.

I sweep up my bows and toss them over the balcony rail and follow them with the quivers. A bloodthirsty roar goes up from the Pit as a couple of prisoners find themselves unexpectedly armed. Then without hesitation I skip forward to meet one of the charging guards and grab his armor at the collarbone. I fall to my back and plant a foot in the pit of his stomach, kick him into the air, and he sails right over the rail and falls wailing into the Pit.

I continue the roll and let it bring me to my feet. The other charging guard has skidded to a stop out on the balcony, and now he looks like he's not at all sure he wants to deal with me by himself. He says, "Hey, wait—" as I jump at him and smear his lips with a stiff jab.

In the instant that he blinks, I wrap my forearms around his head and twist around for the neck-breaking hangman's throw. He clenches his neck enough to save his life, but the leverage sends him, too, over the rail to join his comrade among the prisoners below. He and his partner both had crossbows dangling from their baldric-slung shoulder straps.

Now *four* prisoners below are armed.

The two still in the corridor struggle with their bows; one doesn't even have it cocked yet, and the other is hastily trying to fit a quarrel into the groove, hands jittering with adrenaline. I show them my teeth and beckon, and they exchange a worried glance.

I start toward them along the corridor, and their nerve breaks: they turn and bolt. The instant their momentum is taking them away from me, I spin and sprint back out onto the balcony, heading for Rushall and Lamorak.

More quarrels snap past me, two or three coming close enough to sting me with stone splinters they strike from the wall, one tugging at my leathers as it grazes my ribs. The guards across the Pit are busy with the bowmen downstairs: this flight of quarrels must have come from someone else, new guards answering the trumpet blast, but I don't have time to turn and look.

My shoulder seems to be working well enough, despite the spreading slimy warmth from the wound. The quarrel must have missed the bone, slicing instead through my trapezius next to my neck, missing my spine by maybe two inches. Every step sledgehammers a railroad spike into the side of my right knee.

I round the curve, and Talann's on the floor, keeping her head down as she fights to disentangle Lamorak from Rushall.

"Go go go!" I shout. *"Get the door; I'll bring him!"*

Her head comes up at my shout; she nods and back-rolls away to her feet. Two guards across the Pit track her with their bows as she runs.

I shriek *"Stay down!"* but before they can fire, a pair of flat whacks sound from the Pit floor. Quarrels zip past their heads. They jerk back, and both their shots go wild.

The others by the courthouse door return fire down into the Pit. All I have to worry about is the four guards that come pounding toward me, now joined by the two I'd chased off earlier.

I have fifteen seconds before they get here.

I grab one of Rushall's limp arms and try to drag him off. Lamorak shrieks in sudden agony—that's all right, at least he's awake—and Rushall jerks convulsively and moans; even with five quarrels in the chest it'll take him a minute or two to die.

I see the problem: they're pinned together by a quarrel that had struck through Rushall's chest just below the collarbone.

The racing guards are forty feet away, then thirty.

I wedge a toe between Lamorak's chest and Rushall's back; all three of us cry out as I summon a burst of hysterical strength and yank Rushall upward, lifting him in my arms like a sleepy child. Blood pumps from Lamorak's belly and from a deep ripped-edge puncture next to his right nipple.

"Run you worthless fuck get up and run!" I scream, and encourage him with an ungentle kick in the ribs as the six guards come thundering up behind me. Lamorak rolls over, groaning and starting to drag himself away on his hands and one good knee.

I spin to meet the guards with Rushall still struggling in my arms and throw him bodily into the leader. They meet with a solid thump, Rushall screaming and clawing frantically, clutching at the cursing guard to recover his balance. Their struggle brings them against the retaining wall; they tip, locked in a lover's embrace, and tumble to the Pit floor. Howling prisoners swarm over them.

The remaining five guards skid to a halt and spread out, lifting their clubs to guard position and moving to flank me.

I could run now; I could get away and leave Lamorak to crawl and be taken—these men in chainmail could never catch me, even half gimpy as I am. Instead I wait for them in an open stance, fists up with fingers forward, presenting the meat of my forearms to absorb the coming blows of iron-bound clubs. Crossbows fire somewhere, and men scream in pain.

Past the closing guards I can see corridor mouths vomiting reinforcements onto the balcony as more patrols answer the alarm.

I wait, forcing air in and out of my lungs.

My soul sings poetry within me.

Their eyes flicker to meet each others', preparing to strike.

I attack, letting go of conscious thought.

I spring to one side of the nearest with a passing-leg, and he folds around the impact of my shin, gasping, even while my fingers stab for the eyes of another. I shift my balance and side kick a third stumbling back over the wall into the Pit, before I spin and slice the edge of my palm against the base of the skull of the first. He drops, twitching spastically.

I'm *winning*.

Just as I feel the first swelling surge of victory, one of the bastards pegs me from behind, not squarely but solidly enough to drive the breath from my lungs and buckle my knees: icy fire spreads from the point of impact above my kidney.

Another swings his club at the joining of my shoulder and neck, and I barely get my hands up in time to take it on the outside of my left forearm and the palm of my right hand. The club blasts the feeling out of both of them and crashes through my guard, on target, but instead of breaking my neck it only strikes meteors through my swimming head.

I snarl at the pain and slap his jaw with my doubled elbow, turning in time to duck under the follow-up of the guard behind me. From my bent-over position I hammer an uppercut into his armored groin—which only makes him grunt, but it lifts him up onto his toes—I grab his belt with my numb fingers and yank him forward and down on top of me in time to shield me from the downstroke of the other. I can feel its impact through his chest, but it's not enough to take him out through the padding under his armor, and now the one whose eyes I poked is blinking like he can see again, and I am in deep, deep trouble.

I can't say exactly *why* I thought I could handle five armed and armored men—

There is, y'know, a history of insanity in my family.

I heave and roll out from under the guard; as he struggles away from me one of his boots whacks me in the eye hard enough to shoot more stars through my vision. I keep rolling while my head slowly clears—if I stop moving, they'll beat me to death in a second or two. When I can see again, the first thing I see is a shiny black pebble on the floor about six inches from the end of my nose.

I get my hand on it as the three guards advance on me, clubs up for the kill. A quick glance back—there's Lamorak, only five or six meters away, wheezing and dragging himself along, still maybe ten meters short of the door.

"Lamorak!" I holler. "Catch this fucking thing and give me a hand here!"

He looks behind, and I shoot the griffinstone at him like a marble. It skips and skitters along the floor, then it hits a crease on the rough-cut stone and bounces wildly into the air.

I track the stone with my eyes, the guards above me forgotten.

Lamorak squints like he can't see it, like he's lost it in the uncertain torchlight.

His palsied hand wavers—Where is the damned thing? Did it go over the fucking wall?—and it drops right into his palm.

His fingers close around it, and that dreamy sexual smile comes back to his face.

He says clearly, "Kill them before they kill you."

I know better than to think he's talking to me. I back-roll to my feet, away from the guards, as one of them pivots and swings his club like a baseball bat into the unprotected face of the man beside him. Bone disintegrates under the impact, and the man flips over like a pancake, dead before he hits the floor.

He swings on the other one, who's still too startled to defend himself, and drops him too. Then he races away from me to meet the charge of the ten or twelve guards that are thundering toward us.

Lamorak has to concentrate to keep this going, so I scramble over behind him and lift him with my arms around his chest. Ten meters is all that's left between us and escape. No one's shooting at us; they all seem engaged in the exchange between the guards and the prisoners in the Pit. I look ahead—

Talann has the Shaft door open.

It opens out onto the balcony; she's holding it wide to use it like a tower shield, closing off half of the balcony so that the guards on the other side can come at her only one at a time. The robe I gave her is painted crimson; no way to tell how much of the blood is hers.

I drag Lamorak toward her; now I'm wheezing and limping and this is taking for fucking*ever.*

Our tame guard goes down under a hailstorm of iron, a couple of the advancing guards stopping to stand over him and beat him until they make porridge out of his head. Lamorak is trying to take over another one, but his breathing is ragged and he's lost a lot of blood and the effort is too much for him—more blood bursts from his nose in a bright crimson spray; he sags in my arms.

The guards sprint toward us, more and more seeming to join them with every step. I look over my shoulder—we're almost there.

As I drag Lamorak to the doorway, Talann is using the two knives I gave her in a very complex infighting style that looks vaguely like *wing chun*, a flurry that not only slices the wrist tendon of the guard's club hand, but ends by driving a blade up through the soft underside of his chin.

She kicks his twitching corpse back into the arms of the man behind him, and we're through the door. I drop Lamorak like a sack of meal and grab the back of her robe, yanking her backward into the Shaft. She whirls on me with a shout and recognizes me barely in time to stop the flashing arc of her blade a couple of inches from my eyes.

I step past her and haul the door shut, bracing a foot on the wall beside it to hold it closed against the pull of the guards outside.

"Don't *wait* for you?" she says breathlessly. "You'll be right *behind* me?"

"No fucking lip out of you," I tell her.

With the door shut, there's only a thin line of torchlight leaking beneath it for illumination. They pull a couple times, hard enough that I feel something pop in my wounded shoulder.

"What now?"

"Wait."

I let go of the door and shift my weight onto the balls of my feet while I draw one of my long fighting knives. This time, when they pull on the door, it swings wide, and I lunge like a fencer, stabbing the chisel point into the mouth of the nearest guard, splintering his teeth and slashing sideways to part his cheek back to the hinge of his jaw. He jerks backward and falls, howling. I slam the door shut again and hold it.

"Now," I say softly, "we just have to wait for one of them to get a bright idea . . ."

"What idea?"

Through my hands I can feel the grinding *chunnk* as somebody slides the heavy bar into place. "That one. They've barred the door from outside. They figure we'll be here when they're ready—they've got problems other than us, right now."

The heavy door cuts almost all the noise from outside along with the light; now soft, despairing voices from below begin to ask each other if they can tell what's going on.

The throwing knife from between my shoulder blades will serve perfectly. I pull it out and feel for the crack of the door, slip the blade within it, and pound it home with the pommel of my fighting knife. It's just like pennying shut a door in the apartments where I grew up. It won't stop the guards when they come for us, but it'll slow them down and give us a little warning—we'll hear them pry it open.

I pull Kierendal's lighter from the pocket inside the waistband of my breeches and thumb it alight. From the darkness beyond the tiny pool of wavering light it casts, eyes peer uncertainly back at us.

"What's happening?" somebody whispers. "You're not guards—have you come for me at last?"

Talann's breath catches, and I put a hand on her shoulder. "Don't answer. There's nothing we can do for these people. To speak to them will only give them cruel hope."

And the smell comes to us: bitter sweat and shit and the sweet rot of gangrene, the thick reek of gas escaping from bloated corpses below, a dizzying stench that burns my throat and slaps tears into my eyes. I hand Talann the lighter.

"Lead the way. I'll carry sleepyhead, here."

In the glow, Lamorak looks even worse, and the blood that once had pumped out from his chest wound now only flows sluggishly. I don't know if he's going to survive. Shit. At least I got him out of the Theater of Truth—that should count for something.

"Hang on, you bastard," I mutter as I slap some of Ma'elKoth's unguent on the chest wound; maybe it'll slow the bleeding, anyway. I sling him up into a fireman's carry that makes my own wounds, shoulder and knee, announce their presence loudly. "Hang on. I don't want to have to look Pallas in the eye and tell her you died down here. She'll never believe I didn't kill you myself."

We move down the long, long step-cut slant of the Shaft. The floor is slick with the condensation from the breath of hundreds of gasping prisoners, and now Talann reaches the first of them, all with one wrist chained to the wall above their heads.

The Shaft is maybe five meters across, just wide enough that the prisoners chained in an endless double row down along its walls can't reach us as we walk down its middle. All are naked, clothed only in their own filth and the filth of those upslope.

Prisoners in the Shaft are unchained only if, through some extraordinary mercy, they are to be released from the Donjon. They are kept here, fed a minimal diet, and kept chained to the wall until they die. Their wastes flow downhill, to the sump that is our destination, so the prisoners below are bathed constantly in the shit and piss from those chained above. Rarely—perhaps once a month—

the guards come in here to unchain the corpses and flush the Shaft with barrels of water. The corpses, too, are rolled downhill into the sump and left there to rot.

Our tiny bubble of light reveals men and women in misery so abject that they've become objects, not even animal, only bundles of shattered nerves and gangrenous sores that have no purpose left beyond experiencing the slow, shit-filled slide down to death.

Even Dante would swoon, here; Talann can barely take it. Her shoulders tremble, and sometimes I can hear a faint sob and a murmured prayer that the Great Mother have pity and release these souls from life.

Y'know, I admire Ma'elKoth, I really do—but if I ever start to actually *like* the man, all I'll have to do is remind myself that he runs this place, and he could change it if he chose.

On the other hand, I guess it's not that different from being born into a Labor slum. Shit, as they say, flows downhill at home as much as here—and in the Shaft, it doesn't take as long to kill you.

The growing ache in my chest, that's the strain of carrying Lamorak. The tears, they're from the stench. And the sickening, retching revulsion in the pit of my stomach—

A squeal of hinges from above, and far, far back I can see a pinprick of light. We're out of time.

"I see it!" Talann breathes hoarsely—and she's looking ahead, downhill. She must mean the sump.

"All right. When you get there, don't even slow down. Douse the lighter and hold it tight in your fist. Until Lamorak wakes up, that's all the light we've got. When you hit bottom, move to one side as fast as you can; Lamorak and I will be right behind you."

We reach the sump: it's nothing more than a ragged natural fissure in the stone of the floor. Faintly up it comes the slap of water on rock.

Loud voices and the clatter of boots come from above. It won't be long before the guards are in crossbow range despite the low ceiling: crossbows have an extremely flat trajectory.

Talann's vividly violet eyes hold mine for a moment across the flame of the lighter, then she snuffs it; blackness so deep you can taste it surrounds us.

Her hand touches my arm, and on my mouth comes the quick brush of her lips; then a rushing absence fills the space where she had been.

It seems like a sizable bite of eternity before I hear her call faintly from below. "Go!" is all she says.

I take a deep breath and shift Lamorak's weight on my shoulders; it takes every milligram of courage I possess to step from the stone and plunge into space.

We fall and fall and fall and bounce from stone and slide across shit-slickened rock: nothing can be seen—how far to go, how far we've come—we bounce and tumble and fall some more—

And land, driven deep into a soft pile that makes wooden splintering crackles beneath and around us.

I dig my way out of it, trying not to think about what's smearing in and around the open wounds on my shoulder and knee.

"Talann?"

She strikes the lighter. My god, I hope I don't look as bad she does. It's impossible to say what it is that layers and cakes every inch of her body because my sense of smell shorted out a couple of minutes ago up in the Shaft. The pile in which we lie is an unknowable number of corpses, layered with an unconscionable amount of human waste.

Hah, I can take it; landing here isn't that different from the end of the Ritual of Rebirth.

By the light of the tiny, smoking flame we manage to locate Lamorak. The underground river is only a couple of meters away. That's what's kept this pile from swelling until it choked the sump: some of it is always washing away when it gets too high.

Lamorak is out cold; there's only one thing left to do. I take off my cable-cored garroting belt and tie one end tight around Lamorak's upper arm, the other tight around my own.

"Remember," I tell Talann, "don't swim until you count to sixty."

"One-ankhana, two-ankhana," she says. "I remember."

"Go, then."

She snuffs the lighter and slips noiselessly into the water. I get both hands over Lamorak's mouth and nose, pinch them both shut, and follow her.

The water closes over my head like a blessing of the Mother, and I float in total darkness, without sensation, almost without thought except for the slow beat of the seconds I count in my head. If I were less exhausted, if the water were not so cool and soothing on my wounds, I might be tempted to panic, but as it is, I have no energy left for worry.

Seconds pass more swiftly than the beat of my heart.

I start to suspect that I've been trying too hard, that all my struggle and worry is a mirage, a dream, that I could be happy to simply float along in my life as I float here.

How long has it been? I've lost count, and I don't care anymore. Struggling to hold my breath is too much work, and I know that pretty soon I'll let it bubble out between my lips. I'll breathe in water, and it'll be as cool and soothing in my lungs and on my heart as it is on the leaking hole in my shoulder.

Now a point of light joins the shimmering phosphenes in my vision, and a familiar voice calls my name. I wonder if this is the tunnel they all talk about, if that voice might be my mother's, until a powerful, calloused hand clamps my wrist and hauls me gasping up out of the water.

The lighter sits on the stone bank by the stream, and Talann belts me on the side of the head. "Wake up, damn you!"

I shake my head sharply and remember what's going on. "All right. All right, I'm back now."

Talann treads water beside me. "You're sure?"

The lighter gives me something to swim toward, and by way of answer I make for it with a strong sidestroke, Lamorak trailing limply by my belt.

It takes Talann and me a couple of minutes to pump the water out of Lamorak's lungs and breathe life once again into his nostrils. Once he's breathing normally, we let ourselves collapse side by side on the stone.

"We made it," Talann murmurs. "You did it, Caine. I can't believe we really made it."

"Yeah," I say. Talk about passing through the belly of the beast . . .

"Yeah, we made it, but we have to keep moving. One or two of those guys might have the guts to follow us."

"In a minute or two," she says, putting a warm hand softly on my upper arm.

The water washed away the filth that smeared her features, and she's really spectacularly beautiful, and she worships me.

"No," I tell her. "Now. Come on, get up. The oil in that lighter won't last forever."

She pushes herself into a sitting position. "You can be a real bastard, you know that?"

I shrug. "That's what my mother always said. Now move."

13

TOA-SYTELL CONSULTED HIS tally sheet, checking his addition one last time before speaking. "My best preliminary estimate—that is, without knowledge of the current status of the guards and prisoners who were still alive when taken to the infirmary—is that twelve guards were killed, with fifteen more wounded in varying degrees of severity. Fourteen prisoners died in the riot that accompanied the escape, and eight more were wounded severely; fifty-six slightly injured. One of Arkadeil's apprentices was killed, and Arkadeil himself is half blinded and may not regain full use of his arm."

The stone rail of the Pit balcony creaked under the massive hands that gripped it; Ma'elKoth's beard shifted as muscle bulged at the corners of his jaw, and a cracking sound came from deep within the stone as his grip tightened.

"Their wives, their children—they thought it would be safe for them to raise families, detailed here at the Donjon, away from the fields of battle," he rumbled, deep within his throat. "They must be pensioned, each and every one. None shall ever know want due to My misjudgment."

Ma'elKoth had insisted on coming personally to the Donjon to view the carnage with his own eyes. "It is not good," he'd said to Toa-Sytell in passing, "for even God to sit removed from the pain of His Children; they too easily become abstract, and vague. I must taste the fruits of My commands, all the more so when that fruit is bitter unto death."

By the time the three of them had arrived, the riot was long over. Surgeons had been moving about on the Pit floor, tending to the deep puncture wounds and limbs left shattered by the impact of steel quarrels. Ma'elKoth's first order upon his arrival had been to carry the wounded prisoners up to the infirmary alongside the guards; he, himself, had followed.

With Toa-Sytell at his side and Berne trailing behind with cynical reluctance, Ma'elKoth had stopped at the bedside of each wounded man, spoken with each, and summoned his power to stroke away the pain of every wound with the warm paternal pressure of his enormous hands.

He opened the Imperial treasury to recompense two of the warrior-priests of Khryl, hastily summoned from their beds at their small sanctuary on Gods' Way. Toa-Sytell had watched the creases of empathetic pain deepen across Ma'elKoth's brow as he came upon men with limbs shattered beyond hope of even magickal repair; he saw crystalline tears swell in the Emperor's coal black eyes as he blessed each of the dead.

"Not even I, Emperor and God, can see beyond this portal," he'd murmured, unaware that Toa-Sytell could overhear. "I wish you well, each of you, on your journey, or the peaceful slumber of oblivion, whichever you encounter."

When they had returned to the Donjon, the only remnants of the riot still visible from the Pit balcony were the pools of clotting blood on the floor.

"Quite a piece of work," said Count Berne, sounding bored. He leaned against the balcony rail at Ma'elKoth's side opposite from Toa-Sytell, with his back to the Pit while he examined his fingernails. There was an edge to Berne's nonchalance, though; Toa-Sytell sensed that Berne overplayed it, just a bit, and he wasn't sure why.

"Caine's turned out to be an expensive indulgence, don't you think?"

Ma'elKoth's only answer was a subterranean rumble from the bottom of his chest.

Toa-Sytell coughed pointedly, and then said, low enough to be heard only by the Emperor and his Count, "I have not yet determined what, precisely, went wrong. The sentry from the rooftop guardwalk was found much more swiftly than can be accounted for by the normal routine of foot patrol. Does the Emperor wish me to pursue this, as a line of investigation?"

As he spoke, he kept his eyes on Berne, not Ma'elKoth, and so he caught the subtle flicker in the Count's eyes, the tiny crack in his mask of unconcern. So, indeed: he knew already where such an investigation would lead.

But Ma'elKoth shook his head shortly. "No. You must bend all your efforts as you would a bow, with shaft aimed directly at recapturing Lamorak and the woman, and Caine. Anything less would be unconvincing to Our enemies; Caine must be given every chance for success."

Berne glanced to his side and found Toa-Sytell staring at him; their gazes met for a brief, significant moment beneath Ma'elKoth's chin. Berne forced a friendly, slightly sheepish smile, which Toa-Sytell returned with a bland *I'll be watching you* stare. Berne shrugged and went back to cleaning his nails.

"What if," Toa-Sytell asked slowly, "what if we catch him?"

"I surmise, in that event," Ma'elKoth replied, "that a substantial number of your men will die."

He shook his leonine head in sad disbelief, looking down on the clot-dulled surfaces of the blood pools that scattered across the Pit and on the balcony itself. "Twenty-seven men and women killed. Twenty-five wounded, maimed, some crippled. More strokes added to Simon Jester's bloody account—an account that I must share against My Will."

"The Emperor will pardon my saying so," Toa-Sytell murmured, "but that seems to be an inevitable consequence of associating oneself with Caine."

The Emperor nodded slowly, lowering his head as if in prayer. "Yes. And I knew this when I sought him." He released a long, slow sigh. "Twenty-seven dead . . . such boundless slaughter."

He lifted his eyes as though looking at something deep within the stone, or something far beyond it.

"Caine could hardly cause more damage if he were, himself, an *Aktir*."

14

ALWAYS CLEAN, ALWAYS crisp, brilliant white teeth gleaming within his polished smile. "This is *Adventure Update*, your only Worldwide Twenty-four-hour Source for Studio News. I'm Bronson Underwood.

"It's now noon, Ankhana time, and this is our latest update from the Studio on Caine's progress in his desperate search for his missing wife, Pallas Ril. As you can see by the Pallas Ril Lifeclock graphic in the corner of your screen, our best estimate leaves her with less than eighty hours remaining, plus or minus ten hours—perhaps as much as nearly four days, or as little as less than three. The entire world waits breathless, hoping and praying that Caine can find her in time. Here's Jed Clearlake."

"Thank you, Bronson. Our report from the Studio this hour has Caine still holed up in the Warrens with the native woman Talann and Lamorak—that's the Actor, Karl Shanks. The Imperials are engaged in a manhunt on an unheard-of scale, flooding the city with troops, searching door-to-door for the escaped prisoners. It's making Caine keep his head down, and I can't imagine he's very happy about it."

"I'm sure he isn't. What's the status on the search for Pallas Ril?"

"As you might recall, Bronson, Caine organized last night's unprecedented escape from the Imperial Donjon, at extreme personal risk, in hopes that one or both of Pallas' companions could lead him to a prearranged rendezvous with Pallas herself. This hope has been dashed by the extreme nature of the Imperial response, making it simply too dangerous for them to move about the city. The rumor is that friends of Caine are checking the meeting places even as we speak."

"And, I'm told, the situation there is interesting, politically."

"Politically?"

"*Sexual* politics, Jed."

"Oh, yes—" a dry chuckle "—well, yes, indeed. Most of the world knows by now of the astonishing measures Caine took last night to save Lamorak's life. Caine and Lamorak are in real life quite good friends—I don't know if you know that, Bronson. What our viewers might not know as well is that Lamorak and Pallas Ril are also good friends, *close* friends; perhaps very close friends indeed."

"I've heard some rumors . . ."

"They're not only rumors, Bronson. It's been kind of an open secret for some time, now. The question is, how much of this does *Caine* know? The Studio isn't saying. I think the question on everyone's mind is: what will Caine do when he finds out?"

"That's a good question, Jed—interesting for us. For Lamorak, I'd guess, it's rather terrifying."

"Well, Bronson, as they say, Lamorak's made his bed, and now he has to lie in it." Another dry chuckle. "From Studio Center in San Francisco, I'm Jed Clearlake."

"Thank you, Jed. In our next hour, we'll have a Studio expert on—are you ready for this?—'chaotic perturbation in multidimensional superstrings' here, live, to take your calls. He'll be explaining why we have such a large margin of error in our estimated Pallas Ril Lifeclock, and he'll be answering your questions about the Winston Transfer. I'm Bronson Underwood. Stay with us."

15

ARTURO KOLLBERG STUFFED another cake roll into his bulging cheeks and glared at the huge, curving POV screen. Every time

Caine glanced away from the sunlit street outside to the ragged straw-leaking pallet on which Lamorak lay bundled in dirty blankets, the chant inside Kollberg's head gained force, became a mantra, an incantation.

Die, you bastard, die. Die, you ratfuck, die die die.

But he wasn't dying. When Caine and Talann had finally hauled him up out of the caverns, he was unconscious and shivering in deep shock; he should have died a long time ago. But they'd kept him warm, and now from time to time he woke up and they'd feed him warm broth provided by the Subjects of Cant. He'd pulled magick of some kind or other to help himself recover; they'd even managed to splint his leg while he used magick to dull the pain and relax the convulsive cramp of his thigh muscles around the tearing ends of bone within.

His leg swiftly and efficiently set, Lamorak had claimed he'd be able to walk with a crutch by nightfall, and then he'd promptly fallen back asleep. Caine and Talann and the amateur surgeon from the Subjects of Cant had taken advantage of his unconsciousness to unstitch his thigh and wash the insect eggs from the wound with the strongest brandy they could find, then resewed it and stitched together the deep slash across his abdomen, as well.

Anger had taken Kollberg wholly as he'd watched this, and he knew he couldn't let the negative emotions rule his judgment; he swallowed another capsule of amphetamine and stuffed his mouth with sweets before the drug could kill his appetite, and he began to feel a little better.

And through it all the chant had rung in Kollberg's brain, losing all sense, a meaningless singsong collection of syllables that would have, if there was any justice in the universe, driven the breath from Lamorak's lungs and stopped his treacherous little heart.

Whenever the glowing mushroom of the emergency transfer switch crept into the bottom of his peripheral vision, his chest tightened and his teeth clenched. He wasn't helpless here, he kept reminding himself. Caine's little crack comparing the Shaft to a Labor slum had been nearly pointed enough to justify yanking him. *It's timing, y'see, that's what's important now,* he told himself. *Timing is everything.*

"MAJESTY'S ON HIS WAY," the kid says, and he sounds a little awed. "I never seen Majesty come *out* for somebody . . ."

I look away, out the small window; I don't want to admit that I don't remember his name. From where I sit, here on the sharp terminus of sun and shadow, I can see the spot in the bazaar where I leveled this kid with a mutton leg a couple of lifetimes ago, there by Lum's shack in the curving shade of the stadium wall.

"What about Pallas?"

"Nobody knows where she is, Baron. Tommie 'n' me, we went there, an' nobody's there. I mean, we waited and everything, and Tommie's still there, but I don't know."

A glance at Talann where she sits on the floor near Lamorak's pallet, a glance that she returns with an irritable shrug. "It's the only one I remember. I can't help it."

No, she can't. It's amazing that even one meet point leaked through the shield of enforced forgetfulness of that goddamn spell. She's been getting more and more cranky ever since I explained what Pallas did, and I don't blame her.

"Yeah," the kid says, "nobody's seen her since the big shitfight yesterday."

"You've *seen* her?"

Something that's been squeezing my chest suddenly lets up. I can breathe now, and I gasp, "Is, is she well? Was she hurt? How did she look?"

He grins at me. "Pretty damn good, considering half the damn Grey Cats were chasing her down the street. That's when the shitfight started."

"The shitfight?"

"Yeah, Baron, sorry, thought you knew."

And he tells a pithy tale of Pallas taking on the entire Grey Cats in the Industrial Park; he makes it sound like she blew half the place up in the process of leading them toward the Warrens, and he proudly recounts how he himself had been there, had answered the call, and had personally thrown a wet clod of shit that splashed the face of Count Berne himself.

I can't help but laugh as the kid mimes Berne's astonished outrage at this maltreatment; the story kindles an unexpectedly warm feeling toward this kid—my god, my god, how I wish I'd been there to see it. He plays up to my reaction, doing the take over and over again, broadening it each time, until finally I wave him to stop. Even the idea of Berne taking a fistful of shit in the face stops being funny eventually . . . well, after the hundredth time or so . . .

And there's maybe a little twinge here, a thumb in my ribs beneath my laughter, a ghost of a stab that she's handling everything so well without me. Maybe I've been nursing an ignoble hope that she can't make it without my help, that she needs me more than she's ever admitted. Maybe it stings a little, that she's put herself up against Berne, who nearly killed me, and Ma'elKoth, who could crush me like a housefly in his fist, and she's holding her own. She's free and effective, and the refugees she's hiding are still out there somewhere. If it wasn't for this unexpected side effect, I'd have no reason to be here at all.

"You have any idea how she ended up taking on Berne and the Cats?" I ask. "I mean, how it started? Why she was there in the Industrial Park?"

He shrugs. "I dunno. I think somebody told me something . . . nah, I don't remember. Not important, is it?"

"I guess not. Thanks, kid. Do me a favor: Get back downstairs and keep an eye open for Majesty."

The kid thumps his mailed chest in that silly-ass salute the Subjects favor, then coughs and rattles the hilt of his shortsword, checking that the blade's loose in its scabbard; then finally, having thought of no further excuse to remain in my presence, he turns on his heel in a sloppy imitation of a military about-face and hustles out of the room. I listen to his boots clomp away on the soft and sagging dryrotted floor, and try to remember what it was like to be that young.

It's hopeless: that was too many lives ago. I go back to looking out the window.

Over by the stadium a regular army platoon of heavy infantry fans out, sweating under their cuirasses, looking pissed and mean. They're arresting passersby at random, questioning them, sometimes slapping them around. Heavy clouds move toward the sun, up from the western coast: it's going to rain, again, which should do wonders for the soldiers' moods. Go from sweat-boiling miserable to drenched and chilled and miserable, and have an endless supply of commoners to take it out on—it's a soldier's dream.

"There *is* one thing I remember," Talann says slowly, after a while and in a tone so excruciatingly casual that it makes me think she's been working on exactly how to say this for a couple of hours at least.

"About Pallas. In spite of this whatever-it-is spell. I remember how close she'd become with all of us. How much she cared for us—especially Lamorak."

I've been gut-punched by experts, y'know, once even by Jerzy Kupczin, who was, at that time, heavyweight champion of the world. This doesn't hurt much more than that did.

Is there anyone who doesn't already know about them?

I take a long time answering, a long time to look down at Lamorak's face, still surfer-perfect even under the swellings and the bruises. His face is all I can really see of him; it pokes out of the blankets he's wrapped in, eyeballs twitching spastically behind closed lids; he bubbles a moan and twists within his dream, and I wonder if he's dreaming about the Theater of Truth.

I hope so.

"Yeah," I say. "She's real caring, that way."

"I know she'll be really, really grateful for what you've done." She's drifting toward me. "Especially for Lamorak."

Now I spend another long minute or two staring at Talann, now only an arm's length away. Cleaned up and dressed in the same style of loose cotton tunic and breeches that she wore when I saw her secondhand, she's one of the most spectacular women it's ever been my pleasure to meet.

Even if the cotton of her clothing were heavy enough to leave much of anything to the imagination—which it isn't—I had plenty of time back in the Donjon to appreciate the smooth curves of her form, the play of muscle in her legs and ass. Her platinum hair shines now, stripped of grease and filth, and forms an aureole of sunlight that perfectly frames the gentle curve of her cheeks and her jaw, lightly frosted with down. She's so beautiful, and so courageous, with the singing dash of a real hero, and so impossibly skilled that she must have a dedication to her arts of fighting that far surpasses my own. I could reach out and touch her now, brush along her jaw with my fingertips, and draw her to me.

Her violet eyes are deep enough to swim in. As I watch her, she takes a slow breath, gently arching her back in a motion that's almost imperceptible, to bring her nipples rubbing gently across the shirtfront and draw my eyes.

I've seen it done better—but right now I can't seem to remember when.

She's fishing, just tossing out a line to see if anything rises to nibble. That's what this shit about Lamorak is, too, slapping the water to beat a fish toward her nets, and I guess I'm an idiot.

I must be an idiot, because I don't want to be caught.

"Drop it," I tell her. "I know all about it."

Her eyes go wide. "About—?"

"Lamorak and Pallas. I know what's between them."

She looks stunned. "You *know*? Then why did you—how could you . . . I mean, Lamorak and Pallas, and what you've done . . ."

A very, very strong man who is somehow small enough to fit inside my skull begins to pound on something behind my eyes. He's using a morningstar.

"Can we not talk about this, please?"

"Is it . . . ? I mean, Caine, please, I'm sorry to pry, but—are you and Pallas done, then? Is that past?"

The guy in my head trades in the morningstar for a chainsaw, and it snarls in my ears. "She thinks so."

"Caine . . ." The hand she lays on my shoulder, alongside the bandage strapped crosswise over my trapezius, is warm and strong, and the squeeze she gives seems to reach down into the muscle and start to loosen its knots. I meet those violet eyes of hers and . . . She's not making a pass at me, that's not what this is. This is something far more seductive and lethal than a subtle offer of sex. She's offering me understanding.

"It must hurt."

I deliberately mistake her meaning. "No, the river washed it clean. I don't think it'll infect."

This doesn't fool her at all. She settles back into a Warrior's Seat, legs doubled beneath her, and watches me with otherworldly calm.

I shrug, and pain stabs through my wounded shoulder—it hurts a lot more than I was pretending. I spend a couple of breaths summoning the Monastic version of mindview, the control disciplines. The guy with the chainsaw in my head wanders slowly away—even though I can still feel him in there, off in the distance but still inside my skull—and the pain ebbs from my shoulder. I spend most of my attention on massaging my swollen knee and wishing for an ice pack. By concentrating on that wound, I can talk about my other, more serious one.

"What's between Lamorak and Pallas, that's their business," I say, low. "It's got nothing to do with me."

Talann manages to look skeptical without altering her expression.

"No, it's true," I insist. "It doesn't matter."

Her voice is as warm as an arm around my shoulders. "But, Caine, it *does* matter. It's eating you up. Anyone could see that."

"It's their business," I repeat. "How I feel about Pallas, that's my business."

"Then, for you—" The curves of her face seem to sag, just a little. "—for you, it's not past."

My head feels as heavy as a wrecking ball. "No, it's not past. It'll never be past. I've made promises, Talann, and I keep my word. Till death do us part."

She doesn't know the reference, of course—marriage in the Empire is more a business deal than a sacrament—but she gets the message, nonetheless, and she shakes her head in wonder and disappointment.

"What kind of man will go so far—nearly get himself killed again and again—to save the life of his rival?"

A fucking idiot, that's what kind.

"It's sort of difficult to explain."

She places her hands on mine, covering them there on my injured knee, and waits until I have no choice but to meet her eyes. Deep inside them something is dying, like the last fading scraps of a dream you can't quite remember when you wake up, and she says, "I hope Pallas Ril understands what an extraordinary man she is throwing away."

Now I have to laugh; it's the only reaction possible, short of outright tears. I feel the laugh inside, but I have to force it a little to get it to come out—a bitter chuckle.

"Oh, she understands well enough, I think. That's part of the problem: she understands too well."

I guess there's not much she can say to that, because she doesn't say anything, just sits beside me on the floor and silently watches me work on my knee.

Time passes swiftly in meditation: the angle of the sunbeam through the open window deepens perceptibly. After a while, I'm convinced that the swelling is receding—the pain certainly has— and I swim back up to the surface of my consciousness to find that Lamorak is awake and eating some solid food.

He looks at me from under his brows, oddly shy. "You, ah, washed out my leg, I guess. I can see in mindview that the, uh, the eggs are gone. Thanks." He looks deeply, inexpressibly uncomfortable. I hope it's from guilt.

"Ah, and, ah, thanks for saving my life. I owe you."

Yeah? I snarl within my head. Pay me back by staying the fuck away from my wife! But instead I say aloud, "You owe me shit. If it wasn't for that last surge on the Pit balcony, I'd be rotting down the sump right now. We'll call it even."

He looks away. "We'll never be even."

There's some sort of harsh self-loathing in his voice, and a large, petty part of my soul grins wide to hear it.

"Have it your way, then."

Thunder rumbles, not so distant; I wince. It reminds me of Ma'elKoth's voice. The first swollen raindrops beat staccato time on the windowsill, and I close the shutters. I can feel the impact of the rain through the wood, a tiny fractal drumroll like the footsteps of scattering rats.

Within half an hour Majesty arrives. He slips in through the door, alone and strangely furtive, shedding his wet cloak as he comes. Talann rises, smoothly uncoiling into a fighting crouch—she, of course, has no idea who he is, and she's not taking any chances. I slow her with a hand on her arm and nod to him.

He looks us over, breaking into that wiseass half grin of his, and shakes his head. "Hot staggering *fuck*, Caine, you sure know how to stir the shitpot."

"It's a talent. Talann, meet the King of Cant. Majesty, this is Talann, a warrior and companion to Pallas Ril."

He looks her over with naked appraisal before extending his hand in greeting—his appreciation of feminine musculature is every bit as developed as my own. When I introduce him to Lamorak, Majesty's wiseass grin returns.

"Aren't you the guy that used to carry Kosall? You know Berne's got your sword?"

Lamorak winces, nodding, and Majesty goes on with a low whistle of mock sympathy. "Boy, that must sting. Kinda like gettin' your dick pulled out by the root, huh?"

We make small talk about the manhunt and the general uproar in the city, and of course he's got to hear the story of our escape from the Imperial Donjon. I have a really hard time keeping my impatience under control; wasting time on jibberjabber, when I'm this close to finding Pallas, is just about more than I can take.

Besides, hearing the story of my heroic rescue reminds me exactly how I got into the Donjon in the first place, the metaphoric woods through which my backtrail leads, and I can't think about that too much. If either one of them finds out I've been hired by Ma'elKoth—

I'm not sure I'd live long enough to explain.

And I wouldn't worry about this so much if Majesty would quit sliding me those significant looks, like he knows something I don't.

Finally, as Talann drags out the fight on the Pit balcony, I can't take it anymore. "Listen, is this important?" I ask. My tone leaves no doubt about my opinion on this question. "I have to find Pallas. Today. Now."

"This is a problem," Majesty says. "I'd like to find her myself, but I can't put the Kingdom on it."

"You *can't*? Majesty, we've been friends how long—?"

He waves off my rhetoric wearily. "It's not that, Caine. When the Cats hit her yesterday, they were waiting for her outside the spot in the Industrial Park where she had the *tokali* hidden—"

"They—she's—" I sputter. "You *know*?"

"About Simon Jester and this Eternal Forgetting?" He gives me a patronizing *What am I, an idiot?* look. "Of course. Am I not the King of Cant? Though, y'know, I am curious about how *you* don't seem to be affected . . ."

"It's a mystery," I tell him flatly. "All right, go on. The Cats were waiting for her outside the *tokali*'s bolt-hole."

"Yeah, that's right. I figure the way they found her there is the same way they found her here, three-four days ago. Somebody gave her up."

My heart thumps once, heavily, within my chest. "A Subject?"

He nods. "Gotta be. Nobody else could have known. My source in the Eyes has no fucking clue—whoever it is deals straight to Berne and the Cats. Paslava, Deofad, one of the Barons, I don't know. None of the rank and file would have the knowledge to sell, y'know? No stooges at the bolt-hole; she doesn't trust 'em anymore."

"That's why you're walking alone."

"Better believe it. We're gonna have to move you, and I'll need the names of every Subject who knows you're here. If the Cats come here looking for you, that'll narrow the field a little."

"When you find him," I say thickly, "you make sure he lives until I get my hands on him. Will you do that for me?"

He lifts his shoulders. "No promises. I'm a little irked my own self, you might imagine. Giving her up like that . . . If I get my hands on that cockknocker—"

His fingers flex expressively, and blood surges into his face, pushing out veins twisting around his eyes. I squint at him. Something has changed since I talked with him day before yesterday. Then, this business was *just a little jab in Ma'elKoth's ass*. Now it's deadly serious, and more; he looks like he's ready to spit lava.

"Just get me to her, Majesty. That's what's important right now."

His clouded eyes turn on me with knife-edged suspicion. "Important why?"

I never really noticed before how small and piggy his eyes are. The veins around his eyes swell more, as though rage is pushing them closed. "Hey, Majesty, this is me, huh? Get a grip."

"Yeah—" he says slowly, color slowly leaking out of his face. "Yeah. I know. I'm sorry. But she doesn't need your help, Caine; shit, I'm pretty sure she invaded the Miracle the other night and got away with it."

"Really?"

"Mm. Some kind of Cloak—and then a Cloak that cloaks the Cloak, know what I mean?"

I spent almost a year and a half in Battle Magick at the Conservatory before my transfer to Combat, and I understand immediately. Not even an adept can find her, because he can't track her pull—probably an effect of the Eternal Forgetting.

My first honestly happy smile in days grows across my face.

Everyone stares at me. Majesty says, "What? What is it?"

"I," I say cheerfully, "know exactly where she is."

17

" 'STRATOR, IT'S THAT Entertainer Clearlake, from *Adventure Update*. He wants to put a live feed on the net—of the reunion."

"Tell him, ah . . . no, tell him no. The answer is no."

Arturo Kollberg gnawed the corner of his thumbnail as he watched. Caine, ever the professional, ever conscious of dramatic necessity, insisted that Lamorak and Talann accompany Majesty and himself, despite the increased danger of discovery and capture. Arrangements took some minutes—a horse had to be brought for Lamorak, as well as heavy cloaks and hats for all against the rain that sluiced the alleys of the Warrens. They couldn't risk the caverns, for security reasons; too many Subjects would be down there taking shelter from the rain.

A team of strikers was assembled, twelve Subjects of Cant whose job it would be to fan out ahead of and behind the party, to distract and otherwise interfere with any soldiers who showed interest in the group. They'd be sticking closer than such teams usually do, because the rain had become so heavy that visibility was little more than ten or fifteen meters, but that would also limit the activity of the searching soldiers; in all, the rain was a substantial advantage.

Kollberg had alerted the *Update* staff, of course, only seconds after Caine announced he now knew where Pallas was. This Clearlake boy, he had good instincts; the scene unspooled in Kollberg's mind: the anticipation, the approach, the first look, the meeting of their eyes, a line of dialogue—and cut.

Cut before the kiss, just before the first touch—it would play absolutely *nuclear*. It could *double* the advance orders for secondhand cubes . . .

Risky—it'd be damned risky, with Caine acting up, with the Board of Governors' hot breath on the back of his neck. It'd take the kind of personal initiative rarely seen in Administration, the kind of daring, the boldness that bespeaks—even in his mind, Kollberg could only whisper the word—a *Businessman*.

The speed sang in his veins, whispering reassurance: *Go for it, take the plunge, get it all . . .*

On the 270-degree POV screen, Caine's party had now crossed Rogues' Way, heads down into the slant of the driving rain. Kollberg might have only a minute to make up his mind—but if Caine could hold off for, say, ten minutes—long enough for word to spread through the programming centers of the net—everyone would want a piece of this feed, *everyone*, all over the world . . . Why simply offer, why just throw the feed out onto *Adventure Update?*

They'd pay, *all of them* would pay. They'd go for it en masse like a swarm of lemmings; how could they afford *not* to? No channel could afford to be the only one in a market who's not showing Caine and Pallas live. Licensing fees—the licensing fees for these few minutes could pay the overhead for the whole bloody Adventure, with *millions* left over!

Once his decision was made, Kollberg wasted no time in ordering the Studio comm nexus cleared for incoming traffic. A hundred marks per second? A thousand? He let the boys down in Marketing settle on a price that would make program directors gnash their teeth and tear their hair but stop short of actually fainting dead away; then he cleared a line to the *Adventure Update* office.

"Give me Entertainer Clearlake," he snapped. "This is B— Administrator Kollberg."

But not for long; I can feel it: not a mere Administrator for very much longer.

18

THE VOICES THAT speak from five billion wallscreens across Earth use tones of urgency that are usually reserved for declarations of war. Nearly all of the voices speak English; the few remaining ethnic channels that struggle for market share in their isolated backwaters are too poor to pay the Studio's per-second asking price. The words spoken by these disembodied voices vary from channel to channel, but their meaning is identical: *You must watch this. You must care about this. Nothing else in your life is as important as this.*

And that face, his beautiful, earnest, clean-cut, honest face with the locked-down hair and the eyes with the glycerin glitter. Behind that face there's an emotion so powerful it defies expression, some combination of religious exaltation and bone-deep smugness: *I am here. I know. But you will know only what I choose to tell.*

And there is a power in him; he blazes with it: a furnace of energy that pours into him from the eager eyes of the ten billion people who look at his face *right now*.

"Live, from Studio Center in San Francisco, I'm Jed Clearlake."

19

WHEN MAJESTY SAYS, "This is it," shouting to be heard over the waterfall sizzle of rain on our hats, my heart stammers.

Can I really be this close?

The broken hulk of the warehouse looms shadowy in the fade-to-black grey-scale of the downpour, and a door gapes darkness. A chill river runs down my spine and empties along the leg of my breeches. I look up at Lamorak on the horse and at Talann, who's kept a hand on the horse's bridle throughout this furtive walk:

they're only ghostly silhouettes. I lean close enough to Majesty's ear that our hat brims overlap, providing a handbreadth of sheltered air through which to speak.

"Pull your boys in," I tell him. "Best to keep all your strikers here until Pallas is ready to move—we can't have one of them talking about this to the wrong guy."

He gives me that sidelong look again, the way you check something out of the corner of your eye to see if it looks the same as it did full-on, but then he nods.

"Way ahead of you." He lifts his hand overhead and swings his arm in a long arc to call the strikers in. I can't believe they can see it, but shortly men begin to appear, shuffling shapes with shoulders hunched against the rain. "But, I'm tellin' you, we've watched this place. Tommie's here right now. Shit, Berne himself was followed back here; he went inside to search, right after the shitfight. She's not here."

I allow myself a knowing smile. "You don't know her like I do. She had thirty-some people here, set up with food and water, a place to sleep and a place to crap. She's not going to abandon all that, not when she has nowhere else to go, no one she can trust. The best place to hide is where the hunters have already looked." I look around: a dozen Subjects now surround us. "Let's go in."

I lead; Talann follows, drawing Lamorak's horse; Majesty pauses for one last head count before bringing all the Subjects in behind us. Once inside, Majesty directs us through the maze of tumbled, half-charred beams, back to an interior office from which emanates the cheerfully rosy glow of a small campfire.

Built in the center of the floor, out of scraps pulled from the walls, invisible from outside, the fire's keeping the chill off Tommie. He straightens from his squat when he sees me. "Hey, Caine! What're you—" Then he sees Majesty behind me and straightens farther to do the chest-thump salute to me and then to his king.

" 'Sno sign of Pallas Ril, if that's what you're after," he says. "Didja bring anything to eat?"

"Where were they, a basement? Where's the door?"

"Right there." He points. "But . . ." Now through the empty doorway he can see Lamorak on his horse, which snuffles irritably at the fire, and Talann, and the other Subjects, and he shakes his head in wonder. "Outa all you bastards, nobody's got nothing to eat?"

By this time I've taken Tommie's lamp and lit it with a splinter from the campfire. I pull open the door and start down the squealing stairs; Majesty's right on my heels. I can't breathe—surging adrenaline makes my whole body thrum like a plucked bowstring.

I made it. I made it in time, with time to spare. I can't believe I'm really here, really doing this. My stomach churns in time with my spinning brain, and we finally reach the basement floor.

"See?" Majesty says. "Nobody here."

The floor is stone; it slops with a handbreadth of water that gleams black in the lamplight as it swirls around my boots. Old broken crates and stacks of mossy lumber lie scattered across it, and the combined deepwood smell of mildew and rot plugs my nose like a cork. It's a big room, five-meter ceiling in places brushed by the mountains of old crates, sagging and waterlogged. I move deeper into the room, sliding my feet and feeling my way carefully under the concealing water. There are no doors, beyond the hole cut for the stairwell.

Majesty, out of sight behind me, says, "Dammit, Caine, bring that light back over here. This place is crawling with rats."

Yeah, that's all that seems to live here. I can see their tiny red lamps of eyes staring at me out of the shadows, and once in a while see their sinuous backs writhing through the water past my feet.

"Come on, Pallas," I say loudly. "Quit screwing around. We need to talk."

"Give it up, Caine," Majesty tells me. "There's nobody here—*shit!* Fuckin' rat came halfway up my *leg*! Will you come back here with that fuckin' lamp?"

Could I have been wrong about this? Impossible—this is exactly what Pallas would do.

Isn't it?

"Goddammit, Pallas, you have *no idea* what I went through to get here." A whiny edge of desperation creeps into my voice, against my will. "Drop the damned Cloak. I have *news from home*."

That's a code phrase that every one of us knows.

And a wave passes over and through me, a ripple through my mind, and now I can suddenly remember that I'm not alone.

As though from the bottom of a deep, deep well I can hear Majesty's gasp.

It's dreamlike—it's exactly like one of those dreams where you're out in public and you all at once remember that you've left your pants at home; this remembering comes in a surging rush, as though I've had my eyes closed and was pretending so hard that I was alone that I'd made myself believe it, but now my eyes have opened, and this reeking basement room is full of people.

It seems like they're everywhere, perched on the crates and the roof timbers, men and women with children clinging close by their hips; they wear clothes that run from the sumptuous brocade of a merchant prince to the filthy, stained rags of a street beggar. But all of them are dirty, faces smeared by days without water enough to wash; all of them are silent; all of them watch me with eyes round in apprehension.

There's a little group that I recognize, a man and wife with two daughters: it's the Konnosi. I nearly nod in recognition before I remember that though I know them, they've never met me. I find myself deeply, inexplicably glad that they've made it, that Konnos' funny self-important researcher act has not vanished from the world, that his wife is still loyal and his daughters still lovely beneath the marks of their ordeal.

And—she's here.

She's standing on a ledge of packing crates high above me, her arms folded over her breasts, one trim leg forward and her hips slightly cocked to emphasize the curve of her slim waist in a way that makes me ache to hold her. Her cloak drapes back over her muscular shoulders, and she gives her head that single toss, to swing the spray of her hair back out of her luminous, bottomless eyes—and y'know, she doesn't look happy to see me at all.

"God damn you, Caine," she says distinctly. "What will it take to finally keep you the hell out of my life?"

20

"CUT!" KOLLBERG SHRIEKED, surging up from the stage manager's station. "Cut cut *cut!*" The techs in the booth stabbed at switches, and instantly one reported that the worldwide live feed had ceased. Kollberg fell back into the chair, trembling with victory.

That was *perfect*. That was better than he could have dreamed. Good god, he couldn't have had a better teaser for a marketing campaign if he'd written it himself. *Will Pallas survive?* It wasn't yet certain. *Can Caine save her?* No way to yet tell. *What will it take to win her back?* It was anyone's guess.

He eased deeper into the chair, twitching in every muscle, squirming in a sort of sexual afterglow.

Perfection.

21

MAJESTY BABBLES SOMETHING, off on the other side of a stack of crates—he's out of sight near the stairs. I struggle with a swelling roar in my ears, a thousand petty echoes of my voice, whining in righteous outrage: *After all I've done for you, this is how you treat me.*

"I meant it, Pallas." I keep my tone pretty level, I think. "About the news from home. We need to talk."

She sneers back at me with undisguised hostility. "I know why you're here, Caine, and you can tell those greedy bastards that I'm handling things just fine, thank you. I don't need your help. You can go home."

We both know which greedy bastards she's talking about. "It's not what you think—"

"Then I suppose I should feel lucky to have you here to set me straight. Go on, Caine, tell me what I should think."

It'd be easy, so easy and seductive, to let that tiny, searing spark of anger behind my ribs flare up to full life, to dive right back into the shouting, the name calling, the snarling toe-to-toe gut ripping that poisoned the final months of our marriage. In a way, she trained me for it: at first, it was a problem that I never raised my voice; only later did the problem become that we raised our voices too often.

Now I hang on, hold my temper with both hands: this is her life at stake. My wounded pride is meaningless here.

"Please," I say simply, setting the lamp on a nearby crate to empty my hands. "Please, let's not fight. Five minutes alone, to talk. Then I'm gone."

The hard-set lines of her face soften for a moment: she was winding up for a brawl, and my preemptive surrender has taken her off guard.

She looks down at me from her high perch surrounded by the *tokali*. For an instant I feel her really *see* me; for just that one precious moment when our eyes meet she's looking at *me*, instead of looking at the mental image of me that she carries in her head, the image that's sullen and cynical, that casually homicidal villain who's caused her so much pain.

We both carry those images, those built-up mental constructs. I think we've spent so long talking to ourselves, inside our own heads, arguing with an imaginary Caine, a fictitious Pallas, that we've virtually forgotten the reality that hides behind them.

Yet, here we are, and I can read inside her eyes. I can see that there's still something there when she looks at me, and she must see the same, that it doesn't have to be over for us. Her lips part as she takes a breath to speak—

A voice from behind those crates, from out of sight at the stairs, comes hoarsely. "Hey, Pallas. Bet you never thought you'd see *us* again."

Lamorak.

I can't see him, but she can from her high perch, and her face lights with a radiance that I haven't seen there in years. Her lips move, she mouths part of a name that her conditioning won't let her finish, that my conditioning won't let me repeat—it begins with a *K*.

"Lamorak!" she cries. "Oh great god, Lamorak!"

She scrambles down off the crates and splashes joyfully toward him. "And Talann, you're *alive*, I can't believe it!"

She's forgotten I'm even here.

There is a happy buzz among the *tokali*, and many of them move toward the stairs, crowding toward the returning heroes. The basement echoes with splashing and happy babble, and I stay put for a bit.

I stand there with water lapping up the sides of my boots and stare at the deserted crates around me, and I listen to them all. I don't think I can stand to watch this part, the part where she falls into his arms and covers him with kisses.

So I wait, and I wait, and the longer I wait the more pathetically ridiculous I feel, like an adolescent sulking in a corner at a high school dance. Only a couple of minutes pass before I can't take it anymore; besides, seeing her in another man's arms is something I'm gonna have to get used to, sooner or later.

With effort, I join the others. I move out of the darkness, into their circle of lamplight.

Many of the *tokali* are crying. Many of them try to keep a hand touching Lamorak or Talann, as though ensuring that these are not ghosts, not apparitions that will disappear as soon as their backs are turned. Pallas is between them; Talann is at her side, but Pallas' arms are around Lamorak's shoulders, there on the stairs, where he sits with his broken leg out before him.

I can't help thinking, can't help remembering that in the Theater of Truth, in the Donjon, during the whole escape, he never once asked about her. Not once. From Talann, it was one of the first things out of her mouth: *Did Pallas send you? Is she well? Did she escape?* Not Lamorak.

I wish there were some way I could tell Pallas that without making myself look like a petty, jealous asshole—which, of course, is exactly what I am.

Pallas now looks at me with shining eyes and speaks in a breathy voice. "Is this true? You broke them out of the Donjon? Alone? You?"

I shrug. "It was the only way I could think of to find you." Well, sort of; but the truth would serve nothing, here.

Lamorak murmurs: "He saved me, saved my life over and over. There were plenty of chances; he could have left me behind and no one would have blamed him. Not even me."

That's a painless display of nobility for him—scraps from a rich man's table.

Pallas gazes adoringly into his eyes; then she suddenly glances at me as though she's only now remembered that I'm in the room. She starts to blush as she delicately disentangles herself. Seeing her effort to be considerate of my feelings hurts as much as seeing her arms around him did.

"Caine—I'm sorry, I . . . Well, you know. I thought—"

"Yeah, I know what you thought. Forget about it. Any other time, you'd have been right."

"So, mm . . ." She leans forward uncomfortably. "So there really is news from home?"

"Yeah," I say simply. "You're off-line."

All right, I admit it: it's a childish thing to do, but I'm tired of screwing around. I'll let *her* invent the lie to explain to the natives what *off-line* means.

She couldn't look more stunned if I'd beaned her with a rock. Her face goes white, then red, then white again.

She stammers, "For, for how long?"

"About four days."

She takes in this information slowly and chews it over in her mind, and she's thinking about something that I have a feeling I'm not gonna like. She stares through me, at some internal scene beyond this basement, then glances at Lamorak, then at me, and it's me to whom she speaks.

"You're right. We do need to talk. The three of us."

22

TOGETHER WE HALF carry Lamorak back up the stairs, leaving Talann staring mournfully after us. That red surge climbs back into Majesty's face as he watches us go, and his eyes go toward slits until a quiet word from Pallas sets him at ease. We go out past the Subjects, who are cheerfully chaffing Tommie for being fooled, and move deeper into the ruins of the collapsing warehouse.

I've got my good shoulder jammed up hard into Lamorak's armpit; Pallas carries the lamp and helps him along from the opposite side; and I try not to think about the acid disappointment that's eating the pit of my stomach.

Looks like she won't even give me the chance to talk to her alone . . .

We find a sheltered spot, away from gaps where the drumming rain pours through the roof, and Pallas sets down the lamp. The floor is a jackstraw tumble of rot-eaten support members, and the place reeks with the chemical stench of wet charcoal. As we try to gently lower Lamorak to a seat on a fallen timber, he inadvertently grabs my injured trapezius. I wince and grunt, and Pallas looks at me, our faces only a foot apart, close enough that she should somehow sense my ache to touch her . . .

"You're hurt."

"Crossbow," I tell her with a shrug. I know she hates this macho downgrade of pain, but it's a habit; I can't help it. "Through and through, missed the bone. Not serious."

A silent moment cuts deep with sudden, overpowering shame. I can read her eyes: she can't decide how much concern to show. She doesn't want to be cold, but she also doesn't want to encourage me. She can't find anything to say, and it stings me at least as much as it does her, so I let her off the hook.

"What's up with Majesty? Since when is he your guard dog?"

"I, ah—" She shrugs and looks away; she can't meet my gaze as she says this. "I wasn't sure I could trust him. There was too much at stake—"

"What'd you do, lay in a Charm?" I ask disbelievingly.

Her voice is very, very small. "I had no choice."

"Sure you did," I tell her. "It's *Majesty* who doesn't have a choice." The small spark of anger in my chest is suddenly fanned by memories of countless self-righteous lectures from her. "Shit, you used to tell me *I* was the one with no principles."

"You know, you're right, Caine," she says, heat banishing the shame from her voice. "I should have done it your way, and *killed* him."

"Pallas—"

"You know the difference? You want to know the difference?" She gets right in my face, snapping. "A Charm *wears off*—in a couple of days, he'll *get.over it*. How long does it take to get over being *dead*? I found out he's hooked up with Toa-Sytell himself. What would *you* have done?"

Majesty, in bed with the Eyes? So Kierendal was right . . . My voice is quiet and calm, and all I say is, "Oh?"

But she knows me too well; her quick anger flees, and she sags tiredly. "Don't do it, Caine. I need him, you understand?"

From this range, I can see the red twist of arteries in her eyes, the purple swipes of fatigue beneath them. Her cheeks are sinking into her face, making her eyes larger and more luminous. She's so exhausted she can barely see, and I don't want to fight anymore.

"When was the last time you slept?"

She shakes her head irritably. "I get an hour or two here and there. I'll be ready to move the *tokali* tomorrow morning; I'll have plenty of time to rest after that." She settles back a little; we're so used to shouting at each other that the anger fades as quickly as it grows. "You look like you could use a nap yourself."

I look at Lamorak and find on his face a frown of disbelief that mirrors my own. We both start to talk at once, because neither of us can believe that she meant what we just heard her say: tomorrow? Move the *tokali*? What is she, nuts?

"Stop it." She takes off her cloak, folds it into a cushion, and seats herself on it on the floor. "I've been off four days, that's what you said, right?"

"Yeah . . ." I say reluctantly. I don't want to give her any rope, here.

"So, even allowing for uncertainty and a pretty big margin of error, I have at least twenty-four hours left. That'll be enough to get them out of the city, and well on their way down to the coast."

"That's cutting it awfully close," Lamorak says doubtfully.

"Too damn close," I say. "You've cut it too damn close already. What if something goes wrong? What if you're *caught*, this time? What if you're the one-in-a-million statistic that breaks the lower edge of the boundary? Don't you remember what—" My conditioning locks the words in my throat. "—what . . . it . . . will *do* to you? How are you gonna feel when everything starts to halo out? How long do you think you'll stay conscious?"

I spread my hands, wishing I could find a way to express the throttling horror I feel. "How much time will you have to scream?"

"There are thirty-six people in there," she says patiently, but with the calm finality she's always used to settle arguments. It's her *My mind is made up, don't waste your time* voice. "Innocent people, who will be put to death if I don't save them."

"Fine. Save them. But save them *on-line*. Shit, that's what you get paid for, isn't it?"

"You think I do this for *money*?"

For an instant there's a fresh spark of anger in her eyes—like she's about to step up and start swinging—but then she lets it go. "Caine, you know me better than that." She opens her hands wearily. "I don't even know if I can do it—get back on-line. It's the spell, isn't it? The Eternal Forgetting?"

I nod. "They think so."

"I can cancel it one person at a time. I touch them and tell them they know me, like I did just now with Talann. But who do I touch to get back on-line?"

Me! shouts a primitive part of my brain. *Touch me!* But that's just wishful thinking.

"Break the spell," I tell her. "Cancel the whole fucking thing, and the sooner the better. Nobody knows how much time you have left."

She shakes her head. "I can't do that. The Eternal Forgetting is the only thing that's keeping me effective. It conceals the pull of my magick, lets me walk Cloaked past the best adepts on the planet. And Berne *knows* me, and he knows I'm Simon Jester. I drop the spell, and he and Ma'elKoth suddenly know exactly whom they're looking for. How long do you think I could hide from Ma'elKoth once he knows who I am?"

"Longer than you're going to live if you *don't* drop the spell!"

"But more than my life is at stake, here," she says calmly.

"What if they figure a way to counter it? Ma'elKoth's so far beyond brilliant, he's terrifying. You think he'll never find a spell defense that works? Then while you're still expecting this Eternal Forgetting to protect you—"

"I'm not worried about that," she says with a quick shake of her head. "The man who wrote this spell also invented what's probably the only real defense against it—he's down in that basement right now, Caine. I don't think he's planning to sell his new invention to Ma'elKoth."

"A defense?" Lamorak says. He's got a funny look on his face, like he's suddenly really interested but for some reason is pretending this is just idle curiosity. "What kind of defense?"

"Those silver nets Konnos was using to conceal his family from seeking items," Pallas tells him. "You remember, just before—"

"*I* remember," I cut in forcefully. "And you know what? It's not a new invention. Ma'elKoth already *has* that technology. Fucking Arkadeil was wearing a *whole suit* of that silver mesh while he tortured Lamorak. Tell her."

He gives her a pale, shamefaced look; I guess he doesn't really like thinking about the Theater of Truth. "It's true," he says. "Nothing I could do got through it."

She nods grimly, her eyes fixed on some internal truth. "Not surprising. Konnos freelanced for the government from time to time."

The bottom of my throat burns like I've swallowed acid. "You're going through with it anyway."

"They still haven't made the connection," Pallas says. "They don't realize that it might be a defense; maybe it'll take them another day to work it out. I only need twenty-four hours. It's worth the risk."

"Are you *nuts*?"

"The *tokali*—" she begins.

"I don't give a rat's ass about the *tokali*—"

"You never did. I would never expect you to. That's part of the problem."

The burning in my throat forces its way up into inarticulate snarls. "Fuck. Fuck fuck fuck!"

I stomp around a little bit and bite down hard on my temper. Finally I feel like I can speak again. "Lamorak, *you* talk to her. Anything I tell her, she wants the opposite, no matter what."

"Caine, you know that's not true. That's just childish," she says, and Lamorak frowns like he's been thinking hard enough to hurt his pretty head.

"Caine, I, ah . . ." he says, his voice low and slow. "I'm sorry. I agree with Pallas."

"What?"

"She has to follow her heart, don't you see?" he says virtuously. They exchange a puppy-dog look that makes me want to slap them both. "I support her. I'll help. No matter what."

I lower myself onto the floor, slowly; I'm afraid my head will explode if I move too fast. The stabbing bitterness churns in my stomach. I can't believe it. I can't believe that after all I've gone through, I'm still going to lose her.

Because I *know*, y'see, I can feel it—this is her last chance.

The affair, her thing with Lamorak, that I can handle. As long as she's alive and happy, I can handle it. What I can't face is the thought that she will be gone, snuffed out of the world, that I'll never see her, hold her, stroke her hair, smell the delicate scent of her skin, ever again.

Pallas says, "This is screwing up your Adventure, isn't it?" That suspicious tone is back in her voice.

I lift my head to meet her eyes. "I don't follow."

"Bull*shit* you don't. That's why you're upset," she says, jabbing an accusing finger at my face. "They sent you here to rescue me, and I don't want to be rescued, and it's going to screw with your profit margin."

I sit still for a moment, searching for the flame of anger her tone should have kindled inside my chest, but it's not there.

Ashes, only ashes and bitter defeat.

"Pallas, you can believe me or not, it's up to you," I say heavily. "They didn't send me here to rescue you. They're *allowing* me to rescue you, like in my *spare time*. If anything, they'd prefer that you die—it'll make the story a hell of a lot more dramatic."

She leaves Lamorak's side for a moment. Something in my tone has caught her, and she knows, whatever my many faults may be, I'm not a liar. She crouches just out of arm's reach, and her brows draw together.

"You should explain that," she murmurs.

I shrug and shake my head dismissively. "You ever wonder . . . Do you ever wonder why it is you're fighting so hard to bring down a government that—in broad outline—is kind of like our own?"

She looks puzzled. "I'm not bringing anybody down. I'm just trying to save some lives."

"You're embarrassing Ma'elKoth: making him look like a fool.

304 MATTHEW WOODRING STOVER

His hold on the nobility is based almost entirely on fear of his near omnipotence. But everyone can see that he can't catch you."

Now she frowns, disturbed. "I don't want to topple Ma'elKoth. If anything, he's right"—a twist to her mouth, parody of a smile— "the *Aktiri are* the greatest threat the Empire faces. He's got the wrong *Aktiri*, that's all."

I shake my head minutely, slowly, and I can't hold in the bitter laugh. "If only I could tell you how right you are."

"I don't get you," she says, frowning, puzzled. Then her face clears to understanding, then to wonder, and passes through to wide-eyed horror.

She whispers, *"You?"*

Stupid, stupid, stupid. I'm a fucking *idiot*—I can never seem to remember how *smart* she is. A cascade of denials tumbles through my brain, but none of them can make it to my lips before she reaches out with a tentative hand that holds warm and dry on my wrist, a touch that goes through me like a lightning stroke and stops my mouth, stops my breath, my heart.

"Caine . . ." she whispers. "My god, Caine—tell me I'm wrong. Tell me that's not what's happening."

"That's the deal," I say miserably. "That's what I owe *them*, for the chance to come here. For the chance to save you."

She looks stunned, sickened, horrified beyond words. "Another Succession War . . . and that's the *best* you can hope for; that's what happens if by some vanishingly small chance you don't die a hideous death . . . Caine, I'm not worth that—"

I summon the courage to lay my hand over hers and squeeze. "Yes, you are. You're worth anything."

And there are tears in her eyes, and I wish I had the words to tell her how precious she is to me; she shakes her head, denying it, denying me, denying the infinite value of her life.

"But this is the last one, win or lose, live or die," I tell her. "I fought it—I'm trying to leave that whole part of my life behind, but *they* won't let me . . ."

"You waited too long," she murmurs. "They'll never let you."

Lamorak has been looking from her face to mine and back again, and finally the truth has percolated through the pudding he uses for a brain.

"You've contracted on *Ma'elKoth*?" he breathes. "Fuck me like a *goat* . . . You don't have a chance!"

And he's right, of course. I agree with him completely, but I can't tell him so, because right now, looking at his bruised and battered face, something has shattered an ice mirror inside my head. Its pieces rain tinkling around me, glittering and shining and chilling my back and making the hairs stand up on my arms. The pieces are falling into a new picture, a new mirror that shows a truth I hadn't seen before, and each piece falls into place with a click like the tumblers turning inside a lock.

Fuck me like a goat—it's a common enough exclamation of dismay, or incredulity, I suppose, but I've heard it recently.

From Berne.

Click.

Majesty's voice is inside my head now, repeating, *"Somebody gave her up . . ."*

Louder, more resonant: *click.*

Another *click*, from Pallas' memory that I share: Lamorak at the window, sun glow backlighting his perfect profile as he lights a smoke with just enough pull to be felt outside—a *signal*. And then his own words: *Please believe I never wanted it to turn out this way. I'm sorry, Pallas. And this is where I pay for it.*

And then one more, one that echoes like a boulder down a well, like the final steel-into-wood chock of a guillotine's drop. Ma'elKoth himself rumbles up from the deepest depths of my chest: *I have found that two agents, working separately—even in competition—toward the same end, achieve that end much faster and more reliably.*

Click.

I look into the eyes of this dead man, and say, "You. It's you."

He stiffens; he can see his death on my face, and he doesn't even know why.

"Caine, uh . . . Caine?" he says. "Mm, Pallas, what's—?"

She tries to hold on to my hands as I pull them free and stand. Her words come from impossibly far away. "Caine? What's wrong?"

Her voice is buried by the winds that howl from the abyss in the center of my spirit; their roaring fills my head, presses outward until the entire universe breathes hatred.

I take a step toward him, and I try to bring my voice back from beyond the edge of the world to tell Pallas. I have to tell Pallas—

"It's Lamorak."

My voice is a passionless, mechanical rasp of cinder blocks; no shout, no scream, no howl of rage could ever approach what I feel.

Any chance of expression is snuffed like a candle's flame by the hurricane in my head.

"He's the one. He's the one that—"

But now chromatic, crystalline halos limn Lamorak's face, and the timber on which he sits, and the lamp, and the walls, and Pallas' panicked reach as she extends her hands to me. I turn and I leap for her, to touch her, to complete the circuit, a last desperate attempt to bring her with me, and my outstretched hands pass through her translucent, insubstantial chest, and I fall, gasping and retching out my anger, alone on the transfer platform of the Cavea, in the Studio, in San Francisco.

23

I CROUCH THERE on my knees, fingernails clawing at the seamless flat black plastic, smooth and cool. I'm shaking too hard to try to stand, but I can lift my head, lift my eyes past the row upon row of first-handers, faceless behind the blank plastic masks of their induction helmets, up to the mirrored shimmer of the techbooth panels.

I am in agony, and now, at last, here on Earth, where my conditioning does not block my tongue, I can give a name to my pain. It is the only word that can pass my lips:

"Koll—"

24

"—BERG," HARI FINISHED, full of that indefinable sense of loss that comes from ending an Adventure on the transfer platform, as the senselink was cut off, as he once again became alone, no longer the source of experience for millions. But the loss was a familiar one, and it sank almost without a trace into the ocean of his impotent fury, as all his raging hatred turned and coiled and stabbed him through the heart.

So close—he'd been *so close*. If he hadn't pulled away from her, if he hadn't started toward Lamorak, if he'd been *half a second faster* in his reaction, if his stiffened knee hadn't slowed him—

She'd be here, beside him, now.

She'd be safe.

The bitter wound of this knowledge consumed him: he'd held her life in his hands, and he'd dropped it. For long seconds he couldn't think, could hardly see, could only experience the taste of ashes, the astonishing pain of failure.

All his wounds dragged at him as he struggled to stand: the deeply bruised shoulder joint from Berne's crushing grip; his swollen, fiery knee; the ragged hole in his trapezius that sent fingers of fever toward his neck; the stretched-tight new scar of the healed rip on his inner thigh; the innumerable aches and pains and bruises from being tossed through the air and beaten with iron-bound clubs. Of them all, the one that stripped the most strength from his knees and pressed the breath from his lungs was the knife of regret that lodged in his heart and pounded in time with his pulse.

Only later, slowly, gradually, did the questions start to come muttering through the haze of pain: How did he get here? Why in God's name did they recall him?

What the fuck is going on?

Actors are *never* recalled in the middle of Adventures; it just isn't done. Shit, Kollberg had needed special authority from the Board of motherfucking *Governors* to recall him at the end of *Servant of the Empire*—what could possibly justify *this*?

Why let him try in the first place, if they weren't going to let him win?

He looked up at the blank spreading looking glass of the techbooth wall high above, and opened his hands. He wanted to shout, to rage, to roar defiance, but all that could come from his chest was a ragged whisper.

"Why did you do this to me?"

25

THE TECHS IN the booth sat at their stations but only stared, silently wide-eyed. Not one was brave enough to say a word, to ask any of the questions or make any of the remarks that were in all their minds.

"That," Kollberg said distinctly, "was a malfunction. Am I understood? A *malfunction*. You know your jobs. Do them."

Slowly the techbooth came back to life as one tech, then another, then all of them turned to the tasks of closing down the transfer mechanisms and bringing the first-handers up out of senselink.

Arturo Kollberg cradled his fist to his soft and rounded chest, the fist that he had bruised on the emergency recall switch. He was painfully aware of how little sleep he'd gotten, the amphetamine-masked exhaustion that was the result of the state of continuous nervous excitement of the past three days, especially this last twenty-odd hours since Caine came back on-line.

He'd been drowsing in his chair despite the drug, almost dozing off in the afterglow of the successful live feed, when he'd been yanked bolt upright by Caine's line about *toppling a government so much like our own.* He'd struggled heroically against the fog in his brain as he listened with growing incredulity to the conversation that followed, and he cursed himself for inattention, for waffling. He'd left it too long, let too much go out. By the time his horror finally overcame his natural inertia and he'd slapped the switch, it was too late.

There should be a feeling of triumph, here, however petty that triumph might be—he'd finally *gotten* that bastard, finally showed Caine and Michaelson both who was really in charge around here—but instead there was a taste of dust in his mouth and an uneasy griping in the pit of his stomach.

He knows. Caine knows.

He looked down through the one-way glass at the transfer platform as Michaelson, below, lifted his eyes toward the techbooth.

He's looking right at me. But . . . that's ridiculous. How could he know I'm up here in the booth?

One of the techs whistled to himself, low and slightly awed. "He looks kinda angry."

Another tech forced a weak chuckle. "It's a whole different feeling when he's looking that way at *you*, isn't it?"

Kollberg huffed a sigh through his nose and thumbed the key to connect his intercom mike to the Security office.

"This is Kollberg. Send a riot team to the Cavea. Full gear."

This was one of the reasons that Actors were never to be transferred in the midst of an Adventure: any emotions Caine was feeling right now would be chemically echoed in the bloodstreams of the five thousand first-handers. Even the tranks that were being fed through their simichairs' neurochem drips didn't entirely eliminate the possibility of trouble.

And then there was Michaelson, who wasn't getting any tranquilizers at all.

Even as Kollberg finished speaking, Michaelson pushed himself upright and began to walk slowly and carefully down the long flight of steps at the side of the ebony ziggurat of the transfer platform.

Kollberg pressed his lips together and tapped his fingers against one another in series: index-middle-ring-little, over and over again, obsessively focusing on the inaudible four-beat drumroll. He'd have to say something, do something that would keep Michaelson on the platform, at least for the couple of minutes it would take for the secmen to arrive in their cardinal red body armor, with their stickyfoam and power rifles loaded with gelslugs.

He keyed the mike for general address, and his amplified voice boomed through the Cavea. "Michaelson? Er, Caine? Please stay on the platform. We've had a transfer malfunction. We're trying to correct it right now; there's a chance we might be able to send you back immediately."

That should handle him; Kollberg turned his attention to his real problems. First, he'd have to find some way to mollify the chairmen of the linked Studios around the world; they would probably all call en masse to shout and scream and variously vent their outrage at this interruption of Caine's Adventure. Kollberg expected these calls to begin any second, but this wasn't his biggest problem.

He was also expecting—dreading would be a better word—a call from the Board of Governors. He'd have some explaining to do. Even the thought of dealing with that blank screen and digitally modulated voice twisted his guts into knots that seemed to tie his throat closed as well. He needed that confidence back, that rush he'd had with the live feed; it seemed now that he'd crashed as far as he'd risen. With trembling fingers, he opened the carton and pried out another capsule. He turned away from the techs and dry-swallowed it painfully.

"Uh, 'Strator?" one of the techs said dubiously. "You might want to look at this."

"I hardly have time . . ." Kollberg began irritably, but his voice trailed off to silence and his mouth went suddenly dry as he automatically followed the line of the tech's pointing finger.

Far down below in the Cavea, Michaelson was sprinting up the long slope of the center aisle, heading for the door.

This could be a problem.

But problems were what he was paid to handle. With only an eyeblink's hesitation, he keyed his mike for Security.

"This is Kollberg again. Detail three men from the riot team to meet me at my office. *Not* in the Cavea, *not* at the techbooth, at my *office*, do you understand?"

His assistant would have already left for the evening; they'd have the kind of privacy Kollberg wanted for what was to come.

"And not regulars. Specials. I want three *specials* at my office, and three more specials up here at the techbooth. Order them to take custody of Hari Michaelson and escort him to my office. Authorize the use of force."

He turned to the curious techs and looked into the growing apprehension on their faces. "When Caine gets here—and he will, ah, make no mistake, this is where he's coming—tell him I'm expecting him in my office. Nothing more, nothing less. Three secmen will shortly arrive to take him there. It would be best, in fact, if you speak with him very little. I believe that he's, ah, planning to hurt someone. Don't let it be you."

With that, he waddled toward the techbooth door as fast as his jiggling thighs could carry him.

26

HARI LOOKED UP at the blank mirrored surface of the techbooth as the echoing hollow words died away and realized that through this particular looking glass, he could find some answers.

With the thought came instant action: he sprang off the transfer platform and hit the floor running. The five thousand first-handers who filled the Cavea didn't so much as twitch as he passed, still locked deep in the chemical slumber of the sendep cycle that would gradually bring them back to themselves.

Tuxedoed ushers scattered at his approach, and the broad double doors at the Cavea's rear boomed back against the marblepaneled walls when he crashed through them. His injured knee screamed at him with every step, and his shoulder burned, and neither pain could register through the greater pain that squeezed his heart.

An alarm Klaxon blared as he slammed the crash bar of a service door, and the corrugated steel of the tech stairs rang under his boot heels. The long twisting spiral was tall enough to have him breathing hard before he reached the serviceway that circled the Cavea. Far below the alarm still hooted.

He burst through an unmarked door into the sterile monochromatic compartment of the techbooth.

Four men in tech whites stared at him, frozen in their chairs. They all had that pinched, flinching look of physical fear, but none of them seemed surprised to see him. One of them lifted his hands, palms out.

"Hold it!" he said, and patted the air as though Hari were an angry dog who could be stopped with a strong tone. "It was a technical malfunction, all right? A *malfunction*."

"You don't lie even as well as I do." Hari paced toward him. "What happened? Why was I pulled?" He came closer and bared his teeth. "If you start talking before I get within arm's reach, I won't hurt you."

"Chairman Kollberg," the tech squeaked, then coughed and started again. "Chairman Kollberg is, ah, expecting you in his office—"

"He called down here to tell you that?" Hari leaned on the back of the empty swivel recliner at the stage manager's station—and registered that the leather was warm. "No . . . He was here, wasn't he? He wasn't talking from his office . . . He was *right here*."

The warmth on the leather that he felt now, it had come from Kollberg's soft, moist flesh. The idea of it caught in Hari's throat, and he pulled his hand away with a grimace of revulsion. He saw the mushroom-shaped fist button of the emergency recall switch at the top of the panel in front of the chair. It was dark now, dead, but in his mind Hari saw it glow red, saw Kollberg's round and sweaty fist slap down on it. For a moment he entertained a crimson fantasy of ripping Kollberg's fingers off that hand one by one and jamming them down his throat; he shook his head sharply to drive the image away, but it came leaking back.

"In his office, huh?"

"And, uh, uh, Caine? He's already, uh, already called Security—called them before he left here. They're supposed to escort you down there."

Hari nodded. "Yeah. He would."

He understood that the nervous tech was trying to help by telling him this, trying to keep him out of trouble. He also understood that it was far too late for that. "Thanks anyway," he said, and left.

They were waiting for him in the hall outside.

Three secmen, Studio Security in full riot gear: cardinal-colored body armor of carbon-fiber ceramic backed with Sorbathane, mirrored antilaser face shields locked down on their helmets, canisters of stickyfoam at their belts, Westinghouse power rifles with hundred-round hoppers of gelslugs held diagonally across their chests.

They moved with the robotic lockstep precision of Workers.

There were recurrent rumors that the Studio numbered some of the cyborged felons among its Security force. They made up for their lack of higher cognitive function by their perfect obedience; they could not even consider refusing an order.

When Hari stepped out, one of them said, "You will come with us," in a flat, emotionally dead voice, and Hari suddenly lacked the energy to invent a reason why he should resist. He shrugged and kept walking; the secmen fell into step around him, flanking him to the sides and behind.

The secmen herded him out of the service corridors to the gilt-filigreed door of the Chairman's private lift and keyed a code on a view-blocked pad. The elevator carried them down the long, ear-popping descent to Kollberg's subterranean office.

It was cool here, far, far down below the tower of the Studio. Hari remembered the last time he was here, a lifetime ago, how it was almost cool enough to keep Kollberg from sweating—but not quite. The thought of even looking at Kollberg's grey, doughy face made the whatever-it-was he'd eaten last, back there in the Warrens, rise up in his throat.

The door to the inner office stood open, and Kollberg's voice came from within. "Michaelson. Come in. Don't bother to sit."

The secmen didn't follow Hari through the door, but there were three more inside, as indistinguishable as cars from the same plant.

Kollberg sat behind his desk, looking—if possible—more repulsive than usual. The dim light from the night skyline that showed on the repeater gave his pale flesh a greenish cast and highlighted the dark shadows under his eyes. His jowls hung slack, and there was a bitter twist to his bloodless reptilian lips. Not even Kollberg, Hari noted, was sleeping well these days.

"I just got off the screen with the Board of Governors," Kollberg said, "and I am in, ah, *trouble*."

Hari felt a surge of gratification—the bastard wasn't going to get away with this, after all—which was instantly dispelled by the Chairman's next words.

"I am in trouble because I didn't recall you *sooner*. I was there, in the techbooth. It was my fist on the emergency transfer switch. That responsibility was put into my hands directly from the Board of Governors themselves, and now my career trembles on the brink of disaster because *I was too lenient.* I let you go too far."

Hari was acutely aware of a flesh-crawling feeling on the back of his neck, which probably came from the muzzle of a power rifle being aimed there by the silent secmen behind him; it was this that stopped him from going over the desk at Kollberg's throat.

"Maybe you could explain that to me, Administrator," he said tightly, chewing on the courtesy title.

Kollberg steepled his fingers in front of his face. " 'Those who make peaceful revolution impossible will make violent revolution inevitable,' " he said distinctly. "Do you know whom I'm quoting?"

Hari frowned. "Kennedy—John Kennedy, one of the leaders of the old—"

Kollberg's hand slammed down on his desktop with sudden violence.

"No, you slack-jawed piece of Labor trash! I'm quoting *you!*"

Hari stood dumbfounded while Kollberg recounted his recent conversations with the Board of Governors; the Chairman grew angrier and more impassioned, coming to his feet, waving his hands and spraying spit.

". . . and *finally*, in what was probably the *stupidest* single act I've seen you perform in your entire *long career of stupidity*, you come out and tell *a hundred and fifty thousand first-handers* that the Studio, Adventures Unlimited, an *entertainment* corporation, has ordered you to *murder the head of state!*"

All the hurt, all the anger he carried within, boiled until his chest might explode. They'd pulled him, they'd killed Shanna, over his *politics*.

For their image.

The cords in Hari's neck pulled his head down irresistibly, like a maddened bull's, and all he could say was, "It was the truth."

"The truth!" Kollberg snorted contemptuously. "If you're so concerned with truth, why don't you tell your Ankhanan friends who you really are? Why don't you tell Talann how you found her in the Donjon? Don't whine to me about *truth*, when everything you've built your life on is lies!"

"All right," Hari said. His voice had that cinder-block rasp in it again. "I won't. You just tell me one thing. When that all came out, all the shit about my contract, I was sitting there, *holding her hands.*"

He was panting now, with the effort required to restrain his killing rage.

"If you'd pulled me then, the transfer field would have automatically extended, and she'd have come with me. She'd be here now. Why did you wait? *Why did you fucking wait?*"

"Don't shout at me," Kollberg said coldly. "Remember your place. I have had my fill of your insolence and disrespect. Raise your voice again and I'll have the secmen shoot you. Understand?"

Hari ground out, "Why did you wait?"

"I said, do you *understand*?"

Hari forced a "Yes" through his clenched teeth.

"Yes, what?"

"Yes, Administrator, I understand."

"Very well, then. The answer is simple. You are contracted to kill Ma'elKoth; once that is done, you may save your wife, or not, at your, ah, leisure. Not before."

"That's the price, then. That's the real deal."

"Yes. And, furthermore, if you wish the cooperation of this Studio, I expect you to confront and slay Ma'elKoth *outside* the Colhari Palace. The twenty-seven hours you spent out of contact are troublesome enough by themselves. If the climax occurs, ah, *offstage,* so to speak, we won't get any cube sales or rentals whatsoever. Any more inflammatory remarks along the way, and please believe that I won't hesitate to recall you again. If necessary, I'll have you tried for sedition."

The rage drained out of Hari as though a sluice gate had opened in his heart, and Caine looked out from behind his eyes.

"Maybe I should just kill you. Maybe if I kill you, I'll get a better deal from the next Chairman."

"Don't waste my time with empty threats," Kollberg said. "You'll do nothing of the kind."

"That's what Creele thought."

"Eh?"

"Ask me a question, Administrator. Ask me how I knew those King's Eyes weren't going to shoot me on the spot, shoot me down like a mad dog when I killed the Monastic Ambassador. Go on, ask me."

Kollberg sat perfectly still. "Ah—"

"I didn't," Hari said flatly. "Think about it."

The Chairman's eyes slowly widened, and his lips smacked as he started to speak, stopped himself, started again, but he couldn't decide what to say as it slowly dawned on him that he really could die here, in his office, right now.

"You think about that," Hari told him. "You think about that before you decide you can sacrifice Shanna's life for better ratings, for your fucking *margin*—"

Hari's voice trailed away as he heard the words that he had just spoken.

He stood on the carpet, blinking.

For the second time in half an hour, that crystal shower tinkled around him, and the pieces clicked into a new picture.

The Long Form. Lamorak on freemod, cut off from Studio monitoring. Lamorak the traitor. And Kollberg had said something, something about Shanna's Scarlet Pimpernel act working too well, being too easy . . . And the sudden insistence on rank, standard upcaste bullshit to avoid giving a straight answer to a straight question: Why had he waited until *just then* to hit the switch? What was the final straw?

What had he been about to do?

Tell the truth about Lamorak.

And the only way that the truth about Lamorak could hurt the Studio, could hurt Kollberg, was if he was acting according to the terms of his contract.

If someone had *ordered him to give her up.*

"Oh, my god," Hari whispered in awe. "Oh, my fucking bleeding god."

All this brutality. All this pain. The fear, the loss. All the suffering—not only his, but Shanna's, the *tokali*'s, Talann's, the dead Twins, even Lamorak's torture—it all began here. In this office. Behind this desk. Within the squirming maggoty brain of this evil, evil man . . .

"She was right," he breathed. "Shanna was right. It's all about profit margins. About ratings. She didn't pull enough audience, so you had her sabotaged. You had her betrayed so that I'd have to go for her. You could make it a global event. You. Not Lamorak. You."

Hari felt a twisting in his guts, a shimmering in his limbs: Caine coiled there, inside him, hungry, aching for blood.

"What are you babbling about?"

"What did you offer him? I've known Karl for ten years; what could you offer him that would make him do this?"

Kollberg pressed the meat of his lips together into a rumpled, liver-colored asshole. "Michaelson, I don't know what you're talking about, but I strongly suggest that you do not repeat any of these wild accusations outside this office. The Board of Governors wants you *cyborged*, Michaelson, for merely making passing *comments*; it is only my, ah, my *intercession* that keeps you alive and free. Should you speak such treasons in public, I would not be able to protect you."

And then it was too late: Caine surged up his throat and took possession of his brain, and he leaned forward onto the desk and bared his teeth.

"Kollberg," Caine said, "I'm not gonna kill you. I'm not gonna kill you, because that won't *hurt* enough—"

He would have gone on to list the ways that he would inflict pain, to demonstrate them one by one by one, but Kollberg suddenly dove below his desk, shrieking, "Shoot him shoot him *shoot him!*" and the whine of the power rifles in the hands of the forgotten secmen behind gave him only a quarter second's warning before gelslugs poured from their muzzles like water from a firehose and pounded him into scarlet unconsciousness.

27

TALANN HAD A way of blushing that began with a tiny kiss of rose high on her arched cheekbones, then spread like the dawn around her eyes and down her neck. Her uncharacteristically shy smile, and the way she almost-but-not-quite pulled her hand from Majesty's grasp, and her artfully artless answers to his questions, soon had the King of Cant wondering just who was seducing whom, here.

He was only killing time, passing the night in idle byplay, but the longer he wheedled Talann the more interested he became—and more suspicious that she was playing his game better than he was. An enchanting woman, taken all in all, and by all accounts a devastating fighter, nearly equal to Caine—some said better than Caine. The longer they spoke, the more Majesty found his attention drifting off into daydreams of what his life might be like with a Queen of Cant by his side, a Warrior Queen, feared by his enemies but beloved by his Subjects . . .

Fine as she was, though, she was, of course, no Pallas Ril.

He caught himself drifting off again. No question about it, he was losing—and, after all, wasn't this no-longer-casual byplay between them a kind of infighting in itself? And this was a fight where losing might be more fun than winning.

His idle fantasies of family life scattered abruptly when Pallas came back alone. She appeared at the top of the stairs, backlit by Tommie's campfire.

"Majesty—can you get a couple of your boys up here to help Lamorak?"

"Sure," Majesty said reflexively, then he frowned up at her. "Where's Caine?"

Silhouetted by the firelight, the expression on her darkened face could not be read, but in her voice was a troubled, uncertain note. "He's gone."

Majesty and Talann said together, in almost identical tones of dismay, "Gone?"

"He just *left*?" Majesty said, rising, disentangling his hands from Talann's. "You let him go?"

Talann also rose beside him, taking on a look of bruised disbelief. "What happened? What did you say to him?"

"Nothing." Days of exhaustion leached all the color from her voice. "I didn't say anything. He came to deliver a message. He did it; then he left. I couldn't have stopped him."

"I thought—" Talann began. "I thought . . ."

Her voice trailed off, and she shook her head silently; she sank back down to her seat on the stairs and rested her chin on the heels of her hands. Talann looked blankly out over the *tokali* and the Subjects on their crate-built nests.

Majesty barely spared her a glance—that was fun and all, but this was business. He came up the stairs, took Pallas' arm just above the elbow with a firm hand, and gently pushed her away from the stairwell.

Over at the campfire, Tommie and another Subject still warmed their hands. Majesty said, "Didn't you hear the lady? Go get Lamorak. Now."

With under-the-breath muttered protests at the unfairness of life, the two rose. Pallas pointed them in the right direction, and they slipped off into the darkness. As soon as they were gone, Majesty turned fiercely to Pallas.

"For fuck's *sake*, Pallas!" he hissed. "Have you lost your sense? How could you let him walk out of here? I *told* you what Toa-Sytell said—!"

Pallas' eyes had a distant, almost haunted look, lines of deep thought etched around them, as though it was a great effort to pay attention to what Majesty said to her, as though he was only a distraction, an irritation.

"Toa-Sytell was wrong."

"How do you *know*? How do you know Caine isn't running to the King's Eyes right fucking *now*?"

"I know."

The calm of her utter certainty slowed him, but it didn't stop him.

"*How* do you know? I mean, I know it's not like him, but you and Lamorak . . . Jealousy can make a man do funny things, Pallas. We'd better move the *tokali*, y'know, just to be sure."

Her attention seemed to return from very far away, and she looked deeply into his eyes. "We don't have to move them. Caine won't betray us; he can't."

"Yeah, well, it's all very fine for you to have that kind of trust in him, but this is *my* butt, too—"

She shook her head and gave a soft, bitter laugh, as though at a private joke that was more painful than it was funny.

"Trust has nothing to do with it. Besides, he left an hour ago. If he were going to the Eyes or the Cats, they'd be here by now."

"Shit, I'd never have brought him here in the first place if I thought you'd really *be* here. You can't take that kind of chance."

She placed a comradely hand on his shoulder. "Majesty, you did right, believe me. In fact, you saved my life tonight. Tomorrow at dawn, I'll ferry the *tokali* out of here, and all will be well."

She let her hand fall and drifted away from him, down the stairs, deep in her private thoughts.

Maybe all will *be well*, Majesty thought as he watched her back sway tiredly down the steps.

Maybe it will. But if it isn't, Caine had better have some fucking convincing answers. Some things are too low to stand for, even from a friend.

Day Five

"What's so wrong with wanting to help people?"

"Nothing's wrong with it; there's just no point. You risk your life for a wet-eyed thank-you and a hug. It's stupid."

"It's my life."

"No, Shanna. It's our life, remember? That's why we got married."

"Oh, right—I knew there was a reason, I just forgot what it was."

"Shanna, dammit—"

"No, Hari. No. Marriage is supposed to make you more than you are. It's supposed to add something to your life, not take it away. You want me to be less, you want me to be more like . . ."

"Go on, say it. Go on."

"All right, I will: more like you."

"That shit flows both ways, Shanna."

"Maybe it does. Maybe that was my mistake from the very beginning. I should have known better."

1

AS DAWN LAYERED the Ankhanan sky with crimson and pale rose, the low-lying mist that rises from the Great Chambaygen every morning began slowly to recede, traces dissolving in the warming air.

Most of the workmen, the stablehands and the copy clerks, all those who were employed in Old Town but could not afford to live there, walked through the swirling mist toward Fools' Bridge with breeches tied tight at the calf and trouser legs laced closed at the ankle.

This was a fashion dictated by necessity, for also through that swirling mist scampered other inhabitants of the capital city, nocturnal citizens returning to their dens for the day, far more numerous than the human inhabitants. And anyone who'd done the Rat Dance as a panicked rodent clawed and bit its way up the inside of one's pants leg had no desire to repeat the experience.

One particularly large and lean rat with patches of grey at the sides of its muzzle crouched by the notch where the single-leaf bascule of Fools' Bridge would descend. It watched the dawn ceremonies with glittering eyes that held more than rodent intelligence.

This was far out on the arc of the span over the river, over the slow-rolling oily water, glossy black in the growing light. The rat watched the bridge captain stride out alone behind the reinforced crenels atop the Old Town gatehouse, diaphanous robes of translucent aqua flowing over his uniform.

The bridge captain wore these robes twice a day, at dawn and sunset, when he made ritual obsequies to the legendary river god Chambaraya. At dawn, he poured out oil from a golden cup to ask the river god's permission to lower the bridge; at dusk, the cup held wine, in thanks for permitting the day's traffic.

The bridge came down; the rat twitched back from its path, but as soon as the bridge settled into place, the rat streaked for Old Town. Its movements were somewhat hampered by two thin leather thongs like bootlaces that strapped a small packet of oiled paper to its back; the rat nearly perished beneath the boot of a startled soldier who stomped at it as it passed, but it escaped and vanished into the alley behind a nearby stable.

There it paused, as though uncertain of how to proceed; that eerie look of unnatural intelligence was enhanced by the way it sat up on its haunches and rubbed at its face with its front claws, the way some men do when deep in indecisive thought. The rat, however, was neither indecisive nor, actually, thinking; what little intelligence the rat had currently snarled in the back of its brain stem and lusted to chew through the leather thongs that strapped the packet to its back.

The thought, and the indecision, belonged entirely to Lamorak.

2

JUST BEFORE DAWN, she'd kissed him good-bye. She planned to ferry the *tokali* to the river barge in groups of four or five, the largest that she felt she could safely Cloak and still move swiftly through the streets. She'd nodded and stroked his cheek when he told her how he wished he could be with her, how he felt his place was on the street to help protect them, protect her, if only it wasn't for this damned leg . . .

And when she turned away from him, when she climbed the stairs toward the street, that troubled, half-haunted expression had stolen over her face, the same one she'd worn in unguarded moments ever since Caine's disappearance the night before.

It stung him, that look; he knew he was losing her. She'd seen him in the same room with Caine, side by side, sized them up, and somehow he'd come up short. Again. He didn't understand it, couldn't understand it. Why would a woman—or anyone, for that matter—prefer a sullen, scowling murderer like Caine to his own sparkling eye and heroic dash? But there it was: it was happening again like a recurring nightmare.

Somehow, even now, everyone in his life was conspiring to make him feel second-rate.

Stupid bitch.

He'd seen trouble coming last night when she'd made him stay in that dripping frigging room aboveground and waste a good hour trying to figure out why Caine had been suddenly pulled. And she particularly pricked away at what Caine had been about to say— she simply refused to leave it alone. What was he about to say? What was he about to do? What, what, what, why, why, which—on and on until Lamorak was ready to slap her.

Some women, the only way to shut their mouths is to put your dick in them.

He knew damn well what Caine had been about to say, and he knew even better what Caine had been about to do. And he knew that, unarmed and with his leg busted, all he could have done right then was roll over and wait to die. He knew better than to think Caine would have mercy on him just because he couldn't defend himself.

It was galling, too, that everything had been so carefully planned, so well thought out, well concealed, and Caine had jumped right to the truth without any evidence at all. He'd never be able to prove a fucking thing. There'd be no court on either world that would accept his unfounded hunch as evidence. Crap, forget court; it wasn't even, strictly, illegal. But none of that mattered; Caine wouldn't trifle with any sort of legal authority, with any sort of official procedure at all beyond a swift flurry of his slaughtering fists.

This had been much on Lamorak's mind overnight as he'd sat high up above the waterlogged floor in a nest of empty crates that several of the grateful *tokali* had constructed for him. He'd spent the night working on his leg, pulling Flow and visualizing carefully the layering of calcium across the break, knitting the splintered ends together. He hoped that by the time Caine made his next entrance, his thigh might be strong enough to bear his weight and give him a fighting chance.

Not that he had any intention of fighting.

It came to him, in one of his frequent periods of rest, that exactly as he was using his once-despised magick to heal his broken leg, he was also using this same ability to heal his broken life. He'd never quite understood how he could have gotten to be thirty-four without becoming a major star; he'd been so sure, as a boy, as a student at the Conservatory, as a novice Actor on freemod, that he'd someday be recognized as one of the legendary greats, that his name would be entered on that tiny list alongside Raymond Story, Lin Zhian, Kiel Burchardt, Jonathan Mkembe . . .

Hari Michaelson's name was on that list, or so people said. Lamorak couldn't see it, couldn't understand how Caine's career continued to soar while his own languished; Lamorak had found himself at thirty-four, when most Actors begin to make plans for retirement, without ever having cracked the Top One Hundred. Caine was what, thirty-nine? Forty? But Caine would never retire, not so long as his every Adventure landed in the Top Ten as though it grew there. His career had become self-sustaining, feeding on his past successes, to where it no longer mattered if his Adventures were any good or not. People paid and paid and paid, just to be Caine one last time—who knew how long he could keep it up? Who knew what Adventure would be his last?

Who, Lamorak often wondered, really gave a shit?

Just when another man might have become oppressed by a growing sense of failure and inadequacy, Lamorak had instead become aware that the reason behind his continuing disappointment was marketing—or rather, lack of marketing.

Caine got the best Adventures because the Studio executives *expected* him to have the best Adventures, and so they were willing to put out more effort, more money, more promotion to keep him up in his lofty position. All Lamorak needed was a break, one big shot, one opportunity to show the Studio and the public his real star qualities.

He was angling for precisely that: his shot. His big break.

Although as an Entertainer he was nominally a Professional, this was only a provisional recaste; on the day he retired, gave up being Lamorak and became, finally and for all time, merely Karl Shanks, he would reassume his true caste, his birth caste of Business. He could retire tomorrow and take a position with the family business, SynTech, the electronic chemicals giant, and make five times more money than any Actor, even Caine.

But that would mean leaving show business.

That would mean admitting that his father, the spineless flatterer, was right. That his brothers were right, and his mother. They'd all said he'd never make it as an Actor. It would mean going on his knees to his grandfather, the old bastard who still perched on Syn-Tech like a senile dragon on his mound of gold, to beg for a chance to prove himself a real Shanks.

However much he might despise his family, it didn't stop him from using their powerful upcaste connections to pressure the Scheduling Board. He had the Board thoroughly cowed; they were only a pack of butt-covering Administrators, after all. But even with bigger, more frequent Adventures, he still didn't command the kind of promotional budget—and, hence, public following—that Caine did.

Ironically, it was the one man most responsible for Caine's success who'd come to Lamorak with a plan and an offer: Arturo Kollberg.

"Do this one little thing for me," he'd asked. *"Spice up Pallas Ril's Ankhanan operations enough to get Caine involved, and I'll take you under my wing the way I did him. I made Caine what he is, but he's become increasingly sullen and troublesome. I can make you what Caine is, and you won't treat me and the Studio with disrespect and attitude. You'll know how to repay me: with loyalty, with courage and honor . . ."*

And if Caine ever understood what Lamorak was really up to, down deep, that what he was really doing was *helping Pallas' career*—and at great personal risk, I mean, look at this leg, look at how he'd been nearly tortured to death because he'd been doing his part to turn a mundane, run-of-the-mill Adventure into something exciting and memorable—why, Caine would *thank* him. They'd *both* thank him. But no, instead of gratitude, Pallas was running off with her damned *tokali* and fantasizing about her husband, and

Caine wanted to kill him and eat raw bloody chunks of his flesh. It was all so fucking *unfair* . . .

But he knew how to get back at them, he knew how to pay them out for making him a loser: magick. That's what was making the difference now; that's how he could make them regret their disrespect. He was more adept than either of them suspected, and he was going to use this hidden skill to make sure, once and for all, that everyone concerned got exactly what was coming to them—especially himself.

Once this was over and he was back on Earth, his career would really kick into high gear.

He couldn't think about this too much, the images and the fantasies of finally getting the respect he deserved: they were too potent, they intruded too much into his minute-to-minute consciousness. So he held them tenderly at the rear of his mind, carefully foggy and unformed. They lurked behind everything he thought or did and whispered heart-swelling endearments to him—faint and ghostly mumblings that Lamorak never analyzed, because he wouldn't let himself listen hard enough to really understand them.

They murmured that Caine's time was past, that it was right Lamorak should step up to take over for him. They murmured that Pallas had been only using him, after all, and that even the love she had pretended to feel for him would vanish without a trace as soon as they transferred back and she audited Caine's Adventure. They whispered that Caine had been lying in the first place: Pallas wasn't off-line. That was ridiculous. He was only jealous, because his star was fading while hers was on the rise. Caine was trying to destroy Pallas' Adventure, even as Lamorak worked so hard to make it brilliant.

And the final, most potent whisper, least rational and buried the deepest: They were in it together, against him. Caine and Pallas had concocted this whole fantastic plan to make him expose himself, to draw him out where they could humiliate him before the world and destroy his last chance for happiness.

All of these back-of-the-head whispers combined into a powerful feeling of justice—a conviction that he'd really thought this whole thing through and what he was doing was not only necessary, but was right.

He'd begun to deal with what he privately termed *the Caine Problem* last night, after he and Pallas had come back alone from their conference. After Lamorak had been settled into his nest and

Pallas had gone off somewhere to brood by herself, the King of Cant had climbed up next to him and begun half-casually questioning him about Caine.

Lamorak realized with growing delight that the King—however reluctantly—suspected Caine of working for the Imperials!

Once he understood, it was simple to inflame those suspicions while appearing to attempt to allay them. The way Caine had vanished—as Lamorak was forced to put it, "He didn't explain, he just left without a word"—made everything all the better. Lamorak knew that not only could he get away with betraying Pallas and the *tokali*, but he'd be able to pin it all on Caine.

Majesty half believed it already, against his will; that Charm Pallas had laid on him made him fanatically, paranoically protective of her. He'd take any Imperial interference as proof that Caine had betrayed them.

The evidence of the morrow would remove all doubt.

And so when Pallas Ril left that morning, a half hour before dawn, with her four *tokali* in tow, Lamorak had set to work without the faintest twinge; with, in fact, a swelling sense of righteousness and delight in his own skill and imagination.

It was a tricky business: finding a way to ensure that the Grey Cats would interfere at the docks without exposing himself once again to Berne's lunatic temper. The solution that Lamorak hit upon not only satisfied that requirement, but there was a certain sense of tradition to it as well, a sort of metaphoric *rightness* that lent an additional air of conviction to his assurance of success.

Rats were everywhere in this warehouse; the paper, the oil, and the knife to cut the strips of leather were easily obtained from the Subjects of Cant with the explanation that he needed them for the healing magick he planned to do on his leg. Knowing nothing about real magick, the superstitious mopes hadn't even raised an eyebrow.

He found himself a secluded compartment in which to work, and Talann was more than happy to guard the door and ensure that he would not be disturbed. It was the work of mere minutes to pull enough Flow to trap the will of a suitable rat, which he then sent scampering off toward Old Town. He had to stay there and maintain mindview, continuing to pull in order to keep the rat under control, but even that was no danger. If Pallas returned and inquired about the Flow currents swirling toward his compartment, Talann and the Subjects would tell her he was still working on his leg.

It was perfect; it was easy. The indecision that he faced once the rat had crossed the bridge was not a hesitation to betray—he was simply trying to decide which would be the quickest, safest route to the headquarters of the Grey Cats.

3

THE RAT SCUTTLED along Gods' Way with a back-humping lope. It stayed just far enough beneath the boardwalk to be in shadow, dodging curses, horses' hooves, and the occasional boot or hurled brick; the hazards of this open route were much easier to avoid than the dogs and feral cats that prowled Old Town's smaller streets and back alleys. It barely escaped the steel-bound wheel of a nobleman's carriage as it sprinted past the Colhari Palace onto Nobles' Way, then south off Old Town, across Kings' Bridge to the South Bank.

The closest the Grey Cats came to an actual headquarters was the walled compound of the townhome that Ma'elKoth had granted to Count Berne as part of his ennoblement. The rat slipped easily between the iron bars of the gate and ran for the house. All the doors and windows were spread wide, and men lay here and there sprawled in the elbow-to-eyes posture of hungover slumber.

One of them happened to lift his head. Rubbing sleepily at his face, he spied the rat. The Cat jerked awake with a yip of surprise that brought other heads up with dismaying speed and alertness.

The rat did not see Berne anywhere among them—perhaps an upstairs bedchamber? It dashed for the stairs. Despite what appeared to have been some sort of drunken revel the night before, the Cats were awake in an instant with mocking shouts like huntsmen whose dogs have started a fox.

A thrown dagger *thrumm*ed into the floor only inches in front of the rat's nose, causing an abrupt change of direction. Suddenly the air was filled with a rain of steel, hacking into the floor, the walls, chipping large chunks from the hand-carved woodwork of the banisters—all to the sound of the Cats' delighted laughter.

The rat scampered this way and that, still trying for the stairs, and when a pause came in the shower of daggers—perhaps they'd thrown them all?—it sprinted once again for the bottom step. Something heavy struck it in the spine and drew a line of ice across its back; its hind legs twitched convulsively, beating against the floor, and it twisted and squealed and bit at the knife that had struck through its haunches and pinned it to the floor.

All semblance of intelligence fled; now there was only its last instinctive desperation to wound what had killed it, its attempt to leave a mark of its life behind it when it passed.

4

ONE OF THE Cats bent over the dead rat and squinted blearily at the oiled-paper packet before slicing through the leather thongs that held it in place. He examined it against the morning light. "What do you make of this?"

The other Cats gathered round.

He unfolded the paper packet and read:

Simon Jester moves the Aktiri today on a downstream barge for Terana from the Industrial Park docks. A full hood of silver net, draped over your head, will defeat the spell that hides them all.

His eyes went wide, and his heart surged. "Where's the Count?" he snapped. "Who knows where Count Berne spent his night?"

Instead of answering his question, the others babbled questions of their own: The message on the paper, what had it said? Whom was it for? Who'd sent it? He waved the paper over their heads.

"Someone has given us Simon Jester once again; this time we must not fail! Ride to Onetower; command them to stand ready at the antiship nets—and find the Count!"

5

TOA-SYTELL WAS SUMMONED from his breakfast by a breathless page instructing him to attend the Emperor immediately.

He had no need to ask where the Emperor might be; at this time of the morning the Emperor was invariably in the Lesser Ballroom, constructing the Great Work. Art, he had always said, is done best from dawn to noon, its power rising with the sun; done after noon it becomes decadent and reducing, draining power from the artist to replace what it should get from the fading sun above.

In the Lesser Ballroom, Toa-Sytell found Berne already in attendance. The Count wore his fighting clothes, the formfitting tunic and pants of patchy strawberry serge. His stolen blade was shoulderslung. Instead of his usual hungover surliness at this hour of the day, Berne looked rested and ready for action. The glitter in his eyes spoke of an excitement that, for him, came only from the prospect of slaughter.

The Emperor stood beside him, at the cauldron's rim, clay drying and cracking on his crimson kilt. Barefoot and bare chested as he always was when working here, flushed with the heat of the coals that kept the clay boiling, muscle rolled like boulders beneath his skin as he extended his hand to Toa-Sytell.

"Come, My Duke. What make you of this?"

He pressed a fold of paper into Toa-Sytell's hand, but Toa-Sytell's eyes were caught by the manikin that bobbed gently in the steam-misted air, hovering forgotten over the boiling clay of the cauldron.

It was of Caine, yet again; Ma'elKoth had spent all the time allotted for his Great Work yesterday attempting to fit Caine into the gigantic puzzle-piece sculpture, trying innumerable postures and expressions, but finally coming to frustrating failure. Now he must be trying a new strategy, for this Caine manikin was vastly larger, perhaps seven feet tall, matching the Emperor's own stature.

Toa-Sytell frowned. This seemed faintly blasphemous, somehow, though he couldn't put a reason to his feeling. A fundamental pragmatist, he had long ago accepted his inability to appreciate art, but it was disturbing that Caine had come to occupy so large a place in the Emperor's thoughts in so short a time.

Toa-Sytell looked down at the paper in his hand and read there the message of Simon Jester's intention to move the *Aktiri*, and of the hood of silver net.

"Who is the writer?"

"Lamorak," Berne said tightly. "I know his hand."

"Hmpf." He turned the paper over; the back was blank. He shrugged.

"You don't look surprised."

Toa-Sytell permitted himself a razor's edge of smile. "I've known for some time that Lamorak had been, before his capture, your source close to Simon Jester. My impression, however, was that you have had some, mm, falling out. Breaking his leg, ordering that he be tortured to death—these are not signs of a close working relationship."

Berne spread his hands. "He'd outlived his usefulness."

Toa-Sytell lifted the note consideringly. "Apparently not. Though if I'd used a source as you did him, I would never trust his word—"

"We do not."

Ma'elKoth's distant thunder cut off all possibility of discussion. The Emperor laid massive hands on the shoulders of his two servants.

"We cannot deduce what profit Lamorak can hope of this; we must assume that it is part of some tactic. Berne and his Grey Cats will pretend to be taken in by it; they will watch, and search the barges." ˙

"What of this silver hood?" Toa-Sytell asked. "It seems that I've heard some rumor of such a thing—"

"Mmm, yes. Master Arkadeil from time to time employed a certain artificer, Konnos by name, who constructed some of his equipment for the Theater of Truth. The most recent such piece was a suit made entirely of fine-worked silver mesh that would supposedly render him immune to any of the subtler magicks accessible to a Donjon-bound thaumaturge: an expensive piece of work, for which Arkadeil paid, I believe, by having Konnos denounced as an *Aktir*."

The Emperor sighed heavily. "I Myself considered this creation to be of limited utility—anyone wearing it is cut off completely from Flow, and hence is essentially powerless. I may have been too hasty: My feelings were prejudiced by My own strengths. I have ordered several full-sized versions of this silver net constructed, after which I shall conduct My own experiments. For the nonce, I have sent to the Donjon for Arkadeil's suit, which can be cut into material suitable for three or four hoods, in addition to the one that is already part of it. We shall test Lamorak's message in action, as soon as the hoods are ready."

Toa-Sytell nodded up toward the oversized manikin of Caine. "What word do you have from *him*? What does he think of Lamorak's message?"

Ma'elKoth wheeled on him; the hand upon his shoulder became a grip of iron that lifted him into the air. Sudden fury twisted his beautiful face into a demon's mask, and his eyes flared scarlet as the rising sun.

"I do not *know*!" he roared, so loud that Toa-Sytell's ears felt as though they'd been pierced by knives. He felt the actual heat of Ma'elKoth's gaze upon his skin. All the breath left his lungs along with the strength from his limbs. He hung like a hare in the jaws of a lion.

Throughout the Lesser Ballroom the pages jumped at the crash of the Emperor's voice and exchanged fearful glances; no doubt every sleeper in the Palace awakened in panic as though from a nightmare. Toa-Sytell had a sudden feeling that across the city, throughout the entire Empire, every man and woman and child who had undergone the Ritual of Rebirth paused as the routine of their lives was suddenly interrupted by a rush of indefinable unease. He felt that every Child of Ma'elKoth had a premonition of some unforeseen disaster.

An instant later, Toa-Sytell was returned to his feet. The crushing grip on his shoulder had become a warm and fatherly hand of support to steady him until he could once again stand.

"You have My apology, Toa-Sytell," Ma'elKoth said softly and calmly, though echoes of that titanic fury still hummed beneath his tone. His chest expanded near to bursting and fell again in a long, long sigh. "The Work goes poorly, and My temper is short."

The Duke said nothing, still slowly recovering from the scorching rage with which he'd been struck. Like a child feeling a parent's fist for the first time, he couldn't quite sort through his emotions: he was hurt and frightened and ashamed and uncertain what to say or what not to say.

Tiny beads of sweat prickled out all over his body, sweat that only peripherally related to the Lesser Ballroom's saunalike heat, and even Berne looked shaken.

"Observe." Ma'elKoth turned away from them, so that neither could see his face.

"When Berne first came to Me this morn, I attempted to Speak to Caine, to get his word on this missive. If he is still in Lamorak's company, Caine would be able to confirm this report or tell Me of its falsity. At the very least, I would have a vastly clearer vision of what is happening. Observe the result."

The outsized manikin rose higher over the rim of the cauldron, drifted toward the three, and descended to the floor nearby.

Ma'elKoth extended his right hand as though offering benediction, his outspread fingers shading the manikin's face from the morning sun. An in-drawing tension, as though the palace itself held its breath, and the air around Ma'elKoth heatshimmered with power.

"Caine . . ."

The word echoed within Toa-Sytell's head like a whisper in a cave, but the manikin remained mere blank and lifeless clay.

Always before, the posture, attitude, even the spirit of the target would come to animate the manikin through which the Speaking took place. Ma'elKoth spoke to it, and it would answer as though it were the very man to whom he Spoke. Now, though, now . . . Toa-Sytell squinted and moved closer, bending his neck to look up into the manikin's face of blood-worked clay.

There was something indefinable missing here, something beyond the obvious lifelessness of the Speaking's inexplicable failure. Some quality of life, of truth, of implicit motion was missing from this figure. The manikins of which Ma'elKoth constructed his Great Work always carried an impression of immanent activity, of not-too-deeply buried life, as though they might move and speak and laugh and love as soon as one turned one's eyes away—but this Caine looked as dead as a discarded doll. Though each individual feature appeared as perfect as one would expect, some ineffable crudity of their combination made it merely a large hunk of Caine-shaped clay.

"You can see," said Ma'elKoth, deep in his chest, "that this goes beyond a simple refusal to answer. Somehow, somewhere, Caine is beyond the reach of My voice."

"But how can this be?"

"I am surrounded by mystery. Why can I not penetrate the magick that beclouds Simon Jester's every move? Why is Lamorak so eager to betray that he will forgive a sentence of death? Where is Caine?"

"You think maybe he's dead?" Berne asked hopefully.

Ma'elKoth snorted contemptuously. "Have you no *eyes?*" The manikin swung around the Emperor to bob pugnaciously a hand span from Berne's nose.

"This is not the face of a corpse! This is the face of a man who *never was*! Caine has been wiped from existence as though he were a phantom of our collective daydreams. I will know how. I will know why. I will bend My magicks to this end, but Caine has, in the past, proven too slippery for such a grip."

The manikin suddenly jerked high over the cauldron's rim and splashed down into the boiling mud as though tossed by a careless giant. Ma'elKoth stood between his two nobles and cracked his knuckles like a wrestler.

"Berne, take your Cats to the barges. Perhaps the note is a diversion, a bait; if Simon Jester thinks we have bitten, perhaps he will move openly elsewhere. Or perhaps the note is honest, and we will take him today at the river. Toa-Sytell, you will place every man, woman, and street-child ever associated with the King's Eyes on alert. I wish to know everything that happens in this city today. Everything. And you *personally*," Ma'elKoth leaned close to the Duke, his breath hot and bloody, "will turn your whole attention, Toa-Sytell, to discovering where in the world a man can go that he cannot hear My voice, where it is that My will does not extend. This is, at the very least, equal in importance to the capture of Simon Jester; it is vital to the return of My serenity."

He turned away and vaulted up over the cauldron's rim, walking barefoot across the liquid surface of the boiling clay. He raised his arms, and a new figure arose from the mud, forming again into a man, ten, twelve feet tall. As his will began to sculpt its broken nose and fringe of beard, he turned his face toward Toa-Sytell one last time: his eyes smoked emerald fire, and his voice scraped and rumbled like a mountain avalanche.

"Find Caine."

6

"AND YOU KNOW, I can't figure out if he planned it this way, or not. I can't even figure out if it matters one way or the other."

Because standing still hurt too much, Hari Michaelson sat by the small square window on an uncomfortably hard examining stool.

His right arm was strapped to his chest to partially immobilize his ventilated trapezius. The wound could not be visibly treated beyond debridement and crude stitching; use of advanced medical technology would cause a continuity flaw when he transferred back to Ankhana. He'd taken several injections of timed-release universal antibiotics and had a week's supply of pinhead-sized analgesic caps slowly dissolving within the muscle. His left shoulder and his knee both ached fiercely from the beating they'd taken as well as from the steroids that had been pumped into both joints; and even though an anti-inflammatory had been injected into each one of the innumerable purple-black bruises from the gelslugs that had hammered him into unconsciousness, his entire torso was strapped with surgical tape to help keep down the swelling.

When he returned to Ankhana, he'd be able to explain away the bruises as battering from the fall down the Shaft sump. It was a good story: the media believed it already, and so did the meditechs who'd treated his wounds.

He stared at the rolling lines of raindrops that slid vertically down the windowpane as though his future could be read there. *It always seems to rain, when I come here,* he thought.

"I don't see how it could be going any better for him," he said. "He even opened my infirmary room to the media—they were on me from the instant I opened my eyes. In the cab, on the way here, I couldn't find a channel that didn't have a story about me on it. If they didn't have one of my quotes, they had an interview with the meditech, or they had retired Actors offering odds on my Final Confrontation with Berne, or some flack from Studio Marketing talking about the record advance orders for the secondhand cubes, or some other asshole claiming to know something about the 'malfunction in the Winston transfer mechanism.' "

He set his left fist on the glass and leaned on it, examining the folds of skin on his thumb and forefinger, the thick pads of callus across his knuckles.

"Some guy in Chicago managed to get an interview with Shanna's parents. They, y'know, they—" He had to cough away a sudden huskiness in his throat. "—Alan and Mara can't get seats, y'know? They don't get their next-of-kin comps because this is my Adventure, not Shanna's. They're Trade, y'know. They can't afford a first-hander berth. Shit, *I'd* give them the money, but I didn't even think of it, and they're too proud to ask me . . . So this Chicago asshole, he's asking for donations, a worldwide sympathy plea to get the Leightons on-line for the rest of my Adventure. Doing well, too, they say—makes you wonder who's gonna keep the leftover profits."

Once he'd managed to fight his way free of the media feeding frenzy at the Studio infirmary, Hari hadn't even bothered to do a fly-by on the Abbey: he knew damned well the place would be shoulder to shoulder with news crews. Marc Vilo wouldn't return his calls: he'd left the Studio the night before, while Hari was still unconscious in the infirmary. Hari guessed he'd probably had his usual luck with Dole and was currently happily humping away at some Leisure tail. And Vilo would have only been good for shielding him from the press. Even with Vilo, Hari couldn't have spoken what was in his heart, couldn't have said the things that he needed so desperately to say.

Many of these words, these thoughts, were dangerous; he needed to say things that could get him cyborged if they were repeated to the Social Police. Vilo couldn't protect him, and Hari wouldn't put his Patron in that position.

So he went to the one place he could always go, turned to the only man who could safely hear whatever he needed to say. He went to the Buchanan Social Camp, to the Mute Facility, where nothing he said could possibly be taped, or even overheard, and told it all to his crazy father.

"How could he have put it all together so *neatly*? I mean, was he planning this when he sent Lamorak to betray her? When he approved her Adventure in the first place? How far back does it go? Back to Toa-Phelathon? What does he care about more, eliminating Ma'elKoth or getting the ratings?"

Duncan Michaelson had lain nervelessly in his bed, listening to Hari in silence broken only by his occasional rasping cough. Veins twitched across his forehead, and as always Hari couldn't tell how much Duncan could understand until he spoke.

"Does . . . does it matter?"

Hari looked at his father's pale and ghostly reflection in the rain-streaked window. "No, I guess it doesn't. I'm dead either way."

"Not . . ." Duncan coughed harshly, convulsively, his mouth filling with phlegm. Hari came to his side, loosened the straps that held his wrists, and pulled out a paper handkerchief for his father to spit into. He wiped Duncan's lips gently.

". . . not dead," Duncan murmured painfully. "You're winning . . ."

What're you, nuts? Hari barely kept the reflexive words from his lips, and he had to fight down a bitter laugh.

"Winning? Dad, I'm barely *walking*. Shanna dies in two days. She's in love with the bastard who's going to kill her, and I'm getting crushed between the Studio and the fucking Ankhanan Empire. Even if I can get back to Shanna in time, even if I live that long, she doesn't *want* to be saved . . ."

"What, what about . . ." The effort of speaking seemed to be exhausting him. ". . . what about Kollberg?"

Hari lowered his head. "He's too smart for me, Dad. He's been two steps ahead of me the whole way." His fingers laced together and twisted, cracking his knuckles in a machine-gun stutter.

"When I woke up in the infirmary, it took me half an hour to really believe that I'd been about to kill him. It took me another hour to get over failing."

"Stupid . . . stupid kid. Didn't I tell you . . . didn't I tell you once what your problem is?"

"Yeah, whatever. You're always telling me what my problem is. I'm a slave, right?"

A thin and bloodless smile stretched Duncan's withered lips. "Not anymore . . ."

"What do you mean?"

"He . . . Kollberg, he's not smarter than you, Hari. Very few people are . . . He just . . . He goes for what he wants, y'know? He's always shaving the odds, always taking another baby step toward where he wants to go, even when he doesn't know how it'll all pull together in the end . . . When you do that long enough, hard enough, eventually things fall into place and . . . and you look like a genius, when you never really planned anything . . ."

"I still don't get—"

"Listen." Duncan's trembling hand gripped Hari's wrist with surprising strength. "You do the same; you always have. Caine does it; so do you. When Caine wins, that's how you do it every time. You inch toward daylight, and then when it comes together, you take it all, one fast move puts it all together—right?"

Hari frowned. "Well, yeah, I guess—"

"That's how you'll beat him."

Hari narrowed his eyes, suddenly thinking hard.

"See?" Duncan went on. ". . . not a slave. You're thinking . . . how you can beat him. A real slave can't even *think* like that— slaves *can't* fight back; they won't let themselves fight back. He doesn't own you . . . in your mind. You can fight him now. You've *won.*"

"Hardly—"

"No no no. *Think.* I couldn't teach you much, but I tried at least to teach you to *think.* Beat Ma'elKoth—there'll be other Ma'el-Koths. There'll be other Kollbergs. You've already beaten the worst enemy you'll ever have—that voice in your head . . . It tells you the fight's already over . . . whispers there's nothing you can do . . . If you beat that voice, it's a victory that can't be taken from you. You might die, but you'll die fighting."

Or I might end up here, in the next room in the Buke, he thought. Duncan had taken his own baby steps, had beaten that voice—and had been crushed like a roach under a boot heel.

Hari sighed and shook his head. "I haven't beaten it, Dad. I'm trying, but so far I haven't been able to lay a fist on it."

Duncan's eyes drifted closed, and he allowed himself a rusty chuckle. "You will . . . Identify the enemy—it's half the battle . . . Take that step, Hari. Take that first step, and then just don't stop."

"Easy for you to say," Hari muttered under his breath, looking away. "It's over for you. You lost a long time ago."

"Nothing's over," Duncan said. His brain might have been out of order, but there was nothing wrong with his ears. "And I haven't lost yet. I'm still in there pitching, Hari."

Hari stared at his father's ruined face, at his withered smile that showed a gentle confidence that was so out of place, so ludicrous from this shattered straw man, that it defied argument.

"Still taking those baby steps, kiddo," Duncan said, wiping phlegm from his lips with a crippled hand. "I took another one, just now."

7

HARI SPENT HOURS in Duncan's room that day; he had nowhere else he needed to be. Kollberg had already scheduled his return to Ankhana for tomorrow morning, and Hari had only a single Studio obligation in the interim, a follow-up interview with LeShaun Kinnison on *DragonTales*.

They had much to talk of, father and son. Hari had heard other men speak of finally coming to know their fathers as men; for those other men, this slow process had begun in their twenties. Duncan's madness, Hari's career—any number of things had stripped this opportunity from Hari's life. Nothing he could do or say would bring it back, but that day he felt as though he made a beginning, like he began to have the faintest glimmer of how Duncan's students must have felt about him thirty-five years ago.

He knew, too, that a beginning was all he could ever have; he'd waited too long. Duncan was too far gone in his cycle of madness.

They tried to spend the day discussing Hari's problem, exploring options for getting Hari and Shanna out from under the hammer that poised trembling over their heads. Hari used up a lot of favors that day, promised kilos of cocaine, to keep himself within the room, to keep the attendant passing by with his occasional injections.

Duncan cycled in and out of lucidity according to a very delicate balance of his medications; much of the time Hari spent in that room was taken up with Duncan's fantasies of a different time, of the years before and just after Duncan's downcasteing, when Hari's mother still lived, when they were still a family. Duncan would grill Hari on his geometry lesson or send him to the bedroom to check on his mother's fever. Hari found it frighteningly easy to slip back into that dream-surfing process of riding the advancing wave of Duncan's fantasy, to be precisely what Duncan expected him to be.

Duncan mentioned the same thing, in one of his lucid cycles. "You're so good at playing along, Hari—seamlessly, faultlessly good . . . I know I beat that skill into you with my fists, before you were big enough to fight back—I remember that, sometimes . . . It's made you wealthy, and famous—but now it's going to get you killed. See, you're so good at being what they want you to be that nobody remembers *you don't have to do it*. Not even you. You've fooled them all into thinking that you *are* Caine; you've even fooled yourself. You don't have to solve every problem with your fists, Hari. That's *Caine's* way. That was Caine, down there in the Chairman's office. The Chairman hurt you, and your reaction was to beat him to death with your bare hands—but that was *Caine's* reaction because Caine doesn't have any other option. It's the only problem-solving strategy he has."

"What else is there?" Hari sighed with a weary shrug.

"Plenty. There's plenty. Dammit, you're too smart to kid yourself this way. You've been taken by your own con, Hari. The whole world thinks that Caine is all of you, and you've let them talk you into agreeing. But it's not true. It never was true. Aren't you the one who's supposed to be looking the world square in the eye?"

Hari shifted uncomfortably. "That's the general idea—"

"Well, it's crap. You're pretending to be *less than you are*. You're pretending the world is worse than it is. You're kidding yourself just as much as any Pollyanna optimist does. You know what it is? It's an *excuse to lose*. And you can't afford it. Not this time. The stakes are too high."

"But what am I supposed to do about it? I mean, really *do*?" Hari said tiredly. "I'm fucked from every direction."

"First, quit whining. Then quit kidding yourself. Let the Chairman, let the Emperor, let everybody think that Caine is who you are—just don't let *yourself* think that. That's your edge.

People have been watching you almost twenty years, and nobody knows yet how smart you really are. Take those baby steps, Hari— inch toward daylight. Trust that if you just don't quit, eventually you'll find yourself on the pivot, you'll be in a spot where one bold stroke will lock everything down. You know your enemy, but he doesn't know you. Kollberg thinks that as long as you can't get your hands on him, he's safe."

"Dad . . . you, uh . . ." Hari said, shaking his head. "You make it sound so simple . . ."

"Maybe it is," Duncan rasped. "Hey, being crazy doesn't automatically make me wrong." He rolled his head sideways on the pillow, so that he could look out the window.

He said distantly, "And a man . . . a man can be excused . . . taking a certain amount of pride in his only son."

Hari swallowed hard and blinked past the sudden heat at the corners of his eyes. "Well," he said, "I guess the first thing I need to figure out is who might take my side in this, who's big enough that the Studio can't just step on them."

They'd talked for a long time more; it was midafternoon before Hari left. From the cab on his way home, he keyed Marc Vilo's private number, and this time the stubby Businessman answered.

"Hari! What news, kid?"

"Marc, I need a big favor."

"Anything, kid, anything. You really pulled it through for me. She signed over Green Fields this morning—"

"Is she still there?"

Vilo shook his head. "Back to Kauai. Why?"

"That's the favor," Hari said. "I need an audience with Shermaya Dole."

"That's not a big one, kid," Vilo said with a broad grin. "This's one old widder lady that's real happy to oblige, you follow?"

Hari took a deep breath. *Inch toward daylight,* he thought. "How about this afternoon?"

8

BERNE'S STRAWBERRY SERGE stood out among the grey leather of the Cats. They gathered within the bridgehouse on the Old Town side of Knights' Bridge, nearly two hundred men of closely matched height and build, the entire capital detachment.

Gone was the horseplay and revelry that characterized their nights; every man in the room wore a face of deathly determination. Every man in the room knew that they were about to go into action against Simon Jester; every man in the room felt the loss of the six men who'd been slaughtered in the failed raid less than a week ago; every man in the room had lost a comrade, a friend.

Every man in the room swore in his heart that he'd be the one to avenge them.

Behind Berne stood what he'd decided to call his Catseyes— four of his bravest, steadiest men wearing flat caps draped with veils of silver netting. The procedure he'd improvised to take advantage of Lamorak's tip was simple: One Catseye would accompany each pride, and he'd describe to the pride alpha at his side each and every person he saw. If the tip was true, and this netting rendered a man immune to Cloaks and other mind-altering magicks, eventually one of the Catseyes would begin to describe people and things that the alpha beside him could not see. Encirclement and capture could then begin according to their standard procedures.

"The Emperor wants the thaumaturge alive; everyone else can die," Berne said simply.

This particular instruction had been carefully planned; he had to be able to say truthfully to Ma'elKoth that he didn't *order* a massacre. If the boys got a little out of hand, well, that was understandable, considering the losses and humiliations inflicted on them this past week. It was the *frustration*, don't you see? And anger—all those boys lost friends this week, and I guess they just had to take it out on somebody . . . He was thinking specifically of Caine, hoping, praying deep in his heart that Caine would somehow be there.

He thought, privately, that the reason Ma'elKoth couldn't Speak to Caine was that Caine had truly gone over to Simon Jester— perhaps was himself Simon Jester—and had somehow draped himself with this same magickal fog that still frustrated the Emperor. He planned to keep one Catseye by his own side; he dreamed of facing Caine while the power of Ma'elKoth filled his chest to the very brink of shattering orgasm . . .

And maybe Pallas Ril would be there, as well. She'd escaped him in the Warrens, humiliated him and his men, but today, just maybe, he'd take her. Take them *both*.

This sweet mirage drifted shimmering at the fringes of his mind and brought a faint curve of smile to his lips, even as he issued instructions to the Cats.

"Guard the Catseyes: Simon Jester will go for them with everything he's got. If a Catseye falls—" Berne swept his men's grim, set faces with a smoldering glare. "—the man at his side will take his veil, and become the new eyes of his pride. There will be no escape for Simon Jester, not this time. To live, he must defeat us all in open combat."

He flicked his gaze to a corner of the bridgehouse wall, to where a horns-and-grin graffito of Simon Jester had been scribbled in red chalk. He had, in fact, secretly scratched it there himself, only a few minutes before the Cats had assembled, with precisely this moment in mind.

"Look at that," he said darkly, reaching over his shoulder for the hilt of Kosall. "Look how he defies us. Look how he laughs."

He slowly pulled Kosall from its scabbard. When he grasped its hilt, its high whine vibrated in the teeth of every man in the room. He extended the blurring edge of the blade to tap the stone where the graffito lay, as though taking its measure.

"This is our response."

A flick of Berne's powerful wrist snapped Kosall in a sizzling arc around its point as he lunged into the wall, a *degage* that sliced a cone of shining rock from the limestone; it slid free. Berne tapped it spinning into the air with Kosall's flat, then caught it neatly in his left hand. He held it up, so that the assembled Cats could see the face of Simon Jester upon it.

He said, "This."

An act of will summoned his enchanted strength, and he crushed the cone of rock within his fist with a sound like cracking bones, crumbling it to gravel, to dust that he allowed to trail between his fingers and trickle to the floor.

The Cats greeted this display with a fierce stillness, a silence that was far more profound than any cheer.

He said, "The tale of Simon Jester ends today, in defeat and bloody death. To your places."

As the Cats assembled in their prides and filed silently from the bridgehouse, every man of them swore in his heart to make Berne's vow become truth.

9

"AAAH, LADY?" THE barge captain's whiskey rasp càme from out of sight beyond the hatch at the ladder's top.

"Y' might wanna come up here and look at this . . ."

Pallas pushed herself to her feet, aching in every joint. When the barge captain said *lady*, he was always talking to her. Everyone else was *hey you*, even Talann; he'd told them outright that he didn't want to know any names.

The newly hired crew had done a fine job on the bilge, flooring it with layers of open-worked shipping pallets, to make a slatted floor eight inches above the slop that still covered the bottom. They'd scrubbed the bulkheads and hung lamps from pegs and generally made it temporarily comfortable.

Several of the *tokali* were tall enough to knock their heads on the beams that supported the deck above, and even the shorter ones felt oppressed and confined by the low ceiling; there was very little moving about. The *tokali* sat huddled into their family knots, here and there, and they all looked at her with wide, frightened eyes. *As usual,* muttered some weary and resentful part of her brain.

As soon as she climbed the ladder, they'd start asking each other what was happening, spinning ever-more-alarming fantasies about what might be going on in the daylit topside world; eventually, one of them would summon the courage to brace Talann about it. Talann would assure them that all was well, and they'd return to their family knots, and the whole process would begin again.

She'd Cloak-walked Talann with the last of them from the warehouse in the Industrial Park an hour ago. Lamorak had decided to stay with the Subjects, and that was all right with her. Majesty and the Subjects could take care of him, hide him, and protect him from the Imperials better than she could. Now they waited only for the barge's turn to slip from the docks and head downriver. The captain had bribed the dock boss to move them up the queue, and they had less than another hour to wait.

All Pallas wanted was to get the *tokali* out of town and well on their way downriver. Then she could leave the barge, walk back into the city, find a way to cancel the Eternal Forgetting, and get herself on-line, safe from amplitude decay. She would come back to the city just in case the Studio had prepared an autotransfer protocol, waiting for her transponder signature; she didn't want to be unexpectedly transferred out in full view of the *tokali*, the crew, and Talann.

Then she'd see what she'd see; if the Studio chose not to pull her, she'd make her way back to the barge—a fast horse would catch it in less than a day—and ensure the *tokali* made it safely to Terana. If she found herself suddenly back on the transfer platform in the Studio, well, she'd deal with that when she got there. At least she'd be able to call Hari and find out what in the name of god was going on.

His sudden transfer last night had wakened terrifying images of what might happen to her—and it was a mystery that chewed on the fringes of her consciousness.

Why would the Studio have pulled him in the middle of an Adventure? It didn't make any sense.

And that long moment of stillness, that slow count of ten where he'd sat without so much as a twitch of his finger . . . She'd seen that from him before—the catatonia of thought so consuming that he didn't have enough brain capacity left over to remember to breathe. What had come to him, then? He'd looked straight at Lamorak and said, "You. It's you," with another look on his face, one Pallas had seen only a few times before: his soul-extinguishing rage that brought instant, reflexive violence.

It was the look she'd seen on his face the night he'd come for her at Berne's camp, back in *Race for the Crown of Dal'kannith*. When he'd loosed her bonds and helped bind over the burns and salted cuts of Berne's amusements, she'd whispered, "Take me out of here." When he looked at her wounds, then at the flayed corpses of Marade and Tizarre, still lying in the tent with her, then out through a slit in the tent flap at the men who had done this to all of them, sitting around their campfire, drinking and laughing among themselves, that was the look his face had worn.

He'd looked at Lamorak the same way he'd looked at Berne that night, and she didn't know why.

But she didn't have time to think about it much. Time pressed on her from all sides: how little of it she had, to move thirty-six *tokali* out of Ankhana, to find a way to save her own life. She'd already spent far too much of her limited time thinking about Caine, about the last look on his face when the crystalline prismatic shimmer began to halo his body.

It stuck with her, and she couldn't shake it; she kept coming back to it in unguarded moments.

It stuck with her because he'd been in his killing zone, consumed by that berserk fury that seemed sometimes to rule his life, the state of mind where nothing mattered to him but blood and pain. But when the world had begun to halo out, in that half second he had to act, he *didn't attack*. There wasn't any time to think, to consider consequences, to weigh a choice.

His reflex had spun him away from killing and back toward her.

She knew what he'd been trying to do when his hands had stretched toward her: extend the transfer field, take her with him back to Earth and safety. It shook her; it really did. It didn't fit her image of him at all. It made her think that maybe he was changing, a little, slowly and gradually in her absence; it made her think that maybe it'd be worth her trouble to get to know him again.

She fought these thoughts, recognizing them for the succubi they were, seductive fantasies that could lead only to more heartache. *That was past,* she told herself again and again. *I'm over him.*

Beneath the layers of her resentment, she'd often felt a sneaking envy for his ability to surrender himself to bloodshed. There must be something deeply free about *hating* so much, having so much anger that consequences became irrelevant, the way he hated Berne.

After all, she'd suffered more at Berne's hands than he had. It wasn't *him* who had been bound in that tent, watching friends being tortured to death, feeling Berne's loathsome caress between the kiss of hot coals and the icy pain of needle and knife edge; it wasn't him hunted through the streets, hiding in basements, remembering the swift and efficient slaughter of Dak and Jak. But he was the one who could forget everything, drop his whole life in an instant for a chance to hurt Berne—or really, any of the enemies he'd made over his career.

She'd always been the mature one, the dedicated one, the one who could put her personal feelings aside, the one who had her priorities straight: save the innocents; protect the children; hold back; think, plan, strategize until her brain went numb.

This came partly from the voluntary discipline of her art; effective thaumaturgy was as precise as mathematics, and like mathematics it required a certain coldness of mind, a detachment. But she had a not-too-deeply buried desire—once in her life, *just once*—to let it all go, to cut loose the way Caine did.

All of these thoughts swirled and colored each other as she mounted the ladder, passing through her brain in seconds, chasing each other in the confused and feverish way that comes with bone-deep fatigue. So when she stepped out onto the sunlit deck and saw the antiship nets being cranked slowly up from the river's surface, dripping weeds and slime, she couldn't really register exactly what was happening, or why it was important.

The upper rim of the antiship nets stretched in a deep catenary across the river from the titanic windlasses, down-geared and ratcheted, atop Onetower and the northwest garrison on the downstream side, and from Sixtower to the northeast garrison at the easternmost tip of Old Town, almost out of sight around the curve of the island. The nets were made of huge steel links, each one nearly six feet long and as thick as Pallas' arm, bent to join with each other like the rings in a shirt of chainmail. They sealed off a stretch of river docks and the barges and boats moored there along the whole curve of the bank opposite the towering limestone walls of Old Town, including the barge on which she stood.

For the moment, though, Pallas could only feel the blessing of sunlight and a fresh breeze; ever since her encounter with the Cats two days ago, she hadn't been outside in daylight without being Cloaked, separated from her sensations by the focused concentration of mindview.

The two poleboys—ogre brothers, each a great hulking hunchbacked brute over eight feet tall—leaned on their twenty-five-foot river poles, staring silently west toward Knights' Bridge. In the wheelhouse, the pilot—human, but ugly enough to be part ogrillo—stared in the same direction, and the two human bilgeboys peered out from a gap in the deck-lashed stacks of cargo crates.

The captain nodded toward the high-arching span of Knights' Bridge while he pretended to light a long-stemmed pipe.

" 'S not just the nets, lady. I'm thinking, that up there might be trouble for us."

That up there—Pallas could barely make it out with a squint; the captain must have exceptional eyesight—was two men standing at the center of the Knights' Bridge arch, leaning on the stone rail to look out over the river, the sun very nearly at their backs. In the glare, she had difficulty defining what it was about them that disturbed her so much. One had something on his head, some kind of hat, or a hood, and the other—

A tendril of cloud passed before the sun, and in the sweep of shadow, she could see that the other man wore a shirt of faded and blotchy strawberry and had something that looked like the hilt of a sword sticking up over his left shoulder.

And he seemed to be staring directly at her.

A shock went through her, from the top of her head in a wave down to the soles of her feet. She froze for an endless second before reason took over. There was no way he could pick her out, recognize her from that distance among this crawling mass of boats and barges along the busy dockside. On the other hand, there was no reason to dawdle up here in plain view.

Now, too, she could see men in grey leather fanning out among the dockworkers and the rivermen. They seemed to come from everywhere, casually half stealing into view simultaneously from doorways and alleys all along the dockside.

"Chi'iannon's Grace," Pallas muttered. "There must be a hundred of them."

She turned to the captain. "Keep the crew calm," she said. "Think of this as just another inspection. I'll Cloak the passengers below, exactly as we did for the inspection this morning. They'll look around; they won't find anything; they'll go away."

He shook his head dubiously, sucking on the pipe stem. "Dunno, lady. My boys, they're good boys. I'd put 'em against any barge crew; I'd put 'em against most river pirates. Nobody can ask 'em to stand against Grey Cats."

"It won't come to that," she said, putting a reassuring hand on his arm. "Tell your boys to play dumb; you go on and yessir-nosir the Cats until they're sick of your voice. I'll handle the rest."

She swung back down through the hatch before the captain could render another objection. The huddled knots of *tokali* below raised apprehensive eyes to her with unspoken questions. She lifted her hands.

"It's another inspection, that's all. We'll do this exactly like the last one, all right? Everyone stay still and quiet while I Cloak you, and we'll send off these inspectors none the wiser. It's best to be ready, though. Everybody find a comfortable spot and lie down. Go on. It'll take only a few minutes; try to relax. In less than an hour, we'll be on our way downstream to safety."

She paused for a moment and waited and watched until the *tokali* slowly began to arrange themselves. Lying down was best; when she was doing something so complex as a mass Cloak, sudden movement in her eye plane could distract her.

Talann sat below her on the stairs, sunk in some kind of brown study, resting her chin on her hands. She'd been listless and un-communicative ever since Pallas had returned last night from her talk with Lamorak and Caine.

Pallas sat down beside her and murmured, "I need you alert and with me, Talann. It's the Cats."

Talann looked at her blankly, light only gradually returning to her eyes. "Sorry?"

"The Cats, Talann. And I'm exhausted."

Her gaze gradually sharpened. "Is Berne out there?"

"Yes, he is," Pallas said slowly, with a growing frown. "Why?"

"He fought Caine—he fought Caine *again*, just two or three days ago, in a brothel in Alientown. The Subjects were talking about it last night. Caine lost. Again."

"Let me tell you something," Pallas said sharply. "Facing Berne and living through it? I wouldn't call that losing."

"He ran," Talann said, staring off into some private distance.

"So did I."

"Well, but you're . . ."

"What? I'm what?" Unaccountable anger harshened her voice. "What's that supposed to mean?"

"Nothing," Talann murmured. "It's not the same."

Then she mumbled something under her breath, something that Pallas couldn't make out, something that she wasn't supposed to hear, but somehow she understood the indistinct mutter all the same: *But I wouldn't run . . .*

It was all too clear that Talann was going through some kind of adolescent crisis, and for a brief moment Pallas actually imagined herself talking to the young warrior about it. This distracted sullen-ness and resentment—this had something to do with Caine, and with Pallas herself, and with Caine's disappearance. They'd spent a whole day together, alone except for the intermittently conscious Lamorak . . .

The thought slid into her mind like a hot needle: *Did he sleep with her?*

But this came only from fatigue and the pressure of fear, a mind trick to avoid thinking about the approaching Cats; she shook it off and forced herself to concentrate on the immediate problem.

"Listen," she said. "Don't even think about Berne. Help me keep everybody quiet, and for the love of Chi'iannon don't do any-thing stupid. Don't forget what we're *here* for, all right? We're not here to kill Cats; we're not here to fight Berne. We're here to save the lives of these people." She nodded toward a far corner of the bilge, where Konnos and his wife tried to quiet their younger daughter, who had become restlessly hyperactive, spurred by the tension and the inactivity.

Talann stared at them silently, stared past them, beyond the hull. "I know it. Don't worry about me."

Pallas took her at her word. With a final, comradely squeeze of Talann's shoulder, she stepped to the corner of the bilge and sank into the Warrior's Seat position that Hari had taught her. Though not quite as comfortable as her accustomed Lotus Seat, the Warrior's Seat had the advantage that one quick surge of the doubled legs beneath her would pop her to her feet, already in a fighting stance.

She began the slow pattern of circular breathing that brought her to mindview. All of her worries, her doubts, and her fatigue sloughed from her spirit like dry leaves stripped by an autumn breeze, and now she began the long and intricate process of erasing her mental image of each person in the bilge. One by one they faded from her consciousness, each of the *tokali*, then Talann, finally even herself, and then she wiped away the provisions, the ragged palliasses, the shipping pallets that made the dry-slatted floor, then the lamps that hung from the pegs on the walls, as well as the light they cast.

And as her final touch, which would have been far beyond the skill of a lesser adept, she *added* to the scene: scuffed the walls with mental grime, raised the level of black wastewater, and imaged bits of unidentifiable flotsam bobbing on its surface.

This last was to discourage the Cats from coming down the ladder for a closer look. This water would look real, but there was no way she could disguise the feel of the dry pallets beneath a man's boots. If one of them came down the ladder, the game would be up, and they'd have to fight their way out.

Time passed unnoticed in mindview, and the level of concentration she required to maintain a Cloak of this complexity prevented her from any more than barely registering the sounds of voices and of boot heels on the deck above. She knew that the Cats were here, that even now the barge captain was muttering with his best pretense of simpleminded helpfulness, but she couldn't spare enough attention to comprehend the words they spoke.

A shaft of light speared into her Cloak as the hatch opened, but she was ready for that. Her disciplined mind automatically made the necessary adjustments of light and shadow, and added a glittering reflection from the surface of the illusionary water. Even in mindview, she felt a certain pride at the quality of this illusion. It was unbeatable.

A pair of heads appeared, silhouetted against the afternoon sky; one of them wore some kind of hood, made of metallic-looking netting, and she heard a gasp that came from down here in the bilge itself. She knew the voice: Konnos.

What in the name of god could have startled Konnos so much that he'd give them all away?

There was no way to tell if the Cats could hear it as well—they were up in the breeze and the dockside noises—but now the bareheaded Cat said something, and the one in the hood replied. Both heads withdrew, and the hatch started to swing closed . . .

And Talann streaked up the ladder and threw herself against the descending hatch.

The sudden motion startled Pallas out of mindview. What was that lunatic *doing*?

But now memory surged back, and she understood what the Cats had said, the words whose meaning hadn't penetrated mindview: *"Nothing. It's empty and it smells bad."* And the reply from the one in the hood: *"It's full of people . . ."*

Talann hit the hatch door like a locomotive, hammering it open, ripping it from the grasp of the startled Cats. She reached up through the open hatch and tangled her fists in the leather collars of the two Cats, then kicked off from the ladder and let herself fall into the bilge, her sudden weight pulling both of them in after her.

The bilge rang with shouts and screams of alarm as the *tokali* wailed with a single voice. Talann released the falling Cats before she landed, then skipped back to let them fall in a heap at her feet. As they struggled to disentangle themselves from each other, Talann spun and cracked a heel kick into the back of one's head; he went down twitching. She jumped high and landed with the heel of one foot on the side of his neck. He flopped like a landed fish as he died.

The hooded Cat came rolling to his feet, and Pallas' startled paralysis broke. Even as he drew his sword, she popped out of the Warrior's Seat into a fighting stance and smoothly slipped her bladewand from its sheath along her wrist; a simple twist of her mind triggered it.

For the brief second of its existence, the blue-white energy of a bladewand is as irresistible as Kosall; a stroke of her hand sent the bladewand's immaterial edge through the Cat's wrist. His sword and the hand that had held it fell together to the slatted floor, and a crimson jet fountained from the stump of his wrist as he howled in disbelief.

Talann lunged past him, snaked her arm around his neck as she passed, as though to put him in a headlock. She planted her feet, locked her hands together, and twisted, cracking the stunned Cat like a whip. His neck snapped loudly, audible even over the terrified shouts of the *tokali*.

The bladewand's energy flickered out, and Pallas said numbly, "You killed them both . . ."

Talann offered her a feral grin so much like Caine's that it hurt her heart. "You had a better idea? What now?"

Pallas shook herself and answered, raising her voice to be heard over the *tokali*.

"How many of them are already aboard?"

"Couldn't tell. A lot. Does it matter?"

"No. If we stay down here they'll shoot us like rats. We fight."

She looked at the metal netting that covered the face of the hooded Cat and understood its significance. "My Cloaks have just become obsolete."

Talann spread her hands. "Whenever you're ready."

Booted feet pounded on the deck above, approaching.

Pallas turned to the *tokali*. "All of you: stay here and *stay down*! I don't know what's going to happen; whatever it is, it'll be extreme. Find something to hold on to."

Talann said, "They have the hatch surrounded—they're just waiting for one of us to put our head up."

Pallas nodded. "That's what I'm counting on."

A flick of her wrist produced one of the last two buckeyes she had. Talann's eyes lit with fierce delight.

"Stand back."

The lines of power inscribed upon the buckeye's surface spoke to her mind, and she touched them with a tendril of her Shell. The buckeye began to trail smoke through her fingers, and she lobbed it gently, underhand, up through the hatch. It triggered five feet above the deck with an earshattering *boom* and blew the deck around the hatch to smoldering flinders; the ladder fell in splinters to the floor.

Where the hatch had been was now a smoking hole about six feet in diameter; the waiting Cats would now be scattered across the deck, some unconscious, others madly rolling and slapping at themselves to put out the flames that clung to their leather clothing.

"There'll be others, and crossbow fire as we come up," Talann said.

Pallas nodded. "You'll have to draw fire till I get clear." Pallas made a stirrup of her hands, and Talann understood instantly. *It's almost like working with Caine,* Pallas thought. *As though we've been doing this for years.*

Without another word, Talann sprang into Pallas' hands; Pallas continued the momentum with all the strength in her own legs. She heaved upward while Talann leaped again, and Talann shot up through the hole onto the deck, rolled, and came up running.

Pallas came right behind her, jumping up to catch at the smoking rim of the hole, pulling herself up and out to roll to her feet, so fast and smooth that the smoldering wood could do no more than singe her palms. She dove toward some of the cargo crates lashed to the deck, going over one scorched and unconscious Cat. The whacks of firing crossbows seemed to come from everywhere and were echoed by the loud splintering thumps of quarrels slamming into the deck and the crates around her. Pallas found cover among the crates and cautiously poked her head up.

Talann fought hand to hand against two Cats on the foredeck, springing, leaping, and tumbling to avoid their slashing blades, slicing back at them with the pair of knives she always carried behind her belt. She was safe enough from the crossbow fire for now— the Cats wouldn't take the chance of shooting their comrades—but more Cats sprinted toward the barge along the wharfside. Pallas triggered her final buckeye and slung it overhand toward them without a second thought. It was her last, but they wouldn't know that, and caution would slow them down.

The fireball exploded above them, flattening three or four and sending a couple tumbling into the river. The other approaching Cats scattered toward cover.

We're about as trapped as you can get, Pallas thought. She might be able to escape—especially with Talann along to cover her back— but she was the only hope of the *tokali*. If she could cut away the ropes that moored the barge to the docks and somehow get the barge to swing out into the current, they'd eventually drift against the downstream antiship net, which she could probably, maybe, cut through with the bladewand, given enough time. She didn't have a lot of hope for this plan; this would be a long, slow drift in the sluggish current, and she'd have to hold off the Cats the whole way . . . and pass right under Knights' Bridge.

Where Berne stood.

First things first. She had to get the scorched Cats off the barge. They'd be swiftly recovering from their shock and even she and Talann together couldn't deal with that many Cats in close quarters. A quick scan of the deck visible from her position found the two ogre poleboys squatting behind a stack of crates not far to her right.

"Hey! You two!" she shouted. "Pick up the guys that are down and toss them overboard!"

One of them shook its massive head. "Not. They s'oot uz," it explained in a growl that mushed around the curved tusks that protruded upward from its lower jaw.

"I'll take care of the crossbows," Pallas snapped. "Move!"

They both shook their heads stubbornly and hunkered down even lower behind the crates. Pallas swore. She once again produced the bladewand and triggered it. A handbreadth plane of shimmering blue-white force sliced through the crate just above one of the ogre's heads.

"Do it or I'll kill you right now!"

They flinched, and their leathery faces went pale: they believed her. They started to scramble out from around the stack.

Now Pallas had to keep her end of the bargain.

She breathed herself into mindview, and the shouts of the battle faded. In her powerful imagination, she structured a shining lattice of golden energy, one huge and powerful and curved around the entire barge. It was far larger than anything she could have charged into a crystal; the quartz would have shattered under the strain of holding so much power. It had to be *more*, it had to be stronger, larger, to hold against the crossbows, against the fists and feet of the Cats; she pulled Flow far beyond her capacity, far beyond what she'd ever dreamed possible, far beyond the point where another adept would have charred his brain and fallen dead on the spot with smoke leaking from his nostrils.

She drew Flow into a towering whirlpool of force that passed into her and through her and powered this enormous shield with an energy beyond any she'd ever controlled. Suddenly her mindview shifted; it was as though she stood *outside* herself, looking on.

She saw the rigidity of her body, the frown that concentration twisted into her brow, and the titanic energy that flowed through her. A sense of wonder, of awe that was almost religious, entered her along with the Flow. Fatigue and ultimate necessity had combined to thrust her upward into a higher level of consciousness, where she could sluice power through her body to energize the Shield but leave her mind free to look on with a curious sense of release, with what was almost an indifference to the consequences, to the outcome of the battle.

The purity and beauty of the Shield; the ease with which it absorbed the flight after flight of crossbow quarrels; the astonishing grace of Talann's combat as she dispatched first one Cat, then the other; the slow, twisting arc of the wounded and unconscious Cats that the ogres tossed spinning into the Great Chambaygen; all these combined into an intricate dance that began with the quantum buzz of electron shells within the atoms that made up her body and extended outward to the mighty sweep of the galactic arm, to the endless dance of the galaxies themselves about the core of the universe.

This transcendent blossoming of awareness carried her away; her consciousness vanished within the universal dance and swung there for an instant eternity. She might have hung there forever, blissfully one with the infinite, but she was brought back to herself by a white-hot surge of feedback through her Shield.

Instantly the barge and the river and the wall of Old Town reassembled in her vision, and everything was washed with flame. The flame vanished from the surface of her Shield, but it clung to the decks of the barges nearby, and the crates stacked on the pier. Around the barge, everything burned. The scarlet shaft of power that sprang from the arch of Knights' Bridge and terminated within the Dusk Tower of the Colhari Palace answered her instant question.

It had been a firebolt. From Berne. From Ma'elKoth.

Her Shield had held.

Yesterday—even this morning—a surprise like this might have dropped her from mindview, but she was far beyond that, now. *This must be what Caine feels,* she realized, this serene confidence that his art is perfect, this release from fear of the outcome, this knowing that any result, even death, has a beauty of its own.

Another firebolt followed, a roaring shaft of flame that speared through the air above the river and splashed across her Shield.

All the troops that watched this battle from the fortified walls of

Old Town, all the laborers and common folk who had peered from Industrial Park windows, everyone save the Cats themselves, now found this fight to be vastly more dangerous than it was entertaining. Helmeted heads vanished behind the crenels atop the wall, and the streets and alleys that led away from the wharf were suddenly crowded with fleeing townsfolk, shoving and trampling each other in their sudden terror.

This firebolt *hurt*, and she knew that for all her newfound power, she couldn't hold this Shield forever. She couldn't match Ma'elKoth strength-for-strength—not yet, maybe not ever.

They had to move.

Another shattering roar, and even the sun dimmed behind the fury of the flames that hit her Shield. How could he attack so fast, again and again? She could hold her defense no longer. Blackness danced within her eyes, and her Shield scattered like cobwebs in the wind. Talann was at her side, to catch her as she crumpled.

Pallas clung to her. "Seconds—we have only seconds before he kills us all."

Talann shrugged and bared her teeth. "What would Caine do, if he were here now?"

Pallas looked gratefully up into Talann's vivid violet eyes and drew strength from the solidity of the arms that supported her.

"He'd buy me some time," she answered, "but—"

"Done," said Talann, and before Pallas could say another word Talann whirled and sprinted across the deck of the barge. She sprang onto the pier and across it to the burning deck of the barge opposite, then curved for shore, outracing the flames. Cats angled to meet her across the docks, but she slanted away from them, sprinting with incredible speed along the riverside, west toward Knights' Bridge.

Pallas reached for that inexhaustible source again and poured herself into the Flow, building another Shield to defend the barge against the firebolt she knew was coming. She layered it upon itself, thicker and thicker, angling it toward the span of bridge, but the firebolt that came next battered it into nonexistence and blasted away her consciousness.

When her eyes opened, she picked herself up and knew that she'd been down only a second or two. She caught the last glimpse of Talann as she vanished into the mouth of an upsloping street at the west end of the wharf, and Pallas knew where she was heading:

the center arch of Knights' Bridge. Pallas sighed out a prayer that wished her luck and the blessings of every good god.

Her Shield had done its work: the barge still floated unhurt. Now to get the thing moving out into the stream . . .

She looked around, leaning on the crates around her against a wave of dizziness; none of the crew were anywhere in sight, and she didn't blame them. She only hoped that none of them had gone overboard. She might need them, later.

The Cats who watched the barge from the wharf were in no hurry to attack; some of their number had raced off in pursuit of Ta-lann, and the rest had no desire to get caught on the fringes of one of Berne's firebolts. They contented themselves with firing a crossbow quarrel at her now and then. Pallas once again drew her bladewand. She kept under cover behind the crates as she slashed at the ropes that moored the barge to the pier; they parted silently.

But how was she to move the barge out into the current without the help of the poleboys? Even if they would help, could she protect them from the quarrels of the Cats if Ma'elKoth and Berne kept scaling up the power of their Shield-breaking firebolts?

She refused to give up; she refused to allow the *tokali* to die here.

Now, far to the west, another figure raced out up the curve of Knights' Bridge, a figure with platinum hair and the lithe grace of a thoroughbred, a figure that ran headlong toward Berne. Tears swam in Pallas' eyes.

Talann was buying her this time with her life. She wouldn't waste it.

She began once again the circular breath control that would draw her into mindview.

I will find a way.

10

AS BERNE WATCHED her run, he knew her: she was that wild-ass bitch his boys had taken with Lamorak, the one Caine had helped escape from the Donjon. When she pulled away from the pursuing Cats and vanished up one of the streets that sloped from the riverfront to the city above, he pounded his fist on the bridge wall in front of him and cursed savagely enough to make the Catseye beside him flinch.

The Cats had overcommitted; every one of those bloodthirsty fucking idiots down there wanted to be in on the kill. They'd left no reserve to seal the wharf, and now that wild-ass bitch was going to get away.

Something sizzled in the back of Berne's head when he remembered seeing the smooth curve of her muscle, her golden skin stretched out nude on Master Arkadeil's table. For a long moment he struggled with a compelling temptation to leave the bridge and chase her himself. The sweetness, fantasy rich, of catching her in the crook of an alley, alone, of bending her over against the rough brick of a manufactory's rear wall . . .

Arkadeil had pincushioned her with his silver needles; Ma'el-Koth himself had put her to the question with all the power of his mind. To neither had she given so much as her name.

Berne knew beyond doubt that she'd give him that, and more.

She'd give him everything.

The heat that came to his groin as he imagined it nearly pulled him from the bridge.

But down there on that boat was an enemy thaumaturge of incredible power; he couldn't know for sure, but he dared to hope that this was indeed Simon Jester. Neither he nor Ma'elKoth had truly expected this dock sweep to work, but when that Shield had gone up—that huge fucking thing the size of the Temple of fucking *Dal'kannith*—when it had held against *three* of Ma'elKoth's firebolts, Berne knew that his place was here. Ma'elKoth would accept no excuse for another failure.

After all, half the dockside was on fire down there; he'd damned well better catch an *Aktir* or two to blame it on. With all the fires and explosions and battles and failed raids of the past week, Ankhanans were becoming more afraid of their government than of the *Aktiri*.

And that weasel-dick Toa-Sytell would be right there at Ma'el-Koth's side, whispering in his ear, telling him how Simon Jester should be left to the King's Eyes, that the Cats would be better used in the hands of someone else, someone *competent* . . .

No, Berne would stay on this bridge until his Cats well and truly cornered and *took* whoever that was down there.

A flicker of blue-white force caught his eye, and now the boat rocked slowly away from its mooring. Berne smiled and muttered under his breath, "And just where do you think you're going, pal?"

Louder, distinctly, he said, "Ma'elKoth.".

I AM WITH YOU, BERNE.

And he was: the Presence, the jittering, buzzing power that filled every crack in Berne's soul, the melting edge of explosion like trembling on the verge of orgasm hummed in Berne's ears and stretched an irresistible smile across his teeth.

"Another firebolt."

BERNE: THE POWER THAT I DRAW FROM MY BELOVED CHILDREN FOR THESE FIREBOLTS IS EXTREME. THE LAST ONE ALONE TOOK THE LIVES OF EIGHT OF MY WEAK-ENED CHILDREN. USE THEM WISELY.

"I will," he said through his teeth, on fire with power. "I will. I *need* it, Ma'elKoth, they're getting away."

VERY WELL.

And the jittering buzz smoothed, then swelled into creamy heat and seemed to lift him to his toes. The Catseye at his side stepped unobtrusively away. He felt tiny flames course over his skin, flames that did not burn but caressed him like a lover's fingertips. The barge still rocked ponderously at its pier, moving away by inches, and no Shield was in evidence. Berne raised one fist to the sky and extended the other toward the barge.

"Yesss," he hissed, withholding his power for this last sexual instant. "Oh, oh yes . . ."

"My lord Count!" The harsh cry of the Catseye at his side drew his eye, and he barely managed to halt the stroke. The Catseye swept his hand up to point to the north, along Nobles' Way, the road that divided the Industrial Park from Alientown.

Along it, sprinting toward him, ran that wild-ass bitch.

Ten Cats broke into view in pursuit, pounding after her. Even as Berne watched, four of them split to the roadside, stopped, and fired crossbows. The wild-ass bitch seemed almost prescient, the way she jigged at exactly the right instant to make the quarrels pass in front of her; she came on, hardly having broken stride, and even the six Cats behind her who had not stopped were losing ground.

The power throbbed inside him, and he raised his fist to strike fire along the street and roast her in her own juices. But Nobles' Way was lined with townspeople, fearfully crowded against store-fronts, but still there, still watching; and there was a knot of them around one or two who must have been hit by the errant quarrels and were down on the street. And Ma'elKoth became furious when innocent citizens were harmed.

His instant's hesitation on seeing this, on thinking this, cost him his shot. She'd already sprinted up the long arching span of Knights' Bridge. Behind her, in his literal line of fire, were the pursuing Cats.

He cast a glance back toward the barge. No Shield was up—the enemy thaumaturge was probably unconscious from feedback through his broken Shield—and he could see his Cats cautiously advancing from cover to cover toward it. They'd reach it long before it rocked clear of the dock; why not indulge himself?

He said to the Catseye at his side, "Take her, Mikli. Don't kill her, just take her."

The Catseye smiled through his silver netting as he drew his sword. "My pleasure, my lord Count." He slipped the hood off his head and gave a happy sigh.

He stepped out onto the middle of the bridge to wait for her, balancing his weight forward with his knees slightly bent. Mikli was a superb swordsman; he'd always been lightning fast and very precise, and for the past few months, Berne had personally overseen his training. Berne had no doubt that Mikli would perform exactly as ordered.

The wild-ass bitch never slowed. She sprinted straight for him as though she planned to run him down. At the last instant Mikli slipped to one side and cut at the back of her neck as she passed, swinging with the flat of his blade for the quick knockout. Once again, her almost prescient reflexes saved her: she threw herself under his strike into a dive roll that brought her to her feet with her back to Mikli, only a couple of paces from Berne.

She gave him a grin that held no hint of reason. "First him," she said to Berne, violet eyes burning with manic fire. "Then you. Don't go anywhere."

"And miss this?" Berne said with an answering grin, keeping his eyes on her so as not to warn her of Mikli's swift approach at her back. "Never."

She lifted her hands as though to show Berne the pair of knives that she held reversed, their blades along her forearm; then she whirled and cut at Mikli's leg as he fired a side kick at her spine.

Her knife-edged forearm parried the kick, but the wire that reinforced Mikli's leather leggings turned the blade. He followed with a slanting neck cut that she blocked with the knife along her left forearm as she stepped into him and sliced down with her right, hooking his sword wrist between the blade and her forearm. A push with her left while she pulled with her right twisted the sword out of his grasp, but she paid for it: Mikli was too experienced to try to hang on to the sword. Instead he let it go and slammed his doubled elbow into the side of her head.

She rolled with the blow, letting it drive her to the ground; then her legs shot out and tangled Mikli's ankles, and he fell. As he twisted to turn the fall into a roll, the wild-ass bitch backhanded the point of a knife deep into the base of his skull.

It went in with a crunch; bone and ligament crackled as she twisted it out, neatly severing Mikli's spine.

He spasmed on the ground, flopping spastically, moaning, "No . . . no . . ." as the light slowly faded from his eyes.

Berne watched this for a cold moment before he pushed himself off the wall and reached over his shoulder for Kosall.

"Y'know, little girl, I'm starting to think you might be good enough to dance with me."

She slipped her knives back behind her belt and picked up Mikli's sword as she rose. She nudged his body with her toe. "I'd imagine he'd agree with you, if he could. So would my last four dance partners, back down there on the boat."

"Five?" Berne said, eyebrows lifting, pretending to be impressed as his juices began to flow, his heartbeat picked up, and heat gathered in his loins. He pulled Kosall free of its scabbard by the quillions, and only then did he activate its magick by grasping the hilt; a second later its humming vibrated up his arms and into his teeth.

"Five of my boys already *today*?"

She looked upon this weapon with respect, but no surprise: she must have known already he carried this sword. She nodded toward the other Cats, her pursuers, who now had arrived at the center span.

"Want to go for ten? Fifteen? Want to bet I can't kill every single one of them?"

Berne shook his head and lifted a hand to hold them back. "You already know there's no way for you to get off this bridge alive," he said slowly, his voice thickening with lust. "So I'm not just gonna kill you. You're ready for that, I guess. Instead, I'm gonna *fuck* you. Right here in the middle of the bridge, for everyone to watch. I'm gonna bend you over this wall and fuck you. And when I'm done, each one of them—" He nodded toward the waiting Cats. "—gets a turn. Then, if you're still alive, maybe we'll give you to some of the passersby, y'know? The bridge traffic. What do you think about that?"

She shrugged carelessly. "You have to beat me, first."

He matched her shrug. "Yeah, all right. You know, I never did get your name."

"No reason to tell you now," she said. "You won't live long enough to use it."

"Come on, then," he said. "Whenever—"

She sprang at him, her neck cut so fast he barely saw the blade move. He made no attempt to parry, just shifted his Buckler to protect the joining of his neck and shoulder. Her borrowed sword rang as though she'd struck metal, and her eyes widened.

He shifted his Buckler to his hand and grabbed her blade. She tried to yank the blade away, to slide it slicing through his fingers, but his magickally strengthened grip held it as though it had been driven into stone. He laughed and cut at her arm with Kosall. She released the blade in time to save her arm and dropped into a backroll away from him, coming to her feet and staring with widened eyes out of which that manic confidence swiftly drained.

Berne flipped her sword into the air and sliced it in half with a stroke of Kosall. The pieces rang on the limestone and skittered away.

"Tell me," Berne said in his richest, oiliest voice, "are you starting to think you might have made a mistake?"

11

IN MINDVIEW, PALLAS had examined and discarded options with computerlike speed and dispassion. Only seconds passed until she knew beyond all doubt that nothing in her experience could save the *tokali*—and the barge crew, for whom she'd also now become responsible—from this trap.

She didn't have it, and that was all. No spell, no trick, no power she had or had ever held at her command could save them. This knowledge did not bring dismay, though, or fear, or sadness: it had entirely the opposite effect.

It brought clarity and perfect freedom: the freedom one can only feel on the very knife edge of death.

The fear, that familiar paralyzing apprehension, would have

come from seeing only one chance, one slim opportunity to escape if everything came together just right. A choice between two chances, equally slim, would have been even worse; then she would have been in terror of making a tiny mistake that would cost the lives she had sworn herself to save. Having no chance at all—that allowed her the ice-and-high-mountains freedom to do exactly what she chose, with no attachment to the outcome.

If all paths lead equally to death, what's left to direct you at the crossroads except pure whim?

With a mental shrug, she settled on a course of action based solely on a childish, fairy-tale metaphor: cats hate to get wet.

Seeking a way to move the barge out from the dock, to make them swim for it, she sent a tendril of her Shell downward, into the river. She felt the life there, felt it pulse into her Shell; the tiny flickering aurae of crayfish, sluggish rivercats, gleaming, thick-bodied carp. And she felt something else, faintly, like a bare, fading echo of memory, something that seemed to link all those Shells together, as though it were a field upon which they all played.

Pallas sought that echo, diving deeper into mindview, no longer merely visualizing her Shell but inhabiting it. That same sense of letting go, of releasing her attachment to her body, came instantly and easily now; she shifted beyond her physical self, became a matrix of pure mind, patterned by her body but no longer bound to it, a matrix tuned to the pulse of Flow itself.

Down within the river, everything she found was Flow.

Flow proceeds from life: it powers life and is powered by life, and here in the river, everything lived. As she sought the echo, the field, she seemed to move downward, ever deeper, not in the physical sense of farther under the water, but deeper than the Shells of the carp and the crayfish, deeper than the murky green aura of the trailing weeds, down and down and down, not below but *through* . . .

Through the moss and the algae, through the protozoans, through the bacteria and the most basic molds themselves, she went farther and farther without finding what she sought. Her consciousness expanded, questing outward, following the dimly sensed links back up—

Another level of Flow lived here.

Behind and below was a slower, deeper pulse, far beyond the busy foreground of species' competition. Far, far deeper than the clash of Shells as a carp takes a newt, far deeper than the silent struggle between two varieties of river weeds fighting for the same stretch of sandy bed, this was Flow of a sort she'd never dreamed existed. Tentatively, she tuned her Shell to its pulse, surrendering herself into its powerful rhythm.

Wonder wheeled inside her with the majestic spiral of a galaxy.

The whole river was alive.

She'd found the Shell of the Great Chambaygen itself, the life aura of the entire river system from its farthest springs high in the Gods' Teeth to its mighty delta at Terana on the western coast. This Shell swelled with not only what lived within the river itself, but its entire watershed: the grassy plains it meandered through, the forests that drank from it and returned their rich soil to it, the whole ecosystem that supported it and was in turn supported by it.

The staggering power of the life it contained threatened to burn Pallas' brain within her skull, and would have, had she struggled against it. Instead she relaxed; she surrendered; she sought her own place within that life and found it. The jewel of her consciousness hung there, fit with perfect inevitability into precisely the place where it belonged, slowly turning, regarding the life of the river with awe.

For there was more than life here: there was Mind.

And there was Song.

The river sang its life, from the freshening trickle of snowmelt in the summer of a geologic age ago, from the bubble of a mountain spring to the soft crackle of corn growing in the night, the crash of an oak toppling with roots undermined by the river's flow to the roar of a vernal flash flood, the whisper of reeds and the rustle of cattails in the backwaters; birdsong was there, from ducks and geese, herons, kingfishers and cranes; the splashing flutter of fish, the flashes of color in the muscular arc of trout and spawning salmon, the slow patience of a snapping turtle waiting in the mud.

The river sang of men, too, poling their boats along its banks, sang of the primal folk who spoke to it with songs of their own in days of old, of the stonebenders who dammed and diverted its waters to power their mills.

And it sang of Ankhana, the massive boil that straddled its middle, the aching running sore that poisoned it for miles downstream.

And now into that song came a new note, a strengthening; the song shifted from the murmur of a lonely under-the-breath sighing to the warm, pure notes of the old singer who's suddenly found that he has an unexpected audience. Note slid against note, the echoing call of a distant moose blending with playful chirps of young otters, underscored by the splash of a sudden autumn wind across a ripple . . . and became charged with meaning.

No words flowed in this song; none were required. Melody became meaning, and meaning became Song.

I KNOW YOU, PALLAS RIL, AND YOU ARE WELCOME IN MY SONG.

Where Pallas hung, she had neither breath nor mouth, but from within her came a melody of answer: *Chambaraya . . .*

MEN NAME ME SO, AND IMAGINE THAT THEY KNOW ME. JOIN YOUR SONG TO MINE, CHILD.

And song poured from her, an effortless counterpoint that became perfect harmony. Here within the song there was no dissembling, no hiding or shading the truth of her; everything that she was flowed into the river's song, and the river knew all of her. Chambaraya took all her strength, all her weakness, the shameful tangles of her jealousies and pettiness, the purity of her courage, and accepted them all with the same perfect serenity.

There was no judgment here, *could be* no judgment: all was one single current from the mountains to the sea.

In her song was the melody of her need, of the desperation that had driven her to dive so deeply and search so far. The river did not understand why men wished to hurt her, did not understand even why she feared them; death and life were both parts of the same endless wheel, out of one cometh the other, everlasting. Why should she resist returning to the earth from whence she came?

But she asked, nonetheless: *Please, Chambaraya, save us. Show your power.*

I CANNOT/WILL NOT. THE COVENANT WITH THE LESSER GODS, THAT DAMMED JERETH GODSLAUGHTERER'S REVOLT, CHANNELS ME AS WELL.

Lesser gods? she thought, as though to herself, but within the song nothing separated her from the river, nor it from her; there were no private thoughts, nor need of any.

YOUR GODS: WHO REQUIRE THE WORSHIP OF MEN: WHO CONCERN THEMSELVES WITH MORTAL AFFAIRS: WHO ARE SMALL ENOUGH TO SUFFER BOREDOM AND PLAY GAMES OF POWER TO RELIEVE IT.

Pallas understood with perfect clarity; Chambaraya was far beyond any concern with the lives of individuals. To the river, a human life was no more than the life of a single minnow in a flashing school—but also, no less. To the river, life is life. What could she offer, what could she do to persuade the river? All that it needed, it had already, in perfect sufficiency.

The Covenant of Pirichanthe had bound the gods outside the walls of time, limiting their actions to providing their priests with power and occasional guidance—and perhaps that was an answer.

From deep within her self came her offer: *Make of me your priest. Grant me some small measure of your power, and I shall be your voice. I shall teach men the proper respect for you.*

I NEED NO VOICE: THE RESPECT OF MEN IS WITHOUT MEANING: THIS REQUEST HAS NO MEANING. A SONG DOES NOT ASK ITSELF FOR POWER.

A song does not ask itself for power . . . She was the song; asking the river for power was like requesting of her hand that it make a fist. It had been only the vestiges of her human viewpoint that had created this separation, this I and Thou, this conversation of Pallas Ril and Chambaraya as two separate beings.

While she was in the song, her need, her will, her fierce devotion to the lives that were in her charge, these were all in the song as well, threads of its most basic melody. With this realization, her final remnants of separateness, of personal identity, blew away like cobwebs before a storm.

She herself was the only part of the river that could suffer this desire . . . but there were no parts here. All was one, was wholeness. Her desire became the river's.

While she was in the river's song, she was the song, she was the river, and her will touched its waters with power unimaginable.

She surfaced within herself and regarded this single tone within her song: one small grace note with its curling spray of hair, with this cloak of blue and clothes of grey. It seemed very small, and somehow distant, but very present as well. She felt the lives within the barge with the same sense that felt an early snowfall high in the Gods' Teeth, with the same sense that felt the death struggle of a trout and a carp in the Teranese delta. She saw that the danger that threatened these trembling humans was purely local; moving the barge would remove the danger, and moving the barge was no effort at all—it was precisely her nature.

Was she not a river?

She breathed in, and the flow from mountain to sea stilled along its span entire.

She breathed out, and power gathered beyond any dream of resistance.

12

THE WILD-ASS BITCH drew her knives and came at him again, flourishing them in an intricate flurry, blank translucent concentration on her face. Berne let her come, waiting; when she came within Kosall's reach he cut at her head. She slipped beneath the stroke—for all his magicked strength, Kosall was a large and rather unwieldy weapon.

As she drove in under the cut, Berne whipped a straight-leg roundhouse kick at her ribs while holding his Buckler across his solar plexus to stop her knife thrust. Her point slashed through his shirt and *skirr*ed across his skin, and his roundhouse crumpled her like a doll, lifting her off her feet and sending her rolling across the bridge.

She rose unsteadily, blood on her lips. His kick had probably ruptured something in her midsection. But she offered a grin that displayed her bloody teeth, and she pointed to his leg.

"You're not invulnerable," she said.

Berne looked down. She'd cut his leg, the leg he'd kicked her with, with the other blade. The cut was shallow, only a skin-deep slice: his serge breeches soaked up the blood that seeped into them.

"Maybe not," he replied, "but I'm a long fucking way closer to it than you are."

Now for the first time, he advanced, attacking, slashing. She was a ghost, even injured: with more than human speed and grace she slipped away and around every stroke, never parrying, never blocking, avoiding Kosall's irresistible edge by inches.

It became a dance, a whirling ballet, and sweat began to prickle across Berne's forehead and shoulders. She'd lean back to let Kosall sizzle past the end of her nose, then whip forward, both knives slashing, to score another thin line of blood across Berne's body before he could recover for the backstrike. She was the most extraordinary fighter he'd ever *seen*, let alone faced, but skill is only one element of battle. Her skill wouldn't save her forever—the internal injury that brought a trail of blood down her chin to her chest would tire her, and slow her. Berne had no doubt of the outcome.

It ended with unexpected swiftness. Practically in midlunge Berne saw her concentration slip, saw her mouth drop open and her eyes go wide. He leaned into the lunge, and sweet release flooded his body as Kosall's thrumming blade entered her belly through the golden skin just below her navel, thrusting in to the very hilt.

She said, "Oh, Great Mother . . ."

Berne pressed his body against her slackening flesh, and he kissed her on her bloody lips, savoring their soft fullness and the copper taste of her blood. Then he stepped back and twisted Kosall's hilt so that the blade sliced outward through her side, opening a massive, gaping wound, from which spilled her uncoiling intestines.

She gasped and fell to her knees. Berne stepped back, panting, and watched her fingers gingerly explore the huge extent of the mortal wound, this incredible gape that split her front to back, watched her follow the ropes of her guts out onto the dirt and grit of the bridge span. Her face was utterly blank with disbelief.

"Never thought it could happen to you, huh?" Berne said hoarsely, breathless. "Sorry I won't get to fuck you. Don't really like 'em cold, y'know? But this, this was almost as good."

He thought for a moment she was going to say something to him, but then he realized that she wasn't looking at him, hadn't been looking at him from the moment he'd stabbed her. She looked *behind* him, over his shoulder, east along the river. Berne turned to follow her gaze, and his breath stopped.

He thought, *Fuck me like a goat.*

Coming toward him, along the river, thundered a wall of green-foaming water a hundred feet high, a titanic wave that bore before it boats and crates and the bodies of men. Berne looked up, and up, unable to comprehend the enormity of the catastrophe that rushed down upon him. The sun struck gold on the unutterable mass of water that still grew as it approached, not yet cresting. High up upon its face rode the river barge, sliding down the face of the wave yet borne up by its rolling progress—and high above the river barge, standing like a god at the very crest of this mountain of water, stood a lone figure, a woman . . .

Pallas Ril.

His reaction was instant: he knew he'd never make it if he tried to clear the bridge. There was no time.

He said, with perfectly enunciated calm, "Ma'elKoth."

I AM WITH YOU, BERNE.

High above him, on the crest of the wave, Pallas Ril rode toward him—without any sign of a Shield.

Berne said, "I'll take that firebolt, now."

Flame burst from his skin, and he lifted his fist.

13

SHE SANG IN her mind, without words, without images: pure melody and pure desire. She sang a wave that would carry the lives within that barge far, far to the sea in a single wave, a rolling sweeping falling that would strike bottom only in the Teranese harbor.

And men fired upon her as she rode the crest of this wave, but their target was only a single note of an eternal song. The song had a life of its own that would not allow her harm. She lifted her arms, and water sprang up around her as though it were castle walls. Quarrels plunged bubbling into these walls, lances of air that trailed to nothing.

Far, far below she saw Berne, and Talann's body beside him on the bridge. The westering sun struck off the face of the wave that reared high above him, reflected from it and lit his face as though with fire; she saw the pulse of the channel that linked him to the Colhari Palace, and felt the surge of Flow.

His firebolt clawed toward her.

She could not match their power, even now; but matching power with power was no longer required. A shrug of melody, a twitch of rhythm raised a mighty arm of foam to take the bolt. It exploded into hissing steam, a warm twisting cloud of purest white that broke around her and below her as she soared ever higher on the crest.

Knights' Bridge trembled as the wave approached, and shattered when it struck. With a thunder that shook the Cyclopean walls around the whole of Old Town, the wave rolled on, carrying the barge and half a dozen smaller vessels high over the top curve of the antiship chains, and sent them spinning downstream for freedom.

I did it, Pallas thought. *I did it,* and that second's thought brought her back to herself—

Standing at the crest of a wave two hundred feet high, looking down on the rooftops of Ankhana, looking down even upon the Colhari Palace itself, looking down at incredible destruction along the wharf from the very edge of Fools' Bridge to the ruin of Knights' Bridge: ships and boats overturned, splintered against each other; dozens of men in the water, some struggling, some only floating facedown; front walls of warehouses all along the riverfront staved in, water still pouring out from them; fish flopping desperately on the dockside . . .

She cried out involuntarily at the sight of the shambles she had made. In that instant of shocked immobility, as the wave started to fall and she came down with it, an unknown bowman fired his weapon from the city wall, and his quarrel slammed into her chest, shattering a rib and spearing into her lung.

She fell in a dream, tasting blood that bubbled up her throat along with her breath. Her hand lazily investigated the steel flanges of the quarrel that were stuck hard up against her light leather body armor.

I'm hit, she thought numbly. *I'm hit,* and: *I did it.*

This was all she could think during the long tumble to the river below; when she reached bottom, the impact with the roiling water snuffed her consciousness like a fist on a candle flame, and she knew no more.

14

THE UNIFORMED LABORER who piloted the smooth-humming cabin apparently did so simply by shifting a floor-mounted lever: forward for go, back for stop; otherwise, the car directed itself. Beyond this shifting of a lever, the Laborer's only duty seemed to be to stand at attention and hold himself smilingly available for polite conversation with his passengers.

Neither of his passengers was interested in talking: Marc Vilo had the upcaste ability to make himself selectively blind to anyone below Professional, and Hari passed the ride concentrating on a meditative cycle of breath, hoping that he could loosen the knots in his stomach and swallow the acid tension at the back of his throat.

Marc had picked up Hari in his own Rolls. He had chattered with bluff good-fellowship across nearly a quarter of the Pacific Ocean, nattering on and on about his acquisitions and under-the-table deals, about undercutting this competitor and putting a regulatory squeeze on that one. As the cloud-topped islands came into view, though, his chatter had gone hollow, and finally stopped. Despite his pre-sumed affair with Shermaya Dole, no one was entirely at ease while approaching the airspace of a Leisure compound—and the Doles were one of the original First Families.

Hari took the blessed silence as a gift. Had he always found Vilo this tiresome, and somehow managed to repress his irritation all these years? Did the man never think of anything beyond his balls and his bank balance?

It wasn't until the Rolls was spiraling in for a landing at the Kauai carport that Vilo even thought to ask why Hari had asked for this interview.

His tone made it clear that this was a courtesy question, the way a man might give a distracted pat on the head to his dog in passing. How important, really, could anything be that would come out of the mouth of a downcaster? The question, even the entire trip to Kauai and the interview itself, was an indulgence, and Vilo probably expected Hari to squirm like a happy puppy at this show of avuncular affection.

If so, he was disappointed. As the Rolls settled onto the grassy landing field, Hari had given him a flat stare and answered the question through his teeth.

"I'm gonna ask her to find a way to get Arturo Kollberg's dick out of my ass."

Before Vilo could come up with a response, a uniformed atten-dant had stepped out of nowhere and undogged the Rolls' hatch from outside. He'd ushered them out and across the lush grass of the landing field. Hari had had time to get only a breath or two of the rich, floral-scented air, only a glimpse of the riot of greens that climbed the ridge of mountains before him, before a section of vol-canic stone at the edge of the field swung back, and the attendant led them inside to the waiting cabin.

The cabin moved on a computer-directed path through tunnels cut into the earth, cut through the rock of the ridges and up the mountains. Since the days of Shermaya's great-grandfather, ma-chines more complex than a bicycle had been forbidden in the inte-rior of Kauai. Surface transport within the Dole compound was by horseback. But this was mostly make-believe, a show of back-to-nature simplicity, that let the Doles and their guests pretend to enjoy the raw outdoors without sacrificing the full comforts of a modern home. On Kauai, all those comforts and then some were there. An entire subterranean town complex spread like cancer through the bones of the island, thousands of servants and technicians and every imaginable luxury, carefully concealed but omnipresent.

During the smooth, silent ride to wherever the hell it was that Dole awaited them, Hari managed to quiet his nerves a little bit by observing Vilo's. The stumpy Businessman shifted uneasily in his seat, chewing on the end of his unlit cigar, glancing at Hari from the corner of his eye and glancing away again. Clearly, he'd suddenly become very unsure that bringing Hari here was a good idea, but he also clearly felt he couldn't say a damn thing about it, not in front of the *servant*—God only knows what kind of rumors would spread . . .

When the cabin hummed to a stop and the doors opened, Vilo leaned over to Hari and glared at him, his face as full of threat as a loaded pistol.

Very softly, almost whispering, he growled, "You behave yourself, Hari, and I'm not kidding," then rose and stepped out of the cabin, his face clearing with practiced swiftness into a lickspittle grin. Hari shrugged, sighed, and followed him.

He stepped out into a rainbow.

The door had opened from a mossy stone outcrop onto a broad ledge, two-thirds of the way up the wall of a mist-bottomed canyon. The opposite wall of the narrow canyon seemed close enough to touch. Everywhere he looked there swarmed foliage of unimaginable variety, a vertical rain forest of every conceivable shade of green, shot through with ropes of brilliant flowers and punctuated with the iridescent shimmer of tropical birds that flitted back and forth among the vines.

High above the ledge where he stood, another outcropping divided a waterfall, so that a pair of hushing streams fell to either side and a sun-prismed spray filled the air.

Only when Dole herself rose from behind a twisted knee-height juniper, wearing loose-fitting clothing that was smeared with greens and browns, and calling out a hearty "Marcus! Over here!" did Hari notice that the ledge on which they all stood had been landscaped as a Japanese garden. Carefully cultivated dwarf shrubbery clumsily accented an array of colored stones and a trickling watercourse that must have sprung from underground pumps.

Dole beckoned to them with a pair of sap-stained garden shears. "One of my projects," she called, waving the shears at the garden around her. "What do you think?"

Hari again trailed in Vilo's wake, his wounds making him move stiffly and slowly, and listened silently to Vilo's effusions about the garden. The Businessman sat on a rock near where Dole had once again knelt to hand-trim a bush, as near as he dared without risking her dignity with uninvited contact. Hari stood a respectful distance away and waited to be acknowledged.

Dole's cheeks colored at Vilo's praise, and she waved away his enthusiasm. "Well, you know, one must keep busy. It's work that makes you happy, you know—I've never understood why our Laborers seem to dislike it so. Entertainer," she said, waving Hari closer. "How do you like my garden?"

It's a thumb in the eye of this place, Hari thought, but he said respectfully, "Your entire home is a garden, Leisurema'am."

"Ah, a diplomat. Come, sit with us." Once Hari had painfully settled in next to Vilo, she went on. "I was so enjoying your Adventure, Entertainer. You'll be continuing tomorrow, in the morning? Yes, and I'm sure Marcus will squire me once again; I am so looking forward to a successful conclusion. I've been dreadfully worried about Shanna, you know."

"Yes, ma'am," Hari said. "Me, too."

Inch toward daylight, he thought. "I'm not sure that they'll *let* me succeed," he went on. "That's, uh, that's kind of why I asked to be allowed to come here and talk with you."

"Oh?" she said with a polite lift of the brow.

"Yeah, it's a pretty tough spot," Vilo put in. "Especially now that Berne has all these magic powers and that sword and everything. How do you think you're gonna handle him?"

Hari shook his head. "I'm not talking about Berne. Him, I'm hoping not to handle at all. It's the Studio. They *want* Shanna to die. It'll make a better story."

"*Hari*—! Jesus *Christ!*" Vilo said, choking on his cigar.

"Entertainer," Dole said severely, "that is a very serious charge. If believed, it could harm their business; repeating it in public would leave you open to downcasteing for corporate slander."

"Even if it's true?"

"Especially if it's true. In corporate slander, truth is not a defense. Besides, I hardly think—"

"That *technical malfunction,*" Hari interrupted her desperately, "the one that pulled me out last night—it wasn't a malfunction at all. I had this from Kollberg's own mouth. I was too close to saving Shanna, and they pulled me. Deliberately. Kollberg himself hit the switch."

"I can't be *hearing* this," Vilo said, jerking to his feet. "Don't you understand that what you've just told me is a legitimate *corporate secret*? Do you have any idea how *compromising* this is? Now I have to either report you or face accessory charges—!"

"Oh, Marcus, sit down," Dole snapped. "Stop fluttering. Nothing said here need ever leave this place."

"I notice," Hari said, "that you haven't said you don't believe me."

"I, ah . . ." Vilo shifted uncomfortably, then finally dropped back down onto his rock. "Well, shit—your pardon, Maya. Everybody knows the Studio, kind of, ooches things around, to make the Adventures more exciting."

"And that is," Dole pointed out, "a perfectly legitimate business practice. Shanna is under contract to the Studio, as are you, Entertainer. If the legitimate pursuit of their business requires that they send you to your death, they are perfectly within their rights under contract law. It's no different than if I ordered one of my pilots to fly into a storm; if he is killed, that is simply a consequence of his employment, and I am not criminally liable. Any grievances must be addressed in civil court."

"I *know* all that," Hari said. "I know that legally there's nothing *I* can do to stop them doing whatever they want to her. That's why I came to you. I know you care about Shanna. I came to ask you—to beg you, if necessary—to intervene for her."

"Oh, for Christ's sake," Vilo said. "You think the Leisurema'am has nothing better to do than—"

"Marcus, please." Dole turned to Hari, a look of well-intentioned helplessness on her face. "I'm sorry, Entertainer, but I don't believe that there's very much I can do."

"He—Kollberg—he sent Lamorak over there with *orders* to betray her. He sent someone he knew she *trusted*. Lamorak's been tipping off the Grey Cats at every turn. And you know why? Because she was *too good* at this—she's too smart, too skilled. She was going to be able to save all these people without taking any big risks, without any big battles, without any innocents being killed—and Kollberg wouldn't have been able to sell enough second-fucking-hander cubes!"

Hari trembled with the effort of keeping his fury under control. "He *fucked* her: he sent Lamorak there to betray her, for no other reason than a few extra marks."

"Well, that's reprehensible behavior, certainly, but still . . . Oh, was that it? Right before you were pulled?"

She leaned forward, her face lighting with more interest than he'd yet seen from her. "You realized that Lamorak was the traitor, and you were about to *kill* him! My goodness. That wouldn't have been a very fair fight."

"I don't care much about fighting fair," Hari said. "I'll settle with Lamorak later. What I care about is saving Shanna's life."

"Oh, well, I too, of course, but I still don't see any way I can intervene. They've done nothing wrong."

"They've done nothing *illegal*," Hari said. "They've done a lot that's wrong."

"From your point of view, certainly, I can understand."

"Couldn't you just—*lean* on him a little?"

"I'm sorry?"

"Put some pressure on Kollberg. Make him behave."

Dole spread her hands. "I don't think so. There's very little pressure I can bring. The Studio is a public trust," she said simply. "It was created to be immune to outside pressure. I'm sorry."

Hari hung his head, but at his thighs his fists clenched spasmodically. Caine snarled within the tightness that bound his chest, and for a wild half instant he teetered on the verge of snapping and slaughtering them both.

He ground his teeth and tried to remember that these were not his enemies. His chest burned; he couldn't stop remembering that if he tuned in *Adventure Update* right now, he could watch the seconds tick away on the Pallas Ril Lifeclock.

There had to be something, *had to be* . . .

"Wait a second," he said, lifting his head. "You're Shanna's Patron. She's the spokesman for three or four of your companies. That makes her a, ah, a corporate *symbol*, right?"

"Yes . . ." Dole said dubiously.

Vilo shook his head. "I don't see what that has to do with anything."

Suddenly Hari was on his feet, his eyes alight, his hands grabbing inspiration from the air.

"But, but, but—don't you *get it*? That gives her *intrinsic value* to the companies she represents, value that maybe could be legally *separable* from her employment as an Actor."

Vilo frowned skeptically. "You're going to go after the Studio through *trademark law*?"

"Why not?" Hari said. "Why not? By intentionally planning her death, Kollberg is deliberately infringing upon her value as a spokesman, isn't he? The loss of consumer identification, from shifting to a new spokesman, that could translate to actual damages—"

"It's *ridiculous*," Vilo said. "It's never been done. Shit, even if it worked, a precedent like that could destroy the whole Studio system—I mean, even scheduling an Actor on a few safe, boring Adventures would reduce his value as a spokesman and a trademark . . ."

But Hari had no attention to spare for Vilo's objections; his breath had stopped in his throat as he watched the play of expression across Dole's smooth and kindly face.

There was doubt there, certainly, but she was thinking about it—and she was slowly coming toward some kind of decision.

"It is," she said suddenly, reaching out for Hari's hand, "brilliant! So what if it's never been done? Arturo Kollberg is deliberately reducing the income of a noncompeting business, and from an immune position, as an officer of a public trust. I should be able to get a cease-and-desist on him before the close of business today."

She rose and laid a hand upon the arm that was bound to Hari's chest for a moment, and then drew him, astonishingly, into a hug.

Hari and Vilo gaped at each other over Dole's shoulder until she released him. Tears shone in her eyes.

"I knew you really loved her," Dole said. "I knew it wasn't just an act. I could feel it. Thank you so much for finding a way to let me help you save her."

Hari's whole body tingled, partly from the sheer height from which she'd stooped to touch him—Leisure to ex-Labor—and partly from an early intimation of victory.

Dole's face now hardened. "And I tell you something else: if we can find any hard evidence, any evidence *at all* that will stand up in court, I swear to you that I will not rest until that vile little man is crushed. He will not live to try this again with someone else. That won't be easy; you know their files and procedures are sacrosanct—"

"I know," Hari whispered, because he could not trust his voice. *Inch toward daylight.*

"I'll find something. You'll see. Somehow, I'll get what you need."

"I know you will."

Dole now turned away and spoke to the air. "Robert." Mist jetted out from concealed vents in the rock face, and intersecting lasers formed a full-animation holosculpture of her majordomo.

"Madam?"

She began issuing instructions to be channeled to the Dole

Family's vast galaxy of lawyers. Hari and his Patron were forced to wait while she made her plans and arrangements. A couple of times during those minutes Hari caught Vilo staring at him through narrowed eyes, a sort of newly appreciative squint, as though he was having difficulty reconciling what he saw with what he'd expected to see.

Hari answered this stare with an expressive shrug.

Dad was right, Hari thought. *I don't have to solve every problem with my fists.*

His father had told him to inch toward daylight, but some inches are longer than others.

Day Six

"Hari? Hari, wake up."

"Hurr . . . ?"

"Hari, I've been thinking. I can't do this anymore."

"Shan . . . can't do what? It's four o'clock, for Christ's sake. Can't this wait till morning?"

"I don't like who I am with you, Hari. Do you understand that? Can you?"

"I don't understand anything at this time of the morning . . ."

"Hari, I want a divorce."

1

ANKHANA WENT TO bed with terror and disbelief, but the disbelief fled during the night: at dawn, only terror remained—slow terror, the kind that feels like icy teeth chewing on your bones.

There was no one in the city who did not know of the battle at dockside, no one who did not have a friend or family member who had been there, who had seen it with their own eyes. Some had connected it to the recent explosions in the Industrial Park; it seemed that a day did not pass without a pitched battle somewhere in the streets of the capital.

Those citizens brave or desperate enough to risk these streets this morning did so with frequent over-the-shoulder glances. They strolled or hurried depending on how near they chanced to be to a sheltered doorway or narrow alley down which they could run should battle suddenly erupt.

Ankhana was a notoriously violent city, but even here there had always been limits: a brawl might end in a stabbing, or the constables might clash with a stonebender gang in Alientown, but a pitched battle in the streets was far beyond the pale.

375

Fear was fueled by a problem of *scale*, as well: jets of fire a thousand yards long, the whole dockside burning, that monstrous wall of water—it was insane, incomprehensible. Who could possibly be safe, even in their own homes behind Old Town's massive walls, when such things can occur in broad daylight?

When Ma'elKoth had begun his campaign to cleanse the Empire of the *Aktiri*, only the most childishly superstitious of his subjects had believed that such beings existed. But as *Aktiri* were discovered, slowly, here and there in places of responsibility throughout the Empire, even among the nobility, this disbelief had turned to a sort of nervous suspiciousness.

Neighbors and acquaintances suddenly became conscious of each other's peculiarities—the sort of little quirks of personality and behavior that had seemed harmless before, but now appeared inexplicable and more than a little sinister. After all, how was one to know who might secretly be an *Aktir*?

Rumors began to circulate of certain touchstones that would cry out when pressed to an *Aktir*'s flesh, of characteristic witch marks that could be found upon an *Aktir*'s body. Tales were told of men who woke and found an *Aktir* in bed beside them in place of their beloved wives—the substitution having taken place under a new moon at midnight—tales of *Aktiri* curses, of poisonings and massacres and more. Each was more extreme than the last, as though truth could be found only by topping what people thought they knew. Everyone felt in their secret hearts that the worst was yet to come, and so each fanciful escalation was taken as hard evidence of how bad things would eventually get.

There were conflicting stories about the proper way to destroy an *Aktir*. Some held that a simple ash-wood stake through the heart would suffice; others claimed that its lips must be sewn shut over a mouthful of copper coins, and then its severed head must be buried facedown at a crossroads. Most agreed that to burn the *Aktir* alive on a pyre of wood soaked with oil that had been blessed by a priest of Prorithun would serve as well as any other method.

Out in the provinces, these and many other techniques were widely experimented with on any number of the usual outcast folk—old solitary widows, eccentric men who kept to themselves at the edge of this or that village, all the folk of this sort—and all were found to work quite well.

Later, stories began to filter into the cities of wealthier, more prosperous peasants being accused, and even some gentlefolk, small landholders and the like. The cityfolk nodded wisely to each other at these tales of provincial superstition and speculated— often correctly—that the accusers in these cases somehow ended up in possession of the executed *Aktir*'s land and goods.

Only later did it occur to these worldly-wise city dwellers to wonder how the sum of their own little quirks and pecadillos might appear to their neighbors; only later did they wonder how vulnerable they themselves might be to false accusation; only later did they begin to eye their more prosperous neighbors, wondering how vulnerable *they* might be, as well.

These screws of tension had been driven tight into the heart of the Empire for months now, even while most of the citizens of the Empire only reluctantly, halfheartedly believed that the *Aktiri* were any more than a ghost tale to frighten children. Many of the citizens listened with a sort of sneaking approval to stories of the slippery rebel Simon Jester, who seemed to effortlessly defy the constituted authority of the entire Empire; Simon Jester had become something of a folk hero, a cunning rogue who could thumb his nose at the power of Ma'elKoth himself.

Anyone in Ankhana who still felt that way need only pause a moment and cast a glance at the wreckage of Knights' Bridge, or pay a copper coin to a page of the *Imperial Messenger-News* to hear a recital of the names of the innocent dead along the dockside—a hundred men and more. Sailors, dockers, warehousemen, and clerks wiped from existence without warning. As a kitchen tale, Simon Jester was entertaining, but as a real, powerful, implacable foe of the Empire, he was terrifying.

These liveried pages also gave an account of how the thaumaturge who'd caused such unimaginable destruction had been captured by the heroism of Count Berne. The pages who wore the green and gold of the competing news service, *Colin's Pages and Current Events,* gave a somewhat different story—of the marksmanship of an unknown bowman and the escape of a boatload of accused *Aktiri* downriver. The army had sworn to take them, but thus far they remained at large.

Suddenly the *Aktiri* had become *real* to Ankhana in a way they had never been before. The *Aktiri* really were out there, as powerful and terrifying as even the wildest stories had ever claimed them to be. Not off somewhere in some distant land across the sea, not in the provinces, not even in some other great city on the far side of the Empire, but *right here, right now.*

Those citizens who were given to prayer now prayed for Ma'el-Koth, prayed to their gods to protect their Emperor and strengthen his mighty arm in his death struggle with the unholy *Aktiri*. Many more of the citizenry found themselves kneeling uncomfortably, unused to the position, before the statues in their small household shrines; instead of praying for Ma'elKoth, they prayed *to* him. The Beloved Children of Ma'elKoth had no other shield.

The object of their prayer was busy this morning. He had forgone his daily morning's ritual of constructing his Great Work; instead he paced to and fro beside the bloodstained limestone altar in the Iron Room.

Some of the blood on the altar was fresh: it leaked through the neatly tied bandages that covered the sucking chest wound of Pallas Ril, who was staked spread-eagled across the coffin-sized stone.

The interrogation progressed very slowly indeed; Arkadeil was in no condition to work and Ma'elKoth felt he couldn't trust any of the apprentices in a matter of such delicacy.

His own techniques lacked, perhaps, the elegance and refinement of Arkadeil's art, but he felt sure they would prove equally effective, in the end.

2

THE MOB OF downcasters surged against the Studio gate and splashed back upon itself like a wave against a seawall. This incoming tide of desperate fans was vast—doubling, tripling the record numbers the Studio had expected. They were packed shoulder to shoulder over the surrounding right-of-way, pressed back to the walls of distant buildings. An excited secman, standing atop the gate in the light of the rising sun, babbled into his comlink that he was sure there must be more than two million people outside waiting for Caine's arrival.

This was only a mild exaggeration; the secman had overestimated the size of the crowd, but not by much.

They were all to be disappointed: Caine was already inside.

His blood-crusted black leathers had been carefully removed from his battered, unconscious body in the Studio infirmary and stored overnight in the Studio ON vault. Hari had arrived by cab long before dawn, and it was down in the vault that Kollberg found him.

The vault, with its Overworld-normal field, conferred almost perfect privacy. Its thick walls were innately soundproof, and the slightly altered physics within its field prevented electronic eavesdropping.

Kollberg posted two of the riot-armed Worker secmen at the vault door on his way in. He kept two more with him, with careful orders to hold their power rifles at the ready between him and Michaelson and to shoot without warning if Michaelson made the slightest move to attack.

Michaelson had become so unstable that all of Kollberg's precautions were predicated on the assumption that Michaelson would become psychotically violent at the first opportunity. Kollberg had made the mistake the other night of being in the line of fire; only the shield of his heavy desk had saved him from injury. This was a mistake he did not intend to repeat.

The safest option, of course, would have been to avoid Michaelson entirely, to have someone else deliver the greenroom instructions, but Kollberg knew well that the safest option is often not the *best* one. The instructions he must give were of a delicate nature; the fewer people who knew about them, the better. This was why he'd chosen the Worker secmen instead of drawing his guards from the more flexible and responsive Laborers: testimony by a Worker was meaningless in any court.

Furthermore, he'd been up all night basting in his own juices, in a fury after a curt screencall from a Dole Family lawyer—imagine, a Professional allowed, even encouraged, to disturb an Administrator at his home! The man's tone was so clearly insolent that Kollberg had immediately filed a countercomplaint with the Social Police, but that had done little to ease the acid ball in his belly.

Between this disturbance, the brutal stress of preparing the climax of this Adventure, and the amphetamine he'd taken to give himself the energy to get everything done, he hadn't slept at all.

And he couldn't let an incident like this pass unanswered. No matter how big a star Caine might be, Michaelson was still only a Professional, and he could not be allowed to one-up his betters. In fact, this incident bothered him more than Michaelson's attempt to lay hands upon him; the attempted violence was merely an outgrowth of Michaelson's increasing instability, while this ridiculous legal maneuvering was clearly a calculated insult.

When Kollberg entered the vault behind the lockstepping Workers, Michaelson stood nearly naked before the dressing mirror. Caine's leathers hung from a peg nearby, and the surgical tape that had bound his torso lay in scissor-cut tangles on the floor behind him. He wore only his leather jockstrap, and he watched himself in the mirror as he flowed through a series of complex stretching exercises, scowling and wincing at the aches and pains these produced.

He looked worse than Kollberg felt. Despite the antibiotics, the crudely stitched wound in his shoulder flared an angry red, and his back swelled with the neat blackened discs of gelslug bruises, clustered around a larger, ragged one tinged with red, left by a Donjon guard's iron-bound club. Another red-purple bruise swelled at the outside of his bandaged right knee, and even Kollberg's untrained eye could see the stiffness in each of his movements. From the pasty look of his hollowed cheeks and the shadowed smears beneath his eyes, he'd missed some sleep himself last night.

In the mirror, his reflected eyes met Kollberg's without so much as a glance at the armored secmen.

"Kollberg," he said flatly. "You don't want to be in here, right now."

"That's *Administrator* Kollberg, Michaelson," he replied with a tight smile.

Michaelson's expression didn't change. "Fuck you, shitheel."

A cold tingle shot through Kollberg, as though he'd touched a poorly grounded terminal.

He blinked once, twice, then took a deep breath and answered calmly. "I'll have my due respect or I will have you broken for caste violation."

"That is your due respect, you flabby sack of shit. Do whatever you want."

Kollberg glanced at the cyborgs between them. "Or I could simply have you shot."

Michaelson shrugged. "Then what do you tell the Leisurefolk—what is it, a million of them, now?—that've already paid to be me this morning? Never thought that making me such a big star would whip around and bite you on the ass, huh?"

Kollberg nodded to himself; he should have seen this coming. "I came here this morning to, ah, outline for you the ground rules of this Adventure. I have already spoken with the Board of Governors on this matter, and they concur. The emergency transfer switch will remain active. At the first suggestion of seditious commentary, you will be recalled, and the Adventure will be terminated."

Michaelson made no response. He stared into the mirror with an expression of peculiar concentration; he seemed to be watching his hands, his fingertips, as they lightly brushed first one, then another of the numerous scars that patterned his body, kneading each in turn.

"Seditious commentary," Kollberg continued, "will include any reference to your contracted goal of the assassination of Ma'elKoth. When you face him, it will appear to be the result of a *personal vendetta*, do you understand? Any reference to this being at the direction of the Studio will result in your immediate recall."

As if in answer, Michaelson's hands stroked the flattened diamonds of scar tissue, front and back, left by a long-ago sword-thrust through the liver.

"If you make any reference to Lamorak as the betrayer of Pallas Ril, whether you connect it to his contract—to the Studio—or not, you will be immediately recalled."

Michaelson ran his fingers over a jagged scar across his collar-bone.

"If you make any reference to your mistaken idea that Pallas Ril's difficulties are in any way related to any policy or directive of the Studio, you will be immediately recalled."

Michaelson's hand ran up a long, keloid-knotted scar on his right thigh.

"If you are recalled for any of these reasons, you will not be re-turned to Ankhana. Your wife will be left to fend for herself. The press will be told that the transfer malfunction seems to reflect some peculiarity of Ankhana itself, and it is too dangerous for you to return. Any public contradiction of this story will result in your being broken back to Labor and put out to work in the Temp slums where you came from."

Michaelson slowly pulled on his leather breeches, then slipped into the blood-crusted jerkin and laced it up to his chest, touching each knife in its sheath as he did so.

"When you confront Ma'elKoth, you will do so *outside* the Col-hari Palace. The Studio has invested far too much in this Adventure to have its climax occur offstage. At this confrontation, you will re-move him from power or die in the attempt. If either of these conditions are violated, on your return you will face downcasteing for slander and corporate espionage."

Kollberg smiled broadly, showing his teeth. "Your silly little cease-and-desist order contains information that the Dole Family could have gotten only through you; it's prima facie evidence of corporate espionage. I *own* you, do you understand? I can break you any time I want."

Michaelson pulled on his low boots of soft black leather without response.

"I said, do you understand?"

"I understand." Michaelson's voice was low and flat, almost a growl; this certainly wasn't the tone of submission that Kollberg looked for, the tone he demanded.

"Don't think that Shermaya Dole can protect you, not from the Studio; she can't," Kollberg said. "Don't expect her to even try."

"I don't."

Now, for the first time, Michaelson turned away from the mirror and met Kollberg's eyes face-to-face, and a cold shiver started in the Administrator's belly.

Michaelson said, "Who do you think is going to protect *you*?"

Kollberg's eyes bulged. "Have you heard a word I've *said*?" he spluttered.

"Yeah. Now listen to these words: there is nothing you can do to save your life."

"What?" This was incredible; this was intolerable! Had Michaelson forgotten to whom he was *speaking*?

But as Kollberg looked into Michaelson's expressionless black eyes, he realized he was no longer talking to Hari Michaelson.

This was Caine.

"You crossed a line," Caine said. "You crossed *my* line, and I'll see you dead for it. No one uses Shanna like this and lives. Even if I *win*: if I survive, if I bring Shanna back, if I kill Berne and Ma'elKoth and god knows who else, come back to Earth with no harm done to live happily ever after; even then, there is no happy ending for you. Enjoy these last days of your life, Kollberg. You don't have many left."

Kollberg could only stare, his mouth opening and closing with the moist silence of the last gasps of a beached fish.

Caine stretched one last time, and his joints popped like faroff gunfire. He cracked the knuckles of both hands, one by one. "There's about fifteen billion marks' worth of audience out there waiting for me right now," he said. "You'd better get out of my way."

3

HAIR THAT GLEAMS like metal under the floodlights, lips wet with something like lust:

"Welcome back to *Adventure Update*. I'm Bronson Underwood. Our top story this morning is once again the Adventure of the Decade. Bloody but unbowed, Caine returns to Ankhana in very few minutes from now, for a final desperate attempt to save his wife from the horrors of amplitude decay. As you can see from the Pallas Ril Lifeclock graphic in the corner of your screen, we estimate that she has less than thirty-six hours remaining. However, due to chaotic uncertainty in phase locking, amplitude decay could theoretically begin within the day. Whatever the true limit is, time is very short indeed.

"Pallas Ril's predicament, and Caine's heroic attempts at a rescue, have captured imaginations worldwide, and the Studio has not been slow to capitalize. Here with that side of the story, live from Studio Center in San Francisco, is our chief correspondent, Jed Clearlake."

"Good morning, Bronson."

"Good morning, Jed. This is quite an event, isn't it?"

"Bronson, it's like nothing I've ever seen before. I've been covering Ankhanan operations for *Adventure Update* for a few years now, and I guess you've realized that this is the biggest thing to ever come out of San Francisco. The numbers released by the Studio this morning are nothing short of staggering. The previous record for first-handers on-line for a single Adventure—which, as you know, was set only four days ago at the outset of *For Love of Pallas Ril*—has been shattered more than tenfold this morning. Public demand for access to Caine has led the Studio system worldwide to cancel the majority of their other ongoing Adventures, preempting them to provide firsthand seats for this one. As Caine prepares to make his transfer this morning, official counts have his firsthand audience at *one point six million*. Assuming, as we do, that these are nearly all Leisurefolk and Investors, you should understand that more than *seventy percent* of Caine's potential audience will be on-line. More than *one billion people* have already placed advance orders for the secondhand cubes. This is more than the Adventure of the Decade, Bronson. This is the story of the century."

"Impressive numbers, Jed, impressive indeed. Does the Studio plan to share any more live feed with us, over the course of this extraordinary event?"

"I've been in contact with Studio Chairman Arturo Kollberg's office, and all they're saying is that we should hold ourselves ready. So I'm guessing all signs are good, Bronson."

"Thank you, Jed. We'll be back with you in a moment. Now we go to Chicago, where Jessica Roan has caught up with Pallas Ril's parents, Alan and Mara Leighton, as they enter the Chicago Studio to firsthand this incredible Adventure. Jessica?"

"Good morning, Bronson . . ."

And the whole world waits, and squirms, and drools like a glutton smelling a feast.

4

THE STUDIO'S PERSONNEL tracking system located Kollberg as soon as he left the ON vault, and the nearest wallscreen flashed at him and loudly announced, "Administrator Kollberg! Urgent message from Professional Mona Carson!"

Professional Carson was the San Francisco head of Studio Legal; this could only mean a serious problem. Kollberg muttered a curse and wiped his sweaty palms on his smock before he responded.

"Go."

The screen lit with Carson's bird-boned face, her delicate brows drawn together in a worried frown.

"Administrator, Caine's and Pallas Ril's Patrons are both up in the Cavea's techbooth right now—and they've brought the Social Police. Please confirm receipt of this message, and then meet me there ASAP."

Kollberg felt like he'd been sandbagged; he was about two rungs on the caste ladder too low not to go weak in the knees on hearing that soapies were waiting for him. For a moment, the hallway seemed to spin around him, and he was afraid he might faint.

The dizziness passed, and he fumbled in the pockets of his smock for the carton of speed, shaking out another capsule and dry-swallowing it painfully before sending the Worker secmen back to their racks. It wouldn't do to arrive with secmen in tow; it'd make him look suspiciously frightened.

He glanced at the wallscreen and ordered his private lift, then strode toward it as forcefully as he could manage, as though by pretending confidence, he could generate some.

Carson was waiting for him at the techbooth door when he came puffing up.

"There's nothing I can do about it, Administrator. They hit us with a surprise injunction, and the Social Police have a proper warrant: our public-trust exceptions are unbreakable, but they've dodged around them. I have Legal on their way to court already for a temporary restraining order, but they're ready for us, and they'll make us argue it out. It'll take hours to get them out of here, at best."

"This is about that damned cease-and-desist, isn't it?"

Carson nodded. "They've brought the soapies to enforce compliance."

Kollberg smacked a soft fist against his palm, and hairs began to stand up along his arms: he was getting a surge from the amphetamine already.

"Damn them. All right, I'll take over here. You keep working on it."

"I will, but I'm up against Dole Family lawyers . . ."

She didn't need to say any more; Kollberg understood perfectly. "We'll make the best of it, Mona. Don't give up."

She nodded, then left with a promise to keep up the fight. Kollberg took a moment to inhale deeply several times and smooth his smock before he opened the techbooth door and stepped inside.

Shermaya Dole sat in his chair at the stage manager's station, holding court among the dazzled techs like a queen. They'd never been this close to Leisurefolk before, and they were stammering and falling over each other, blushingly obsequious.

Standing at her side like a prince consort was Marc Vilo, and behind them stood a pair of soapies in their sky blue jumpsuits and their silver-masked helmets.

Kollberg pasted a smile across his meaty lips and said, "Leisurema'am Dole, Businessman Vilo, it's an unexpected honor to find you in my techbooth."

Vilo snorted, openly contemptuous, and Dole said, "Marc, please. Be gracious." She sat a little straighter in his chair and spoke regally.

"Administrator. I'm sorry that we must meet again under these . . . adversarial circumstances. I hope that you understand that none of this—" She waved a finger at the soapies behind her. "—is directed at you personally. They are only here because of some disturbing reports that are becoming common knowledge on the nets, and I feel that I must take steps to protect the interests of the Dole Family and our undercastes."

"Common knowledge on the nets?" Kollberg said with a pretense of polite surprise. The upcaste bitch was trying to slip Michaelson off the hook, and there really wasn't much he could do about it, here and now.

"Oh, yes. And while I understand that the Studio's records and contracts are sealed, any observations made by social enforcement officers will be legally admissible as evidence."

"You seem very well informed on Business law," Kollberg murmured.

She shrugged coquettishly, a gesture Kollberg found gruesome in a beefy woman nearing middle age. "I have my little hobbies," she said. "One must keep busy, you know. Now, I believe we must be on our way. Marc is squiring me once again in his private box, and Caine will be mounting the transfer platform at any moment. Thank you for your time, Administrator, and I do apologize for the inconvenience. Come, Marc," she said, rising, and they left without another word.

Kollberg eyed the soapies; they hadn't moved, and he felt a little queasy about sitting in the stage manager's chair with these blank silver faces peering over his shoulders.

He turned to one of the wide-eyed techs. "Two chairs for the Social Police. Now."

The tech scurried off.

"We'll stand," one of the soapies said. They stood close enough together that he couldn't tell from which one the digitized voice had come. "When we feel the need to sit, we'll sit. Now get on with it."

Kollberg coughed into his fist and settled tensely into the chair, painfully aware of hidden eyes behind him.

"All right," he said tightly. "Fine. Signal the greenroom and tell Caine he's on in five."

5

THE CLOSET THAT materializes around me is barely larger than a coffin, and it leans at a crazy angle: it's set into a wall that's in the midst of a monthlong slow-sagging process of falling over. A little grey cloud-light leaks in from a rent above my head, and the closet reeks of moldy plaster and wet charcoal.

I put my shoulder against the moist and swollen wood of the door opposite the hinge side; it squeals briefly, muffled like a piglet in a burlap sack, then sticks fast.

All right. Screw being sneaky.

I brace my back along the angle of the wall behind me and kick the door sharply in the middle. The sodden, rotting wood tears more than it breaks, separating with a shriek of rusty nails, and I step out into the ruins of the same Industrial Park warehouse from which I'd been recalled.

Roof tiles litter the puddled floor around me, and shreds of the ceiling drape like the long arms of a dying willow. The thick fractal curves of steel-grey clouds press low above me, and the remains of recent rain still drip through the holes in the roof. In with the rain comes the clop of iron-shod hooves on paved streets outside, and the occasional shout or snarled exchange of curses from passersby.

I lift my arms and turn my face up into the pale light; I breathe in Ankhana and breathe it out again, waiting for that swift rush of freedom that Adventuring always brings.

It won't come.

All I feel is weight, dragging at me, pressing on my shoulders as though those clouds above are stones that I carry on my back, and a nagging, gnawing awareness of the tick of each passing second.

That freedom, it's gone, and I'm starting to suspect it'll never return. They've stripped it from me . . .

My father would say: freedom that can be taken away was never real in the first place, and maybe he's right. Maybe that freedom was always only a figment of my imagination—but it was an illusion I cherished.

Shattering an illusion is the insult we never forgive.

I shake my head and set off, picking my way through the debris, threading deeper into the ruins. I'll pick up the trail at the place where I lost it; though she told me she would be gone by now, there is no better place for me to begin my search.

The little sheltered office area is empty save for the dead coals of Tommie's campfire, and the basement door stands open. I glance down the steps—most of the water seems to have drained off. I should maybe go down for a last look around.

But the creaks and groans of the settling warehouse become just a little too insistent.

I'm not alone, here.

I fade silently against the wall, alongside the only door. Busting that closet door must have made enough noise to draw watchers in to investigate; these are no innocent explorers. No honest man moves with this much care for silence.

A hoarse voice barely whispers from the other side of this wet-dough wall of plaster at my back.

"Caine? Baron, is that you in there? It's Tommie."

They've got me boxed. "Yeah, Tommie, it's me. What's up?"

He steps into the doorway, relief painted across his cheerfully ugly face.

"Was hoping it was you, Baron. Figured it was—figured you was the only guy could get in here, past the dozen Subjects we got watching this place."

I take the undeserved compliment with a shrug. "Watching for what? Where is everybody?"

He shakes his head, and his face darkens.

"It's bad, Caine. Pallas is shot and taken by the Cats, and that fighting girl with her, that Talann? She's dead."

He sees something in my face that makes him spread his hands apologetically. "Berne emptied her guts all over Knights' Bridge."

Ahh . . .

God, I'm old.

That's all I can think for long seconds, all I can feel, every god damned day of my life piled onto my back.

You have to be young to take shit like this. You have to still be young and adaptable, and full of optimism. You have to still believe in happy endings, to believe that suffering has a point, that death is not a meaningless extinguishing of consciousness.

You have to be young enough to still hope that shit happens for a reason.

So maybe they get their wish, all those executives who put me here. Maybe there's nothing left for me but revenge.

The weight of days presses me down like I'm slowly being flattened under God's own millstone. I slide down the wall to sit on the floor; I search within the sick emptiness in my guts, looking for my anger.

If I can recover the rage that has always lived there, it'll put enough strength back into my legs that I can get up and walk again. But I find only ashes.

Tommie says, "And the King wants to talk to you. We been

waiting here since yesterday. Tell you, I din't think you'd come back here, but Lamorak said y'would. He was pretty sure, I guess, and here you are."

Lamorak . . .

Still here, of course, still under the protection of the King of Cant . . .

Ahh, there it is, a spark kindling among this bitter ash, starting to trail smoke down there around my heart.

When I look up at Tommie, there are more Knights behind him—a lot of them. Naked blades gleam dully from their fists. My lips press through a thin smile. "Thanks, Tommie."

He frowns, puzzled. "For—?"

"For giving me a reason to get up."

I suit action to the words, and he steps back, taking a short coil of rope from one of the other Knights.

"Why so many of you? Majesty think I'd fight?"

Tommie twists the rope between his hands. "Aw, nah. 'S to keep each other honest, y'know? The King ain't the only one wants to talk to you. The Eyes bumped your bounty a bunch and all. With us all together like this nobody can turn you in and collect."

"Did they? I hadn't heard."

"Oh, yeah. Thousand royals . . ."

His gaze and voice go off to some distant place, some fantastic realm where they belong to a man a thousand royals richer; then he comes back to himself with an apologetic cough. "I'm, ah . . ." He clears his throat. "I'm supposed to bind your hands."

I show him my teeth. "You'll die trying."

"Baron, c'mon, it's nothing personal . . ."

"I'll explain it to Majesty. He'll understand."

"Won't try to escape, will you? Hate to have to cut you."

"Escape?" I snort a cold laugh. "You're taking me right where I want to go."

6

ARTURO KOLLBERG BROODED in his seat, the faceless soapies still staring over his shoulders. He barely watched Caine's progress. He rose out of his chilly self-contemplation only when Tommie led Caine into view of the tumbled wreckage that had been Knights'

Bridge and the soldiers who still picked over the shattered dock-side, searching for survivors.

"Pallas did this?" Caine half whispered in awe. *"Shit a brick... Where did she get this kind of power?"*

"Barge got right away," Tommie told him.

"Yeah, I'll bet."

To judge from its aftermath, the battle had obviously been spectacular, extraordinary—and Kollberg hadn't had an on-line Actor there, not one. No one had it on cube.

It might as well have never happened.

This did nothing to improve his mood.

He composed and dictated the press release right there in the techbooth, all the while keeping the red glowing emergency transfer switch in his peripheral vision. The huge curved POV screen now showed Caine hiking through the caverns beneath Ankhana under the guard of the Knights of Cant.

Kollberg was pleased with himself, pleased that his press release flowed out smoothly. He let the public know Pallas Ril had been captured in a calm and level voice that held no hint of his fury within.

In the very few minutes that had passed since the confrontation in the vault, his shock at Michaelson's naked threats had transformed to cold rage. They were all after him, all of them: Caine, Lamorak, Pallas, Dole and Vilo, and the damned soapies behind him. But he didn't have to lie down and take it.

He wasn't helpless, here.

He resolved, right here and now, that Michaelson's career was over. Two can play that *It's too late* game. If given the slightest, faintest ghost of an excuse that would pacify the Board of Governors, he'd take away Michaelson's whole life.

Where would his arrogance be then? How tough would he sound, begging for work on a Temp netboard? Take away his money, his home, his friends . . . And, of course, the cut that Kollberg relished in imagination the most: he dreamed of being present, watching Michaelson's face, while Pallas Ril slipped out of phase with Overworld and went to her hideous screaming death.

He only hoped that Michaelson lived that long. It'd be a bloody shame if he died on Overworld before Kollberg got his chance to crush him.

7

IT'S A LONG climb up the mucker-shaft ladder from the caverns to the pissoir, and Tommie holds the door for me when I step out into the pale, cloud-filtered light.

"On the sand," he says curtly; it gives me a twinge. I've seen a couple Subjects called onto the sand for King's Court. It ended badly for them, both times.

"You sure you can't tell me what this is about?"

He shrugs and shakes his head grimly. "Would if I could. Sorry."

Tommie and the other Knights follow me down over the curving rows of weathered stone-cut benches, into the deep bowl of the Stadium.

Majesty's already there, up on what used to be the royal dais in the midst of the seats at the south end, on the comfortably over-stuffed old armchair he calls his throne. Deofad's on one side . . . On the other, in the place of the absent Abbal Paslava, sits Lamorak. His splinted leg—a splint that I bound to that leg with my own hands—is thrust out stiffly before him.

I let my gaze skate off his surface. A lingering glance would yank me toward him, helplessly berserk: I'd go for his throat like a wolverine. As it is, I can feel him there, even with eyes averted, feel his presence as though he burns with a fierce actinic light that scorches my face.

The Brass Stadium . . . It's always unsettling to be here in day-light, to see its shabby disrepair under the unforgiving sun. My memories of this place are of bonfires and dancing, good food and endless drink, the backslapping fellowship that was the most pow-erful glue binding me to the men and women that use this place; memories of a sense of belonging, a sense of family—the family that I've never had.

But the Kingdom of Cant is a night family; now here in the day-light, deprived of the seductive glamour of firelight and friendship, the house we shared is as depressing as a flop in a Temp slum. The rings of benches that rise above me are stained and broken. The sand in the arena is still damp from the rains—blackened here and there by the abandoned humps of bonfires and littered with mutton bones, apple cores, fish heads, cherry pits, and mounds of less iden-tifiable detritus. A few large and tardy rats scavenge fearlessly in the growing light. They dodge the hooked beaks of squabbling gulls and the straight ones of crows that croak and hop aggressively at the gulls, the rats, and each other.

The birds lift off in a parti-colored cloud as I vault the ragged arena wall and alight on the sand. One bloated rat that's too fat to waddle out of my way gets a sharp kick that sends it rolling across the sand, writhing with a high thin squeal.

The dozen or so Knights of Cant who brought me here follow me down onto the sand, and Tommie steps forward at a sloppy attention to begin the ceremony. He intones: "I bring before the assembled Court of Cant the Honorary Baron—"

"Shut up," I tell him, and enforce this advice with a sharp slap to the back of his head. He stumbles forward a step or two, then wheels on me, his face ablaze with embarrassed anger.

"Caine, dammit, you can't just—"

I ignore him, lift my face to Majesty and the Court.

"Save the horseshit, Majesty," I say, full-voiced. "I'm here. Tell me what you want of me without the fucking make-believe."

From the Knights around me come the sharp steel-on-steel scrapes of blades being drawn, but Majesty lifts a restraining hand.

"All right," he says thickly. He leans forward, his face suffused with blood. "All right, you bastard. Where did you go the other night? When you left the warehouse, where did you go?"

"None of your business." Shit, I couldn't tell him if I wanted to.

I can see where this is leading. I glance around at the Knights who cage me, estimating my chances of fighting my way out.

"I've *made* it my fucking business, you shit," Majesty barks. "I think you went straight to the Cats."

"You're out of your head." I'd tell him who the traitor really is . . . but I can't. Not yet. "Can you see me walking in to shake hands with Berne?"

He comes up out of the chair with a snarl of rage and raises his fist as though he would smite me with a thunderbolt if only he could.

"*I know you work for Ma'elKoth, you pigfucker!* You hear me? I *know*!"

In the silence that follows his shout can be heard the wings of the gulls, startled off again, and faint street sounds from the Warrens beyond the walls. The Knights around me look away, wincing. They might not ever have seen Majesty this far out of control; I never have. But I've been bellowed at by bigger voices than he can command, and it takes more than rage to impress me.

"Yeah?" I answer quietly. "Maybe you might want to explain here who it was that would've told you that?"

His eyes bulge, and he makes a faint choking sound in the back of his throat. He sure as death doesn't want to let gruff old Deofad and these Knights hear how he's been in bed with the King's Eyes.

Lamorak murmurs something in a voice too low for me to hear; my lipreading skills are pretty rudimentary, but I catch the words *question* and *answer*. Majesty doesn't seem to hear him, but now he says, "I'm asking the questions, Caine. You're answering them. You got that?"

I pause for one calculated second to make sure he knows I've heard and understood him, then I say, "Is Pallas alive?"

Majesty says through his teeth, "Maybe I'm not making myself clear—"

"Tommie, here, says Pallas was shot yesterday, and taken by the Cats. Is she alive?"

"How should I know?"

"Screw the games, Majesty. You and I, we both know how you should know. You want me to spell it out?"

He wavers for a second, and I wonder if he's about to just say *fuck this noise* and have the Knights cut me down. He looks away.

"Yeah. She's alive."

All right, all right, huh. I can breathe again, and some of those days that burden my shoulders brighten and relax. Now I only need to figure out something to do about it.

"What are you doing to rescue her?"

Now he looks startled, as though the thought of a rescue had never entered his head. What in hell has happened to that Charm of hers? Has it worn off already? "Well, I, ah, I mean, the word is Ma'elKoth's holding her himself, interrogating . . ."

I let a little of the furnace in my chest leak into my voice. "You son of a whore, you're more interested in pinning this horseshit on *me* than in saving her *life*! What the fuck is *wrong* with you?"

Y'know, come to think of it, that's a good question . . . This isn't like him, Charm or no Charm. If nothing else, Majesty is a reasonable man, pragmatic, a planner. And he's known me for years. He knows goddamn well I'd cut off my own balls with a rusty knife before I'd do anything like what he's accusing me of.

Another question slowly filters through the solid bone that I use for a brain: if he really wants the answers he's going after, why doesn't he turn Lamorak loose on me with that Dominate of his, try to force the truth out of me?

Lamorak murmurs something else. I catch *trust* and *business first*, and Majesty says, "I can't trust you with any plans until we settle this business first."

Son of a motherfucking shit . . .

I get it.

I understand now.

Lamorak hasn't turned that Dominate on me because *he can only do one spell at a time*.

So much for the voice of reason.

Okay, maybe I don't have to solve every problem with my fists . . . but every once in a while, a situation arises that is substantially improved by the judicious application of force.

Majesty was saying something that I missed, and now everyone's looking at me like they're waiting for an answer. I shake my head and say, "Sorry—my mind was wandering. What was that?"

He begins, "I said—" I miss the rest of it again, because as soon as everyone looks back at him for his reply I whip into a spinning kick that brings my heel against the cheekbone of the Knight at my right rear flank hard enough to snap bone and flip him into the air. He lands half against the Knight beside him, and they both go down.

Ten more to go.

But I don't need to drop them all to escape the arena. For half a second nobody moves while they comprehend what it is I've just done. Tommie recovers faster than the others, but he's also the only one who doesn't have a sword in hand. I jump him as he claws at its hilt and get one hand on his wrist. A sharp twist and a blow from the other hand breaks the bones of his forearm. It's a more difficult technique than breaking the elbow, but I like Tommie, and I don't want to cripple him.

He howls as jagged bone rips through his flesh, and his knees go slack. I shift my weight and slam my forearm up into his armpit, then twist like a tennis champion delivering a backhand smash. Tommie tumbles into the other Knight right in front of me, spraying blood into his face from that forearm. They fall in a tangled heap.

The other Knights hesitate. Nobody wants to be the first one to get within my reach, and I don't blame them. I take advantage of their eyeblink of indecision to run like hell.

A quick leap over Tommie and the guy he's struggling with, and I've got a straight shot right at the dais. My wounded right knee snarls at me as I sprint. When I get to the nine-foot-high arena wall, the knee makes its displeasure fully felt by buckling exactly when I need it to leap.

I barely manage to avoid braining myself when I crash into the wall. I don't have time for another attempt: the Knights are right on my ass.

The lead Knight tries to slow his headlong charge when he sees me whirl back toward him, but it's too late. I skip out to meet him and foot-sweep his ankle while slapping a backfist into the nape of his neck. He goes headfirst into the pockmarked limestone wall and collapses to his knees.

The other Knights fan out to try to come at me from a couple directions at once. The stunned Knight shakes his head dazedly. He's on his hands and knees at the base of the wall, so I use him like a footstool: I jump up onto his back, and before he understands what's happened I jump off again. The two-foot advantage this gives me is more than enough to let me catch the rim of the wall and haul myself smoothly over.

"Get him kill him!" Lamorak shouts, and the edge of panic in his voice brings my blood up like the surge of a tidal bore.

I gain my feet in the lowest ring of benches. Deofad towers over me, his enchanted blade Luthen upraised and glowing like a bar of steel white-hot from the forge.

I have no desire to try conclusions with this tough old bastard, so I throw myself sideways into a shoulder roll as his blade descends to strike searing sparks from the stone. I come to my feet out of swordreach and bound up the bleachers toward Majesty and Lamorak. Majesty comes down to meet me, foolishly: he customarily goes unarmed, and if Lamorak wasn't controlling him, he'd know better than to come at me barehanded.

When he closes with me, I let my knees bend and drop my shoulder to catch him under the ribs, letting his momentum flip him off his feet and over my back. He tumbles down the steps, and I keep moving.

While he's trying to rise behind me with the anxious help of Deofad, I reach my objective.

Lamorak's face is as white as a toadstool.

"Caine . . ." he whispers, and that thousand-yard stare of mindview steals into his eyes. "Don't—"

"Shut up."

My right hook catches him precisely on the hinge of the jaw, just in front of his ear, and the joint breaks under my knuckle with a deeply satisfying crunch.

"Stay with me, Lamorak." I shake some light back into his eyes by a handful of his shirtfront. "I'm not through with you yet. Try another spell. Go on. Try."

He puts his arms up to shield his head and averts his eyes so he won't see it come. "No . . ." he says though his numb mouth. "No, pleass—y'broche m'zhaw, shit."

I raise my fist and give myself a slow count of ten to think up one reason why I should let him live.

I'm up to eight when Majesty bellows, "Caine, *stop!* Everybody stop! *Nobody fucking move!*"

In the long silence that follows, I keep my eyes on Lamorak. If he starts to summon mindview, I'm gonna pop him.

Behind and below me, men curse in low voices as they pick themselves up and gingerly explore the extent of their wounds. Lamorak cups his broken face with both hands and avoids my eyes.

Majesty says, low and close behind my shoulder, "You mind telling me what the *fuck just went on here*?"

Lamorak flinches back from what he glimpses in my eyes. I mutter, "How much do you remember?"

"All of it, Caine, shit. I just couldn't stop—and, you know, it made perfect sense at the time. Fucking *creepy*, is what it was."

He steps around to where I can see him and lowers himself onto the bench beside Lamorak, staring into his face with aggressive concentration. "You wouldn't mind borrowing me one of those big knives of yours, would you?"

I shake my head; I've come to a sudden decision. It's a hunch, a feeling, irrational but powerful. "Let him live."

"Yeah, right."

"Please. As a favor to me."

"I don't get it," Majesty says. "I thought you guys were friends. Why would he want to do this to you? And why are you gonna let him get away with it?"

I look down at Lamorak, and now he looks back at me. I give him a faint lift of my brows, a minute nod toward Majesty, a *Do you want me to tell him?* kind of look. His eyes plead with me, and I shrug carelessly.

"The other night, remember we had that long talk?" I say slowly. "Pallas told him she's coming back to me. He took it badly."

"Yeah, no kidding."

Lamorak's eyes bulge in disbelief. "You . . ." he sputters. "A lie! Thazz a *lie*! He, he—"

I say, "Thought I told you to shut up." My swift side kick spreads his nose with a crackle of smashing cartilage and bounces his head off the front edge of the stone bench behind him. His eyes roll up and he sags, blowing blood bubbles through his open lips, out cold.

Great Grey *God*, that felt good. For one long moment I struggle with a nearly overwhelming lust to just go ahead and finish him, but I master it. Barely.

"Do me this favor. Hold him for me. Lock him in that apartment where you met us after we came out of the Donjon—but make sure no Subjects are within the sound of his voice."

"No shit. All right. But when you're done with him, he's mine."

"Yeah, whatever."

Majesty grunts and pushes himself to his feet. "What are we gonna do about Pallas?"

"That's the attitude I've been waiting for." No way to tell if this question comes from Majesty's own heart or if Pallas' Charm is still operating. Y'know, in the end, I guess it doesn't really matter. "I think it's time for you to come open."

He squints at me warily. "What do you mean?"

"I know what you want, Majesty. It's not here in the stadium. It's not in the Warrens. You're playing for higher stakes than that."

"I don't know what—"

"Horseshit. You didn't risk the whole Kingdom of Cant to support Pallas' Simon Jester act out of the goodness of your heart. You don't give a rat's ass, one way or the other, about the *Aktiri* or any of the rest."

He doesn't answer me, just stares grimly down upon his wounded Knights in the arena.

"I know what you had in mind," I tell him. "I know that you planned to roll up Simon Jester's network and sell them to the King's Eyes. What were you playing for, a title? Or just orders from Toa-Sytell for the Eyes and the Constabulary to look the other way while you operate in the city? Maybe some covert Imperial action against the other Warrengangs?"

When he turns to me, his eyes are bugged as though my hand's around his neck. His mouth works, and only a strangled croak of denial can come up his throat.

He flinches away from the hand I put on his shoulder, but all I give him is a friendly squeeze. "It's all right, Majesty. I'm not mad."

"I, I, Caine, I swear, she said she *dumped* you—I thought you'd *thank* me . . ."

"Yeah, well, shit's never quite that simple, is it?"

"But it's *different* now," he insists. "After I got to know her . . . Shit, Caine, I'd never do anything to hurt her. Never."

"I'm giving you a chance to help her. You help her, and I'll help you. You get it? I'll *outbid* Toa-Sytell. You'll get more from helping Pallas than you ever could from betraying her. You do this for me," I say slowly, convincingly, "and I'll put Ankhana into your hands."

He turns to me, and there's a glimmer of ambitious lust in his eyes. I have his full attention.

"Do what for you?"

"I need so much going on in the streets that Ma'elKoth can't spare any attention trying to figure out what I'm up to, you follow? I want a *riot*. Not a little disturbance in the Warrens, understand? I want the Constabulary, the King's Eyes, even the bloody army all tied up trying to get things under control. I want the city in flames."

"You're asking a lot. You're asking more than a lot. It could expose the whole Kingdom."

"Listen, you don't have a lot of choice. I mean, Pallas can't hold out under interrogation forever. When Ma'elKoth breaks her, he's gonna learn who's been bankrolling her operation. He'll have the goddamn *army* in here to mop you up. It spun out of your control the instant Pallas was taken alive. It's too late to roll up her network or whatever because Ma'elKoth is going to do that without your help, and then he will fall on you like the wrath of a god, and that's no fucking exaggeration. You have to hit *first*. You have to hit now. It's your only chance, Majesty. Like the saying goes, opportunity is a nettle—grasp it boldly, or get stung."

He stares consideringly into the middle distance, and I give him the space of a breath or two to think it over.

"We can set fires," he says finally, "but that won't be enough. The kind of riot you want has to get plenty of support from the straights. It has to be self-sustaining after my boys start it up. People need to be angry, and afraid—"

"That's easy," I tell him. "They're already afraid. Ma'elKoth's got them all whipped up with his *Aktir* hunt. Turning fear into anger is the easiest thing in the world."

"Yeah? How?"

This part, at least, I already have figured out.

"We can beat on Ma'elKoth with his own stick. Ma'elKoth—" I spread my hands like I'm preparing a conjuring trick. "—is *one of them*."

Majesty frowns, and I grin at him.

"He's an *Aktir* himself," I say. "The whole *Aktir* hunt is a dodge, a cover, a point-at-you-so-nobody-looks-at-me *con*."

Majesty's eyes go wide, and his hand clutches blindly at my sleeve. "Hot staggering *fuck* . . ." he says breathlessly. "Is it *true?*"

"Does it matter? When you tell a story loud enough and long enough, a story that plays right into people's worst fears of betrayal, it grows its own truth."

"But, but . . . Could it actually *be?* I mean, if there was such a thing as *Aktiri* . . . It'd make sense; it'd make perfect sense. It'd fit together just right . . . With some kind of proof, some kind of evidence, you could bring him down all at once. The nobles hate him anyway; they'd turn on him in a light breeze. The army wouldn't fight for him . . . But without it . . ."

I can see now what I have to do.

This is gonna hurt like a bastard. This is gonna hurt for years.

But a choice between my integrity and Pallas' life is no choice at all.

I clasp his shoulders with both my hands and gaze into his eyes with every ounce of level, direct, plainspoken sincerity I can muster.

"All right, Majesty," I say slowly. "It's true. Think about it: Ma'elKoth came out of *nowhere* during the Plains War. How can you look like that, be that size, have that face and that kind of raw power, without anyone ever hearing a whisper of your name until you're what, forty? Where *was* he all those years? How in the name of every living god did he end up Emperor less than five years after he dropped out of the fucking sky? Where did he come from? Where are his boyhood friends? Where's his *family*? There's your answer: no family, no friends, no history. He's an *Aktir*, Majesty. He's one of them."

"I can see it," he says softly. "Tyshalle's *Blood*. I can see it! But I'd need *proof*, Caine, something I can take to the nobles, make them rise against him."

I say, with the perfect conviction of an honest man: "I'll get you your proof."

His eyes go vague, looking past me. He's looking at the view of the Great Hall of the Colhari Palace, as seen from the seat of the Oaken Throne.

"Put that evidence in my hands, and you'll have your riots."

I shake my head. "It'll take a couple of days. We need the riots *now*. Two days from now Pallas will be broken or dead, and Imperial troops will be camped all over the Warrens. The whole Kingdom will be wiped out. We have to hit *now*, today, within the hour. Act boldly, act now, and you win it all. Fire those riots, and you'll have all the proof you need within two days. I swear it."

He looks into my eyes, searching for truth that he's not gonna find there. I look back at him, trading more than ten years of friendship, trading all the trust I've earned at his side for one massive act of betrayal.

By the time he finds out I'm lying, Pallas and I will either be home, or we'll be dead.

Even if it's wearing off, the residue of the Charm will make him inclined to help, but his natural pragmatism tells him he'll be wasting the lives of his men in a lost cause. He balances on the knife edge between them, teetering.

He weighs our years of friendship and trust for a long time. He weighs his mental image of my reputation—*Caine would rather kill a man than lie to him*—then finally he nods, sharply, as he falls from the edge of the knife into the abyss below.

"All right," he says firmly. "I believe you. The riots will start within the hour."

I can only nod.

I look down at Lamorak's unconscious face, which seems to sneer back at me with malicious contempt.

Go ahead and sneer, asshole, I mutter inside my head. *I never claimed to be any better than you in the first place.*

"Burn the whole city," Majesty muses, shaking his head in slow disbelief. "That's pretty extreme for the life of one woman."

"Fuck the city," I tell him. "I'd burn the world to save her."

That, at least, is not a lie.

8

THE WORD WENT out like an impulse through the nerves of a human body, a body whose head was the Brass Stadium in the Warrens. A Knight patrolling the border with the Face spoke with a family of leprous beggars. One of the beggars ambled onto Rogues' Way and had words with a pack of dirty-faced street urchins. One of the children skipped into the Industrial Park to find a playmate who picked up pocket money paging for *Colin's Pages and Current Events*. The page spoke to a workman lounging with his mates in front of Black Gannon's Charcoalers at the corner of Lackland and Bond. The workmen scattered through the dockside. One of them murmured to a carter who carried the word with his goods across Fools' Bridge and onto the island of Old Town.

They knew the drill, these clandestine Subjects of Cant: each of them spoke with at least three others. Within the hour, a beggar at Nobles' Beach on the south bank of the Great Chambaygen said to a passing patron, "Y'know what I think? I think Ma'elKoth pushes a *little too hard* on this *Aktir* thing. You ever wonder where he *came* from? You ever wonder if maybe he's *covering something up*? Thieves fall out; that's what *I* think."

Almost the same words could be overheard in taverns and inns from the Snakepit to the Financial Court. Most who heard them scoffed. It was inconceivable. It was ridiculous. But when they'd laughingly tell their friends of this outrageously silly rumor they'd overheard, there was someone in nearly every group who could say with an honest frown, "Well, I dunno. I heard it somewhere else already today. Maybe there's something to it. I mean, you gotta admit it's not *impossible* . . ."

The story took on a life of its own, though it might very well have died a natural death in a day or two. A few days of calm and quiet lets sudden fears relax and outrageous rumors dissipate.

But only an hour past noon, on that short autumn day, flames licked up the back of the Nobles' Playhouse on the south bank. Even as a bucket brigade engaged that fire and began to quiet its roar, an apartment block half a mile away burst into flames. Half an hour later a stable burned in the shadow of Thieves' Bridge. By that time, the bridge captains had already begun detailing regular troops to fight the fires and sending requests to the garrisons for replacements.

By midafternoon, soldiers were spread throughout the capital, sweating and red faced from the heat of the scattered fires they fought. More than a few of them griped to each other that *"the Emperor can send rain to save a few peasants' crops in some province a hundred leagues away, but he can't spare even a squall to put out these damned fires? Maybe he wants the damned city to burn."*

The captain at the gatehouse of the shattered Knights' Bridge pulled his men off their salvage duties and sent every one of them to help; he led them personally. He was overheard to observe to his aide as they quickstepped across the island, "There's a bad smell to this, a bad one for sure. This'll be worse before it's better, no mistaking."

No one in the city needed to be told this; they could feel it for themselves.

The entire city drew in a breath of fearful anticipation, and held it for the shout that everyone knew would come at nightfall.

9

KIERENDAL SAW THE current in the Flow a full minute before the knock came on her apartment door. This current resembled not at all the stringy lace of the pull of a thaumaturge; this was something vast and turbulent that seemed to organize all the Flow around her into something oceanic, something tidal; the current that rolled through her walls seemed only the tiniest portion of some unimaginable leviathan.

Perched on the back of the chair behind her, braiding Kierendal's fine silver hair, Tup sensed her mistress's tension through her tiny fingertips. "Kier? Is something wrong?"

"Get Zakke. He's in his room." Kierendal uncoiled from the chair like a releasing spring, her long pale limbs stretching into an arc as graceful and as tense as a bent longbow. Her money-colored eyes looked far beyond the walls. "Wake him up and both of you take cover. Something's about to happen."

"Kier—"

Kierendal whirled on her tiny companion. "Don't argue! Go!"

Tup's bandaged wing didn't allow her to fly, but her arboreal people were also as agile as monkeys. Infected by the urgency in Kierendal's voice, she scampered and sprang from the back of the chair to a sofa, then skittered across the carpet and through an inner door.

Kierendal draped a robe over her angular form, afraid to spare the concentration she'd require to hold an illusion of clothing. She extended her Shell and tapped into the rushing pressure of this cur-

rent, gasping as power entered her like a rough lover. It had a curious flavor, this Flow—one that she couldn't quite identify, but
felt she should somehow recognize . . .

She put these thoughts firmly aside and patterned the Flow with
her powerful mind; when the knock came in one of the Faces'
codes, she was ready for anything.

She reached out with an imaginary hand, and Flow flicked back
the door bolt and opened the door.

In the hall, their Shells lemon with nervous energy but overlain
with amethyst triumph, stood a pair of her coverts, one human and
the other stonebender. "Pardon, Kierendal," the human said, "but
we caught this one coming in the back, and we thought you might
want to talk with him."

Between them, his hands bound by manacles of steel and his
Shell pulsing dangerously with lethal ebon life, stood Caine.

His Shell was vastly darker than it had been before: he was
barely visible within the midnight shadow that surrounded him.
Kierendal's mouth opened in silent awe as she saw the shift in the
direction of Flow: it moved *toward Caine*, as though he himself
were a thaumaturge of godlike power. It didn't pass into him as it
would an adept; it swirled and eddied around him and beat back
against the incoming currents. She could see that he wasn't doing it
purposefully—he wasn't even in the mindview trance that humans
needed to perceive and direct the Flow. What, then, could this be?

"Security's gettin bettar, nah Kier?" the stonebender said.
"Caught un dis time, didna we?"

"Don't be idiots," she snapped. "Cease this ridiculous act, Caine.
Show them."

Within his cloud, Caine shrugged, and the manacles dropped
clattering to the floor. The two coverts jumped like they'd been
goosed and went for their weapons. Caine raised his hands.

"Do we talk? Or do I break your puppies, here?"

"Leave him be," she ordered. "Caine, come inside. You two,
guard the door. And do a better job of it, this time."

Caine stepped casually within, his half smile blurred by the raging
Flow that whirled around him. He closed the door behind himself
and leaned against it. Those shadow forms were back again, those
ghostly Caine doubles that his every motion seemed to spawn.
He was so utterly prepared for any possible action that the ghost
doubles took on a solidity in the Flow around him. She could *see*

them now, vague shifting patternings of force, where before she had only imagined them.

"Stay there," Kierendal told him sharply. "This is a new day, Caine, and I am ready for you. Any threatening move will be your last."

He spread his hands. "Don't come all hostile, Kierendal. I'm here to apologize. I let them take me so I wouldn't have to hurt anyone on my way in."

"Apologize?"

"Yeah. Busting up your place like that—belting your houseboy, knifing the little treetopper . . ."

Kierendal squinted. His expression was half hidden by the ghost-Caines around him; she couldn't decide how sincere he might be. "Money is love, Caine," she said. "If you meant it, you'd say it with gold."

"I plan to."

"You cost me five hundred royals."

One black-brushed eyebrow arched. "That's a lot for a broken table and an eyepatch."

"That's how much I'd fronted to Berne. After your . . . departure . . . he cashed out and left."

"I'll double your money back," Caine said with an easy shrug. "Turn me in."

For a long frozen moment Kierendal could only blink. Had she heard him correctly?

Caine went on. "I'm serious. You know my new head-price. Send a runner to the Eyes, and I wouldn't be surprised if Toa-Sytell himself shows up to put the gold in your hand."

"I don't understand."

"Look, somebody's gonna collect that money. Might as well be you, huh?"

"What kind of game are you playing?"

"That's not your business. You want the money or not?"

"What I *want*," Kierendal found herself saying with unexpected heat, "is some damned idea what's going on."

Caine grinned at her. "Don't we all?"

"My agents report that there are fires all over the city; that everywhere they turn someone's arguing over whether or not Ma'el-Koth's an *Aktir*—a rumor I hear was started by the Subjects of *Cant*, by the way. And everyone says there's a riot heating to a rising simmer. Yesterday, a human thaumaturge raised the whole bloody Great Chambaygen to half drown the dockside and wipe out Knights' Bridge—something that I would have sworn was impossible. *And* I hear that this thaumaturge, who has more power than any human has a right to, turns out to be your old girlfriend Pallas Ril. Now you show up at my place, asking to be turned over to the King's Eyes. Why do I get the impression that this is all connected, somehow?"

"You have good sources," he said impassively. She waited for him to offer more, but he might as well have been carved from stone: he didn't even blink.

"Why do you want this?"

"I have to get into the palace." He winced as though at a sudden shooting pain. "Ahh, bad pun, sorry." At her blank look, he shook his head irritably. "Forget it. You don't have to understand. You want the money?"

Kierendal hissed frustration through her overly sharp teeth. "If I don't?"

Caine's words were throwaway casual. "Then I go someplace else." But the Flow that boiled around him darkened and roiled alarmingly, and Kierendal suddenly wondered why she'd resisted the idea; she'd never been averse to easy money. Watching the Flow pattern itself around him, she found herself suspecting that by far the safest course was simply to do whatever Caine wanted. Opposing power of this magnitude might crisp her like a moth in a candle flame.

"All right," she said quickly. "I'll send the runner, and I won't ask any more questions. Someday, you'll sit down and tell me the whole story."

"Yeah, whatever."

"There are," she said carefully, "powers at work in your life that beggar my imagination. I see them, a small part of them, but I don't understand them. You are at the nexus of forces beyond comprehension."

He gave her a cynical, knowing smile. "Everybody is, Kierendal. We just don't notice, most of the time."

"I pity anyone who gets in your way."

"Yeah, me too. Let's do this, all right? I don't have all fucking day."

10

WHEN HE HEARD Berne enter the room behind him, Toa-Sytell turned away from the window only long enough to acknowledge the Count's presence with a cold flat stare, then turned back.

This window overtopped not only the Sen-Dannalin Wall around the Colhari Palace, but the intricate spires of the neighboring Temple to the Katherisi; it commanded a fine view of the western reach of Gods' Way. Close enough to be visible below the glare of the sinking sun, an iron-caged carriage drawn by four black horses rolled slowly through the heavy traffic. With Knights' Bridge destroyed, all the poor folk and subhumans that resided on the north bank were forced to crowd toward Fools' Bridge to beat the curfew at dusk. The day was unseasonably hot, and ending far too swiftly; it was clear to Toa-Sytell's eye that there was no way for all these folk to crowd out of Old Town before nightfall. Fights had already broken out in several places along Gods' Way alone, as a sweating townsman had his foot trodden upon one too many times, as another took one too many elbows in the ribs, as another took a gentleman's whip across his face for blocking the path of a horse. The few constables in view looked nervous and harried. The army should have been out, helping to maintain order, but most of the available troops were occupied fighting the fires scattered across the city, which sent thick smothering coils of black smoke toward the cloudless sky.

Berne spoke from behind him. "Not here yet?"

Toa-Sytell twitched his chin vaguely toward that approaching carriage. "On his way. It's a long way around, you know," he murmured blandly. "Perhaps you hadn't heard that Knights' Bridge is down—?"

For once Berne didn't rise to the bait. He said only, "Ma'elKoth wants him in the Iron Room."

"I'd like to see him in the Iron Room myself," Toa-Sytell muttered. "Any idea where he's been?"

The Duke shrugged irritably. "He fell off the world. Then, this afternoon, he fell back on. Beyond that, I cannot say."

He sighed within himself, waiting for Berne's needles to begin their pricking. He couldn't even retaliate: Berne's Cats had done *their* job. Even though the *Aktiri* had escaped, Ma'elKoth knew where they were and could reach out his hand and take them when he chose, and the thaumaturge who had protected them was even now on the altar of the Iron Room.

The King's Eyes, on the other hand, had uncovered no trace of Caine. It had been left to the elvish whoremistress of Alien Games to do his job for him. Berne was far too childish to resist such an opening, he believed, but now the Count surprised him. He took a place at the window beside Toa-Sytell, leaning with his palms on the sill and staring blindly out over the crowds that packed Gods' Way.

"There aren't any words . . ." Berne near-whispered. "There just aren't any words to say how much I hate that man."

Toa-Sytell stared at Berne's profile—no longer flawless with the swollen bend of his broken nose, his face painted bloody rose by the setting sun—and was astonished to find within his breast a sudden flash of sympathetic fellow feeling. "Perhaps Ma'elKoth will let you kill him, now."

"I hope so. I hope so. But . . ." He turned to Toa-Sytell and shrugged fluidly. "I don't know. I'm worried, y'know? I have a feeling that there's too much going on that I don't know about. I have a feeling things are out of control. Not just for me: for us. For everybody."

Toa-Sytell studied him for the millionth time, but it seemed as though he'd never really seen Berne before. Berne had come through the destruction of Knights' Bridge without so much as a bruise—only a few now neatly stitched scratches from the knives of that girl he'd killed—a reminder of the power of Ma'elKoth that defended him, a reminder that here was the favorite of the Emperor. His masculine beauty, his powerful build and pantherish grace, all these were familiar to Toa-Sytell; new to his searching eye was this unexpected depth of concern for Ma'elKoth, perhaps concern for the Empire itself. Yesterday, even this morning, Toa-Sytell would have wagered his immortal soul that Berne was incapable of the very feeling that he now fleetingly displayed.

He had, during this week, wondered how much of Berne's hatred for Caine might spring from jealousy, from the fear that the assassin might be replacing him in Ma'elKoth's personal affections. Now he wondered how much of his own contemptuous malice toward Berne might have been prompted by the same petty emotion; after all, until Berne had been created Count and given command of the Grey Cats a few months ago, Toa-Sytell himself had been the Emperor's closest advisor and confidant.

How peculiar, he thought, *that I, who make a profession of knowing the minds of men, should be such a mystery to myself.*

"I have felt this, even as you have," Toa-Sytell said, coming to a sudden decision. "Berne, we have never been friends. I do not believe we ever will be. What I do believe is that we have spent too much time and energy bickering and backstabbing each other—jealous like rivals in romance—and the rift between us has given aid to the enemy. We each serve the Emperor in our own way; let us try to be content with that. Let there be peace between us."

He held out his hand. Berne stared at it as though it were some alien thing, then shrugged and took it.

"All right," he said. "Peace."

Berne turned again to the window, staring moodily toward the sliver of sun still visible above the horizon. "But we have to do something about Caine. I thought, y'know, I thought that him disappearing like that . . . Well, I thought if he ever turned up again, Ma'elKoth would just let me take his head. But when I told him that sub bitch in Alientown had claimed his head-price, he laughed—that kind of rich-uncle laugh he has, you know what I mean—and told me to have him sent to the Iron Room, alone, as soon as he arrives. I think Ma'elKoth *likes* him, y'know? And maybe it's more than that, too. There's something between them that I don't understand, something deep."

Toa-Sytell nodded. "I agree. I recall Ma'elKoth saying only last week that he'd give Caine to you. I believe he meant it at the time, but now I do not think he'll ever do it. Have you watched him at the Great Work?"

"All the different Caines he keeps trying to fit in there?"

"Yes. Since that night on the Dusk Tower, images of Caine have been his only subject. The first evening Caine spent here, Ma'elKoth spent the entire night examining him magickally. Since then, his obsession has only grown. Caine has taken over nearly his entire attention; it's excessive, and inexplicable."

"I should have killed him at Alien Games," Berne said distantly, staring out the window.

"I agree," Toa-Sytell said. "But it is too late, now. We must find some way to break this mesmeric hold he has upon Ma'elKoth. To do that, we must discover what it is. How much do you know of Caine's past?"

Berne shrugged. "Only the same stories that everyone knows. But I'll tell you where to go for more: the Monasteries."

"Really?"

"Yeah. You know my father's Monastic? An Exoteric. Well, they're a little crazy about records. They write everything down; I mean, *everything*."

"Yes, I've heard that," the Duke mused. "They'd let me examine these records?"

"Not ordinarily, no—they're supposed to be secret. But, y'know, the Monasteries might be a little perturbed with Caine right now . . ."

Toa-Sytell leaned against the window to look down into the courtyard's thickening twilight as he thought about this. Far below, five heavily armed Household Knights stood at ready while a King's Eye unlocked the cage door of the iron carriage. Torches flared around the courtyard in the gloom. The tiny figure of Caine stepped nonchalantly out into the shadow of the Sen-Dannalin Wall, apparently unmindful of the manacles on his wrists and the steel bilboes that held his ankles.

"Any number of people," Toa-Sytell murmured thoughtfully, "seem to be a little perturbed with Caine. Come. We'll await him in the Dusk Tower."

11

AT DUSK, A company of mounted constables started to sidestep their horses west along Gods' Way, pushing against the rear ranks of the crowd to force it along from behind. Voices were heard to mutter and complain. Why should they be forced off Old Town just because it was getting dark? Whose rule *was* that, anyway? Ma'elKoth's? Why were these vicious bastards *pushing* so hard?

The street, already crowded, swiftly became choked. Children cried out, crushed between larger adults. Men and women shouted at the mounted officers to *ease off, people are getting hurt,* but the constable captain was as nervous as any. He wanted the trouble that he knew was brewing to boil over on the north bank, not here in his own district. He ordered his men to press harder. The sooner the streets of Old Town could be cleared of this rabble, the better.

It wasn't long until the crowd began to push back.

The horses came to a stop against a solid mass of living resistance—human, stonebender, and primal bodies forced together until they might as well have been fused into a single organism. An ogre pried up a cobblestone with its long hooked claws and shied it at the captain, missing widely but giving the rest of the surging crowd an idea.

Rocks began to fly, and the mounted constables now unlimbered stout clubs that rose and fell upon heads and shoulders with cracks like drumbeats.

Someone in the crowd shouted, "Why you beating on *us*? Why aren't you off protecting us from the damned *Aktiri*?"

Someone else answered him, "They takes their orders from the damned Aktiri *themselves*, that's why! Why not put assfuck *Ma'el-Koth* to the question, eh?"

The captain snapped swift orders that this treasonous agitator was to be arrested at once, but no one seemed to have seen him. Now other voices joined a growing chorus. *"Aktir! Aktir! Put Ma'elKoth to the question!"*

The first two speakers, the questioner and the answerer, were Subjects of Cant. They elbowed their way toward the mouth of a nearby alley, well satisfied with their work, encouraging the crowd that they shoved through with a simple chant: *"Ak-tir, Ak-tir!"* Voices echoed them, then took over of their own accord as the two slipped away.

The chant of the crowd grew, swelled dangerously: *"Ak . . . TIR! Ak . . . TIR!"* and they pushed against each other's backs, surging against the line of horses, forcing them to retreat step by step along Gods' Way.

Once the crowd realized that it had the power to move in this direction, it became unstoppable.

The captain could have pulled back his troops in an orderly retreat and maintained some control of the situation. He could have ordered his men to attack full force, slain a few in the crowd with club and sword, and perhaps broken the rising spirit. He did neither. Young and inexperienced, he dithered, shouting at his men to hold the line, for it seemed to him that he had no other option. Retreat equaled disgrace, and he felt he could not order his men to slaughter the folk they were sworn to defend. He hesitated, and was lost.

One of the constables was suddenly pulled from his horse; he vanished under the fists and pounding feet of the crowd around him. A roar went up like a great carnivorous beast giving tongue at the scent of blood.

A simple shift in perspective, an epiphanic flash of a shared singleness of purpose, and the crowd was no longer a crowd, was no longer a mass of individuals who chanced to stand together on this street on this day. Each man, each woman, dwarf and elf, ogrillo and sprite, had all become single cells in some massive hive mind, almost a single organism—an organism that was hungry.

In seconds another constable was down, then another. And then the company had broken, and they turned to flee under a pursuing hail of flying cobblestones and jeers.

When full darkness fell, the mob owned the street. The flames of buildings would be its sun, and the stores of the rich would be its table.

It was hungry, and it had all night in which to feed.

12

TWO HOUSEHOLD KNIGHTS pushed him ahead of them into the Shifting Room, and one of them yanked the bellpull for the ninth floor before joining the others within. A whip crack came faintly up the shaft, followed by a slow-oiled creak of rope as the ogres below pushed against the donkey wheel and the Shifting Room began to rise.

Caine rode it silently, hands clasped behind his back, avoiding the eyes of the soldiers around him. For their part, they watched him intently, occasionally licking nervous sweat from their upper lips, hands moist on the hilts of their scabbarded shortswords. They knew him by reputation and were taking no chances. Once he jangled the chains of his manacles, just to watch them jump; they did not disappoint him. He chuckled dryly, without humor.

He felt too old to laugh.

Old and frightened: not for himself, not fear for his own life. He'd always known he'd die on Overworld. He'd had a few days to get used to the idea of dying *soon*, dying now, dying like Talann, like the priest of Rudukirisch at the Ritual of Rebirth; dying because he was utterly overmatched.

He was afraid he was going to screw up, somehow.

On the sand at the Brass Stadium he could act without hesitation because he'd seen his goal before him, solid in front of his eyes, and the path between where he was and where he needed to be was physical, was an actual expanse of dirt and stone.

But now, though his goal burned like the sun before his eyes— Shanna, safe on Earth—the path from here to there was only a thick fog of possibility. He was vastly too far from his goal to choose the safe path toward it, and deep within his chest he knew that there was only one that threaded through to Shanna's life, one among a million choices. Even that single safe trail was lined with quicksand and pits full of sharpened stakes, and it was patrolled by monsters that hungered for her life.

Inch toward daylight, he told himself, along with his other subsurface mantras: *Pretend you know what you're doing. Never let them see you sweat.*

The thick-beamed ninth floor slid down across the doorway of the Shifting Room and stopped; two more Household Knights met his keepers at the door. The first soldier to get out had to step up, but the room lifted a few inches when each man left it. By the time Caine came out they had to help him down. The steel bar between the bilboes that held his ankles wouldn't let him take that large a step.

They exchanged passwords with the guards who stood by the door to the Dusk Tower, then stooped to remove the shackles from his legs. It was a long climb up spiral stairs.

Going up with two soldiers in front of him and two behind, Caine slowly became aware of a smell up there, an electric scent of charged metal that brought a bitter tang to the back of his throat. As they came closer to the top, to the open door, he also caught a whiff of sulphur and decay, like a corpse half mummified by the fumes from a volcanic fissure.

Two men stood in the room at the top of the stairs, sidelit by a languidly wavering lamp flame, watching him approach: Toa-Sytell and—

"Hey, Berne," Caine said, faking cheerful mockery. "I wondered what the smell was."

"Keep laughing, goatfucker," Berne replied evenly. "Your turn'll come."

"That's what my mother always said."

Toa-Sytell spoke colorlessly to the lead soldier. "Unbind his hands."

The soldier frowned. "You're sure—?"

"Ma'elKoth wills it so. Free him and go."

The soldier shrugged and unlocked the manacles, then he and the others trooped away down the stairs. Caine listened to them go while he made a show of picking the shreds of skin off his wrists, where they'd been scraped by the manacles' rough edges.

"Where have you been, these past two days?" Toa-Sytell demanded.

Caine ignored him, walking to the window and peering out. Clouds had come in with the twilight, and now they took on a ruddy glow from the fires beneath. Far-off shouts came clearly on the wind, and in some of them he could hear the faint chant *"Ak-tir . . . Ak-tir . . ."*

The Subjects were holding up their end of the bargain; if only he could find a bare chance to hold up his own . . .

"Nice view," he said.

"I want an *answer*," Toa-Sytell said, with more heat than Caine had ever heard from him.

Caine turned and sat against the windowsill, regarding the shadowed, backlit faces of his enemies. "Here's news, Duke. I don't have to tell you shit. You can get your answers from Ma'elKoth, if he feels like giving them."

Berne took a step forward, his hand creeping up his chest toward where the hilt of Kosall projected above his shoulder. "You little fuck. I should kill you right now."

"You look kinda stiff, Berne. Did Talann cut you a couple times?"

Berne's pale eyes darkened dangerously, but his voice came out light. "Was that her name? She died before she could tell me. Her last words were 'Please, please, Berne, fuck me like an animal.' "

Caine shook his head and fought to make his snarling bared teeth look like a smile. "You're such a baby. It's a shame I can only kill you once."

Berne took another step forward. Caine grinned and lifted his hands, turning them this way and that as though displaying jewelry. "Too late. You should have done me while my arms were still tied. You might have had a chance."

He poised himself bonelessly against the windowsill. One wild lunge from Berne, and Caine was fairly certain he could topple the sonofabitch right out the window at his back. *Let's see how that Buckler of yours works when you hit the street at terminal velocity.*

Toa-Sytell laid a gently restraining hand on Berne's arm. "Answers from Ma'elKoth?" he said. "Are you saying that Ma'elKoth *knows*? That my search has been a, some kind of a, an *entertainment*? Is this merely for amusement, or part of some larger game?"

Hey, why not? Caine thought, *confusion to the enemy.* "Don't get pissy, Toa-Sytell. God, you may have heard, moves in mysterious ways."

"He's playing you," Berne said. "Ma'elKoth doesn't work like that. He's always been straight with us, and you know it."

Caine looked from one to the other. *Berne and Toa-Sytell have suddenly become an "us"?*

That alone was enough to twist his stomach even tighter.

He nodded toward the massive black iron door that dominated the north wall, its cold-worked surface incised with gleaming silver runes. "Ma'elKoth's in there?"

Berne smirked. "He's not the only one—"

Toa-Sytell hissed him to silence. "Let him learn for himself."

Caine's mouth went dry and chill as though he breathed a wind across an arctic desert. Blood sang in his ears. "Pallas . . ." he murmured, and for the stretching eternity between one thundering beat of his heart and the next, all the rational parts of his mind were driven off by the bloody imagery of half-forgotten tales of the Iron Room.

There wasn't a tavern in Ankhana, maybe not one in the Empire, where you couldn't raise a pleasing shiver and goose bumps on a warm night just by mentioning its name. The knots in his guts would have been far less tight if he'd learned they'd put her in the Theater of Truth.

On the other hand, the thought of walking in there himself didn't bother him at all, not if going there gave him the shadow of a chance to help her.

He pushed himself off the sill, but Berne and Toa-Sytell together blocked his path to the door.

"When Ma'elKoth desires your company, he will summon you," Toa-Sytell said.

Caine replied, "You want to get out of my way."

"Wait till you're called," Berne said, stepping close to tower over Caine. "He doesn't like to be interrupted."

Caine looked up into Berne's ice blue eyes, close enough that with a simple twist of his head he could sink his teeth into the swordsman's throat. Though the old familiar fury still burned within his chest and the diamondine lust to tear Berne's limbs ragged and spurting from his body had not slackened, he was a world away from doing anything as reckless and stupid as he had on the gaming floor at Kierendal's. Instead he found within himself a cold and level purity of intention: everything for Shanna.

"Funny how things change in just a couple days," he said casually. "I can imagine a future in which you're still alive tomorrow, Berne."

Berne snorted contemptuously, his breath heavy with meat. "Just stay away from that fucking door."

Caine leaned to one side to frown at the door around Berne's shoulders. "What, that one?" He flicked a humorous glance sideways at Toa-Sytell, reached out, and tapped lightly with two fingers upon the Duke's chest.

"Hey, Toa-Sytell. Thought you told me once that I shouldn't bother to hope that I'd ever catch you within arm's length."

For one brief second, Toa-Sytell stiffened, remembering Creele's death in the Monastery. In that second Caine was able to straight-arm him out of the way and slip past Berne's shoulder.

He reached the door and grasped the enormous Ouroboros ring of the knocker, lifting it with a grunt of effort—

"Caine, *don't*!" Berne gasped from behind him, an unexpected note of honest panic in his voice that sparked, for Caine, a real smile.

He grinned back over his shoulder: Berne and Toa-Sytell both stood where they'd been, faces identically pale, their hands out imploringly as though they'd stop him if they dared, but feared to make a sudden move that might startle him into letting the knocker fall.

"You don't know . . ." Toa-Sytell said hoarsely, "you don't know *what might be in there*—!"

"Shit," Caine said with a laugh. "All right, relax, you big babies. I won't knock."

Instead, he yanked the door open.

The smell from within was all blood and old shit, washed down with salt water, and sharp cedar from the coals that smoldered in the braziers. The high-ceilinged room was broad enough to throw back an echo from the scrape of Caine's boots, but when Ma'el-Koth rose and turned majestically toward the door, the room shrank like a receding dream, as though there was no place within it beyond the reach of the Emperor's arm.

"Caine. Come in. Shut the door behind you."

Caine flicked a shrugging glance back at the two behind him. Berne and Toa-Sytell each managed to look awestruck and vaguely alarmed and deeply suspicious all at once.

He winked at them and went in.

13

THE DOOR'S SLAM behind him made the whole room ring like a gong.

Ma'elKoth drifted toward him, a human thunderhead. "I have been awaiting your return."

He wore a veil, a drape of some kind of mesh that covered him from head to foot like a kid playing ghost with a sheet over his head; from the lower hem of this mesh sheet hung four large, irregular, shiny black rocks that looked like griffinstones. Beneath the transparent mesh he was naked save for the tight leather knee breeches that he'd worn beneath his robes for the Ritual of Rebirth. Sweat glistened across his breathtaking musculature as though he'd been oiled like a bodybuilder, and it darkened the ends of his bristling beard as well as the lower third of the mane of chestnut hair that curled to his shoulder blades.

"I will be interested in some answers from you, Caine," he said, and there remained no trace of his usual paternal indulgence. If distant thunder could be made into precise words, broken into clipped and overarticulated speech, it would have the impersonal, dispassionately threatening sound of Ma'elKoth's voice.

"Pallas Ril is your lover. Pallas Ril is Simon Jester."

The Emperor towered over Caine like a mountain poised on the brink of avalanche. His mask of calm began to break, cracked from the inside by the swell of outraged veins in his massive neck. "You will regret having deceived me, Caine."

Caine barely heard this threat. It had no meaning for him, could have no meaning. Beyond the Emperor, a slim form, bound nude upon the table-sized block of bloodstained limestone, held the universe's hope of meaning upon its still and silent breast.

Her eyes were open, staring blankly at the circle of grey-brown exposed stone of the ceiling above her. Her hands had been tied together stretched above her head; her ankles were tied similarly, by ropes that looped through heavy iron rings on the floor nearby. Her body was mottled with bruise, so many small insults upon her precious flesh that they'd blended together into one. Linen that once had been white stretched tight across her chest; it was now crusted with brown, shading to wet-gleaming crimson. But mostly what held Caine was her eyes, those eyes—

They were open and they did not blink, and he could not make himself care what Ma'elKoth might be about to do to him.

It seemed that he stood there forever, motionless, timeless, unable to think, unable to breathe. Even his heart paused for an eternal instant while he lived wholly through his eyes.

And then *her chest rose*, slowly, gradually; when it fell again, Caine felt the dawn of a new day. With her breath, his own returned, and the world began to make sense once again.

"But first," Ma'elKoth said, so close now that Caine could smell corruption on his breath, "I will know *where you have been*!"

Caine shook himself back to the present. "What are you, my mother?" he said, trying for the cheerful mockery he'd used with Berne. A flash of movement gave him barely enough warning to begin to roll with it as Ma'elKoth's open hand slapped him spinning irresistibly, tumbling and skidding across the iron floor.

Holy shit, he thought dizzily as he tried to unravel the stunned tangle of his limbs and reach his feet. *This is a problem . . .*

Ma'elKoth pounced on him like a hunting cat. The Emperor yanked him into the air by huge handfuls of his leather jerkin and shook him the way a terrier shakes a rat to snap its spine. Every single one of Caine's wounds screamed pain at him, and the shout of agony seemed to clear his mind.

All at once, he became aware of a number of things:

One: He was about to die, here. If Ma'elKoth didn't get an answer that satisfied him, he'd beat him to death with his bare hands—and there was no answer that Caine could give.

Two: Ma'elKoth was using his bare hands not merely from rage, but because *his magic was inaccessible*. The net—this was silver mesh that he wore over his head, just like the suit Arkadeil had worn in the Theater of Truth, just like the veils that Konnos had invented. It must be cutting him off from the Flow. This was how he knew who Pallas was and knew that she was Simon Jester: the silver net protected him from the Eternal Forgetting.

Three, most important, dizzying, staggering in its implications: Cut off from the power that made him what he was, Ma'elKoth was vulnerable.

Caine could kill him.

Right now. Right here.

He'd never get a better chance.

Even without the knives that the Household Knights had confiscated, despite the enormous power of the sheerly physical sort held within Ma'elKoth's massive body, despite being a foot and a half shorter and about half the weight of this man-god, Caine had a chance, had a good chance.

Maybe his only chance.

Right now.

Ma'elKoth shook him again—the room spun and jittered crazily around him—and roared into his face. "*Where? Answer me! Where have you been?*"

"All right," Caine said, "all right—"

Ma'elKoth shifted his grip to hold him in the air by only one hand, while he drew back the other in a fist the size of a catapult stone. Caine got his own hands, both of them, up in front of his face in time to absorb some of the thundering force of this punch. Instead of breaking his neck, it only shot stars through his vision. A hot rush of blood filled his mouth from his smashed nose and teeth-cut lips.

"Ma'elKoth, stop!" Caine said with as much force as he could press through his half-stunned slur. "You'll kill me . . . and then *you'll never know*—"

Ma'elKoth held him there, his feet dangling loosely below him; his mighty chest heaved like a bellows as he worked air in and out through teeth clenched so tightly that scarlet patches overlay his bulging jaw.

"I *trusted* you, Caine," he ground out. "I do not give My trust lightly to any man. I will have My answer, or I will have your life."

Caine met his smoldering gaze with a flat stare of his own. "Put me down."

Ma'elKoth's face went from red to white with rage. For a long moment Caine's life teetered on a knife's edge, but Ma'elKoth suffered from a curse that plagues all brilliant men: he had to know.

Slowly, struggling with his anger, he lowered Caine to the iron floor; slowly he opened the fist that held Caine's jerkin.

"Speak, then."

Caine pretended to straighten his clothing; he pretended that wiping the blood from his lips really mattered; this gave him the space of two breaths to rake Ma'elKoth with his eyes, deciding where to hit him first.

His knee, the joint vulnerable behind the tight leather; his bulging groin; the nerve cluster behind his solar plexus—? No: the bare hint of skin-covered cartilage that showed between the cabled muscles of his throat. A handspear or a phoenix fist, either one, quick and sharp. Even if the larynx didn't break, the muscles around it would clamp down in reaction: he wouldn't be able to yell an alarm. Then it would be flesh against flesh, bone against bone, man against man: on those terms, Caine would not allow himself to lose.

Ma'elKoth would die before the altar on which he'd bound Pallas Ril.

And yet, poised here on the cusp between killing and dying, knowing full well that if he did not attack, Ma'elKoth would give him no other opportunity, looking up into the rage-poisoned eyes of this giant man-god, Caine thought inexplicably of Hamlet coming upon Claudius the King at prayer: *Now might I do it pat, now he is a-praying . . .*

Images cascaded through his mind: the fight, the death of Ma'elKoth, freeing Pallas Ril, opening the door of the Iron Room—to find Berne and Toa-Sytell outside, whom he cannot kill before their shouts alert the Household Knights at the foot of the stairs. Ma'elKoth is not the Wicked Witch of the West, that his retainers would cheer his death and let his killers go merrily on their way. He was loved. He was revered . . .

He was, in fact, a damned good Emperor.

And he's one of the few men I've ever met that I respect, Caine thought, *and one of the fewer still that I kind of, even, admire.*

A good man? No, clearly not; but then, neither was Caine, and he well knew it. But Ma'elKoth was better than most; intellectually honest, at least, aware of his own brutality, and with the good of his subjects at heart . . .

Kill him now, kill him here, what happens? Ma'elKoth dies, Caine dies, Pallas dies, maybe Berne, maybe Toa-Sytell, maybe hundreds of thousands more in the Second Succession War that will surely follow. Who wins?

The Studio wins: a massive, destructive civil war is exactly what they've been hoping for.

Kollberg wins.

That, Caine decided, was not an acceptable outcome.

His father had told him to forget the rules. He'd shrugged it off. He'd never paid much attention to rules in the first place. But now he found that there *were* rules he'd lived by, rules that had made Caine what he was, patterns of behavior, trip wires of which he wasn't even aware. Now it came as a startling revelation:

Maybe I don't have to kill him.

Not only did he not have to kill Ma'elKoth here, he didn't *have* to kill him at all. That was a Caine pattern: when threatened, kill. But he could choose not to be a slave to his own past.

Maybe here in the prison of the Iron Room, he'd found another kind of freedom.

Everyone thinks Caine is all of me; that's my edge.

Step outside the Caine patterns—he'd already begun. Maybe if he stayed outside, circled *around* them, so to speak, used the patterns themselves as a weapon—those patterns that determined what friends and enemies both expected of him, what they thought he was capable of—he could have it all.

Why settle for less than everything?

Save Shanna. Save himself. Pull the King of Cant out of the shit-hole he'd dumped him into. Get Kollberg. And screw the Studio: save the Empire from another Succession War.

He saw a chance, a vague and misty path through the fog, so dangerous that the mere thought of it stopped his breath. But he'd already started along that path—he'd been pushing through it blindly, picking his way among the pits and the mires—and now the sun had risen within him, and the fog had begun to burn away. He saw that he was *already doing it right*: he was already on a path that led to everything, if he only had the guts to risk it all. The slightest hesitation, the vaguest stirrings of fear, and he'd be lost. The demons that patrolled this path would close in and rend him at the first hint of uncertainty, but he didn't mind that at all.

There was one Caine pattern that he'd never change: when in doubt, go for it.

A wild grin took over his face.

"You know what?" he said brightly into the teeth of Ma'elKoth's expectant fury. "I don't think I'm going to kill you."

Ma'elKoth's eyes widened, then his brows drew together. "Of course you won't. What makes you think you could?"

"Let me put it this way: I'm hoping I won't have to."

"No games, Caine. I am waiting for your answer."

"You've been here all day, haven't you? Must be frustrating, questioning her with that net over your head. No wonder you're in a temper. Kind of funny, if you think about it: With the net, you can't use your magick to force the answers out of her. Without the net, you can't remember what questions you want to ask, or even why you've tied her up here. So, what are you left with? Pain? You know in advance that won't mean much to an adept."

Ma'elKoth grunted. "I haven't touched her. The bruises are from her capture."

A knot loosened in his chest. "Then what's wrong with her?" he said. "Why does she just stare like that?"

"Caine, I am a patient man," Ma'elKoth rumbled dangerously, "but not today."

"Yeah, no shit. Me neither. Listen, if you keep that net on, I might just go ahead and beat you to death."

One eyebrow lifted, and a corner of Ma'elKoth's mouth quirked; fury had become amusement without transition. "Oh?"

"Yeah. You know I can; I mean, for all your size and strength, you're no warrior. Without your magick, I'll drop you like a bag of rocks."

"You would never escape the palace."

Caine shrugged. "I've done it before."

Ma'elKoth pursed his lips while he considered that.

"Just so," he said at length. "And why is it that you tell me this?"

"Making a point, Ma'elKoth." *And getting your attention off where I've been.* "If I meant you harm, I could have your life. Right now." He opened his hands, showed them to Ma'elKoth in a gesture of innocence. "I also want you to *take off that net.*"

"And why is this? Do not hope that this spell that protects your lover will win her release. I may forget why she is bound here, but I will not forget the use of this net, and that by putting on this net I re-learn the identity of Simon Jester."

"Nah, nah, nah, that's not it at all. First, she's not my lover. She dumped me months ago. Second, she's not Simon Jester—not in the sense of being the mastermind who's protecting the enemies of the Empire."

"Come now, Caine. Berne himself—"

"Is an idiot, and you know it. He *assumed* she was; she never bothered to correct his mistake. She's protecting the real one."

"Hmpf." Ma'elKoth looked away now, then back. "At one time, he thought that the real Simon Jester was *you.*"

Caine snorted. "I'm not that smart. Neither, obviously, is he. But I can tell you who is."

Ma'elKoth folded his massive arms. "And?"

The lie came out smoothly, without hesitation. "It's the King of Cant."

"Impossible," Ma'elKoth said instantly. "Duke Toa-Sytell—"

"Has been completely fooled. I have it from the mouth of Majesty himself."

"But . . . but . . ." Ma'elKoth frowned, sputtering.

Caine almost laughed out loud; he'd never imagined he'd see the Emperor at a loss for words. "Do you want to know what they're doing right now? Take off the net."

"I don't see—"

"Of course you don't," Caine snapped. "You've spent the whole fucking day in a room with no windows, a room that makes everybody crap their pants just thinking about *knocking* to tell you what's going on outside! And then you can't feel anything in the Flow because you've buried your head in this damned net of yours. You want to be a god to your Children, Ma'elKoth? Well, there's thousands of them *screaming* for you as we speak. You want to step outside and *look*? *Half your fucking city's on fire right now!*"

"Fire?" Ma'elKoth said, sounding suddenly young and vulnerable, like a small boy caught half asleep. As though they moved of their own volition, his hands lifted and caught at the netting from the inside, pulling it down over his head, taking long strands of his curling hair with it, dragging them across his face, ripping the hairs from his head with faint tearing sounds that Caine could barely hear but that must have buzzed like harsh static inside Ma'elKoth's skull.

When it came free he cast the net blindly aside. He lifted his head like a hunter who's heard the far-off call of his prey, and he froze in that position as though he'd been turned to salt.

He said once, softly, "Ahhh . . ."

Caine took a breath, then another. Ma'elKoth wasn't moving, wasn't even breathing: he stared into some impossible distance, his face as blank as a river-smoothed stone.

For a long moment, Caine was held every bit as tightly as Ma'elKoth; then he forced himself to look away, forced himself to turn and move, to walk over beside the altar upon which Pallas Ril was bound.

Her eyes stared wide and vacant; they looked as empty as Caine's chest felt, hollow and lifeless. Dried blood crusted her nostrils, and her hair was matted, still tangled with twigs and scraps of weed from the river. His hand went to her face, to gently pull a weed from her hair, but some savagely cynical part of his brain sneered at him, *Sure, you can touch her now, now that she's tied down.* He jerked his hand back, his face heating up with unaccountable shame.

"Pallas . . ." he murmured, softly so that Ma'elKoth might not hear, and he lowered his head over her to gaze into her empty eyes. "Pallas, where are you?"

At his words, her chest filled as though with an incoming tide, and she inhaled consciousness along with her breath.

"Caine . . ." she said. In her voice were distant inexpressible echoes of meaning, far beyond anything he'd even attempt to interpret. "You're so alive . . ."

His eyes stung madly. "I don't understand—"

"I'm safe, Caine," she said, barely audible, looking at him as though from far, far away. "I cannot be harmed . . . Save yourself . . ."

"Pallas . . ." he said helplessly.

As the light faded once more within her eyes, she said faintly, "I understand now, so many things . . . We should have been happier . . . I'm so sorry for your pain . . ."

She returned to whatever mysterious place within herself from which she had just come, and she took all of his heart with her.

I swear to you that I will make it right. All of it. I swear.

He could only stand and stare, immobile, frozen with agonizing dreams of happiness, until a step came behind him and Ma'elKoth's monstrous hand closed on the back of his neck like the jaws of a dragon.

"What have you DONE?"

The weight of the Emperor's arm forced Caine to his knees beside the altar. The power of his grip strangled Caine's voice. "Ma'elKoth . . . what . . . ?"

"My Children scream in pain and fear; they writhe in panic and bleed out their lives in misery and terror; and *you have done this*!"

Maybe I should have killed him while I had the chance, Caine thought with a sickening lurch.

And then, belatedly: *How does he know?*

He tried to struggle, to speak and deny the truth, but Ma'elKoth's grip had crushed the speech from his throat and blocked his blood flow like a garrote; the room darkened around him.

"Their torment echoes within My heart; it tears like savage talons into My belly. I brought this upon them, I, I who would hang from the Tree of Gods for them! This has happened because I brought you to Ankhana, because slaughter follows you as inevitably as crows pursue an army. I, who knew this, Drew you to My city to rid Me of a minor irritant, something less than a thorn, less than the prick of a spider's bite, and now I am undone . . ."

His voice scaled down from apocalyptic fury to a kind of puzzled anguish, and his glorious eyes filled with gemlike tears. "My people cry out to Me to save them, to ease their suffering. Others plead with their lesser gods, but to whom do I turn? To whom? I have set Myself among the gods, and now there is no one upon whom I can call to bear witness to My pain."

The hand released his neck, and Caine collapsed bonelessly, sucking in great gulps of air while the room brightened within his eyes.

He understood now: Ma'elKoth didn't know of Caine's direct involvement, here. This was some sort of metaphorical responsibility; Ma'elKoth seemed to think that Caine had caused this simply by being here, and Caine didn't see any reason to correct this delusion.

Towering above him like the titanic icon in the Great Hall, the Emperor raised a fist as though to crush Caine like a roach and lowered it again. His face sagged into painful loathing, as though Caine were a mirror in which he saw himself and could not bear the sight. "I will make of Myself something worse than you, if I slay you for this, My crime," he said.

Caine pushed himself back up to his knees, waited another moment for the spinning in his head to subside, then rose and dusted himself off again.

The trick to handling this guy, he thought, *is to keep him so pissed he can't think straight. All the brains in the world do you no good if you're too angry to use them.*

"What I want to know is," he said deliberately, "when did you turn into such a whiner?"

Ma'elKoth's mouth opened, then closed again. His eyes bulged like the veins in his neck. "You *dare?*"

"I dare fucking near anything," Caine said. "That's why you need me. Why don't you stop whimpering and *do* something?"

"Do—?" Ma'elKoth said, while lightning flickered within his eyes. "I will show you what I can do."

Ma'elKoth reached for Caine with such smooth inevitability that he couldn't even think of dodging the Emperor's grasp. His fingers once again closed upon the front of Caine's tunic and lifted him into the air.

Y'know, Caine thought numbly, *I'm getting pretty damn sick and tired of being manhandled like this.*

Ma'elKoth raised his eyes to the ceiling and gestured with his free hand; then without warning his knees bent and he *leaped*, springing upward as though Caine's weight and his own bulk had no meaning to him, up *through the solid stone of the ceiling*.

Caine flinched involuntarily as the limestone rushed down toward his head, but he passed through it as though it were nothing more than thick pale mist, up into the smoke-reeking air of the city's night. Ma'elKoth set him gently on the once-again-solid stone beneath him; they now stood together atop the Dusk Tower of the Colhari Palace.

From the city around them volcanic columns of smoke and ash boiled upward, straight toward the clear, still stars—stars that faded one by one behind the thickening pall, until the only light on the streets of Ankhana was a frenzy of nightmare orange cast by the flames of burning buildings.

"Not the faintest breath of breeze," Ma'elKoth growled to himself, "and still it spreads. Still it grows."

"Yeah, no kidding," Caine said dryly. "Did you think any of those are *accidents*?"

Ma'elKoth drew himself up, and his chest expanded as though it would burst. Something wild and elemental entered his eyes; they cast a light that Caine could see upon stone around him, green as sunshine through an emerald.

"Do they think I'll stand idly by and let them burn My city?"

Before Caine could answer, Ma'elKoth raised his hand to the heavens as though grasping power from above. Caine had seen this gesture before in the Great Hall, and he threw himself out of the way as Ma'elKoth's fist stroked forward. Thunder cracked around them so loudly that the very stone trembled beneath their feet.

Far, far away, at the easternmost tip of Old Town below Six-tower, the flames that leaped from a huge building suddenly stilled—snuffed as though they had never been; not even smoke rose from its hulk.

Christ Almighty, Caine thought, shaking his head against the ringing in his ears that was nearly as loud as the thunder had been. He couldn't even *imagine* the mechanism behind this feat. Nothing he knew of magick would allow it.

Does he have any limits at all?

As Ma'elKoth once again lifted his hand to the sky, Caine said, "That's kind of stupid, don't you think?"

The Emperor wheeled on him, his hand still upraised, and his glare smoked green. "Have a care, Caine—"

"Yeah, yeah, yeah. Threaten me some other time, all right? Think about what you're *doing*, Ma'elKoth! Are you planning to stand up here all night and throw power around for *nothing*? An hour from now, *less* probably, every fire you snuff will be burning again, bigger and better than before."

His hand slowly lowered and the light in his eyes began to fade. "This is true. This is too true; I attack a too-limited area of the problem. A *storm*," he said desperately, "a storm is the answer, a thunderhead to douse the fires and drive the rioters indoors, but . . . but I have sent the weather to Kaarn. It will take *hours* to call a storm . . . And meanwhile Ankhana burns; I cannot snuff the fires while I call the storm, and I cannot call the storm while I . . ." His voice trailed off; Caine could almost feel sorry for the man, for the real anguish he so obviously felt.

"Yeah, too bad. I got news for you. That's not the worst of your problems."

"There's *more*?"

Caine nodded. "See, you're only looking at the outside. All you're seeing is the results. You have to look deeper for the causes. You know where these riots come from?"

"From, from, I suppose from fear—"

"That's right," Caine said. He squinted out over the city and took a deep breath to time the pause just right.

"Fear that you're an *Aktir*."

He swung his gaze back toward Ma'elKoth, letting it sink in.

The Emperor looked like he'd been clubbed. Some constriction of the throat allowed him only a monosyllabic gasp. "How?"

"You did it to yourself," Caine explained, trying not to look like he was enjoying this. "Your *Aktir* hunt has your people terrified. You did such a good job, whipping up fear of the *Aktiri*, that it was pretty simple to twist that around into fear of *you*. I'm telling you, it's the King of Cant behind it all."

He squinted at the Emperor's face, trying to read comprehension behind the pain. Was he getting through to him? He had to deliver this information now, while it still had value as intelligence; the King's Eyes would be reporting all this within hours, and then it would be too late.

"It's easy to spread a rumor in this town: at least half the beggars in Ankhana are Subjects of Cant," he went on. "And it's no wonder people believe it. Your *Aktir* hunt has trained people to be suspicious of anything that is unusual or inexplicable about their neighbors, trained them to be constantly on the lookout for *Aktiri*. And, y'know, there's a lot of stuff about you that people find a little creepy."

Was he buying it?

"But this is *absurd*—!" Ma'elKoth insisted. "Why would I, who have done so much . . . ?"

Caine reached out and laid a hand on the Emperor's sweat-slick arm. He looked into Ma'elKoth's eyes and shook his head pityingly. "You're looking at it *rationally*, Ma'elKoth. You're looking for a reasonable answer to an unreasonable situation. You'll never get there from here."

"But surely, eventually, they'll remember—"

"Yeah. *Eventually*. But by that time, the city's in ashes, and every last surviving noble is openly at war with you. The whole Empire goes down in flames. The way I see it, you have one chance. Break the Kingdom of Cant. You have maybe twenty-four hours, no more."

Ma'elKoth's hand blindly sought Caine's and engulfed it. "Twenty-four hours . . ."

"You have to stop him *now*, before it gets out of control. You have to stop him before the nobles get into the act."

"I will. I *will* stop him. I will flood the city with troops; I'll burn the Warrens to the ground if I must. This should have been done years ago."

"And you'll fail." Caine licked blood from his lips and forced down a creeping smile.

It wasn't so different from fighting, what he did here on this tower—combat of another sort, perhaps, but still combat. He was fighting for his life, for Shanna's life, and for Majesty's. Hours ago, he had thought he was betraying his best friend; now, if he could only swing Ma'elKoth in the right direction, he would reverse that betrayal. He'd make every lie he had told Majesty into the truth.

He had to keep Ma'elKoth away from the military solution for one simple, awful reason: it would work.

Think of this as combat, he told himself. His usual tactics would serve him as well here as they did in hand-to-hand. Attack attack attack—come at your target from every possible direction and press until his defenses overload. Never give him time to recover his balance: never give him time to counter.

Looking at this like a fight gave him confidence. He knew that every solution Ma'elKoth offered was only a parry, a block, and like their combat equivalents these parries and blocks created other openings through which he could strike. An all-out military assault on the Kingdom of Cant would certainly succeed; Caine had to ensure it wouldn't be attempted, at least not yet.

"You can't catch the King with the army," he said. "The Subjects of Cant are masters of the caverns under the city. There're miles of them, y'know. At the first hint of military response they'll go underground—literally—and it'll take days, maybe weeks to root them out. You don't have that much time."

"I do not need it," Ma'elKoth said. "I can Draw this man as I Drew you, Caine. I will put forth My power—"

"Yeah? If it's so easy, why couldn't you find *me* this past day or two?"

A vein pulsed in Ma'elKoth's forehead. Muscle bulged at the corners of his jaw, and he made no answer.

"I'll tell you why," Caine said. "I was with the King of Cant."

"*Where?* Where was this? Where were you?" Ma'elKoth lunged and once again those gigantic hands shot out to grab him, but this time Caine slipped aside and skipped behind the Emperor's rush. Ma'elKoth wheeled on him, and Caine stepped back with his hands up.

"Now just fucking *stop it*," Caine said. "You don't want to put your hands on me again, Ma'elKoth. I've been very understanding so far, but don't push me. You're starting to make me angry."

Ma'elKoth drew himself up. "You will give the answers I require or I shall teach you what anger is, Caine."

"Guess I should have known better than to expect an apology, huh?" Caine said without humor. "It's like this: you know how the rock around the Donjon impedes Flow? All the rock beneath the city acts the same way, and the Subjects know it—that's why they use the caverns. The King of Cant's house thaumaturge, Abbal Paslava, is a sharp character—a lot of this has been his idea from the first—and he's found some caves that are so deep that Flow never touches them at all."

"The power of My will, foiled by mere *rock*? I don't believe it."

"No? Then how come you couldn't find me?" Caine said simply.

Ma'elKoth scowled and didn't answer.

"It's this simple: the only way you will root Majesty out of those caverns is by brute force, and you *don't have time*. Go for him now with the army and you're throwing away the one real advantage you have right now: *He doesn't know what you know.* He doesn't know that you know he's Simon Jester, that he's behind the whole thing. It's your shot, Ma'elKoth. It's your big chance. You have to bait him out."

Ma'elKoth looked out over his city, and its fires burned within his eyes. "But how? How can I do this in time?"

Caine chuckled. "That's the easy part. You have Pallas Ril, right?"

Ma'elKoth turned to him, frowning, his eyes clouded once again. "Pallas Ril? Yes . . . yes, she is here. What has she to do with this?"

"There's no way to explain it, Ma'elKoth. You'll just have to trust me on this. She's in this up to her neck. She was captured while helping the *Aktiri* escape, remember?"

"Yes, ah, yes. This is the action of that spell . . . I feel its pull—"

"Anyway, listen, this doesn't matter. I'll tell you what does: Majesty is counting on that spell to frustrate your interrogation. He has no way of knowing that you've got a way to beat it with that silver net of yours."

"Right, yes, the net—"

"You're still the Emperor. When you talk, people will listen. You have all the pages of the *Imperial Messenger-News* to carry your word. You can summon the storm. Save the city. Then at dawn, you send every page and crier out with this call: At noon, you will answer your critics. You will show who the evil genius behind our current troubles truly is. And you'll do it this way: At high noon, you'll take Pallas Ril out into public somewhere—say, the new stadium, Victory Stadium on the south bank, where thousands upon thousands of your citizens can bear witness—and you'll do that spell on her, the one that you used on the *Aktiri* that you captured within the palace. You'll kill her and magickally capture her memories. You're doing it publicly so that everyone can see. You have nothing to hide, right?"

"But, but what good will this do . . . ?"

"None at all. You won't learn anything that you don't already know, *but Majesty doesn't know that.* See? He'll have to act to cover himself. He can't afford this kind of exposure. If he's publicly associated with the *Aktiri*, the nobles won't rise with him, and none of this comes off. You load the crowd with Grey Cats in civilian dress, and they take him when he moves."

"You think he'll try to rescue Pallas Ril?" Ma'elKoth asked skeptically.

"Shit, no," Caine said. "She's not even really the bait. You are."

"Ah . . ." Ma'elKoth's eyes went distant again. "Ah, I think I begin to understand . . ."

"He's not interested in her at all. Oh, sure, he'll kill her if you give him the chance. But what he'll really go for is the chance to kill *you*."

"Will he *have* a chance, Caine? Is this Paslava a thaumaturge of Pallas Ril's strength?"

"Maybe, but I'll handle him tonight. Listen, I have a better idea," he said, as though it had only now occurred to him. Caine knew Ma'elKoth would think of this on his own soon enough; he might as well bring it up himself and score another point or two. "Why put yourself in danger at all? You're too important to the Empire to do anything reckless. You can do those substantial illusions—Fantasies—can't you? Like what's her name, that elf dyke who runs the Faces?"

"Kierendal," Ma'elKoth said musingly. "Yes . . . yes, I believe I can."

"Then there's no real reason for you to expose yourself at all. From right here on the Dusk Tower you could create an illusion of yourself and make it move and speak and breathe just like the real thing. You'd never be in the slightest danger. You could do the whole operation as a Fantasy. Shit, you don't even need Pallas there: you can project an illusion of her, too. That wouldn't be too complicated for you, would it?"

Caine watched the wheels turn within Ma'elKoth's mind as he imagined the event from every possible angle and through every conceivable outcome. "No," he said slowly. "No. Pallas must be in the stadium in truth; there is a limit to what even I may convincingly accomplish with an illusion. The play of light and shadow, the touch of a breeze in My hair, even My voice. Heard only with the mind, it must perfectly counterfeit what would be heard by the ears. We can afford no slip; the slightest flaw would signal Our ploy to Our enemy."

"No, you can't," Caine said, his voice low and desperate. "You can't put her there. It's too dangerous. Please." *Please,* he thought, *don't throw po' li'l me into that briar patch . . .* "I can help you, Ma'elKoth. I can make this work for you. But if there's any danger to Pallas, we have no deal."

Ma'elKoth stepped close to Caine to tower over him and gaze

down deeply into his eyes. "So. In the end, it comes down to the woman."

Caine didn't answer; he didn't trust words to come clearly through the hammering of his heart.

"I have nearly killed you twice within the hour," Ma'elKoth murmured. "The King of Cant is, or was, one of your close friends. He has made you an honorary Baron of Cant, sheltered you, shared bread, wine, and perhaps his inmost thoughts. And you betray him to me—for a woman. For Pallas Ril."

"You have her. I want her," Caine said hoarsely. "When this works, you won't need her anymore. Give her to me."

"Why? You said that you are no longer lovers."

"That was her choice, not mine." Caine squared his shoulders and looked up into the Emperor's face with level frankness. "I love her, Ma'elKoth. I always have. Alive, there's a chance she'll change her mind about me."

He let the truth of his words carry him away; if Ma'elKoth read that truth in his face, it would paint over the cracks in his lies.

"Even after you have betrayed the King of Cant?"

"Yeah. Even then. He betrayed her, first." Caine stepped back and wrapped the truth around himself like a flag. "She was never in this to be against you, Ma'elKoth. She never opposed the government. She never hurt anyone until the Cats started pouncing on her everywhere she went. All she wanted was to save the lives of some innocent people."

"None too innocent—" Ma'elKoth began, but Caine cut him off.

"Bullshit. She's not political, all right? Whatever reasons you had for starting this whole thing, those people aren't *Aktiri*; you know it, and so does she. She's a . . . a, well . . ." Caine coughed through a sudden thickening in his throat. "She's a hero, Ma'el-Koth. A *real* hero, not like me—or you either, no offense. She couldn't stand off and let innocents be killed, and that's the only reason she's involved in this in the first place."

"Mmm," Ma'elKoth rumbled. "If she is such a hero, how did she come to be the lover of a man like you?"

Caine shook his head and looked away. "I don't know. Maybe she thought she could save me, too . . ."

He realized that Ma'elKoth had led him off his thread, and he forced his mind back onto the business at hand. "The point is that the King of Cant saw an opportunity to strike at you through her; through your *Aktir* hunt, he saw a chance to bring down your whole house. She wouldn't go for it, not at all. That was never why she was in this game in the first place. They quarreled, and she threatened to expose him. That's why he gave her up. He couldn't betray her through Toa-Sytell—that would reveal his complicity. So he had Lamorak do it."

Ma'elKoth's brows lifted. "Indeed? Lamorak has been in the pay of the King as well as the Cats? How very enterprising."

"Didn't you wonder why he blew the riverboat to you after you nearly had him tortured to death?" This was a risk, but only a slight one; Caine was almost positive that it was Lamorak who had brought the Cats to Knights' Bridge.

"Yes," Ma'elKoth said slowly, "yes, I did. Now many things begin to come clear . . ."

"You screwed Majesty's plans for real when you took her alive. That was one outcome he hadn't planned on. To kill her himself would have been too raw for the rest of the Kingdom. They still have some illusions of honor. He was gonna let Berne do the job for him, but Berne fucked it up. Pallas is still alive. That's why he's had to move. That's why the riots, the story about you being an *Aktir*. He has to hit you hard before you break her, so that by the time you know who to hit back at, it's too late. You get it, now?"

"I see . . ." Ma'elKoth mused. "And once my illusionary Emperor has apparently slain Pallas in the stadium, any of her surviving enemies will believe her dead, thus protecting her from reprisal."

"Exactly," Caine said. "And we can go off and live happily ever after."

"But if the King of Cant is her enemy, why does she still protect him then? Why does she resist Me?"

"She's a hero," Caine said simply, his mouth dry. "She can't do anything less. That's why I love her. If you want my help, keep her here in the palace, out of danger."

"I have explained to you the difficulty with this," Ma'elKoth began, but Caine cut him off with a slash of his hand that was all too close to a killing strike.

"Don't bitch to me about your problems," he said. "You're the one who wants to be a god; are you telling me you can't do a simple fucking illusion to save your empire?"

The Emperor scowled darkly. "You doubt My power?"

"*You're* the one with doubts," Caine countered.

The Emperor's eyes went vague, his thoughts drifting far to a noontide in a sunlit arena on the south bank.

"Perhaps it can be done," he said at length. "Difficult; nearly impossible. No mortal could hope to accomplish such a feat—an interesting challenge. But I can take no chance with Pallas; her power has become extreme. Without My will to block her, she may find a way to pierce My wards and reach the Flow once more."

Caine shrugged. "Put her in the Donjon."

Ma'elKoth frowned musingly. "I suppose—"

"It's the safest place," Caine said easily. "And the rock will keep her from pulling Flow."

"Yes ..." Ma'elKoth said slowly. "She can be kept in the Donjon safely enough, I believe."

You just keep on believing that. He'd given in too easily on this; he had other plans for her. *That's all right,* Caine thought. *So do I.*

Ma'elKoth's eyes focused on Caine once again. "It shall be done. Even if the Fantasy fails, little will be lost. No matter the outcome, I will still have the huge public forum in which to accuse the King of Cant; the risk is small. Caine, I have underestimated you. You are thoroughly brilliant."

The consideration in the Emperor's features hardened into resolve. "We shall do this thing. It will be a simple matter to contrive to 'lose' the apparent corpse of Pallas Ril before it is burned, or to find another corpse of strong resemblance to consign to the flame. Caine, you have My gratitude. Once this affair is complete, you shall have more: you shall have a title, and lands, and vassals to do your bidding. And you shall have the life of Pallas Ril."

Holy shit, Caine thought in wonder. *I did it. This might work.*

14

CAINE STOOD CLOSE to the altar where Pallas was bound while Ma'elKoth spoke to Toa-Sytell and Berne. He wished impotently that there were something he could do for her, right here and now, some way that he could, at least, cover her naked body. This was more for his own comfort than for hers: she was far away still, in that distant mystic place of her own, utterly dissociated from what went on around her.

He watched the eyes of Toa-Sytell and Berne as Ma'elKoth paced around the Iron Room, issuing his orders. Berne's kept flicking wetly to Pallas' naked, bruised body tied to the altar. Once when he caught Caine looking at him, he slowly and with obscene deliberation ran his tongue around the rim of his lips.

A sole regret burned within Caine's stomach: his plan included no opportunity to personally murder that sick motherfucker.

Toa-Sytell's eyes, however, remained fixed on Ma'elKoth's impossibly beautiful face. Behind the Duke's habitual mask of polite blankness lurked concern that bordered on fear. When Ma'elKoth revealed that the true enemy was the King of Cant, blush flooded the Duke's face. "I don't believe it," he muttered. "I don't believe it for one second."

The Emperor rounded upon him. "Belief is not required of you, Toa-Sytell. Obedience, however, *is*."

"But, but . . . you don't understand!" Toa-Sytell stammered. "What word do you act upon but Caine's? Have you forgotten the destruction that follows him everywhere? Have you forgotten the Donjon? Have you forgotten the *Succession War*?"

Ma'elKoth stepped to him, towering over him, his face darkening as though a cloud had passed before the sun.

"I have not. Take care that *you* do not forget: I am Ma'elKoth. The Empire is Mine to risk, should I choose. As is this city; as is your life, Toa-Sytell."

The Duke didn't flinch, but he could not abide the Emperor's gaze. As soon as he dropped his eyes, though, Ma'elKoth relented, laying an avuncular hand on Toa-Sytell's shoulder. "I understand your concern, My Duke, but you should also recall that the destruction attendant upon Caine's presence has always redounded to My benefit. It was the Succession War that brought Me to power; the slaughter in the Donjon has brought Me to the brink of victory over My most troublesome adversary. I do not ask you to place trust in Caine's word, but rather in My judgment."

Berne stepped forward, a half sneer on his face as he chewed the inside of his lip. "And where'll Caine be during all this? Ask me, I'd lock him up here where you can keep an eye on him."

"I did not ask you, Berne." Ma'elKoth bent down and lifted the net from where it lay piled on the iron plates of the floor. He wrapped it about itself with a flick of his powerful wrist—the griffinstones knotted into its hem gave it plenty of heft—and he tossed it as a bundle to Caine. "Caine has a part in this, as well."

Caine caught the net in one hand and tied it into a bundle as he spoke. "The one sticky point in the plan is Abbal Paslava.

They call him the Spellbinder—he's sort of the house wizard for the Kingdom—"

"We all know who he is," Toa-Sytell cut in dryly.

"Well, he's a problem. He's a specialist in illusions and shit like that. He might be able to detect Ma'elKoth's Fantasy somehow, or even dispel it. That would blow the game for real."

"And what do you intend to do about him?"

Caine hefted the netting. "Kill him. It'll be easy enough. I'm trusted there, remember? I get him off alone, throw this net over his head so he can't defend himself, and one breath later our problem is solved. I know more than a few ways I can kill him that won't leave a mark. Paslava's not a young man; if I tell Majesty that he suddenly collapsed and died in my arms, everyone will believe me."

Berne directed his appeal to Ma'elKoth. "How do we know that he'll do what he says? Why take the chance of letting him go? Ma'elKoth, I'm telling you—"

"Fear not," Ma'elKoth rumbled. "I have taken Caine's measure and not found him wanting: he will be true. Toa-Sytell, you will give the necessary orders for all other arrangements; you have complete authority in this matter. Berne, you will have the Cats ready and present. Once the King of Cant is in My hands, we will raise the matter of Pallas Ril."

Play it out, Caine thought. "Ma'elKoth, you promised—"

"I did not. My word was given conditionally: *once this affair is complete.* Nothing is complete until I have determined to My satisfaction that Pallas Ril is no longer a threat to the Empire. When dusk falls tomorrow, if the city is calm again, I shall continue My examination. If I can make certain that your tale is true, she will be released."

"Released?" Berne looked stunned. "You can't!"

"I can. I will. Caine, you have much to do. Go with Toa-Sytell and arrange to escape from the iron carriage as you are transported to the Donjon. You are to be convincing, but—" thunder gathered upon the Emperor's brow "—kill no one. Reserve your slaughter for Our enemies, and you shall be rewarded. Take the lives of My loyal soldiers, and you shall be punished. Am I understood?"

Caine shrugged irritably, showing plain displeasure. "Yeah, whatever."

"Go then, all of you. I also have much to do; I must summon back the storm from Kaarn to save the city. It will be work of some hours, and then I must prepare the Fantasy for the morrow. Go."

The three men exchanged a glance: Caine's was grim, Toa-Sytell's bland, and Berne's openly venomous. Caine took a deep breath and reluctantly headed for the door. It required a physical effort for him to step away from Shanna's side. He set his teeth and didn't look back.

Toa-Sytell beat him to the door and pulled it open for him. As they both stepped into the entry room, Ma'elKoth rumbled behind them, "Berne, bide a moment."

Caine turned back instantly. The image of Berne left behind in the Iron Room with Shanna while Ma'elKoth wandered off to do his weather magick was so sickeningly potent that he couldn't help himself. Ma'elKoth made an absent flicking gesture from across the room, and the door clanged shut in his face.

He stood for a moment, staring at the silver runes that spidered across the Ouroboros knocker, trying to breathe, trying to recover his mental balance.

"Caine."

Toa-Sytell's voice had an unfamiliar intensity. When Caine looked back over his shoulder at the Duke, Toa-Sytell's normally bland face had gone white with suppressed fury.

"You've made me play the fool once before, Caine," Toa-Sytell hissed, "and a hundred thousand people died in the Succession War—including my sons. I know you, Caine, and I will not be made the fool twice. I do not know how it is that you've gulled Ma'elKoth, but I tell you this: I am not deceived. I am watching you, Caine, and at the first hint of treachery I will see you dead."

Caine met his fury with bared teeth. "You're just pissy 'cause I do your job better than you do. Majesty conned you exactly the same way Lamorak conned Berne."

"Be warned, Caine—"

"Y'know, if I were you, I'd be paying less attention to me, and a little more to covering your ass, Toa-Sytell," Caine said, conspicuously backing off from the confrontation, becoming almost friendly. "I'm going to give you some advice, Duke. Not because I *like* you, you understand, but because I think that fundamentally, you're a decent man. You should be remembering who your friends are. You should be thinking about what you'll do if Ma'elKoth falls."

"He will not fall, not while I live," Toa-Sytell said.

"Don't make that promise. If Ma'elKoth goes and you go with him, who would that leave in charge? At least until somebody kills him and takes over?"

Toa-Sytell frowned; then his eyes widened and he started to go a little pale. A moment later he shook his head and murmured, "But . . . but no one would follow *him*; he's only a Count—he has no authority, no real power . . ."

Caine offered an openly cynical smile. "Hey, there are people in the world who just need someone to tell them what to do, and they're not particular who it is."

Toa-Sytell looked grim, but then he shook that distressing image out of his head. "But Ma'elKoth will not fall. He cannot fall."

"Don't bet your life on it. He's been acting a little strange lately, don't you think? These sudden rages, this obsession with me, with where I've been, what I'm doing. I'm starting to think he might be cracking up."

Toa-Sytell narrowed his eyes, and his gaze became distant; Caine could see that he'd been thinking along these lines already.

"Sure," Caine went on, "we'll handle this particular threat tomorrow. But I think you can already see that Ma'elKoth isn't untouchable. If we can see it, so can his enemies."

"Caine—"

"I'm sorry about your sons, Toa-Sytell. I know it doesn't mean much at this late date, but I swear to you that nobody knew how bad the Succession War was going to be. The Monastic Council would never have sent me in here if they'd thought it would get like that. I don't want to see another one any more than you do, all right? Think about it. Someone has to be in place to keep order if Ma'elKoth goes down. I can't think of anyone who'd do a better job than you would."

Muscles bunched at the corners of Toa-Sytell's jaw and relaxed again, and slowly his vision regained its focus. "Come. We must arrange your escape."

15

"I CAN'T BELIEVE you're trusting him," Berne said, pacing furiously, stabbing at the air with his stiffened hand. "And I can't believe that you're going to let her go! After what she did to me? Do you know how many of my boys she's killed?"

"Hush, dear boy," Ma'elKoth rumbled. "Recover your center. I do not trust Caine. Nor will Pallas Ril be released. Her feat at the docks—" A fleeting shadow crossed his perfect features. "—I My-self might not be able to surpass. She has become a Power; vastly too dangerous to be allowed to live."

"But you told Caine—"

His massive shoulders lifted and fell again. "She, after all, suf-fers a sucking wound to her chest. Life will slip away from her soon enough, I think; she shall live only until We have no further need of Caine." He smiled into his beard. "It may be instructive to perform that pretended spell on her in truth, instead . . ."

"Need him for *what*? Why did you let him go?" Berne's voice took on a rising, petulant edge. "Why won't you let me kill him?"

"I may do that, even yet." Ma'elKoth laid a hand on Berne's shoulder. "The tale he brought to Me is a convincing one; it fits every fact, and he had an answer for every question. This alone would make Me suspicious: only fictions tally so neatly. Life is less orderly."

He turned majestically, a ship of the line tacking against the wind, and drifted over to the altar. He looked down on the still, blank face of Pallas Ril, and his hand extended to absently stroke her eyelids closed.

"And I have reason to doubt the word of Caine already," he went on. "His plan, however, suits My purposes so well that I wonder at it: a tremendous gain for no risk at all. It may be that he is true. I ac-cept the possibility, but I do not rely upon it." He looked up, and the sleepy cast of his musing cleared from his face; he fixed Berne with a stare of sudden intensity.

"Give me your knife." Ma'elKoth held out his hand; Berne pulled his dagger from its sheath and handed it to Ma'elKoth without hesitation. The dagger was dwarfed by Ma'elKoth's hand as he raised it to the level of his eyes; it looked like a pocketknife. "The net that I gave to Caine—as I lifted it from the floor I put my mark upon it."

His eyes glowed green. He smothered the dagger in his fist, staring at it with transcendent concentration. The dagger shone with the emerald reflection of Ma'elKoth's eyes. When the light faded from his face, the dagger still glimmered faintly. He handed it back to Berne, who cradled it gingerly, savoring the remnants of Ma'elKoth's touch in the warmth of its hilt.

"Point this dagger toward Caine, and it shall grow warm within your hand and shine green to the eye. Follow him, and learn his purpose. Take a team of Cats with you. If you should see a chance to capture or kill the King of Cant or any of his followers, take it. Do not follow too closely. I cannot spare a Cloak, as all My energies must bend toward calling the thunderstorm."

"I'll do it, Ma'elKoth," Berne said, clutching the dagger as though it were the symbol of his oath. "You know you can count on me."

"I do know that, Berne. I rely upon it." Ma'elKoth turned away, and Berne's gaze slid onto the naked body of Pallas Ril. The vacant look in her eyes, the bruises that covered her slim form, the blood-stained bandage that bound her breasts, even the chains that tied her hand and foot to the altar—Berne had never seen anything so erotic in his life. He wanted her so badly that it squeezed the breath from his lungs.

"Ahh, Ma'elKoth?"

"Yes, My son?"

"When you're done with Pallas, can I have her? I mean," he said hastily, "I caught her, after all. It's only fair."

"Mmm, yes. Yes, it is: only fair."

16

"CAINE'S BACK ON-LINE."

Kollberg came bolt upright like a hound scenting game. "How long was he off?"

"One hour, seven minutes, Administrator."

"Perfect, perfect." He leaned forward with a glance at the soapies; they'd finally sat, a couple of hours ago, in the chairs he'd provided. Neither one was moving. For all he could tell, they might be fast asleep.

The POV screen at the end of the techbooth was lit with the view inside the iron carriage. No Soliloquy, yet. Caine spoke offhandedly with a man Kollberg recognized as that Toa-Sytell guy, the Duke. There were two other men inside the carriage; they wore the uniforms of Household Knights. Caine kept glancing out the barred window at the fires on the streets and the people that ran back and forth—some armed, many bleeding, some carrying boxes and barrels and jugs, some savagely attacking the thieves to steal their loot for themselves.

"This is good," Kollberg whispered. "They're taking him right through the middle of the riot. I'm *loving* this . . . Damn, Caine, I knew I could count on you. I *knew* it."

Kollberg giggled out loud at the blank shock and horror on the faces of the Household Knights when Caine's manacles dropped off. He produced a tiny blade from somewhere, a small hooked knife that he held to the throat of the Duke.

"Kill him," Toa-Sytell snarled. *"Never mind me. Don't let him get away! That's an order!"*

"Yeah, go ahead," Caine told them. *"Then who'll be left alive to tell* Ma'elKoth *it was an order? You think he'll believe you? Open the damned door and step aside."*

The Household Knights were in no mood to take chances with their lives. They opened the door, and Caine dragged Toa-Sytell backward into the riot. The Knights who rode guard on the carriage shouted in surprise as the two tumbled to the street, but they were no more adventurous than the ones inside. Caine and his hostage were able to back into a nearby alley.

"Is this far enough?" Toa-Sytell asked softly.

"Yeah. I practically grew up here. They'll never catch me."

"All right." Toa-Sytell suddenly started to struggle and shout. He wormed his way loose from Caine's grip, yelling for the Knights. Caine kicked him to the ground. He stood over him with the knife raised, long enough for the Knights to see him there as they charged toward him from the carriage, then turned and fled into the red-shadowed darkness of the alley.

Kollberg chuckled to himself as Caine dodged through the riot. All his jitters, all his bitter determination to destroy Caine, all the back-of-the-neck pressure of the soapies in the booth, all was forgotten. This was shaping into a spectacular Adventure.

No corner of Old Town was calm that night; from everywhere came shouts, sounds of fighting, and the splintering crash of breaking glass and pottery. Trust Caine to find a way to stir things up— that was, on reflection, perhaps his greatest talent. He skipped around a storefront where an embattled platoon of regular infantry struggled to hold off a mob of several hundred rock-throwing citizens; even as he passed, someone set fire to the building where the platoon had made their fort.

Caine slipped inside a nearby pissoir and startled a miserably squatting townsman when he splintered the mucker-shaft door away from its locking hasp with a strong side kick. He slid down the mucker-shaft ladder and found the concealed door at the shaft's base that let him into the caverns below the city. A moment of digging in a pocket produced Kierendal's lighter; its wavering flame provided enough illumination for him to keep a steady pace.

He filled in backstory as he walked silently through the caverns, rolling out imagery with his usual skill. There was an odd note to it, though, and Kollberg sat up straighter and cocked his head like a spaniel, trying to listen more closely, trying to determine what the unfamiliar element was. Something just slightly strained, a tiny bit stilted . . . Ahh, that was it.

Kollberg smiled satisfaction to himself. Caine was overcontrolling his Soliloquy. That's what had caused the change. He must be making a conscious effort to leave out anything that might be controversial, so of course it didn't flow with his usual free-associating style.

Kollberg smiled in spite of the lessened quality of the entertainment: he smiled because he had Caine running scared. *On the other hand,* he thought, *he might be leaving out something* else, *as well . . .* Where had that thought come from? Did he really think Caine was concealing something? What could he possibly be hiding? Kollberg smiled at himself again: this was purely the natural paranoia of the perfectionist.

Here and there in the caverns, the flicker of firelight reflected on rock came distantly to Caine's eyes. He circled wide of several such places where the murmur of distant voices blended with the blurred plash of water, seeping through the limestone and dripping into pools below. He crept past a couple more where going wide would have taken him into unfamiliar places. In the knotted three-dimensional maze of caverns below the city, a wrong turn could possibly have required hours or days to correct. Finally he came upon one toward which he walked boldly. Three men who looked like beggars and one in the painted mail of a Knight of Cant lounged around a small fire built on the naked rock.

They didn't seem overly concerned at Caine's approach. He identified himself and exchanged brief recognition signals with them, and they nodded him along on his way. As he passed he said softly, *"Could be unfriendlies on my tail. Be wary. You might even want to clear out."*

The Knight rose to his feet with confident ease, one hand on the hilt of his shortsword. *"Want them stopped?"*

"No. I don't want anybody hurt. Just be alert, is all."

He left them there and found a mucker shaft nearby; he climbed out of the caverns through a pissoir and into the firelit night of the Industrial Park.

He kept as close to the shifting blue-black shadows as he could and still move at speed. The streets could be deserted at one moment, then an instant later flood with shouting, struggling, looting mobs. At the mouth of an alley he tried to duck into, he was accosted by a pair of men brandishing broadswords. *"Declare yourself!"*

"Declare myself what?"

A sword point came perilously near his throat. *"Are you for the Emperor or the damned Aktiri?"*

"Loyalists, huh? You boys are in for a bad night, I think."

While the loyalist tried to decide which side that meant Caine was on, Caine leaned around his point, grabbed his wrist, and twisted the blade out of his hand. His weight already shifted, he was able to stop the shout of the other with a whipping heel to the jaw. He let the momentum of the kick carry him around in a tight circle that ended by braining the first loyalist with the flat of his own blade. The blade quivered in his hand and sprang back straight, not bent: a decent grade of steel. *"Huh,"* he said. *"Not bad."*

He held on to the blade as he dodged into the dark-shadowed alley away from the downed loyalists, even as they gathered breath to plead for their lives.

He loped through the streets, avoiding trouble and skirting crowds of any size or description, and finally arrived at a darkened apartment block that looked vaguely familiar to Kollberg. A quick glance at the on-screen telemetry assured him that this was Caine's destination: his adrenal production had soared, and his heart rate was ramping up toward redline. A door hung slack from a single hinge. Caine went in and up two flights of darkened stairs.

At their top he called out a soft repetition of the recognition signal he'd given to the Subjects in the caverns and got a low-voiced response from the shadows beyond. He stepped out into the hall to find two Knights.

"Majesty sent me. He wants you both back at the stadium right now."

The Knights exchanged a dubious glance. *"I, uh, I dunno,"* one of them said. *"We're supposed to stay here unless Majesty tells us personal, y'know?"*

"He's a little busy right now. Maybe you've noticed?"

"Sorry, Baron," the other said. *"He was pretty clear on this."*

Caine sighed and spread his hands in a gesture of surrender. *"All right. It's like this. I need to have a talk with our boy Lamorak in there. This'll be the kind of talk that you don't want to be witnesses to, you follow? Head back for the stadium and just pretend you believed me about the phony message. Majesty'll understand."*

"But, but I don't think—"

"I'm telling you, Majesty will understand. He wouldn't expect you to, like, give your lives here," he said with a significant twitch of the naked blade he held. He paused a moment to make sure they understood him perfectly. *"You follow?"*

They exchanged another long look and decided that absenting themselves would be the better part of discretion, but Kollberg was no longer paying attention.

Lamorak, he thought, oddly calm and obscurely pleased by his unexpected serenity. *This is the safe house in the Industrial Park.*

He made a fist and held it upraised, trembling above the emergency transfer switch; the chubby underside of his fist reflected an ominous red in the switch's glow.

One slip, Caine. Just one—and it doesn't even have to be from you. Let Lamorak so much as hint at a confession, and my fist shall fall like the Hammer of God.

His liver-colored lips quirked at the image, and he squirmed briefly in the stage manager's chair, settling his weight in to get comfortable—but he couldn't, not quite. He itched, here and there; he felt like ants crawled on his skin; and he couldn't seem to relax his shoulders or slow the sudden racing of his heart.

Just a little while longer, he told himself. *It won't be long now.*

17

WHEN I OPEN the door, he's at the window, staring out, the light from fires in Alientown dancing red across his battered profile. As he starts to turn toward me I spring across the floor and lunge like a fencer; my fleche stops with the broadsword's point a finger breadth from his throat. He freezes in the act of rising from his chair. I guess that splinted leg of his can now bear some weight.

"Don't say a word," I tell him softly. "I'm not here to hurt you."

Slowly he takes his weight upon his arms and lowers himself back into the chair. Some thoughtful Subject has immobilized his broken jaw with a large bandage knotted on top of his head; he looks like a cartoon baby with a toothache. "Y'not?"

I sigh deep and long, then reverse the sword and offer him the hilt. "No. Try that Dominate, though, and I'll break another bone in your face, you got it?"

He reaches tentatively for the sword, like a child for candy that it fears will be snatched away. Once his hand closes on the hilt, most of the tension drains out of his shoulders and neck. The relief that smooths his face is so strong I can almost feel it myself.

"Caine . . . Caine, I—"

"I know all about it." I turn away to light a lamp and set it so its glow will be visible outside. "We're gonna have words, you and me, back home, but that's not important now. I know what you've done, and I know why."

His eyes bulge, and the sword point twitches up toward my face as his other hand takes the hilt as well. "I, I, but I—"

"You don't have to say a word. I'm telling you, I know, and I understand."

His lower lip quivers. "I never meant for anyone to get hurt—"

"I know. Lamorak, believe me, I know what it's like—the kind of pressure they can put on you. I've been there, all right? I've done the same, and I didn't like it any more than you do."

Now his eyes start to moisten, and the revulsion in my chest nearly chokes me with the effort to keep it off my face and out of my voice. "Her career . . ." he whines. "Her Adventure—"

I cut in strongly. "The only thing that matters now is prying her loose from Ma'elKoth, all right? Help me now. Help me save her, and nothing else matters. I'll even make sure that Majesty doesn't kill you for what you did to him."

"Caine . . . Caine, that was—"

"I'm telling you, Lamorak, I *understand*." What a fucking whiner. "I scared you back in the warehouse the other night. You thought I was going to kill you."

I give him a shrug and a moderately sheepish half smile. "And I was. Without the recall, you'd be dead, but hey, that was temper, y'know? Once I had time to calm down and think it over, I understood. Listen, we don't have any more time to waste on this. I need your help."

"For what? I mean, anything, *anything* I can do, to make this right, Caine."

I show him the net, and his eyes fasten on the griffinstones in its hem with naked lust. "I'm running a deep game on Ma'elKoth, and I think the Cats might be tailing me magickally. I need to know, one way or the other; if so, I need to know if the tag's on me, on my clothes, this knife, this net . . . You get the picture. I can't have them following me everywhere; it'll blunt the hook."

"Tailing you?" he says, alarmed; his gaze skates nervously back toward the street outside.

"Relax. They're not close. They don't have to be, if there's a tag on me."

"How would they tag you? Where did you get this net?"

"Ma'elKoth." I chuckle dryly. "Ironic, huh? This morning you tried to get me killed by making Majesty believe that I was working for Ma'elKoth—and I was. I am. Or, at least, Ma'elKoth thinks so."

"*Damn,* Caine . . ." Lamorak says in a tone of awe. "Damn . . ."

"The point is, I have Ma'elKoth convinced that Majesty is Simon Jester, and that he can draw Majesty and the whole Kingdom out of the Warrens by performing a sort of public ritual on Pallas, where he'll magickally wrench the true identity of Simon Jester out of her in front of twenty thousand people at Victory Stadium."

"But why would Majesty—?"

"He wouldn't. But I've got Ma'elKoth thinking that Majesty and the Kingdom will be on hand to take a shot at killing him, so Ma'elKoth and Berne are going to load the crowd with Cats and King's Eyes and soldiers in mufti, to lay in wait for him—but Majesty and the Kingdom won't be anywhere near the place."

"So what's the point?"

I show my teeth. "The point is, Ma'elKoth won't be there, either. He's going to run the ritual by remote control, using a Fantasy, to keep himself out of danger. Now, the reason for all these riots today is that Majesty and I, between us, have half the city thinking Ma'elKoth's an *Aktir.* Put twenty thousand people in that stadium, and let them watch while I drape that piece of silver netting over Ma'elKoth's illusionary double."

It takes him a second or two, but then his eyes widen and his mouth hangs slack. "My *god* . . ." he murmurs. "My bleeding god . . . The net cuts off the image from the Flow, so it fades and vanishes exactly like *an* Aktir *is supposed to* . . ."

"Yeah," I say warmly. "Nice, huh?"

"All the Cats, officers of the army, thousands of citizens—"

"All the King's horses and all the King's men. Yeah. Ma'elKoth's government goes down in flames. It'll be a matter of hours until he's besieged in the Colhari Palace."

"Caine . . . it's brilliant. It could actually work."

"It's going to work. I have a couple more arrangements to make, and everything will be in place."

"What about P-Pallas?"

"She's as safe as possible, right now. Once the fighting starts, I can get her out."

"Out of the Victory *Stadium*? How do you figure?"

"She won't *be* in the stadium; she'll be in the Donjon."

"Holy shit—"

"Yeah. It's the only place Ma'elKoth can keep her, where she can't pull enough Flow to blow his lights out."

"But . . . you think you can bring her out?"

I give him a solid nod. "I know the way in," I remind him, raising my right hand. "In all the confusion, it shouldn't be too difficult. And to get out, all I need is to get within arm's reach."

He gives me a sharply speculative look that the bruises from his broken nose and jaw make kinda comical; I beckon to him. "Now, come on. She's running out of time. So get started. Check me over and find the tag."

I keep a close eye on him as he breathes into mindview. If he tries, even now, to turn that Dominate on me, he's a dead man; I'll find a different way to make this work.

A minute or two of under-breath murmuring as he examines me, then he nods and looks up, his eyes clear of mindview. "You were right. It's this net. They can track it somehow. I don't know the spell, but there's definitely some sort of patterned power here, not just the leak-over from the griffinstones."

Huh. Ma'elKoth must have tagged it in the instant that he picked it up, before he tossed it to me. He's pretty smooth, that one.

Come noon tomorrow, I'll show him what *really* smooth looks like.

I step over to the window and peer out. I can't see anyone outside watching the place, but if they're there they can see me. "Thanks, Lamorak. I gotta go now, but I won't forget this. I'll square things with Majesty, all right? He won't lay a finger on you."

"Caine, I . . ." He sounds all choked up. "Thanks, uh, thanks for not killing me, y'know?"

"Don't mention it. We get back home alive, maybe I'll get you in a ring somewhere and take it out on you then."

"It's a date." He holds out his hand, and I force myself to shake it without breaking his wrist.

"See you later." I bundle up the net again and go.

18

THE DOOR EXPLODED in a shower of splinters. Lamorak leaped from his chair with a shout through his tied-shut teeth, and his blade snapped up to guard; without hesitation he lunged from his splinted leg, and the first Cat through the door took a foot of steel through his thigh.

Lamorak was a fine swordsman, able to compensate for his immobilized leg and recover his balance before the following Cat could swing past his falling comrade. But even as Lamorak whirled his broadsword back up to guard, another Cat crashed through the window at his back and kicked him in the spine with stunning force. He spun hard to the floor but held on to his blade, rolling onto his back and hacking at the legs of every Cat in range. He said nothing: there was nothing to say. With grim, silent desperation, he fought for his life.

The blade's edge hit a leg that it didn't cut, that made the blade spring back and ring like a bell, made it sting Lamorak's hand. Not a leg in grey leather; a leg in heavy serge that once was red, but was now faded to the blotchy shade of an old bloodstain. Lamorak lost his breath, and for an instant his grip slacked; before he could move the blade again, a boot heel came down hard on his wrist, and the matching boot kicked his sword away.

He looked up without hope, even the grim determination to survive bleaching from his face.

"Berne . . ." he murmured. "Berne, don't . . ."

"Don't speak," Berne said, his amusement colored with deeply satisfied malice. "I heard about your little trick with Master Arkadeil."

He reached back over his shoulder and pulled free Kosall. Its whine sighed a freezing breath up the back of Lamorak's neck as Berne took its hilt and whirled it singing through the air. "You know, I never really *properly* thanked you for the gift of Kosall. Sure did a job on that fighting girl of yours: spilled her guts all over Knights' Bridge. I hope you weren't too attached to her."

He dangled the blade point downward over Lamorak's crotch. "You think if I drop it, its magick will fade before it cuts off your dick?"

"Berne, wait, Berne—"

"Shut up. I don't have time for your treacherous little cock right now. I have to keep up with Caine."

"Berne," he began again, but the Count wasn't listening; easily, casually, he reached over and tapped Lamorak's mouth shut with the flat of Kosall's humming point, and held it so. The blade's song made his teeth buzz and fuzzed his hearing like a storm wind.

"Carry this sack of shit back to my place—no, don't. If he can fight, he can fucking well walk. March him back and lock him in the den. I'll make time for him later." He looked down at Lamorak, and his smile pulsed wide into a grin, growing like a stiffening penis. "Mmm, yeah. I will make time. And, if he tries to talk to you? Kill him."

He pursed his lips and made a smooching noise. "It's all the same to me, so long as I make it back before you're cold."

He spun Kosall back into its scabbard and stalked off before Lamorak could summon the words to stop him, stepping over the Cat who sat pale on the floor, clutching his spurting thigh. "Pero, tie off Finn's leg before he bleeds to death, huh?" he said, and was gone.

The other Cats he'd cut had only scratches, the wire that reinforced their leggings having mostly withstood his weakened blows. Without bothering to bandage them, the Cats prodded him to his feet at sword point and marched him, limping and in great pain, out the door. He drew breath to speak, not to Dominate, just to beg them to carry a message to Berne, that things were not as they seemed—

"Don't," said the Cat behind him and enforced this order with a jab of a sword point hard enough to slice skin over Lamorak's kidney. "Talk, and you don't live to cross the river, get it?"

Lamorak started to answer, caught himself, and nodded miserably. The Cat jabbed him again, and he lurched forward toward the stairs.

19

THE KING OF CANT, attired in a fashionable slashed-velvet singlet and satin pantaloons of matching silvery grey, strolled through the crowd around the knucklebones pit that dimpled the floor within Alien Games, one hand on the decorative scrolled hilt of the short blade at his belt. He shifted and bumped around shoulders, admiring the magnificent dark walnut of the dice table, its blond burled maple inlay that caught the light like brushed gold under what must have been several coats of buffed lacquer. "Nice," he muttered under his breath. "Wonder how she got it here so fast. I heard Caine busted the shit out of her old one."

"*This* is *the old one*," came the whispered reply from inches behind his ear. No one in the push of the crowd around the bones pit could have heard it; and no one in any of the pits, at any of the bars, on the stage, or seated for dining could have seen the man who spoke.

"*It is magicked, even as I am,*" whispered Abbal Paslava, who walked at his king's shoulder, fully Cloaked and using a pair of crystal-lensed Truesight spectacles to pierce the illusion of opulence. "Everything here is magicked; this is why I need fear no detection of my Cloak's pull. This room, this entire building pulls Flow constantly. Nothing in this room is truly as it appears."

"Huh," Majesty grunted, a grim smile baring his teeth. "Including the customers."

No windows allowed moonlight onto the gaming floor, where a view of the sky might have reminded the gamblers of the hours that passed in the outside world, but the ruddy glow of burning buildings angled through the street door. Alien Games was crowded, astonishingly so considering the rioting that still flared here and there across the city. Well-dressed South Bankers mingled with trickles of workmen coming off shift in the Industrial Park; for some, the pleasures of drink and dice come before all else, even safety.

Far from diminishing these pleasures, the riots *added* something, a certain zest in the cast of dice or the slap of a card. Everyone seemed to laugh a bit louder, talk a bit more. Here and there across the floor, knots of spontaneous dancing would suddenly break out and just as suddenly fade. The riots outside gave the evening's gaming a festive, insular atmosphere, a carnival spice, as though nothing done here tonight could have any relation to everyday life: a sense that here was a small island of brightly indecent pleasures in the midst of a huge and bloody ocean of night.

There were a few faces, here and there, that the King of Cant did not recognize. He mentally estimated their number, coming up with a total of only fifty or so. Of these probably fifteen were covert guards in Kierendal's employ—human Faces.

He ambled off the gaming floor to one of the bars, passing an appreciative hand over the glossy, hard wax finish. "Y'know, it's a shame that I didn't come here before," he murmured. "This woulda been a nice place to relax, once in a while."

"Pity," came the whispered reply.

"Yeah. Don't know what you got till it's gone, huh? And, y'know? I'm kinda looking forward to meeting Kierendal. Should have paid a call under social circumstances."

"Too late now."

"Yeah."

He beckoned to the bartender, a short and slender elf, ageless as they all were, who mixed drinks and measured narcotics with a speed that made him seem to have an extra arm or two. The elf narrowed his eyes at him, a fleeting frown passing across his feathery, translucent brows; then he stepped lively toward Majesty, his face now a mask of neutral cheerfulness.

"Does he see you?" Majesty muttered.

"No," Paslava whispered, *"but he may see an odd eddy in the Flow around you. He will know there is magick at work here."*

"Hey, so what?" Majesty said. "That's not a secret."

The bartender leaned on the back rail in a friendly fashion and gave him a professional smile. "First time in AG, sir?"

Majesty nodded. "You have a good eye."

The bartender took this as a given. "It's what I do, sir. You look like an alcohol man, am I right, sir? I have a very fine Tinnaran brandy, if you're interested?"

"Mmm," Majesty said, pretending indecision, "not exactly what I had in mind . . ."

The bartender nodded back over his shoulder at the rows of bottles and phials and baskets of herbs stacked up behind him. "If you want to try something and you don't know its name, feel free to just point. If you'd like something you don't see here, please ask and I'll bet I can get it for you."

"Bet? For real?"

The bartender's grin became more honestly friendly. "Why not? This is a gaming establishment, sir. Shall we say, for a royal?"

Majesty gave him an ugly grin. "Sure, all right. I'd like a skinny fucking elf bitch dyke, about this tall. Goes by the name of Kierendal."

That trace of a frown flitted across the bartender's brow once again, as his smile congealed into a flat chilly stare. "Be assured that she is already on her way, sir," he said coldly. "And you may find it wise to reconsider your tone."

"Yeah? Or what?"

"Or the fellow behind you might open your skull—to adjust your attitude from the *inside*, sir."

Majesty turned to find himself nose-to-sternum with a chest roughly the size of a river barge, and he slowly lifted his head until he stared up into the protuberant fist-sized yellow eyes of a troll, a nocturnal cousin of the ogres that worked here in daylight hours. Those huge lambent eyes spread a rich golden cast onto the brass-capped tusks that thrust up through slitted gaps in its upper lip. The troll wore chainmail painted in the scarlet and brass motif of the Alien Games uniform and carried a morningstar the size of Majesty's head. It snorted down at him, its breath the exhalation of a late-summer slaughterhouse.

"Yeah," it rumbled thickly. "Adjust y'attitude."

"You're ugly, and you stink," Majesty said precisely, "and I think you should be falling down, now."

"Huh," the troll huffed, blowing a blinding gust of stench into Majesty's face. "I don't think—"

Its voice cut off an instant after Majesty heard the faintest of whispers, the rustle of the cloth on Paslava's sleeve as the Cloaked thaumaturge reached past his ear and touched the troll with a spell that caused all of its skeletal muscles to lock into maximum contraction. Majesty fancied he could hear the creaking of the beast's oversized joints as they took the stress; the troll swayed like an unmoored statue. Majesty placed a palm flat on the creature's chest.

"I repeat," he said, with a gentle shove that sent the troll toppling like a felled oak. It hit the floor with a thunderous crash that drew every eye in the room.

Majesty grinned into the sudden silence, waiting only a second or two for the last faint pitter of dice and clatter of numbered wheels to fade away. "I'm here to see Kierendal. Anyone else want to get stupid with me?"

Paslava whispered behind his shoulder: *"She's coming."*

"Where?"

"I can't see her. I can feel her. She's here."

Three more liveried trolls converged on their fallen comrade with the ponderous threat of warships at full sail. They stopped a pace short of the one on the floor, their massive backs forming a wall against the crowd that pressed curiously around, and each held in his two clawed hands a morningstar with a haft as long as Majesty was tall. They glared at Majesty, growling low thunder-rumbles, but made no further move.

As though an invisible door opened edge-on in the air, a slender female elf stepped from nowhere into view. She bent down and stroked the face of the fallen troll, and the creature relaxed into unconsciousness with a sigh like a fresh-bunged keg of beer. She straightened and stepped around her fallen bouncer, coming near enough to Majesty that he could smell the curious spice of whatever unnameable dish she'd been eating.

She was taller than Majesty, and she hadn't troubled to put on her human face. Her halo of platinum hair framed features that were purely alien: huge golden eyes slitted vertically, high chiseled cheekbones that swept back to ears as pointed as the carnivore teeth that gleamed through her pack-hunter's fighting grin. "Why have you come here? Why do you assault my staff? Why shouldn't I kill you for this?"

"I am the Ki—"

"I know who you are, cock. Answer my question."

Majesty was tempted, just for a moment, to match her aggressive tone, but instead he only shrugged and offered her a friendly smile. He'd have a chance to play interpersonal power games on their next meeting; for now, he had to tend to business.

"Your problem, Kierendal," he said slowly, "is that you're not Warrens. You run a Warrengang, sure, but you're not *from* there; you don't know how things are done. If you have a problem with one of my people, you come to me, we work something out. That's how things are done. You don't give them up to the Imperials. That's how wars start, y'know? People get hurt. Places get burned."

"This is about Caine?"

"Your fucking *ass*," Majesty said. "That's what it's about. Caine is a *Baron of Cant*, you stupid bitch, and you sold him to the Eyes for a lousy thousand royals. I'm cutting you *slack* for this, you understand? Instead of slashing your fucking dyke throat and torching this shit-hole with you and everybody else in it, I'm going to let you slide a little, because I figure you don't know any better."

"You don't understand—"

"*You're the one who doesn't understand!*" Majesty roared her down. "You got *five minutes* to get your people and your customers out of this fucking whore palace. After that, it's gonna be too late, and they're gonna die in the fire, you follow?"

"If you would only listen to reason," she said mildly, stretching forth a gently supplicating hand, her palm turned up, her fingers curving in a precisely defined pattern.

Paslava whispered, *"Spell."*

Kierendal went on, "We don't have to be enemies. Caine came to me as a *favor*; he owed me some money, and this was his way of paying it back. Let's work something out, can't we? You and I?"

"Some sort of Charm," Paslava whispered. *"I grounded it off."*

Majesty met Kierendal's yellow stare; her expression never altered, only momentarily froze as she watched her spell fail.

"We might have had a chance to work out something, I guess," Majesty said. "Too late now. Anybody ever tell you what I do to people who try to put magick on me?"

Kierendal drew herself up, and her gown swirled around her like smoke. "Then the time for explanations has passed," she said.

Paslava whispered, *"She's signaling with Flow."*

The charged silence in Alien Games suddenly sparked with the scrape of weapons being drawn from scabbards. Every bartender bore a club, every waitress a knife. Some of those unfamiliar faces among the customers now grinned as they moved through the crowds, advancing on Majesty with swords in hand.

He took all this in with a bored glance and gave Kierendal a contemptuous snort. "Rookie," he said, then raised his fist and shouted, *"One!"*

Fully a third of the sumptuously dressed South Bankers slid daggers from their sleeves as they drew pragmatic, razor-edged swords from scabbards that had appeared purely decorative. Now all the armed waitresses, bartenders, and covert guards had at least three blades leveled toward their throats, and six men with knives stood at the backs of the three armed trolls.

Majesty chuckled. "That's half of us," he said warmly. "Wanna go for Two? And maybe you can guess what Three's gonna be."

Kierendal's eyes blazed. "You invite a massacre."

"Yeah. But it's your call," he said. "Nobody has to get hurt."

She measured him for a moment, and Majesty sighed to himself. She was going to cave. He was almost sorry; he kinda liked her style.

"Another signal," Paslava murmured.

Now a new rhythm underscored the restless silence: thumps of window shutters closing and scrapes of doors being barred. The distant shouts of rioters faded to muffled mumbling as the building was sealed.

"Now. Have your people sheathe weapons and exit through that door," she said, pointing. "If anyone starts anything, I shall burn this place *myself.*"

Majesty clenched his jaw to keep from nervously licking his lips. "Horseshit."

"Perhaps. But imagine a fire in this crowded building: Imagine flames raging up the velvet; imagine burning beams crashing down from the ceiling. Imagine a fire when there is only a single door, and far too many people need to use it. My staff knows other ways out of this building. Does yours?"

That pack-hunter smile was back around her wickedly sharp teeth. "As you said, it's my call—but I raise, instead. Bet or fold, cock."

For the space of one long indrawn breath, Majesty could think of nothing to do. He couldn't back down, not in front of his men, but he saw in Kierendal's eyes that he couldn't push her. This was a bluff, he told himself. It *had* to be a bluff: Some of the men in this place were real South Bankers. If a few of them died in an arson fire, her business would never recover—not to mention that one or two might be minor nobility, which would put her in line for hanging.

But he couldn't count on it.

As he looked at her skeletal grace and her razor grin, he became acutely aware of how *unhuman* she was; he had no way to gauge how crazy she might really be. What should have been a simple, safe little object lesson in manners had inexplicably escalated wildly toward a holocaust.

As though Paslava could read his thoughts, he whispered, *"She is aware of me; there will be little I can do that she cannot counter."*

Majesty nodded, as though to himself, and gave a chuckle that sounded far more confident than he felt. "All right," he said with an appreciative smile, "I apologize for calling you a rookie."

"You're most gracious," she sneered. "Now get out."

"It's not gonna happen," Majesty said sadly. "Caine was a Baron of Cant, and you gave him up."

"At his own *request*," she said through her teeth.

"I wish I could believe you." Majesty looked around the room and shook his head. "You also should be thinking, here, that your boys and girls are outnumbered two or three to one. If shit starts to fly, most of them will die here. Secret exits or not."

Her head came up like a cat's, as though she heard the scratch of rat claws in the walls; her eyes lost their predatory focus, looking past him, through him, as though he wasn't there at all.

Got her, he thought. "You're not bad at this, Kieren-dolly," he said kindly. "You just gotta understand that when you get in a pissing contest with giants—" He laid a pious hand upon his chest. "— you're gonna get wet."

She gave no sign that she heard him; instead, she stared glassily over the knots of armed and nervous folk who crowded the gaming floor, past the massive trolls that made a wall at her back. Everyone in Alien Games returned her stare: Face, Subject, and civilian. Each was suspended on a knife edge of action, a balance as dangerously unstable as a cocked crossbow, waiting for the slightest sign or word from either of them. Swords trembled in sweaty hands, and folk on both sides shifted their weight, seeking the best position to fight or run. She murmured, in a voice so subdued that even Majesty, a bare pace away, could barely make out the words, "No wonder all this spins out of control . . ."

Majesty scowled at her; he didn't like this at all. What in fuck was she looking at?

"Something is happening." Paslava's whisper sounded vaguely awed.

"Yeah, no shit," Majesty said from the side of his mouth. Hairs prickled along his arms and up the back of his neck; his heart pounded, and icy sweat trickled down from his hairline. He suddenly felt like someone had dosed his wine with rushweed: the floor seemed to rock just a bit under his feet. His head buzzed; it felt kind of carbonated, like fresh beer. He didn't know what he might do in the next second—if he would launch himself at Kierendal's throat, burst into tears, or drop his tights and crap on his boots. "What is this? Is this some kind of attack?"

"I don't know," Paslava whispered. *"I don't think so. It's some kind of Flow effect; I can see dark currents drifting in from all directions.* There! Over there!" he nearly shouted, forgetting himself, forgetting to whisper, forgetting that Majesty could not see which direction his Cloaked finger was pointing.

The excitement in his voice could not be told from panic, and in Majesty's growing confusion, that was signal enough. He drew breath to cry the attack, to bring it all down, to let the slaughter begin just because straight-up bloodshed would be so much easier than this stretching, twisting, edge-of-the-cliff windmill-the-arms shit.

Kierendal reached for him and caught his elbow in an astonishingly powerful grip. *"Don't!"* she said urgently, pleadingly. "Don't—*he's here*."

Majesty tried to yank his arm away, but found her grip was not so easily broken. "What? Who's here?"

"Weapons down!" she cried. "Everybody, put them away!"

From the direction of the single unbarred door came a splintering of wood and the sound of bone meeting bone through intervening layers of flesh.

"What? What?" Majesty couldn't seem to make sense of what was happening. Who was fighting? What was Paslava talking about? Who was Kierendal trying to say was here? "What—?"

"Majesty, tell your men to *put their weapons down*! Do it!"

"Ah—"

"Yeah, do it," somebody said in Caine's voice. "Let's everybody play nice, huh?"

Majesty turned. Caine stood in the far doorway. His battered black leathers looked even dirtier than usual and shadows dark as bruises ringed his eyes, but it was unquestionably Caine.

"But—but—" Majesty sputtered, gaping, "but you were *arrested*!"

"That's right." He walked slowly onto the gaming floor, limping, heavily favoring his right leg. "And there's a lot of people out looking for me, right now, so I'd appreciate it if nobody left this place. Can the two of you manage that?"

"I, ah . . . yeah. Yeah, sure," Majesty said stupidly, then he raised his voice. "Hear that? Nobody leaves. Nobody."

Caine kept on limping toward them, fixing Kierendal with a searching look. "And you?"

She pulled her head back, the whites of her eyes showing around her golden irises like a spooky horse. "We were quits, Caine. Even. You said you would leave me alone."

She'll face down a hundred fifty Subjects of Cant without blinking, Majesty thought with a puzzled frown, *but Caine shows up and she's about to piss herself.*

At his shoulder, Paslava whispered, *"It's Caine."*

"What am I, an idiot?"

"No—that Flow effect. It's Caine. He's part of it, somehow."

Caine said, "I can make it worth your while."

"Another thousand royals?" Kierendal snorted and waved her

hand at the roomful of armed men. "You see what the last one almost bought me."

"How about an alliance with the most powerful Duke under the new Emperor?"

"What?" Majesty said, for what seemed like the thousandth time. Too much was happening, too fast; he couldn't make sense of any of it. "What new Emperor? What Duke? If you're handing out alliances with Dukes," he said, "don't you think you should be thinking about your old friends, first?"

"I am." Outwardly, Caine seemed grim as a hangman, but behind his flat black eyes danced some secret glee. "You're the Duke I'm talking about. You will be."

Majesty and Kierendal exchanged equally dumbstruck looks.

"But . . ." Majesty struggled to sort through the hundred questions that crowded his brain, to find one or two that would be most pertinent. "But how can I be a Duke—? And no, fuck that; start with how you managed to *escape*."

Caine grinned at him, and his teeth seemed edged with fresh blood. "Two questions, one answer: I gave you up to Ma'elKoth. I told him you're Simon Jester."

"You what?" The room seemed to darken and rock dizzily around him.

"Sure," Caine said. "Why not?" He leaned close to the King of Cant, peering deeply into Majesty's eyes as though cryptic runes might be read there. He said with slow, deliberate precision, "That's how you will help me save Pallas Ril."

"Pallas . . ." Majesty murmured. Of course he would; nothing was more important than Pallas Ril's life, than her happiness. Majesty felt as though he was awakening from a dream: what foolishness had he been undertaking here, picking a fight with Kierendal, while *Pallas* was in danger? He passed a hand before his eyes and fervently thanked his every god that Caine had come along in time to remind him of what was *really* important . . .

Whatever Caine had been looking for, he apparently found, though this finding seemed not to please him. His mouth twisted briefly, a spasm of nauseous distaste. But an instant later his face cleared, as though he drove some evil thought from his mind by force of will.

"So, Kierendal," he said cheerfully. "Who's a guy have to maim to get a drink around here?"

The bartender who Kierendal summoned looked at Majesty and

said in that infuriatingly superior tone that is acquired by a lifetime in fine food service, "You, sir, owe me one royal."

20

"BUT IT'S NOT *proof*," Kierendal says stubbornly. "It's a trick, not real proof."

Sometimes, the toughest part of a revolution is deciding to start one.

"But it's a *good* trick. A good trick is better than proof," I say with an easy grin. I nod toward Paslava. "Ask him."

Paslava doesn't wait for Kierendal's question. He leans forward and clasps his skeletal hands judiciously on the tabletop near his mug of beer, and the table lamp's flame paints deep shadows in the hollows of his cheeks. "It's true. With twenty thousand witnesses, Ma'elKoth will never be able to deny, never be able to explain. It will shatter the morale of the army; without the army to keep order, control of the city—and the Empire—falls into the hands of the first man prepared to grab it."

They exchange looks, lust sparking to life behind their eyes. Here in Kierendal's sitting room, the air is still as a tomb's; the flame of the lamp might as well be cut from shining glass. My faked ease is getting to them; infected by my perfectly feigned confidence, they're starting to believe that toppling Ma'elKoth might be doable, after all, and the pure *possibility* makes it nearly irresistible.

The riots were one thing—they're self-sustaining now. When the riots are crushed under the military's heel and the main agitators are arrested, none of them will be found to be Subjects of Cant. This is something else: they're *seeing* it now, in their minds, in their hearts; they're seeing the Empire without Ma'elKoth, the army without leadership, Ankhana without law.

It pulls them like a river's current, like the gravity of this world. The four of us, sitting around an ordinary dining table—an icon of Ma'elKoth watching us from the corner shrine—*could take down the Empire*. That lust in their eyes, it's the same hunger that drives a kid to smash his only new toy on his birthday afternoon; it's the same hunger that drives riots in the Temp slums, where we torch our own homes and dance around the flames; it's the same hunger that drives a conquering army to loot and burn.

Sometimes, we destroy simply because we can. Because, when

you come right down to it, it's the kind of fun you just can't get any-where else.

Don't get me wrong. I don't disapprove of that lust.

In fact, I'm counting on it.

Majesty leans forward to weigh in. "Then why put troops there at all?" he says. "We'll need every man we have to hold the city once the fighting starts. Why risk every Knight and half of the Subjects?"

I settle for being cryptic. "Chaos creates opportunity."

He doesn't give up that easily. "But opportunity for *what*?"

Every time Majesty's natural pragmatism surfaces, all I have to do is reach out and tap on his weakness, that trump card that always seems to be there in my hand, no matter how many times I play it. "I told you before," I tell him. "I'm going to rescue Pallas Ril."

His eyes glaze over a little bit; the Charm still has him, even if it's fading. "But how?"

"I can't tell you that."

"Why not?"

"Because I can't." That'd give too much away to you viewers back home. "What this does for me is gives me a smaller, more concentrated version of the riots. I need someone to keep the Cats and the constables off my ass while I save Pallas. The rest is all gravy. The revolution? That's just the come-on, to give you a little something for your trouble."

He winces. "The Cats—"

"No, you *want* them there," I say significantly. "All of them, or damn near, all gathered into one place."

"Waiting for us."

"Sure. Waiting for a small, elite strike team. With the whole Knights of Cant in the stadium, you can bury them."

"Bury them under piles of our own bodies," Majesty grumbles.

"You *have* to deal with the Cats," I tell him flatly. "The Cats are the best troops in the Empire—not just man-to-man, but running small-unit tactics, too. Everybody's afraid of them: shit, they can hold the army together by sheer terror, if they want. Nobody wants to cross the Cats."

"Especially not me," Majesty agrees grimly.

"On the other hand, they might not even fight."

Majesty shakes his head. "You don't know them. The Ma'elKoth bit won't break their morale; Berne has them believing they're more than human."

I turn to the Spellbinder. "Your *specialty* is crowd control, isn't it? You can whip up some sort of magick that'll take the heart right out of them."

"In theory," Paslava says slowly. "But I don't have that kind of power, to search them out in a huge crowd and hold their spirit down—especially not if Ma'elKoth smells what I'm up to."

I chuckle. "How much power do you need?"

I dip two fingers into the thigh sheath where one of my throwing knives used to be and come up with one of the griffinstones from the hem of the net. I flip it skittering across the table, and Paslava's hand strikes like a rattlesnake; breath leaves his lungs in a long hissing sigh as he holds the griffinstone up and regards it in the lamplight with naked, wet-eyed lust. Kierendal's eyes widen, glittering in the lamplight, and flick from the stone to me with pure golden envy.

"Ahh," Paslava says with breathless reverence. "Ahh . . . I've never even *seen* one this size. It's flawless. It's beautiful."

"Will that do it?" I ask, knowing the answer.

"Oh, yes," he says. "This will do it very well, indeed."

"We'll never get our men into the stadium," Majesty interrupts gruffly. "They hardly look like real South Bankers, and there will certainly be a weapons search at the gates."

"You can do it," I tell Kierendal. "You can do an illusion that'll hold up just fine." I pull another two griffinstones out of the thigh sheath. "With a little sliver knocked off one of these on every Subject to power them, you can put illusions on them that'll hold till next week."

Paslava's mouth drops open. In a second or two he'll be drooling on the table. Kierendal reaches toward them with a tentative hand, and she sighs like in sexual afterglow when I put them into her palm.

"Here's your alliance. The Snakes, the Dungers, and the Rats aren't going to fade away. When the government goes down, you're gonna have to fight them—and they'll be recruiting deserters from the army, you can bet. With the Faces and the Kingdom of Cant together, the other Warrengangs won't have a prayer." I smile cynically. "They won't have a prayer to *Ma'elKoth*."

"What about Berne?" Majesty asks. "So what if Ma'elKoth's not there? The kind of power Berne throws around these days, he can turn the battle by himself."

"Don't worry about Berne. He won't show up."

"No?" He makes a face. "What, he's gonna be taking a snooze after kicking your ass again?"

I let him see all my teeth. "A long snooze. A permanent snooze."

"I don't like it," he says decisively. He pushes himself up from the table. "It doesn't make sense."

"It can work," Paslava interjects, each of his eyes reflecting an image of the griffinstone he twirls between his fingers. "We can do this."

"Sure we can," Majesty says, "but what *then*? Who's gonna rule the Empire? *Us?*" The derisive edge in his voice makes it all too clear what he thinks of this idea. "Who's to say whoever ends up in charge won't be *worse*? And the Cats might be monsters, but they're still Imperial troops. You're asking me to commit the Kingdom of Cant to open rebellion—to *regicide*, for shit's sake—because *somebody* has to storm the palace and kill that bastard; he's too powerful to leave alive. And who else is there but us? Whoever winds up on the throne will *have* to wipe us out just to keep the Ma'elKoth loyalists happy; otherwise they'll start working on their own revolution as soon as shit calms down."

"Majesty, Majesty, you forget: you're *already* committed," I say. "If Ma'elKoth lives out the day, he'll have your balls in his teeth by sundown."

"I should kill you for that," he says grimly.

"Too late, buddy. It won't help you any, and you know it. Besides, didn't I promise to make you a Duke? All you need is an Emperor who owes you a big favor."

"And you've got one in your pocket?"

"No," I say with a grin, "but you do."

"Huh?"

"Sure. Toa-Sytell," I offer, then grin into the deathly silence that greets my suggestion. Majesty's eyes bulge with the effort of restraining a curse, and he glances around the small back room as though to make sure we are still alone. Kierendal nods in grim self-satisfaction at this confirmation of her long-held suspicion. Paslava's mouth drops open.

"Am I the only one who doesn't know about this?" he says incredulously.

Majesty shakes his head at him. "I'll explain later."

"You'd better," his thaumaturge says feelingly.

I go on. "Think about it. You need somebody you can trust. Despite the Kingdom's loyalty, despite the position you've held in this city all these years, you're a commoner. Your kingdom is one of spirit and devotion, not of birth. The nobles won't follow you. Toa-Sytell, on the other hand . . ."

Majesty's eyes go distant and calculating. "I see it."

"He was created Duke by Toa-Phelathon, the last legitimate ruler of the Menelethids. That makes him a Duke for real, in the eyes of the nobles; they might deny titles conferred by Ma'elKoth, but not by their beloved Prince-Regent. Toa-Sytell also controls the King's Eyes. You want to run the Empire, you need him."

"Who says I want to run the Empire?"

"Screw running it," I tell him. "When shit blows up, all you have to do is come to Toa-Sytell with an offer of support. The Kingdom of Cant will be the only real, organized troops that can keep order in the city. By being the first to come to his side, you could make him pretty grateful; I should think he'd express his gratitude with a title—maybe even a Dukedom and a seat in the Cabinet. Say, maybe, Commerce and Taxation?"

That cold calculation in his eyes starts to ring up stacks of gold coins.

I go on. "I mean, you guys already have a relationship, right? You trust each other?"

"More or less," Majesty allows. "But Ma'elKoth—holed up in the Colhari Palace, he could stand a year's seige . . ."

I lean forward and let all the easy humor drain out of my eyes, let my face go as passionless as an ice sculpture. "You can let me handle that."

Majesty gives me a frankly scornful look. "You?"

"I've done it before."

"So, let's see if I've got this plumb," he says sarcastically. "These are your plans for tomorrow: Get up, have breakfast, kill Berne, sneak into Victory Stadium and discredit Ma'elKoth, grab some lunch, sneak out of Victory Stadium and into the palace, kill Ma'elKoth, sneak back out of the palace again, have dinner, maybe a couple of drinks, go to bed. Is that about it?"

"Roughly," I tell him. "You forgot one thing."

"What, your afternoon nap?"

"No." I reach out with my words to tap that trump on the table one more time. "I'm going to rescue Pallas Ril."

Her name siphons the color out of his face, and his eyes drift closed.

While the Charm keeps him off balance, I hook him and reel him in. "The point is that Toa-Sytell is a fundamentally decent guy with a stake in keeping things calm. He has both power and a reputation for ruthlessness. He's exactly what you need to keep the Empire from dissolving into civil war; on the other hand, he can't hold the city without you until he brings the army to heel. He'll need you as much as you need him. He's perfect."

"He's also devoted to Ma'elKoth," Majesty points out.

I grin. "I think we'll take care of that part of the problem tomorrow. He's devoted to the throne, not the man."

"God damn you, Caine," he says. "God damn if you don't have it figured to the butt end. Paslava?"

The thaumaturge can barely tear his gaze away from contemplation of the beauty of the griffinstone in his hand. When he does, his eyes are pools of fiery possibility. "We can do it," he says.

"Kierendal?"

Unnoticed, her face and form have shifted throughout this conversation; her eyes have shaded from gold to hazel, and her platinum hair to a dirty blond that borders on chestnut; the harsh lines of her razor cheekbones have softened into an easier, more human oval. She gives Majesty a look that makes the air between them smoke, just a little. "I can help," she says slowly, in a husky voice that reminds me, inescapably, of Pallas. What is she playing at? Can she read the Charm on him, somehow?

What she says next removes my doubt. "I'm with you, Majesty, but we must . . . cement our alliance, in a more, mmm, *formal* way," and her tone is suggestive enough that she's giving *me* a hard-on; I can only imagine the effect she must be having on Majesty.

He looks like he's been sucker-punched; a moment passes while he remembers that there are other people in the world. He reddens, coughs, and looks at me, shaking his head. "And you get out of this . . . what? The gratitude of a new Duke? But you don't even really care about that, do you?"

I shrug. "No, not really."

"You're telling me," he says slowly, "that you're bringing down the Empire just to get a shot at saving Pallas Ril?"

"That's what I'm telling you."

"All right," he says, suddenly grinning like a maniac. "I'm in."

I almost gather him into a hug before I remember myself and settle for sticking out a hand.

He takes it. "And thanks. I mean, really *thanks*, Caine."

"For what?"

"For giving me a chance to help you save her. That means a lot to me."

"Yeah," I say, feeling just a little sick. "I knew it would."

A long, slow, mediative silence drifts into the room like a shadow of tomorrow's war. All we can do, for this eternal instant, is sit and contemplate the enormity of what we have decided, here tonight.

Finally, Paslava breaks the silence with a cough.

"And I am also curious," says Paslava, "about this silver net of yours. I would like to examine it, with your permission."

"That, ah, that won't be possible until tomorrow. I stashed it."

"Do you think that wise?" Paslava asks with a sudden frown of alarm. "The success or failure of this entire plot depends upon that net! If it is stolen, or lost—!"

"It's perfectly safe," I reassure them with a secret smile. "You'll get a chance to look it over tomorrow. For tonight, I, ahh, have somebody watching it for me."

21

CURSING SILENTLY, BERNE rappeled down the natural chimney to the very limit of the torchlight above and peered down into the black abyss below him. How deep did this fucking shaft go? How in fuck's sake did Caine get down here without leaving a rope behind? And why was he hiding out down here? How did he even *breathe* down here in these reeking goatfucking fumes?

Before continuing down, he wrapped his wrist in the rope and used his now-free hand to draw the dagger Ma'elKoth had magicked for him. He swung it in a short arc, and sure enough its green glow was strongest still when it pointed straight downward. In fact, it was brighter than he'd yet seen it.

Bright enough, it was, to illuminate the bottom of the chimney only a few feet below and the untidily piled net that lay on the rock as though it had been carelessly tossed there.

Berne's curses were no longer silent; they echoed off the stone loudly enough that the Cats waiting above startled like spooked horses.

Caine *knew*, somehow that slippery little fuck knew, and he'd ditched the net on purpose. Berne released the rope and dropped the rest of the way, taking the shock of landing with a slight bend of his strengthened legs. He bent to pick up the net, then hesitated and changed his mind. He grunted to himself, then swarmed back up the rope to the torchlit cavern above.

"You four," he snapped, picking them out at random from his followers, "you're staying here. He'll be coming back for this. Don't interfere with him. As soon as he shows, one of you come for me at the Colhari Palace. The others, follow him. Don't let him know you're there; if he makes you, he'll make you dead."

"The palace? You're not going home?"

"Probably not tonight," Berne said with a grimace that reflected a sharply twisting knot of apprehension in his guts. "I have to go tell Ma'elKoth that we've lost Caine."

22

LAMORAK SAT AT a broad scarred writing table in the den of Berne's house and stared out the window at the approaching storm, a massive wall of cloud that blocked the polar stars. Lightning speared almost continuously in the north, and the thunder was loud enough already to rattle the windows. Big freaking storm, big as he'd ever seen, but he watched it with only a scant corner of his attention.

What it really came down to, see, was survival, he told himself. Sure, he didn't want Pallas to die, but having Pallas alive wouldn't do him any good if he wasn't around to enjoy her, right? And Caine . . . Well, fuck Caine. Caine knew that Berne and the Cats were tailing him, and he'd led them right there to Lamorak's room. Caine might as well have locked him into this den personally.

Lamorak cherished no fond illusions or hopes of mercy from Berne. His only hope was to buy his freedom, to get himself at the very least out of the Cats' clutches and into the care of the Constabulary or the King's Eyes—and to do it before Caine stirred the shit-pot tomorrow. Even if Berne himself died in the inevitable riot at the stadium, the Cats would cut his throat before they'd let him go.

No: he had only one chance. He had to make a deal while there was still a deal to be made.

He couldn't speak to his guards; they'd been well prepared against him. Instead, he ransacked the den until he found a sheet of lambskin parchment and a pen. A few minutes' further search found an ink pot that still sloshed faintly when he shook it.

He wrote:

> *Berne:*
> *You left before I could tell you. I have news to sell, news of Caine that may save the Empire, if you act upon it. Come with Duke Toa-Sytell or the Emperor himself to guarantee my freedom, and I will reveal all of Caine's sinister plot. You will not regret it.*
> *Urgently,*
> *Lamorak*

He folded the parchment and wrote on the outside:

> *Give this message to Count Berne, and he is sure to reward you*

He held it in his hand for a moment, weighing it briefly; it was no heavier than any other parchment, and it meant nothing at all.

He hobbled to the locked door and slid the parchment beneath it. Somebody should find it there by morning. He turned and leaned a moment to rest against the door before the trip back to the chair at the writing table. Outside, lightning flared and thunder crashed. The first scattered drops of rain mixed with a spurt of rattling hail clattered against the window. The rising wind howled like wolves in the wilderness.

Going to be one big bastard of a storm, he thought. *Glad I'm not out in it.*

DAY SEVEN

"Do you, Professional Hari Khapur Michaelson, take this woman, Professional Shanna Theresa Leighton, to be your lawfully wedded wife, to have and to hold, to love, honor, and cherish forever, for richer, for poorer, in sickness and in health, to cleave to her only all the days of your life, until death alone doth part you?"

"I do."

1

THE THUNDERSTORM BATTERED Ankhana from midnight until an hour before dawn, breaking windows and cracking doors, peeling roof tiles off houses like a fisherman scaling a trout, kicking over trees like an angry child stomping through his mother's garden.

The blinding downpour drove the mobs shivering to shelter; the streets belonged to the army. Between the smothering rain and the military bucket brigades, the fires were soon brought under control.

The riots, though, weren't over: this was only a pause, a hitch in the breath between inhale and shout. All over Old Town, every sheltered spot was filled with North Bankers caught in last dusk's initial chaos. Men and women, primals and stonebenders, ogrillos and trolls huddled in shattered storefronts or stretched out beneath overhanging eaves. Plenty of whiskey was still to be found: jugs passed hand to hand among drowsy folk who waited with a sort of sullen excitement for the end of the rain.

The army and the Constabulary were still too busy fighting fires and their own internal dissensions to engage in street sweeps and mass arrests; everyone knew that more trouble lay ahead.

Runners from the *Imperial Messenger-News* had braved the storm to summon every one of the pages that the *IMN* employed,

467

hammering on their doors and yanking them from beds in the middle of the night. By the time the storm ended, they were all assembled and had received their instructions. When the first rosy glow pinked the summits of the eastern mountains, they streamed forth to take positions throughout Old Town and many more waited patiently on the ways for the bridges to lower at sunrise.

When the uppermost spires of the Colhari Palace were kindled by the first rays of the morning sun, bells began to ring all over the city, from the mighty brass clang out of the Temple of Prorithun to the intricate silvery chiming of the Katherisi's carillon, from the crash of shields struck by swords in the Sanctum of Khryl to the hand bells of the *IMN* pages. An instant later the bells were joined by all varieties of horns, from simple bugles to the massive three-man *bruhti* atop Victory Stadium. The skull-splitting cacophony kicked citizens from their beds and drove them to their windows; it shocked dozing rioters scrambling from their improvised bedrolls and brought every soldier to attention.

The pages roamed the streets, swinging their bells and calling out their news. They did not wait for the coin and the nod that is usually required to get a story: this was an Imperial Announcement and was free to all.

The Emperor enjoined his citizens and Beloved Children to stay at home and remain calm, to hold fast to their faith in him. This day was declared a holiday; no store would open and no business would be conducted. The streets were ordered to be vacant until midmorning. From midmorning until noon, all who wished could make their way to Victory Stadium on the south bank, where the Radiant Emperor would greet his subjects and allay their fears. All were welcome, all would be safe, and the Emperor would calm every heart and answer every doubt.

The Subjects of Cant were still out in force, under orders to keep the pressure on. The rain had forced some changes of plan. The fires that began now started from *within* the still-damp buildings—from their dry interiors—and there were, perhaps, not quite so many. Nonetheless, a pall of grey-black smoke soon struggled with the lingering clouds above.

The army also took advantage of the curfew, reasoning that all honest folk would obey the Emperor's order and stay indoors: all the troops that could be spared from fire fighting were organized into small units of ten to fifteen, and they roamed the streets at random in search of looters. Some were arrested; many more were surrounded and beaten to death.

The army took some losses as well, though; the looters began organizing into larger bands for self-protection, and many of these bands were well armed, especially in Alientown. There was longstanding, almost traditional bad blood between the humanoids and the authorities there. Much of that bad blood soon flowed through the gutters.

And a new story was on the street this morning, a fresh rumor about the *Aktiri* that afflicted the Empire. It spread from rioters to bartenders, from stevedores to carters, and it was muttered, whispered, and argued over wherever a knot of citizens might gather: The tale was of a magickal net whose merest touch would slay the most evil *Aktir* and send it screaming back to the hell from whence it came.

Also, in the new light of dawn:

A Grey Cat, lounging at the far end of a long upstairs hall, saw a folded slip of parchment lying on the floor in front of the door he'd been set there to guard.

In a cautiously neutral-ground room filled with the accouterments of the most luxurious bedchamber imaginable, Majesty and Kierendal gazed upon each other. The dawn light sparkled like lust in Kierendal's eyes; Majesty's smile had the sleepy satisfaction of a well-fed lion's.

Berne reclined in the palace bedchamber he maintained and watched his twin nude valets. The brother and sister—both still musky with the sweat of sex and marked with bloody stripes left by the switch with which Berne still toyed—brushed his slashed-velvet tunic, making fearful glances back over their shoulders to be sure of his approval. He watched closely for the slightest flaw. The tunic must be perfect before he would set them to shine his boots: today would be a formal occasion, and he intended to look his best.

Ma'elKoth stood alone in the Lesser Ballroom and stared up at the Great Work. The room was silent around him; no clay boiled in the cauldron nor coals glowed beneath it. He had no leisure for art this day. He squinted at the emerging structure of the face that he'd built there, seeing something new in it, something he'd never intended—seeing one of those artful accidents that give great works their life.

It was to have been a model of his own face, but now, as he

looked at it, he realized that without altering the existing structure one whit, a mere change of intent could make the Great Work into the face of Caine.

2

TOA-SYTELL RUBBED HIS gritty eyes and snuffed the lamp at his elbow. The window at his back in the scriptorium of the Monastic Embassy had an eastern exposure, and the rising sun was vastly easier on his eyes than the lamp had been. He grimly tried to bring the tiny letters on the page before him into clear focus.

He shook his head, surrendering. He rose and stretched, and his spine popped in a wave from his neck to his waist. He sighed and crossed his arms to rub his aching shoulders. He'd been at this all night and still had more questions than answers.

He'd gone to the embassy directly after Caine's arranged escape. He'd had some difficulty getting in; the embassy was designed and built to be a fortress in the middle of the city, and it was buttoned up tight against the riots. But eventually, his calm-voiced reasonableness got him not only inside, but into the presence of the Acting Ambassador. This man he recognized: the Acting Ambassador was the grim-voiced older friar who'd been present at Caine's arrest and the murder of the previous Ambassador. The Acting Ambassador had become deeply thoughtful when presented with Toa-Sytell's request.

"Our records are our own," he'd said slowly. "But here there are some special circumstances. The matter of Caine has been brought before the Monastic Council, but it is too early for a decision. It is possible that his death will be ordered; it is nearly certain that he will be cast out from Brotherhood, if not actually outlawed. I think that perhaps I may be forgiven for opening his record to unsworn eyes."

"You have them? You have them *here*?" Toa-Sytell had asked, surprised. "I'd thought we'd be forced to send for them to, to, er . . ."

"Garthan Hold," the Acting Ambassador had supplied absently. "No, his records are here. After the Battle of Ceraeno, Caine's transfer to Ankhana became official, and his records were forwarded here. They may not be entirely up-to-date, but if you will wait in the scriptorium, they will be brought to you."

Toa-Sytell had bowed his thanks and done as the Ambassador had suggested. Shortly two novices had arrived, each bearing a massive leather-bound book. One of them was full, and the other had been filled to a third. The Duke was astonished—how could one man have done so much in a single short life?

Through his night of study, his astonishment had only grown. Caine had been everywhere, had done everything; he had an unsettling tendency to abruptly appear in the middle of important events with little or no explanation of why he was there or even how he'd made the journey. In between these battles and assassinations and adventures so incredible that Toa-Sytell dismissed most of them as fantasy, he didn't seem to be anywhere at all. He had no fixed home; there were no records of him spending any significant amount of time at any Monastery after he'd completed his novitiate and left Garthan Hold nearly twenty years ago.

His youth was equally puzzling. He'd arrived at the gates of Garthan Hold with a tale of having been born to a Pathquan freedman and sold to a Lipkan trader as a body servant during the Blood Famine—but it was recorded that he spoke Pathquan with an accent that no one had ever been able to identify. No attempt to contact his family was recorded; the Abbot at Garthan Hold had assumed the story was fabricated, that Caine was an escaped slave or a runaway serf of one of the local nobles. The Abbot had thought it significant that Caine displayed no particular aptitude, liking, or understanding for either horses or ironwork—seeing as how his supposed father allegedly was a farrier and the village blacksmith.

Toa-Sytell began to understand the Emperor's fascination with this man; Caine was like some force of nature, some wind or storm that would suddenly appear and blast the land for miles about, then vanish again. No one knew where he came from, no one knew where he went: his only tracks were the indelible scars he left on the lives that he touched.

And Caine was more than this, more than a mere elemental power—the elements, after all, Ma'elKoth had shown he could control to a nicety. Caine was like a griffin or a dragon, a supremely dangerous animal that could be befriended but never tamed. At any moment his thin veneer of humanity could burst to reveal howling destruction within.

Thin veneer of humanity . . . It was true that there was something not quite human about him: his astonishing luck, his preternatural confidence, the way he could come from nowhere and go at will, as if by magick . . .

Like an Aktir.

Toa-Sytell froze in midstretch, his mouth open to yawn—but his breath stopped in his lungs as though the air had become stone.

Like an Aktir . . . Toa-Sytell himself had said it, again and again, reminding himself and others of the destruction and death that followed Caine wherever he appeared. Even Ma'elKoth had said it, down in the Donjon as he leaned on the rail around the Pit balcony: *Caine could hardly cause more damage if he were, himself, an* Aktir.

The truth had been there, before their eyes; every one of them had looked right at it but had refused to see.

There was more than this—small coincidences of timing, tiny reactions that had seemed inexplicable then, but now made sense. Toa-Sytell needed none of these.

He *knew*.

He knew beyond the possibility of doubt, he knew with the faith of a saint: Caine was an *Aktir*. Caine intended the destruction of Ma'elKoth, of the Empire, of all that was good in the world. Caine had to be stopped. He had to be killed.

One convulsive gesture—his fist smacked down upon the open page. He stood for a moment, breathing hard, thinking. Then he turned away, leaving the books open on the table, and he ran from the room as though pursued by wolves.

Berne, he thought, running. *I have to find Berne.*

3

THE PALLAS RIL Lifeclock graphic had ticked a steady yellow at the corner of the *Adventure Update* transmission for six days. At dawn it clicked over to scarlet and pulsed bloody light from wallscreens across the Earth.

That meant, explained the perpetually smiling Bronson Underwood, that Pallas Ril had entered the margin-of-error range on the phase-locking capability of her thoughtmitter. The time she had remaining was no longer possible to predict.

This announcement was followed by an extended feature on amplitude decay, including never-before-released images of the re-

mains of the very few Actors who had suffered this fate and left any
remains to be viewed. The unconscionably hideous nature of these
images provoked a storm of protesting screencalls to Studio Central; but even larger was the flood of calls requesting that the feature be replayed, so that people who'd missed it the first time could
record it properly on their home netplayers.

The Studio staffers who fielded the calls smilingly apologized:
the feature would not be replayed, but copies were available for a
low, low, one-time-only discount price . . .

4

TOA-SYTELL WASTED NO precious time searching for Berne himself. After warning the Acting Ambassador—and receiving full assurance that in the unlikely event that Caine presented himself for
Sanctuary he'd be not only denied but detained—Toa-Sytell and
his small contingent of personal guards galloped straight for the
palace office of the King's Eyes. There he spent only very few minutes quietly but forcefully giving a precisely detailed set of orders.

He defined Caine as an immediate threat to the Empire and the
primary target of the King's Eyes: every Eye in the capital was to
drop his or her business to search for him. Toa-Sytell himself dictated the updated description, and he sent politely worded orders to
the commanders of the Constabulary and the capital detachment of
the army requiring their assistance. Caine was to be taken, no matter
what the cost. If he resisted, he was to be killed—a shoot-on-sight
order was permissible, at the commanders' discretion.

Ma'elKoth would be furious, Toa-Sytell knew; but his loyalty
was not to Ma'elKoth personally. His duty was to the throne, to the
Empire, and he knew in his bones that the Empire would never be
safe so long as Caine lived.

When he inquired for Berne, he learned that the Count had returned in the early darkness this morning, had spoken briefly with
Ma'elKoth before retiring, and was now enjoying a late breakfast
in his palace apartment. Toa-Sytell went straight there.

On his way up, he had time to marshal his thoughts, to arrange
his evidence and organize his argument. He expected Berne to
deny this revelation out of sheer contrariness, and Toa-Sytell was
determined to overwhelm any resistance with a flood of facts.

Moving at a near run even within the palace, he nearly collided in the corridor with a grim-faced Grey Cat who hurried away from Berne's apartment. When Toa-Sytell burst into Berne's outer chamber, the Count was at table in his silken lounging robe. He smirked up at Toa-Sytell and began to offer the Duke a place, but Toa-Sytell waved him off. "I have no time for this," Toa-Sytell said. "I must find Caine. *We* must find him."

Berne's fine-drawn brows pulled together. "Oh? That might be a problem . . ."

"It *cannot* be a problem. Berne, he's *one of them*. Caine is an *Aktir*."

Berne stared up at the Duke for one long second of stillness, then the corners of his mouth quirked toward a smile that grew into a grin.

"All right . . ." he said, considering. He mopped his mouth with a linen handkerchief, and some inexpressible energy drew him to his feet and lit his face with joy. "All *right*!"

Toa-Sytell was astonished. "You *believe* me?"

"Of course I believe you," Berne said happily. "I don't care if it's true or not; I still believe it. Because this means we have to kill him. Right now."

He snapped his fingers. A young valet appeared in the bedroom doorway, carrying an array of formal wear draped over his arms. "I was," he said, "preparing to dress already."

While Berne selected clothing and donned it, he related to Toa-Sytell how he'd been given the task of following Caine and how Caine had slipped him.

"But," he said, showing as many teeth as could fit into his grin, "one of my boys handed me this, just now, before you came in." He flipped a folded sheet of lambskin parchment at Toa-Sytell, who caught it neatly, unfolded it, and read the message in Lamorak's spidery hand.

Toa-Sytell's face lit up. "You have him!"

"Yeah, Caine led us there. I'm guessing he anticipated Ma'el-Koth's tag, and it was Lamorak who identified it on the net. He's smarter than he looks."

"Which one?"

"Both of them. Come on, let's go see what he has to tell us."

"Ma'elKoth," Toa-Sytell said. "We should see him first—he should know this. We need to tell him before we go."

"Fuck that." Berne shook his head and ticked his points off with raised fingers. "One, he's busy preparing that illusion, and if we interrupt him it could blunt the hook. Second, he's in the Iron Room. If you want to break in on him there, well, be my guest, but don't expect me to be standing behind you. And last, if we tell him this, *he won't believe it*. He's known Caine for years—longer than I have. Even if he does believe us, like as not he'll make up some excuse to order us to leave Caine alone. You know how he is—he'll probably think it's more *interesting* if Caine's alive, or some fuck-me-in-the-ass thing like that. Better we find Caine and kill him *first*, don't you think?"

Toa-Sytell compressed his lips and nodded. "I agree. Give me five minutes to assemble an escort."

"Fuck the escort, too."

"The streets still aren't secure—"

"Sure they are: you're riding with me." Berne slid his arms through the harness that held Kosall's scabbard, then fastened the rope-worked silver buckle across his chest. His fingertips brushed the hilt, and Kosall answered with a buzzing rattlesnake's threat inside its steel scabbard.

"We don't need an escort. Let's go."

5

TOA-SYTELL STUDIED LAMORAK minutely while he listened to the traitor's tale. Lamorak's features appeared so open despite the swelling of his broken jaw and the crust of blood below his pulpy nose; Toa-Sytell could see that without these injuries he'd be ruggedly handsome. His was a face to inspire almost automatic trust.

Toa-Sytell found him fascinating in an abstract sort of way. A man's features follow his character closely, as a common rule. Toa-Sytell found it extraordinary that he could find no hint of weakness in Lamorak's, no clue to the void where the man's spine should be.

When they'd entered the upper-floor den of Berne's townhome, Lamorak had flinched like a guilty puppy; he cringed whenever Berne stepped close to him and twisted to keep his splinted leg as far from the Count as possible. He'd refused to speak until Toa-Sytell had given his personal guarantee that Lamorak would be taken from the hands of the Cats. Even after having received it, he spoke hesitantly through his tied-shut teeth, a guilty flush on his beardless cheeks. Toa-Sytell squinted at him, absently stroking the hilt of the poisoned stiletto concealed in his sleeve.

Outside the door, Berne had warned him: "Lamorak's a crappy thaumaturge, but he has one trick that he does well enough to be dangerous. It's a Dominate. Watch for it."

Watch he did, but he saw no hint that Lamorak summoned power of any kind. A moment later all of these considerations were driven aside as Lamorak revealed the climax of Caine's insidious plan.

Lamorak stammered out his betrayal, wincing now and again when the linen strips that bound his jaw cut into his swollen cheek, when his eagerness to prove the value of his news made him forget his wounds.

". . . and, and then, you see, all he has to do is throw the net over the illusion, and the net cuts it off from Flow. It'll *vanish*, don't you get it? Twenty thousand people will see Ma'elKoth disappear exactly the way the *Aktiri* are supposed to. It'll be *proof*. Ma'elKoth will never live it down."

"That net, that goatfucking *net*!" Berne snarled. Veins twisted in his neck. A chair that got in the way of his furious pacing exploded to splinters under his kick. He wheeled on Lamorak. "What about *Pallas*? How was this supposed to help him rescue Pallas?"

"It wasn't," Toa-Sytell said, rising. "Don't you see? He doesn't care about her. Pallas is a blind, a decoy. *Caine* is the danger. The Empire has been his target from the beginning."

"I don't believe that," Berne said. "You don't know what he's gone through for her."

"But it's all a *game* for them," Toa-Sytell insisted. "Don't you remember? Ma'elKoth learned this from the ones he captured in the palace. It's a game, a play, just a *story* for them somehow. Entertainment. We suffer and die for the amusement of the *Aktiri*."

"Entertainment or not, he'll still try for her—" Berne went on, but Toa-Sytell lost the thread of what he was saying. He once again stared at Lamorak.

From the instant Toa-Sytell had spoken the word *game*, Lamorak had stared first at him, then at Berne, in eye-bulging panic. His lips hung slack as a blubbery child's, and a guttural sound of breathless choking came from his throat.

"What is it?" Toa-Sytell asked. "Lamorak, what's wrong?"

Lamorak waved him off with a trembling hand. "I, I, nothing, I just, I can't—"

Berne sneered contemptuously. "He's about to piss himself, isn't he? Aren't you a little old to be afraid of *Aktiri*?"

"I, no, I—" Lamorak's chair scraped backward; he was blindly trying to press himself back with his good leg.

"No, it's more than that," Toa-Sytell said, stepping close. "I've seen this before. It's like a sickness. Some men fear spiders in this way; another man I once knew could not even mount a stepladder for his fear of falling."

"Yeah?" Grinning, Berne suddenly jumped at Lamorak and grabbed his shoulders. He hauled him up out of the chair, holding him off the floor and shaking him like a child.

"Are we a little *scared*, then? Have a little *problem* with this?" He laughed drunkenly. "Say it with me: Caine is an *Aktir*. Go on, *say it*! Caine is an *Aktir*."

Lamorak shook his battered head wordlessly, struck mute with terror.

"Berne," Toa-Sytell said with a hand on his arm, "this serves no purpose. He can't help himself."

Berne turned only his head toward the Duke. The look on his face was that of a puma challenged over its kill. "Take your hand off me if you want to keep it attached to your wrist. He'll say it, or I'll pull his fucking arm off."

Lamorak moaned as Berne pulled him close and shook him again. "You think I can't? You think I'm not *strong* enough? Say it! Caine is an *Aktir*. *Say it!*"

Lamorak's eyes rolled like those of a horse caught in a barn fire. His face went red, then purple. "C . . . C . . ." he forced out through his teeth, choking, "C-Caine . . ."

Toa-Sytell felt a chill flame climb his spine. His mouth dropped open, then closed again, and opened to say, "Berne, wait! He *can't* say it! Don't you see he's trying? *But he can't!* Remember that spell, the one that blocks the tongues of the *Aktiri*? Remember? You must have heard Ma'elKoth speak of it—!"

Berne frowned at him; for a moment Lamorak dangled forgotten from his fists. "I don't see what you mean."

"Don't you? *Lamorak is one of them!* He can't tell us that Caine is an *Aktir* because *he knows it's true*!"

"I'm *not*!" Lamorak said shrilly. "I *swear*! I'm not, I swear it! It's not true, it's all a lie, I—"

"Shut up," Berne said absently, emphasizing the order with a shake that snapped Lamorak's head back. Without transition he'd become calm and bonelessly relaxed, with a sort of luxurious satisfaction like sexual afterglow.

"Well. How about that? Fuck me like a virgin goat. Thieves fall out, they say."

Toa-Sytell nodded grim agreement. "They do say indeed. Do you understand what this means?"

Berne shrugged. Lamorak whimpered, and Berne slapped him with stunning force on the purple-black swelling over his broken jaw. "Quiet."

"It means we've found a *test*. Set him down in that chair."

Berne did so.

"Take his hand," Toa-Sytell said.

Lamorak tried to cower away, but Berne's strength was irresistible.

"Now," Toa-Sytell said, "pull his fingers off one by one until he repeats the phrase, 'I am an *Aktir*.' My guess is, he'll lose all ten."

Lamorak began to howl, his screams muffled and distant behind his teeth, even before Berne twisted and yanked his smallest finger from his hand. The bones crackled like crumpling paper, and the flesh tore with a sound like the ripping of heavy cloth. Berne tossed the finger over his shoulder like a gnawed-clean chicken bone. Blood sprayed his grin, and he licked it from his lips.

Toa-Sytell stepped in and tied his belt around Lamorak's wrist, tightening it until the crimson spray trickled to a sluggish drip.

"Why don't you just go ahead and say it?" Berne asked. "I can do this nine more times without any trouble at all. It's easy enough to say, no? I am an *Aktir*. I am an *Aktir*."

Lamorak shook his head and drew breath to speak, but Berne covered his mouth with his bloody hand. "Think about what you're gonna say, Lamorak. Anything that comes out of your mouth that's not *I am an Aktir* is gonna cost you another finger."

He took his hand away. Lamorak said nothing, only looked a silent plea at Toa-Sytell. The Duke shrugged—Lamorak would be of little use to anyone if he was in deep shock or dead from blood loss. "We've learned what we need to know here, Berne. Now we must take Lamorak to Ma'elKoth. This is a way we can prove to him the danger of Caine. With the evidence of Lamorak, Caine's true nature no longer rests on speculation."

Berne nodded. "You go on with that. Some of the boys can escort you. Me, I'm thinking that for his plan to work, he needs that *net.* I posted four men to watch it and follow him when he comes for it. They might know where Caine is right now. I'm gonna go and ask them."

He reached back over his shoulder and touched Kosall's broad quillions as though he caressed a lover's thigh. "If I can catch him, I can solve all our problems with a single stroke."

"Time grows short," Toa-Sytell said with a nod toward the rising sun, now high above the rooftops. "Waste none of it."

Berne held out his blood-soaked hand. "Good luck with Ma'elKoth."

Toa-Sytell shook it without hesitation. "Luck to you, Berne. And good hunting."

6

KIERENDAL COULD FEEL each blink as though the leading edges of her eyelids were dusted with broken glass. Cautiously, extending her Shell wide and deep so that the pull would be difficult to detect, she allowed fatigue-suppressing energy to trickle in from the Flow. She'd have plenty of time to rest once this show was over.

Beside her, the King of Cant stared out the window at the crowds below. His Shell swirled with silver that glittered with rosy, dawn-colored highlights. Some of those highlights, no doubt, sprang from his appreciation for the face and form she presented to him. Over the past night and day, she had tuned the illusion of her appearance in careful, gradual increments—shading her hair toward curls in richer shades of chestnut, her eyes toward hazel, layering her skeletal flanks with the look and feel of lean tawny muscle, to capture just that hue in his Shell.

Any man is easier to control when you can lead him by his dick.

"Those guys, there, they're ours, aren't they?" Majesty's voice thickened with excitement. "Gods, those too, *they* could be ours. See them? Didn't you do a couple with the plumed cap and tights look?"

Kierendal twisted to glance lazily out the window, not really interested in the thronging crowds massing to file into Victory Stadium. For her, the real action was taking place right here in this room with Majesty.

"I don't know," she said. "They could be. I did so many, really, that I can't remember them all."

"And you can't tell, right? You can't look down there and tell which are ours? Even though you did the spells yourself?"

Kierendal shrugged. "The griffinstones power the illusions; they draw no Flow. Undetectable."

"Good thing, too. Fucking body searches—without your magick I don't think we'd get a toothpick in there." When he looked at her, the thrill in his eyes made him almost attractive. "You sure you don't want to join me? Gonna be a fucking spectacular show."

Kierendal smiled like a cat. "I'm a lover, not a fighter."

She had no intention of being anywhere near the stadium at noon.

If she could help it, she never wanted to be that close to Caine again.

The energy that surrounded him, that oceanic, tidal current of Flow that somehow followed him—she couldn't tell what it was, or how he did it. She was fairly certain that he had no idea of the power that rolled through his life. Perhaps it was a human thing; perhaps, as a species, they had more power below the surface of their consciousness than did any primal mage, and she had only become aware of it through her close study of Caine's oddly black Shell. That power seemed to grow on him, to gather into itself, doubling and redoubling like a river piling up behind a weakening dam. She had some clue what effect it might have when released: she had seen the hints of it during the standoff with Majesty at Alien Games.

It would be chaos. Pure destruction.

She suspected that it was that dark current in the Flow that had so nearly escalated the situation at AG out of anyone's control; she suspected that Caine, by his very existence, piled up potential forces like snow and rock in the Gods' Teeth. Where peace had reigned for years, one shout from Caine might bring down an avalanche.

She had no intention of being downslope from him. Not this time.

No point in trying to explain this to Majesty. He'd never believe her. Besides, if he died today, she'd have a fair chance at gathering whatever survived of the Kingdom of Cant under her hand. On balance, of course, she'd prefer that he lived, and that Caine's plan went perfectly; she was well on her way to permanently cementing her relationship with Majesty.

Speaking of that, she thought, glancing at the entourage of mingled Subjects and Faces that littered the rest of the room. "I think," she said slowly, "that we should empty this room, so that we can, mmm, *negotiate* some more."

The hand that she laid on Majesty's arm was warmer than a human's, and it sparked some answering heat in his smile.

"I'm not sure we have time," he answered.

Three minutes at most, she thought, but kept that thought off her face. "Mmm, if you say so." She sighed as though disappointed; his attention had already been drawn away by the scene outside. "Where are your Dukes?"

"Deofad's already inside the stadium. Paslava . . . well . . ." He turned to her again, and his grin got wide and slightly malicious. "Paslava'll be here later. Right now, he's got some business in the caverns."

7

ARTURO KOLLBERG MOPPED sweat from his upper lip and leaned close to the chairscreen's mike to half whisper hoarsely, "No, dammit! No feed, not now."

The VP for Marketing frowned a Businessman disapproval through the screen at him. "They're all over me on this, Art. They want another feed, just like the other day." He lowered his voice to a whisper. "I've just heard from the Board . . ."

Kollberg twitched involuntarily—that ants-on-the-skin feeling was back again. He glanced over his shoulder at the two soapies. Their face shields seemed to be directed at the phosphene kaleidoscope of the POV screen, but he had no way to know for sure.

"You'll just have to *wait,*" he insisted. "All of you, you'll have to wait. *Nothing's happening right now, for Christ's sake!*" His eyes bulged and he spoke through teeth clenched so hard his jaw hurt. "Nothing's happened for *hours*! He's *asleep,* all *right*?"

"Jesus, Art, calm down. Okay, he's asleep. No problem. But I want an assurance that we'll get a feed for the big blow-off, yeah? This thing he's supposed to be pulling on Ma'elKoth—we want this live on the net. That Clearlake guy, the Board's very up on him right now. They want him hosting."

Kollberg's hand trembled as he wiped perspiration back into the thin strands of hair that were already pasted down with his sweat. "You'll kill our cube sales. You know that, don't you? That's the climax of the whole damned *Adventure*! Caine's the *best* at this— you know he is. I've been running Caine's Adventures for fifteen years. This is his *trademark*. He's pulling everything together for this show at the stadium. It's all going to happen at once. Put it out live and everyone in the world will know how it comes out!"

"We're okay with this. The Board's okay with this, Art. The fees for the feed will cover any drop in the cubes—and we're projecting that any drop will be minimal. This is a *collectible*, Art. Especially if he dies."

8

IT WAS HEARING distant voices speak the name *Caine* that brought Pallas drifting upward like a bubble through the layers of Chambaraya's song. There was no knowing how long she had let the currents of song carry her gently away from the awareness of her body; her last clear memory was of speaking to Caine, here from the body that was tied upon the altar.

He shone like a star, she thought. There was some power within him, something not Flow-based—but perhaps Flow-related— some dynamic energy of life that had called to her within her river dreams. It hadn't come from the Flow or from any outside source; the very room had heated up at his entrance as though he carried a furnace within his chest. How could she never have seen this before?

Had it never been there?

All of their struggles, all the wounds inflicted and taken on both sides, his endlessly simmering anger, her tangled envy, all seemed so distant, so trivial. She couldn't comprehend, from this perspective, how they could have made each other so unhappy.

There is nothing easier than happiness; it's the feeling that comes when you're open to the life that flows through you, when you know that you are the river and the river is you. She and Caine, they had somehow never found that. Cut off from each other, cut off from themselves, they had clutched at their lives, had scrabbled for them like misers hugging gold, pretending that life itself could be hoarded, or spent.

Ridiculous.

No wonder they couldn't live together.

If only she could tell him that, somehow get through to him, tell him how easy it is to be happy.

She knew that she didn't have much time, that this body was dying, that the life she had borrowed through thirty-three years was leaking out through the hole in her lung. This prospect didn't distress her. It was nothing more than the little rivulet called Shanna Leighton, called Pallas Ril, slowly drying as its water returned to the river. She only worried about Caine; she hoped that she could hold life inside this body long enough to speak with him one last time.

She wished she could ask the river how much time she had left, but that way was blocked for her. She could still hear its song, could still let the mingled melodies float her away. No wall of stone or steel or magick itself could sever this link, which was as much a part of her as her heart and her spine, but some immaterial barrier prevented her from adding her own voice to the song, from drawing its power through herself.

She knew from whence that barrier came: from the same source as the voice that now said, *You cannot ask Me to accept this without proof.*

Him, she could see without opening her eyes: a gigantic foaming Kharybdis of Flow, sucking energy in from every direction, draining it to power his massive body and to light his extraordinary mind. The Iron Room rang with its echoes, and every stone of the Colhari Palace resonated with the beat of the Emperor's heart.

She knew, vaguely, of the fires and turmoil, of the riots and the fighting in the city outside. From her vantage it seemed that Ma'el-Koth's distress was not the product of the chaos, but was its source. His internal furies had somehow broken out, spilled over, sparked the disorder as though the city itself was an extension of his body.

She would need her eyes to see the others, but she wasn't up to that level yet—still rising, registering now the beats of her heart and the pain that came of struggling to breathe. They continued to speak of Caine, though—spoke in voices that she knew.

And they named him as an Actor.

She knew in a disconnected way that this was a bad thing, that it would be a problem. As her attention gradually sharpened she heard more of some plan of his they'd discovered, of a silver net and griffinstones, some plan to paint Ma'elKoth in the colors of the *Aktiri* before thousands of his subjects.

Ma'elKoth's voice now came to her in tones of weakness, of self-doubt and inner pain unlike any she'd heard from him.

Is it possible? I cannot comprehend the depths of . . . No, no, it cannot be! This is impossible! My entire career . . . My rise to the throne, all planned, all the work of an Aktir *. . .*

I cannot believe it. I do not believe it.

As Pallas' consciousness rose to the surface, she recognized the voice of Toa-Sytell, every bit as neutral as it had been that night she'd overheard him with Majesty.

"It is an unconscionable risk. You must cancel the ceremony."

"Cancel? Now? My Children enter the stadium already; to cancel the ceremony would be an admission of guilt; the result would be the same in the end."

His voice became thready with unaccustomed self-pity. "To be tumbled with one swift stroke from the mountaintop unto the depths of a dung heap. Had the other gods hated Me from birth they could hardly have used Me worse. To believe that it could have been *planned* from the very beginning, that seven years ago Caine brought Me the crown of Dal'kannith to start Me along a path to bring me here, where with one stroke he can shatter the Empire itself . . . Can he *be* that brilliant? Can he be so far beyond even Me? You—you know him. You are his companion; you have brought Me this news. Speak, now. Tell Me the truth of this man."

Pallas wondered fuzzily, *Is he talking to me? Does he think I'll start talking now just for asking? He can't force my voice by torture or magick, and so he's decided to be* polite?

A rustle of footsteps, the half-tearing sound of stressed cloth, and she opened her eyes.

Ma'elKoth faced three-quarters away from her. The oiled muscles in his bare back were rigid as stone. His fist held the tunic of a man, held this man high in the air. Pallas had a vague flash of memory, of Ma'elKoth holding Caine in precisely this fashion—but this wasn't Caine.

This man had a broken leg tied to splints with dirty linen, had manacles on his wrists and a bloody bandage tied around one hand, had knotted linen tying shut a painfully swollen, purple-black jaw, his nose equally swollen and spreading blackened rings of bruise around his eyes.

Not until he spoke did she recognize him.

"I don' . . . I can' . . . All I know I already tol' you . . ." Lamorak said miserably, his eyes wet and blinking.

I held this man in my arms, she thought, marveling. *Kissed him, made love with him. And now I can't remember why . . .*

But her Olympian perspective made everything clear. Looking back, the answer became obvious: She'd turned to him because he wasn't Caine, because he was Caine's opposite in every way. Tall, and blond, beautiful to look upon and clearly heroic, a *good* man in every sense of the word, caring and compassionate, romantic and brave.

And hollow inside. A beautiful shell, fragile as a blown egg.

This was the final opposite: Caine, at least, was all of a piece. What you saw was what you got. That's why Caine would never break the way Lamorak had so clearly broken: he was solid, through and through.

"This, then, is what shall be done," Ma'elKoth said, turning once again to Toa-Sytell, who stood with respectful stillness nearby. Lamorak dangled trembling from his fist, forgotten. "I am Ma'el-Koth. I do not run. I do not hide. If Berne cannot recover the net, I will meet Caine face-to-face upon the arena floor."

Toa-Sytell looked alarmed. "Ma'elKoth—"

"No. If I cower within My palace, Caine's plan succeeds. I shall reverse this with a single stroke of My own: *I will truly be there.*"

He opened his fist, and Lamorak dropped clattering to the floor. "I have never been comfortable with the idea of employing a Fantasy. It would be a fake, a pretense, and I do not lie to My Children. I shall do this ritual *in truth*. I shall take these lives upon the arena floor. I shall have the memories of Pallas Ril, and of you, Lamorak, however distasteful it may be to absorb such revolting worthlessness."

He stepped close to Toa-Sytell and looked down upon his Duke. "Continue the search for Caine. If he can be taken before the ritual, do so. If he must be killed, so be it. I suspect, however, that you will not find him. He's too resourceful; too ruthless. But I am more than he is. I am Ma'elKoth. Whatever happens, I shall be ready."

He clasped his mighty hands together and twisted them against each other, popping his knuckles like a string of firecrackers.

"I shall be ready, and I shall kill him with My own hand. And then I shall have *his* memories, as well."

All the rich and boundless energy that had drained from his voice before had now rushed back; the maelstrom of Flow that fed him gathered unimaginable power.

"Then all questions shall, at last, be put to rest."

Oh, Hari, Shanna thought, as her eyes drifted closed. The death of this body she could accept with a certain equanimity, but the new star that had shone within Caine was so unexpectedly lovely, a surprise of beauty: a perfect rose in a wasteland.

I'll hold on. I'll find a way. To warn you. To help you. Somehow. I can live that long, I think.

9

BERNE CLENCHED HIS teeth and resisted the urge to cut his way through the surging crowds.

The curfew had lifted at midmorning, and it seemed that the whole city had streamed onto the streets. More than one citizen received a bone-crushing kick from Berne's horse, a spirited animal that disliked breasting through the crowds. It rolled its eyes toward anyone approaching its flanks or rear, and Berne let it have its head a little—a few bleeding townsfolk flat in the street behind him went a long way toward clearing a path before him.

Finally he struggled through to the pissoir closest to the shaft where he'd left his Cats to watch the net. He loose-tied the horse at the post outside, looping the reins through the topmost hook. The lock on the mucker-shaft door squealed and snapped with a simple twist of his wrist. A moment's work with flint and steel lit the lamp that he took from a peg just inside the door; he strapped the grip to the outside of his hand and went down the ladder into the darkness. He curled his lip against the smell as he sloshed through the puddled urine across the pissoir's shaft base; he ducked through the cavern entrance and moved at a fast crouch until he could stand upright again.

Soon he edged along a ledge midway up the curving wall of a gallery that disappeared into darkness below him and fought off the temptation to take the shortcuts that seemed to offer themselves. He kept exactly to the route he'd marked on his way down here before—he well knew that the easiest thing to do in these caverns was to get irretrievably lost and wander until the oil in the lamp died. He clambered down a narrow shaft to a lower cavern. For a moment, he thought he glimpsed lamplight reflecting from rock somewhere ahead. Tiny stalagmites broke away under his boots and skittered loudly across the stone, and the light went out before he could be sure it had ever been there.

He shook his head. He'd told those idiots *No lights*. They had each other for company in the darkness, and any lamplight would warn off Caine.

He arrived at the spot, the broad bowl-shaped depression with the well to one side, and looked around. No sign of his boys; he nodded approval to himself—they were properly remaining covert until sure of his identity. "All right, boys. It's me. Come on out; there's a change in our plans."

And he stood there, listening to the fading echoes of his voice and the lonely plash of millennial water seeping through the limestone.

With a sudden curse he remembered the dagger that Ma'elKoth had magicked for him, that still rode his hip in its leather sheath. He drew the knife; the green light from within the blade was faint, barely visible in the glow from his lamp. As he swung it around at arm's length, he found that it only barely brightened—while pointing diagonally up and away.

"Bastard," he muttered. "Bastard. He's already been here."

His boys should have left some sign of which way they'd gone. He couldn't just follow the dagger, not down here. As he circled the chamber, he passed the mouth of the well—the vertical shaft where the net had been—and from its mouth breathed the smell of shit and rich metallic blood.

Berne let his eyes drift closed as he stood at the rim of the well. He didn't have to look down there to know what he'd see: the piled bodies of his four Cats.

But if they were dead, whose lamp threw that light he'd seen?

He spun, trying to whirl away from the well's mouth, but it was already too late.

He got no warning at all. No scrape of boots, no breath of breeze, nothing except silent and invisible hands striking his back at his center of balance while an invisible tether held his ankles. Before he could understand what was happening, he found himself falling headfirst down the well, tumbling as he bounced from wall to wall, crashing into the yielding cold-meat bodies of his men.

Light flared in the chamber above him, and five heads became visible as men above peered down the shaft at him.

Slowly, Berne disentangled himself from the nerveless clasping limbs of the corpses, picked himself up, and made a show of brushing dirt and blood from his clothing, all the while digging his feet around to find stable footing on the stone below the bodies.

"I am Abbal Paslava," said one of the men above. "Men call me the Spellbinder. I thought you might be interested to know who has killed you, Berne."

Berne bent his neck to look up at him and nodded with an expression of professional appreciation. "Good trap, Abbal Paslava the Spellbinder. Nicely done, indeed. Now I expect those men with you will be shooting me with crossbows, or dropping rocks on my head, or something like that." Berne chuckled warmly. "This was Caine's idea, wasn't it?"

"Why yes, in fact, it was," Paslava said with a broad malicious smile. "He told us of your magickal enhancements, and he decided that this would be the best way to kill you, to draw you down here into the caverns where your magick will not function. Not your strength, not your invulnerability, and most especially: not Kosall. With a griffinstone pulled from the net your men so thoughtfully kept watch over for us, I have more than enough power down here to slaughter you."

"A good trap," Berne repeated. "He's smarter than I thought he was. But there's something Caine doesn't know."

"Mmm," Paslava hummed judiciously. "Caine said you would try to bargain for your life. What information do you have that could possibly be of greater value to us than your death?"

"Information?" Berne laughed out loud. "I'll give you information," he said, as he reached back over his shoulder and drew Kosall.

Once the blade cleared the scabbard, he took its hilt, and Kosall whined to tooth-grinding life.

Paslava's eyes bulged.

Berne grinned and waved up at him with the humming blade. "You're not the only one with a griffinstone."

Paslava shouted, *"Shoot! Shoot him now!"* but before the Knights of Cant with him could bring their bows to bear, Berne bent his knees and sprang out of the well with a single leap. The Knights all ducked as he shot upward like a quarrel from a crossbow's slot. He arced high over one ducking Knight and split the man's skull from base to crown with a single backhanded swipe of Kosall.

He somersaulted in the air and landed gracefully poised. The dead Knight collapsed slowly to his knees, then tumbled forward into the well behind him.

He turned and leveled the blade at Paslava while the other Knights scrambled back and went for their swords.

"Come on, then," he said cheerfully. "Fight or run. You're dead just the same. I don't have all day."

Berne did not consider himself an intellectual, or even an intelligent man; he preferred to leave thinking to men who were good at it, like Ma'elKoth or Toa-Sytell. Nonetheless, a question of the sort that he generally didn't bother to consider sparked within his brain as he killed first one, then another of the terrified Knights of Cant. By the time he casually, rather distractedly slaughtered the third, this question had acquired real significance: it was a puzzler, and he suspected that its answer was somehow vital in a way he could not, yet, understand.

So it was that when he pounced on the fleeing Paslava and sliced the thaumaturge's leg off precisely through the middle of his knee joint—so that Paslava tumbled to the ground in a screeching spray of blood, skidding his jetting stump along the jagged limestone—Berne did not finish him immediately.

Instead, he seized the thaumaturge by the thigh on his half leg, his strengthened grip cutting into the muscle until the arterial spray of blood diminished to a trickle. He lifted Paslava into the air, head downward to keep his blood pressure up so the wounded man wouldn't faint.

Holding him out at arm's length, Berne frowned into the Spellbinder's upside-down eyes. "So tell me, before you die," Berne said slowly, with a growing premonition that things were somehow going hideously wrong, "exactly how Caine knew I'd be coming down here to get that net."

10

WELL BEFORE NOON, Victory Stadium was full, dangerously full. A close-packed sweating mass of humanity squatted on stone benches and crouched in the aisles. Some stood in knots around the closest man with a jug. Many struggled in disorganized masses at the doors of the grandstand pissoirs.

The Imperial official in charge of the stadium, himself sweating and wringing his hands, told the Commandant of the constables to shut the gates. Then he turned to kneel in front of the small icon of Ma'elKoth that stood in the corner of his office to pray that there wouldn't be a riot.

When the constables swung closed the public gates, the crowds outside recoiled upon themselves like worms encountering hot brick; a ripple passed outward from the stadium to the farthest reaches of Games Way and the street that joined it, Long Way, as people began to reverse direction to fight back against the press of bodies behind them.

A reinforced cavalry brigade began driving the commoners off Nobles' Way and away from Kings' Bridge: soon Ma'elKoth himself would travel this road.

11

HIGH ABOVE THE city in the Iron Room, Pallas Ril had paid little attention to the Household Knights that draped a linen shift over her and transferred her manacles from the altar to a jointed frame of oak—no more attention than she had paid to Lamorak's single miserable plea for forgiveness. They were bound identically under the thoughtful supervision of Ma'elKoth himself. A silver net had been tied over Pallas and her frame entire; this had at last captured her attention, as the twisting lace of Flow vanished from her mindview. Now when she looked upon Ma'elKoth, she saw only a man of great size and surpassing beauty, instead of the godlike whirlwind of power that had stood at the altar's side for two days.

Cut off from the Flow, she tumbled out of mindview and groaned weakly at the pain that chewed at her.

The Household Knights carried the frames upon which she and Lamorak were bound as though they were stretchers, down and down and down the endless flights of stairs to the front courtyard of the Colhari Palace. There a huge processional was being organized—hundreds upon hundreds of Knights and musicians and acrobats, pretty girls with garlands of fresh flowers, strong young men with baskets of sweets and pastries to throw to the crowds. The centerpiece of the parade was an enormous open wagon. It was hung with flowers until its frame could not be seen, and upon it were bolted a pair of freestanding iron racks. The jointed frames upon which Pallas and Lamorak were bound were swiftly unfolded into wide X shapes and hung upright upon the racks.

Being vertical for the first time in two days caused Pallas to nearly black out; as her vision dimmed and the scene swam in the brilliant sunlight, she saw Ma'elKoth leap lightly from the ground to the center of the wagon. The paraders around him, the Knights, everyone present in the courtyard or looking down from the windows cheered—a happy racket that he acknowledged with a sweeping bow and a grin that brought more cheers and applause.

Even without mindview, Pallas could see how he fed on their love, how it elevated him far above the concerns of mortality. His doubts and grim determination of this morning had vanished without a trace; here in the presence of his Children, Ma'elKoth rivaled the sun itself, all power and supernal beauty.

She looked over at Lamorak, at his battered body crucified like her own, his eyes closed on his private misery. She looked down at herself, at the linen shift that was already showing crimson stains of the blood that leaked through the crusted bandage around her chest, then again at Ma'elKoth, who now waved for the gates to be thrown back. She tried to summon mindview, to recover some of the serenity that had sustained her in the Iron Room, but the pain in her wrists and ankles, the agony of drawing each breath into her punctured lung, the tumult around her, all combined to prevent her from reaching that sanctuary.

She was alone, without even the faintest beat of life's song to comfort her.

The gates swung wide, and Ma'elKoth's face seemed to cast a dazzling light of its own. The waiting crowd outside answered his appearance with a full-throated roar.

12

HIGH IN THE stands within the stadium, the King of Cant looked down. Over a thousand Subjects of Cant were seeded through this crowd—every man, woman, and youth of them armed. They would fall upon the Grey Cats like an avalanche. Even now, as he sat with his palms pressed together between his trembling knees, the Faces were spreading through Old Town, taking strategic positions to cover a retreat, if a retreat became necessary. It wouldn't, though: this Majesty knew beyond doubt.

There would be no retreat.

By nightfall, he would hold this city in his hand, ready to deliver it to Toa-Sytell—in return for, ah, certain considerations . . .

The tremor in his knees and the fluttering in his guts, these had nothing to do with fear: they were pure anticipation. Only one thing troubled him as he squinted upward to check the near-vertical angle of the rising sun.

Where in fuck is Paslava? He should have been here half an hour ago. If he's not around to do his crowd-control stuff, a lot of people are going to get hurt.

From outside, far beyond the walls of the stadium, he heard the voice of crowds that roared like an approaching hurricane.

13

TOA-SYTELL MET THE parade at the south end of Kings' Bridge. A handful of King's Eyes forced a path for him through the crowds, and the Emperor paused in his joyous acceptance of his Children's adulation long enough to wave him aboard the wagon. He clambered up and stood close to Ma'elKoth's side, yelling at the top of his lungs to be heard over the crowd that Caine was nowhere to be found. Every person who'd entered the stadium had been searched, and every man who answered Caine's general description had been detained. Toa-Sytell himself had looked over the detainees, and Caine was not among them. Caine had not entered the stadium, and there was no way he could get in, now that the gates were sealed.

Ma'elKoth bent his neck to look down on his Duke. Sudden silence surrounded them, though Toa-Sytell could see that the crowd lining the streets still shouted as lustily as ever.

The Emperor smiled and said gently, "You misspeak. You mean to say: Caine has not entered the stadium since your search began. Mark Me: he will be there."

14

"ALL RIGHT ALL right allright *allright*," Arturo Kollberg muttered, chewing the words around the ends of his nail-bitten fingertips, still in his mouth. His heart beat double march time against his ribs, and blood sang in his ears. His face felt swollen, bloated with the pressure inside his brain, and it glowed with the same malignant flush of rose as the fist button of the emergency transfer switch.

After two swift glances, one over each shoulder, back at the impassive mirror masks of the soapies, he again faced forward and checked Caine's telemetry as it scrolled across the darkened POV screen.

"All right," he said again. "He's awake. He's moving. He's making a move. Start the feed."

15

EVEN THE SMALL-MARKET, ethnic-language channels buried in the non-English-speaking backwaters of the world carried Jed Clearlake's summation of the tale; their poor advertising revenues did not give them the funds necessary to carry the live feed itself, but they could go this far. They would break into their programming at intervals with whatever updates became available.

Clearlake's summary was a model of clarity; other broadcasters could only helplessly envy his characteristic blend of emotional intensity and suave good nature, his air of being on the inside, of being a player.

"Now, after this message, we'll return with *Caine: Live!*"

The following message was from the Studio itself, sixty seconds of opportunistic self-promotion, worldwide and free. Their slogan, *Adventures Unlimited: When you need to be somebody else* faded slowly from screens around the world; then the feed began.

And the world ground to a halt.

Foot traffic was gridlocked in Times Square as shoulder-to-shoulder pedestrians stared up at the ring of Jumbotrons. Tokyo was in a similar state; London, Johannesburg, Kabul, New Delhi ... Those citizens fortunate enough to be carrying handscreens stopped in their tracks to watch, and all the others rushed to their homes, to taverns, to storefronts where at least they could look at the pictures. Trading on the commodities and stock exchanges was suspended; air traffic was maintained only in the computer-directed slavelanes.

Nearly every breathless human being on Earth heard Caine's Soliloquy:

Seems like I spend most of my life climbing up out of other peoples' shit.

16

THE TOILET SEAT makes a dimly backlit ring above me as I clamber up the side of the shaft, get my hands on it, and quickly chin myself to get a look around. The latrine is empty, as I expected it would be; the Eyes who searched this place were too fastidious to climb down into the shaft—it figures that they wouldn't spend more time here than absolutely necessary.

I push the seat up and pull myself out of the toilet. It's a struggle not to groan out loud when every single one of my injuries acutely reminds me of its presence—from the fever that's scratching my eyeballs all the way down to the bone bruise that stiffens my right knee.

Tyshalle's Bloody Axe, I'm a wreck. Spending a few hours sleeping in petrified shit at the bottom of a latrine shaft didn't really agree with me.

Could have been worse: if Ma'elKoth hadn't banned gladiators, there might have been guys using this shitter while I was down there.

Daylight leaks in through the vents at the joining of wall and ceiling, and the rising thunder of the crowd's roar tells me that Ma'elKoth will be coming through the outside gates anytime now.

Those vents up there perforate the arena wall. The gladiator latrine is right next to the glory hole, to handle the nervous bladders and spastic sphincters of men walking out to die. I spend a nervous moment myself when I go to the doorless arch and peer out into the glory hole itself.

It's empty, thankfully, and dark—an iron door closes it off from the gated shaft that leads to the arena—and I go back to the vents, jump up, and chin myself to look out. I don't have to worry about making noise; with twenty thousand Ma'elKoth fanatics howling over my head, I could set off a bomb in here and attract less attention than a fart in a brothel.

The arena wall's about three feet thick here; I wriggle headfirst into one of the vents to get a decent view. I have to struggle to hold down some incipient claustrophobia—I can feel the weight of the stone an inch above the back of my head, and my elbows brush stone on either side. I'm in black shadow cast by the noonday sun, invisible.

The mouth of the vent frames the golden glare of sun off sand. Across the arena the bright holiday clothes of the spectators—

shoulder to shoulder in the stands—make a splintered mosaic of random color that shifts and ripples like a patchwork flag.

I spend one more moment looking out at the crowd. Some of them are nervous, some seem angry, some of them look sincerely happy.

A lot of them will be dead within the hour.

My field of view no doubt includes any number of Grey Cats in mufti and probably more than a handful of disguised Subjects of Cant. I'm not worried about them; they're all here to fight.

I wonder, though, if any of the civilians out there had a premonition, a queasy feeling about coming here today. I wonder how many won't be surprised when the shit explodes, how many will feel only a sickening stomach-drop of recognition, how many will die with *I knew I should have stayed home* echoing in their heads.

I wonder how many homes will echo with keening for the dead tonight.

Y'know, if the situation was opposite, if someone I loved died because some guy did what I'm about to do, I wouldn't rest until I'd hunted that man down and killed him with my own hands.

But: if I could buy Pallas' life with the deaths of every man, woman, and child in this stadium, I'd do it. Cheap at twice the price. Even so, I'd be inclined to haggle—in fact, today I'm gonna drive a hard fucking bargain.

Maybe I'm getting thrifty in my old age.

The roar that rocks the stadium notches up another five decibels or so, cutting short my seesaw of second thoughts.

Ma'elKoth has arrived.

He's brought a whole parade, hundreds of revelers in holiday costume; they come dancing onto the sand, casting sweets and coins up into the grandstands as they circle the arena, urging the crowd to join them in the singing of Ma'elKoth's anthem, "King of Kings." There are a few pretty girls among them, but most of them seem to be men—not young men, either. I can pick out weathered creases beneath the holiday face paint, and behind the smiles are the cold eyes of career soldiers, veteran killers.

So: he's ready.

Good.

The crowd isn't really going for the song. The voices that do join in are nearly drowned by the ever-increasing general roar.

And then the Rose Parade wagon rolls across my black-framed field of view.

It moves without visible means, powered by Ma'elKoth's will alone. That's him, there in the middle—the one who looks like a hero of legend, a god from myth, standing like the figurehead of a battleship as it rolls to the center of the arena floor, fists on his hips, head thrown back. And for those of you who are new to this story, the fellow at his side—the one looking very natty indeed in the ruffled doublet and pants side-buckled down to his thigh boots—that's Toa-Sytell, the Duke of Public Order, for which read "head of the secret police." Very competent. Very dangerous. His face is characteristically blank as he scans the stands.

He's probably looking for me.

He shouldn't be here; I was hoping he'd know better. If he gets killed today, Majesty and the Kingdom are deep in the shitter.

Yeah, oh well—too late now to worry about Majesty. I have other business. Business up there on that wagon with Ma'elKoth.

Hard as I try not to let myself register the twin X-shaped frames on either end of the flower-decked wagon, there they are; I can't look away. From one, Lamorak hangs limply, head down. He looks like he's already dead, which would be a pity.

I'd hate for him to miss this.

From the other, inside a drape of silver net, hangs my wife.

A chill opens in my belly, like I've swallowed ice, a freezing void that spreads to my chest, to my arms and legs, to my head. In that icy emptiness it seems that I'm watching myself lie here, hearing myself think. I can't feel my heartbeat, just a sizzling hiss behind my ribs that crackles in my ears like lightning on a radio.

Pallas has her head up. She looks alert and worried: she's a long way from that private mystic bolt-hole where she'd kept herself safe. The shift of white linen that covers her is stained with a crimson trail from her ribs down her left leg. Her blood drips from her heel into the flowers below her feet.

That rack she's hanging from—that's going to be a problem. Somehow I didn't expect to find her crucified . . .

Maybe I didn't think this through quite as well as I could have.

No Berne, though: that means his body's cooling at the bottom of that well in the caverns even now. Shame I couldn't be there myself to watch the light go out of his eyes—but I can settle for knowing I've outlived him.

Ma'elKoth lifts his bridge-girder arms, and silence bursts from him like the shock front of an explosion, as though God has reached down and spun the volume dial on the world.

He begins to speak to his assembled Children.

I guess that's my cue.

I pull myself scraping forward and roll headfirst out of the vent. My hands grip its lower rim so that I can flip neatly forward and land on my feet.

There's no hesitation now, not even time for a slow breath. There's no profit in any second thoughts: there are no choices left to make.

I hook my thumbs behind my belt and stroll out across the arena floor.

And this is it.

I'm here. On the sand. In my last arena.

Twenty thousand pairs of eyes swing curiously toward me: *Who's that idiot in black? What's he doing here?*

And hundreds of thousands more, all of you here with me inside my skull, all of you who think you know what I'm about to do. Maybe I've got a couple surprises for you, too.

A few of the costumed mock revelers see me now and still themselves, hands drifting toward folds of clothing for the weapons concealed there.

I keep walking toward them, slowly, offering a friendly grin.

The golden sand of the arena crunches as it shifts slightly under my boot heels. The sun is hot, and it strikes a reddish glow onto the upper reaches of my vision, where it glistens in my eyebrows.

All my doubts, all my questions fly away like doves in a conjurer's trick. Adrenaline sings in my veins, a melody as familiar and comforting as a lullaby. The thunder of blood in my ears buries all sound except for the slow, measured *crunchch . . . crunchch* of my footsteps.

Toa-Sytell sees me now; his pale eyes widen and his mouth works. He tugs on Ma'elKoth's arm, and the Emperor's head swivels toward me with the slow-motion menace of the turret of a tank.

As I walk toward him, my chest swells with some inexplicable emotion; I'm nearly there before I can tell what it is.

It's happiness, I guess.

I am, right now, as happy as I will ever be.

I look up at Pallas and find her eyes on me, full of horror.

I acknowledge her with a droop of my eyelids that is almost a bow, and I mouth the only words I can give her: *I love you.*

She's trying to say something back to me, something about Ma'el-Koth. I can't read her battered lips, and I won't have the chance to figure it out.

It's time for the killing to begin.

17

THE COMMANDER OF the northwest garrison had only just lain down, heading for a richly deserved nap after thirty solid hours on his feet. He was stretching his exhausted body on an obscenely comfortable pallet in a back room, his eyes drifting closed, when the entire building trembled and shook as though struck by a giant's fist.

Outside his room, men shouted in confusion and terror. He scrambled to his feet and staggered to the peg where his scabbard hung on the wall. He clawed numbly at the hilt of his sword, but before he could draw, the door burst squealing around the bar that locked it and fell in rattling splintered fragments to the floor.

The man who stood panting in the doorway was covered in moist and clotted blood, as though he'd been swimming on a slaughterhouse floor. His eyes burned fiercely within his red-smeared face. As he gasped for breath he snarled: "Call your men . . . all of them. And I need . . . a horse. Your *best fucking horse*. Now."

Slowly the commander's fatigue-dazzled brain registered who this was, and he stammered, "I, ah, Count *Berne*—! Count . . . my lord Count, you're *hurt!*"

Berne's teeth were nearly as red as his bloody lips. "It's not my blood . . . you stupid . . . sack of shit. Get that horse. And sound the alarm. Every man, every fucking trooper, I want the *whole shit-eating army* at Victory Stadium *right fucking now!*"

"I, ah, my lord Count, I don't understand—"

"You don't have to understand. Just do it. He talked; I knew the sonofawhore would talk."

Berne strode into the room and took the commander's shoulder with a grip powerful enough to make the commander wince as the joint popped. "All your men, all the men from the other garrisons. Get them to the stadium and arrest *everyone*. Anyone who offers resistance, kill them."

"But, but, what's going on?"

Berne leaned close, and his eyes smoldered. The commander

nearly choked on the rich meaty scent of blood on his breath. "Fucking *Caine*—the whole goatfucking thing's a *setup*!"

Without effort he lifted the commander off the floor and snarled into his face. "Now do I get that horse and those men, or do I tear your fucking arms off?"

18

FAR BELOW, HE was only a stick figure in black, a sharp contrast to the golden sand and the brightly costumed revelers, but to Majesty's eye he was unmistakably Caine. The slight, unconscious swagger, the flash of teeth in the swarthy face, the leisurely walk that drew out and stretched the awesome silence of the Stadium. *Too late now for Paslava to arrive,* Majesty thought, his heart sprinting.

His white-knuckled fingers dug painfully into his trembling knees. Without Paslava, this was going to be bloody, but there was no going back, not now, not when victory was *this close* . . .

He caught the eye of Deofad. The grizzled warrior sat twenty rows away, and he returned Majesty's look of sizzling anticipation.

Majesty mouthed, *Ready?*

Deofad's reply was a barely perceptible nod.

Majesty lifted one finger and held his breath.

Now, everything waited for Caine.

19

A LANGUID WAVE of the Emperor's hand parts the sea of revelers, and they allow me to pass. I don't have to look back to know they're closing in behind me, but that doesn't matter. All that counts is how close I can get before the shitpile explodes.

Slowly, with the same kind of deliberation my father used to use when he'd take off his belt to beat me, I untie the silver net from my waist and coil it around one fist.

"What news, Caine?" Ma'elKoth booms with hokey feigned surprise. Whatever his other talents might be, the sonofabitch sure can't act. Toa-Sytell at his side watches me expressionlessly, one hand stroking his other wrist up the sleeve of his blouse. Pallas croaks some unintelligible raven sounds, her breath stolen by her punctured lung.

I stick my free hand through the garlands of flowers that hang over this huge wagon to get a grip on its wooden underframe, then climb up aboard.

Now the silence from the crowd is no longer enforced by Ma'elKoth's magick: everyone stands, and stares at me. This is obviously not part of the show.

Boy, are they wrong . . .

"I can see through the eyes of this image," Ma'elKoth says, "and speak with its voice. Why have you come here, Caine?"

I get up onto the platform and uncoil the net. From outside the stadium, a thousand voices shout in distant confusion and outrage, overscored by the sound of brass trumpets. Toa-Sytell turns his shoulder a bit toward me, his hand still up his sleeve. Pallas croaks again, and now I can understand her. *". . . it's a trap . . ."*

I smile up into her black-ringed desperate eyes. "Yeah, I know."

The Emperor towers over me, a mountain of meat; I can smell the oil that curls his hair and smooths his beard, hear the faint rustle of his kilt as he steps close.

"I ask again, why have you come here?"

If he bent his neck another inch, if I stood on tiptoe, I could kiss him on the lips. The cold hollow that has opened around my heart spreads to my arms, to my legs; I've cycled between exhilaration and dread so many times in these last seconds that emotion has become abstract; I can no longer feel anything except a chill empty stillness. I look deep into his bottomless eyes.

"I'm here to save my wife."

"Your wife?" A certain mild astonishment enters his face. "You never told Me you were married."

"There's a lot of things I haven't told you."

Now that I'm here, now that I'm committed, I'm inexplicably reluctant to begin. I've aimed the gun, but I can't seem to pull the trigger. As long as I draw this moment out, Pallas and I, we're Schrödinger's cat, equipoised between life and death, and my first move will collapse our wave function into history.

"Indeed," Ma'elKoth murmurs smugly. "Like, for example, that you are an *Aktir*."

An invisible hand closes my throat. Even if I were cool enough to take this in stride, which I'm not, my conditioning won't let me answer. I settle for a small smile that might look confident.

"What are you waiting for?" Ma'elKoth says. "Here is My

image. The net is in your hand . . . Second thoughts? Now, when you face the moment to strike at God?"

I force words through my half-choked throat. "You know what a dead spy is, Ma'elKoth?"

"A dead spy?"

"Yeah. It's a name a writer from back home gave to the guy that you feed false intelligence to, when you know he's gonna be captured by the enemy. When they break him and he talks, he tells them exactly what you want them to know. He thinks it's the truth. See?"

Ma'elKoth's lips quirk oddly, and a glow enters his eyes. "Lamorak . . ." he murmurs.

Rather than being dismayed by this concept, he's clearly amused and appreciative. His amusement grows as he murmurs down the chain of reasoning.

"Of course. That's why you do not strike with the net . . . You know I am present in truth, not in image. You planned things so. How else could you draw us both out of the palace, which is defended against *Aktiri* magick by the power of My will?"

Lamorak makes a choking sound from up there upon his cross. *"You knew. You did this to me—!"*

I nod up at him. "Yeah. I was counting on you. Shit, Lamorak. Just the other day I killed a better man than you'll ever be for doing less than you did. Did you really think I'd let you live?"

Now, all I have to do to make this work is get Pallas down off that cross. Toa-Sytell is sidling closer to me, his hand still up his sleeve—on a weapon, of course: he's too freaked to be subtle.

"But what now?" Ma'elKoth murmurs. "You are here in the midst of My power. How can you possibly hope to escape?"

He rumbles on in this vein, but I lose the chain of his words. I'm looking up into the light of the only eyes that have meaning for me now.

Even the most flexible thinker in the world takes time to shift her paradigm. When I walked out upon the sand of the arena, all Pallas could think of was the appalling danger to me—that horror had shouted from her eyes. She'd given up on herself, and by the time I climbed up onto the wagon, she'd given up on me, too; inside, where it counts, she'd left us both for dead.

But she's too smart, the life within her is too powerful. This is the point of my pointless jabber with Ma'elKoth: it gave her time to adjust. Now, as I pull the griffinstone from my pocket, holding it by my side where she can see it but Ma'elKoth and Toa-Sytell can't, when I look up and with my eyes I ask her *Are you ready?*, I see a response that is fierce and potent and still somehow serene.

Her answer: *When you are.*

Ma'elKoth is still talking, burbling on with the cheery unconcern of a whodunit fan mulling over the clues. When I turn back to him, he's saying ". . . and why carry this net, when you knew it would be useless?"

"Oh, that." I give him a cold chuckle. "It's not useless. It's the signal for the Subjects of Cant to attack."

"What?"

While he's parsing this revelation, I whip the net over his head. He bats at it with condescending annoyance, but it drapes over him nonetheless. Toa-Sytell lunges at me like a fencer, in his hand a dull flash of steel. I twist away from the blade and stamp the side of his knee; it breaks with a dull crunch, and he pitches toward me, grunting in sudden agony. The revelers below the wagon draw their blades and charge as I skip away from Toa-Sytell—and Ma'elKoth's arms reach toward me within the net.

I smile at him. "Didn't I tell you about putting your hands on me?"

He's not thinking about what he's doing, not registering that the net cuts him off from his magickal defenses.

My smile grows to a wild grin as I haul back my leg and kick the Emperor in the balls.

His testicles squish against my instep, and his eyes bug out like baseballs jammed in the sockets, and his jaw drops open as all his breath leaves him in a whoosh, and the look on his face makes me laugh out loud.

While he's still bending over, his hands twitching blindly toward a clutch at his injured groin, while he's stuck in those timeless seconds between impact and discovery of how sickeningly intense the pain will become, I whirl away from him and leap onto Pallas' cross. I tangle my fingers in the silver net that covers her and haul myself up, and we come face-to-face for an eternal instant.

My eyes ask another question, and she says "Yes."

I kiss her, once. Our mouths meet hungrily through the net. I have lived every day of my life only to bring myself here to this moment, and it's been worth every second.

I press the griffinstone between the strands into the palm of her upraised hand. Her fingers close around it, and I speak against her lips.

"What do you need?"

Tears surge into her eyes. "Buy me time."

"Done."

Quarrels snap past my ears as I drop back to the wagon's platform. I feel an instant's sickening conviction that Pallas has been shot, but a glance upward shows the net sprung outward, tight over an enormous sphere of semisubstantial glass with Pallas at its center. She's gotten a Shield up, and the quarrels bristle from its surface. But even with the griffinstone, she can't do two magicks at once, can't hold the Shield and get herself off the rack at the same time.

I need to buy her a break.

Down here beside me, Ma'elKoth snarls wordlessly from his knees. His face strains purple as he claws at the net over his head. I chamber for a kick, but then change my mind and drop my foot again.

Some things cry out to be done by hand.

I lean into an overhand right.

My chest expands with raging joy as my knuckles smear his perfect nose sideways onto his perfect cheekbones and his eyes cross and flood with the pain. My blood's up and I'm gonna kill him now while I have the chance, but an icicle spears into my left thigh.

It's that little fucking knife of Toa-Sytell's. He's a lot tougher than he looks, still going for me, dragging a shattered knee. He looks up at me with an expression of savage completion on his face: he's done what he needed to do with his life and he's ready to die.

That expression makes no sense; it's barely even a flesh wound. I pull the stiletto out of my leg like a splinter and toss it away—and let him have a roundhouse in the side of the head hard enough to kick the light out of his eyes, but not to kill him. He flops bonelessly onto his side, still semiconscious—he *is* tough—and I make sure of him by dropping to one knee and slicing the edge of my hand to the base of his skull.

Quarrels still fly, but none come close to me here—they're shooting from the seats, and they can't take the chance of hitting Ma'elKoth. He's getting a grip on the net, now. I have to finish him and damned fast, too. Any second those mock revelers are gonna be all over me.

Trumpets blare, too close by. The gate, the gate on the tunnel that leads outside, it's *open*—!

Shit. It's the cavalry.

Half-armored lancers flood through the gate at a gallop and fan out across the arena floor. Sunlight splinters from their steel-bladed spears, except for one group—five of them riding behind an unarmored man who's covered with blood, who waves a bastard sword as lightly as a conductor's baton.

Our eyes meet across the sand, and Berne shows me his bloody teeth.

And now fingers of liquid fire spread through the large muscle of my left thigh, and I understand where that mysterious look of satisfaction on Toa-Sytell's face came from.

The little cocksucker poisoned me.

With a dull ripping sound like the tearing of flesh over bone, Ma'elKoth shreds the net and casts it aside. He comes to his feet in a surge like a tidal wave. I leap into the air, chambering my leg for a side kick at the point of his chin, but the purple blood is draining from his face. His magick is back and he's already too fast for me: his huge hand strikes like a snake and wraps my ankle before I can fire the kick, and he slams me down to the wagon hard enough to splinter its bed.

Meteors shoot across my vision and I can't breathe. Ma'elKoth picks me up by the ankle, so that my head dangles near his knees.

He purrs, "Now, you will learn what it means to trifle with My wrath."

This isn't working out quite as well as I'd hoped.

But there comes a shout like the end of the world, and the wagon bucks as though it's alive. Ma'elKoth staggers.

His hand opens and I fall. For one brief instant the air is filled with metallic snicks and clacks: Ma'elKoth's belt buckle springs open, and the manacles that hold Lamorak to the cross over my head burst wide and he falls toward me. Throughout the stadium pieces of armor fall as their buckles unclasp; even locked doors slam open and gates bend wide.

The wagon bucks again, and this time I can see it's not the wagon that's moving—it's the *whole fucking stadium*. Horses stagger and men fall and screams rend the air—fading behind the grinding roar of the earthquake.

Pallas floats above us, hanging in the air five feet above the cross on which she'd hung. She is the only motionless thing in the pitching world. She extends her hands, and the linen shift that covered her burns away in a flash of pale fire, a fire that burns ever brighter until I can't look at her, burns to a pure white streaming light that melts the last remaining shreds of the net that had restrained her power. The grinding roar of the earthquake gets louder, beating against my ears, rhythmic—

And becomes a Voice, as though the world itself speaks to us.

"HARM MY HUSBAND, LITTLE MAN, AND I WILL TEACH YOU TRULY WHAT IT IS TO ANGER A GOD."

20

EVERY TECH IN the booth was on his feet, eyes riveted to the POV screen. Arturo Kollberg was right behind them, breathless, trembling.

"Jesus stinking Christ on a *stick*! That's *Pallas*! The earthquake, the voice . . . My *god*, if I'd known she'd show this kind of power, I'd never have . . ."

He felt a presence behind his shoulder. Kollberg bit off the sentence, wincing, suddenly aware of the chill sweat that trickled between his shoulder blades down the curve of his spine.

A digitized voice said flatly, "You would never have what?"

He flicked a glance at the soapy's mirror mask; a fisheye-distorted image of his own black-bagged, red-veined eyes leered back at him. He licked his lips and tasted the salt sweat that had moistened them. The speed muttered in his veins and leaked into his head until he thought his skull might burst like an overblown balloon.

"I'd, ah, never have let her take on a mission of such, ah, limited audience appeal. I'd have pushed for something, ah, more, you know, bigger, more like, well, more like *this* . . ."

Impossible to tell if that satisfied the mirror-masked face or not. This was a nightmare, and he couldn't wake up. He wiped his sweaty palms on the legs of his jumpsuit and prayed that Carson would come through with her restraining order before something really damaging slipped out.

Damn that Dole cunt, he prayed to a god in whom he did not believe. *And her lawyers, and her damned soapy goons, and Marc Vilo, and damn the frigging Studio too while you're at it, and yes, most of all: damn Caine.*

Kollberg's rolling eye fixed upon the emergency recall switch. *Especially Caine.*

21

EVERYTHING WAS GOING wrong.

Majesty had stayed at his vantage in the upper reaches of the grandstand. He'd signaled the attack when Caine threw the net. Loyal old Deofad had gone diving onto the arena floor, his enchanted blade Luthen upraised and shining like a bar of white-hot iron in his fist. He had already cut down one man to spill out his life onto the sand and was fighting another before any of the Subjects following reached the sand behind him. None of them saw Majesty's frantic wave of negation, nor heard his throat-clawing screams of *"No! Come back!"* when he saw that Caine's lunatic plan had failed. Ma'elKoth was *really here*, and though he was currently occupied with killing Caine, it was all too clear that this was the time for all prudent folk to be finding an exit.

Then the gates had opened, and the Ankhanan Horse Guards had thundered in. Deofad could still be seen down there, his blade scattering gouts of molten steel that it cut from the lancers' armor—but the lancers charged, spearing Subjects and mock revelers alike. And the earthquake began, and that awful voice that seemed to come from everywhere and nowhere.

He kept his head, Majesty did, in the midst of the screaming, staggering townsfolk around him. He kept his eyes open for a chance to get away, looking away from Pallas Ril, who shone like the sun.

A shadow fell across him, and the heat of the sun vanished. Curving within this huge shadow that painted the stadium in dark greens were twists of purest gold, like the sun seen on the bottom of a rippling pool of clear water. He couldn't understand what cloud could cast this sort of shade, and he looked up—

And saw the river, up over his head.

22

THE MOST FRIGHTENING part of this is that Ma'elKoth isn't afraid.

He looks up, shading his eyes against the stinging actinic light that streams from Pallas' nude body, and he grins the grin of a rich kid on Christmas. There is some deep sexual anticipation in his voice.

"Chambaraya, I take it? I had always thought that you were a myth."

The Voice that answers him shapes itself of birdsong, of cracking stone and splashing water, of the very shouts of the fighting itself that storms around us.

"NO MYTH, LITTLE GODLING. STAND AWAY FROM CAINE, FOR HE IS OURS."

Chambaraya? My mouth flops open a little wider. The freaking *river god*?

"Stand away? Most assuredly," Ma'elKoth responds with silken courtesy. He steps back from where I lie helplessly watching, and he dusts his hands like a workman finishing a well-done job.

"I have been waiting for the Old Gods to come and stand against Me. I had been hoping for someone more . . . impressive. But you will do."

Pallas closes her fist, and the flowers that garland this wagon suddenly writhe to life—snaking over and around Ma'elKoth, pinning his arms to his sides, wrapping his neck. Even the wooden platform beneath his feet squirms and shapes itself to manacle his ankles. For a moment he tests his purely physical strength against them, his robes rippling with the play of parahuman muscle. They creak but hold him fast. He looks down at the riot of flowers making a jungle of his massive body, and his grin spreads.

He shrugs, and thunder rolls.

He laughs, and the sun goes dim.

He lifts his head, and lightning spears from the darkening sky, crackling energy that transfixes him; flames explode from his body, igniting the wagon, charring the vines to blackened ash in the blink of an eye.

The thunderclap that follows blows away my hearing, and Ma'el-Koth stands triumphant amidst the flames.

He raises his fist, in that gesture I remember from the Ritual of Rebirth in the Great Hall. I roll away, shouting a wordless warning for Pallas.

Ma'elKoth's fist strokes outward. A blast furnace ignites the air with a shattering roar, a shaft of power that strikes my wife full upon the breast—and she opens her arms to receive it as a flower opens its petals to the sun.

Her laugh is full of alien power. She points north, over the wall of the stadium, angled high into the noonday sky.

A pulsing crystalline mountain rises there, blocking half the sky, emerald with algae and sparking with the silver-mailed flickers of darting fish. The river itself is spilling *upward* against all reason—

It shapes itself higher, and higher yet, a globe the size of a village growing upon its end. Then the globe unfolds, like a flower, like a starfish—

It's a hand.

The Hand of Chambaraya descends upon the stadium. All around us fighting men, seasoned veterans of a hundred battles, cast aside their weapons and throw themselves to the ground, covering their eyes and screaming like children. Civilians clutch each other and wail. And I . . . I can't look away.

What has Pallas become, that she can do such things?

The hand is the size of a battleship, a freaking *aircraft carrier*, and it closes upon us. The flames of the burning wagon hiss and boil through it, sending a cloud of bubbles skyward. For a long, astonishing instant I am underwater, face-to-face with an equally astonished carp that's bigger than my head. Then the surface leaves me, lying here upon the smoking dripping reeking ruin of a wagon, wet through, with the poison still spreading through my fiery leg.

High, already so high above that the sun glares through it, the hand holds Ma'elKoth within its watery grip—it's a globe of water again a hundred meters through—I can barely see him deep within its center.

Sudden steam bursts boiling around him as he spreads his arms and begins to burn.

He hasn't given up yet, and I'm not all that sure that Pallas—Chambaraya, whatever—I'm not sure they can beat him.

I'm not sure that anybody can.

I roll over, coughing out a throatful of thick greenish water, and find myself staring into the ruins of Lamorak's face. We've really done a number on him, over the past few days—broken leg, broken jaw, shattered nose that has his eyes nearly swollen shut. Those swollen eyes meet mine and begin to drift hopelessly closed; if I choose to take his life right now, there's not a goddamn thing he can do about it, and he knows it. He's letting go of consciousness because he knows me too well to waste his breath begging.

"Stay with me, you worthless sack of shit," I snarl, twisting my fingers into the bandage that ties shut his jaw. The sudden sharp pain of the linen cutting into his swelling brings him back, and his eyes roll like a spooky horse's.

"Stay with me. I want you awake for this."

"Wha . . . but, but Caine . . ."

I'd love to lie here for another day or two, but I drag myself to my feet. My poisoned thigh has gone numb around the wound now, and a creeping wave front of fire enters my pelvis.

I've got maybe five minutes to live.

I stumble over Toa-Sytell's unconscious body—hope he drowned, the sneaky little shit—and barely make it to the X-shaped framework that Pallas had hung from.

She's up there, over my head, shining like the sun.

She's the only light left in the stadium. Black clouds have come out of somewhere—huge rolling granite boulders of storm clouds licking the sky with tongues of lightning.

All I have to do is get to her, get my hands on her, and I can save us both, but she is far out of my reach, floating, borne up by the air itself—

I shout her name, over and over again, but winds have come, gale winds that rip the sounds from my mouth and cast them carelessly away. She can't hear me; she'll never hear me. Maybe, maybe if I climb the rack, I can balance on the top, and jump—

Both my legs are killing me, my right knee and my burning left thigh. I groan as I pull myself up onto the cross . . . and that's when I see Berne.

He's down on the arena floor, shouting and cursing and kicking the soldiers that cower on the ground around him. I can read his twisted lips, screaming for somebody to *just shoot that fucking bitch*, but none of the men nearby have bows and none of the bow-armed Cats that still struggle with Subjects here and there in the stands can hear him.

He lifts his head, and the light from her body blurs his face into featureless white, and he's calculating something. He reaches a decision, and Kosall comes up like his cock, his legs bend—

And he leaps.

So do I.

He shoots upward like an arrow. I jump up and out to intercept him, with all my failing strength. I'm starting fifteen, twenty feet above him, but it doesn't matter, it's not enough, I'm too late, too slow. I stretch forth my hands . . . and my fingers find his boot top as he soars past me, and I hang on.

The opposing angles of our momentum jerk us into a crazy

tumble in the air. I fall down, down, and down, losing my hold on him as we twist apart, and the sand slaps all breath from my lungs.

I can only lie there, limbs twitching like a dead man's, while I try to drag air into my chest. Even as it comes in a great whooping gasp, Berne looms over me, backlit by the lightning-shot storm clouds above us.

"What the fuck," he says, raising his voice above the wind. "I'm nothing if not flexible. You first, then."

He lifts Kosall and regards its shimmering edge. "Y'know, I've been waiting a long time for this."

"Yeah, me too." I hook his ankle with my instep and stamp the side of his knee, but he's seen that one and it nearly costs me my leg. He bends the joint to absorb the impact, slicing down toward my thigh with Kosall, and I only barely throw into the back-roll in time. I go over my back to my feet while he's pulling an arm's length of Kosall out of the sand.

I back away from him, glancing at the ground around my feet so that I don't trip over one of the cowering soldiers. He comes for me, stalking cat-footed, holding the blade loosely canted at a high angle between us. The smile on his face looks like what people must see on mine before I kill them.

It's not much fun from this side.

Thunder cracks over our heads, and the flashing glare of lightning above tells me that the other fight, the important one, is still going on: Pallas and Ma'elKoth, duking it out in front of twenty thousand terrified witnesses.

Nobody's watching Berne and me. Nobody cares about this dirty little grudge match.

No blaze of glory for me.

He's vastly stronger than I am, inhumanly fast, his technique and balance are better than mine, and he has a sword that'll cut through anything. Not to mention that this Buckler thing of his makes him virtually invulnerable.

I'm gonna kill him anyway.

I have to. Because Pallas has no attention to spare for him, and there's nothing but me between them.

I glance around, and he comes for me in a lightning lunge, covering three meters in less than an eye blink; Kosall's point sizzles through my tunic, parting the leather without resistance, as I twist aside barely in time. I take his wrist lightly as he passes me, pulling him along to draw his balance, and then clothesline him with a forehand chop at his throat.

He drops his chin and takes it on the mouth—I don't even draw blood—but his boots skid on the wet sand and he goes down on his back. No point in trying to take advantage: I can't hurt him and he can muscle out of any pin. I whirl away and run as fast as my limping legs can carry me.

"Hey, Caine?" he calls mockingly from behind me. "You used to be able to outrun me!"

And he's right on my ass already. I can hear his booted lope, but I'm almost there, almost to the spot I'd found with that risky glance. His Monastic training saves my life—as he swings for the back of my neck, he exhales a sharp *chuff*, like a *ki-ya*. I dive into a forward shoulder-roll. Kosall hisses through the space that my neck just vacated, and when I come up, the net is in my hand.

Berne stops and cocks his head, still smiling. "What do you think you're going to do with that?"

"Recognize this, Berne?" I say. "This is the one four of your boys died watching."

"So?"

I draw a long, chisel-bladed fighting knife from its scabbard below my armpit. "So I've been saving it to kill you with."

He snorts. Lightning flares and thunder crashes.

"Come on, then."

So I do.

I don't cast the net over him, as I did to Ma'elKoth. Berne is a born fighter, a natural warrior, and I'd never catch him like that. Instead I use his incredible reflexes against him: I snap the net like a whip at his head.

He disdainfully blocks it with Kosall, but he hasn't carried this blade very long, not long enough to retrain himself: he blocks the net with Kosall's *edge*. It slices right through, so instead of wrapping around the blade, about half the net splashes across his face. In that half-second reflexive blink, I lunge with the knife.

He knows how I fight. He knows I favor the heart, and so I stay away from it—that's where he will have focused that Buckler of his. Instead I lowline him and shove a foot of cold steel through his groin right into his hip joint.

The hilt vibrates against my palm as the blade grates on bone. Berne gasps and gives a lover's low moan. I jam the knife in deeper, right into the joint. As his superstrength muscles clamp down around the injury, I wrench the knife downward, leaning on it with all my weight. The hilt snaps off in my hand.

He looks at me in white-faced astonishment: he can't believe how badly I've hurt him.

I drop the hilt with its stub of blade. I reach inside my tunic for my other fighting knife and between my shoulder blades for my wedge-pointed thrower.

And Kosall flashes down toward my head.

I throw myself to the side out of its path, but I feel an impact on my boot as I dive away: half my boot heel and a thumb-sized chunk of my own heel are sliced away in a fraction of a second. I scramble back, and Berne comes for me, snarling his agony with every step.

I can't believe he can even *stand*, let alone walk, and now, beyond reason, he breaks into a *running fleche*—!

Again I throw myself sideways and roll away. My god, my god, *that was my best shot.* Any normal man would have fainted from the pain, and this would have been over . . .

"Run, Caine," he rasps, hoarse with agony. "I can still catch you. I can still kill you. Go on, run."

I believe him. Despite the knife blade scoring the bones and slicing the cartilage in his hip joint—causing what kind of pain I can't even imagine—he doesn't seem slowed at all.

I'm gonna have to take him inside.

I stand and wait for him.

Kosall is a heavy weapon, and Berne's magickal muscles don't entirely compensate; swinging a blade that size shifts your balance in ways that have nothing to do with strength. He's not lunging this time—maybe that knife blade in the joint has that much effect.

He slides his feet forward, keeping his weight perfectly centered as he lifts the blade in a short semicircular arc.

"That fighting girl, that friend of Pallas'," he says, straining for a conversational tone, "she was better than you are."

I shrug. "She was worth both of us, Berne."

"Pretty, too. Did you fuck her?"

I let him think it's working, the cretin: I force heat into my voice. "You sonofabitch, I'll—"

And that's all I have time for as he comes for me again. He thought he was taking me off guard, but in fact it's the other way around. I slip Kosall's lethal humming edge and step into him, knife blades reversed along my forearm. There are a couple things that you just can't learn in abbey school. One of them is *kali*.

Suddenly I'm close enough to kiss him. As he tries to step back and slice with the sword, I stay right with him, my body against his, blocking at his wrist with the blade of my knife while the other one slices at his neck. His Buckler turns my blade from his neck, but the other cuts deep into his arm.

He snarls into my face, but he's nothing if not adaptable. When I try the same trick again, only this time at his face and his heart for the death stroke, he drops Kosall and gets his hands in close, taking the cuts on his wrists. We stand nose to nose for one eternal second while our hands fly in lethal flurries; blood sprays, and it's not mine, but he's faster than I am and he slips a short hook onto the side of my head that shoots stars across my vision, follows it with a twisting roundhouse knee to my side that breaks a couple ribs with dull internal pops, and the next thing I know he's got hold of my head and he's gonna break my neck. He's too fucking strong, I can't hold him but there's Kosall upright in the sand—I get my hand on the hilt and feel the buzzing tingle. I can just barely drag it across his foot, and his toes fall away, and I'm flying one way while Kosall goes another.

Flying, tumbling through the air, I land skidding through the sand. He cast me aside like a bored child throws a doll.

I struggle up, coughing blood—the sharp ends of those broken ribs must have ripped into my lung—but he's not coming after me. He's got Kosall again, and his back's to me because he's limping over toward Pallas.

She shines above us, a star against the storm, the center of a firestorm of lightnings and energy bolts that fly freely, seemingly from all directions. Berne, Tyshalle damn his rotting heart, has somehow matured enough to get his priorities straight.

Once she's gone, I'm no threat at all.

He's too strong; he's too fucking good. Nothing I do seems to matter to him.

I couldn't beat him on my best day.

I have one trick left, an old one from my childhood, from long before there was a Caine, from a bootleg video my father showed me once. It's just that I was really hoping I wouldn't have to do this.

Ahh, what the hell: after this one, I won't be in any shape to care, anyway.

I drag myself to my feet, my feet that seem a mile below me now. I can't even really feel them as Toa-Sytell's poison spreads through my body. I draw my last two knives, the little five-inch leafblades from my boot tops, and check my grip on them. I hold them as tight as I can, the one in my right tanto style, the other reversed, its blade flat against my forearm.

This had better work.

I have to lean forward to get myself moving, because my legs seem to belong to somebody else. Whoever he is, though, he's still letting them operate instinctively to keep me upright. As I lean farther and farther forward they finally break into a clumsy, lumbering run.

Even over the earthshaking roar of the battle above our heads, he hears my boots on the sand at the last second. He whirls, instinctively leading with Kosall's point, which enters my belly as smoothly as a hot knife into butter.

It slides in just below my navel, and he continues the thrust until its humming point comes out the middle of my back.

It doesn't hurt, but it's very uncomfortable, a buzzing ache I can feel in my teeth.

He's killed me.

Our eyes meet. His face goes slack in astonishment: after all these years, he can't believe he's finally done it.

For one stretching second, his mind whirls back through every time he's dreamed of this, a cascading flutter of his dreams of revenge. In that slack instant I lean forward, forcing my body onto the blade until its hilt at my stomach stops me, and I stab him below the solar plexus.

My knife doesn't go in as smoothly as his sword did, but we stand there, locked together, our blades within each other's bodies. I work the blade, sawing upward to slice muscle, using the feel of the knife to search for the beating of his heart. Suddenly the blade locks in place; I can no longer move it at all—he's shifted his Buckler down into his torso. Our eyes meet again, for one last instant, because he knows he's about to die.

The other leafblade, held reversed in my left, I windmill overhand into the top of his head.

The blade crunches through his skull into his brain. The bone crackles as I jerk the hilt back and forth, taking Berne's life, all his memories, his hopes, his dreams, his lusts, and his joys and twisting them into scrambled eggs.

An instant ago he was a man. Now he's just meat.

His eyes roll up and he convulses. He finally releases Kosall's hilt as he falls at my feet, and the buzzing blessedly stops.

I stand in the middle of the arena, the sword sticking through me. I try to step away, just a few steps, anything to get me away so that I don't die on top of Berne, but I can't feel my legs at all anymore. I can't tell if it's from the poison in my bloodstream or if Kosall went through my spine.

My knees buckle, and I twist toward the ground.

Spine, I guess—the buzzing in my teeth said it hit bone in there.

I splay my arms so that I fall faceup. A foot and a half of Kosall is forced out of my belly by the impact with the sand.

Pallas' star still shines above me, and it's all right.

I don't mind so much, so long as I go out with her light being the last in my eyes.

23

THE TECHBOOTH STILL thundered with the sounds of the battle playing out on the POV screen, but within, all was still.

Kollberg tried to control his shaking, but he couldn't. His whole body trembled and itched, and one eye winked spastically.

"My god, my god," he kept repeating, over and over again. "He did it. He finally did it."

One of the techs murmured, "I've never seen anything like it. This ought to be the biggest seller since the Caste Riots. The biggest *ever*."

Another tech, of a more thoughtful bent, murmured in reply what a privilege it was to be present, how he'd be able to tell his grandchildren that he sat in the booth and watched Caine die.

Of everyone there, it was—surprisingly—Kollberg who prayed for Caine to hold on, to keep drawing breath.

His reasoning was simple: Pallas still fought Ma'elKoth in the skies over the Stadium. If Caine died too soon, he wouldn't have any recording of the outcome.

The subvocal murmur of Caine's Soliloquy whispered in the techbooth's speakers.

I understand now. I know what he meant. My father told me that knowing the enemy is half the battle. I know you, now. That's right.

It's you.

Kollberg blanched at the words. It was as though Michaelson spoke directly to him. He mopped his mouth with a trembling hand and eyed the emergency recall switch. He could do it; he could pull Caine right now, out of the middle of the battle, and he'd goddamn well *do* it, even now, if he got the first hint that Caine was straying into forbidden territory.

But an instant later he made himself relax. How much could Caine really say? His conditioning would stop his mouth before he could say anything really damaging. He squirmed in his chair, trying to get comfortable, trying to find a position from which he could give Caine's death the attention it deserved; he'd been waiting a long time for this, and he intended to enjoy it.

24

IN THE SKIES above Victory Stadium, two gods met in battle.

The water of the river discomfited Ma'elKoth only in that it interfered with his vision. Within the sphere, he called upon the love of His Children and stretched forth his hands, and lightning from the sky danced to his gesture. The fire of his body boiled the river around him, sending clouds of white upward to meet the rolling grey above.

A holocaust of lightning and fire together struck that small part of the Song of Chambaraya that was the body of Pallas Ril and passed through as though her body were a lens, striking outward at Chambaraya itself—and harmed the god not at all. Fish died, trees withered, grass burned black away from its bank; an otter and its family choked and died in a boiling pool, and a scalded deer fell into the current. In all, the extreme power of Ma'elKoth could not affect Chambaraya as much as could a single brushfire, or an early frost below the mountains.

Pallas sang with the Song, and the Song flowed through her, and the Song was her; she was transparent to the Song; just as she was to the power of Ma'elKoth.

And through her, Chambaraya struck back: not with fire, not with lightning, but with the power of the life that it served.

Boils festered instantly upon Ma'elKoth's perfect skin, and algaes flourished within his lungs. Leprosy ate away his flesh. The tiny symbionts that still lived deep within his guts suddenly grew and grew, swelling his belly, swelling his chest, and would certainly have burst him from within—but Ma'elKoth, like Chambaraya, was as much an idea as an entity. The powerful love that he drew from the lives of his Children burned within him; soon his guts, his skin, his lungs, his blood, all were as sterile as the face of the moon.

As the two gods strove together, they conversed. Ma'elKoth's voice was a choir of thousands, from the cries of newborn babies to the whimpering rattle of consumptive old men: *Why do You not strike at My Children? By this you know you can weaken Me: shake the earth, topple their buildings, flood their homes. Is not this where Your true power lies?*

The answer came in the roar of a waterfall, the trumpeting of geese, the ice crack of a shifting glacier: *THEY HAVE NOT OFFENDED ME.*

And Ma'elKoth understood: Pallas Ril was more than a simple conduit for the power of the god. Her will colored its Song; they were one . . .

He didn't have to defeat Chambaraya, only Pallas. Concerns that would be less than dust motes to the river might loom large indeed for the woman through which its power flowed.

Come then, you and I. Let Us finish this.

He spread wide his mighty arms and poured power at her; not fire, nor lightning, nor wind, but power. Pure power, raw Flow that he drew from the lives of His Children, focused and sluiced into her without end.

She accepted it all. It passed into her and through her, and as it came, she felt within it the source from which it sprang: she felt the lives of the Children of Ma'elKoth, one by one, wink out like fireflies in the frost.

25

Now that it's too late, now that I lie here dying on this blood-stained sand, I finally get it.

I understand, now.

I understand. I know what he meant. My father told me that to know the enemy is half the battle. I know you, now. That's right.

It's you.

All of you who sit in comfort and watch me die, who see the twitch of my bowels through my own eyes: You are my enemy.

Corpses lie scattered around me, gleanings left in a wheat field by a careless reaper. Berne's body cools beneath the bend of my back, and I can't feel him anymore. The sky darkens over my head—but no, I think that's my eyes; Pallas' light seems to have faded.

Every drop of the blood that soaks into this sand stains my hands and the hands of the monsters that put me here.

That's you, again.

It's your money that supports me, and everyone like me; it's your lust that we serve.

You could thumb your emergency cutoff, turn your eyes from the screen, walk out of the theater, close the book . . .

But you don't.

You are my accomplice, and my destroyer.

My nemesis.

My insatiable blood-crazed god.

Ah, ahhh, Christ . . . it *hurts*.

26

WITHIN THE SONG, Pallas's heart broke. As the power of Ma'el-Koth flowed into her and through her, she knew the men, the women, the children whose lives were snuffed by its drawing, knew each and every one of them as a mother knows the lives she brings forth from her body. Each death lashed her with the world-ending grief of a mother who watches her children die, one by one by one.

Perhaps if they had come in a mass, she could have borne it; a single shattering extinction could have blended these people into some huge and abstract mass, a Stalinist statistic; but instead she knew the individual tragedy of each and every one.

Her soul sagged beneath the weight of clasped and loving hands, and sudden weeping, and despairing last glances exchanged through closing eyes.

What had brought her here was her devotion to innocent lives; the inmost core of her being was the defense of innocence; to withstand this grief would have required that she be someone other than Pallas Ril, other than Shanna Leighton.

Even the aeonic serenity of the river could not carry away this pain.

Though she knew it would cost her life, and Hari's, she could not allow this distant and passionless slaughter to continue; their two lives for thousands—thousands that were as close to her as family, thousands that resided permanently within her heart. This was a bargain that she was prepared to make.

Slowly, with searing regret, she muted her melody within the Song.

Ma'elKoth sensed the change within the Flow, and his attack dwindled as the water of the river deposited him upon the sand of the arena. It withdrew, flowing away along its bended arm above the stadium wall, and returned to its place within the banks.

Pallas stood facing him, across the blood-soaked sand.

"You win," she said simply. "I surrender."

He sprang forward and seized her, holding her limp and unresisting arms in his mighty hands. He looked down on her with disdain.

"Compassion is admirable, in mortal man," he said in tones almost kindly, but then his voice sharpened into cutting contempt. "In a god, it is a *vice*."

She made no answer.

He looked about himself, compressing his lips as he surveyed the carnage and the men and women who now began fearfully to look up. He raised his eyes to the heavens, and the skies cleared and the sun shone down brilliantly upon the earth.

"This has been no more than a delay," he said. "An amusing diversion, but the end is the same."

He hummed to himself, distractedly muttering, "Now, where is Caine?"

She saw him first, lying with back bent over a corpse that could only be Berne's. A double span of Kosall stuck out of his belly like Excalibur in the stone.

She felt that sword stroke herself, punching into her guts, and her breath left her.

Ma'elKoth followed her eyes and hummed his satisfaction. "So, he lives yet. Excellent."

Through the tears that flooded her vision, she saw: Kosall's hilt shifted back and forth, swayed above his body in a hitching, ragged rhythm that could only be Hari's breath.

Ma'elKoth's grip was oddly gentle as he dragged her across the arena to where Caine lay, and the noonday sun was warm on her river-moist skin. He cast her to the sand beside the corpses.

Hari's eyes rolled toward her. "Pallas," he murmured faintly. "Dark . . . It's cold . . ."

His arm twitched, lifting his wrist an inch from the sand, dropping it again. "Take . . . take my hand . . ."

Pallas held his hand; she folded her legs beneath her and cradled his precious head on her lap. "I'm here, Caine. I won't leave you."

Her tears had dried; they had come from the stinging realization that he was still alive—that at least she'd have a chance to say good-bye. Now as she knelt upon the sand with his wet hair cold on her bare thighs, she had no tears, no agony of grief, only a deep, calm melancholy.

She had been here too many times in her career, had held the hands of too many dying men; she had only the acute perception of something unique, a single irreplaceable life, leaving the world; and the world becoming less, in its absence.

I believed he was indestructible, she thought, gently stroking his beard. *Everyone did. But wherever it is he goes to, I'll be with him soon enough.*

I'm sorry, Hari, she thought and could not say. *If I'd had strength like yours, we wouldn't be here now, soon to die.*

"Ahh-hh," Ma'elKoth said abruptly, above her, a hitch in his voice that approached a sob. She looked up. His face was tragic, skin still flecked with the marks Chambaraya had left there, blood that streamed from his broken nose painting scarlet into his beard.

"Ah, Berne," he murmured. "Ah, My Child, you deserved better."

He became aware of her regard and mastered himself instantly, drawing up to his full height.

"Now." He walked in a slow circle around Pallas and Caine, and his hands worked, clenching to fists and opening again. "Now," he repeated. "Now, indeed. I shall learn . . ."

His eyes clouded.

"The mystery of Caine," he muttered softly. "How you have held Me, these past days. When I Drew you here, you Drew Me; you reversed My grip and used it to chain My own hands. But now, it is I that have you, again, and I shall have you wholly, as I did your foul *Aktiri* servitors. I shall extend My power and taste your mind as it fades within your dying brain, as a hound might scent a passing breeze. I shall read your memory as though it is a book; I shall have every bit of you. I shall know the truth, and that truth shall break your hold forever.

"It shall make Me free."

"Lll . . ." Hari said, cords bulging in his neck as he struggled to speak against some unimaginable resistance. Ma'elKoth stepped closer and leaned down politely to hear.

"Yes?"

"Lll-Llllamorak . . ."

"Mm, yes," he said, straightening. "Yes, indeed. Thank you for reminding Me. Lamorak is himself one of you vile *Aktiri*; his memories are likely instructive, as well."

He scanned the arena, looking almost cheerful. "Now, where has he gotten himself to?"

The Emperor strode off across the field of corpses and moaning wounded. A lancer officer who'd managed somehow to keep hold of his horse cantered up to him, asking for instructions—Pallas couldn't hear what orders he gave. The officer in turn relayed orders to his men. Through the broad tunnel gate now marched a column of armored infantry bearing pikes and crossbows. The lancer officer gave them instructions as well. They spread out across the arena, helping the wounded, and up into the grandstands, keeping order, disarming demoralized combatants, and keeping the terrified citizens in their seats.

Hari's back arched once. His eyes rolled and he forced out words once more.

"Lamorak," he said clearly, "is the one who betrayed you to the Cats."

27

"*WHAT?*"

Arturo Kollberg's voice cracked like a whip.

"That bastard!" he raged. "That slacked-jawed piece of Labor trash! *How dare he!*"

He stood in front of his chair and shook his quivering fist at the POV screen.

"You rotten *shit*! This is going out *live!*"

The techs stared at him, at the sweat that poured down his face, at the white foam that flecked the corners of his rubbery lips. A digitized voice said from behind his shoulder, "Why so upset, Administrator?"

"I, ah, I ah, nothing . . ."

If only this buzzing in his head would subside, let him *think*!

Was there anything else Michaelson could say, anything that his conditioning wouldn't prevent—oh *god*, the Board of Governors were watching this *right now*—could he say anything that would implicate the Studio?

His skin crawled with trembling, and large muscle twitches began to distort his face. He stared at the red glowing recall switch as though it were the muzzle of a gun pointed at his forehead.

28

PALLAS GAZES DOWN at me out of the gathering darkness. "Yes, Caine. I know."

The world blinks—I think I passed out for a little bit. We're still here, though, still in the arena.

It didn't work.

I came all this way . . . I gave my life to reach this instant . . .

And it didn't work.

I guess I should have known better than to think that sack of maggots would keep his word.

It's getting cold, *really* cold, freezing for this time of year in Ankhana. I try again, searching for the words that'll bring us home.

"He *had* to," I push out. "*Ordered* to . . . contract, his contract . . ."

"Shh," she says, stroking my hair. "It's all right. Shh."

It's *not* all right, it's—

Darkness.

I swim back up into the world of light again.

We're still in the arena.

I should just let this go.

If anyone had ever asked me how I wanted to die, I'd have told them: exactly like this, with my head on her lap and her hand stroking my hair.

Something's going on, here, though.

It's gotten quiet, and it seems that we're in some kind of spotlight. Lamorak's here, right beside Pallas. Ma'elKoth's got all three of us together for this. There's Ma'elKoth; he's talking to the people in the grandstands . . . That rolling, reassuring thunder of his beautiful voice . . .

Darkness, and when the light comes back he's beside me, *right here beside me*. His voice is warm and gentle, and he's telling me to just let go, to relax and let it go.

He stops talking. His face blanks out into that thousand-yard stare of mindview.

The spell!

I remember now . . . I remember the spell.

And strength comes into me from somewhere.

Fuck letting it go.

Never surrender.

Never.

I roll back my head and search the murk. "Lamorak . . . Lamorak—"

Pallas leans close, an angel from a fairy tale. "Shh, Caine, I know. It's all right."

"No . . ."

I gather more strength, I focus it. Concentrate. When I concentrate I can move my hands—don't need to be strong, but I have to be able to *move*, do it all with surprise . . .

"Lamorak . . . Lamorak, please, I have to tell you . . ."

His broken face resolves out of the gloom; I whisper nonsense to make him lean closer, closer. That's right, you shit, right there . . .

"Lamorak . . . no Iron Room . . . no Theater of Truth . . . you have to take care of Pallas . . ."

"It's all right, Caine," he says. "I will. I promise."

"Promise, do you?" The surge of adrenaline clears my vision and pours strength into my arms. "How do you figure to *keep* that promise *without your fucking head*?"

His eyes go slack in surprise. In a single unstoppable instant, I place one hand on the hilt of Kosall above me to awaken its sizzling magick while I tangle the fingers of the other in Lamorak's long blond hair and yank his neck against Kosall's edge.

His head comes off, *zzzip*, like a sheet of paper torn from a notepad.

Blood fountains; Pallas jerks beneath me and cries out; Lamorak's mouth works soundlessly; he stares at me in horror, still alive within his brain.

I flip his head like a soccerball, right into Ma'elKoth's lap.

Ma'elKoth grasps the bloody head instinctively. His whole body jerks, his eyes go wide, and a cry of shock and despair bursts from his lips.

Not Ma'elKoth's shock, nor his despair, but Lamorak's.

"My name," Ma'elKoth gasps, his eyes still wide and blank. "Karl Shanks, my name is Karl Shanks! I'm Lamorak . . ."

"Lamorak," I snarl with all the sharp strength I have left, *"who ordered you to betray Pallas Ril?"*

"Kollberg," he says, dazedly but clearly. "Chairman Administrator Kollberg . . ."

Before the words can even fully leave his lips, the halos of crystalline rainbow color outline the world.

And in the half second of recall, I reach out—

And take Ma'elKoth's hand.

29

KOLLBERG'S FIST SLAMMED down again on the recall switch, and again. His screamed *"No! No! No!"* kept time with the impacts; he beat the switch until his flesh tore, and his blood sprayed the interior of the techbooth.

The tech flinched away from him and stared. The two soapies exchanged a blank, mirror-masked glance. "I think we've seen enough," one of them said.

"But it's a *lie*," Kollberg said with wild desperation, "I *swear* it's a lie! He can't prove it, he can't even *testify!*"

One of the soapies seized his wrist. "You recalled Pallas Ril in front of native witnesses; by exposing her as an Actor, you've willfully damaged her career. You're under arrest."

He tore himself free and jumped to the techboard, stabbing at the mike switch. "Michaelson!" he howled. His own voice echoed back through the booth speakers: Caine was still on-line, down in the muddle of bodies that lay on the transfer platform.

"I'll see you dead for this! *I'll see you dead!*"

As the soapies finally restrained him and dragged him away, he heard Caine's Soliloquy whispering in the booth.

Yeah. And pretty soon, too, I guess.

30

THE HARSH, UNFORGIVING stage lights that frame the transfer platform break into a prismatic halo through Ma'elKoth's mane. Silhouette that he is, I cannot see the expression on his face, and I'm glad of it; the choking horror in his voice is bad enough as he looks out at the row upon row of faceless induction helmets, the reclining zombied sweep of first-handers that are stacked to the ceiling of the Cavea.

"Your world," he whispers. *"Oh, abandoned gods, you've brought me to your hideous world . . ."*

And this is not an instinctive xenophobia, not the helpless terror of an unsophisticated native; it's not the alienness of Earth that is choking him.

It's the *familiarity*.

He spoke in English.

These are Lamorak's—Karl's—memories he's correlating within his massive brain; he sees that his world, Overworld—that place of brutality and pain and sudden death—is the dreamed-of, soughtafter paradise of this one, where now he's trapped.

I've brought him with me into hell.

I cannot imagine the horror he must be feeling, and I can't bring myself to care very much.

Kosall, quiescent now and probably forever, still sticks up out of my belly. Berne's corpse lies on the transfer platform beneath my legs.

I won.

He bends his mighty neck to look down on me, on us.

"You have destroyed me. Why, Caine?"

His heartbreak cracks in his voice. *"Why have you done this to me?"*

I shrug. It hurts. "Because you had the bad luck to be on the wrong side of Pallas Ril."

There's a slam in the back, high up. It's the doors to the Cavea. The medics' crash cart is coming for me; some on-the-ball tech had the presence of mind to call them.

Warm salt rain splashes lightly upon my cheeks; it's Shanna's tears.

"Hold on," she says. "Please hold on."

I try to squeeze her hand, but the darkness is closing in again. "Don't leave me."

"I won't. I swear."

Ma'elKoth sounds lost and helpless and very, very young. "What comes next? What will become of me?"

I don't answer; that's not my problem.

I guess I'm still on-line; nobody's thought to cut the feed. You're all coming down with me, into the night.

Shanna bends close and puts the warmth of her cheek against the chill of mine. She whispers in my ear, *"Hold on, Caine."*

"Fuck Caine," I tell her painfully. I fight off the darkness for one closing line: "Forget that asshole. Call me Hari."

And the shuttering night turns slowly to dawn, and I inch toward daylight.

Once an hour, worldwide:

The hair, of course, is perfect, and the chiseled cheekbones have a Leisureman's tan—but there is a hint of cold desperation in the delicate, semivisible tracery of lines around the glycerine eyes, and the lips that part over the polished teeth have a faint, barely half-detectable twist of bitter self-contempt.

"Hello, I'm Bronson Underwood. For the past ten years, I've brought you the best of Studio action from all over the world, as the host of *Adventure Update*. Today, and for a short time only, I'm proud to bring you this special offer, direct from where it all began, the San Francisco Studio of Adventures Unlimited:

"*For Love of Pallas Ril*, the Limited Edition Boxed Set."

The eyes go glassy and the smile sets like gelatin as he numbers the special features of the Limited Edition Boxed Set: excerpts from *Race for the Crown of Dal-Kannith* and *Servant of the Empire*; several hours of *The Pursuit of Simon Jester*, leading up to the Eternal Forgetting; deep-background interviews with Caine, Pallas Ril, and Ma'elKoth himself, speaking on both his own behalf and that of Lamorak;

". . . and, direct from the Confidential Archives of the San Francisco Studio, *exclusive to the Limited Edition:* 'When the Lifeclock Stopped!'

"You remember that incredible instant, when Caine brought his beloved out of the blazing noon on those arena sands, back to Earth, back to safety. You saw it live; you may have even experienced it as Caine.

"Now, it can touch you *all over again* . . . for in that instant 'When the Lifeclock Stopped,' the recording of Pallas Ril *started once again*.

"This special offer will *not* be repeated; this Limited Edition

527

Boxed Set is your *only opportunity* to receive this precious moment. *This is your only chance* to step inside the heart of Pallas Ril, as she kneels upon the transfer platform, saved from certain death by the only man she has ever truly loved. This is your only chance to see what she sees, feel what she feels, as her tears touch the face of her fallen hero."

The eyes seem to recede, just a little; perhaps dust has settled upon them. The smile becomes fixed, as though the lips have been stapled to the teeth.

"And to commemorate this incredible offer, in honor of this extraordinary Adventure, if you order before *midnight tonight*, you will also receive the Special Edition Personal Pallas Ril Lifeclock!

"Calibrated by Studio scientists using *your personal actuarial data* compiled from the global medical database, including data from as many as *six generations* of *your* ancestors, the Special Edition Personal Pallas Ril Lifeclock will accurately number the hours of *your* life! This handsome unit fits attractively on a nightstand, on an office desk, even a kitchen table . . ."

The advertisement, which runs until most of the world has forgotten why they should care who any of these people are, includes a subtitled disclaimer: *Special Edition Personal Pallas Ril Lifeclock is not intended as a predictive tool.*

For Entertainment Purposes Only.

EPILOGUE

THERE CAME A day when Hari woke up and found Shanna sitting at his bedside.

He lay on his gelpack pillow and gazed at her through half-opened eyes while awareness leaked into his brain with the morning light.

She sat staring idly out the window, toward the clouds, toward the ocean, high over the shantytown of media vans that invested the hospital like the siege engines of an Overworld army. She was thin, her cheeks still hollowed and her eyes dark, and she still carried her left arm stiffly at her side—and Hari thought he'd never seen anything so beautiful in his life.

He didn't speak, for fear that the sound of his voice might dispel the dream.

She coughed a little, with wet discomfort, when she felt his gaze on her. She smiled and touched her ribs where the quarrel had smashed through them into her lung. "Pneumonia," she said apologetically.

He ventured a tentative answering smile. "Yeah, me too—think I caught it in here, though."

"I, ah . . ." she began, then said, "How, how are you? I mean . . ."

She nodded vaguely toward the gunmetal bulk of the MRNS unit that covered him from thighs to ribcage; she didn't really want to look at it directly.

Hari shrugged and patted its side. "I don't know. Not so bad, I guess. They're telling me I should get some feeling back in my legs within the next couple of weeks. They're gonna hook up one of those computer-bypass things so that I'll be able to walk in a year or so, by pretending to wiggle my toes or something, even if the regen doesn't take . . ."

He sighed in a deep breath for courage, sighed it out again. "Mmm, they say I'll probably walk with a cane for the rest of my

529

life; I told them I knew that already," he offered with a crooked smile.

She turned away, toward the window again, and lowered her head.

"Yeah," he murmured, "bad joke, I know."

"Oh, Hari, I'm so sorry—"

"Stop it," he told her. "Don't even start."

"Your career—"

"Fuck my career. All I—all *Caine* ever wanted to do was to die in your arms. That's his happy ending, and it's good enough for me."

He rolled his shoulders forward and back again and wished the thousands of hairlike probes that ran through his skin from the MRNS unit to his severed spinal cord would let him shift his hips—he was getting a hell of an ache.

"And I got out of it alive. How many living retired Actors do you know?"

Her voice was barely a whisper. "You've given up so much for me . . ."

"Nah."

"Hari—"

"I didn't do it for you—you should know me better than that by now. I did it because a world without you in it is one I'm not all that interested in living in, y'know?"

He slapped the cold side of the unit. "My legs? My career? Cheap at twice the price. You're worth ten of me."

She said softly, still looking away, "I used to think that, too . . ."

And the hand that squeezed his heart wouldn't let him think of anything to say.

LATER, SHE ASKED, "Have you been following the trial?"

"Are you kidding? Watching that rotten fuck go down in flames is several of the high points of my life. Hand me the remote—let's see what they're up to now."

He keyed the pad, and the screen above his head lit up with a scene outside the San Francisco Corporate Court. One of a long line of limousines disgorged a knot of Attorneys who circled their client like bodyguards, even though not one of them was as tall as their client's shoulder.

"Hey, that's Ma'elKoth," Hari said. "I guess they're gonna let him testify after all."

His Attorneys held off the mob of reporters so that he could mount the steps, then he turned and favored them with a smile that seemed to brighten the sunlight. He wore an immaculately tailored suit of an appropriately classic Eurocut double-breasted style that emphasized the enormous breadth of his shoulders. The taupe-colored weave set off his richly burnished hair, which was now drawn back into a conservative ponytail.

Clean-shaven now, with the noble jut of his jaw, with the wide brow above his clear and serious eyes, he could only be believed when he turned to the tapers and rumbled, "My interest here is to see justice done. Arturo Kollberg robbed me of my throne and conspired against my life, as well as the lives of Pallas Ril and Caine. Only the truth, ugly as it may be, can serve to guard society against such crimes."

The cameras followed him on his stately march into the courthouse.

"Amazing how well he's adapted," Shanna murmured. "He sounds like he's running for tribune."

"I'd vote for him."

"I suppose I would, too. You think the Studio will ever let him go back to Overworld?"

"Doubt it. I can't imagine he'd want to—the way I took him out branded him as an *Aktir*. He wouldn't have much of a life."

"He doesn't have much of a life now. He can only leave the ON vault for a couple of hours at a time. To have come so far, he must spend all his time watching the net."

"He had a head start," Hari said.

She dropped her eyes.

"You notice?" he went on. "He's got Karl's accent."

"Hari—"

"I'm not gonna apologize for that. I've done some shitty things in my life, but that wasn't one of them. It was better than he deserved, and you know it."

"Yes, I do know it," she said faintly. "You . . . you just have to understand that it's a little hard for me. There was a time when I thought I loved him; no matter what I know about him now, nothing changes that . . ."

That fist within his chest came back and squeezed his heart; he couldn't look at her. "We're not gonna live happily ever after, are we?"

"I don't know, Hari. I really just don't know."

* * *

DAYS PASSED. VISITORS came and went, interviewers, most of whom wanted to know how Caine had managed to execute his bewilderingly complex plan to such a nicety; none of them believed him when he said that he didn't know either, that he just kept inching toward daylight till he finally made it.

Marc Vilo called every day to check his progress; he remained blindly certain that Caine's career was not over, as though with his billions he could buy new legs for his pet star.

Some news of Ankhana leaked through from various Actors around the Empire; the story was that the King of Cant and his Subjects had saved Duke Toa-Sytell's life at the stadium that day when Ma'elKoth had been revealed as an *Aktir*. With Kierendal's Faces, they held the city and were gradually gaining the loyalty of the military. In light of this, much of the nobility was pledging fealty, and it looked like the Empire would stand with Toa-Sytell in control.

It was impossible to get more details than this because the Empire had become, for Actors, very dangerous indeed. Toa-Sytell carried on Ma'elKoth's *Aktir-tokar* with a vengeance. A number of Actors had been caught and executed.

Hari appreciated the cold irony: the Studio conditioning that was intended to prevent them from betraying themselves or others was the very means by which they were caught.

From there in his hospital bed, Hari watched in quiet exultation as the Interim Chairman announced over the nets that the Studio was suspending Ankhanan operations until a solution could be found.

Arturo Kollberg was hung out to dry by the Studio; the official line was that this had all been his own rogue operation. Downcasted to Labor, he was moved to a Temp block not far from where Hari grew up.

Hari had won; Caine had won.

They'd killed him, but it didn't matter; he'd beaten them all.

Then, one day, Shanna came back.

"CONGRATULATIONS, ADMINISTRATOR MICHAELSON," was the first thing she said. "I hear your upcaste came through."

Hari shrugged. "Hello to you, too. Yeah, the Studio got behind me, and they pretty much get what they want."

"The Studio?" she said, looking puzzled. "Why would they want you upcasted?"

"Because they offered me Kollberg's job."

She went absolutely blank. "I don't believe it."

"I didn't either, but when you think about it, it makes a lot of sense. I'm the most famous man on the planet, right now. Even though I'm—I was—only a Professional, I could cause the Studio a shitload of trouble. I'm virtually untouchable, and I could tell some stories. I could deliver the knockout to follow up the black eye they got from the Kollberg business. So they want to keep me in the system."

"They really think you could do them that much damage?"

He spread his hands. "Hey, I've toppled one government already this month."

"You don't seriously think—"

"Well, maybe not. All I can say is, they better not piss me off."

Her face had become more full, and the shadows had disappeared from under her eyes. She suddenly seemed vastly uncomfortable; she made tentative *I think I'd better leave* movements.

"What's wrong?" he asked.

"Hari, I . . . I don't know. That's great, your news, your upcasteing, all that, but I . . . Maybe I'd better just let this go."

"What? Let what go?"

"I don't want you to think this has anything to do with your upcaste—"

His heart leaped into his throat, and blood sang in his ears. "This what? Come on, you're killing me: Talk."

She hand-combed her hair away from her eyes and turned to gaze into the misty distance outside the window; she spoke hesitantly, with obvious difficulty.

"There at the last, I was a god," she began, and sighed as though she didn't know how to continue.

"I remember . . ." Hari said softly.

"And, you know, it wasn't really me—I mean, it was me, I was me, but I was also him, it, Chambaraya. I was only a little part of the god, but at the same time I was all of it, and I know this isn't making very much sense . . . Words are kind of inadequate, I guess; the only way you could really understand is if it had happened to you."

"You miss it, don't you," Hari said. This wasn't a question; the truth of it was all too clear, and it stabbed him inside. *She's leaving me again,* he thought. *Leaving me for the love of the river.*

"Yes. Of course I do. But I'm *here* now, and this is where I need to be. I need to be where I am, and whatever I'm doing, that's what I need to do. Do you understand?"

"Not really . . ."

"You saw the power," she said, "but power has nothing to do with being a god. They, the gods, they *look* at things differently. To join with Chambaraya, all I had to do was see the world the way it does. And when the world looks different, it's because you've *become* different—you're not the same person that saw it in the old ways."

She spread her hands, shaking her head with a weak smile of surrender. "I can't seem to get close to the point."

She rose and paced about the room; Hari's gaze followed her helplessly.

"You know, the gods don't understand us, either," she said. "Mortal folk are as much a mystery to them as they are to us. And what they understand least, what they just can't figure out, is why we choose to be miserable. It seems to them that we *insist* on being unhappy . . . When I was with Chambaraya, it seemed that way to me, too, and I couldn't understand it any more than the river could."

She straightened. Hari could see the faintest tremor in the hand that smoothed the seam of her tunic. She breathed deep, as though drawing in courage from the air.

"I've been giving this a great deal of thought, looking it over from every side I can find," she said hesitantly.

Hari squeezed his eyes shut. *I don't need to hear this.*

"You're going to be going home soon."

"Yeah . . . ?" was the best he could force through his closing throat.

"I'd like to . . . I'd like to be there, when you do. And after."

He couldn't speak, couldn't breathe, couldn't even blink.

She sat down and once again turned away. "Businessman Vilo, he's got this simichair . . . He and Leisurema'am Dole, are, well, y'know, and so I've . . . Over the past week, I've been, sort of, first-handing your Adventure."

"Shanna . . ."

"I understand so many things, now. And, and Hari? Through it all, through everything, the separation, everything, I never doubted that you loved me. I guess I just thought you had to love me *my way*—or something equally petty and stupid. I don't know. I guess it's not important, now."

"I, I . . ."

"I don't know if we can make anything work between us, Hari. I really don't know. I'm not the same woman you married— different things are important to me, now. And you're not the same man, either. Maybe, maybe we could . . . get to know each other again. You think? Because I love you, and I want to try to be together, again. I want us both to try to be happy."

"Shanna, my god, Shanna . . ."

And as he reached out to take her hand, a team of doctors with a crashcart burst through the door of his room; his telemetry had set off six different alarms.

DAYS LATER, WHEN the doctors had been satisfied and he was loaded into the levichair that would be his mobile home for the next few months, he held her hand and gazed into her eyes and thought, *Well, shit, this is all right: in the end, I even get the girl.*

She walked beside his humming chair as they left the hospital and entered the open air.

The sky arched high overhead, and the shining golden spark of an approaching cab arced down toward them.

He looked up at her. "You really think we can make this work?"

"I hope so," she said. "After all, I promised I'd never leave you. And promises are important."

"Yeah," he said, "yeah, they are . . . Y'know, you just reminded me of another promise I made."

When the cab landed, she helped negotiate the loading of his chair inside. He leaned forward, tapped the CANCEL RUN key, and told the driver to enter a course for the Buchanan Social Camp.

"The Buchanan?" Shanna asked. "Why are we going to the Buchanan?"

Hari smiled, just a little; his heart was too full for anything bigger. The greatest joys are expressed in the stillest, smallest, quietest ways.

"There's someone that I want you to meet."

A Conversation with Matthew Woodring Stover

Matthew Woodring Stover lives in Chicago, Illinois, where he works as a bartender at a private club in the United Center, home of the Bulls and the Blackhawks. In previous incarnations he's been an actor, a theatrical producer, a playwright, a waiter, a barista (okay, what the heck is a barista?), a short-order cook, a telemarketer of fine wines, and a door-to-door vacuum cleaner salesman. With his partner, noted painter and up-and-coming fantasy author Robyn Fielder, he was cofounder and codirector of the Iff Theater. In addition to being a recreational marathon runner and amateur kickboxer, Stover has studied a variety of martial arts, including the Degerberg Blend, tae kwon do, aikido, English boxing, English quarterstaff, the Filipino sword arts (kali/escrima/arnis), savate, and muay thai (reviewers, take note!). Somehow amid all this exhausting activity he finds time to write fantasy novels—three to date—with more on the way.

Q: *Tell us a little about how you became a writer . . . and why an SF writer.*
A: Two words: Robert Heinlein. I read *Have Space Suit—Will Travel* when I was about twelve, then got ahold of *Glory Road*, and my fate was sealed. From Heinlein to early Zelazny to Fritz Leiber to Evangeline Walton; they got me started, and I've never stopped. Much of my life has been an obsessive inquiry into philosophy, mythology, magic, religion, and the concept of the Hero (in the Joseph Campbell sense). SF—fantasy—is the only branch of literature that lets you look at all of those at once. As to "how I became a writer," I did it on the Ray Bradbury plan: a thousand words a day, six days a week, rain or shine, even if you have to throw it out because it's so bad that burning it would violate the Clean Air Act.

He claims that by the time you've written a million words, you start to have some idea what you're doing. He's right.

Q: Your first novel, Iron Dawn, *was published in 1997. Its sequel,* Jericho Moon, *in 1998—which is also when* Heroes Die *was published. Three novels in two years—all of exceptional quality. Are you an incredibly quick and prolific writer? Do you work on different projects simultaneously, or do you have a lot of material stockpiled from over the years? In other words, should I just slit my wrists now?*

A: Save your wrists: it was pure stockpile. May the gods witness my wish that I really could write that fast. I wrote *Iron Dawn* in 1993 and early '94. I sent it off unsolicited and unagented, straight to the slush pile. While I was waiting for a response, I wrote *Heroes Die* (which is actually a massive revision of an earlier, vastly longer, completely unpublishable book). In late '95—through the kind intervention of a perceptive editor—I finally got a great agent, and he had *Iron Dawn* sold at auction within about a month. By that time, *Heroes Die* was finished—but my editor at Roc Books offered a contract for a sequel, at which I promptly jumped; *Jericho Moon* was a story I'd been wanting to write for a long time. So *Heroes Die* had to wait for *Jericho Moon*, which I finished in early '97 . . . and then there was a long round of revision on *Heroes Die*. So, actually, these three books took me five years to write—eight years, if you count the three I spent working on the early version of *Heroes Die*. The "three books in two years" is entirely an optical illusion.

Q: Whew! It just wouldn't be fair for you to be so good and so fast! Your answer will be of special interest to aspiring writers, I think, because (if I've understood correctly) Iron Dawn *was discovered in the slush pile by an editor who then pointed you toward an agent. What advice would you give to writers looking to break into the field in terms of agents, editors, and submissions?*

A: I think the ideal way to get an agent is exactly the way I did it: a recommendation from an editor who'd like to buy your script. Agents tend to be vastly interested in projects where a sale is more-or-less guaranteed. In my case, the wise and perceptive editor provided me with a list of agents she knew represented my kind of fiction. The best advice I can offer to aspiring fiction writers in any field is to read two books: *Zen in the Art of Writing,* by Ray Bradbury, and *Writing to Sell,* by Scott Meredith. Between the two, they'll tell you just about everything you need to know. As far as advice specific to the fantasy field goes, well, that's obvious: the easiest way to break into fantasy fiction is to write a novel about an Innocent Adolescent Who Suddenly Develops Powers and Now Is Destined to Defeat the Dark Lord, Save the World, Cure Dandruff, and Wipe Out the Scourge of Acne.

Q: Iron Dawn *received an unusually strong response for a first novel. What sets that book and its sequel apart?*

A: I can't really say what sets those books apart. All I can tell you is what I like about them—and that would begin with the characters. That's how I start a book: I get interested in a character, and I try to pull together a story that will show that character to his/her advantage. In the case of *Iron Dawn,* I became fascinated with a character that my partner, Robyn Fielder, had developed, this female Pictish mercenary named Barra. I had been developing an idea for a historical fantasy based on the premise that Homer's *Iliad* was history, rather than fiction, and when Robyn started telling me about Barra, I just fell in love. She became the axis of the book. All three of the heroes are outsiders, expatriates in a foreign culture, and Barra is the most alien—a female warrior from the far side of the world, a land so distant that most people think it mythical—but she is also the most at home. She's the inside-outsider, the link between the various cultures that interpenetrate the story. She speaks the language, she knows the city, she has an adoptive family that lives there; it's her fierce passion to defend her adopted city that drives the plot. I'm really only interested in people who have that kind of passion, that fierceness; there are plenty of others who write about pure-hearted knights and Innocent Adolescents Who Are Destined, et cetera. Which brings me to the other thing that I like about my first two books: they're not about the conflict of Light Against Darkness, or Good versus Evil. They're about people trying to protect their homes, their families—and they're about Barra, who has an unfortunate tendency to get emotionally involved in the jobs she takes on. The whole concept of Good and Evil as an abstract moral dichotomy doesn't appear in historical thought until Zoroaster, five or six hundred years after these books are set. Barra herself puts it this way: "One of the things I've learned in all these years is that just because someone's your enemy, he's not automatically a bad man."

Q: That was one of the things I liked most about Heroes Die: *your focus on characters and situations of a certain, shall we say, moral complexity all too rare in fantasy. Is this your strength as a writer?*
A: I don't really know what my strengths as a writer might be; judging from my mail and the reviews I get, the things I think I'm good at are often not what people like in my work. So let's just say this: I'm thorough, I love my characters, and for me, evil is entirely a matter of perspective. Everyone's a good guy, in his or her own mind; even serial killers, Nazi concentration camp commanders, and "ethnic cleansers" the world over don't think of themselves as evil.

Q: Well, unless of course they get a big kick out of defining themselves that way! Hitler never thought of himself as evil for a second; on the contrary. But there are men and women, I believe, who consciously set out to embrace and embody an idea of evil: 'It's better to reign in Hell than serve in Heaven,' as someone once said . . .
A: But now you're shifting into aberrant psychology, as opposed to metaphysics. You quote from *Paradise Lost*—in that work, Lucifer is a tragic hero, a magnificently flawed character. And what's his flaw? Basically, he refuses to Do What He's Told— which, to a more modern sensibility than Milton's, is hardly a flaw at all. In fact, given the history of the twentieth century (i.e., the Nuremberg trials: "I was only following orders"), it's a positive virtue. What I'm trying to get at with that element of my work is this: reality has no moral dimension.

Morality is an arbitrary human creation that supports culture-specific social orders. Not to say it's not useful, even necessary, but to pretend that it derives from supernatural authority is childish: "This is wrong because Daddy (God, Jesus, Mohammed, pick one or make up your own) says it is." Similarly, to pretend that behavior we don't like in others (or desires and drives we've been taught are bad in ourselves) is the result of some supernatural force of evil is just a way to shift the blame: "The Devil made me do it."

Outside of the wackos who use evil as an excuse to justify their actions, those embracing "evil" are usually defining evil as opposition to a specific social code; it's an act of rebellion—and they're actually rebelling not against God, or Truth, or Justice, or whatever but against society's restrictive view of what these things have to be. Chat with a Satanist sometime; most of them are really nice folks.

Q: What writers have influenced you most? You've already mentioned Heinlein and Leiber; Heroes Die *put me in mind of Michael Moorcock as well. Not just the sword and sorcery aspect of it, but the science fictional idea—well, more science factional now thanks to quantum theory—of a multitude of realities harmonically related to varying degrees.*

A: Michael Moorcock is one of my heroes, naturally; the decadence and moral ambiguity that runs through the Elric stories . . . Kierendal (and her brothel) in *Heroes Die* is pretty much a direct nod to Moorcock. Fritz Leiber—it's no coincidence that my first novel, *Iron Dawn,* is set in Tyre, which was the setting of "Adept's Gambit," the only Fafhrd and the Grey Mouser story (as far as I remember) to be set on Earth rather than Nehwon. Roger Zelazny— the original version of *Heroes Die,* all those years ago, was inspired by Zelazny's *Isle of the Dead* . . . and, of course, *Nine Princes in Amber.* Stephen Donaldson's Covenant books were a powerful influence; I read them back in college, and they were my first look at the possibilities of really adult fantasy. He showed me how a fantasy hero can be a long way from conventionally heroic but still capture the imagination and emotion, so long as he or she cares. Outside the genre, I guess my greatest influence would be Joseph Conrad. He convinced me that you don't really find out what you're made of until you discover that there are no rules; my characters usually find themselves, at one point or another, in situations where the boundaries they've set for themselves break down. They have to act—and usually, act fast—without recourse to the structure of behavior that they have relied upon to carry them through their lives. The characters who win are the ones who are flexible enough thinkers to find right action in a moral vacuum.

As far as the quantum mechanical part of it goes, well . . . let me put it this way: a few years ago, when I was first reading Michio Kaku's *Hyperspace,* I looked up at Robyn and said, "Holy crap! You won't believe this: Overworld is theoretically possible!"

Q: How would you describe Heroes Die?
A: It's a piece of violent entertainment that is a meditation on vio-

lent entertainment—as a concept in itself, and as a cultural obsession. It's a love story: romantic love, paternal love, repressed homoerotic love, love of money, of power, of country, love betrayed and love employed as both carrot and stick. It's a book about all different kinds of heroes, and all the different ways they die. It's a pop-top can of Grade-A one-hundred percent pure whip-ass.

Q: Yee-hah! Makes me want to read it all over again! How much of your experiences as an actor and playwright, as well as a martial artist, informed the events and characters of Heroes?
A: There is a kind of creative tension between Hari Michaelson, the actor, and Caine, the character he plays, that I touch upon in this novel. I was a stage actor; when you play a character night after night, it begins to infect your offstage personality. Not in the cliché sense of the actor who gets "lost in the role" but in a subtler way. You entrain your reflexes with the character's mannerisms, for example, and you might find yourself standing like the character, gesturing like him, even using his voice without really thinking about it. When a character you are playing also reflects something fundamentally true about yourself, you can find yourself reacting instinctively from that character's point of view—thinking like the character. This is what has happened to Hari; part of his struggle in the novel is to find a way to break out of Caine's self-destructive patterns without losing the positive parts of that persona. One of the lessons actors learn is how incredibly powerful "make-believe" can be. That's what acting is, after all. As a playwright, you find that there is no feeling in the world worse than to be sitting in the house at one of your own plays and discovering that you've lost the audience. You can always tell—when people start to get bored the theater is suddenly filled with subtle creaks of people shifting in their seat, coughs, sniffles, the crackle of after-dinner-mint wrappers . . . That's why the book is structured as an adventure novel. *Heroes Die* has been described in print as "energetic," "vigorous," "hard-hitting adventure," even a "furious, gory hack-em-up." All true. If you want to keep your audience's butts nailed to their seats, the story has to move.

I've been studying various martial arts intermittently for almost twenty years; I've done dozens of styles without ever becoming really proficient in any of them. In the process, I've accumulated a vast theoretical knowledge of personal combat—and I've done a little fighting, in the ring and out of it. I know what it feels like to get my ass soundly kicked; I also know what it's like to fight someone who's a lot better than I am and beat him anyway. Part of what I wanted to achieve with Caine is to get across that feeling; Caine is a long way from the Bruce Lee/Remo Williams/Sir Lancelot myth of the invincible martial arts superman. Everything Caine does in *Heroes Die* is real-world fighting; every move he makes can be duplicated by a reasonably skilled fighter. He's not the best fighter in the world—he's not even the best fighter in the book. But there's a lot more to combat than skill.

Q: Is the caste-ridden capitalistic society of actor Hari Michaelson's world something you see as possible in our own?

A: In a word, yes. Hari Michaelson's Earth is the triumph of American capitalism, stripped of its egalitarian pretense. Don't get me wrong; I like capitalism. But any social system becomes pernicious when taken to unchecked extremes, and Americans are extremists by nature. We have to push the envelope. The novel postulates a catastrophic event a couple of hundred years in the past (that is, in our near future) that essentially frees the multinational corporations from even the shadow of governmental control. The resulting society is caste-based because that reflects the curious psychological phenomenon of the industrial age: You Are What You Do. Caste systems are by far the most stable form of social organization—the members of each individual caste have a vested interest in maintaining the status quo. The upper castes can depend upon the lower to participate in their own oppression. This particular system also holds out the old capitalist dream of self-improvement: it is possible to buy one's way upcaste. No one wants to rock the boat and screw up their chance of someday joining the ruling classes. Of course, these days it looks like the catastrophic event might have been superfluous. All you really need to bring about this future is a few more years of the Republican Congress.

Q: Perhaps the Republican Congress is the catastrophic event.
A: Hey, what are you trying to do, get us both audited?

Q: The Overworld—Caine's world—is a wonderfully realized creation. There's a complexity and sophistication to your portrayal of Ankhana's inhabitants, their cultural practices and beliefs, their private fears and desires, that, once again, reminded me of Moorcock and Leiber. Even magic is treated with the same gritty realism as, say, Caine's fight scenes. In fact, in many ways the Overworld seems more real than the "underworld" that is home to Caine and the other Aktiri.

A: Overworld is a step closer to the fundamental reality of existence; the whole concept of Acting, in the book, is to give the audience the feeling of having been to a place more raw and exciting than their everyday reality. I'm hoping to give the reader an analogous experience. And yes, Ankhana—especially the Warrens—owes a lot of its feel to Leiber's Lankhmar.

Q: How exact are the parallels between Overworld and underworld? When I first looked at a map of the city, a nagging familiarity convinced me that I was looking at the Overworld equivalent of Paris. Are there analogues of places, of people? Could Caine, for example, meet an aspect of himself?

A: The parallels are more metaphoric than actual; even the geography has only rough similarities. For reasons that will eventually become apparent, Caine won't be meeting aspects of himself. He is unique. Ankhana's resemblance to Paris is pretty much a matter of story mechanics (the island enclave of human rulers, the river that separates the wealthy from the ghettoes that hold the poor and the nonhumans being the central spine of the city, et cetera). It also came about because I originally conceived the plan of the city while reading *The Hunchback of Notre Dame*; you might also have noticed a certain similarity between the Night of the Miracle in *Heroes Die* and Hugo's Heart of Miracles . . . Hey, if you're gonna steal, steal from the best.

Q: Can you talk a bit about actors and Aktiri? There are similar mirror images all through the book—ideas of reflection, reversal, opposition, splitting in two . . .

A: Let's just say that a lot depends on your point of view. Ever wonder how Han Solo must look to, say, the wives and mothers of those Imperial Troopers he so casually slaughters? As far as the imagery goes, I'm really not comfortable talking about my use of literary devices and stuff like that. Some things are harmed by exposure. Pay no attention to the man behind the curtain . . .

Q: Will there be a sequel? If so, what can you tell us about it? I'm hoping we'll see more of Ma'elKoth . . .

A: Yes, not much, and you will. All I can say is that the sequel will be an entirely different animal from *Heroes Die*; I'm using many of the same characters to look at a very, very different group of interconnected themes, from the clash of individualism versus social responsibility to the essentially chaotic (in the sense of chaos theory) nature of reality. But there will still be a fair amount of serious butt-kicking, and several brutal murders . . .

Q: You mentioned earlier that your stories begin with characters. Do your characters, as you come to know them, suggest the themes of your books, or do you consciously set out to examine certain themes?
A: Some of both. It's a little difficult to describe. They feed off each other: Characters suggest themes—in fact, most of the viewpoint characters in *Heroes Die* carry their own individual themes—but themes also alter characters. As I play around inside the characters' heads, whatever I happen to be obsessing about that week tends to be reflected somehow in their personalities or their histories, but each character is also a kind of perceptual filter; I could never use Caine, for example, to address a theme of overcoming timidity and self-doubt, or dealing with shyness or any of that kind of thing. Those emotions are too alien to him.

Q: I was fascinated by the magical force of Flow and its relationship to the wave functions of quantum physics; i.e., a link between the science of one world and the magic of the other. Is that something else you plan to explore?
A: Flow is a fantasy expression of the Earthly concept of the Tao—which can be interpreted in many ways, as a metaphoric representation of the force described as the GUTE: the Grand Unified Theory of Everything. It is the fundamental force, of which electromagnetism, gravity, et al., are the differentiated expressions. It is also—in the Teilhard de Chardin sense—the consciousness of the universe. On Overworld, "energy" is equivalent to "mind"; since matter is a form of energy, everything in the Overworld universe partakes to some degree in the Universal Mind. If you read much Eastern philosophy—or much in the Western mystical tradition—you will have recognized this idea already. So, yes, there is a direct relationship between the way the physical laws operate in the two universes. This becomes a crucial element of the sequel, as we discover that there are some forms of magic that will operate even on

Earth, and some forms of technology that work perfectly well on Overworld . . .

Q: Any chance we'll go further afield than Earth and Overworld? There must be an infinite number of alternate Earths reachable by means of the technology that sends Hari to Overworld, or by other (perhaps even magical) means.

A: There must be . . . and not only other alternate Earths. The Winston transfer technology seems to be able to transfer a person to any spatial coordinate on Overworld . . . and Einstein contended long ago (and Hawking confirms) that duration—Time—is only another spatial dimension . . .

Q: And who's to say that Hari's Earth isn't itself the unwitting stage upon which otherworldly actors are performing?

A: Who's to say our Earth isn't?

ALL ACTORS HAVE A PRECISELY
DEFINED ROLE—
to risk their lives on Overworld
in interesting ways.
It's not personal; it's just market share.

Caine has long been the best of the best.
A generation grew up watching the
superstar's every adventure.
Now he's chairman of the world's largest
studio and he's making changes.

Higher powers of Overworld and Earth don't
approve. It's just business.

But for Caine, it's his wife, their daughter, his
invalid father, his status, his home.

And it's *always* personal.

FIST OF CAINE

by Matthew Woodring Stover

Published by Del Rey Books.
Available at bookstores near you in Summer 2000.